who

DIVIDE THE DAWN:
FIGHT

by Eamon Loingsigh

SHANACHIE51 PRESS - NEW YORK
For questions, comments or concerns - artofneed@gmail.com

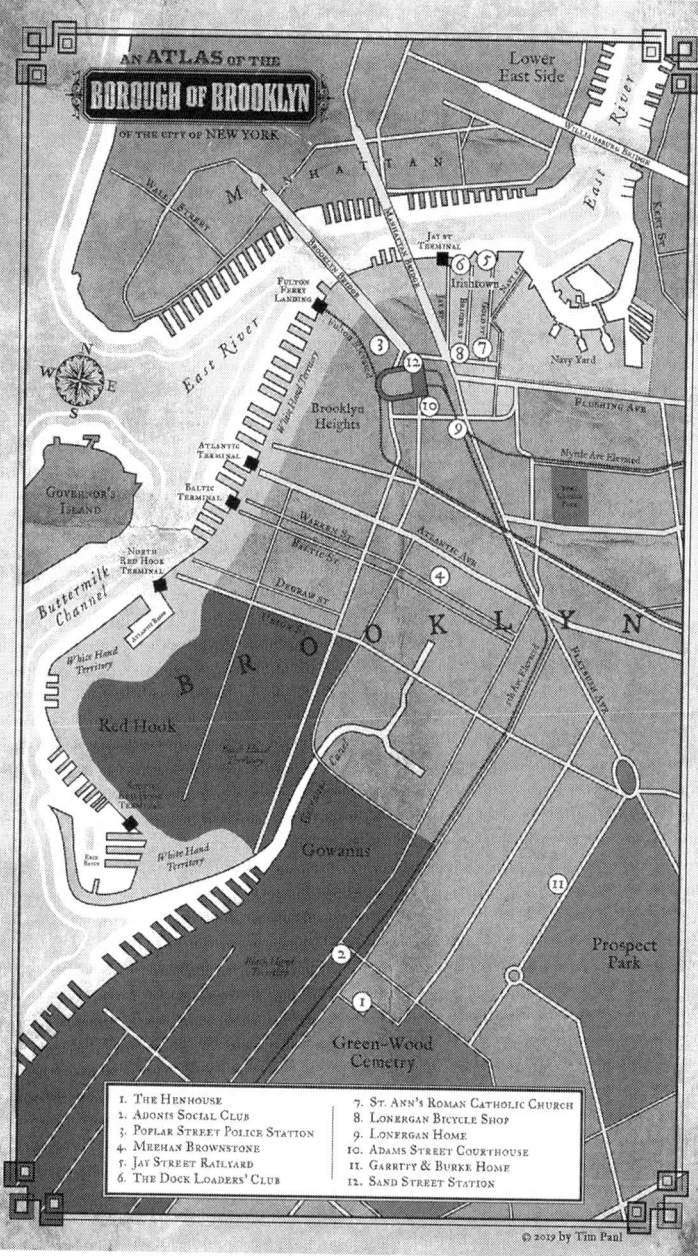

Main Characters

Meehan's White Hand
Dennis Dinny Meehan - Leader
James The Swede Finnigan - Enforcer
Vincent MasherMaher - Enforcer
Liam Poe Garrity - The Thief of Pencils

Dockbosses
Harry The Shiv Reynolds - Atlantic Terminal
James Cinders Connolly - Fulton Ferry Landing & Jay Street Terminal
John The Lark Gibney - Baltic Terminal
Cute Charlie Red Donnelly - Navy Yard
Dan Dance Gillen - Atlantic Terminal

Others
Beat McGarry - Old gang member, storyteller
Thomas Burke - Downstairs neighbor of Liam Garrity
Tanner Smith - Westside Manhattan leader of the Marginals
Whyo Mullen & Will Sutton - Ten year old Irishtown moppets

The Swede
by Guy Denning

Lovett's White Hand
Wild Bill Lovett - World War I vet
Lieutenants
Richie Pegleg Lonergan - Anna Lonergan's brother, killed Mickey Kane
John Non Connors - World War I vet
Joseph One-arm Flynn - World War I vet
Frankie Byrne - Longtime Lovett follower
Trench Rabbits
Darby Leighton - Banished Whitehander
Abraham Abe Harms - The mole in Bill's ear, former Richie Lonergan Crew member
Petey Cutpurse Behan - Former Richie Lonergan Crew member
Matty Martin - Former Richie Lonergan Crew member

The Law
Detective William Brosnan - Longtime Irishtown cop
Patrolman Daniel Culkin - Son-in-law of Brosnan, Doirean's husband
Patrolman Ferris - Culkin's partner
Captain Sullivan - Police Captain at Poplar Street Station
Commissioner Enright - New York Police Commissioner

The Black Hand
Sixto The Young Turk Stabile - Owner of The Adonis Social Club, Harvard grad
The Prince of Pals Frankie Yale - Owner of The Harvard Inn, Coney Island
Lucio Lucy Buttacavoli - He of the aquiline nose
Stick'em Jack Stabile - Sixto's father, former owner of The Adonis

The Waterfront Assembly
Jonathan G. Wolcott - President
Amadeusz Wiz the Lump Wisniewski - Muscle
Garry fookin' Barry - Wolcott's chosen leader, former Whitehander

The International Longshoreman's Association
Thomas Quick Thos Carmody - Treasurer, New York
T.V. O'Connor - President
King Joe Ryan - Vice President
Paul Vaccarelli - Vice President

Other Mains
Anna Lonergan - Richie's sister, Mary & John's daughter
Sadie Meehan née Leighton - Mother of John, wife of Dinny, cousin of Darby
Mourning Mother Mary - Mother of fifteen, including Anna & Richie
Ligeia Guida DeSantis - Italian immigrant, fiancé of Darby
Doirean Doe Culkin - Brosnan's daughter, Culkin's wife
Maureen Moe Egan - Former best friend of Doirean Culkin
Grace White - Prostitute at Adonis Social Club
Kit Carroll - Prostitute at Adonis Social Club
Charles Pakenham - Reporter
Father Larkin - Irishtown Priest at St. Ann's Roman Catholic Church
Dead Reilly - Irishtown attorney
The Leech Vandeleurs - Brooklyn landlord
Eleanor Allerton - President ,Woman's Christian Temperance League

*For all other characters, go to back of book

Special Thanks
The Cesario family, the Meehan family, Jade Visos-Ely, Rochelle Deans, T.J. English, OpenX

~***The Hearse Song*** or ***The Worms Crawl In*** was a popular song during World War I, credit unattributable.
~***Dear Ol' Skibberreen*** was written by Patrick Carpenter in *The Irish Singer's Own Book* (1880)
~Lyrics to ***God Save Ireland*** was written by Timothy Daniel Sullivan (1867)
~***Down by the Glenside (The Bold Fenian Men)*** was written by Peadar Kearney (1916)

Divide the Dawn is a work of fiction, though many characters retain original names and monikers. Many scenes are based on historical events. Still, the work is a product of the author's imagination.

artofneed.com

Cover art by Guy Denning (guydenning.org)
Cover design by Martin Beckett (martinbeckettart.com)
Map by Tim Paul (timpaulillustrations.com)

Copyright 2020, Brooklyn, New York
ISBN: 9798622209321
Ebook ASIN: B0848R85PF

Prologue
Eight Becomes Seven, None One

TULLA, IRELAND
Feb. 1908

Down the hilly and slanted fields of childhood I run through the realm of the Otherworld. The great gray mist has brought us the shanachie storyteller, but if I don't get back by dark my Da will massacre me, so he will.

It is here in the fog that the deities and the dead generations relive life's eternal struggles through us. Over the ages their unending battles transform into the mythical and our own difficulties are but mere images of their like. The shanachie is a witness to the past himself, so I know it's true. He told me. The heroic vows, promises and honor pledges, the loyalties and bitter vengeances all become symbols, runes, stories resurrected in us. To be shown again in our day.

Out of breath I scamper through the foggy dusk, though the way home is well-worn into the muscle of my memory. For I am led by a sense of the land and the people before me, you understand. But even so, the wet weighs down my clothes. And the earth sucks at my boots to slow me, but still I must hurry for it's almost dark.

The thick mist had fallen over us two days past and many in the swaths of farms round Tulla fear a great blight again. What else could it mean? But I know it's the Otherworld because the shanachie has come to us! The seer! right here in West Ireland this very day. We know him to be such because the mist is his door, you see. The threshold to crossover into our world to give us what he's seen.

I plummet down the rounded hillocks and in my hurrying I almost run right out of the floppy farm boots. Our family's region has long been here in the lowlands between the Maghera mountain bogs to the north, and the Moylussa peaks in the south where the browned February rushes and ling heather cover the deep peat. But nothing slows me because I have the excitement loaded up inside.

This land, the land of our people was once thick with oak forest and woodlands, but was cleared away by the English. Not only was our virgin timberlands given free to our ancient enemy for their long ships and reconstruction after the great London fire, but the land was cleared to remove the Irish rebels' hideouts too, my own ancestors the woodkerns and descendants of the Fianna. Everything is done for the benefit of the English, my Da says. But he taught myself and Timothy, my older brother, the secrets of our ways. For one, when traveling through the farmlands and the countryside we aught never trek along the roads and boreen lanes. Like the old days we keep to the countryside. It's long in us, the old ways. I suppose that's because things haven't changed much here in seven hundred years.

Along rivulets and rain-dappled lakes where crannog ruins lay listless in the gloaming I run as straight as the crow flies. I hop over the low stonewalls that partition the small acreages to ancient properties that people once bitterly fought over, but have been left empty for generations. When I come to a narrow dirt lane I peer in both directions and cross quickly into the lines of conifers and low hazel trees and the alder and rowan brush. In these parts we were once known for our cider. Although demand has waned, the odd apple tree still slouches forlorn and forgotten. And as I run, a long and silver-colored branch lashes at my face with a lone apple at the end of its reach.

"Hello Mr. Cudmore, Mr. Ryan," I yell out to the two aging countrymen who hadn't seen me canter through the low haze between their farms.

"Helloooo Liam," they offer back, blinded by the graying mist but knowing my shrill voice, even with a mouthful of apple. "Get yerself home bhoy, almost black now. If I know yer father he'll have yer arse in a—"

I continue on as there's no time to answer. Through tussocks of moor grass I can think only on how best to convince Da on my plan of going to see the shanachie. Emerging again from the rushy pastures to a tree line of willow and birch scrub with their drooping winter catkins, I cross another boreen behind Father Daly's carriage that trots along in the ethereal fog without his noticing me.

At Mass Father Daly says the heroes and the dead generations are in heaven above for eternity. But the farmers say they are preserved beneath our feet in the boglands forever. The storytellers though, they assure me that the dead generations of the Otherworld descend in the mist and the storms or even through the portals in the ancient burial grounds. But since it's so often the adults speak of them I am assured at least that the dead watch me. So when I scramble behind Father Daly without his notice I imagine it gives them a chuckle up there. Or down there. Or in there. I'm only seven years old so I'm not really sure where they mingle, but between their souls above or the bodies below or the ghosts in the mist, I can certainly feel their lingering eyes amidst the deep fog. But it makes me want to be a good boy because nothing I do happens that they can't see anyhow. Even through the fog.

Along my way are the Poor Law Roads, or at least that's the local name for them. Rude rock paths strewn aimlessly along sloping cottongrass, left during the Great Hunger. Others call it the road works scheme. Some plan hatched in the comfort of London to put the Irish to work so we didn't get free handouts because we were feckless, the English said. But many died of the famine fever and the elements right there while breaking the stones alongside the rocky roads that trail off mysteriously as if the world had suddenly come to an end. They're odd to me, those patchy stone roads, for the Irish of East Clare never quit on a job until it's finished. And done right.

Finally I come to the scariest part of my journey when I walk between the old brick walls of the disused Tulla Union Workhouse and the soggy banks of Garruragh Lough. On this day I have no time to climb the ten-foot rock walls and stare upon the old haunted, three-storied edifice. So I jog through without hesitation.

A year earlier, the guardians of the dilapidated Workhouse voted to use it as an auxiliary asylum, since both the Tulla and Scariff districts' lunatics were overcrowding their facilities. I myself think it's a silly idea to put lunatics in a house full of ghosts. But no one asks children about that queer plan and I've found it difficult convincing grown ups of anything. Even when its obvious the insane won't feel at home with the unsettled spirits of a starved people.

Some people say they hear the Workhouse itself moan at night, begging us for food. In 1847, back when the potato went black on the vine and the English used the calamity to move us off the land, it was built because the landlords had evicted everyone from the local farms. That's when people lived in scalpeens, if not on the roadsides, starved and choleric. And the children my age were green at the mouth from eating grass, their mothers gaunt and boney.

The Tulla Workhouse was built by the English foreigners. It was called the Soup School at first, to attract all the hungry with the name of it. But it never lived up to that name, no it didn't. And instead it became a place for the people of Tulla to die. My uncle Joseph says there must be two thousand bodies in unmarked graves round the back of the building where you can still see humps in the ground when you look over the rock wall. I even heard Father Daly during his homily quote from the 1901 census that the population of Tulla is still nowhere near what it was before the hunger came.

"Mam," I yell as I run across the fields. "Mam, guess what?"

With my two baby sisters Abby and Brigid forever lingering behind my mother's dress with big, watchful eyes, Mam turns round to see, "Liam! For the love o' god, it's dark. Yer father—"

"Mam, there's a shanachie at the O'Dea farm," I reel off, half out of breath. "I worked with him all day and he's a real storyteller and he knows how to thatch roof with a needle better than Miko, and tomorrow after Mass everyone is going to the O'Dea farm to listen to him, can we go?"

But she just smiles.

In County Clare it did my mother little to no good being the smartest girl in her class. It hadn't even landed her the eldest male in the Garrihy family until my father's older brother suddenly "fell off his trolley," it was said. Which meant he went mad and left my Da and Mam the Garrihy family plot. Before that stroke of bitter luck, they were forced to sub-let a room behind the O'Dea farm. Two sons were born and died there. Sean and Colm were their names, I'm told. But their deaths put my parents in debt paying for proper graves in the old cemetery. Mam never speaks of them, but the boys weigh heavily on her heart because I see her cry when she kneels in front of the candles and prays at St. Mochulla's church on the hill. And everyone says her vibrant eyes had dulled a bit in their memories. Maybe she thinks they watch her all the time, too.

"Liam child," she says, still trying to capture all the words I throw at her. "I don't know if we can go see this storyteller-man. We'll have to ask—"

"Bhoy!" Da yells from the turned field he's tilled with Timothy and uncle Joseph.

But before I run off, my mother gives me a bottle of milk, "Here ye are, give it to the man, yeah?"

I run with the bottle of milk and hand it up to him. Da takes off his cap with the vapor coming out of his mouth in the cold and takes a long pull of the milk right out of the bottle. Timothy and uncle Joseph and I watch and wait, until finally he speaks.

"Why're ye late?" He looks at me through sharp cheekbones, a twisted blackthorn tree looms behind him like a dark shadow over the field.

He stands over me awaiting an answer. I think of lying, but he is a severe man. And it's not just me who says it. Six months prior Dierdre, the farm dog, had become fat with pups. My sisters and I snuck into the barn where she lay during her gestation and gave her extra dinner scraps mixed with milk. Mam warned us not to get too close to the notion of Dierdre's motherhood, but dared not tell us why. When Dierdre gave birth, Abby, Brigid and I watched as she licked her pups clean of the blood, squirming against each other to suckle on her belly. Abby even cradled one that slept trustfully in her arms and gave them names. The next day, Da took Timothy and I to the barn. He put the pups in a sack and walked us to the closest river and had me toss them in like stones.

No, I cannot lie to my father. He would have the truth from me. But that does not stop me from hating him.

When he was my age, Da went by night to burn the landlords' property and maim their cattle; a longstanding tradition in the West. In the times of past they were called Moonlighters and agitated for the right to own their property. Some people called it the Land War, though my father said we'd been fighting for centuries and it was for freedom in general, not just about the land.

Looking up at him I try to start from the beginning, but I feel nervous and it comes out all wrong, "I was talking with Miko O'Dea and, I mean we were working on their thatch roof while we were talking, and he told me—"

"Here by dark is the rule," Da interrupts. "Ye'll give up a week's worth o' yer mother's sweet bread, an' lucky it's only that and not the belt. Now listen here bhoy, we're finally able to buy the farm legally."

"Oh, oh that's good," I say.

"It's a waste o' time," Uncle Joseph bleats from behind like a sullen goat.

Da glances over his shoulder, "I s'pose ye'd think that, seein' as though ye haven't farm nor family."

Uncle Joseph is a thin and spindly man with a slope in his shoulders and a large bald spot for a man in his early thirties. Though small of stature, he is bitter of tongue, and my father has often been summoned to the local pub late of a Saturday evening to quell a drunken quarrel his younger sibling had inspired. But Da is strangely tolerant with his brother's sour talk of late, ever since the announcement of my uncle Joseph's intentions to emigrate to New York. They are building a new bridge there, the Manhattan Bridge it's to be called, and it's cheap Irish labor they need. These are to be the last days we would see uncle Joseph, though we secretly count them with endurance.

"I'm just like Liam there," Uncle Joseph says, standing some three inches shorter than my father. "Born the youngest son and without land. Not our fault, is it Liam?"

"I, well—"

"Liam bhoy," Da says. "We'll be headed to the Maghera bogs to pull the peat and sell it every Sunday. It's been generations we've fought for the right to buy our land, and the day has come. But it's the money we need now. We start tomorrow morn."

"Start tomorrow?" I say, almost in tears.

"Yes," Da turns back toward the house with Timothy on his heels.

"I want to listen to the shanachie at the O'Dea farm tomorrow," I blurt out with all the courage I own.

"A shanachie?" Timothy turns round. "Who said he was a shanachie? He's just an itinerant laborer. Pavee traveller, more like."

I want to tell my brother to shut his gob and to stop tripping over Da's heels, but I just grit at him and tell the truth of it, "Miko says the man is a true storyteller—"

"Miko is twelve years-old," Timothy says.

"That's four years older than yourself."

Uncle Joseph cuts in, "We got better things to do than sit round an' listen to stories about sham heroes, ghosts an' lost rebellions. Why dwell on the histories?"

"If the past is as unknown as the future, it is alive, and therefore volatile," says I.

My uncle's face pinches, "Where'd ye hear that one?"

"The shanachie told me to say it if someone asked, and then you asked, so I said it. Da!" I yell at my father's back. "The Brennans'll be there. So too the Leddy's. Both the Halloran's *and* the O'Halloran's. The Cudmore's, Ryan's and even the McNamara's and the Neylan's. And what would it say about us if the Garrihy family doesn't show?"

But Da doesn't answer and continues walking away from me.

"Maybe we could celebrate for owning the farm?" I yell in desperation.

"T'is a fool who celebrates bein' given what is rightfully his," he calls back without even a glance.

I stand in the turned field as they pull the horse plough toward the barn in the dark, my uncle and brother shaking their heads at me.

"Liam child," My mother calls out. "Dinner is ready, come help set the table."

"I won't eat tonight," says I, then look away in shame, stomping toward her. "But I'll help set the table, of course."

"Ye understand that the Land War has lasted in East Clare longer than in other parts? Men died in the unrest so that we could own our own land one day."

"I know Mam, I know," I answer as my eyes flood, doubling my vision.

"Oh with the tears runnin' down the apple cheeks on ye," she wipes them away and runs her fingers through the hair over my ears. "Ye'd have us all at the O'Dea farm just fer stories, ye would? I don't blame ye fer thinkin' about the world beyond, Liam. In this far-flung place? But ye have to try and remember that it's yer home and yer family who cares most about ye. We'll always defend ye, Liam. Yer father has always been there fer ye. Always fought to have a better life than what he's had, which includes the upkeep o' this property to make a stable home fer us. Are there any other families that'd do that fer ye? Do ye think o' that?"

"I understand, Mam. But. . . Maybe if I promise to work double hard next weekend, then I can go by myself tomorrow?"

"Double hard is it?" she chuckles. "Ye know Liam, ye already worked hard. Mendin' the roof o' the O'Dea's today. An' what did ye get fer it? Why not ask Miko if he'll come with ye next Sunday in return fer lettin' us go tomorrow?"

"That's a great idea, Mam. I'll go tell Da now—"

She grabs hold of my arm, "It's better heard from myself than a child, such a request is. I'll speak to the man, ye'll go an' set the table as I asked."

I hug my mother at her waste, "You're the best Mam that ever was, Mam. I love you so much."

~~~

The smartest thing about Mam is that she never takes credit for being smart. In fact she's always the first to blame herself for things. With that, my father believes all emanates from his own thoughts. And so, it was his idea from the start that we should all go to listen to the storyteller and have Miko O'Dea bring his slain tool and come with us next weekend to pull the peat in the bogs.

I know it's not right, but I love Mam more than Da. But it's no secret that I favor her because Timothy calls me "Da's eldest daughter" and Miko O'Dea says I'll make a lovely bride one day.

As I bend to sit on the wood floor in the front row I notice a strange man who warms me with the look of him. The peat fire bathes the old fellow in an amber glow from behind and a smile forms across his face when he notices me stare at him.

"Who is that?" I whisper to Miko.

"That's the shanachie, Liam. Are ye so shattered from work that ye can't recognize him? That's the auld wan we worked with all day, t'is."

"The itinerant man?" I say incredulously. "He looks different now."

"Aye," says Miko. "Now he's the shtoryteller."

I turn to the man, "Are you a druid here to interpret the mist? Or are you a god from the Otherworld?"

I hear Mam's laugh behind me, but the old man storyteller hadn't heard me. I look on him again as he leans forward in the rocking chair, his eyes alight with the happiness of many children at his feet awaiting tales. A man's eyes says loads about him, Da says. And even as the shanachie's face droops and he appears sad and old, his eyes are as bright and hopeful as a young child's, even as they are half-covered by a wild patch of bushy brows. But atop his head is a tangle of white hair in the shape of crown and in the slow gesture and thoughtful glance on him I recognize both great wisdom and a mischievous guile.

"Ah well," the old man's voice fills the room to silence his listeners' bantering, while his mouth is all smiles. "I'm not much fer the newspapers, but these days all the talk in Dublin-town is of the un-veil-ing at Leinster House of the statue erected in remembrance of their Jackeen queen, Victoria."

When he draws out the word 'un-veil-ing,' we all snigger because he says it in the smug accent of the lordly English. His big knuckley hands and growly sandpaper voice intimidates the wee children, but his jowly smile is the heart of him.

"Maybe it's in Dublin they use words to describe such a thing as un-veil-ing, but out here in the West we've a way o' gettin' straight at the truth of it. And so we've always called the auld woman exactly what she was, 'The Famine Queen'."

Even Da allows himself a smirk at that crack as he stands like a sentinel among the other impassive men in the back of the room with pints of pure in their fists. Timothy wants to stand with the men too, but my uncle Joseph shoos him off, then puts a hole in his stout quicker than all and summons a second before yet even the story's begun.

Only Mam understands the magic in the storyteller's voice. With Miko in front, I look back at her and as always she's right there with the winking eye and the big proud smile as my baby sisters Abby and Brigid sit on her lap with owl eyes.

"Oh and it's the ways of us that make ye wonder, to be sure," he rocks in the chair and throws out his arms. "In the auld days our laws came from within us. From the bottom. Risin' up from us, all judgements were made accordin' to the culture. The outsiders though, they believe that everythin' important comes from their aristocracy at the top an' decisions should be disbursed at their whim an' fancy," he laughs a sad laugh. "When honor clashes against power, power always wins, which in turn immortalizes honor. Yet they say we're a beaten people. If that's so then why is our music so happy? If we are to be hated as the outsiders claim, why are we loved everywhere? If we lose all rebellions, why do we still hope for freedom? An' if we truly are beaten, hated and hopeless, why do we elevate our heroes to such great heights? Brian Boru, Finn MacCool and his son Oisin an' Niamh, Cú Chulainn, Wolfe Tone, Emmet and more. Every generation has a hero one part man an' another still myth. Even as he is begrudged durin' his lifetime, showered with treachery, abused by the lust fer power, menaced by cruel cunning while outsiders are invited to break his body. It has been this way since the stone age, it has," he lowers his voice and one eye too. "An' still today it plays out like a theatre show with many characters who must play their roles."

He laughs again, the old fellow, and rocks back and forth before the crackling fire, "But what is a hero, really? An Irish hero? In the old tongue, he was known as the *laoch* who comes to care for them what need it most, summoned by seers known as *Sean Dream* it's said; the Old Folk. But who is the hero to us? An' why must we always summon him like an apparition in our time o' greatest need?"

Myself and the other children think on these questions with an urgency in us, but we're just children and we want to learn the things, not to answer them.

"Oh it reminds me o' a ghost story!" The words roll off his tongue and quickly he sits high in his rocker.

The fire moils and churns. The shadows shimmer. The children look at each other with bright eyes and mouths gone small. And here I am about to take flight in the story and I can barely hold my breath. In fact, I can't breathe at all until I burst out, "What's the name of it?"

"The what, child?" The old fellow asks, but I'm ashamed now, so Miko speaks for me.

"The name o' the ghoshtory, he's arskin' ye."

"Ah the ghost story? Yes, yes, well, it's had many names over the years. Some call it, *A Song to Divide the Dawn*, but I always preferred *The Keenin' Croon an' the Risin' o' the Moon*. But let me assure o' one thing, child. Every myth, every aged lore is no more than a fool's mur-

murin's if they do not contain elements o' great truths. A great story exists in a time before even time existed."

Oh but I can't help but be carried away by the manner in which the shanachie speaks. The charm of him! The one-lowered eye and the voice that moves in a singsong pattern, up and down in levels like open-winged birds dip and rise with the sea winds.

He looks round the room menacingly into each and everyone of our eyes and gently begins, "Those who survive are chosen, and so *we* are a chosen people. Some say we were chosen to suffer. But whatever the case, we've proven that we can flourish under the greatest duress an' the worst o' troubles an' tragedies. We are survivors, but we don't just survive alone. We have survived because o' our communion an' fellowship. An' it's been proven over hundreds o' years that no one can suffer as beautifully as the Irish."

A round of laughs comes from the parents behind, while we children listen intently.

"Monsters!" He suddenly yells, the kindness of him disappeared, his eyes affixed upon the rafters and the shadows of the dancing flames above. "They come to turn us. To turn our souls too so that a shadow falls over our hearts. To turn our people against each other so that we can never trust again. The honor corrupted."

"Monsters," his voice drops low into a gloomy sadness. "The labors o' their trade are but rape, war, theft an'. . . starvation. But turnin' us into them is their evil dream, ye hear it? An' fer those who refuse? They move us off the land. Banish us to the westernmost island. But fer the monsters, this far-flung island is not far-flung enough fer our like. So they send us into the sea! Yet still we endure. But how?" He pleads. "How is it possible fer a people to've survived centuries o' invasion an' attack? It is impossible! Improbable! If t'were a story, not a single listener would believe it. How is it possible that we are still here an' with the love in our hearts?"

We children look at each other, but we know by now he isn't asking us to answer his questions.

"Because love saves the soul. Where there is no hope. . . then an' only then does the heart sing the song. We may forever an' always lose, yes, yes, but forever an' always we must fight. T'is a song, as I've said," he sweeps his smiling eyes along the line of children. "A bygone song that is long in the Irish. We look to hear it, so we do. Because there is no thing so egregiously beautiful as a glim of light in the envelopin' darkness. Twinklin' like a distant song in the beleaguered soul. An' in the depths o' us there is the ancient prayer; fertile hope springs from despair."

The shanachie bows his head and wipes away a raw tear with a sandpaper, calloused palm. I stand among the whole crowd to comfort him, but Miko places a hand on my shoulder, "He knows what he's doin', Liam. Shtay put."

In his gloom the shanachie manages these words, "T'is but the dream o' a hero in that song an' in that dyin' light. A hero who appears throughout our history. He may have different names but the hero is there when we need him, risin' like the moon. Yes, the moon. Before St. Patrick brought us his faith, t'was to the harvest moon an' the trees we prayed, an' a portent to the hero's comin'.

And the old fellow turns his sea-green eyes down to me and gives only but the slightest smiling nod. His voice croaks out in a low and despairing calm, "When the great hunger came, so did the monsters. Again. Slinkin' back through the black, laughin' shrill with rotted teeth corrupted from the defilement o' their souls within. They let us starve, they did. Howlin' and snappin' amongst each other at what they called a great opportunity. An' how can starvation equal a great opportunity, ye ask? Change, they crowed to us. Change or starve an' begone. *That* is the great opportunity monsters exult in. Fer when the mist rolled down from the hills an' smelled o' death, t'was the mornin' moon what stared from above knowin'ly like the evil eye. An' we knew that our greatest tragedy was now begun. Yes, the mornin' moon! The aura o' the past felt to be within our grasp an' endlessly repeatin' itself in the now.

"I was but a teen. The eldest male in me fam'ly. T'was on a cold night that the black mist rolled down through the Moylussa mountains an' the Maghera bogs into the lowland villages an' farms o' Tulla an' East Clare. T'was the smell o' death came in that mist. Some in Tulla immediately knew the horror to come an' keened on the spot where they stood. An' some walked all the way to the coast to fling themselves from the Cliffs o' Moher, so they did, for they had not the heart to fight the monsters. The next mornin' when the mist finally cleared, there t'was!" He points toward the ceiling and stares into the distance. I look up too, but only see the rafters.

"The mornin' moon! Starin' from above knowin'ly, the evil eye lookin' down through the barren trees. That was when they appeared, the monsters did. There were so many o' them those days, but not-a-one was more deceitful in his approach, devilish in his comparin' the blight to divine providence, no one more fraudulent in his assistance nor as cold in his reliance on the aristocracy's whim an' fancy; he was Charles Trevelyan, the Famine Queen's henchman."

At the sound of that terrible name, a name we all know from stories of that time, the younger children begin to cry round me. And so the mothers look upon the storyteller with anger. Though the fathers are unfazed as they drink the dark stuff and mumble to each other in the back. I don't care about being scared though because I want the truth of it. I want to know of the past so I can see the future, like the shanachie.

The old fellow speaks, "They came in packs with official uniforms an' signed papers an' drove us from our homes. They burnt the thatch roofs an' pulled down the walls to send us to the roads, starved. We had no shoes upon our feet an' no more than patched wool over our shoulders. Weakened we became, until the roamin' dogs licked their salivatin' grins at the sight of us."

His face twists in anger and with a bent finger he points toward the northeast, "We waited with the masses outside the Tulla Workhouse, so we did. Hundreds of us as day turned to night, night to day, until we swelled to thousands! All with the same names your neighbors carry today, an' many others whose surnames died off forever. The state of us was a wretched sight, fer t'was disease that killed the most. Children's eyes gone white with blindness, groups o' boney figures with blackleg, the stench o' putrifyin' flesh was overwhelmin', an' then there was the typhus an' the dysentery. Some o' the people's limbs would swell so horribly that they would burst. Entire fam'lies with smallpox an' the famine fever. Every night outside the gates we rattled an' moaned an' the aged would fail to wake from sleep. Babies too, an' children. The weakest of us leanin' up against the Workhouse wall only to stare into nowhere. The look o' hunger on our faces; an indictment o' Trevelyan's policy on its own. Then rumors came to me fam'ly's ears that the soup the monsters offered inside would either kill ye, or worse; that if ye drank it, ye would lose the faith forever, an' in its place ye'd be left with the soul o' the monster," he hisses and stares with bulged eyes. "When we looked over the wall an' saw they were burying our people in shallow graves behind the Workhouse, we knew it to be true.

"We had no choice. Me mother an' father an' me three sisters an' a younger brother, we left the gates o' the Workhouse grounds. Ye must know, it meant certain death. There was nowhere to go, so we dug a scalpeen in the earth along a hillside, the whole fam'ly o' us. We were to die there, though that went unsaid. But then it came. . . A storm! At dawn when the veil between life an' death is thinnest an' the powers o' darkness an' blight are in the ascent, our only hope bein' the old proverb; from whence death is wrought, life is due. A paltry prayer, to be sure. But how could it be that we deserved this? Starved, we had no food an' at the moment the monsters had beaten us, the freezin' cold an' snow comes to finish us off? Why, by god? Are we cursed?"

Indignantly, I yell out to him, "But you said we were chosen. Why ask if we're cursed then?"

My mother bursts out in laughter until the other mothers hush her with taps to her crossed knee.

"Fertile hope springs from despair," he reminds with a chuckle. "But the snow was everywhere. Taller than I was. T'was 1847, the year the song would come to my ear. The wind whistled cruelly an' the snow came down for weeks on end. Me father had fed us any scraps we came across, an' so he was the first to die. That was when me mother began to sing. She sang over our father's body as I watched. She had us clear a path o' snow from the entrance o' our scalpeen an' I helped her drag me father's body out by his shoeless feet. Then, on a frozen night, we saw what comes o' the storm; visitors came a-rappin' on our hovel. They were one o' us an' had our tongue. Surely they were not my enemy, an' so I begged alms. But they must have changed at dawn's storm, fer they had turned. Their eyes were mere holes o' black an' the bones in their shoulders poked through their rags an' when they spoke, the blood spilled from their mouths an' the sores on their faces leaked."

"Monsters!" The children yell fearfully.

"They had made their minds. In all our hearts there is the eternal struggle to decide, fer we are fixed in that constant position o' change between right an' wrong, an' between the remembrance o' night an' the unknown day. The contradictions pull at our souls. These visitors chose the lyin' life against a truthful death, can ye blame them? Can ye?" The old man is at the edge of his rocker now, searching for our eyes until he sits back, defeated. "Well they knew we wouldn't turn by the honor in our eye. So they took our last morsels, the only rags we had to cover our bodies, an' the sod we had pulled for a turf fire, as well as our blankets. They took it all. Me sisters an' younger brother died within a couple days, an' so me mother sang. She keened the auld way. So heartfelt, t'was! So powerful! She sang by night. An' she sang by day. T'was a song so strong, it had the strength to divide the dawn!"

My fists are balled up and Miko has the look of fear in him as we both turn back to our own mothers.

"In her dyin' breath, she held me. Summonin' that last bit o' strength she had, she produced one last song. As she sung I was taken away by a fascination that I had never seen or recounted in this world. I could hear somethin' in that song that I hadn't before. An' fer good reason. T'was not me mother who was dyin'. . . T'was me! An' this was the prophecy, so listen as ye must an' ye may see. Listen close an' listen well, fer within these words is the true story to tell," he looks above with the words falling from his mouth as if a spirit had overtaken him:

DIVIDE THE DAWN

T'is dawn,
When the darkness o' the past
An' the light o' the future clash,
Dividin' them in the amber flash o' song,
Where death gives life to the seein',
A hero is born to provide our well-bein'.

Summoned from a dead heaven,
In their calumnies,
Five archons make him known as the demiurgic son,
An' come together with his three orphans,
Until eight becomes seven,
An' none becomes one.

But just as they create him,
So too do they destroy him.
For t'is at dawn
that this keenin' song's
Lonely croon lifts our hero,
Like the risin' o' the moon.
An' so the people o' Irish towns everywhere chant aloud,
'My soul is pure, a cloud in a mountain shroud.'

And then the itinerant shanachie stands from his chair as we children gape at him. In a trance he walks through us, and we struggle to make a path for him. Then he walks through the mothers and finally past the fathers, all of us watching in awe.

"But what does all of that mean?" I yell to the man as he opens the door to the whining wind. "Why are there five archons, and why are there three orphans? And how do they lift the hero?"

"I have already told ye child, ask yerself. . . 'What *is* an Irish hero?'"

"But why don't you just tell us?"

He stops and looks through a mesh of gray eyebrows, "O' the five archons I can say that they have always represented our enemies. But when the souls o' our people turn, it is ourselves who become the enemy. An' of the three orphans ye ask? O' the three orphans I say that one will beatify him. . . One will betray him. . . An' one will become him."

"Is that why eight turns to seven, because one becomes him?"

"No," he turns his face back to the crowd and lowers an eye to me, "Garrihy is yer name, is it not?"

"It is," says I.

"Ye," he smiles. "It's ye who must see with the inner eye of an auld man havin' the gift o' vision. An' seein' as ye can the age-old struggle to survive in this ever-changin' darkness to day, ye must find the five an' the three, fer ye are the witness of a *laoch* an' will one day be a man to open the door fer many. An' on yer journey to find, ye must also resist. They will demand ye to change. They will even change yer surname. But the anchor o' honor is weighted heavily in ye, child."

"But how did you survive when your mother sang for you? When so many others didn't?"

"Meself?" The itinerant man lifts the hood of his cloak over his head, but no shame blots his face. "How much o' ye can truly survive after such a tragedy? Survive? I did not."

He slowly closes the door behind him, which was immediately opened again by my uncle Joseph who berates the old man for scaring the wits out of the children. But he is yelling into mere air, he is. For outside the door there is no one at all, at all.

We rush outside to look for him and find that the great mist had broken and the giant night sky was again starry and alive.

"I told you all and none of you would listen!" I scream through the black fields. "He comes with the magic mist and goes when it lifts."

Man, woman and child search for him, but gone, is he. To time and memory. Never to be seen again.

The Veil

BROOKLYN, NEW YORK
Feb. 1919

Dawn, and three of us appear gently as if from a blank past. Out of the night we come to the corner at Nevins Street and look down Warren Street to the long bed of snow, white, thigh-high and unblemished.

"Liam? Do ya think Mickey came here?" Thomas Burke whispers.

"Maybe," I mumble, then look to Harry Reynolds. "Let's just fix the window and get out of here."

The storm that thrashed New York the past five days had finally wearied. Heavy snow had come slanting down in a driving wind to turn Brooklyn a heavenly hue. But at this hour the city has not begun to dig itself out. Even the trolley rails remain buried, and the street cleaners have yet to show.

Like the Great Blizzard of 1888 it was, so the newspapers report. Many of the ramshackle, pre-Civil War buildings had collapsed under the weight of snow and the pressing wind with children and the aged trapped inside. Whole families falling prey to a homeless night in the frenzied storm. The recent coal shortage means if they don't tumble down in their tenements, then they'd freeze inside them. In

Green-Wood Cemetery a hundred trees have been felled and the police have confirmed thirty-seven dead so far.

Mickey Kane can be added to that number. Though many say he is but missing. The wise among us, however, know that he is not only dead, but that it was no accident.

"Stay behind," Harry says with a glance round the corner.

In the distance there is an echo of words, but they are hard to hear.

Are we being watched? I wonder.

I can feel someone. Something. Up in the windows or on the roof. In the sky. Yet no one is there. No one.

Then why do I feel I am being watched?

"They let us starve," the echo simply says. "They let us starve."

It must be my own thoughts that I hear, I realize. *I have heard those words many times before.*

I had lived on this block for three years with Dinny and Sadie Meehan, but it had never been this quiet. Here, now, a cool peace floats after the storm like a child who naps deeply after a great and teary-eyed tantrum. But I know, we three know, the quiet will not last. I can see it in Harry's eyes and smell it in Burke's fear.

Holding the rough wet brick wall for balance, the icy snow crunches under-boot and hugs at my legs. I take a deep breath and find Harry's eyes for a moment, then to the untouched, bright white morning snow between the buildings. The row houses and brownstones stand wet in the air above with little whitecaps atop the metal handrails and doorknobs and cornices. And the bare ivy vines that snake along the brick facades are coiled with frost and look like white slithering bones strung up on the walls in some strange message. As a wedge of whiskey-colored light sneaks through the buildings at our left shoulders, the three of us look on the scenery with foreboding.

"I don' see nobody," Burke whispers again, then exhales and looks to his own breath as if to assure himself that he truly is alive. "We should go back."

Harry's mouth twitches and his head slightly turns to the side to hear. He is a stern man of twenty-seven years and few words. I should know, he has been my mentor ever since my last mentor, Tommy Tuohey was murdered.

Though Harry has the countenance of etched stone, I know that his curiosity is piqued. He should not be here, Harry shouldn't. Of all places Harry should be, the Meehan brownstone while Dinny is incarcerated is the very last. If I know this, Harry certainly knows that his presence here and now means he will assuredly endure Dinny Meehan's swift consequences. If ever Dinny is released, that is.

Between Dinny and Harry there is a mystery. No one will tell me the real story. And I've asked. Though I have heard tell of something bad that Harry did in the year 1913. That was when Dinny was last manacled by Detective Brosnan in the streets and jailed, until recently.

Although he is here to help the Meehans in their time of need, somewhere else in Harry's mind there is a curiosity long buried in him. I can see it in his eyes. In coming here for the first time since his treachery, while again Dinny Meehan is jailed, Harry Reynolds has dared step out of his years-long servitude.

A cool, gentle wind gathers and softly sucks a lace curtain out of the broken window in the Meehan brownstone on the third floor.

"We should go back," Burke whispers again. "No one's been around here. Anybody wit' a mothball o' sense could see that if we leave, everyone'll be better off."

Harry's eyes narrow without regarding Burke's pleas. I believe he senses something too. Though he is not quite able make out what it is. Normally the chaos of the waterfront rings in our ears. Even from this distance between Nevins and Bond streets. But now the quiet reigns. It's as if we had fallen asleep during a cacophony of sound and suddenly awakened because it stops.

The Meehan room upstairs is empty. Sadie is safe in hiding now. Before the storm, with Dinny in jail and his enemies harassing her, Sadie and their son L'il Dinny were forced to run. They came to me on Eighth Avenue for help. And when their wide, hopeful eyes swung up to mine, I was honored they'd called on me. So I sent them to Long Island where they'd never be found. As luck would have it, they fled just in time. When the snow endlessly fell amidst the lashing wind to spring death out of winter's biting breath, Dinny's cousin Mickey Kane had disappeared. And Wild Bill Lovett, returned from the Great War where we were all told he'd been killed, had swept down on us in much the same way.

If Harry spoke more he would say it's a fool's fancy to believe in coincidence. Back in 1917 when Dinny quashed Bill's revolt, he replaced him with Mickey as the dockboss of the highly profitable Red Hook territory. Now Bill has come with the driving snow as Mickey has gone. Rolling down in it to take Red Hook back by storm.

No, Mickey Kane is not disappeared. And this spectral stillness we sense is merely the peace before another storm, the gang war. Worse yet, since Bill took the life of Dinny's kin, a primal, old-world call can be summoned. Dinny may in fact declare a Blood Feud now. And from there, one of them must die.

"Harry?" Burke says. "Let's go home. Jesus on the cross, Harry. We should go before somethin' happens."

Harry says no word. But across the whitened street I see Boru. The old draught horse waves his long face out of Mr. Campbell's stable door with smoke tumbling from his nostrils. The light of life appears anew in me, and like a boy again, I run.

"Liam," Burke calls to me.

I high-knee it through the snow, holding the Frommer M.12 pistol inside my right pocket, a lead pipe stitched inside of my coat.

"There you are ol' bhoy," I say to Boru, who whickers at my approach.

He seems both sad and happy to see me. His eyes look away, then back into mine. They are distant and detached, yet emotional.

I wish his mouth knew how to smile, I think.

But he puffs and stamps in place, then smells the back of my hand for food and the memory of my scent with his big, dry nostrils that grab at the air.

"I knew you'd remember me," I pet his face and run his whiskers through my palm and notice his mouth again, wise and slightly downturned.

"I love you Boru," I tell him with the whole of my heart out.

Across the street I point at the Meehan brownstone and ask him, "What have you seen, bhoy? Tell me what you've seen. Has anybody come by Dinny and Sadie's room lately? Yeah?"

A man's voice reverberates off the buildings, "Nobody's been over there in the last few days. Not since the storm."

I search above for the voice, but Harry comes up from behind me with Burke and has already spotted Mr. Campbell who peers down from a window adjacent the steeple of the stable house. He has a blanket over his head like an old monk.

"Dinny can't help us no more, can he?" Mr. Campbell asks, but we don't answer him on that.

Mr. Campbell then looks down to Boru, "The horse. I've had to spread his feed out over the last few weeks. Help a man feed his horse? Can yaz? Maybe a few dollars for myself? There's no food here an' the coal shortage has kept the pot-belly stove barren an' the fireplace dark. It's colder than Trevelyan's heart in here."

Two more heads pop out of windows above when they hear Mr. Campbell, and even more across the street. As Boru rests his long face on my shoulder, I wrap my arm back round his ears and kiss close to one of his faraway eyes.

"You hungry?" I ask him. "You are, aren't you?"

Harry digs into his wallet. He takes out a few bills, reaches over the half-open stable door and slips them into Boru's headstall. Mr. Campbell quickly ducks under the window and disappears. The sound of descending footsteps ring through the wood-framed tenement until he reappears at Boru's flank.

He steps into the breaking light and says, "We're goin' hungry. Dinny's been gone awhile now. He gettin' out o' what? There's rumors that—"

The words freeze in Mr. Campbell's throat when he sees what Harry has spotted.

Across the way, toward the corner of Bond and Warren streets three men stand and glare at us. One holds a gas can. For a moment we stare at each other, the three of them and the three of us as Mr. Campbell slips away. The silence is only broken by the rhythmic nickers deep in Boru's throat.

The man who holds the gas can is a giant with thinning hair, thick shoulders and a broad forehead. The one next to him has a face so disfigured that it seems to have been torn in two and sewn back together. When I catch the eyes of that one, a shutter runs up through my spine.

I know those eyes, I realize.

Even from across the street and through the inflamed and festering scar, I recognize him. On the night of the explosions on Black Tom's Island those eyes appeared out of some dark, wretched hole. An assassin with a knife and Dinny Meehan in his sights. He had failed, like all those who've tried to kill Dinny. But the disconnect in those brutal eyes had reminded of something deep and terrible inside myself.

"Who are they?" Burke's words break the cool silence. "I don' wanna kill nobody."

I hear a click at the end of Harry's extended arm that holds the ten-round .32 pocket pistol. From Harry's queue I pull out the M.12 and hold it at my thigh threateningly as they stand one building away from the Meehan brownstone.

Between them and us is the stone-white snow ablaze in a bright tremor under the new sun. As if the morning sighs, a delicate breeze moves among us. When it touches my face, I hear the three men mumble amongst each other without breaking focus on us.

"Don' do it Harry," Burke says.

The scarred man yells toward us in a nasally voice, his eyes inert and sullen, "Eighth Avenue!"

The giant looks to his comrade and says something we cannot hear.

"Shaddup," the scarred man mumbles at the giant, then yells back toward us. "Liam, Burke. Yay live on Eighth Avenue. When I kill Dinny Meehan an' take—"

A gunshot rings out. I duck instinctively and Boru bucks and whines in fear. Across the street the giant and the third fellow pick up the man with the disfigured face who had taken a bullet in the shoulder. Harry wades through the snow toward them, his weapon smoking and pointed. I follow as Burke cowers by the drifts.

"Ya can't kill me!" The man declares. "I am Garret Barry! Yaz cannot kill the destined one. I am your leader! Garret Barry! Garret Barry!"

The giant takes Barry over his shoulder, drops the gas can and quickly strides through the snow back from where they had come up Bond Street. The third man takes cover and follows in a crouch until all three disappear round the corner.

"They're gone," Burke concludes quickly.

"Stay behind," Harry rounds the corner onto Bond Street with his pistol lowered until he lands in a squatting position with his back against the side of a stairwell. "C'-mon Liam."

"They must be Bill Lovett's," Burke says.

"I know the big man," I say, as Harry looks at me. "I met him once. At the New York Dock Company when I went there with Dinny. He was in Wolcott's office. I remember the man because he's so big. A Polish fellow, is he."

Harry nods and looks round the corner again, "Wisniewski's his name. Amadeusz Wisniewski. Garry fookin' Barry's the one who caught the bullet and the last guy's James Cleary, Barry's lone crony."

"I thought Garry Barry was dead," Burke pulls down nervously with both hands behind his head like a petulant child not wanting to hear any more words. "He was dead, right? The Swede an' Big Dick Morissey killt him wit' Dance Gillen, from what was said, at least. That's what I heard."

"I heard that too, but he don' seem dead," Harry says.

"Jesus on the cross," Burke sits in the snow behind the stairwell, mouth open. "He knows where my fam'ly lives.

He called it out to us. Liam? He knows where we live. He called it out to threaten us. To threaten your mother an' sisters an' my fam'ly. Eighth Avenue, he said. Ya heard him."

"I heard him," I say.

"He's going there now," Burke stands up.

"Get down," Harry grits his teeth and pulls him by a sleeve. "He's not gonna go there now."

"How do you know that?"

"I know," Harry stares at him, then peeks over the stoops to make sure they've gone.

"Ya think they're dead, but then they show up," Burke mumbles to himself, then peers up to Harry. "These guys, they work wit' Lovett now?"

"Nah."

"Well who are they wit' if they ain't wit' us or Lovett?"

Harry looks away distressed in hopes Burke will end his blathering.

Half-tilted in the snow by the sprays of Barry's blood, a gas can comes into focus.

"Were. . . Were they here to burn down the Meehan home?"

"Seems that way," I say.

"But, I don' understand," Burke squats again with his back to the stairwell. "If they don' work for Lovett, what are they doin'? What does it mean?"

"It's not supposed to mean anythin', it's just supposed to be what it is," Harry says.

"This is gettin' to me," Burke shakes his hands and scratches at his neck with nails. "Maybe Mickey Kane will come back? Maybe?"

"Burke," I growl, but I don't know what to say next other than, "You're getting on my wick. Mickey's dead, alright?"

"So was Bill," Burke pleads. "So was Garry fookin' Barry."

Harry leans down and grabs Burke by the neck with his left hand, "I'm tellin' ya to shaddup right fookin' now. Don' talk no more. Ya never saw Lovett dead. Or Barry. So ya don' know if they ever really were dead, got it?"

Harry let's him drop, but Burke looks into the distance and whispers to himself, "I never saw Mickey dead either." Then to me he speaks, "I'm not in it for this, Liam. I just wanna work. I got fam'ly, I don' need this shit. I gotta son wit' the palsy an' I'm out here doin' this shit wit' guns? Ya know what happens if I die? They'll separate my wife from the kids an' put them all in the poorhouse. That's what they do when people can't pay rent an' go homeless. I didn't want any o' this. I don't wanna die. I can't die."

"Dinny will be there to help you and your family," I say.

"Dinny's in jail," Burke implores.

"I'll be there for them then. If you die, I'll adopt your son Joseph and take care of him. I'll take care of all the kids, I'll be eighteen soon."

Burke gives a fearful smile in my direction then looks to Harry, "For months I came for the shape-up at the Atlantic Terminal an' ya never once chose me."

"Ya're too small an' scrawny. Ya're a fookin' sniper's nightmare," Harry says. "We didn't know ya then... an' ya had scared eyes."

"It wasn't until I got lucky and Liam moved upstairs that I could get regular work."

"We brought ya in because we wanted to help ya fam'ly an' ya son Joseph 'cause we knew no one else would," Harry says. "When ya accepted work wit' us, ya knew that it meant bein' a soldier, not just a laborer. Now the time has come to defend our hold an' ya say ya never got into it for this?" Harry shakes his head. "Why's it always the desperate that turns into the coward?"

"I'm scared o' everyone," Burke looks at Harry with big eyes. "I'm scared o' everyone."

Harry drags Burke by the back of his coat toward Warren Street, "I told ya to stop talkin'. I don' want ya to go home wit' a broken face, but I'll do it if ya keep talkin'."

"Hitting him isn't going to make things better," I yell at Harry.

Harry quickly turns to me, "Either is gratifyin' his fears. We need to be ready. Do ya understand what's happened? Do ya? Mickey was the future for us. Bill knew that."

"I know," I say defensively.

"Now this?" Harry broods and points toward Bond Street in the direction where Garry Barry and the others had disappeared.

Burke and I don't have an answer for him.

In response, he gathers himself, stands upright and pockets the pistol. As a matter of duty, he pushes through the snow and stands in the middle of Warren Street. He then raises his handsome face and yells into the watching windows, "All o' ya that saw what happened here this morning, remember who we are," the voice echoes off the tenements in a mournful, yet confident resonance. "We are the White Hand. The hand what feeds yaz. If the tunics come here askin' questions about what happened, do not bite us. Ya give them silence, but if they ask who was here an' why there is blood, ya tell them it was Patrick Kelly did this. We're all Patrick Kelly, remember it. . . Clouts for touts, the old way."

Out his window Mr. Campbell nods in harmony with Harry's words, knowing very well our codes and that the name Patrick Kelly stands for all of us, and none of us. The only name anyone in Irishtown ever gives the police.

Harry then pushes toward the Meehan brownstone and leaves Burke by the abandoned gas can in the snow.

Above I look closely at the broken window in the Meehan brownstone. The reason we came here in the first place.

"Come on," I say to Burke, who sits dumbly in the snow.

I make him stand-watch at the bottom of the stairwell inside the brownstone where it is warmer, but I don't dare give him the M.12.

"Just yell if you see anybody," I tell him over a shoulder as I walk up to the third floor in the darkness with Harry. We leave him on the third step as he stares into the window light amidst the shimmer of dust, slump-shouldered.

I had climbed these stairs many times while living with the Meehans, but never had I walked up them with Harry Reynolds. Oddly, he too had lived with them here once.

Years before I had, the first of the three orphans Dinny and Sadie took in, raised and trained to become loyal gang members. I was the last, the homeless immigrant whose name was changed at Ellis Island from Garrihy to Garrity. Now we walk up them together as if brothers.

I still have the key and when the door swings open a flood of memories rush through me. Everything in the room seems shrunken, though it's me who has gotten bigger. My boots clop on the wood floor and the round carpet. The same round carpet where L'il Dinny looked up at me for the first time on Christmas Eve, 1915. He was only two years old then.

Inside, the fireplace is empty and hanging within it is the pot where Sadie used to make her soups that warmed me and brought me back from a great hunger and weeks of homelessness after my uncle Joseph put me out to the street in a drunken rage. I peer into the kitchen where Sadie cut my hair just days after I was beaten by Petey Behan, my nose all lamped up and the scar that slices through my left eyebrow to this very day was red and gleaming and open under her care.

Dear Sadie, the mother who nourished me in my own mother's absence. I hope you're alright out there. I hope you're safe.

I miss her so much, but I'm happy I can help by cleaning her home while she's out.

She's not out, she's in hiding, a voice in my head corrects.

Harry stands by the door to the Meehan bedroom and reaches into his coat for his pistol, gravely aware to any sounds inside. He holds it in his hand, a gentle finger caresses the trigger while he lays an ear to the door, then opens it. But there is no one inside. Afterward we signal to each other in the cold quiet when all rooms are cleared.

In the kitchen a large rock had found its way under the small dining table where once Sadie and L'il Dinny sang me the American Happy Birthday song. The rock had traveled through the front window that faces Warren Street. Thrown by Sadie's own cousin, the shadowy Darby Leighton and the evil Anna Lonergan. It was they who had berated Sadie from below for hours while Dinny languished in jail. Afraid, Sadie picked up the child and left with only what she could carry and came to me.

Glass litters the floor by the open window, fresh snow has settled on the ledge and the curtain is slowly being drawn out by a gentle wind.

A pigeon gargles a throaty cooing sound from within the room. It had brought in a loose collection of sticks and brambles and made a nest on a table in the corner where a candleholder had once resided, but now lay sideways on the floor. The belly-weighted bird flaps all of a sudden and smartly flies across the room and directly through the broken window as if it had done so many times. With it gone, I wet a rag in the sink and rub out the droppings from the floor and the table.

Harry watches until he turns back round to measure the window. Although his face is deadpan and distant, I know that he is a true friend because of all the things he has taught me, and the many hours he spent helping me renovate the room on Eighth Avenue before my mother and sisters arrived from Ireland. But his concern worries me. Harry Reynolds does not suffer anything without good reason.

My breath mists due to the cold air of the room as I look down at the circle of sticks. With one quick swipe, the nest crumbles apart and breaks the silence in the room with the clangor of hollow, metallic sounds when they land in the bottom of the garbage can.

Sadie had left in such a hurry that the table still has plates of food on it and there are dishes in the sink. So I clean it all up. Afterward I walk into the room that L'il Dinny and I once shared. My old bed is smaller than I remember it. And L'il Dinny had outgrown the crib, but still it sits in the room as if awaiting a new baby. Dinny and Sadie had always wanted a large family, but no more children came for them. I change the sheets on the crib and make sure there are no creases and that the pillow is fluffed and ready as if doing so might help bring a new child to the Meehan home.

At least their home will be clean when they come back, I smile, proud of my work.

Harry walks in and looks at the crib. In the doorway his face hardens as he stares at the floppy animal toy in the corner. He then lowers his dark eyes under hard brows.

"It's been a long time since you were here. In this place, right?" I say, half-joking, half-prodding.

"Six years," he answers.

"Longer than I've even been in New York," I feign innocence. "Why don't you, um, why don't you ever come back here?"

He pivots away and walks toward the parlor, "We better be goin'."

"I can tell Dinny that it was just me and Burke that came here," I say, following him.

Harry disparages me with a glance, "Ya know as well as I never to lie to the man."

I nod admittedly, then ask more questions since he is talking now, "Dinny and The Swede and Vincent. . . they're not getting out anytime soon are they?"

When he doesn't respond, I turn and place my palms on the sill, as Sadie used to, and stare across the street at Boru and speak my mind whether Harry answers or not, "The Dock Loaders' Club and Irishtown and the terminals and all the territories and the hundreds of families that depend on us. . . We're going to lose it all. We've never been this vulnerable. Bill and his men down in Red Hook, they'll see opportunity and attack us. We'll have to fight them without Dinny, and without his enforcers. It's all right though; I'm ready to fight. Tommy Tuohey taught me how to brawl like a Pavee gypsy after Petey beat me up, so I'll be ready. But I'll have to give this gun to someone else," I turn round and drop it on the table. "I won't kill anyone, Harry. I made a vow never to kill again after," I swallow hard at the memory. "After what I did to my uncle Joseph. And I mean to keep it. I do."

But to speak with Harry is like throwing a rock into the swirl of a current; he takes it in, but gives nothing back. He opens the front door for me to walk through and looks back into the Meehan room. He won't admit it, but I know that he has fond memories of the place as I do. But what those memories are, and what he had done to deserve Dinny's disdain churns in the depths of him, never to be salvaged.

We come out the front of the brownstone with Burke and look toward Bond Street again, then to Nevins. Our tracks lead to Boru through the thigh-high snow, then to where Garry Barry, Wisniewski and Cleary ran from us. The bloody trail puddles in some of the foot spoors.

With troubled eyes, Burke shies away from my gaze.

"No one will ever take your family away," I assure him. "I won't let them."

He gives an unbelieving smile, "Ya told me once that maybe our ancestors are always wit' us, Liam. Informin' us. Watchin' us. But maybe ya're wrong. Maybe it's our offspring. Maybe our children and their children an' beyond who will one day be able to peer into the past. To see us. Maybe they're watching us now," he raises his eyes past the tenements and up to the blue of sky, then back at me. "Don' ya think that's more likely?"

"I hope not," I say.

At Harry's approach, Burke lowers his eyes and shuffles from his way.

"Wolcott," says I to Harry. "If Garry Barry is with Wisniewski, it means he reports to Wolcott, the president of the Waterfront Assembly. Why would Wolcott reach out to the lowliest, wretched piece of trash like Garry fucking Barry? How would they have even come to work together?"

"Same way we came to make a deal wit' the International longshoreman's Association and the I-Talian Black Hand, I s'pose," Harry says. "Everyone's choosin' a side an' wit' Dinny locked up an' less shippin' contracts now that the war's over, Irishtown's up for grabs."

"We have Irishtown," I say proudly. "Dinny, The Swede and Vincent will get out soon. We just have to hold on until then."

"Hold on, eh?" Harry looks at me with those taciturn eyes. "We once had Brosnan an' the police at the Poplar Street Station in our service, now that's Wolcott's too. How long do ya think we can hold on wit' both Wolcott an' Lovett comin' after us?"

"We have to get in touch with Thos Carmody of the ILA and Sixto Stabile of the Black Hand," I say. "We have to call on our allies. Now is the time."

"They're all comin' for us. All o' them," Harry leans close and finds my eyes. "I wouldn't count our allies loyal either. The ILA is like all the unions; just tryin' to hang on, an' everyone knows I-Talians keep their enemies closest to them, right? Listen to me, ya have to leave Brooklyn. Liam, are ya listenin'? Because all o' this what's happenin'? It's all goin' in a straight line and it's real easy to see where it's gonna land, if ya're lookin'. Are ya lookin' Liam? Because ya need to look wit' ya own eyes now. Not through mine, see?"

"I know, I know, I can feel it too," I say. "I can feel it in the air, I truly can. But it's not so easy to just pick up my family and leave when—"

Harry shakes his head, "Ya have to leave here, don' be stupit. We're all in danger. Everythin's changin', but we're not. This ain't a matter o' fixin' broken windows, Liam. Ya could get hurt. Ya could die. We can't afford to take care o' everybody like we used to, an' right now all the people we care for in Irishtown need more help than ever before. Best thing is for yaz to leave."

"But Dinny helped me when I needed help," I say. "So did yourself, Harry. And I'm no poltroon—"

"What are ya then?"

"I—"

I don't know, you're supposed to tell me that, Harry.

Harry raises his voice, "Take ya mother an' sisters an' leave here. T'day!"

I look away, *I have failed him somehow. He doesn't trust that I can help in the coming wars. He doesn't think I'm ready.*

"But Dinny wants me to stay," I cross that imagined line between he and Dinny.

Harry's head seesaws slowly up and down while he stares into my eyes, regarding me with a willingness to listen.

"My mother and sisters wouldn't even be here if it wasn't for him and everyone else in the gang. I'm staying.

We are staying. I will honor those who helped my family. I will. And you can't stop me."

"It's not just that. There are things—" He looks for my eyes. "Things ya don' understand. Things none o' us understand."

"Like what?"

But Harry has turned and walks with his back to me. Walks through the snow toward the rising sun at the east-end of Warren Street. And in the breaking light I can see a shape in the sky that reveals itself slowly. I blink to make sure I see it right. It is not the sun, but a morning moon that had been there all along without notice.

I am Come

The stoicism in Darby Leighton's eyes betray the curiosity above as he stands in the hip-deep snow amidst a slew of some fifty onlookers at Red Hook's North Terminal.

Up there, Bill Lovett's body is kept amidst a snow bank on a bench along the railing of an overlook roof of the pierhouse. His arms and feet are crossed. His lips are a cyanotic, plum-blue. Next to him, an old torch that has hung unused for many years on the upper pierhouse wall is upside down, unused and weatherworn.

"Is he alive?" A man in his fifties with a droopy face whispers close to Darby's good ear.

Many had shown early to see if it was true, only to be left wondering how a man can sleep in fifteen-degree weather, while on the bench Bill Lovett reposed like a winter king. Rumor had spread quickly north from the windy Irish shacks along the terminals and up to Brooklyn Heights, eventually reaching Irishtown, that Wild Bill'd come back when Mickey Kane disappeared.

Among the onlookers Darby watches as Bill's men mumble to each other. They are dressed in strange pelts over military uniforms.

"Wake him up ya'self," Non Connors says to the one-armed Joseph Flynn and flicks a cigarette over the railing.

Flynn looks down to a slew of men where Darby Leighton looks back up to him. Flynn then walks over to Bill, "Can't sleep all day soldier, sun's up."

Darby and the others shuffle to the stairwell like slack-jawed sightseers while neglected dogs weave through them. A shit brown hound rubs its mangy coat against Darby's leg and sniffs his fingertips for food. Darby pulls his hand away and rubs the cold off of it against his trouser-leg, then looks round his old haunts.

When Mickey Kane was dockboss here in Red Hook, only true Whitehanders were chosen for work when ships arrived. And so the castoffs, who have gathered here today, whispered about the old days when Wild Bill Lovett was boss in this territory. When the rumors of Bill's reappearance came to them it could scarcely be believed. It was as if they had summoned him from the dead by their hopes.

Darby's windburnt face tilts when he overhears the mumble of men. He then searches round him for their moving lips. Deaf in one ear, it is difficult to put the words together in his mind without seeing their mouths move and their facial expressions.

"Is it true?" Darby sees a man say among three others who bandy about a hand-rolled cigarette between them.

"*Can* it be true?" The older man answers with a question.

"He came to me," Darby tells them, eyes fixed above. "He gave me the gun. An' I gave it to Richie Lonergan."

From the deck of a bobbing lighter-barge tied up in the Atlantic Basin, four bundled sailors stare up at the pierhouse roof along with everyone else, while all round them the harbor wind blows through their clothing.

Bill Lovett sits up as the onlookers gasp and a morning moon floats softly in the new sky over the returned soldier. He rests his elbows on his knees and slumps groggily, eyes down at his boots. He kicks some snow from his way and stands in place and stretches his back. Slowly he turns to the north and pants for air. His face and neck are pocked with pustules and blisters, his hair shorn close except on top where it is whipped back, black and slick above a couple fawn ears. His half-round black eyebrows look painted on his pale face like some crepuscular carnival clown.

Though the air is frozen, his face is dewy and his collar is damp with sweat. He grits through a cough and turns to the opposite direction toward the South Terminal of Red Hook, which was lost to the Italian Black Hand while he was gone to war. He then winces inwardly as his stomach muscles stifle another deep cough. The onlookers watch him and stare with dread in the low morning light, for a great grippe still tears through the waterfront neighborhoods like the black plague of Medieval Europe.

"He is a dark angel. Do not be fooled. He is a demon," the older man with the thickly wrinkled face warns.

Bill Lovett wears a rudely sheered sheepskin over his Army uniform with one large hole cut for his head and two smaller holes for his arms. The animal had been butchered by his own hand for its meat and warmth in the wilds of France. The shearling coat is now darkened from exposure and was tanned with the wool intact in the forest where his Metropolitan Division was surrounded for weeks, taking heavy casualties.

The pelt is blackened in the front because he had to crawl on his belly under German fire to draw water from a ravine, Darby would later learn. Bombarded not only by the Hun, but his company had also caught a barrage from their own side when inaccurate coordinates were sent through carrier pigeons. Seven hundred of them had been surrounded, only one-hundred and ninety four would escape with their lives. With the dead all round them, they suffered from pleurisy and gas poisoning. Bill had been shot through the right arm and right leg in a nine hour standoff that left charred and dismembered bodies strewn among the churned earthen craters from German shells. As he dragged himself off his machine gun post after an order to retreat, a faint yellow cloud overtook him. He heard the canister hiss, but could not move fast enough. He eventually lost consciousness.

In a report written by 2d Lt Sidney Delvin, Bill was dragged for a quarter-mile, but had gone cold and unresponsive. The company, under perpetual battering at both flanks from trench mortars and rifle fire, resumed their retreat without him. In Delvin's report, Non Connors was mentioned as "causing great distress among the ranks," by protesting the decision to retire without Lovett's body, but he too had been wounded and was hauled off despite his unrest.

In the end, Bill Lovett's remains were left in the rushes amidst a hilly grouping of white birch trees in the forest of Argonne. A burlap sack covered his upper body and face.

Five weeks later Bill's name was included among many others in the New York newspapers as "Missing in action, presumed dead." Father Larkin of the parish of St. Ann's appeared at his parents' room on Jay Street in the Bridge District of Brooklyn, the priest's hands clasped, his head bowed. Two uniformed men flanked him, hats under arms. Pt. William Joseph Lovett was dead.

But death need not prove fatal, and like some motley assemblage of reluctant death worshipers Darby Leighton and the others see him risen here and now in Red Hook. And under Bill's sheepskin is a Distinguished Service Cross pinned to his 77th Infantry uniform, as well as a crude patch on the shoulder of a halo-crowned lady liberty who holds up a flame, which matches the statue just beyond Governor's Island on the water behind him.

Bill takes in the snow covered industrial view as one-arm Flynn sidles up to him, "This is our home, Bill."

"No one tells us what to do," adds Connors. "Ever again."

Bill looks round himself, then at the two men he fought with in France, "Smells like piss and diesel."

Flynn crows out a laugh.

As the men below await his noticing them, a doleful smile crosses Bill's face as he finds the feral hounds below tip-toeing on the frozen ground and yawping into the cold air.

The teen Richie Lonergan, the one with the delay in his leg, limps forward and steps in front of Darby, who moves from his way. Innocently, and without the superstitious reverence of the other onlookers, Richie stares with ice-blue, high cheekbone eyes up to the three uniformed veterans surveying their old territory above Red Hook's North Terminal.

Bill then looks from the hounds to Richie, and summons him with a slow wave. Richie wears trousers he'd outgrown two years ago, hiked high by suspenders. He labors up the stairwell and yanks at one leg and leans heavily on the handrail so as not to put much weight on the wooden peg strapped to his thigh where his lower leg had been severed years earlier by a streetcar trolley.

Approaching Bill, Richie pulls the .45 from his belt and hands it back, grip first.

Darby observes the teen melee fighter with envious eyes, *I'm the one who gave that to him.*

"Richie," Bill says above, vapor streaming over his shoulder.

"Yeah."

"Help Connors an' Flynn get the men against the pierhouse wall," Bill commands, stopping to catch his breath. "Ya wit' us now. Ya're my lieutenant. Understand?"

Richie's pale blue eyes focus on the men below, "Yeah."

Connors and Flynn briskly walk past Richie, their heavy boots clop down the wooden stairwell as they yell toward the men below, scattering them. Richie irritably looks down and reaches for the handrail to begin his slow, labored descent.

"Richie," Bill calls again.

The teen turns round in short steps to keep his balance and looks over a shoulder.

"Good work."

Darby's upturned face remains fixed on Bill. The long creases in the returned gang leader's Army issue slacks ripple in the gusts and the woolly fleece flattens as Bill stares along the coastline toward Gravesend until the sensation of a cough bends him in half. Chest rattling, Bill hacks heavily until he puts both hands on his knees to regain regular breathing.

Troubled glares come from the men below. For months, ships have arrived in the New York Harbor with the Yellow Jack flag signifying contamination. When Mickey Kane ran Red Hook for Dinny's White Hand gang, many were stricken with the great grippe, and the influenza spread across the country and the world over a few months' time. In Brooklyn, soldiers had come back from the war with a simple wet cough like Whitehander Johnny Mullen, only to drown in their own lungs within a fortnight. And amidst the men Darby heard mention that James Hart the teamster had recently been rushed to Cumberland Hospital in dire straights. He was supposed to haul a truckload of coal ash and cinders from the Navy Yard, but collapsed wheezing with the grippe in his lungs.

"Against the wall boyos!" Connors yells at the onlookers who stare at Bill as he descends.

"Shoulders, asses an' ankles," Flynn yells. "Get in formation. Stand at attention. Ten men against the pierhouse wall at arm's length. Good, good. Now make rows."

Hopping through the snow a pair of wet rats wiggle between the lines of men to get from one pier to another.

"Looky there," Flynn chuckles. "That's a good sign. Trench rabbits can survive just about anythin'. If yaz prove half as tough as trench rabbits, ya might be wort' the moniker."

As the pack of hounds descend on the rats and sink their teeth into the rodents' backs and necks and run off with them through the lines, Bill laughs with wet and hoarse chortles.

Darby stares incredulously at Bill. Barely able to decipher the orders, he hears only mumbles while his focus remains on the man coming down for him.

It had been six long years since Darby had been banished to the shadows by Dinny Meehan for something that was not his fault. Six years alone. Darby hopes they were not for naught.

Back then Dinny had outsmarted Pickles Leighton, Darby's younger brother, and had him sent to Sing Sing. But Darby too was made to suffer his brother's effrontery, since loyalty always leans to lineage before clan. Twenty-nine years old now, and Darby has spent the majority of his life hiding in abandoned basements, behind factory walls, observing from row house rooftops along the waterfront neighborhoods of Brooklyn and fighting the creatures that sprung in his own mind. Banished from working on the docks, even with him being a Meehan man, Darby was forced to live with the rats and roaches in the shadows where the White Hand gang had chased him.

Until this moment.

But shadows need light for life to spread a darkened reflection. And like a shadow, Darby Leighton is caught somewhere between.

Only twelve short hours ago, Darby's daughter was born. Twelve strange hours. He had held the child in dismay, while the muffled cries of happiness from his fiancé echoed in his head. As he clutched the swaddled creature delicately under a hallway gas lamp, an epiphany swelled inside him. A guiding light, she would be. A message from some god, a true god, that he had been found. Illumined, he could finally emerge from his darkness.

In celebration, Darby took to the drink as men often do at the birth of a child. His older brother Frank had come with him and spoke into his good ear. Frank mentioned that he and Darby's fiancé and newborn daughter should consider a move to the burgeoning suburbs of Connecticut with him to start a new life. But when Darby turned to look at Frank's face, he was not there. Drunk, Darby had unwittingly migrated to one of his hideouts; a shack on the roof of a row house where once pigeons were bred. He could not be seen there. He could not be found. The snow came down thick as thumbs and swirled outside the coup, breaking apart in front of his eyes, slicing through the chicken wire. He looked at the bottle of whiskey in his hand, but it was empty. He remembered the baby and the echoes in the hospital hallway, and remembered feeling illumined by light. He wondered why he had come back to his old haunts after having an epiphany.

Was it habit? Did the drink make me fall back to my old comforts? Was it fate? But I don't believe in fate. I don't believe anything I can't see with eyes. He shakes his head, *I'm not even sure what I believe.*

Inside the pigeon shack, the door opened and a black figure handed him a gun.

"Give this to Richie Lonergan," the figure said.

"Bill?" Darby wondered.

It appeared as though the figure was wearing a black mask that covered his eyes and had a long, phallic nose.

"Tell him I need to know who he really is. Tell him this is for Mickey Kane."

Now, after daybreak with his wet boots in the snow, Darby Leighton looks up to Bill Lovett whose mouth moves without words.

Epiphanies are as fleeting as flakes of snow.

He blinks impassive eyes as men are yelling and scrambling in formation all round him. Still coming down the stairs, Bill Lovett's mouth moves again, but Darby cannot make out the words and tilts his good ear at him.

"What?"

Impatient, Non Connors punches him in the side of the head, waking Darby to Bill's orders, "Up against the wall ya fool!"

"Me? But Bill came to me—"

Connors then kicks Darby's legs out from under him, "Now!"

"Extend ya arms ya bunch o' fookin' navvies," Connors continues as Darby rises to stand with the others. "Get in formation. Do it. Do it now, we don' got all day. Now drop ya arms an' look straight forward. I catch anyone lookin' at the captain and yaz'll end up just like Mickey Kane in the drink. Don' look at him Matty, I'll fookin' kill ya. Timmy? Ya got it?"

"Yeah yeah yeah."

"Shaddup then," Connors looks at Leighton one last time and points in his face. "No one looks at the captain. Just stand still." Connors then steps back and surveys the lines. "A'right, there all yours Captain."

Bill Lovett nods toward Connors and Flynn to stand behind him. Richie falls in with the rest after finally descending the stairs. Bill stops as a crackling sound emanates from his lungs until he spits red into the white snow and grunts as Darby's eyes move to the ruddy splotches at his feet.

Bill peers into each man's eyes as he stalks the lines. Teens Richie Lonergan and Abe Harms. And neither look back. Petey Behan, Timothy Quilty and Matty Martin, they all stare ahead obediently. All is quiet but the crunching of snow under Bill's feet. As he crosses in front of them a tugboat *hoo-hoos* in the waterway distance. Best friends Joey Behan and James Quilty, both Army vets too, stand bolt upright. The experienced Frankie Byrne and his followers Sean Healy and Jidge Seaman. And Richie's father too, old man John Lonergan and forty others are lined up along Commercial Wharf.

More like prisoners than soldiers.

In a raspy voice, Bill speaks out, "Ya know what he done to us. Dinny Meehan. . . But it won't happen again."

He said the name, Darby thinks. *You're not supposed to say that name.*

Bill turns at the end of the men and paces back, "Meehan sent Pickles Leighton to the stir," he sulkily nods toward Darby, then to Non Connors. "An' set up Connors afterward. And to crown it off, he gives the South Terminal to them guinnea-fookin'-wops, lettin' them cross the Gowanus into our territory," he turns on his heel southward and points. "To this very fookin' day, they are allowed into the territory I used to run. 'Til he set me up too, for murder. I had to go to war on another continent to show this country my loyalty to it. An' for what? Because Dinny wanted me outta the way, that's for what. A man what speaks highly o' honor, yet bends low to demean us."

Cool grumbles float through the lines of threadbare and scruffy men.

"But Dinny Meehan fights more than mere men. He fights fate," Bill's voice is commanding, almost ceremonial. "He may imagine himself made outta clay, but' I am fated to lead from the Dock Loaders' Club atop Irishtown."

Bill criticizes Dinny for believing in divine right, but believes he is fated?

"The rightful King o' Irishtown has come back," a man in the back of the line voices his support.

"Hear, hear," others agree with the sentiment, but Bill shoots a look back at them.

"I ain't no king," the words are half-drown in phlegm until he clears his throat. "But the power o' the seat above the Dock Loaders' Club can make life. Or break it. It breathes into lungs an' it suffocates. It feeds babies an' starves them. It is heat against the ice an' shelter against the storm," he turns with an arm pointed north. "That seat above Irishtown is pure revelation! An' is fated to me. Fated to all them who would bleed wit' me. All o' yaz here t'day were lost to Dinny Meehan's plan. Some o' ya like the Leighton fam'ly been lost for years now. But we shall rise! Together. An' through me is the way among the lost people reborn and ready!"

He knows, he knows me. Darby's skin tingles with goose prickles and his eyes fill with cold diamonds as the men burst with excitement and call out his glories.

"An' now?" Bill moves his pointed arm toward the channel. "Now Dinny Meehan has killt his own cousin. What kind o' wretch murders his own kin?"

Caw-caw, Flynn quarks in laughter at Bill's words.

The man in his fifties next to Darby turns to him, "He is a false prophet, I say. An archon of death." He then breaks the formation and thrusts in heavy strides through the snow toward Imlay Street and the north.

"Old man!" Connors yells at him.

"Let him go," Bill interrupts and cups his mouth to project his voice toward the old, scared man. "Ya tell the leaderless men at the Dock Loaders' Club what comes for them! While Dinny an' his inner circle are in jail. We come t'day for them!"

Darby's head is tilted. He wonders if he had heard Bill correctly a moment earlier. He turns to Abe Harms behind him in the line, "Did Bill say the man killt his own cousin? Mickey Kane?"

Connors growls and hurls himself at Darby. He punches and wrenches him to the ground for all eyes to see, "Ya can't keep ya mouth shut, can ya?"

When Darby lifts his head from the snowy ground, the barrel of a gun is held to his nose at the end of Flynn's only arm.

"Ya gonna be the one I make a example of?" Bill says as the wind-tossed fur on his sheepskin pelt tousles in waves. "Ya gonna be the one?"

Unable to hear exactly what Bill says, Darby asks, "Why would the man kill his own cousin?"

Bill walks among the men on the wall, "I bet everyone here knows but ya'self, Darby. Richie c'mere."

Richie breaks formation and limps to the side of Bill.

"Answer the question," Bill demands.

Richie's eyes go from Darby to Abe Harms, who mumbles to him, "To blame it on Bill."

Richie turns to Bill with his eyes to the ground in supplication, "So to blame it on ya, Bill."

"That's right," Bill stares daggers at Darby and pivots confidently to the men along the wall. "That's to what lengt' Dinny Meehan'll go to to make sure we never have the right o' things with the people o' Irishtown. He's a sick, sick man, Dinny Meehan. He's taken everythin' ya have. Even ya'self Darby, didn' he? Was it fair when he banished ya? All them years ago?"

But it's a lie. It's not right. Darby shakes off his thoughts and instead says, "Well, no—"

"Then why do ya act the fool? Why? Never mind. It don' matter, because the rest o' these guys are tired o' bein' taken for a ride. They wanna work. We've all been through the shit, haven't we?"

The men along the wall and in line nod their heads, doing their best not to look at Bill.

"We learn. Learn about loyalty. I was loyal to Dinny once," Bill proclaims and points to the bullet scar that streaks across his temple through his hair and over an ear. "Look what I got. My loyalty wasn't appreciated. But I know now that *I* was the one that was wrong. I learned somethin' important. . . About loyalty to Dinny Meehan. I made my mistakes an' I own up to them now. I even shot a man for pullin' a cat's tail once. Ya think that little pussy appreciated my loyalty?"

A few men snort through the nose at that, until Bill glances at them.

"Nah," he says. "But dogs? A dog'll go to war for ya. So dogs it is. I need dog-men who bark and bite 'cause it ain't about who's right or who's wrong. There's only one right, the right o' conquest. Fuck all the rest. Nobody's gonna give ya nothin' in this world, an' if ya ain't got the sand to go an' take it, then this is the time for ya to leave from here," Bill ends and points an arm toward the street now. "G'ahead."

Darby feels his claim to a leadership role slip further away. Bill had come to him, after all. That must have meant that in some small way Bill trusted him.

But now I'm thrown in line with all the rest, Darby turns his eyes away from Bill's cold stare. *Why haven't I earned a spot as one of his lieutenants? What did I do wrong?*

He raises his eyes from the snowy ground to the gun pointed at him and calls out, "But no one's gonna believe that, Bill. That he killt his own cousin to blame it on ya."

Bill angles his face down to Darby in the snow as Flynn pulls back the hammer. "Put him on his knees, tie his hands," Bill commands. "Gather all the men around us in a circle so no one can see. Frankie Byrne! C'mere an' help get the men in a circle. I saw'r ya a kill a man for me a couple years ago, ya're my fourth lieutenant, understand?"

"I do," Byrne says obediently.

What about me?

As Flynn, Byrne and Richie Lonergan order the men out of formation and into a circle round the prisoner, Connors ties Darby's hands behind his back and forces him to his knees.

Looking toward the water, Darby sees the lighter-barge bob and yank slack from the mooring lines where four sailors stare back at him from its deck. But the men ordered to surround Darby come together in a circle and block the sailors from his view.

"I just had a daughter," Darby pleads. "Her name is Colleen. Colleen Rose Leighton."

"Then why don' ya think about her before openin' ya mouth?" Flynn responds as Connors ties a piece of cloth over Darby's eyes.

"She's not even a day old," Darby says, his vision blacked. "She needs me."

Darby hears the hammer of Bill's Colt .45 caliber, which sounds heavier than the Army issue revolver Flynn has. Then he feels a nudge at the back of his head. The cold of the barrel thrusts a shiver through him as his teeth begin to chatter.

That's the same gun that killed Mickey Kane just a few hours ago, he realizes.

"This is what we do to traitors," Bill shouts.

In the black, Darby hears Bill, but the words die off in his mind without piecing them together. Disoriented, he searches for Bill with his good ear. But without sight or the ability to hear in one ear, half-words linger in his head.

I had such high hopes. The cruelty of it. Of everything. Six years in the shadows for a moment of light with my daughter.

With his knees in the snow, moisture soaks through his trousers up to his hips. He searches with his fingers to loosen the knot that hold his hands behind his back, but all he can feel is his own forearm.

Thoughts flash through Darby's mind so quickly that it's hard to make sense of them. He has a few visions of his childhood in London. Then how he was abandoned in Brooklyn when he was five years old with his little brother Pickles. They lived under a pier. All of those experiences will be lost forever. Gone to time and memory. Coohoo Cosgrave's face comes to him. Coohoo taught Darby and Pickles to steal from ships in the middle of the night and run them through the sewers under Irishtown. The memories rush through him. There was a storm. A terrible storm and an upturned ferry in the East River in 1900. Then, Dinny Meehan appeared as the old-timers of Irishtown chanted of a prophecy. What does it all mean? Then into his mind comes an image of blood. Rushing out of a man's stomach. Pickles had stabbed a man in Darby's view. And then The Swede comes into his mind too, when he beat and banished Darby after Dinny was exonerated for murder in 1913. The memories are a confusion of time.

They must mean something. They can't just go into the unknown.

Darby doesn't remember what his mother looked like back in London. He doesn't remember her telling him that she loved him or that he was a good boy. The only mother he ever had was his aunt Rose, but she left them to the streets of Brooklyn. Then there was his cousin Sadie, but she left him too, for Dinny Meehan. Darby searches for what he felt was missing in his life. But how do you search for something if you don't know what it is?

I'm tired of sifting through misery for an answer. Maybe I am ready to give up.

He thinks again of Dinny Meehan. A noble and just leader. Dinny would never do something this cruel. Even if Dinny set men up, and had others killed, the reasons were always for the benefit of all the people he cared for in Irishtown and beyond. Not to make an example of his power to intimidate his own men. Bill would never follow Dinny's lead. Dinny was always there to offer the one thing people like Darby never had; hope.

That's what's missing, Darby realizes. *That's what I've been searching for; hope.*

He concludes then, finally, that he wants to be a father and cursed himself for leaving his fiancé and Colleen Rose at the hospital while he went out for drinks.

All I need is hope, Darby thinks. *Hope is all. And Bill Lovett, as crazy as it may seem, offers me hope. Hope to feed my family. I'd prefer Dinny Meehan over Bill Lovett, but Dinny would never have me. It wasn't my fault Pickles tried to kill Dinny back then.*

Again his brother Pickles comes into his mind, *Pickles?*

"Pickles!" Darby yells out desperately. "Pickles has a retrial! Pickles! In May o' this year!"

Darby cannot hear what the reaction is to his yelling his brother's name aloud. Silence is the only response.

Am I dead already?

He can't see his own breath, but he feels his wet and frozen legs and his hands tied behind. Then, the blindfold is ripped off.

"What about Pickles?" Bill mumbles as Darby watches his lips.

"I have to right the lie. The lie that changed my life. An' yours and everybody's! Pickles never killt Christie the Larrikin back in '12. It was someone else, but the witness lied. She was bulled by The Swede an' she lied on the stand. I have to fix it. I have to right the lie about my brother. I made my cousin Sadie pay for an attorney to get Pickles a new trial. To right the lie!" Darby throws the words out so quickly that it takes a moment for all to comprehend it. "Ya know what that means, Bill. If Pickles is released it means paroled soldiers for ya. A hundret soldiers. Maybe more. We can't attack t'day, we don' have enough men. We have what? Fifty? Even though the man an' The Swede an' Vincent are in the Poplar Street Jail, they still have more than a hundret men loyal to them up in Irishtown. If ya want to take the Dock Loaders' Club, ya need more men. Ya need *me*."

"We will take the Dock Loaders' Club t'day," Bill waves his .45 round in the air. "We will take it t'day. That's the whole purpose o' this. I survived so that this could happen. I am come o' the hope o' the people. The fertile hope o' the despairin'. Fate cannot be undermined. I am come of fate! I have risen! Yaz don' even know what I been through to arrive at this moment, right now! Yaz got no idea," Bill's wild and woolly eyes turn to Darby. "That's a cute story ya tell. A story that'd save ya life if true. But o' course Pickles is way up in Sing Sing an' can't confirm it."

"There's no such thing as fate," Darby shoots back. "A king isn't born, he makes his own way. When we get the lie about my fam'ly exposed to the light o' day, we will win Irishtown an' ya will have domain over every one o' the five main terminals from atop the Dock Loaders' Club in Irishtown wit' the truth empowerin' ya. But we do not have the manpower to do it t'day, Bill. Listen to me for just a moment," Darby turns on his knees in the snow. "Dead Reilly can confirm this story—"

"Dead Reilly?" Non Connors squints incredulously. "Dinny's lawyer that sent me up to the stir?"

"Yeah, I hired him. He's got no loyalty to the man. He's a slave to the dime, that's all—"

Bill cuts in holding up fingers like a V, "Two things: First, stop callin' him 'the man.' His name is Dinny Meehan, their code o' silence means nothin' to us. Second, ya hired Dead Reilly an' made ya cousin Sadie Meehan, Dinny's own wife, pay for it?"

"That's right."

Bill looks at Darby and lowers the gun, then laughs so hard that he coughs and turns his back and bends down until he gags and retches up a red mass.

Richie stands over Bill amidst the circle, "An' ya're a vet'ran too Bill."

"So what?" Bill struggles to say.

"Ya're a vet'ran," Richie simply repeats himself until Abe Harms comes to his ear.

"What are ya tellin' him?" Bill loosely holds the gun in Abe's direction. "Tell me what ya're tellin' him? Yeah you, ya fookin' little mole of a man. I don' know what's worse about ya, the Jew side or the Hun side, ya fookin' Jew-Hun. What are ya tellin' my lieutenant?"

Harms clears his throat. Self-conscious of his German accent, he keeps his eyes away from Bill's, "You're a veteran, Bill."

"What of it?"

"That's your edge," Harms continues. "You're a var hero. You even von a medal for your bravery against America's enemy, Bill. If you show up vith guns at the Dock Loaders' Club now, while Dinny's in jail, they von't know to respect you. The men you allow to live, they'll haunt you for killing Mickey Kane. You're a bull, Bill. But show them you're uniform. Show them the medal your country honors you vith and they vill turn away from Meehan. And come to you. You don't have to run down the hill like a crazy bull to fuck a cow. No Bill, valk down. Valk down and fuck them all."

Bill stares into the eyes of Harms, who looks away obediently. He laughs under his breath and clears his throat.

With his hands still tied behind his back and on his knees in the snow, Darby speaks out, "Bill, name me the Fifth Lieutenant. You'll need five dockbosses when we kill Meehan. I have proven my worth to you. Two years ago when Meehan made a deal wit' the Black Hand and sent Sammy de Angelo to kill ya, I tackled him before he could put a bullet in ya head. I held him down when ya killt' him an' to this very day I can't hear outta one ear because o' it. My brother has paid the ultimate price for loyalty to ya, an' my cousin was abducted by Meehan and betrothed to him in order to marry our fam'lies together. An' me, I spent six long years in the shadows. Banished. I wasn't even allowed to work wit' ya down here in Red Hook, remember that? My success is tied to ya, Bill. None o' us can move up unless ya win Irishtown. Now I'm here provin' my loyalty to ya. I come to ya wit' the gift o' a hundret soldiers, Bill. I ask ya, name me Fifth Lieutenant. But more importantly, we all ask ya, all o' us standin' here in the freezin' snow, what do ya have for those who are loyal to ya? What does it mean to be loyal to Bill Lovett? A bullet to the back o' the head?"

The men in the circle look from Darby on his knees, to Bill, who stands over him. They see that Bill is perturbed for having lost control. That he feels helpless and outwitted by a deaf fool who questions him. Begrudgingly, Bill waves with the back of his hand toward Darby, "Untie him."

Darby rubs at his wrists and comes to his feet. He loosens his shoulders and awaits an answer to his request.

"Let me make one thing clear to all o' yaz," the waterfront gales blow over Bill's pelt. "I don' trust no one who I ain't seen kill. We're goin' to war an' we're surrounded. Look around yaz. Black Hand to the east an' to the south o' us. White Hand to the north an' we got our backs to the water. If ya ain't killt someone for me, I don' name ya as my lieutenant," he looks defiantly toward Darby Leighton. "Ya wanna be my lieutenant? Kill Dinny Meehan, or The Swede, or Vincent Maher. Hell, kill that fookin' Liam Garrity kid, I don' care. Prove to me that ya're loyal, like these men have."

Connors, Flynn, Richie Lonergan and Byrne stand behind Bill proudly.

"Some men are valuable in other ways," Darby exchanges a nod with Abe Harms.

"A man can't kill for me, he's got no place as my lieutenant," Lovett repeats, "Ya're alive, Darby. Say a prayer or light a candle or somethin', but shut ya fookin' mouth up."

Bill suddenly looks away. Across the snowy street Darby finds what Bill sees; three women in dresses staring back at them.

"Look at these savages," Non Connors says.

Flynn cackles, "Wish we could ride them into battle."

Grace White and Kit Carroll are gaudily-tinseled in second-hand, pleated gowns of worsted wool with discolored shirtwaists and ruffled, low-cut necklines to reveal discount jewelry. To keep warm they wear shawls over their buns along with imitation furs while their hemlines are wetted and sullied by the soot and grime of snow and street puddles.

Flynn caws out a laugh and points with his lone arm toward Grace, "That one there could nourish an entire division wit' them swolled utters."

Anna Lonergan walks in front of Grace and Kit to stare at Bill. The gown she wears is an off-white drop-waste dress, fitted to her slight curves with flares round her hips to accentuate them. She even bears makeup; a smokey orange-brown eyeshadow to bring out her eyes with rouge and red lipstick that offsets her thick fox-colored hair. And her skin, a marbled porcelain with a blend of milky shades.

Strikingly gorgeous, Darby focuses on Anna who has always been known as a tomboy, until now. As he stares, a deviant breeze contrives to set her gown aflutter.

When did she get so elegant?

She turns her mouth and blinks her eyes like someone unsure of what they see, "Bill? Ya're back?"

"Back?" Kit blows cigarette smoke out the side of her mouth. "Regurgitated more like."

The last time Darby saw Anna was when the two of them had called up into Sadie Meehan's window on Warren Street before the storm. It was her idea. In a rage she told him to take her to the Meehan brownstone when Dinny was arrested for the robbery at the Hanan shoe factory. And when they got there, Anna was wild with fury and berated Sadie from below. Then she picked up stones and broken cobbles and fired them at the windows. Eventually one hit the mark and went right through the window, raining glass on the sidewalk below.

After that, she disappeared. Even her brother Richie didn't know where she'd gone. Sadie had disappeared too, along with the funds she was giving Darby for the lawyer and Pickles' retrial. Though he dare not bring that up to Bill.

Darby steps from Anna's path and notices the difference in her appearance. She even wears an elegantly fitted gown, but most telling is the crestfallen gaze of her. She stares at Bill in a seemingly distraught state made beautiful with the pouting bottom lip and the disbelief in her eyes at Bill Lovett's resurrection.

Round her finger is a ring made of leaves. Gold leaves. She strides past Darby with Bill in her eyes and a cold strength to her.

"Looks nice from afar, but she's far from nice," Darby hears one of the men say about her.

All eyes watch, but Bill's pierce her. She stops in front of him and holds her palm behind her, motioning secretly to Grace and Kit to stay where they are.

Of a sudden, Bill breaks through the circle of men and stomps through the snow to meet her. Face to face, they stop.

"Welcome back Bill," courage overcomes her shock, then she nods toward her father and her brother who stand with the rest before slowly raising her eyes up with a matter-of-fact assurance. Coming to her toes, she gently places her chest to his. "I'm eighteen now."

Bill stares dumbfounded at her as if he'd never seen a young woman before. His expression then changes to one of near desperation as if she were some creature of fantasy or a goddess.

"Bill?" She snaps him to attention. "What happened to Mickey Kane?"

He grunts and turns away from her, then back toward the pierhouse on the water, "Went for a swim."

Anna swallows and shifts her feet in the snow.

"Non?" Bill calls out.

"Yeah?"

"Get the men to work. That lighter-barge is waitin' to be unloaded."

"Come wit' me," Bill grabs an arm and marches Anna away from the men. He looks behind and catches eyes with Darby. "C'mere," Bill motions to him. "The two o' yaz worked together right?"

Darby looks past Bill into Anna's eyes, "We did."

Bill stumbles through the snow and whips Anna round and again searches her up and down with wild eyes, leaving her confused. With an index finger Bill opens her coat and slowly pushes it off her shoulder. It crumples in the snow behind her as she looks up again with the same eyes as her brother, yet hers are filled with blue flames that flick back and forth. Bill undoes the brown shawl that covers her head, freeing her hair to swirl in the wind like red tentacles in the white backdrop.

Darby stares until she glares back at him, weary of his eyes on her. Yet all the men behind them fixate on the red beauty in the snowy scene as if their leader's ascension is now complete by a royal pairing with this crimson wife.

"Ya goin' somewhere?" Bill asks. "Why ya all dressed to the nines for?"

Anna swallows again and screws her face up to appear innocent of any emotion, "I'm here for ya, Bill."

"Who are them two?"

Anna looks back toward the street, "Grace an' Kit."

"Bedraggled-lookin' slatterns—"

"They were there when Pickles killt Maroney back when," Anna says angrily.

"They're old women, drug addicts."

Anna catches that comment with a screw face, "They're like twenty-two years old, the both o' them. They're younger than ya'self, Bill."

"Why ain' they got husbands?"

Anna's lips part and Darby can see that fiery glimmer in her eye again, "Ya want them wit' husbands an' babies, or ya want them makin' ya money? Ya're gonna have a lotta people comin' to pledge support to ya, Bill. Ya're a war hero an' Irishtown's been starvin' since Dinny's on a stint an' this storm came. Was bad before even that."

"I ain't a pimp."

"Bill," Anna steps closer to him with the calculated patience Darby came to know her by. She lowers her voice and bites her lip, "Ya know they work for the I-talians down at the Adonis Social Club below the Gowanus? Ya know who runs that, right?"

Without an answer, Bill refuses to admit he does not remember.

"The Stabile fam'ly," Darby says.

Anna picks it up from there, "Those girls live in the Henhouse; a buildin' owned by ya enemy, Bill, the Black Hand," Anna spells it out for him gently. "Some o' the Whitehanders go down there, like Vincent Maher. Wouldn't ya like to know what he says to them? I don' know if ya remember Vincent, but he likes to talk. 'Specially to girls."

Anna watches Bill as he studies her.

The wheels are turning, Darby thinks.

Bill breaks eye contact and turns his eyes over a shoulder to the men working, then back to Anna.

"Soldiers need spies, advisors an' insiders, Bill," Anna assures him. "Ya've got no reason to question my loyalty. Ya were there for my brother when he got run over by the streetcar, an' ya've been there for him ever since. Ya want my loyalty, ya got it 'cause ya've been there for us Lonergans all along."

And there it is, Darby remembers. *That dogged and determined will. A will power stronger than any domineering bull male.*

Anna surveys Bill's eyes to try and figure his thoughts, but there is nothing but a black mirror, devoid of humanity or kindness. The same thing Darby had found.

Abruptly Bill reaches out to her. Anna's breath catches as he palms her left breast. She allows it, and moves her eyes to the men unloading the barge. But they are too far away to see Bill's pale hand grope at her off-white dress. Anna then looks back to Grace and Kit, who witness it all with quiet concern.

Bill slowly gazes up from her breast to her face and drops his hand self-consciously, "Ya been down there? The Adonis?"

She nods in admission.

"Are ya still pure?"

She laughs unskillfully and turns on her hip, "What does that mean?"

Bill's lip curls as he comes face to face with her, "Are ya pure? Simple question. Did ya keep ya'self pure for me while I was gone?"

"None of us are pure anymore."

Bill grabs her by the arm, "Maybe ya're not understandin' the fookin' question, so lemme spell it out for ya. Has any man fucked ya? Put his cock in ya?"

Anna rips her arm away from his grasp and pushes at his chest, "Let me remind ya o' somethin' Bill fookin' Lovett, I went to ya god'amn funeral. I comforted ya parents. I put flowers on ya grave. Candles on the altar for ya. They tol' me ya was dead. All hope was lost. Gone, Bill. There's been a coal shortage, an' these last two winters were the coldest I've ever known. Now the docks've dried up 'cause wit' the war over, there ain't so many contracts for goods comin' in or leavin' Brooklyn no more."

"So what's that got to do wit'—"

"Tiny Thomas died!" she yelps.

A few men peer over their shoulders at her voice.

"Then it was the grippe that came for us. Hundrets o' people died in Brooklyn. Thousands. An' it took my little sister Ellen, too. She couldn't breathe, Bill. It got in her lungs," Anna clenches her teeth recounting the pain. "An' maybe it's in ya own lungs, Bill. Ya don' look so good ya'self, so don' come back here wit' ya ignorant notions on the purity of a female. None of us are pure any longer. We never will be again."

Bill looks at her, "Where'd ya get the money for all this then?" Bill runs his finger up and down her gown. "Huh? So ya go down to the Adonis an' give ya'self up to I-talians. Gave ya'self away. Didn' ya? The most important thing ya got."

"Ya was dead, Bill," Anna points into his chest. "I stand by everythin' I do. I might not be able to find work like a man, but there are things I can do to ensure no one in my fam'ly starves, or dies again."

"Who was it?"

"None o' ya fookin' business."

"Richie?" Bill motions for her brother to come over.

Richie holds two crates in his arms and stops in front of the lighter-barge and turns round to walk toward them.

Anna beams at Bill with warning in her eyes.

"Richie," Bill taps him on the chest. "Did ya know ya sister's a slattern?"

Richie turns emotionlessly to her. She watches as her brother places the two crates down and awkwardly touches his own eyebrow and begins to speak, but words fail him. He looks at Darby for a moment, then away.

He doesn't know how to answer that question.

"Did ya know she slept wit' a man for dime, Richie?"

Anna punches Bill on the cheek, then rears back again until he catches her by a clump of red hair and forces her to the ground. Richie takes one step forward, but Abe Harms suddenly appears to whisper in his ear. The men unloading the ship stop and turn dumbly toward the spectacle.

"Anna!" Grace and Kit pull up their dirty hems to run through the snow.

"They left me in the forest," Darby reads Bill's lips as he whispers into Anna's ear. "I had nothin'. Nothin', do ya understand? I had nothin' but memories."

Bill lays his weight on her as she digs her fingernails up into his face and neck, "Fuck you. Get off me!" Anna screams.

"Bill, maybe you should—"

But Bill talks over Darby, "Just a naked forest. They even took my sidearm an' my rations. Even my boots. I had nothin'. Nothin'."

Bill straddles her and takes both her hands and holds them behind her back and whispers into her ear, "But I had you. I was in the darkness, Anna. I was gone. All the world was empty, but I had the memory of you. I known ya my whole life an' never did I think it'd be ya what saved me. An' now this? It was all for this? This fookin' sick joke? I crawled back to life for this? To find out that the girl who saved my life is a slattern? What kind o' world is it when hope is proven as futile as a fool's errand?"

Anna struggles against him until his hand appears on her throat.

Her eyes begin to bulge in fear. Darby and Non block Grace and Kit, who scream for her. Under the shadow of the lighter-barge her father sullenly turns away. But Richie steps forward again when he hears his sister choking. He opens his mouth, but Abe catches him again. Richie's body begins to shake and he holds his fists over his thighs as Petey Behan laughs and slaps Matty Martin on the shoulder, who is pale and distressed.

Bill sits on top of her and reaches back with his right fist. When he connects under her jaw, Anna goes limp and her hands drop to the snow.

"Anna!" Grace screeches as Bill slowly stands over her.

Richie unclenches his fists and drops his arms to his side. Beyond the lighter-barge, a tugboat again *hoo-hoos* out on the water as if nothing has happened.

Wild Bill Lovett then turns to his men. From his belt he pulls out his .45 and checks the chamber.

"No!" Grace screams over Non Connors' shoulder.

"Shaddup ya slattern!" Bill holds the gun to the sky and fires.

"We will not wait until Pickles is released," Bill announces. "We will not wait to show these men at the Dock Loaders' Club that I am a decorated veteran. We will show them who we are wit' our force an' our might!"

The men who wanted to attack earlier walk closer to Bill. Joey Flynn has his revolver out and stocky Petey Behan a cudgel at the end of his arm. Non Connors and others have bail hooks and knives and pipes and broom handles even, and wave them in the air and yell for their leader.

"We will take the war to them now!" Bill yells. "We need territory! We don' need hope, we need war! Are yaz ready to take back the land o' our people?"

The men roar in approval.

"The Irish have ruled Red Hook since we arrived seventy years ago!"

The men yell as Grace and Kit kneel in the snow over Anna as Darby watches on.

"Let's go then!" Bill leads the way.

"Anna," Grace has tears in her eyes and holds Anna's limp hand. "Are ya okay? Anna?"

"Where's Neesha?" Anna asks, disoriented.

Neesha? Neesha who? Darby wonders.

Even Grace and Kit are stumped by the question.

"Who is Neesha?" Grace gently asks Anna.

"Wha. . . What happened?" Anna slurs her words as if drunk.

"Bill hurt ya, Anna," Grace says as Kit gently pets Anna's red hair.

"Oh, oh yeah," Anna sits up in the muddy snow, her gown soaked through the back. She notices blood on the front of it and tries to wipe it away as more blood drops from her mouth. She tries to focus and wobbles and peers up to Grace with confusion in her eyes. "What happened?"

"I just told ya. . . oh never mind," Grace pulls Anna's face to her chest for a hug and rocks back and forth.

Before Darby turns to join the men, Anna's muffled voice comes to him one last time, "Where's Neesha?"

A Slew of Mendicants

The morning moon sits white and half-faded like a rune painted on the blue canvas sky. It hangs there as if watching like an unblinking eye. Staring through the naked trees and peeks round buildings. Following us. A symbol of the past, some might argue. Or maybe a portent of what comes. I cannot say, yet high in the sky it watches, wholly impassive of the theatrics below and the interpretations we attach to it.

Burke said, "I'm tired o' sloggin' through this snow. I'm goin' back to Eighth Avenue. There's no work today, an' I'm starved. An' I wanna check on my son an' my fam—"

"Ya leave us now and I'll kill ya myself," Harry says.

Burke frowns back, "A true seaman weathers the storm he cannot avoid, an' avoids the storm he cannot weather. My father was in the United States Navy an' had the sense o' the seas. We'd be wise to heed them words an' head home."

"Spare us your memorizations," Harry chides. "If we were on the seas t'day, I'd want to avoid storms, sure. But we're not. Our home an' our way o' life are under attack by mortal men. An' we gotta face up to them. The storm ain't our enemy; men are."

Things ya don' understand. Things none o' us understand, Harry had warned me. I remember the words, but now he seems to have forgotten.

No, he hasn't forgotten, I realize. *He's just concentrating on what he can control.*

"The storm breathed life into those men," Burke mumbles. "The Bard o' Irishtown predicted it."

I turn to Burke, "The Gas Drip Bard fellow? Have you been back to listen to him since we went with the kids?"

Burke nods worrisomely and whispers, "Their eyes are mere holes o' black. . . an' when they speak, the blood spills from their mouths."

I tilt my head at those words as they bring on some foggy sense of a memory.

Inside the Hanan boots my feet are wet and freezing and it's hard to think on memories with the cold everywhere. But the Bard I can never forget. After my mother and sisters arrived from Ireland I had taken them with Burke's family to listen to the aged shanachie storyteller in the oldest part of Irishtown. We went for the entertainment in it, of course. At first he gave us yarns of drunken goats and buxom biddies that amused the children.

Afterward, he told of the gangs of old Irishtown. How they had long protected the borders without, and enforced the old Brehon codes within. He elevated Dinny Meehan as a hero on a hero's journey. Cut from the mold of the old days, Dinny brought back the old ways after the evil Christie the Larrikin had sold Irishtown's secrets to the Anglo-American ascendency. He called us, the followers of Dinny Meehan, "Soldiers of the Dawn," so he did. He meant it in a poetic way, I believe, which can be interpreted any manner a listener may lean, just like the moon above.

I turn my eyes back up to the sky, and the one-eyed waning moon stares back.

"It warns us," Burke comes to my ear. "It gives us heed; the white moon born o' the morn. After the storm. It's a signal that we should—"

"It means nothin'," Harry turns back to us as trails of vapor billow from his mouth. "It's only a moon. It's as meanin'less as a brick or a shoe or a fart. Do ya see omens in a mornin' fart too? Or is it just gas an' wind built up overnight?"

"But there should be—"

"Stop sayin' *should* all the time," Harry cuts him off again. "Everybody believes in *should*, who wouldn't? There *should* be enough food an' jobs for everyone. There *should* be justice for all too, but there ain't. Let's all pray to *should*, the new god o' gods. Why not?"

Burke glowers at Harry like a boy at his correcting mother.

Out of the silence comes a voice in the distance.

"Who is that?" Burke has turned round.

From the south, a figure runs through the snow between low-rise buildings on either side. It's calling to us. Waving to us.

"Should we run?" Burke asks.

Harry shoots a glare at him for saying 'should' again. "Nah," he answers and turns to face the oncoming man but does not take out a weapon.

Beat McGarry struggles through the hip-deep snow. When he reaches us, he stops and stands with both hands on his knees, out of breath. The old fellow has a face like a melted candle with little mouse eyes hidden in the waxy folds. But what we can see in his eyes, is fear.

"I saw'r Bill Lovett," he finally says, the fearful countenance gives him the appearance of a man older even than the fifty-seven years he has.

"So it's true," Burke taps my arm. "See!"

"They're headin' toward the Dock Loaders' Club, I heard Bill say it, I did. They got weapons. Bill's back! I saw'r him. He's comin'!"

Harry turns to face north, "We have to hurry. We have to warn everyone at the Dock Loaders' Club."

"What's that gonna do?" Burke shrugs.

"Save lives, let's go."

Harry grabs Burke by the lapel and we high-leg through the deep snow. Soon enough we are blowing hard. Sweat inside my coat turns to ice, but we can't stop.

"We have to beat them," Harry whips us with his tongue. "Keep goin', keep goin."

"Did Bill admit to killin' Mickey?" I ask Beat, who is falling behind us.

Beat calls up toward us, "Darby Leighton told me that Bill came to him and gave him a gun to give to Richie. . . Richie Lonergan."

"Richie did it?"

"He did," Beat says dispiritedly. "But that ain't the all of it."

"How many men do they have?" Harry asks.

"Fifty, fifty-five maybe."

"Run faster," Harry tells us all. "We have probably half that right now at the Dock Loaders' Club."

"Probably less."

"They're doomed," Burke says as white smoke billows out of his mouth.

"Look," I interrupt them both before they take up arguing again. "The White Wings. They're cleaning the snow off the trolley rails and sidewalks."

Men with white hats and white uniforms furiously shovel snow from the middle of the road and pile it six feet, eight feet high where the street meets the curb. Snowy passageways are left for passengers to enter the trolley cars from sidewalk to street. Against the buildings, snowdrifts reach higher still and creep up to second-floor window ledges. Up ahead the Fulton Elevated Line is already in service, albeit at a snail's pace. It plods along and pushes heavy clumps of snow down onto the street along the iron girders to clear the tracks.

"We can take the El at Duffield Street to Sands Street and we'll only have a few minutes walk to the Dock Loaders' Club."

From inside the car on the Fulton Elevated Train we can see the heavenly whiteout across the dirty old industrial city.

"It's like a ghost town," Burke's voice echoes in the empty train car.

Windows are blocked with snow that has collected on the ledges and all the streets are coated with the puffy white stuff. On the streets there are no trolleys running and there will be no labor work to accomplish this day. There are hardly any ships in the slips either, which means no goods will be unloaded here, prolonging the hunger and foreboding.

"There has to be some purpose to all this," I say incredulously. "There has to be."

Harry's voice is a gravel of dour, stoney words, "The grocers will be robbed soon."

"Always cheerful news wit' this one," Burke shakes his head at Harry.

"They'll choose jail over starvation, logically. There's not enough to feed everyone, so the quickest, boldest thieves'll benefit."

The gigantic, three-story Sands Street Train Station, the busiest in all of Brooklyn, is completely barren save a few itinerants who stare off into the air or mumble prayers. A family of refugees huddles closely together in a lean-to and a few sparse morning riders bundle up against the gusts that rattle the broken second-floor windows. Unmolested by thick crowds and the accompanying cutpurses that normally clog the train platforms and narrow halls, we jog four-abreast. Under our feet, joints in the wood-framed train station creak and moan like an old schooner ship upon the open ocean. Beyond that there is silence but for the whistling wind.

"Let's go, hurry, hurry," Harry runs ahead toward the exit with Beat following as we rush down the snowy stairwell.

Through the snow we trudge along Sands Street in front of a saloon situated between the bridges, which has twenty regulars inside. Regardless of the weather, it is only the drink that worries the men inside. Next to it is a lot with some charred remnants of a building covered in snow. Outside, we walk by one man with a pallid, sleep-fallen face, his body stretched on its side in a drift. Rust-colored vomit stains have melted the snow in front of his hairy gob.

"Isn't this where Pickles killed Christie Maroney, the Larrikin back in 1912?" I call out, pointing at the dilapidated framer.

"It is," Beat assures, blowing harder than the rest of us. "Ya sure got a good remembery, Liam."

"A good what?"

"Ya good at rememberin' things, is all I'm sayin'."

"It's memory, not remembery."

"Oh yeah, yeah," Beat continues. "It was a fateful morn. Foreseen by the ol' timers. I remember! One shot an' the old ways was resurrected in Irishtown. It led to the Adams Street Riots a year later after Dinny was exonerated. Riots o' celebration, that is. To honor their new leader the revelers dragged Maroney's followers out of Jacob's Saloon, their gang's headquarters, an' set the building alight."

Now old and small in number, dead Maroney's remaining adherents have migrated next door to whet their softening memories with hard whiskey. And Jacob's Saloon is now but a place where boys go to piss in the rubble.

But Harry doesn't talk about those days. Ever. Or what it might mean that we pass in front of the charred bones of Maroney's old headquarters now.

A drunkard with a bedraggled old derby hat stumbles through the door of the saloon and spits at our feet. "Fuck all o' yaz, White Hand scum," says he.

At that the man sleeping in the snow gags and smacks his lips.

The derby-helmed man sloppily persists, throwing a cigarette toward us, "Ya day'll come too, yaz'll see! Ya fookin' pieces o' shits. Ya reap what ya sow."

But Harry ignores the soused and swaying man.

"Oh they're comin'," Beat assures us. "How do ya reason wit' someone who thinks they're touched by fate?"

Breathing heavily now, Beat and Burke turn to Harry, who gives them the answer, "Ya don't."

What if we arrive too late? God forgive me for what I am about to do, my mind races and summons on its own the god of my childhood. *Forgive me. The M.12 is still in my coat pocket.*

Just then, Harry hits a second wind that the old fellow cannot equal.

"G'on," Beat says. "I'll meet yaz there."

As we turn onto Bridge Street, behind us the gigantic Brooklyn Union Gas tank hangs three stories above the tenements and elevated tracks. Down the hill we edge through the snow and pass in front of the empty Lonergan bicycle shop. Burke cranes his head up and flinches when a lone gull twists across the sky and clamors in a guttural shriek. The white bird with a gray-winged cloak squawks again to remind us that we are approaching the waterfront.

Just as my toes are about to freeze, in the distance a low chant comes to our ears. Over the rooftops the cold blue-gray steel towers of the Manhattan Bridge looms over our destination. Down the whitened slope of the Bridge Street hill a clanking sound grows louder with the chants.

What are they yelling?

"Why are there so many outside the headquarters?" Burke asks through ruddy cheeks. "There must be two thousand o' them."

"Are those Bill's men?" I wonder. "How did they get there before—"

"They're starved," Harry says, pacing ahead. "It ain't Bill's men. It's Irishtown faithful. They don' wanna loot the local stores, so they go to the one place that's always served them."

"Maybe they all came because Mickey's back?" Burke puts in as we fall to a slower stride.

"Mickey's dead," There is a finality in Harry's voice that cools my spine. "He ain't comin' back. Now stop sayin' otherwise."

As we push through the periphery of the crowd, the begging of alms comes to our ears when we are noticed.

"We're hungry!" Yells the sable-shawled widow of Johnny Mullen. Her hands hold the hands of children with frayed gloves, exposing most of their tiny blue fingers to the cold. Mrs. Mullen's lonely eyes are half-veiled and she is clad head to heel in black. Her youngest child, a little girl, has Vincent Maher's eyes, so it's said. The eldest, Johnny Jr., is a randy little ten year-old who swoons as we pass. His cap is tilted so precariously that he is forced to constantly right it, while all along a lit cigarette smolders from the corner of his mouth. "Poe," he calls out, and it's only then I see Mullen's cohort shadowed over his shoulder, the Sutton boy from High Street.

Banging pans with wooden spoons behind Mrs. Mullen are more black-veiled widows, they of Quiet Higgins and Gimpy Kafferty who died in the Great War. And then there are the large families of the Simpson brothers, Whitey and Baron who also died in some rainy ditch in France. The widows clack their pots and pans noisily and have the shame in their eyes for us.

"We'll never go 'way," Mary Lonergan screeches with her brood of snot-faced moppets gathered round her time-worn sack dress. Her lopsided face and bulged fish eyes ogle us defiantly. "We'll starve to death right here at ya door 'til we're sated, we will! We want the honor price that's due us!"

"Poe!" I hear a boy's voice call out. "Look it's Poe and The Shiv!"

The children of Irishtown throw us up as heroes and long to become us one day.

If only they knew how fragile we truly are, they would never claim us as heroes.

Mrs. Lonergan lunges for my arm, the burn-scar along half her face gives her the appearance of some traveling carnival oddity.

"Liam child! Please, please, I haven't seen me Anna. She's been winnin' us food since before the storm but she's gone now for days. Liam please, just a few dullars." She holds my arm and blinks with the eye on the misshapen side of her face, then blinks the other as if the two sides of her face are disconnected altogether.

I reach into my pocket but before I can take out any bills, Harry grabs me by the back of my coat and drags me away from her.

"We need to make a plan first," he yells into my ear over the chant of the mendicant crowd. "They'll rip ya to shreds if ya pull out any bills."

The three of us push through the endless flock of hands that claw for us until we come to the front where we are allowed passage. Coming through, Burke can't close the door behind him. Inside Eddie Hughes and Freddie Cuneen pull it open and Harry yells through the doorway, "Let us talk and we'll find a way to help yaz!"

Finally the door slams shut.

From behind the mahogany trough a Kilkenny lilt is barked out, "They'll be after breakin' the glass on the front window soon, ye know," Paddy Keenan warns. "We can't deny them forever, like. It's not right."

Just then Beat barrels in, "Bill's comin'," he announces as Ragtime Howard turns his eyes to us from the whiskey glass at his lips.

"Jaysus," Paddy reels and points to the stairwell. "Yez g'won 'hopstairs to the second floor then. The bhoys are up plannin' a plan fer these hungry people as we spake. G'won, tell them Wild Bill comes."

Harry turns for the stairs while Paddy catches my eyes, "Fer feck's sake, when Bill shows up it'll be a bloodbath. T'is true Mickey's stiff?"

I nod, abashed to admit it in front of the other Whitehanders at the bar.

Paddy throws his towel and reaches underneath for his revolver, empties it of bullets and blows into the cylinders.

At the top of the stairwell Harry gives the office door a coded knock and Red Donnelly opens it wide with a look of relief on his big red box face, "Oh thank god yaz are here."

"Rebels are to descend on the Dock Loaders' Club this very minute," Beat blurts out again, the two little beans he has for eyes half-hiding the horror within the melted face on him. "Bill and his boyos are on his way to kill us. An' he's got some dark devilry on his side too."

Cinders Connolly stands from behind Dinny's desk where the Manhattan Bridge and the New York skyline fill both of the arch windows in the background. "What did yaz see out there?"

Harry doesn't answer but stands forth and turns to Beat McGarry. "I want ya to go downstairs."

Beat stops in his tracks, then nods in my direction, "What about him?"

Harry stares and takes another step forward.

"Cinders is the boss while Dinny's in the stir, not ya'-self," Beat's flushed and fleshy face pivots. "Cinders, I can stay can't I?"

Cinders leans both palms flat on the desk, "I ain't the boss. Dinny said Mickey was in charge an' I was to help him. I'm no man for the job alone. Do as Harry says. Go downstairs an' gather all the weapons we got in the rear-room. G'ahead."

Beat warily turns round for the door and leaves me with a sour look of half-jealousy, half-resentment.

The other sullen-faced men assembled in the dark corners of Dinny's office moue at me like a litter of cornered refugees. There is The Lark Gibney with his tree-trunk thighs and broad waist. He is dockboss of the Baltic Terminal and his right hand is the burly, barrel-chested, black-haired Big Dick Morissey. Henry Browne is Red's righthand. He was once the ILA leader in the Navy Yard before the deal to join forces with the Italians of South Brooklyn whisked him into our midst. And half-black Dance Gillen is in a chair with head in hands, "I shoulda went down there wit' Mickey," he mumbles.

"I shoulda never let Mickey go," Cinders answers him, with the fool-mute Philip Large behind his shoulder, short arms at his side.

With a low whistle of wind through wood-slats and iron shutters, Cinders recounts his last moments with Mickey in muted tones, "I couldn't stop him. Harry, I dunno why he left. He was dead set on goin' to Red Hook even though the storm was comin' down sideways, everywheres. I needed him here, but he just went off into it."

"Did he say why?" Harry asks.

"Nah, he was just pacin' an' pacin' in circles up here, like he. . . like he needed to be somewhere."

"He knew he was supposed to die," says a dejected Burke. "He knew he had to be there for it. He knew that was his role."

"The fuck are ya sayin'?" Cinders takes that statement as an affront, while feeble-minded Philip recognizes Cinders' angry voice as a cue that violence looms.

"An' there'll be more," Burke presses on. "I had a dream the other night, durin' the worst o' the storm, that. . . that a man would see wit' his own eyes, his body only a few feet away. . . wit'out a head. But at that moment, his last moment, he knew it was his callin'. As if it were written beforehand, or known. That *death* was his duty all along. Same as Mickey!"

Harry takes three steps and is in front of Burke, who looks back at him sheepishly. With one quick swing a clout lands under Burke's jaw that puts the small man to sleep with an unnerving ease. Harry then catches Burke before he hits his head on the wood floor and drags him effortlessly to a corner for a nap.

"He's been spookt all mornin'," Harry says with a somber assurance.

The spectacle of Harry's cold, brutal performance bears mute testimony until a sound downstairs turns all of our eyes toward the floorboards.

Are they here?

But it was just a chair being moved.

"Burke don' know what he's sayin'. That's what happens when dread o' the unknown is allowed to run rampant in ya," Harry turns as the chant strikes up again for those outside that protest their hunger. "Cinders, what are we doin' for all these people?"

"We have to help them," says I.

"That's the thing," Cinders' broad shoulders obscures Philip as he moves from the desk and wipes a shock of sandy hair away to tuck it behind an ear. "The tunics came here 'bout an hour ago. Patrolmen Culkin an' Ferris."

"In here?" I ask disbelievingly.

"What about Detective Brosnan?" Harry's eyes are on the floor in thought.

"Nah, just Culkin an' Ferris, but they were escortin' that fookin' leech, Vandeleurs, the slumlord. Apparently his rent-collectin' thugs went to each an' every home recently, passin' out eviction letters."

"So now they threaten to evict our people while they're hungry?" I complain. "What good will it do to put them on the roads?"

"Some things never change," Cinders' gloomy realization sparks Harry to action.

"Everybody empty out ya pockets on the desk. We'll sift through every dollar to determine what we can and can't give them downstairs. It won't be much help, but we gotta do somethin'."

"Wait," Cinders says. "Before we do that. . . We need to determine who our leader is now."

"Ya're the leader," Harry waves off. "Dinny left ya an' Mickey in charge. Ya're in the hot seat now."

"No, he left Mickey in charge. I was only to help him. I'm not a leader, Harry. Dockboss o' the Jay Street Terminal an' the Fulton Ferry Landin', sure. I give ya that, but I ain't a long term solution. We need to vote on the leader o' the White Hand movin' forward wit' Dinny gone. An' I for one am votin' for ya, Harry."

"Aye," Dance Gillen tallies his support and stands at the ready.

"True," The Lark and Big Dick agree.

Harry turns away, "I can't."

"You are the most obvious candidate Harry," I step forward. "You're the smartest, you're experienced and the most capable, it's clear to us all. Why wouldn't you want this?"

"Dinny'll see it as a insurrection," Harry says. "I've already been to his home t'day."

"And shot a man to defend it," I point out. "Why would Dinny see it as an insurrection if you're the most competent to help while he's out?"

"He didn' choose me. He didn' want me to supervise the White Hand in his stead. Ain't that enough for ya?" Harry's words are like the lyrics to a dirge over the harmonic chants outside. "He trusts Cinders more than he trusts me. No. Cinders Connolly is the leader 'til Dinny comes back, an' I won' hear another word on it. I'll do anythin' that's needed to help these people outside an' to hold Bill's thrust, but don' give me any titles. I won't have them."

Cinders turns round and faces the open iron-shutter windows, as Dinny always had. The men's faces turn long as well.

Dance sits down and shakes his head, "I shoulda been wit' Mickey, goddamnit. Goddamnit."

"Ya'd've been slaughtered wit' him," Harry says. "Another thing everybody oughta know. We saw Garry Barry out there."

Dance picks his head up, his dark face darkened more by the shade of shadow, "That can't be true."

"It's true," I say. "I saw him, but his face is all lamped up."

"It's true," Burke is still on the floor in the corner, but comes to his elbows. "Like a woman's wound, but sewn up an' with an arsehole for a mouth. That's who Harry shot, but he just got right back up again."

"No one coulda survived what we gave Garry fookin' Barry at the Hoyt Street Saloon," Dance raises a hand to Big Dick, who along with Eddie and Freddie, wrecked his head and left him for dead. "I was pullin' brains outta my boots for two days after I danced on his face. . . fuck, ya're kiddin' me? What the fuck's goin' on here? Shit's fuckt lately."

"He was wit' Wisniewski," Harry says.

"Wolcott's lump," I put in.

"So lemme get this right," Cinders sits on the edge of the desk, but Harry finishes the sentence for him.

"Barry's workin' wit' Wolcott an' the Waterfront Assembly now."

"Damn Harry," The Lark slumps in the corner. "Ya really know how to kick the wind outta a guy, don' ya?"

"It's just what it is, is all. I'm not tryin'a tell ya nothin' except how things are."

When the room goes silent we can hear the hum of voices rise and fall out front.

Burke fidgets, "I'll put in five dollar bills for them."

"Ya need that money for ya son. To feed ya fam'ly," Harry says. "Turn in two and keep three. What about the rest o' ya?"

The slew of mournful mothers and half-starved children outside becomes unsettled. Harry turns his head to listen as a wave of gasps sounds off from below. The arched windows of the second floor overlooks the Belgian block alley and the lot beyond, leaving us to wonder who it is that comes to the front of the saloon.

"Wild Bill is here," Burke holds his jaw. "Beat was right. If only Dinny an' The Swede an' Vincent were here. . . An' Mickey. Good fortune's not on our side."

Harry hushes him while the other Whitehanders in the room listen.

"How many men do we have?" Harry asks Cinders.

"The men in this room, an' downstairs we got Paddy, Ragtime, Beat an' Needles."

The Lark and Big Dick shake their heads, "A bartender, a whiskey drunk, an ol' man an' a drug addict? Laughable. Bill'll overrun us if he's got fifty men."

"Eddie an' Freddie are down there," I say. "They're fair fighters. An' I saw Chisel McGuire an' Dago Tom too. An' Paddy's got a pistol."

"I don' know for sure he'll pull the trigger at a man," Harry says, as outside the slew again stirs until a woman's scream cuts through the morning.

Harry yells at Red Donnelly, "Get the door! Get the door! Tell them downstairs to bar the door. Go! Liam, gimme the M.12!"

I pull it out of my coat and hand it over as men yell downstairs to block the entrance.

Harry quickly puts the pistol in the hands of Dance, "Now's your chance to kill them that killt Mickey."

"This is as good a place as any for a last stand," I hear The Lark say who suddenly has a bail hook in his hand as Big Dick Morissey grips at a cudgel.

Dance walks up to a pouting Burke and flips the brim of his cap up with the barrel of the M.12. "Get off that an' get ready."

Philip Large stammers until Cinders whispers in his ear. Philip then transforms and lowers his wide shoulders and round eyes in preparation for the fight to come.

Harry comes to me, "Ya still got that yoke?"

From my coat I reveal the pipe, "I do."

"Ya said ya'd fight for this place, is it true?"

"I told you, I'll fight and die for those what helped my family."

"Good, we'll fight. Cinders, we need to prepare, an' quick. We'll need to tell Paddy to get all the strongest homebrew an' grain alcohol, wet some towels wit' it and plug the bottles an' keep matches close," Harry looks round to everybody in the room, Red Donnelly and Henry Browne, The Lark and Big Dick, Philip Large, Dance Gillen, Thomas Burke and myself until he draws the gun in his righthand and a shiv in the left. "We're a shadow of our former selves, but if Bill thinks he's gonna take this place wit' a simple thrust, he's mistaken. Our ways are the ways o' honor and Bill Lovett has never valued that."

Waves of screams come from the crowd outside as Harry puts a hand on the desk, "The Dock Loaders' Club has been our headquarters since 1848. The power in Irishtown has always resided here except durin' Maroney's time. But we had it out wit' him an' took it back. We will burn it to the ground before losin' it again. An' we'll always be remembered as standin' up for honor's sake, hopefully," he allows for doubt in that statement. But then resurges with an angry assurance. "Bill Lovett would sink Irishtown in the East River if he could be the captain to go down wit' it, see. An' the pain that ya may feel before death? It will be a small price to pay for the cowardice ya fam'ly will know o' ya if we back down to Bill Lovett. To the end, we will stand up for our people. To the end, we lie down for no one. I ask yaz this question, why is Dinny Meehan in jail right now? Why?"

"Because he stole thousands o' dollars worth o' boots from Hanan & Sons?" Dance answers unsurely.

"That's right," Harry agrees in a hoarse growl and a pointed finger, then wheels round to the men. "He stole it to help those that need helpin'. That's what Dinny Meehan does, he uses his might to help people. To make right. He has always been there for them. I know I ain't much for talkin'. An' what I done. . . I have paid for my mistakes. Paid dearly, ya have no idea. . . But Dinny has been fair wit' me. Even in punishment, he is fair. I was a orphan wit' nothin' an' nobody but an ol' nun named Sister Reynolds who I was named after, but Dinny reached his hand out to me an' gave me life an breathed life into me. An' I know for a fact that all o' yaz have a similar story as mine. An' so too all o' them people outside. We are the forgotten, we are the unneeded, but Dinny always remembers us. No one cared for ya, but he did! If ya die today, ya die fightin' for everythin' that's right in this world, even if it is against the law. Ya die fightin' against what we know is wrong. I don' care if no one ever knows about me a hundret years from now an' I'm completely forgotten. For me. . . this is more than enough."

Every man in the room stands and barks in accord. The ceiling is too low, so we can't raise our fists and weapons. But we bark and howl like rabid dogs in husky, rhythmic punchy sounds, *REW, REW, REW,* and stamp in unison. Ready for death and a scorched earth plan. Refusing ever to secede our headquarters to Bill Lovett.

In a horrible hymn, and with a pulsing rhythm, *REW, REW, REW*, we trample down the stairs in a great calamitous war chant.

Over a shoulder I see Burke, who has not dared to make a move.

I turn round to him angrily, "Do you think you're safe up here?"

"I. . . I might just crawl out the window and jump down. Make my escape out back and maybe I can—"

"We have a hundred men who aren't here," I interrupt him. "Go get some of them as reinforcements. You know where the local men live here in Irishtown. You can run through the snow. Now go."

I make him go ahead of me down the stairs. Behind the bar, Paddy and Cinders collect match boxes and plug bottles with towels as Burke and I walk by. Philip stands next to them with his mouth open.

"Go wit' Liam," Cinders tells Philip, who waddles round the bar.

We file out the front door together as a band, barking and stamping, *REW, REW, REW*. Outside, we stand in the snow along the perimeter of the saloon. Above us, frozen spikes hang from the low roof that glitter like crystal glass in the morning sun.

The slew of mendicants that have braved the weather fall back away from the Dock Loaders' Club when they hear us bark and see us with weapons wielded.

"Please Liam!" Mrs. Lonergan's shrill voice cuts through our deep chants. "Just enough to get us t'rough the day! A few dullars!"

Beyond the edge of the crowd people are being shoved by something, though I can't see who or what it is. Whatever it is, it heads straight for the Dock Loaders' Club. Some cheer and shout as it gets closer. With the back of my foot against the wood frame of the saloon, I hold the pipe tight in my right hand.

I will not kill, but I will beat them back. I will not kill.

"For Mickey!" Dance Gillen pulls the bolt and barrel back to chamber the first bullet on the M.12.

REW, REW, REW, we chant and stomp and bang cudgels and pipes against the wood-framed headquarters.

Philip Large stands next to me and I pat him on his thick shoulder and make a fist as he nods back to me with his round eyes and tiny mouth while Burke slinks away and runs round the corner.

"Where's he goin'?" Harry demands.

"He's goin' to get more men that live nearby," I yell over the crowd noise. "But if he doesn't come back, well—"

"Good thinkin'," Harry nods.

The bodies in front of us begin to part. Some realize that a gang war is about to erupt and wrench their children by the hand in panic and push through the crush.

REW, REW, REW! Louder now, meaner, eyes bulging, teeth gritting.

"The king is here!" Mrs. Lonergan screams. "The king o' Irishtown!"

The entire crowd jumps in glee as Harry and I look at each other. The slew opens in front of us to form a clearing as up ahead the gaunt and elongated face of The Swede appears, while his long body casts a ghostly pall a head taller than all else. Angrily he drives people from his way with one arm and berates them. His other arm hangs uselessly at his side.

Cinders runs out with a flaming bottle in his hand, "What happened?"

"I've never been so happy to see such a ugly mug," I yell in Harry's direction, pointing at The Swede.

"Vincent!" Red Donnelly runs ahead and lifts Vincent Maher onto a shoulder in elation.

In the air Vincent is all sly smiles and piercing eyes. When Red lets him down he musses Vincent's mane and hugs him from the side. Behind them the Mullen and Sutton boys throw their small fists in the air. Vincent quickly has a hand-rolled in his teeth as he cuts through the slew with a libertine's swagger. The Masher, as he is monikered, surveys the crowd in a slim-fit long coat that hugs his lithe build. He then purses his lips and adjusts his cock down along his left leg. The length of his famous manhood plainly shows in his thigh-tight, belt-less trousers while the suspenders hang round the knees.

As Vincent and The Swede step aside, Dinny Meehan emerges and dawns through a clearing of the hungry Irishtown faithful. I can't help but smile when I see his powerful frame stride toward me while Feeble Philip embraces me so hard that I drop the lead pipe into the snow. The throaty words that spill out of Philip's mouth are indecipherable, but it's clear he is as elated as I am. It is then that the chanting falls into bursts and fits as Dinny's people claw at his clothing and pull at him. He moves forward with a manful gate and unflinching eyes. And sees me. Sees through me, even.

I turn to Harry to share in the relief, but he has gone. In the offing I spot the back of him as he moves through the thick slew away from us.

From the side Mrs. Lonergan falls to her knees and cries to Dinny and clutches at his thighs. He stops and touches her disfigured face, leading her back to her feet with a gentle hand on her cheek. Among the wild horde round them, her many children hold tight to her sack dress and eye the man who helps their mother stand.

"Please don' kill me son Richie," she implores. "I beg ya! Oh god, please fer once. Listen to me. Please don' do that to me. Not me Richie. Ye will be saved!" She suddenly screams out as she watches him walk through the crush. "When god comes back again, ya will be saved from the second death! Blessed are the dead what die in the name of our lord! On such his followers the second death hath no power!"

"What is she, some fanatic now? It's gods an' kings all the time wit' her," Big Dick laughs.

"Is that Tanner Smith?" The Lark wonders. "Why is Tanner goddamn Smith wit' Dinny an' them?"

"And Dead Reilly too," I say, the attorney tiptoes through the muddy snow in pointy black patent leather shoes and a pin-stripe suit.

"Tanner paid our bail," Vincent motions to me. "He got us out."

"He fookin' backstabbed us a couple years back," Cinders says. "He betrayed us. All o' us."

As Dinny walks toward me, my knees shake. He stops as I hold the door open, and looks at me with his green-stoned eyes and shakes my hand.

"Grab me a couple stools, would ya?" He says humbly, so I turn round and grab two from the bar inside and hand them to him through the door.

He takes the stools and sets them in front of the coal-soot windows of the Dock Loaders' Club and stands upon them. When the crowd sees him above, they cheer, though the widows spoon at their pots and pans noisily. Now joined by his enforcers, The Swede and Vincent, the rest of us, dockbosses and righthands and myself, surround him below.

"I should be going, fellows. Thank you so much, I'll be leaving now," Dead Reilly reaches out timidly to shake our hands goodbye.

"Wait here awhile," Tanner tells Reilly.

"I really should be going now—"

"Wait here," Tanner holds the sharply dressed attorney by the upper arm. "Why ya wanna run off so fast? Ya got a client more important than us?"

Reilly looks shaken as Dinny looks down at him, "Well do ya?"

"Eh, no I don't," Reilly washes a kerchief across his forehead and nervously mumbles to himself.

Dinny motions to the crowd and asks for silence by lowering his palms. But the hungry people are in hysterics.

"They're like to evict us," A father holds his young son on his shoulders to see the the man known as King of the Exiled, King of the Diddicoys, King of Irishtown and of course, King of Kings County.

"Where's Lumpy?" Cinders asks Vincent.

But Tanner Smith laughs when he hears that name, "Lumpy Gilchrist, the bean counter. . . Someone had to take it on the chin for the rest o' them to get released. Best it was him."

"Is that true?" I ask Vincent.

He shrugs. "Guess so."

Poor Lumpy Gilchrist, the savant.

Lumpy could do but one thing in life; count numbers in his head, for which Dinny put him to good use. We want no record of our earnings, so Lumpy's talent served our needs. In a time of relative peace, Lumpy was a valuable member of the White Hand. Other than that lone talent, however, he was as helpless as a baby.

I look with concern to the feeble-minded Philip Large. The White Hand protects the weak and the defenseless, and for that I am proud, but at least Philip can fight like a wild boar. Knock-kneed Lumpy was as lily-livered as a lamb, but having him spend his remaining days in Sing Sing is a fate worse than death.

Dinny stands over us and surveys the crowd of Irishtown faithful as a host of smokestacks and water towers stand sentinel in the east. He waits for them to quiet with cool patience as the currents of wind rush through his coat and snap behind him.

"Me girls an' me bhoys are hungry," Mrs. Lonergan screeches. "I've already buried two childers! An' now we've no food an' facin' eviction from that leech o' the land, Mr. Vandeleurs an' his own band o' thugs. What will ya do fer us, man?"

"Uhright, uhright," The Swede growls as the clank of pots and pans chorus over him. "Let the man talk!"

Dinny's voice booms out over the heads to shepherd their attention, "I am here t'day to announce that our enemies are at the gates. The siege o' Irishtown has begun!"

The people jostle among each other in the cold to get a better look at him. From the cobblestones that reach down into the railyard on the water half a block away, to the street and sidewalks that lead up to the Hanan & Sons shoe factory in the opposite direction, the people move closer to hear him.

"But when a people are forced to their knees, it's not proof o' their weakness. It's proof only that their strength is to be feared. They have taken the life o' one o' our own, my own relation, Mickey Kane," his voice cracks when he says the name.

Sympathetic faces stare back to see if he will cry.

"A golden prince, was he!" A woman howls.

"The heir to Irishtown!" Another voice calls out.

"T'was Bill Lovett!" A man yells out the bitter words we know to be true.

Dinny roars out over them all, "They took his life to instill fear among us. To take our heart. To divide us!"

"But we are hungry *now*!" Mrs. Lonergan demands as one hundred wooden spoons clap on one hundred pots to take up her claim.

"I will feed ya," Dinny looks in Mrs. Lonergan's direction with kindness in his eyes. "It is my life's work. I have always cared for the people o' Irishtown an' the elders what came from the old country, have I not?"

It's a fair play to him on that point. Not a single face can disagree.

"An' I always will until my dyin' breath. But we who are here now, within the walls o' Irishtown an' the long riverine territories have a great decision upon us. For seventy years gangs have kept outsiders out. But now the enemy is. . . Ourselves. The outsiders, the foreigners, they have burrowed their way into our hearts an' crept into our fam'lies within the walls. One o' our own, Bill Lovett has turned against us."

"Again!" A woman holds up a fist.

"Black bastard!" The Mullen boy yells.

"Some o' ya are related to his followers. Sons that ya love, or Grandsons even. Beloved husbands an' carin' fathers. . . I could not ask ya to turn against ya own family, for that is what Bill Lovett asks. We have a choice now, each an' every one o' us. Will ya turn against ya own people an' join Lovett?"

The crowd stirs.

"I am loyal. I pledge a bunch o' fives to ya!" The Mullen boy bows up and stands forth with two fists held up. His ferocity is joined too, by chants of "Patrick Kelly, Patrick Kelly, Patrick Kelly!"

"The auld ways!" A toothless man sings out with spittle in the air. "Honor the ways of our forebears!"

Dinny's voice carries in the wind, "If only we could turn to one man for blame, but we cannot. Our enemy is fivefold an' gainin' power. I cannot make ya mind. I cannot give ya the courage to put ya lives up against our enemies. I have neither the right nor the arrogance to do so. An' on my honor there will be no punishment from me if ya decide in ya heart that our enemy gives ya a better life. I simply ask ya a question," he bows his head, then slowly brings it back up to the faces that watch him. "I ask ya to search in ya heart. Is there a-one o' ya this day who believes Bill Lovett would do the same for yaz as what these men an' myself have tried so hard to accomplish for our people?"

"Bill Lovett only cares for hisself!" A woman announces. "He would never care for my fam'ly!"

"We love ya, sir!"

"Our people have survived much worse than Wild Bill Lovett," they answer the call with cheers. "We will stand together as we have in the past. We will set aside our petty squabbles an' accept our neighbor's needs as our own. Do not come wit' ya hand outstretched. Come bearin' gifts, however meager they may be. That is our way."

"But we are hungry *now*!" Mrs. Lonergan repeats.

On the stools, Dinny nods his head in the air and points down toward Tanner Smith who stands below and at his side, "Thanks to a ol' friend, we are here in front o' yaz today. Life as we known it will be forever changed. We no longer can make the money we once did since the war's ended an' no more European contracts to be had... For each family I have cash to give for meals this week," Dinny meets their request. "An' as far as the landlord Vandeleurs is concerned, we will pay that leech your rent for the next two months."

Cinders whispers in my ear, "Where'd Tanner get all that money, payin' for bail an' all these handouts? We banished him for good reason. Now he shows up like a hero wit' a bag o' money? Who gave him all that money's what I wanna know."

Mrs. Lonergan blurts out, "What about Mickey Kane! What will be done about ya cousin's, eh. . . disappearance? An' what about the Red Hook territory?"

Without answer, Dinny pans across the gathering to Mourning Mother Mary, as she is known. The burn scars on her face give her the mask of a woman perpetually sad, or insane. Yet Dinny looks upon her with great generosity.

But Dinny Meehan does not warn his enemies before he strikes out at them. And so nothing is said in return. The silence itself is blacker than any words. In time the metallic moans of the Manhattan Bridge and its banshee screeches fill the void as a train passes overhead, *cha-chum, cha-chum, cha-chum*.

"We should attack before they come at us," The Swede whispers among Dinny's inner circle. "Beat McGarry says Bill's on his way now. Here!"

But Dinny ignores him as he steps down from the stools and turns to my direction, "Where are the McGowans? Why are the McGowans not here?"

I try to answer, but my heart gets caught in my throat when I think of Emma McGowan. It's said that first love never dies, but when Emma died of the grippe, my willingness to love seemed to have died with her. I can no longer fall head over heels for a girl, and that might hurt worse than any beating Bill Lovett's men could give me.

Cinders answers Dinny, "The McGowan's left the city. I couldn't stop them. Rochester, I think."

As Tanner hands money to the needy, the mendicants send humble thanks to the white hand that feeds.

"Did you know that Garry Barry is alive?" I come to Dinny's ear. "And he is working with Wolcott and the Waterfront Assembly?"

But he seems overcome with the idea that the McGowan family left Brooklyn while he'd been incarcerated.

"I know you and McGowan went way back," I speak up after swallowing my shyness. "Too brave, too pure they say of him. But he's been dead for almost four years. You did right by him. You buried him with dignity and took care of his family. You even found them all jobs. But we have important things—"

"Sadie an' my son?" He interrupts. "Where are they?"

"They are out on Long Island. Darby and Anna hounded them while you were gone and broke the window in the brownstone," Through the crowd Harry glances over his shoulder at us from a distance. "That's when we saw Barry and Wiz the Lump."

Mrs. Lonergan's boisterous voice breaks in again for Dinny's attention, "Thank ya so very much, man. An' what 'bout the bikecycle shop eh?"

"That biddy ol' hag ain't worth a flamin' bag o' dog shit to us now," The Swede puts in for Dinny's consideration. "Her husband an' her eldest son are both Bill's now. Let that bicycle shop pay its own way."

"Tanner," Dinny calls out. "Give her some extra for the bike shop. Two mont's rent. She's got a business to run."

Tanner nods his head and peels off a few more bills for Mary as she leaves us with a pug ugly smile and handfuls of cash.

For once I agree with The Swede's logic. Over the crowd I look with a cold eye, for some here would take the Hanan boots, the handouts of cash and our good will and ask Bill Lovett to better it.

At that moment Burke comes round the corner with twenty men behind him.

"Let Bill come for us now," The Swede clutches the handle of a wooden cudgel. "An' we'll cut him down in the snow."

Little Riddle

"Kill, kill!" Non Connors yells over his shoulder and thrusts a cudgel into the air.

Darby Leighton strides through the deep snow at the ass end of Bill Lovett's new gang. As the wind lashes at the florid bruise over his eye he blocks the gusts with the back of his right hand. Through his fingers he eyes the Statue of Liberty between a brick rail house and a decrepit clapboard stable. But his hands burn like ice in the cold, so he shakes them out and pushes them into trouser-pockets. Under a flat cap tears freeze on his cheeks when the wind rushes over the snow.

I have to convince Bill I can be his Fifth Lieutenant, Darby's thoughts race as he struggles against the elements. *He has to understand. I have a family to support now. Everyone has a role already, but me.*

Inland, on the left is the corbeled brickwork and arched windows of the half-buried Pioneer Iron Works factories.

Empty this morn. Everything is empty this morn. Even my stomach.

Up ahead Connors again belts out to a solemn morning, "We're gonna fookin' grind them down to dust! Whose territory is this?"

"It's ours!" fifty men chant back. "Always been ours."

DIVIDE THE DAWN

"Who do we name for losin' this ground?" Connors calls out again.

"Meehan! Dinny fookin' Meehan!" they raise rope in response, and kitchen knives, spades and blackened two-by-fours pulled from burnt-out storehouses.

You're not supposed to say that name, the thought comes to Darby as a matter of routine.

"We take this back t'day," Connors growls through clenched teeth, the veins in his neck coursing blue with aroused blood.

"Kill, kill, kill!" the gang hoarsely chants in the bitter cold.

Bill's gang is lined up in phalanx formation from sidewalk to sidewalk between the buildings and cuts through the snow like a spear through white skin. At the head of them all is Bill Lovett with his weather-worn sheep's pelt over a pressed Army uniform. He is flanked by his lieutenants on the left and right—one-arm Joey Flynn, Frankie Byrne, the limping Richie Lonergan and a rabid Non Connors goads the crowd with hymns to homicide.

The grunts who form the weight of Bill's force follow along. Many deem themselves the Trench Rabbits and have taken up the moniker proudly. The crew of teens that follow Richie Lonergan includes Abe Harms the little German Jew, Petey Behan the Cutpurse, Matty Martin and Timmy Quilty, but since there are so many Tims and Toms and Jims and Johns, the men call him Timmy Bucks, since he has a face-full of buck teeth. Lagging behind them all like a lost soldier, Darby pulls up the rear.

The angry mob passes P.S. Thirty, but the primary school is barren of children on this day. On the right comes the Lidgerwood factory. Inside, foundries normally melt steel into liquid and cast it. An assembly line then manufactures electric hoists for miners in Pennsylvania or even loggers out in Washington State as well as heating boilers for ships and modern buildings. But today it is vacant as if the industrial age had ended and only the shells of buildings past remain.

"Kill!" Connors yells into an echoless air. A shirtless blacksmith holds crucible tongs and watches the men pass from arched iron double-doors as steam emits from the forge and furnace inside the brick facade.

Four wild hounds slip by Darby and hop through the snow baying along to the men's song, joyful to join the hunt. Bill had fed them enough meat scraps to whet their love for blood, and to assert his status as pack leader. Just as he'd done with his new gang members. Just enough to want for more.

"Kill, kill!" The incessant chants goes on as Darby's stomach bubbles in fitful churns at the words.

"My god," he mumbles as John Lonergan, Richie's father, thrusts a stevedore's hook in the air. "Someone will be killt today."

"Vhat did you say?" Abe Harms falls back to Darby and pushes a broom handle into his chest. "Here, you need a veapon."

"Does it really need to come to this?" Darby leans his windburnt face down to Abe and speaks in a lowered tone.

But Abe does not respond in-kind and moves his close-cropped eyes away from Darby, "Keep your head up, Leighton. This is the best thing that could have happened to you."

"I don't need advice from a teen," Darby shoots back.

"Yet you ask," Abe coolly glances upward. "Vhat opportunities did you have after Mickey Kane took over Red Hook? You had none. And now you valk among Bill's men pouting like a petulant little parasite. Are you just a hanger-on like shit on a dog's tuchis?"

"I ain't poutin'," Darby snaps back and picks at the icy tears stuck to his cheek. "I just don't think it needs to get bloody."

The thought of blood makes Darby's stomach churn again. When he witnessed his brother Pickles go hilt-deep with a knife in a man's belly back in 1910, Darby had turned as white as the dying man. And when he watched Bill's gun transform Sammy de Angelo's face into a meaty ruin, he felt the tension in the body loosen and—

Oh, Jesus on the cross, Darby grits and winces just thinking about it.

After he witnessed that murder up close, Darby stood woozily until his stomach threw its contents out of his mouth so quickly that it shocked him. And when he smelled the deep scent of iron and saw the puddle of blood slowly spread round de Angelo's collapsed head like a red halo, his legs wobbled, his body shook and all went black. Moments later he was awoken to men dragging him, while a cacophonous roar had taken over one ear that dogs Darby to this day. That was back in 1917, Bill's first revolt against Dinny Meehan's White Hand Gang.

How much blood must be culled in the second?

Abe leans into Darby's good ear as if to answer, "Vhen the resources dvindle, the cruelest zurvive and the compassionate must step aside. Those who have the ability to plunder and kill at will may live longer days than those who hesitate. It may be a hard truth, but in the grand zcheme of things, Bill Lovett is doing great acts of benevolence."

"I'm sure Mickey Kane'll take great solace in that," Darby counters.

"In this vorld men like you and I must find a vay to become valuable. Parasites will be purged. Here, a man is judged by his value. And value you have, Darby Leighton. You are marked, you know. You have a very important role to play. More important than any of us, except Bill. Do you even know vhat it is? Your role?"

I will be Bill's Fifth Lieutenant, and you will be my underling.

But instead of admitting his desire, Darby says, "I know all the narrow alleys and courts, back entrances, dark corners an' hidden passages through the mazes all along the waterfront from the Navy Yard down to Red Hook. I know where Detective William Brosnan goes to collect his stipend from Jonathan G. Wolcott's lump, Wisniewski. I know where Vincent Maher goes to get his cock stroked and I know where Liam Garrity's mother and sisters live." Darby eyes the short teen. "I know all the comin's an' goin's o' the White Hand an' if a slattern farts in Brooklyn, I can tell ya if ya she puts butter on her potatoes or milk, so don' pretend I don' know that rightin' the lie about my brother

Pickles an' gettin' him outta Sing Sing is in Bill's best interest, as well as yours and mine."

"Good, good. Then the only question is, can you accomplish this? Because vhen ve look into your bevildered eyes, we do not know if you can. And if you are able to do it, then you must know how to leverage it for your benefit. Do you know how to do any of this? I can help you, if you require it. You need but ask, and I vill be there. There is great danger ahead. Mortal danger to your person."

And now he threatens.

Darby leers wordlessly back at Abe, a wee fellow with little eyes and little teeth, a floppy cap and the round shoulders of a nosey little mole, yet his words are sharp as shanks.

Is this little mole on my side? Or is he my competition?

"I don' need ya help," Darby says. "But ya can bet ya bottom dollar on this. Bill hasn't been in Brooklyn for close on two years, an' watch. . . when he needs to know somethin', he'll come to me. Not some cagey foreigner."

Abe says, "Didn't you come here from London vhen you vere young?"

"I was born Northern Ireland," Darby says proudly.

"But are you Catholic-Irish?" Little Abe's breath is cool as winter mint on the ear. "Or maybe worse than a Jew, are you a Prod?"

"Keep guessin'. At some point ya might get somethin' right," Darby says. "Knowin' things is what *I'm* known for. It was me who got my cousin, Dinny's wife Sadie to pay for Dead Reilly, Dinny's own attorney. Now we got a retrial for Pickles in May. What've *you* done for Bill?"

The men call out ahead, "We take back what is ours t'day! Kill! Kill!"

"Yez, yez, you have convinced your cousin to turn on her husband. Zuch a talent you have," Abe says in a tone that is half-whisper, half-indictment. "But it is not talent alone that has convinced Zadie Meehan to help free Pickles, I vould bet. There is more to it than that. You must know zomething, yez. Zomething that she is deeply ashamed of. A zecret, maybe. Yez, zecrets are more valuable than zlungshots. Zecrets are as dangerous as a drunkard with a loaded pistol. I vill give you this, if you truly do possess the ability to vield that type of cruelty, Darby Leighton, you may yet zurvive. Blackmailing your own kin? A lethal veapon indeed. Tell me, what shame do you hold over poor Zadie's heart?"

"Ya sponge up lies like a bride does seeds; hopin' they quicken," Darby waves him off. "Keep guessin'."

"You are a ztrange man. Cruel, yet naive enough to believe you can trust Dead Reilly."

"His motives are easy to read. He may play both sides, but we'll see how that shakes out. I tell ya what though, the man knows his way outta a murder conviction. But if ya do get convicted, he'll lower the sentence. Shit, if ya broke a mirror, Dead Reilly'll get ya off wit' only four years bad luck. He's got value for us. But ya gotta give him the dime. The dime is all. Point is, I'm the one turnin' Dinny's pockets inside out. What were ya doin' when I was buildin' Bill's army? Ya're known only for whispers, secrets and rumors, but everyone knows whispers are louder than screams around here. How's Bill gonna trust a fella who can't speak his mind aloud?"

Abe leans in again with a furtive smile, "Is it ztupidity, or a lack of common zense that allows you to believe a vhisper is more zuspicious than a shadow? Charity requires hope for the latter."

"I need no charity," Darby snaps back as he trudges through the snow.

"No I zuppose you have been very busy," Abe turns his head sideways. "You've even found time to make a daughter, yez?"

Darby chews on those words.

I should've never spoken about Colleen Rose openly. I can only hope that this little mole does not find a way to use her against me. Or worse; find out who her mother is.

"Darby, Darby my little friend," Abe tisks him with soft horse-clicks and a calm authority. "If you were given two bits every time you didn't know what vas going on, you'd vonder vhy you had zo many bits. You do not know the Irish, even though you are one, zupposedly. The Irish have a head-full of ghosts. It can happen to anyone though:

Irish, Italian, German, African, Indian. It makes no matter. When an entire generation zuffers great tragedy, war. . . Your people call it *An Gorta Mór*, yez? The Great Hunger? The famine?"

"Don' call it famine," Darby corrects. "It weren't no fookin' famine."

"The next generation and beyond experience living nightmares, and in zleep the dead visit in dreams. These are zad times your kind lives. Dark times. Times of mystery and zuperstition. But you have zpent too much time alone in the shadows, Darby Leighton. I speak vith you not as an enemy, but to help you, yez. Now listen to this. Think on this, I ask you. Think of who it is that has power among Bill's men. Mathematics advises that the power of numbers is ztrong. And zo is the power of love, for there is nothing zo assured than a red-haired girl's revenge."

"Whose revenge?" Darby asks. "For what?"

"First you must lower your voice, my friend. Think on this, I ask you. You are zmart, believe it or not. You can zolve this little riddle, I'm sure you can, yez. Listen to the words I give you. Very important, yez. Ve all hope for your zuccess, yez ve do."

As the fervor of the Trench Rabbits ahead wanes over the long push through the snow, Darby leans down into Abe's ear, "Who wants revenge?"

"Darby, Darby, my little friend," Abe's eyes slowly move up to meet his. "You have zeen much from your place behind blind corners and atop factories, it's true. But even you have missed the beauty of hidden love inside the heart of an evil little girl, think on this, I ask you."

"Riddles ya got?"

Abe shrugs one shoulder and tosses his hand at the wrist. "Ve need your help, Darby. But you don't listen vell. You can't see vhat is happening below the zurface. Vhen a riddle is zolved there is a zubtlety that is understood, and the expanse opens. Only then you vill see the bigger plan at vork. Only then can you help us."

I'll have to outsmart this one in order to get ahead, Darby bites his lip. *But can I do that? I've revealed too much to him. If I am to become Bill's Fifth Lieutenant, I'll need an edge. I'll need to. . . kill someone.*

At that moment Darby sees the quizzical eyes appear in the low-rise tenement windows above. A yawning, rusty wind rushes through the narrow alleys as the eyes look down at him and the gang that pushes through the cold morning snow. Yet they fix on him, mostly. Or so Darby believes.

They know me. They know my struggle. Those eyes know everything about me.

Hunger bites at the inside of Darby's stomach. He hasn't slept all night and a euphoria swims up his body in strange pulsing surges as the eyes watch him.

Should I even be here?

But Darby is having another spell. He places a palm on his temple. When he is nervous or anxious, the spells come to him. Overtake him and fill him with dread and despair and guilt and terror and. . .

Hopefully it will soon pass.

But his teeth chatter and his eyes flick back and forth.

Please make it go away. Please, please.

He shivers under the eyes that stare. The eyes that watch. He hears his mind replaying the riddle: *The beauty of hidden love inside the heart of an evil little girl,* the words repeat, overcoming his own determination to stop them.

Up in the windows, the needy eyes stare. Those eyes. Those judging eyes send wiry tendrils through his body as he slides his flat cap low over his weatherworn face. Between the buildings one block away the brackish green channel slaps hard against the bulkhead and sends saltwater and foam spraying into the snow.

Non Connors' voice rips through Darby like the sound of two ship hulls scraping and shearing against each other, "Fookin' beat them down to a whimper! This is our territory!"

Darby's feet and legs are wetted through to the skin and the only thing that stops him from feeling completely frozen is that he keeps moving, trudging, yanking and pulling at his legs through the thigh-deep snow.

Then he notices Abe's eyes on him too. He gathers his thoughts and turns to the little narrow-eyed teen, "An' what's ya value? What is it that ya want?"

"I vant zimply to help Bill to the zecond floor of the Dock Loaders' Club, leader of the White Hand. The man in control of Irishtown and all the incomes from the terminals and territories," Abe says as if he's memorized the response.

"An' how ya gonna help him win it?"

"Best vorry how you yourself can help Bill vin Irishtown," he says without looking. "You are the one marked for greatness, not me."

High in the blossoming blue morning sky languishes a white three-quarter moon as if it had waited for Darby to notice all along.

The morning moon, he beams.

When Darby was a boy his Aunt Rose had taught him moon phases, which had been taught to her by her Romani father in Ireland.

"Ye was born under a wanin' gibbous," Aunt Rose had told him through brown teeth and whiskey breath. "Ye will be a healer. Maybe a spiritual healer or even a teacher. Ye may cure ignorance or heal the soul, but yer message will not always be well-taken, nay, t'will oft-times be too difficult fer yer students to hear the words an' the visions."

Darby believed her then, though he could not see the evidence over the course of the next twenty-odd years of his life.

A teacher? I don't know who I am now. And at this moment I cannot even feel my body from the cold or hear my own footsteps from being half-deaf.

He kept fond memories of his Aunt Rose, who travelled with him from London. His own mother, he never knew. But Aunt Rose had shown him kindness, humored his innocence and spoke with him at length as no other grownup had ever done. He even remembers crying to her once as she held him at her soft bosom. Though all that was before she abandoned him and Pickles to the Brooklyn streets when he was but five years old.

In the sky the morning moon stares back at him.

Who am I? Why am I here? Please tell me. Bill needs to know. He needs to know what I know in order to win. I must teach him, even if he refuses to heed me. Is that why I am here? Should I kill to become his Fifth Lieutenant?

"Kill, kill!" the men sing, but the lyrics catch in Darby's throat when he tries to join the melody. The staccato chant reminds him of stabbing motions. And it reminds him of Pickles, of course, his psychopathic brother. "Kill, kill, kill!"

Up ahead the last turn comes into view.

We're almost there.

Anxiety creeps over Darby's skin. The thought of blood and death shoots another pulsing surge of dread, startling him.

In truth, I should be with Colleen Rose, Darby wipes his cold nose with a sleeve.

He had told his fiancé Ligeia that he was going out to celebrate the birth of their daughter with his older brother Frank. But that was many hours ago. And Ligeia feared being left alone. She had travelled by her lonesome at sea from Southern Italy, stopping at strange ports with strange languages. And at the end of seven grueling months, the ship at last fell into the New York Harbor.

But loneliness hung over her like a dark cloud from the day she was born. In telling her story to Darby, Ligeia spoke in absolutes and with hand gestures that eloquently accented her points as when she declared her berth at Ellis Island here in New York the very first day of her life. Her new life. The horrors before that, in Italy, she could only hope to forget. Here in America, Ligeia is a pretty face among many pretty faces. But in Italy she was an ugly family secret, exposed, hounded and forced away.

And now, after giving birth, she rests at Long Island College Hospital with no one by her side. Unmarried and with broken English.

I should be with her, Darby shakes his head. *But I will make us a steady income first. Then I will be there for her and our little Colleen Rose. I must provide, as a father should. But if it were to be found out that Ligeia is Italian,* Darby hears his teeth clack together. *No, please not that.*

"Ginzo hunt!" The bantam Petey Behan calls out. "Beautyful mornin' for a ginzo hunt!"

Darby's stomach churns as he side-eyes Abe Harms.

"Here t'day, gone tomato!" Flynn quarks in laughter. "Hey Frankie, when was the last time ya killt a I-talian?"

"It was only a dago," Frankie Byrne answers with a half-smile.

At Coffey Street Bill is at the head of the van and is the first to cut to the right at building's edge. His lieutenants and the rest round it in a wide tide of men with waves of snow crashing at their thighs.

"Terror," Abe touches Darby's arm and smiles. "It was the Conquest of Gaul when Julius Zaesar zaid that it is dread of the unknown that inspires terror. And all this time the White Hand thought we were coming for them today. . . But it is zurprise that will win us back Red Hook instead."

Up ahead a small outpost of less than twenty Italian longshoremen are huddled and linger by an engineless barge on the water. Caught unawares, they lazily turn when they hear the chants a block away. But when it is realized that the men are coming for them, a few bow up their chests and grab for broken gear shifters and long shards of glass.

Until one of them yells, *"Pulcinella!"*

And with that word they scatter and break apart, but can go nowhere but north.

"Guinea-negroes on the run!" Connors yells and sprints ahead.

The fastest of Bill's men split off in a sprint and close in on them, supported by yellow, shit-brown and black dogs twirling tails high and yawping chattily at the Italians. Connors leads this group as Bill takes a cache of men to cut off the south. Flynn takes the lead of the largest band to assault the belly of the enemy and push all the way back to water's edge to cut the enemy in two. Darby does not share the happy savagery the lieutenants, Trench Rabbits, Lonergan Crew and howling hounds enjoy. He follows Flynn up the middle and haplessly swings his broom handle ahead of him, hitting nothing but air. He even feigns a swing at a man he has no intention of hurting. Darby realizes that the little mole takes note of him again. Abe then presses on and joins an assault to take down and subdue the lone rowdy Italian man with enough dignity to go down swinging. Though the round, olive-skinned man is beaten like all the rest by Bill's boys, he is not so badly bloodied for the sake of respect. When the man is fully restrained Abe kicks him in the ribs and glares at Darby.

Where Coffey and Van Dyke streets end on the water, a small inlet opens at the elbow of Red Hook. There, a pier slices through the middle of it out beyond the bulkhead. When Flynn's assault force reaches water's edge overlooking the inlet, the Italians are rounded, bound and forced to the ground. From the south Bill's men drag more through the snow. All prisoners then have their ankles strung to their wrists behind their backs and forced to sit along the coping of the bulkhead on their knees. Minutes later the baying of hounds intensifies until Connors and his group appear with more bound and bloodied prisoners and sat next to the rest. There the prisoners' feet hang off the edge of the bulkhead and behind, the water churns and bulbs up to wet them. Fearful, they look back over their shoulders with foreboding.

A frightened mutter comes to Darby's ear from a prisoner, *"Pulcinella il morto."*

On their knees the whole lot of them peer in fear at Bill with his dark gun-powder eyes, cherub ears and sheep's carcass over an Army uniform. With the murderous Lovett ahead, the channel churns behind hungrily, eager to swallow the prisoners whole.

"Pulcinella il morto è tornato" Darby hears.

"Stop sayin' that," Connors pushes a man over the seawall and holds him there by the thread of his coat. "I hear that word one more time an' I'll let ya go."

The man screams as the current reaches up to his hips, the rest of them stare with round, pale faces until Connors and Byrne pull him back up to his knees.

Flynn and Lonergan have unfastened the small engineless barge from the bollards and tossed the mooring lines into the channel and wave it off, "Go to the North Terminal o' Red Hook, or fuck off somewhere else," Flynn cackles in laughter. "Yaz came to the wrong terminal. As o' t'day, the Black Hand's gone from all o' Red Hook. This is Irish White Hand again."

"Do you speak for both the Black Hand an' the White?" A sailor cups his hands and yells across the bow.

"Nah, Wild Bill Lovett," Flynn answers. "The true leader o' the White Hand."

The sailor stares back with a confused look as the current pulls his barge out to the choppy harbor with nothing to power them.

Inland, Bill follows the footpaths through the snow from the dock to the street where the Italian longshoremen were loading automobile trucks. Five teamsters watch as Bill tracks the footprints closely and raises his eyes up to them. The teamsters scatter and jump into their trucks and turn over the engines in haste.

"Ya want I should stop them?" Frankie Byrne asks Bill. "We could sell the goods in local stores for half price."

"We ain't river pirates," Connors sneers.

"Go get me one o' them trucks," Bill cuts in. "An empty one. An' make the driver wait here, but don' beat him so bad he can't drive, uhright?"

Bill turns back and walks toward the dark-haired prisoners as five of his men rush past him to stop one of the teamsters.

Bill walks past Darby and the toothy smiles of the Shit Hounds and points at the men along the seawall, "Who among yaz speaks English?"

Fret-faced Italians look at each other, then back to Bill. One of them outright cries and sniffles and pleas with strange sounding words. Even as Darby's wife-to-be speaks the same language as these men, he does not know their words. It is Ligeia who has spent day and night learning English instead.

"Bring that one here, the crier," Bill points to the ground in front of him for the crier to be laid.

Connors and Byrne pick the man up by the upper arms and pull him through the snow, his knees drag behind. They turn him round to face his countrymen so they can see his tears and fear.

"Darby?" Bill looks round him.

Darby's stomach turns as he comes forward.

"The fuck ya got in ya hand, a dustbroom?"

Darby shows him, "Broom handle."

"Dustbroom Darby," Bill deems him with a crack of a smile on his blue lips. But Bill's snickering stirs a sodden cough in his chest that outlasts the chuckles his jape inspires. He bends and gags three, four times until he culls up a mouthful of red and green spittle and discharges it in front of the prisoners. After which, Bill gazes into their scared eyes as long lines of bloody slather dangle from his open mouth and swings in the gusts off the southern Buttermilk Channel.

With a nasally, sickly chortle, Bill wipes the slaver with a single finger and whips it away while leaning on the fearful prisoner's shoulder, "I thought I asked a question. If I don' get a answer I'm gonna shoot a guy to show yaz how serious I am. Who the fuck among yaz has English?"

"I could speak it," A hogtied man says with a thick South Brooklyn accent.

Bill comes to Darby's good ear, soft peach fuzz brushes against his cheek, "When I point at ya, ya hit this man in the knuckles wit' that dustbroom. Ya do what I say. Show me what ya can do an' we'll talk."

The crier's hands are connected tightly by a rope to his ankles. Darby grips the broom handle, then loosens it.

Can I do this?

The crier gazes with kitten eyes at the broom handle, then turns away in sadness when he hears the voice of *Pulcinella*.

"Translate this," Bill announces while walking along the line of bound prisoners on the bulkhead. "Ya will leave here this day an' never return. This is the territory o' the White Hand, led by me, Bill Lovett."

The translator busily chatters behind Bill, "*Dice che dobbiamo partire oggi e. . .*"

"Understand somethin'. Since the 1840s this territory's been Irish," he turns sharply when he reaches the last bound man. "Only when a weaklin' gave it to yaz as the price o' turnin' *me* out did yaz receive this territory. The price o' peace, so ya thought. It was a three-way deal between ya Prince o' Pals Frankie Yale, Dinny Meehan an' Thos Carmody o' the ILA union. Ya may have thought the war wit' the Irish was over when ya made that deal. I am here to tell yaz that it's peace that's finished. An' the war is back!"

Flynn smiles and scratches his chin with the barrel of his revolver. Bill turns and points at Darby as behind him the translator trails off. Darby's teeth clack and clap in his head as he grips the broom handle. As he rears back and holds it behind him, Darby catches the prisoner's eyes and hears the pleading tone of holy invocations in Latin. He grits his teeth to make the clatter stop and hears the call of prayer while between buildings the wind wheezes. He then lowers the broom handle and slaps at the hands softly, without so much as a peep of pain from the prisoner.

Bill's ears turn red in fury, "Not like that!" He charges Darby, yanks the broom handle from his grip and elbows him from his way. "Like this!"

Bill rips the broom handle downward as if it were a war hammer until a crack echoes through the wood.

"*Ayoooo!*" the prisoner yowls and flops on his side, wiggling in pain like a fish on a cast line. The shit-brown hound's dander goes up with the excitement and bites at the Italian's pant leg and tears rabidly back and forth.

Flynn laughs uncontrollably, *caw-caw-caw-caw*, while Connors sneers with disgust at the crier.

"That's a good puppy," Abe mutters.

"The peace ya paid for has expired!" Bill proclaims, high on the pain he's inflicted as the translator translates in an echo of foreign words. "Dinny Meehan's in jail an' Thos Carmody from the union? Well it just so happens that he fought in the Great War wit' me and some o' my men here. Fought valiantly too, an' was injured like we was. An' we talked about Brooklyn, me'n Thos did. What we was gonna do if we ever got back. An' made a pact. So here it is, I declare war on ya fookin' ginnea-wops—"

Mid-sentence Bill looks at Darby and walks in front of him and snaps the broom handle across the crier's knees.

Irate, he hurls the handle over the other prisoners' heads into the shaggy whitecaps that beard the choppy channel.

"*Ayoooo!*" the crier screams again as the mutts growl, then snap at him until they turn on each other. Two of the animals bounce against one another's chests and wriggle in the snow until the shit-brown hound asserts itself as the dominant while the yellow dog paws upward from the snow in supplication.

"By the end o' this day we will push ya people back across the Gowanus Canal. From this day on, if ya need work," Bill points to the south. "Go to the BushbTerminal or the Grand Army Terminal, south o' the Gowanus border. All o' Red Hook an' the North Brooklyn docks is Irish again!"

Bill's men hoot and throw their fists and weapons up.

"But still yet," Bill yells while men whoop and clap sticks and cudgels against the side of a building. "I don' believe yaz understand me well enough. I don' think yaz know what I'm sayin'."

Bill pulls up his sheepskin pelt to reveal a large handgun as a glint of cold sunlight flashes off the barrel across Darby's eyes.

"This man here wants to be my lieutenant," The translator trails behind Bill's English with Italian. "In my gang, death elevates a man to the heights he hopes to achieve. For only when ya own a man's life does his soul strengthen ya."

Richie Lonergan and Frankie Byrne shoo the mutts that guard the crier and right him back on his knees. They hold him still as the dogs snap at him. Then they blindfold the man and stand back amidst the rest of the gang men.

In some ceremonial change over, Bill clicks his heels and turns the .45 caliber in his hand. He holds the barrel in his palm over his forearm, and hands it over to Darby Leighton with a demeanor of officialdom.

"This is ya day come," Bill announces. "The day ya take the future in ya own hands. Today we will reclaim all o' Red Hook. Tomorrow Irishtown. Many men will die when we assault the South Terminal at the Erie Basin, but one must die now. To show yaz. To make yaz understand that I am not just some *Pulcinella*-clown, but the man to take Brooklyn, one o' yaz must give ya life. Yaz need to know deep in ya. Not by words, but by blood as blood feeds hearts and minds. An' now," Bill turns. "Darby Leighton, a new father who has shed the shadows o' his past, wantin' nothin' more than to take part in the feast o' his own future for the right to feed his family; this man will make blood an' stand at my side as my Fifth Lieutenant an' soon-to-be dockboss, wit' all the attendin' incomes an' graft."

Bill steps back as Darby holds the frozen gun loosely in hand. All eyes are on him.

This is for us Ligeia. And you Colleen Rose, Darby warrants.

Behind the Italian he takes a stance with his right foot between the prisoner's feet, arm extended. He feels Bill's eyes on him; red-rimmed and black and angry. Then raises the gun and rests it on the back of the man's head.

"*Aspetta, cosa sta succedendo? Ho una famiglia,*" the man says into the air blindly. "*Ho una figlia, figlia, figlia.*"

"He says he has a daughter," the translator speaks out from the bulkhead.

"Ya shaddup!" Connors answers him. "Nobody told ya translate that."

Darby's eyes go soft and glass over with water when the wind blows in them. His mouth nervously twitches as he licks quickly at his dry lips.

The sly and glottal words of Abe Harms comes to Darby's good ear, "Do it. You know how, my little friend, yez."

Pangs of hunger bleat at the inside of Darby's stomach. And throughout his body rings a deep and feverish shiver. His eyes are heavy with lack of sleep and all he can think of is a warm bed with Colleen Rose between him and Ligeia. He imagines himself lift the baby when she has fallen asleep to gently place her in the crib just steps away from the glow of a soft-crackling fireplace.

If I don't kill this man, that day will never come. I must win work on the docks and with the coal shortage and this wretched long winter. . .

"*Figlia, figlia,*" Darby winces at the man's rhythmic pleading. His teeth chatter on as if he has no control of them while his eyes waggle back and forth yet again. Hunger has left his mouth dry and his tongue with the taste of cardboard. The .45 feels like a heavy piece of ice in his hand, burning it. He pulls back the hammer.

"Fookin' hell, Dustbroom Darby's fookin' slower than a turtle swimmin' backward in molasses," Flynn cackles, *caw-caw*.

"Get it over wit'!" Bill yells as a mutt drops its ears in sadness upon hearing his new master's angry voice and tucks tail through the snow.

Twenty frozen Italians watch from the bulkhead, hogtied and half-hung over it. The translator swallows and licks his lips to speak out in English. Richie Lonergan stares at him with a peg in the snow. His father John eggs at Darby impatiently, "C'mon, c'mon."

Abe coolly whispers, "Do it."

The bound man chats away blindly, "*Figlia, figlia. . . figlia, figlia.*"

There must be a better way to help my family without ruining another's.

He lowers the gun as the wind ripples through his clothing.

"Bill," he turns his head toward them. "Bill there's gotta be another—"

But Bill storms over and takes the gun from him, "That was ya only chance."

The blinded man turns his head toward the words he does not understand. Still on his knees, he smiles at Darby in thanks. With the cold barrel no longer pressed to the back of his head, he is relieved. But without his knowledge Bill points the gun at his temple and fires.

A deep crack bursts open the morning with the sound of the .45 caliber. For a few seconds there is no reaction. Darby blinks and falls back into the snow. Next to him the crier spurts out a red stream from the side of his cranium. Then it stops. Then again it squeezes out the pressure, raining red onto Darby until he squirms to back away.

Above, Bill's eyes are wild with frenzy and his gritting teeth almost look like a smile. With a burst of energy he turns the gun to the translator and blasts another charge.

This one into the man's chest, which flares his white linen shirt open in a red splotch and fells him backward into the water with a ker-plunk.

The Italians lined up along the seawall lower their heads in prayer and supplication in the foreign tongue. One man screams as Bill ravenously gnashes his teeth and walks toward them with his hand cannon loose in his right hand. The screaming man loses his balance and sways backward, then tumbles into the turbulent channel; his hands and feet tied behind him.

Caw-caw, Flynn howls. "Look at him. Looky there, he's tryna swim. He looks like a flounder wit' palsy," *caw-caw*.

Darby wipes the dark blood from his face with frozen fingers. He looks at the clumps of red gooey warmth that rushes down his hands as it spreads into the fabric of his sleeves.

Is this my blood?

In his shock he had forgotten already until a dim and bubbly spurt struggles out of the open skull in the snow next to him. Only then, when he sees that death had plunged a busy hand into the Italian's brain, did he remember.

"Watch out ya fuckwit," Darby is told as Connors and Lonergan drag the dead and blindfolded man by the belt buckle. Darby kicks backward through the snow to move from their way with red palm prints spotted on the front of his linen shirt. At the bulkhead they toss the body in with the others as if he were not a father of a little girl, but a beat cigarette.

"Load the rest o' them up in that automobile truck," Bill orders and points at the teamster that had been detained. "Drive these half-niggers back across the Gowanus Canal an' leave them there, bound as they are, understand?"

The teamster does understand and runs to assist in loading the human cargo.

"Darby," Bill stands over him. "Get up."

Darby does as told.

Bill tucks the .45 in his belt and takes a long sniff, "Good day for ginzo-huntin'.

They got half the men they'd normally have at the Erie Basin due to the weather. But weather is our greatest ally. We can storm the South Terminal wit'out much o' a fight, but ya'self? Y'ain't to come wit' us."

"But—" Darby comes to his feet.

"Shaddup an' listen. To win wars ya need more than just soldiers, ya need eyes. An' ya need them behind enemy lines in reconnaissance missions. Ya lived in the shadows six years, now be an agent for me from there."

Darby's eyes swim with tears of happiness.

"First part o' ya mission: Ya get up into the enemy, understand? Ya sow doubt amongst Dinny's ranks. Make them believe it's in their interest to think o' themselves an' their fam'ly's safety now. Make them see death, an' tell them we are comin' to the Dock Loaders' Club."

"Really?" Darby asks as Abe Harms sidles up behind Bill.

"Sneak up an' get word to one 'o them that we come under a white flag, no weapons. We come to talk. They're too choked up wit' honor an' the Brehon codes to kill a war vet'ran, so I'll be safe."

Darby looks to Abe, *Your whispers go into Bill's ear and out his mouth now, I see.*

"If silence is the gate that guards Irishtown, we'll slip inside an' slit their throats in their own home," Bill says, then holds up two fingers. "Second part: Get ya brother outta prison. I want them soldiers he can give us. Tell him I ain't happy he won't give them soldiers to me now on credit, but I know he knows I wouldn't need him no more. Startin' tomorrow we're loadin' an' unloadin' ships," Bill declares. "Ya will get a stipend for bein' my agent. But ya don' get Pickles out? I'll cleave off ya twig an' berries, understand me nature boy?"

Abe gives a single snigger at that.

"I understand, Bill."

"Go to Dead Reilly's office an' start workin' wit him," Bill orders. "Keep payin' him the money Dinny's wife gives ya."

I have to find Sadie now, Darby's stomach turns. *Where could she be?*

"Darby," Bill takes Darby's lapel in his fist, which he lets loose almost immediately; a restless look upon his face. In fact Bill appears to have a burst of energy and strength he hadn't had since he appeared after the storm.

Darby stammers, "Wha. . . What's the third part o' the mission?"

Two Shit Hounds slink behind Bill and sit at his feet, ears down, tails wagging. The big brown one is closest to Bill's knee. That one moves its eyes coldly to Darby and shows him teeth in a low growl.

"I can trust ya?" Bill looks up and down Darby, unsure of the answer himself. "This last part is, eh, sensitive."

"Yeah Bill, ya can trust me."

"Ya do good things, ya can move up in rank an' distinction. An' if ya keep ya mouth shut about this, I won' make ya take a brodie off the Brooklyn Bridge," Bill says with black eyes, then shrugs and tilts his head. "The higher ya rank, the more ya make."

"I can do this," Darby assures him.

"C'mere," Bill takes him by a shoulder away from Abe and peeks behind him, then whispers grimly into Darby's ear. "Did ya ride Anna?"

"What? Me?"

"Ya spent time wit' her while I was gone, breakin' windows an' whatnot, I hear."

"No Bill, she's not like that."

"She *is* like that, she admitted it. A man rode her an' gave her money for it. If it wasn't ya, who was it?"

"I dunno Bill."

"I thought ya knew things?"

"Well I. . . I don' know that."

"After yaz broke the window at the Meehan brownstone, where'd she go?"

"I eh, I—"

"Well find out who rode Anna so I can kill that man, got it?"

How do I do that?

Bill cranks his head up to the sky, then down to Darby's eyes, "Now move underground from here on out an' report ya findin's directly back to me, understand?"

"Right," Darby says with a distant smile. "I'll fight for ya until ya sittin' in the catbird seat above the Dock Loaders' Club, King o' Irishtown."

"I ain't no king," Bill says with a gruff sadness. "Kings claim god's divinity, but there ain't no god. I know that from what I seen in France. We're just bags o' electricity runnin' around untethered, is all. There's somethin' else out there though. I dunno what it is. Somethin' cruel an' indifferent. But it found me. It brought me to this moment, an' it keeps showin' me signs o' good favor. It ain't no god though, not like we know. We don' need god, anyhow. We need discipline. I ain't no king. I'm a captain Darby, nothin' more than a captain."

Bill turns round and walks away with Abe toward the water and barks orders at his lieutenants. Suddenly the Trench Rabbits run into formation under the morning moon for the battle to take the rest of South Red Hook. Illuminated by a rising sun in the blue sky, they begin to march in step.

As the soldiers about-face and move south with Lieutenants Connors and Flynn leading the way, Bill yells back to him, "Right the lie, Darby! Right the lie an' ya will change the past."

Sublime Surrender

"Nothing beautiful can grow out of this trash heap, this forsaken industrial port city," Neesha whispers in Anna's dream. "But somehow. . . the *most* beautiful girl in this world, sprouted right out of the cement."

She lay over his powerful shoulders like a fur stole. In Anna's dreams her fox-colored hair floats round his neck, across half his face and meets behind his back as she flows about him. Bulbs of daffodils and amber water lilies have drifted into her hair too and cover her breasts from his watchful, amber eyes. And in her dreams Neesha lives again, even as she knows her love is gone forever.

I'm dreaming, but I don't care. I don't care.

She blinks and reaches up to him until her hands disappear in his flaxen mane. Neesha tilts his head and speaks these words, "I am the prince, but I will be king. The lion of Irishtown. But you must crown me, Anna. It's up to you. You have the will of a prophetess, and the future is yours to shape. Make me king and you will be Queen of Irishtown."

"I. . . I have heard this before," Anna furrows her brows to try to remember, but cannot. "But what does that mean? How do I make ya king if," she blinks again and exhales. "If ya only live here now?"

"No, I exist inside another."

"Another? Who?"

"I can't tell you, you have to find me for yourself."

"How do I do that?"

"First you have to surrender to keep me alive, only then can you crown me."

Outside the snow storm rages. But inside their bodies are warm together. When dawn finally shows through the window in a faint orange light amidst the terror of the black and snow-specked night, he says, "You must let go. To keep me alive, you must trust me. You must surrender in order to live another day. To get rid of me, they will call you evil. They will say your heart is black as coal. They will name you a slattern, but you must keep your heart open for me. I am Neesha, your love. Surrender to me. It's the only way. But if you listen to them, they will take the thrown away from us. Surrender to me Anna. It is a surrender so sublime that the world will quake at your approach and our reign will begin."

Am I going mad? Anna wonders.

She bites her lip as she looks up, her wild red hair caressing the nape of his neck and his elegant face like the motion in a great ocean's current.

"I can't," she finally says. "I don' wanna let go. It's the only thing that serves me now. I'll never let down my defenses, that is who I am. I surrender to no one."

"Don't let me die, If you close me off you will never find who I am inside of now."

"I don' wanna surrender to nobody. Men always want me to do that," her temper flares and blue flames flicker in her eyes. "Why must ya be the same as all the rest, even in dream? I don' wanna love, ever again."

Anna rears back, afraid he will leave her if he sees her angry. She softens her voice and holds his face in her hands, "But ya can stay here, right here in my dreams, for always an' ever. I'll visit ya every night. Right here, in the past. An' in my dreams we can live together forever, warm against the storm. I. . . I don' want a future out there."

"That is not how it works," Neesha answers.

"So tell me then—"

"Continue on, and ya will learn, I promise," says he. "Surrender, and you will find me. Shut me out and—"

A flash of yellow and orange light bursts through the window as outside the wind whistles and the slanting snow buries the city. Anna turns her eyes to the window and holds up a hand to shield them from the bright light.

"What is that?"

When she looks back at her lion, he has changed. He now wears a black mask with a grotesquely phallic nose; limp and long-sloped. She can still see his mouth, but it too has changed. A mortal scar has appeared over his upper lip and one side of his face is pockmarked with hundreds of small, open wounds as if a shotgun's pellets had strafed him. Another bullet scar streaks over his ear by the temple where hair can no longer grow.

"Neesha? Neesha! What happened to ya?"

He does not answer.

Just then the window explodes and she is covered in snow. The wind whisks her hair away from his face to reveal the weeping wounds. A viscous-like red string mixed with pus sloughs off his open scar and stretches in a goopy string as he holds her down. Anna turns her head so that it doesn't land on her face, but she can't stop it.

It's about to break, she realizes, but she can't move from his grip.

"Stop!"

"Anna," he grows over her, stronger than ever before. The string of bloody pus gathers at the end, then separates and falls through the air toward her face.

"No stop! Stop it!"

"Anna!" His voice changes, and turns into her mother's voice.

When Anna looks up again her mother stands over her and jerks on her shoulders to wake her up.

"Anna! What's wrong wit' ya, Anna"?

Her mother's face is also disfigured, but hers is from the burning grease her father had thrown at her years ago.

"Was it ya face I saw'r in my dream?"

"What dream, Anna? Ya've been talkin' nonsense all morn."

She sits up and looks round.

I was sleeping right here on the floor on Johnson Street? How did I get here?

"Anna child, there's three childers need diaper-changes. Be a doll an' help ya poor ol' Ma, would ya? Now that the man has helped us, we don' need to move. We can stay here, we can."

I must have been sleeping for days.

"Where have ya been anyhow, Anna. Anna, do ya hear me? Answer me, Anna."

"Ma, how long was I out?"

"'Bout an hour 'bout. They tried to hide from me, them slatterns. But I saw'r them, I did."

Grace and Kit, damn them. They must have left me here. They left me.

"Where've ya been Anna? Ya was gone durin' the whole o' the storm, then ya show up here drunk as a shithouse rat wit' them two slatterns. Anna, are ya listenin' to me? Are ya gonna be a drunk like ya drunkard father? Is that it? An' why's yer jaw all black an' blue, eh? An' who bought that dress for ya, Anna? Eh? It's a beautyful dress, I'll give ya that, but I think ya've pissed in it. Who bought it for ya?"

"I'm not druuuunk," Anna's voice howls in a high-pitched yawing sound.

I shouldn't be here, she wipes sleep from her eyes.

"Stop bein' such a pill, Anna. Help wit' the diapers now, come now. Ya can't sleep the day 'way. I've been to Holy Communion wit' Father Larkin already. An' he has things to say concernin' the state o' Irishtown these fateful days."

"Of course he does, wit' a flock o' bleatin' widows an' mournin' mothers crowdin' his pews? He's a regular shepherd, ain't he?"

Anna stands and bends her back. Her head pounds to the rhythm of her heartbeat and her thoughts are displaced by the pain. She holds onto the back of a chair and shakes her head, then turns to her mother, "Ma, what did ya say about the man? Do ya mean Dinny Meehan?"

"Oh child, don' say his name aloud. But yes, he gave us money s'mornin', so he did. The Dock Loaders' Club was overwhelmed by our numbers an' when he was released—"

"He was released?"

Mary stands up straight, "He was, an' so all the fam'lies appeared—"

"Ma, Bill's back ya know."

"Well surely I heard it."

"Bill's gonna win Irishtown," Anna leans on the chair with both hands now as spots appear in front of her face. "Richie pledged himself to Bill an' when Bill wins, Richie will become a dockboss, or maybe even an enforcer. He'll make enough—"

"Child, don' beg for breeches from a bare-arsed man," Mary interrupts. "Bill might have a hist'ry wit' our fam'ly, but it's not him who has helped us t'rough the years. Why fix what ain't broke, Anna?"

"Yeah an' look at us," Anna spreads her arm along the tiny, first floor room. "We're just drowin' in dime, aren't we Ma?"

"Well enough to keep the wolf from the door, at least," Mary stamps a foot. "An' what about ya'self? Where was it ya got the money to pay rent while the man was in jail? How'd ya get the dime for that dress, Anna?"

I have to get away from here. I have to go back to Grace and Kit at the Henhouse. Why did they leave me here?

"I have to go, Ma."

"In this shnow? Anna, It's freezin' outside. Ya've no coat on ya'self. Help me wit' the childers, Anna. Ya're me eldest daughter an' ya're under me roof here. Anna! mind ya place!"

When the door closes behind her, Anna sighs and takes her first step in the snow.

At least I have these Hanan boots. Thanks for that at least Dinny Meehan.

The door opens again behind her, "Anna Lonergan ya get back here now. Don' leave ya poor ol' Ma alone wit' all these childers now! Anna!"

Anna now runs with the wind. Through the snow she sprints as fast as she can. A half block past the Lonergan tenement on Johnson Street where the slanted approach to the Manhattan Bridge reaches above. Then she sees the cold eyes that stare out from tenement windows.

They think I'm psychopathic. Good. Fuck them. But I should've listened to my mother and grabbed that coat, damnit.

Two blocks away and she can see that her mother does not follow, so she slows her pace. Men who shovel heavy snow from the sidewalks stop and stare as she walks by. She can feel their eyes grope down her gown at the waist and hips, then move up to her breasts. A shiver runs down her shoulders and just as she crosses her arms to ward off the cold, she slips in an ice patch on the pavement. Before she realizes anything, the back of her head smacks the icy, unforgiving slate of the sidewalk.

The next thing she knows, a man helps her up by the arms and back, "Ya uhright, eh. . . mam?"

"Don' touch me ye fookin' deviant," she screams and pulls away in shame and fury. "Keep ya fookin' hands to ya'self, god'amned toothless hare-brained eejit."

"I was just—"

"I know what ya was doin'," She turns to the three women and five men that have rushed out of the grocery store at her screams. "All women know what ya're tryin' to do. Catch a quick feel, ya fiend, wit' ya. . . wit' ya fookin' claws an' ya pointy nose."

"I'm sorry, I was just—"

"Leave me alone!"

The shocked onlookers then turn to the man as Anna makes her escape.

What did I dream? I can't remember my dream now. What did Neesha say? she strains to remember as she clops toward a train station in her gown and untied boots. *What did he tell me?*

On the elevated train she rocks back and forth to keep warm and brushes her hands down her exposed arms.

I just want to go back to sleep. Back to sleep so I can talk to him again.

At the Twenty-Fifth Street Station she walks down the snowy stairwell as the wind tosses her hair in the air like flames against a city in white.

On Fifth Avenue by Green-Wood Cemetery there are no grocery clerks to shovel the snowy sidewalks. Entire trees have fallen over the wrought iron fence and are now covered in snow that leaves the whole scene as if it were the end of the world. At each step her boots get wetter. Her feet, colder. The lower half of her dress is completely soaked in both melted snow and frozen piss.

I'm going to freeze to death if I don't get inside soon.

Atop the hill on Sixth Avenue she turns round but her eyes water in the wind and freeze on her face. When she tries to wipe them away, it pulls the skin off her cheek. Eventually she focuses in the distance where smoke billows out of Red Hook.

"I hope it burns, all of it!" She screams against the cold.

When she recognizes the business sign she stops and reads aloud, "Yale & Stabile, Undertakers."

I can't go in there though.

She looks up to the third floor window, then searches the ground to find a rock. But there are none. None that she can see. Everything is buried in white.

Behind the undertaker there is an old stone wall. Without tying her boots, she climbs up the wall by holding onto protruding rocks. As she grasps for balance, the mortar chips in her hand.

At the top she reaches an arm across to grab hold of something. Then she slips and falls backward and screams. Before landing she tries to look behind her to see what she might fall on, a metal handrail? A garbage can? But before she can see below, the snowy ground comes up to smack her in the back.

"Anna?" A voice calls down from a third-floor window. But Anna can't respond.

"Anna is that ya layin' there? What happent?" Grace White yells down.

"Why did yaz leave me?"

"Leave ya?" Grace yells back. "We didn' leave ya, this mornin' ya wanted us to take ya home after Bill Lovett hurt ya. 'Take me home, take me home,' ya bellowed. That's all ya would say, 'Take me home, take me home.'"

I don't remember any of that.

"Grace," Anna mumbles. "Help. . . help."

"Jaysus on a stick, look at that mad woman," Kit pops her head out and takes a long drag from a cigarette. "Ya hair looks like a big blood stain in the snow. Looks like a fookin' crime scene down there. I wish I had one o' them macgillicuddy's, what o' ya call them things? Photygraphic picture makers?" Kit flicks an ash that is taken away by the wind. "Anna ya tryna to kill ya'self or what? Why not get a pistol, it's easier that way."

"She's hurt I think," Grace says.

"She ain't got nothin' wrong wit' her but a broken heart's all. Anna, get ya spindly little arse up outta the snow."

"We should help her," Grace disagrees in the window next to Kit.

"Why? She ain't no royal Stuart or Lancaster or York, she's a fookin' Lonergan," Kit flicks the cigarette into the wind. "Anna *get up!*"

And Anna does. She takes a deep breath and gets to her knees. Then eventually to her feet and wipes the freezing snow out of her hair and down the inside of her gown.

"I'm up," Anna yells back.

"The drama wit' this one," Kit ducks back in the window.

"I'm comin' down for ya Anna," Grace says and ducks in too, but Anna can still hear her talking up in the third floor. "I have a warm coat for ya an' coal in the potbelly. We ain't no shleps up here. Call it what ya like, Henhouse, slattern house, whatever, it's warm."

I just want to go back to sleep. . . So I can talk to him again.

What Comes of the Storm

A match is struck in the dark doorway illuminating Detective William Brosnan's large, jowly face and droopy eyes under beetle brows. He twists the gallery and mantle and raises the wick with gnarled fingers, then gently turns the knob and lights the wick on both sides until he has an even flame all round. Shaking out the matchstick behind, he turns up the flame on the gas lantern as yellow light blooms through the glass chimney to reveal that he stands in a narrow hallway at the top of a steep stairwell.

Brosnan takes out a silver watch from a vest pocket with a fancy hunting case that was gifted him on his 25th year on the force, checks the time, and then snaps it shut. The old cop then turns his attention to the buttons on his dark blue tunic. Swollen joints leave him struggling to push the buttons through the buttonholes. At six-feet, two inches and with his police tunic on and a keg belly out ahead of him, he looks like a bear standing on hind legs. But what he had witnessed over his years as a Brooklyn beat cop left deep furrows in his face.

"*Paw-paw, paw-paw!*" A shoeless child stumbles through the doorway and grabs for Brosnan's pant-leg, the first step of the stairwell only inches away and disappearing into an unseen darkness below.

"C'mere to me, don't fall down them stairs an' break yer crown Little Billie Bear," Brosnan bellows in the booming, resonant North Dublin brogue he never did lose, then picks up the toddler who straddles his belly. "Ye know what they'll call ye if ye break yer crown? Do ye?"

"*Paw, paw,*" the child repeats, and stuffs four fingers into his teething mouth.

"No, silly, they'll call ye Billie Box o' Rocks," Brosnan laughs and swings the child over the dark stairwell. "Do ye wanna be called Billie Box o' Rocks? Do ye?"

"Yes!" little Billie screams.

"Dad, what are ya doin'?" His daughter Doirean yells at him through the doorway.

"Oh we're just havin' a bit o' fun's all."

"I mean why are ya all dressed up? The snow's hip-deep out there and ya got the day off."

"Ah my Doe, I can't even begin to tell ye the whole of it," Brosnan kisses her forehead and holds her shoulder gently as he looks down at the bump where her third child warms inside her. "Things to care fer, is all."

"Is it because Daniel's shift ended hours ago?"

"No, no," Brosnan shakes his head incredulously, but knows very well that his daughter sees right through him as if he were a glass door. Brosnan had learned years ago that when he lies to Doirean, she finds yet more evidence in his choice of words and his seemingly unabashed expressions. In truth, she is twice the investigator he could ever wish to be.

"I. . . I just," Brosnan feels her eyes piercing him, judging him, searching.

"Then why go out now?"

Brosnan's chest rumbles in response.

"Don't ya growl at me, ya ol' curmudgeon," Doirean wags a finger at him with one hand and balls up a fist in the other. "Thirty-one years on the force an' ya've earned the right to let the young men like Daniel work on snow days. I know a lotta people've died 'cause o' this storm, Dad, an' ya wanna help them. But that's not it, is it? Ya not goin' out there to help people, are ya?"

Little Billie Bear squirms in Brosnan's arms under the yellow mantle light of the narrow hallway. He fiddles with his grandfather's badge and then undoes one of the buttons on his tunic.

"My Doe," Brosnan begins.

Doirean folds her arms over the bump, "Don't call me that, just tell me why."

"I. . . I've finally got the answer I was hopin' for?"

"Well? What was the question?"

"It's good news all round is what I can tell ye at the moment, my Doe. Rest assured—"

"An' what's that got to do wit' goin' out on this day in the god-forsaken snow? Ya don' even make sense when ya lie, Dad."

I cannot tell you yet, my sweet. But soon you will know.

Brosnan takes a deep breath. There is no one in this world who can cause him great pause but his little Doe. No man could ever hope to wield the power she has over him. When she looks up at him with those sweet brown eyes, his voice warms and softens. No one knows that voice but her and it even surprises him when he hears himself. But some things men must keep close to the chest. Women will worry, mothers even more, but Doirean is right now with-child and there's just no need for her to get into the middle of his plan. Not now.

He had worked on this plan for her and Daniel many months now, but only recently had it all come together. Everything was thought out carefully, calculatingly, and on this day it will all come to light. To clue her in now would be silliness. He longs to tell her and share in her delight, but it would mean revealing his innermost secrets and superstitions. For it is secrets and superstitions what comes of the storm.

"It's Daniel ya're after," she says resolutely. "Ya're worried about him."

My god, she knows so much. God bless her. But she does not know all.

She would not agree. But there's too much wickedness out there for her to know it all. Things of late have become dire in Brooklyn, where life has long been held cheaply.

But there ain't no pockets in a shroud, Captain Sullivan once advised.

Worse though, are the signs he has seen of late. The symbols, everywhere. Then came the storm and rumors of dead men returning. Again. The worst of them hangs over his family like a black specter, returned now. Returned again.

"No, no," he shakes his head again until Little Billie reaches up and grabs hold of his loose jowls as if to stop him from lying, then lays the side of his face on Brosnan's barrel chest and plops a thumb in his mouth for comfort.

"Has he gotten himself into trouble again?" Doirean asks in whisper.

"I have good news, I say. But I have to go now. Billie? Can I play trumpet on yer face again?"

"No!" He yelps and writhes at his grandfather's tunic to get away.

"C'mere 'til I tell ye," Brosnan blows into Little Billie's fat cheeks to make the funny flatulent sounds, which transforms the boy's giggles into screeches of happiness.

"Ya get him all riled up an' then ya leave," Doirean scolds and takes Billie away from him. "Ya just leave an' ya don't even say why."

"I bleedin' love ye so much my Doe."

"Just go," she turns away with Little Billie in her arms.

"Wait."

Brosnan turns back from the first step of the stairwell to allow his daughter to straighten his badge and button the button Billie had undone. He waits with patience, long enough to see the tear that has welled up in her right eye. When done, she pats the button and spins round with a sniffle and slams the door behind her.

"Remember Doe," Brosnan yells through the door with a great bellow. "Dignity is the strength we hold in our name, the Brosnan way!"

As he carefully steps down the narrow stairwell the wrinkles round the fifty-five year old man's eyes move into a pensive glare. For Doirean hadn't been a Brosnan close on five years now, she is a Culkin. He had raised her as a single father. A proud father. A patient, open-handed father. A father who gave her so much affection and love that she felt smothered and grew spiteful of it. Until something terrible happened—

At P.S. Five where Doirean went to primary school, her best friend was a chipper little redhead named Maureen Egan. The girls were inseparable. Their classmates called them "Moe and Doe." But Maureen's father was a follower of Christie Maroney, the King of Irishtown back then. Snake Eyes they called him. And for good reason, that man had a poison tongue that spat hatred everywhere he went. When Moe and Doe turned nineteen and graduated, Maureen confided something Doirean never knew or could have ever considered: Maureen's father had taken liberties with her body for many years. Raped her.

Brosnan had roughed up Snake Eyes and arrested him, but he was soon released. Afterward he tried to help the young woman to escape her father's wrath. Worse though, she needed to escape her own thoughts. Brosnan couldn't help her there, and that was when she fell: To drugs and the drink and Christie Maroney, her father's boss. And she never got up again. Her new home was above Jacob's Saloon on Sands Street between the bridges. But it was more like a prison where heroin and cocaine and alcohol were her bars and rough men in derby hats her guards. Maureen Egan, Doirean's best friend, was lost to Brooklyn.

It wasn't until then that Doirean began to appreciate her father. His presence over her and the protection he provided when she was most vulnerable as a little girl made her feel blessed. She had come back to her father's loving arms and from then on, nothing could get between them.

Doirean's eyes watch him from the window above as the old fellow wades through the snow. He can feel her watching, but does not look back. Even though motherhood has endowed her with powers, she cannot sense the wraiths that come out of the storms. She cannot know. For he has never told her the truth about the death of his wife, her mother. And the terrors that await Daniel Culkin.

Brosnan wipes his brow as he struggles through deep snow.

You can do this old man. You must.

"G'mornin' Detective Brosnan," Patrolman Ferris emerges from a group of four tunics standing in front of a Navy Street tenement. "Ya really goin' out to Manhatt'n?"

"No choice, ye said it was Wisniewski ya saw with Daniel durin' the storm, that only means one thing."

"Well that *is* Wolcott's lump, after all. Wiz the Lump, they call him."

"Daniel never came home last night," Brosnan wipes his mouth as frost billows in front of his face.

"Doe know what's doin'?"

"She knows but she don't."

"Mind if I tag along? We don' get to jaw so much since ya was promoted to big shot."

"Big shot my arse," Brosnan smiles. "Sure c'mon then."

Patrolman Ferris had been broken-in by Brosnan some fifteen years ago and turned out to be a dependable partner. The son-in-law of Captain Sullivan of the Poplar Street Police Station, he paved the way for Brosnan to bring Daniel Culkin onto the force when Doirean settled for the sly, petulant younger man. And when Brosnan was promoted to detective, he could still keep his eyes on his son-in-law by naming Ferris his partner.

Inside the wooden train that rumbles over the Manhattan Bridge commuter rails, Brosnan grips the straphanger and turns to Ferris, "Ye sure t'was Garry Barry that left with Daniel?"

"Ya told me to tail him when I could, so I did," Ferris answers from the side of his mouth. "He met up wit' Wiz the Lump, walked into a Hoyt Street tenement an' they came out wit' Barry an' his lone crony, James Cleary."

"I'll tell ye what Doe does know," Brosnan leans toward Ferris while he keeps his eyes on the train patrons. "She knows he's up to somethin' now that even I won't suffer. Did ye know last weekend Daniel had a brand new sofa delivered to our room on Navy Street? What patrolman salary allows for such a luxurious items, I ask? An' all the gold he buys? Real gold too! At least yerself an' I know to tuck our dirty money in a savin's account. But Daniel Culkin? No, he wants it flaunted for all to see."

Ferris leans in too, "I put my wife's name on my account. Just in case, ya know?"

Brosnan smiles, "I just spent all that money."

"Yeah? On what?"

"Never mind. Ye'll find out in due time," Brosnan changes the subject. "Not even Daniel knows. I might've taken him under my wing when he married my daughter, but I don't trust him worth a shriveled shite. He's too quick to the blackjack, he's got no dignity about him an' now he's up-jumped himself to a dangerous height. To work directly for Jonathan G. Wolcott an' the Waterfront Assembly? Oh no, no no. Now he's gone too far an' I'm after convincin' Wolcott to release him from his employ, for good an' ever."

Patrolman Ferris nods, tilts his head and sucks through his teeth, "Ya ever worry that ya shelter the kid too much? Sometimes a guy's gotta learn about his follies the hard way, ya know?"

The bear growls, "It's more than that, Ferris. It's the hand o' destiny we're up against here. My fam'ly's destiny. History, prophecy, blood an' dreams all inform me. As much as it pains me, there's nothin I am more certain of than the task at hand. This terror I must face dauntlessly, selflessly. It is all for my little Doe. *All.*"

"Destiny eh?" Ferris stares at a bearded Hasidim wearing a yarmulke with long ringlet-sideburns that hang to his shoulders. "I known ya a good long time now, Brosnan. An' any time Garry fookin' Barry's name comes to ya lips, ya get all fidgety an' spookt."

"Because I saw him dead, *twice*," Brosnan makes a fist and whispers angrily through his teeth. "To save Daniel, my son, I have to alter destiny. A task way too big for the likes o' me. I have to untangle the trap Wolcott dragged him into. Daniel's now caught in the same nightmare that took Doirean's mother."

Ferris purses his lips, "Didn't she die givin' birth to Doirean?"

Brosnan lowers his head, *This is why I have never spoken with anybody about this. They won't believe.*

Ferris turns to Brosnan with a straight face, "Is Daniel pregnant?"

"I don't blame ya for makin' light o' my situation, but if t'was yer own daughter that was facin' life without her husband—"

"I understand that part," Ferris interrupts. "I just don' know what's got ya all spookt. Talk to me, eh? I'm just a guy."

From a breast pocket Brosnan anxiously pulls out a small packet with the words *Na Bocklish* scrawled on the front. He taps it and quickly withdraws a black cigar and holds it between his teeth. He lights the end of it with a matchstick and drags hard. Then turns round, "Look out there."

Ferris turns with him and looks out the window.

Brosnan holds his face close to the glass until he points toward the whitened Jay Street Railyard on the waterfront below. Beyond lay the poorer quarters from Bridge Street all the way to the old wall of the Navy Yard. Irishtown, his beat since 1888.

"There," Brosnan points through the passing suspender cables and tower bases. "Out over the river, the white mornin' moon in a bright blue sky. It's back."

"Back? They're kinda common, ain't they? What do ya mean *back*?"

A shudder pulses from the back of Brosnan's hair down his spine, through his legs and back up. It hovers unsettled in his stomach as goose prickles pebble on his skin.

"I don't give a fiddler's fart if ye think me psychopathic," Brosnan side-glances a woman with indigenous features and a child swaddled inside her alpaca poncho while speaking to Ferris. "Just don't ever repeat what I tell ye, understand?"

"Yeah, ya know me for my word."

A plume of smoke flitters above Brosnan as he stares down toward Irishtown, "I was but a wild child on the streets o' North Dublin when the president o' the Supreme Council o' the Irish Republican Brotherhood, James Francis Xavier O'Brien himself, had raised funds in a recruitin' measure. Fifty street urchins were sent to the west o' Ireland for a summer. No more than a fledgling lad o' seven years, was I. The year was 1871. So long ago an' so strange, it may have been another life.

"Into the west, I'd gone. The only thing I knew o' that lot was that they were bog savages an' culchies, but what I found was that West Ireland was a portal to a feudal past where an agrarian way o' life remained unchanged for centuries. Where the industrial revolution that had taken the world's economy was but a rumor. Where cattle was still a form o' currency an' the countryside was a vast crisscrossin' o' Medieval boreens and stone fences stretched about the wild, windswept hills. Nought but hints o' homes here and there. Vacant, roofless places pockmarked the landscape; a reminder o' Ireland's long-idlin' tragedy. Battles that took place durin' the Dark Ages still lingered on the lips o' locals, an' superstitions that could not survive an ever-changin', enlightened world yet thrived out there still, rehashed by aged augurs an' blind seers. It was out there I was first called a 'Souper.' A word derived from the times o' great hunger, pauper's graves an' exodus. For in those days Catholics were offered soup if they gave up their faith."

A horn blows up ahead as the train begins to descend the Manhattan Bridge toward the big city.

"To a barren farm I was sent, my only companion was an ashen-faced, field-hardened distant cousin eight years my elder. I began to adjust to the new surroundings an' all seemed well. Until a shanachie appeared of a silent night to speak over a peat fire.

"The storyteller told o' dead generations an' cycles o' Irish heroes who died for honor's sake against horrific monsters who sought to change them. Transform them into ghouls an' murderers. To turn the sick an' the old, children even, into the monsters themselves. There are many ways to do so, the shanachie proclaimed. But when the storm comes and exposes them, an exchange happens. A life passes on, an' a dead man comes back in his stead at dawn, when the veil between life and death is thinnest. The shanachie had shifted in his seat and found my eyes across the fire, 'Awakened from death,' he said to me. 'The mornin' moon looms on the monster's shoulder. But so too death is due when life is wrought, an' on an' on together they ride the same path.'

"The stories had sent my head into a spin. In tears I vomited on my breeches, the only pair I owned. Raised among the rookeries an' the clatter o' urban Dublin life, the void o' the west an' the ghosts that haunted the survivors after the famine left me with grim visions o' skeletal mobs solicitin' alms. An' in the candlelight shadows I saw a wraith with a baby's face that visited my dreams for many years."

"A wraith?" Patrolman Ferris's voice is colored with doubt.

"That face," the words from Brosnan's lips make steam circles on the train window. "That face. It haunted my dreams an' sometimes, if I listened close enough to the gusts that crawl up the Navy Street hill, I could hear the ol' shanachie's words like birds whistlin' in the wind.

"But when my wife became pregnant, the fear came back to me. An' the baby's face reappeared in life form one terrible morn in the year o' 1888, my first on the force. Its eyes stared up at me when I found it, yet the light in them had been extinguished. It's little arm extended in my direction as if reaching. His little palm open for alms."

Detective William Brosnan scans meekly along the faces in the sway of the train. Russian men with open shirts. Dark brown women with angry cat's eyes. All with that same cruel New York stare.

Patrolman Ferris tilts his head toward Brosnan without looking, "What happened next?"

"T'was the Great Blizzard o' 1888 when a tenement had collapsed in Irishtown from the wind an' the weight o' the snow. In the wreckage the child was bleedin' from the skull an' ears an' even its open eyes. Limp-limbed an' breathless, the poor creature was dead. But with my own child on the way, I was filled with the love an' the compassion, so I ran it all the way to Long Island College Hospital in the drivin' snow. But while I was out there, my wife had to be rushed to the hospital when she'd suddenly been struck with pain."

Patrolman Ferris hums to show he is following along.

"We had our whole life ahead o' us," Brosnan's chin quivers until he gathers himself and straightens his tunic until his voice sounds sedated and calm again. "While at the hospital I was notified that my wife died givin' birth. Now I don't know if ye're a religious man, but I believe in the spirit o' Christ an' that he died an' come back. He was summoned for a reason, Jaysus was. Destiny. An' that pattern o' destiny can be found in our lives as well. Always repeatin' itself. The exchange o' life for death happens everyday on this earth. It's a fact. Someone lives, another passes on. But there are gods o' death an' despair out there too. Some call him the devil, others Mephistopheles, Satan, an archangel, Beelzebub an' even the demiurge, whatever it is, that god often wins in our world, here between heaven and hell," Brosnan looks hard at Ferris. "My love. My love had been taken. I'd fallen to the floor o' the hospital an' was howlin' like a crazed man. But then a nurse came upon me an' said that the baby I had pulled from the tenement wreckage had survived. That outta the horror o' losin' a life, another had been saved. The baby that'd haunted my dreams for so long had its own destiny, do ye see it now? Ye know what the name o' that baby was? Do ye?"

Patrolman Ferris turns his head sideways.

"T'was Garret Barry. Garry Barry took life from my family back then when he was assuredly dead. I prayed for god to intervene so this curse or prophecy, as some in Irishtown call it, would never return for me. But now he's back. Back from the dead again. The wraith is back."

"So ya're worried that—"

"Death is due when life is wrought," Brosnan turns and grabs Patrolman Ferris's arm. "If I don't talk Wolcott outta releasin' my son Daniel from his employ, he will be next. Or worse!" Wolcott's eyes go wide as he strains the words through clenched teeth. "My Little Doe is pregnant."

An Asterism

"So Pope Clement excommunicated Henry VIII for marryin' Anne Boleyn, right?" explains the man behind the counter with the bloody apron. "Not long after that the Pope was poisoned to death by a mushroom. Them Protestants even got their evil fingers in Rome's doin's. But Pope Clement got the last word, ya know what it was?"

Thos Carmody hides his face as he mumbles, "This doesn't taste right?"

"What?"

"He was poisoned, right? An' died?"

"Yeah, poisoned by a mushroom."

"Famous last words. Anyhow it wasn't Clement VII who excommunicated Henry VIII, so he couldn't've got the last word. It was Paul III. If I was a nun I'd clap ya ears like they did me at St. Veronica's."

The cook stares open-mouthed with a hand on the counter next to a disheveled newspaper with a headline that reads:

Volstead & Anti-Salooners
Contemplate Dry Law

The White Wings and the Sanitary Department had worked all morning to shovel out the freight tracks and the sidewalks on the West Side of Manhattan. No one wants a day off these days, so the small business owners were out there right next to the city workers piling five and six-foot snow banks along the sidewalk ledge to make paths for possible customers.

Thos pushes at the kippered herring and the shad-roe omelet on his plate and looks out the window to the wet cobblestones of Laight Street a block from the Hudson River, then turns a cold leopard-like eye to the dirty-aproned man, "An' why talk to me about poisonin' food when I'm tryin' to eat?"

"Sorry."

"Yeah well, the thing about bein' a well-meanin' fool is that ya're ignorant of it. An' anyway, conspiracy theories are as likely as findin' gold in a glitter mine."

"Gee sorry, Thos."

Ever since Thos had returned from the war, the taste for food had been lost to him. Avoiding it, he has grown weaker of late. But even when he forced himself to chew and swallow the copper and metallic-tasting items, he never felt nourished. It was as if he ate nothing. Weaker and weaker he has gotten since his discharge from the Army, though his mind is sharper than ever. A torture all its own.

Maybe the Army took my strength too, he pushes the plate away, and that is when Tanner Smith comes to mind.

Thos looks out the window for his informant, who is late. There will be much to learn about Tanner Smith through the informant.

There is no way to make peace with Tanner now. Back in 1916 allegiances were very different and Tanner had been hired by Dinny Meehan to kill Thos. But Tanner had parlayed it instead. He told Thos to go on the lam, then told Dinny he killed him. By saving Thos's life Tanner wanted to be named Vice President of the ILA in return. An impossible, desperate demand.

Thos had always believed that to weaken your enemy you must turn his friends against him. And so Thos came back to Brooklyn and exposed Tanner's lie to Dinny. That of course got Tanner banished from the White Hand.

Tanner then vowed revenge, another desperate act, but by that time Thos turned the tables completely when he proved himself an ally of the Brooklyn gang by brokering a monumental deal where he got the Black Hand and White Hand to shake under the ILA's banner. A masterful succession of chess moves performed by the fellow many on the westside of Manhattan call the Tenth Avenue Prodigy.

Like a hunter, Thos had already outmaneuvered his prey by taking the high ground.

Now I have to move in for the kill. Because if I don't kill him, he'll kill me.

All Thos's thoughts seem to go back to Tanner Smith recently. The weaker he gets, the stronger his desire to murder him becomes.

But why? It's as if I'm being driven by something, or someone else.

With Tanner under White Hand protection again, Thos turns his attention to another pressing need.

I only have one job, per the International Longshoreman's Association: To keep ALL of Brooklyn's waterfront loyal to the ILA.

But to do that Thos must choose between the two Irish factions: Dinny Meehan or Bill Lovett. Both demand he take their side, but he can only choose one.

Meehan had sent Vincent Maher as his emissary. A tactical move. Vincent had taken Thos on his very first murder. And the ability to murder is a good thing to have notched on your belt before a war. But a common thing in the 77th Infantry, which pulled from the Lower East Side and other parts of the city.

Yes, he and Vincent go back. And a killer like Thos Carmody never forgets his first. That fluttering feeling in the stomach. That sense of winning against death. Silverman was his name, Jonathan G. Wolcott's follower. Silverman had begged Thos for his life and put up a hand in front of his face as if he could stop the bullet, but it went through the hand and into the brain.

Now Silverman's soul resides inside me, Thos thinks.

The elation he felt in killing was better than sexual climax, and he had Vincent Maher to thank.

Brooklyn, Thos shakes his head. *The biggest challenge of my life.*

Manhattan is bad enough, but Brooklyn is like reasoning with rhinos. Even the weather is worse despite the proximity; you get on the train in Manhattan and there's a bit of cloud cover, you get off in Brooklyn and it's been raining two hours.

Bill Lovett is back one day and he kills Dinny Meehan's cousin in north Red Hook and takes south Red Hook from the Italians to obliterate my peace deal, Thos laments with an elbow on the counter and a hand on his forehead. *Now The White Hand is split in two, the Black Hand has a finger cut off and Wolcott and the Waterfront Assembly want to sever them all off at the wrist.*

The rumors Thos had always heard that Dinny Meehan never sleeps makes a pound of sense when you see how hard it is to take a nap when the crown of Irishtown is on your head.

How do you get three hands to shake? Picking the right man to sit atop the Dock Loaders' Club will be like milking a unicorn.

A motor car's horn blows Thos Carmody out of his daydreaming. The Klaxon horn had wound up like some wounded animal in its last gasps, bleating in his ears. He glares over his upturned lapel through the diner's front window at the man in the convertible Studebaker Big Six with the boater's hat and the pencil mustache.

Even the cold won't stop a guy from showin' off his convertible.

The gold limousine with the whitewall tires had been waiting for the old industrial rail cars to round the snowy tracks in the street. But the train is stopped halfway into the brick freight station building of the Grocers Steam Sugar Refining Company because a side door had been left open in one of its cars, spilling thirty pound bags onto Laight street and blocking the roadway. The horn bleats and bleats as the man cusses the workers.

Thos wraps his hand round the coffee so the man with the bloody apron behind the counter doesn't see it shaking. He sinks back into himself. Into his coat and his thoughts. Lowering the floppy cap to hide his war-wounded face.

The easiest thing to do is to have Lovett killed. But then all the men who follow Bill would rally behind Richie Lonergan. I'm not sure I can ever bet against Bill Lovett again. He's already fooled me once when we warred together. Twice, and shame on me.

He brings the cup of weak coffee to the left side of his mouth and looks out the front window through the snow drifts from a cloaked face.

It was a Cricket Ball grenade that changed Thos Carmody forever. He never saw it. He woke up after multiple surgeries as if he was in another time and space. In another man's body. Everything felt different. The grenade that sent him cart-wheeling through the air had exploded on his right side, shooting hot metal into him, leaving small bald spots in his head and, most noticeably, ripped open his lip which had been hastily sewn only after his more concerning wounds to the head, heart and major organs. It had turned a once handsome man into a grim stranger all too aware of himself when people glower at him.

When he awoke in a field hospital, he had surprised the surgeons. They had told him that during surgery to remove metal fragments from his body his heart stopped and he was pronounced dead. They placed a bloody sheet over him and the nursing staff moved on to the next patient. When the Graves Registration Unit came to take his body away, they were shocked to find his eyes open.

"I died?" Thos had asked the field surgeons.

"You and that one over there," the doctor turned and pointed at Bill Lovett a few beds down. "Weren't you in the 77th too? He had gas poisoning, shot twice. He was left for dead miles behind the gap your infantry courageously held. You're heroes, you know? How anyone survived what your companies were put through, the world will never understand. I've never seen anything like it. Dead men, walking. . . Chosen, you could say."

Chosen? But why? For what?

The surgeons sewed him back together, but the nuns brought him back among the living. When he wanted to die, they gathered round him and told him he is marked for greatness. They touched his neck gently.

"You have an asterism," Sister Alice told him. "A grouping of stars on your neck in the shape of the Big Dipper. You've been scarred for greatness. It's god's autograph on you. It has to be from god, it is formed around your jugular. Completely improbable. If one of them nicked your jugular, you would not be here with us. You have been reclaimed, now you must find out why. Look to god."

Thos looks round the diner, *It isn't god who haunts me, it's something else.*

When he got back to New York he didn't waste time wearing his Army uniform in the city. He threw away the crude sheepskin pelt as soon as he got a suitable replacement; Coal gray coat with a long lapel to hide his face, a tweed waistcoat, E. & W detachable linen collar and a starched white shirt with a narrow black tie over workman boots. The uniform of the longshoreman union rep. He didn't want the attention of being a veteran. None of it.

Out the window, across the street at 79-101 Laight Street, his informant finally appears outside the refining factory he manages and stands between the freight tracks in the cobblestoned street. Thos leaves a half-crumpled dollar bill by the coffee cup and pushes the glass door open and walks between great hills of snow on the sidewalk.

"'Ow are yu Thos?" Says Frank Leighton in a thick East-end London cockney. "Yu know, I was readin' the ova day about the lost battalion, the 77th Infantry. That was yu company, yeah? My god Thos, what 'appened to yu face? Wounded, were yu?"

"Yeah," Thos pops his lapel to obscure Frank's view. "When the nun saw me she said I scared her half to death, twice."

Frank looks at him confusedly, so Thos changes course, "What did ya hear about ya brother?"

"Which one, Darby or Pickles?"

"Either."

"Well, it's true what yu 'eard about Pickles, 'e's got a retrial for the Maroney murder. 'Ere's the funny part, me ova bruva Darby got me cousin Sadie to pay for the attorney. Wild, innit? Well Darby's a plonker, yu know that yeah? But he's come out into the light after all them years in the shadows, I s'pose. Like Darby, a lotta gormless muppets 'ave turned to Bill Lovett. I 'ear Bill's got more than fifty men an' a brood o' wild dogs supportin' 'is claim for King o' Irishtown. Bill 'as always been known to love animals, yu know."

Thos rubs a thumb across his nose, "So does a butcher."

"The word is Pickles promises Bill a hundred scofflaw soldiers if 'e gets exonerated in the retrial."

"Interestin', that'd give Bill an edge."

"An' makes me bruva Darby's role important."

The conductor of a locomotive nods toward Frank as the train rounds the freight tracks into the brick building from the street.

The sound of wet metal wheels scraping against the rails causes Frank to speak louder, "Dark days loom down Brooklyn way. I'm glad Dinny sent me away. 'E was always good to me when I managed the Kirkman Soap Fact'ry, Dinny was. Good to me wife Celia too. Good man, Dinny Meehan is. But for what I done; speakin' wif the eighty-sixt Darby. . . Dinny let me off light. Let me leave Brooklyn on the quiet. I still feel bad about it. What's wrong wif me? Why do I still feel bad for double-crossin' Dinny?"

"Those are two very different questions," Thos answers. "Dinny makes exceptions for fam'ly matters. Fam'ly makes a big difference when it comes to the White Hand's code o' silence."

"Bill Lovett wouldn't've let me off light. It's touts for clouts in Brooklyn, but I got lucky," Frank smiles and taps Thos on the shoulder. "Yu gonna back Meehan, aren't yu? Yu sound like yu put respect on 'im."

"If respect won wars, mothers would rule the world. How did Darby get Sadie to pay the legal fees for Pickles' new trial? Why would she do that?"

"That's what's eatin' me up too," Frank scratches a clean-shaven chin.

He knows but won't tell me. Darby must be blackmailing her. But with what?

Thos nibbles at the edges to get more information, "Is she still in hidin', Sadie?"

"Yeah I s'pose so. . . I 'aven't spoken wif 'er though," Frank looks up and to the right.

"I didn' ask if ya had," Thos shoots him hunter's eyes, yellow and cruel.

He's lying, he definitely has spoken with her recently.

Frank clears his throat and changes the topic, "I 'eard Tanner Smif bailed Dinny out. Ya 'eard that, Thos?"

"Yeah," he groans at Frank.

Another of Thos's informants let him in on that one, Henry Browne.

"An' now Tanner's in the inner circle o' the White 'and, true innit?"

I wish you would tell me something I don't know, that's what I pay you for.

Frank continues, "That must complicate things, eh? Did ya call the Blood Feud on Tanner before yu knew 'e was in Dinny's inner circle?"

"That don' matter. The business between Tanner an' I goes back to 1916 when he tried to muscle me to get into the ILA. What happened back then can't be smoothed out. It's blood an' only blood's gonna solve it."

"Well now that ya proclaimed a Blood Feud, someone's gonna die. I got me money on Thos Carmody, though," Frank comes in closer for a whisper. "I got somethin' yu can use, Thos. Yu're gonna like this one. Word is Tanner Smif is in deep wit' a shylock 'ere in Man'attan."

"The Dropper? Or Johnny Spanish?" Thos asks.

Frank smiles, "Spanish. They always called ya Quick Thos for good reason."

So that's how he got Dinny to take him back, Thos looks away in thought, then asks, "Wasn't Johnny Spanish the fella that shot his pregnant wife an' when the baby came out it was missin' three fingers?"

"It is."

Thos turns an eye up to Frank with the masonry block quoins on the corner of the solid brick building in the background. Along the tracks in the cobbles, a locomotive driver blows smoke from his mouth while trying to get a better look at the disfigured side of Thos's face.

"Dark days," Frank mutters. "One more thing. Goin' back to me bruva, Darby. 'E 'as a child now. I was wif 'im the night 'is fiancé gave birf."

"What about it?"

"She's. . . Italian. Yu know 'ow much Lovett 'ates the guineas, yeah?"

So the shadow has secrets too, eh?

"When is Pickles' retrial?"

"May. On top o' that," Frank continues as they both step out of the cobblestones when an automobile truck approaches. "I think Darby's lost the plot altogeva. 'E told me 'e sees. . . angels."

"Angels eh, plural?"

"Two."

"One for each shoulder," Thos grumbles and looks off, weighing the informant's words.

So Sadie is not just hiding from her husband, but also her cousin.

Thos turns cruel eyes to Frank, "Why do ya feign innocence an' give me all the dirt I need to know about ya brothers, Frank? Then lie to me about ya cousin Sadie?"

"Thos, I—"

"Ya movin' to Connecticut, I hear?"

Frank laughs and shakes his head again, "Quick Thos knows all."

"I know ya're lying, but why?" Thos eyes Frank, "What's the secret Darby has over ya cousin Sadie?"

"Quick Thos—"

"If ya keep callin' me quick, my enemies'll come to expect it. It's best when they believe they can out-quick me, see?"

Frank's voice changes to sound as if he is pleading, "I'm sorry, Thos—"

"Answer the question."

"Which one Thos?"

"What is Darby bribin' Sadie over?"

"I dunno, Thos—"

"Liar."

"I dunno, really I don't. We. . . Celia an' I just don't want any trouble is all, yu know? I 'ate danger."

"Ya hate danger, eh?" Thos groans at that, "Ya wife Celia, she still eh—" *What is the word I am looking for? Barren?*

"We have not been blessed wif children. . . yet."

Frank speaks as if even he doesn't believe they'll ever come. This leads Thos to believe it's probably the wife who holds out enough hope for the both of them.

"That's good reason to take in Sadie an' her child," Thos says.

"We're not—"

"An' yet ya don't give two shits about Darby's baby wit' the I-talian. That at least is smart o' ya. Anyhow," Thos shakes his head realizing he is being cruel to Frank. "I'm. . . I'm sorry to hear about the kids gimmick, Frank. I know ya've always prayed for a large fam'ly."

"What about yu'self, Thos? Ya ever gonna get married? Start a fam'ly?"

Never, it's not for me. Not now. "I don' know."

"Yu just got back from the war, Thos. Take some time off. That's a good idea, innit? On 'oliday maybe?"

"Holiday? Nah, I don't need fam'ly or holidays, I just need trouble. Someone's gotta go in and make sense o' it. I like trouble. Trouble is my Juliet."

"Trouble, or tragedy?"

"Yeah well," Thos shrugs and looks out onto the Hudson River and New Jersey in the distance. "If everythin's goin' ya way, it's a sure sign ya probably in the wrong lane, ya know what I mean?"

"Not sure I do, but that's alright."

"Frank!" A man yells from a third-floor arched window of the refinery. Frank and Thos crane their heads up from the street.

Frank looks at Thos, "I'm sorry Thos—"

"Don' worry," Thos interrupts and pulls his hand out of his coat pocket with a folded twenty dollar bill in it and shakes Frank's hand, passing it to him, "Thanks."

"Might be the last time I ever see yu Thos. In a couple weeks me wife an' I will be in Connecticut for good. We bought a 'ouse up there," Frank rubs the twenty dollar bill between his fingers before slipping it into his pocket. "Safer up there, it is."

"Well good luck."

"I got one last thing for yu. Yu bosses King Joe an' T.V. O'Connor are gonna invite yu for a sit-down in the Chelsea ballroom, but it's a ruse. They're 'avin' a banquet in yu honor. They're to give yu an award in front o' everyone to prove 'ow patriotic they are. The papers keep mixin' the ILA up in their Red Scare an' callin' them Bolsheviks. So they feel like they 'ave to—"

"I get it," Thos cuts him off. "Thanks for the heads up."

Thos turns round coldly and puts a handrolled cigarette in the left side of his mouth before calling behind him, "Thanks again, Frank."

"It's yur world, Thos. We're just livin' in it."

Thos stops.

If this is my world, it's nothing but a dream. I should be dead. Why aren't I?

He takes a long drag as pedestrians walk round him on the snowy sidewalk. When he looks back, Frank has disappeared.

Maybe I am dead and this is a dream?

Since he'd returned from the war he'd had a sense that nothing was real. He didn't eat. He didn't sleep. He was getting weaker.

Maybe I am right now dying on the battlefield and time has stopped, while a dream of living has begun.

Like in a dream, Thos reasons, he can conceive and perceive the world at the same time without realizing it's not real.

But if I can conceive everything, then I might be able to control what happens. Yes, I can create my own reality. But am I really in control? Or is someone else?

Thos looks round himself, then remembers what the doctors said of him in the armory where he had been transferred after being released from the field hospital.

"Shell Shock," they said.

"I ain't shell shocked, goddamn yaz," Thos angrily disagreed. "I ain't no fookin' poltroon coward! I'm a killer. I got sixty-seven confirmed kills an' one back home in New

York. That means I'm beatin' death sixty-eight to nothin'. I'll always be a killer, but—"

"But what?" The doctors ask.

Is that the right score? Or did I actually die? Sixty-eight to one?

Thos slowly unbuttoned his hospital gown to stand naked in front of the doctors, bearing the thousands of shrapnel wounds along the right side of his body, "I'm haunted."

"Ok so you're haunted, fine," the doctor pleads. "Call it what you will. Just please eat. You're getting weaker and weaker, Mr. Carmody. Eat something, don't whither away."

On the sidewalks of Manhattan, Thos pulls up his lapel and begins to walk with the crowds that are now forming, but he cannot. He leans against a brick wall and looks down to his shaking hands. Almost losing his balance in the icy slate sidewalk, he pushes off the wall and gathers the bits of strength he has left.

I'm going to get you, Tanner. Sixty-nine to one.

Born for this

A crackling sound comes to my ears as the clouds rush through me. From up here they move faster than I ever realized. They are colder and wetter too. And dense on the skin like white shadows.

I am fast at work. . . dragging corpses. I know that I am dreaming, but too busy to palter with that I continue my work dragging the malnourished and emaciated corpses. Carefully I organize them as they stare off with shock on their faces. Frozen forever in disbelief. They wear eternal masks of mistrust that had taken shape in their very last moment as if they doubted death would ever truly come for them.

No. . . I am not dragging the corpses. I am. . . I am stacking and linking them together. The broad-hipped women fit perfectly with the broad-shouldered men like cargo in a hull. Yet I am atop a mountain amidst the movement of clouds. In this dream I am back home high in the Moylussa peaks southwest of Tulla. Below, when the gray mist parts and opens enough for me to see down toward Tulla town, instead the East River appears with the Manhattan and Brooklyn bridges spanning it.

Diligently I stack the corpses like cordwood. When I look away, turning to grab hold of yet more, I find that the neatly stacked bodies have transformed, becoming the earthen soil on which I stand. Each body lifts me higher into the clouds. Higher and higher still. So high my ears sizzle and pop from the pressure. A dizziness takes hold and interrupts my work. If I should fall I will land in the river, my mind rationalizes, but most likely I'll wake up just before the water rushes up and smashes me.

I must have known there was something important to be done, and with that in mind I continue my work, stacking and organizing. As I lean to grasp the next lank and lifeless body under the arms, its blank eyes move and find me.

"Liam?" Through its throaty gargling sounds I recognize the voice of my uncle Joseph.

Says he to me, "Ye took me life, an' ye have me soul. I live here now, inside ye. I understand though. Why ye killed me, that is. I understand it. Ye're buildin' somet'in'. I just didn't know that the dead are important elements o' the bigger story. That it was all written out beforehand. Turns out I was made to die regardless o' all me hopes an' dreams. The fulfillment o' me life's direction is but a stepstone fer others."

"But Dinny says there's no such thing as fate," I squat over my dead uncle.

"The *laoch* prepares his people fer life without him, but a shanachie? Ah yes, a shanachie resurrects the dead. Fer to create is to truly rule."

"*Laoch*? *Shanachie*?" I say with incredulity. "Those are Irish words. Words you would never have used in your living days, save in mockery. Why do you speak to me in kindness now when in life you were cruel?"

A wan smile comes to uncle Joseph's face, "True, now I am dead. An' ye are in-dream."

"Dinny is the one who creates. And it's Dinny who rules. I am merely a teenage boy, ignorant and naive. Loyal but callow."

"Ye're almost a man proven. Look not at yer youthful age but at yer journey. Separated from yer loved ones, ye were initiated into another world; overcame it an' summoned back yer fam'ly. Stand tall Liam, ye are more man than most. Now look round. See that ye're born for this. See it! That is why the Bard waits fer ye an' the Ghost God watches."

"The Bard? From Irishtown? Why does he wait for people in dreams? And who is the Ghost God who watches?"

"One is man. One is myth. An' on earth he sees with eyes. The witness! While in the Otherworld he shows, both at once together. Forever they ride.

Among the clouds I rub my forehead with an index finger, "So they wait and they watch, then they see and they show? At the same time?"

"The witness is not he who heard, ye understand. It is he who saw. An' there is a subtlety that is understood when visited in dreams. Somethin'—" he searches for the right word. "Eternal. The magic o' myth can reveal the inner maze o' a thousand generations worth o' truths. An' just now archons and orphans bud like flowers over earthen corpses. As the miracle o' life is forever threatened with the tragedy o' death, so too a great and terrible thing this way arises. An' ye shall bear it witness."

I place him on the soil as gently as a mother puts her newborn down for sleep. His hair is thinner than I remember and is no more than flaying dry wisps across his pate. And his cheeks are so sallow that it seems the skin is but paper over his jaw.

I stand over him as the wet clouds pass through me and give a chill. Then I see it. Protruding from his throat is the blade of a knife that had been pushed through from behind. It's Harry's knife, I remember. The knife Harry gave me to kill my uncle Joseph.

His eyes search for me, "Ye're alive, Liam."

Prostrate, uncle Joseph looks away in thought but does not blink. Then tries to swallow but cannot. "Alive but ye don't know what anyt'in' means yet. In yer world mortal sin is only forgiven by a great contrition o' charity. But ye were always charitable. An' ye did this to me in the name o' yer fam'ly so that they might have a new chance for a better life in America. Yet still ye'll seek out absolution as yer good mother advises. But I want ye to know that I forgive ye, Liam. I forgive ye, so I do."

~~~

In the black of morn my eyes flick open and at once I have risen, dressed and tied my boots in the cramped quarters.

Harry and I had built a second wall in the Eighth Avenue room no bigger than a closet with enough room for a single bed where I sleep. A narrow window above provides a shaft of light.

In the darkness I run my fingers along the oaken top of the table Harry handmade for us. The dropleaf table fits perfectly between the wall and the cabinetry.

In the moonlight I walk the room as my boots set the wood floors to creaking. Harry too had taken the time to help rebuild the flooring as there was a giant hole when we moved in. By hand we sanded the floors, rebuilt the plumbing, painted, replaced the windows, mortared the hearth and built a new mantle to place photographs upon.

Over the sink I hold the white lace curtains between a finger and thumb and gently rub.

What a hopeless feeling we would be left with if it were all to be lost. All that work. All the conversations we have in here. All the love. We built it ourselves. And we made it our home.

Still haunted by the night's dream, I freeze in place when I see movement in the blue-black of the moonlit room.

In the doorway to the larger bedroom the silhouette of my mother appears as she silently ties her robe. My stomach turns at the thought of the trouble I have put her and my sisters in.

If I was smart, I would make us move. It's too dangerous here. But this is our home. Our creation.

"Some toast Liam?" She whispers, then moves for the coal stove. "I'll wet some tae fer ye."

"No bother, I have to be going."

"Yes, going," her mouth squiggles as behind her Abby and Brigid reposition in the squeaky spring bed they share until soft sighs quieten them.

"Yes, yes, going," she repeats, a mother's mockery. "Between yer father, yer brother Timothy an' yerself, ye were the only one that never rose an hour before dawn. My how things change. What type o' longshore werk is done this early?"

Murder, theft and intimidation.

Guilt wriggles through me like eels under the skin. "We're uh. . . to meet at the Atlantic Avenue Terminal this morning. Last night a ship from China arrived and requires unloading. Since there aren't as many ships as there were during wartime, our uh. . . closest friends are doing the job."

She gazes out the kitchen window through the lace curtains where beyond are shadows of rooftops and obscured water towers and the fingers of leafless treetops swaying in Prospect Park. I reach for the door in desperation to exit, but hold my hand over the handle.

"Do you have trouble sleeping, Mam? With all the noise round here? I know you're accustomed to the silence of Tulla and—"

"Are ye associated with a man named Wild Bill Lovett?" she asks all of a sudden.

Even she's heard of him.

"I know who he is."

"I. . . I read an article in the daily about him a few days ago. Did ye know he beat a Swedish man with a razor-ring awhile back, before he went to the war? The man's blinded fer life," she says with sympathy in her voice. "There are consequences in life when violence flares up ye know, Liam. Here ye can read it yerself. It's called Tilda's Tears," she points at the newspaper.

"You are being naive, Mam."

"He can't werk an' his mother, her name is Tilda, she's facin' the poorhouse. But this Lovett man walks free. In fact he's a war hero just returned an' has a new longshoreman gang that's taken over the Red Hook section. Do ye work in Red Hook, Liam?"

"I don't," I say over a shoulder, wanting nothing more than to slip out the door.

"So what happens if yer maimed like Tilda's son? Eh? Or worse. I read that the gangs control all o' longshoreman labor. Been that way fer many years an' it's too dangerous fer a citizen to enter the maze o' docks an' piers an' storehouses along the waterfront because the gangs hate outsiders an' strangers. An' when they kill the people, no one ever talks with the police fer fear o' bein' called a 'tout.' Now the unions support the gangs, the article says. But king o' all the wild ones is this Dennis Meehan fella. Dinny, they call him."

Whatever happened to our code of silence? Who's behind this article?

She comes close through the darkness, "He steals t'ousands o' dullars werth o' merchandise from ships an' local fact'ries an' sells it fer profit. He's the leader o' the White Hand. . . Killed many men. An' fer no reason t'all, it's said. Other than talkin' with the wrong person. Do ye work with this Meehan man, Liam?"

"I don't know any man with that name," I say by rule and rote.

"Don't ye?" She whispers in resignation, though it screams of disbelief. "They're enemies, those two. Which side is yerself on, Liam?"

"Mam, the newspapers don't tell the all of it."

"The newspapers lie? It's all lies then? The whole thing? Tilda's Tears an' Lovett an' Meehan? I'll have ye know that I'm not one fer believin' whole-heartedly in anythin' most men say, particularly in newspapers. But there are kernels o' truth in everythin'. So I ask ye, Liam. Concernin' this business o' murderin' men. Have ye been involved in any murders round here over the past t'ree years? Have ye?"

A soft rap comes to the door.

"It's Burke," she turns to me as Abby and Brigid sit up in bed. "We always know who t'is by the coded tappin', don't we? Him with the fearful eyes. An' if it's not him it's the stoney stare on Harry Reynolds, is it not? My god Liam, what price must we pay fer our passage to New Yark? Eh? The noise round here is not what keeps me awake, son. It's the werry."

I dig into my pocket and pull out the Saint Christopher she had given me back in October of 1915 as I was being sent 'way for reasons untold to me. "Remember this Mam?" I hold it up to her face.

"Of course I do—"

"Not to worry, you told me. That I'd be grand with it. Safe-keeping, you said. May trouble be always a stranger to you, remember? That's what you said. I was a boy then, sent on a man's journey—" Burke taps on the door a second time and my sisters are now out of bed. "I had no idea what grief and woe was in store."

She cuts in, "But I wanted only to pass the virtue o' safe travel to ye. It wasn't my decision to—"

"I have kept this on me the entire time, Mam. Everything I have done since coming here has been for us. Everything. I survived the crossing and overcame all obstacles. Just to bring you and the girls here. I was a boy and ill-prepared for any of it, yet I have prevailed and you stand here in front of me now, safe and sound."

That's a lie, no one is safe here, but I can't stop now.

"All of this I have done only to have you question me? Question my decisions and the people I associate with? I won't have it. No I won't. Especially since all you know about them and what I do is what you've learned through the willful lies of the owning class and the deceitful gossip they curry up as yellow news."

"Now ye sound like yer father," says she.

"But I'm not him, am I? He's gone, missing. Goes off to fight and leaves his family for a teen to care for everything."

Abby and Brigid watch by the doorway with tousled hair.

"Don't ye speak ill o' yer father. I knew what I was gettin' into when I married the son of a Moonlighter."

"Is that why ye never worry about him and put it all on me? You think it's easy? What I've done? What I have to do everyday?"

"What have ye done? Are we in danger here? Should we leave?"

All three turn their eyes to me. But I look at the wood floor we refurbished, the new hearth, the table Harry built and the lace curtains.

I created this with the same people she would have us run from. No, no way.

"There's not enough money to go round. Especially with the rich people who hoard it all up in their mansions. The only way immigrants like us can make it is by working together," I come closer with bitterness on my face. "Work with us, Mam. You're supposed to be an ally. Do not be an enemy."

"Liam—"

"There's nothing else to be said, Mam. It is not a bad thing to want what I want."

"It's not what ye want what scares me, it's what drives ye, Liam. That engine inside ya chest that pushes into danger further an' further an' then further still."

"Aye, apparently I am my father's son after all."

"Don't ye open that door!" She screams.

I open it quickly and come into the dark hallway where Burke jumps from my way. As we step down the stairwell shame rushes through me like the clouds in my dream. And it's only then, as Burke and I step into the wind that knifes across the gray slate sidewalk that I realize I've left her worse for wear with my words.

I'm not really asking her to be an ally, am I? No, I'm convincing myself to keep what I created, against my own instincts. I truly am the fool.

I twirl a pebble between my fingers and stop in the street and look back to the third floor room. Back to the window where assuredly my mother looks out over the dark streets.

"What? Ya goin' back?" Burke asks.

But I just exhale and throw the pebble against the cobblestones as we cross the street and head toward the waterfront.

Then a strange feeling washes over me. A feeling that we are being watched. I turn my eyes up and see something slip behind the line of cornices along the row houses.

"Are we goin' or what?" Burke asks.

But I can't speak to him. *He has his fill of anguish already. And I with shame. I just want to get to the Atlantic Terminal for the meeting.*

When the train rumbles in at Ninth Street I can feel the eyes watch me again.
Am I mad?

Ace in the Hole

"This where the Waterfront Assembly is? Wall Street? Jeez all the sidewalks've been shoveled out already. How come they get the white gloves? Even wit' Enright's new retirement system he got for us, I could never afford to live around here."

Detective William Brosnan looks round himself at the winding, cavernous streets canopied by rows of gargantuan buildings that shadow this part of the earth, "Well, now that Europe fought against itself to ruins, this. . . this is the new empire, isn't it?"

Ferris laughs, "Sometimes ya're a straight talker, Brosnan. Then other times I think ya're haunted by mad theories o'—"

"Ferris," Brosnan stops him.

Patrolman Ferris turns as behind him paperboys yell out the morning's headlines, "Yeah?"

Brosnan stares up to the top of the looming skyscraper in front of him, "From here I have to go it alone."

"Yeah?"

"The things I told ye?"

"I know, I know, don' repeat it. I'd never get people to talk to me if I betrayed their trust. I'll keep it zipped. Don' worry ol' fella."

"Not even to yer father-in-law, Captain Sullivan?"

Ferris scratches his chin, "Thing is, the captain wanted me to follow ya, Brosnan. He says ya been actin' strange the last week or so an', ya know, I gotta agree wit' him. Plus there's that report ya gave him yesterday—"

Ah, I see, I suppose you were being nice to set the bait, now you close the trap.

"It's, it's just information, in case. . ." Brosnan trails off.

That's my ace in the hole. Hopefully I don't have to pull it out.

Brosnan then changes direction. "I'll go to him this very day an' tell him if I want it to be officially filed or not."

"Uhright, what did ya spend all that dirty money on then?"

"A house."

"A house?"

"In Peekskill," Brosnan admits, though what he says next is a lie. "I don't want to retire in Brooklyn, I'm goin' upstate."

Ferris purses his lip again and backs off a bit.

"I thought you were bein' friendly all along," Brosnan sheepishly looks at the patrolman.

"I was," Ferris leans back on his heels and looks up to the gargantuan buildings above. "Big things are comin' Brooklyn's way. The captain an' me, we're worried for ya."

They shake hands and Ferris walks backward while staring at Brosnan, then turns and walks along the five-foot high snow banks until crossing Wall Street.

Brosnan peaks up one more time at the great height before walking in.

Wolcott'll be up there working, I do not doubt.

Jonathan G. Wolcott may be of ill repute in Brooklyn, but no one could say the fat man born into old money is lazy or lackadaisical. No, Jonathan G. Wolcott prays to the god of efficiency. He will be up there now working harder than ever, hatching schemes to win the bounty of the Brooklyn waterfront from the old longshoremen gangs and unions that own it.

I'm not mad. I'm not mad, Brosnan tells himself. *You can do this old man, You must. Daniel must be released of the fat man's clutches, otherwise. . . Death is due.*

Inside the warm elevator Brosnan struggles to undo the buttons on his tunic. He stares down at them with his bottom lip sticking out and growls. The scent of rusty water comes to him as he rubs his itchy and dry nose. The electric boilers that warm the newer buildings are a marvel, for certain, but far too hot for a bear's liking. In Irishtown, such luxuries are unknown. Only but a few of the tenements along the waterfront where he lives even have electricity. The people there warm themselves by the hearth or at the foot of coal-fired stoves in the pre-Civil War wood-framers. There is even less coal than there is wood these days in Irishtown.

But Wall Street never suffers the elements. Oh no. Brooklyn does though. Brooklyn will freeze even though the boilers are manufactured in the smitheries and forged in the waterfront industries there.

The heat in the office on the twenty-eighth floor hits Brosnan like thick soup. A wide, uncommonly clean fireplace gently crackles in the waiting room even though the radiators under the row of windows are in perfect order.

Over the tight bun of the secretary are perfectly placed letters that read "New York Waterfront Assembly." He smells fresh paint and brewed coffee, and the carpet looks as if it had been laid that same morning.

"Hot as hades in here," Brosnan bellows to no one in particular.

The secretary observes him with flinty eyes. His soiled boots. The darkened ring at the bottom of his tunic. The swollen knuckles upon bent fingers like winter branches. The mannerisms of a commoner. "How can I help you?"

"Ye know who I am, Detective William Brosnan," he announces in his North Dublin accent. "I am here to see Mr. Wolcott, President o' the—"

"Do you have an appointment?"

"Listen, I need to speak to yer man—"

"My man? I am not Mr. Wolcott's—"

"I don't need a bleedin'—" he stops himself and grunts. "I do not have an appointment, but he—"

"Is busy, I do apologize," she reaches for a large black book and opens it. Without looking at him again, she withdraws a pencil from her tight bun and sedately wipes the page clean with the back of her pinky finger. "I suggest you make an appointment. Which ward are you from?"

Brosnan steps back, shoulders out of his tunic and drapes it over an arm.

"Sir? What ward are you from?"

"An' I apologize to yer grand self. . . In advance, that is," Brosnan briskly walks passed her desk. With a *whoosh* he swings the door open where he remembers meeting Wolcott previously.

The secretary slams the big black book closed, "Sir!"

Inside, Wolcott sits at his executive desk with two bespectacled men at each corner.

"I need to pull on yer ear, now," Brosnan folds his arms high on his broad chest; a low and threatening growl simmers within it.

One of the men who sits opposite Wolcott is dressed in a suit reminiscent of the gay 90s with a polished silver watch-case hanging from a waistcoat pocket.

Vandeleurs, Brosnan recognizes. *The Leech landlord.*

The other man is Charles Pakenham, a reporter Brosnan has seen many times down at the Adams Street Courthouse in Brooklyn, as well as the Poplar Street Station.

"I see Brooklyn is well-represented on Wall Street these days," his booming voice breaks the mousy hush in the executive office where a wheeled chalkboard in the corner partially obscures the view east toward lower Manhattan with Brooklyn in the distance.

"Complete with honest cops and all," Pakenham says. "I'll have you know that it was me that—"

"Ye don' have to talk about yerself, Pak," Brosnan interrupts him. "We'll do it for ye after ye leave, get it?"

The reporter sniggers as he walks by with papers under his arm. At the coat rack he drops a beige boater cap over his comb-back hair and pushes out the door, the Leech Vandeleurs worms behind him.

"Bleedin' bowsies, them lot," Brosnan grumbles toward Wolcott. "That's the feller wrote about me in the article on police corruption a while back, is it not?"

"Might be," Wolcott shrugs as the door closes behind Brosnan.

"T'was yerself told him to write it, I'd wager."

"You would win that bet," Wolcott retorts. "You simply needed a gentle nudge to join the right side. Or at least to accept money from the right side. Simply put, you were in need of civilizing. It was for your own good. I'm sure you realize that now, don't you?"

This isn't going to be easy, Brosnan sighs.

"I never wanted the White Hand's money. Same goes for the money yerself gives. Which reminds me that ye owe me a nice handful for lockin' up Dinny Meehan on the boot theft gimmick."

"Gimmick?" Wolcott's face turns sideways. "Strange word."

"Ye owe me."

"I remind you, sir, that no payments are exchanged here. You will meet Mr. Wisniewski at the agreed-upon Union Street location. That being said, Hanan & Sons is more than appreciative for bringing those thieving little monkeys to justice," Wolcott motions toward the door. "And now even the newspapers have joined the right side. I'm sure you have not missed the recent editorials concerning the gangs and their misdeeds."

A cock fight you want, is it? I can play that too. First one to get mad, loses.

Brosnan sits in the wooden chair across Wolcott and leans forward. "Why not tell us how ye pulled off the miracle o' yer sudden rebirth? Go ahead then. Go ahead. Riddle me that one, at least. Why not?"

Wolcott rolls his eyes and folds his fingers to allow the old Dubliner his say.

"Dinny Meehan an' his troupe o' turf cutters wiped ye up clean in both battles when ye was with the New York Dock Company. So they fire ye for it. Now look at ye. Sittin' up here like a god representin' *all* the waterfront businesses in Brooklyn. Down in the workin' class neighborhoods where I come from, it's a strange notion; to receive somethin' ye've not earned," Brosnan's jaw moves under his angry eyes. "I started out with next-to-nothin' when I came to this country. An' I still got most o' it. But yer-very-self? The truth is ye've never had to earn a thing in the whole o' yer life, have ye Johnny G. Wolcott? An' here ye are now, a man well into the winter o' his days still workin'? It's not for the money, that's plain to see, I never knew a fat man to be poor. The only reason I can come up with is pride. Pride, it must be then. Because if ye died this very day, ye'd be forever known as a man who never once succeeded on his own merit. Ye've failed yer entire life, yet ye were given more opportunity than the great many o' us. Isn't that the truth of it?"

"All this from a man who was promoted from patrolman to detective for naming Non Connors the leader of the White Hand instead of Dinny Meehan."

Brosnan sits back and adjusts his copper badge.

Wolcott looks outside and runs his tongue along the top of his teeth, "I expect you came to my office across the bridge to appeal for some recourse? I try to avoid people who are in. . ." he flicks fingers in Brosnan's direction, "reduced circumstances, but you seem famished for favor."

"I've tried to explain it to ye, but ye don't listen to an ol' gumshoe," Brosnan says. "The gangs are like the Kilkenny Cats, they'll fight themselves into their holes if ye let them. I—"

"You are right, they just need a little help," Wolcott interrupts. "A house divided cannot stand, it's true, but maybe hanging the cats upside down by their tales next to each other would irritate their grievances?"

The bear's chin quivers, giving away his deepest fears, "An' to do it, ye turn to my son, Daniel Culkin. To scare up that, that. . . *wraith*! Ye don't know Garry Barry like I do. An' I know ye have eyes on burnin' down the Meehan home too."

Wolcott's right eyebrow lifts with interest, "And you know all this how?"

"Do ye think anythin' happens in Brooklyn I don't know about? Pertainin' to my own family on top of it? My son has always been after impressin' the well-to-do an' quick to the blackjack, but ye don't even understand what's at stake here for my family. In this storm?" Brosnan points out the window. "Garry Barry should've been dead twice over, do ye understand me? Ye're toyin' with destiny here."

Wolcott grunts, "Some day a real storm will come and blow all the rats and roaches off the Brooklyn streets. So, nothing happens in Brooklyn that you are not aware of? That's what you are saying to me, correct?"

"T'is."

"Go ahead, then. Look out that window. Look to the south and tell me what you see."

Brosnan wrinkles his brow and stands from the chair. In the distance he sees the bridges and the long bluff along the waterfront from Brooklyn Heights down toward Atlantic Avenue. Further south he sees Governor's Island on the Buttermilk Channel and then—

Wolcott smiles, the fatty folds amidst the fleshy pouch under his chin quivers. "Black smoke."

"What is it about?" Brosnan moves closer to the glass. "That's down by the Erie Basin. Italian territory ever since the White Hand an' Black Hand made an agreement with the ILA union."

Wolcott pretends to hold a conductor's baton between his thumb and index finger and waves it as if to lead an orchestra through an imagined symphony, "What is that black smoke you ask? It is war. The gang war is here. White Hand against Black Hand. Both hands against the ILA. But most importantly, it signals White Hand against itself," Wolcott smiles. "Now Mr. Brosnan, come sit down. Say what it is you have come here for, or be gone."

The wooden chair creaks as Brosnan rests in it, "I am here for one reason, to make sure that ye release my son from yer employ." The chair creaks again when he leans back.

Wolcott allows a slight smile to cross his soft, fleshy pink face, "*Na Bocklish*, isn't it?"

"That's what I smoke. What of it?"

"It's a brand from Ireland, correct?" Wolcott rolls back in his leather chair. "But you haven't been to Ireland since you were, what? A teen?"

"What does that matter?"

"You smoke that brand because it reminds you of the old days. The scent of your childhood. The old country. I find that interesting. I've always found you interesting, Mr. Brosnan. The Dubliner that lived between the great progress of England, and the new-caught, sullen peoples, half-devil and half-child."

"I don't know what ye're—"

"It's a poem. A famed poem. I'm sure you've never heard of it."

"Well—"

"Does your cigar brand go well with coffee?"

Brosnan turns his head, "Better with whiskey."

"I don't believe we have whiskey here, scotch maybe?"

"Why not. But I'm neither here to smoke cigars nor for the drink, I'm here—"

"I enjoy cigars too, but not the black ones," Wolcott stands, opens a desk drawer and pulls out a wooden box with the words 'Ybor Gales' drawn on it in large, orange lettering. "Try one?"

"I will, but we need—"

"And can you bring that bottle and two glasses over here?"

Brosnan looks over his shoulder, stands up and fetches the crystal bottle and two rocks glasses, sliding them onto Wolcott's desk.

A plume of thick smoke roils round the fat man's face with an ember glow in the middle of it. He hands Brosnan a lit cigar across the desk.

"A toast," Wolcott offers with a cigar in his mouth and a quarter-filled rocks glass in his right hand raised in the direction of the window, "As one war ends, another begins; may Grey's Faith reward us with the division of Brooklyn: To the future!"

Brosnan gives a quizzical glare, "What do all them words tell us?"

"Only that Brooklyn is a diseased portion of the state of New York that must first be cured and reformed before it can be in a position to appreciate the good and sound laws of business. Oh come now, a simple cheers," Wolcott smirks happily. "To the future!"

"To the future," Brosnan reluctantly drinks and curls his nose.

"You don't appreciate aged scotch?"

"It's got a bleedin' ashy aftertaste," Brosnan says as Wolcott sips from his glass and drags long on the cigar through floppy lips and a gin-blossomed nose.

"To each his own," Wolcott settles in his chair. "Now, we were on the topic of getting to the point, were we not?"

"Yes, the reason I am here—"

"About the future," Wolcott finishes his sentence. "That's the point isn't it. No one knows this truth like two old-timers. Why else do the dying turn to god but for hope of an afterlife? The future is all! But it is controlled by those who have the power to make people powerless. Did you know that the law of competition was created by slave owners and monopolists?"

"Eh—"

"Irony," Wolcott chuckles. "Of course the victims of the past are written about by their victors. My point is; to control the future you must have power, understand?"

"I believe I do."

"Very good. In the process of controlling the future and writing the past, you must find associates who provide useful service. I myself, am in the business of changing power over industrial labor from violent gangs and red-Bolshevik unions to something much more American in character, and agreeable to the interests of Brooklyn business owners, my clients. Mr. Brosnan, you no longer provide useful service. From the Poplar Street Police Station in the jurisdiction of Irishtown and the waterfront territories we need more of a viceroy, or someone who furthers our interests. You have simply failed at that role, which is why we enlisted Daniel."

"But ye don't understand—"

"But I do," Wolcott breaks in. "Of course the law is quite slow, as you are. Even still, you must always be perceived as respecting the law if the future is to be—"

"The law? There is no law but self-preservation in Brooklyn, an' the Irish are well-equipped for they have suffered great hunger, pain, fear an' the darkness o' ill will. We do our best, but I can tell ye that the law is *not* here to serve only the people in high towers an' their notions," Brosnan's chest puffs out. "It's here to serve all. Now just because ye're fat as the butcher's dog—"

Wolcott chuckles and begins to say something, but can't get a word in edgewise.

"An' yer nose is so high in the air that ye think yer arse smells o' *chypre* perfume, still ye're not above the law."

The fat man's laughing sets his midsection to jiggling in fits and starts.

"Ye scoff at that notion," Brosnan lowers his voice and bows his head. "The oaths a policemen takes to protect an' serve? For yerself, they are but the silly slogans o' duty-bound soldiers. We can't control who's right and who's wrong. But for yez and yer like, the only thing that matters is who's left standin' to serve yer needs."

"So prescient," Wolcott rolls his eyes. "You truly do understand."

Brosnan lowers his eyes at Wolcott and growls. "Ye could butter parsnips with words like that."

"Could I? The funny thing is, you don't even know to fear me," Wolcott ashes. "But you will."

"A threat? From a man beaten twice by Dinny Meehan?"

"The third time will be charming. I have learned a few valuable lessons. You are one of them."

"Garry Barry's going to help ya this time?" Brosnan laughs. "Ye'll never beat Meehan, an' I'll tell ye why. Down at the Dock Loaders' Club there's a single photograph on the wall behind cracked glass. It's an old yellowed thing, torn and decrepit. But the man in the photo is the great Abraham Lincoln an' his values are as old as the flood. Just north o' here in Manhattan, up at Cooper Square, Lincoln said somethin' in a speech many-a-year ago that I put to memory. Talkin' on the fight to end slavery he said, 'Let us have faith that right makes might, and in that faith, let us, to the end, dare to do our duty.'"

Brosnan takes a deep breath and lets it out slowly, "In Irishtown, they have faith that right makes might. But Johnny G. Wolcott? Ye can't help but think ye can control the future from above Wall Street," Brosnan growls. "Ye should be scarlet with shame, but look at ye."

Wolcott leans back and draws from his cigar, never taking his eyes off Brosnan.

"Ye can't have my son," Brosnan flatly states.

"He is your son-in-law, if I remember correctly."

"Here's what we're goin' to do," Brosnan stands above the desk, "Dinny Meehan, leader o' the White Hand, which is closely allied to the main union in Brooklyn, the International Longshoreman's Association, is right now sittin' in my jail at the Poplar Street Station," Brosnan pulls out his police issue revolver, holds it, then slowly places it on Wolcott's desk. "To better serve ye, I will take care o' Mr. Meehan myself."

Wolcott touches his lower chin, then slowly shakes his head, "And yet you believe the gates of your heaven will be flung open for a corrupt cop who takes bribes from a man for years, then offers to kill him? A true Roman Catholic, aren't you? Forever with your hand out asking to be forgiven."

"God up in his high heaven has naught to do with this bollix. All I want is for ye to leave my son out of it," Brosnan growls. "I want ye to disassociate yerself from him an' refuse his offers. That's what I ask in return. Deal?"

Wolcott wraps five little sausage fingers round the rocks glass and slowly brings it to his lips, then gently places it back on the desk, "What makes you come to such an extreme decision? Is it love? I seem to have a blind spot to such things as love when it comes to understanding what drives a man."

"Pimps too," Brosnan grumbles. "Pimps can't account for love, like yerself as ye say. But yes. It is love that motivates me. An' Garry Barry."

Wolcott turns his head in interest and opens a palm, offering him the floor to explain.

"Thirty-one years ago, it began. Thirty-one years ago, the love of me, to whom I gave my vows and heart, became pregnant. It was the best moment o' my life, and the worst. It was the year of the great blizzard of 1888," Brosnan points out the window. "I was on duty. A rookie in Brooklyn and was sent into the lashin' wind and snow to a tenement that had collapsed. In the wreckage I found a baby with its eyes starin' back at me and its head smashed open. Believe me, or don't. It does not matter to me but I. . ." Brosnan moves in closer. "I had dreamed of that moment for twenty years before it came to pass. I swear on the Virgin mother o' Jaysus, hand on the Bible! I had dreamt o' the future. But it was more a nightmare."

Brosnan lowers his voice and refills his glass with scotch, tossing it back. "Less than two years ago, if ye remember, Barry was beaten to death by the White Hand Gang off Hoyt Street. I do not blame the gang for doing it to him, Garry bleedin' Barry has bats careerin' round his belfry. But there he was, I saw him! lyin' on the pavement with his head once again burst open an' face mangled, his eyes lookin' up sightless at me. He had a couple ragged breaths, then silence. A few days later the papers reported that the doctors had pronounced him dead. That same day my daughter, Daniel Culkin's wife, gave birth to a baby boy. Billie he is called, named after myself. Barry died and I became a grandfather. That's when I knew. Finally I knew what my dreams were about. The circle had closed," Brosnan slowly raises his eyes to Wolcott. "So I thought."

Brosnan tilts back the empty glass and takes in the last drops until Wolcott refills it. "Now. . . a storm comes our way again. . . An' suddenly Garry Barry appears? Do ye read the Bible, Mr. Wolcott?"

Wolcott does not answer.

"The cowardly, the unbelieving, the vile, the murderers. . . the idolaters and all liars, their place will be in the fiery lake o' burnin' sulfur. This is the second death. Do ye see it now? This world is Garry Barry's lake o' fire. An' on the way here I saw again the white moon o' the mornin', an' knew. I knew the terrible curse on my family had returned. An' this is it; another exchange must happen an' I desperately, *desperately*! cannot allow my son to be taken away from my daughter an' their children. He's out there now with Garry Barry. Worse than all, my daughter is expectin'! Do ye understand me? Do ye understand me now? I will offer myself in their place, do ye see? Do ye see it now?"

Wolcott stares back into the panicked eyes of Detective William Brosnan and ponders the story. He tosses his head slightly back and forth as if to weigh the pros and cons and taps his desk with one finger. "I see," Wolcott looks toward the police issue revolver on his desk, lying on its side. "So you plan to kill Meehan, then turn the gun on yourself."

Brosnan looks down at the revolver too, then up into Wolcott's eyes, "I do."

"And you want an answer on Daniel?"

"I'm not askin," Brosnan flattens his hand out and washes it across the air. "Ye'll need to release him this very day. I can't take no for an answer. He is my son, and mine to look after. Ye've got no rights over him."

The obese man behind the desk runs his tongue along his teeth again and gives over his attention to the cigar that hangs between two short fingers.

He best make it easy for us both, Brosnan sits back. *I don't want this to get ugly.*

"Mr. Brosnan? I always saw you as different than those gypsy thieves on the waterfront," Wolcott rights himself in the leather chair. "Those shanty Irish are hairy at the heel. They believe in death. All of their heroes are dead and encourage them to choose death over assimilation. I never understood how so many people could lay their faith in martyrdom. That just makes them death worshipers, don't you agree? I hate to admit this though. . . I was wrong about one thing."

"We all are sometimes," Brosnan's voice is deep and assuring.

"Yes, I was wrong," Wolcott says. "You truly are just like the shanty Irish, overcome with heathen folly and not worth your salt, I must say. Curses and leprechauns, pookas and hero myths."

DIVIDE THE DAWN

Brosnan groans, but Wolcott continues, "You are no different. You offer to kill Meehan under incredulous pretenses. And of course that would mean there'd be no gang war. There could possibly be some killings, but there would be fewer casualties down there than if Lovett has a true enemy to fight."

"It's only casualties ye're after?

"You miss the point. How can we divide them if we kill one, and prop up the other?"

"It sounds like ye're the one who believes in death."

"No, I believe in terror," Wolcott smiles and yells toward the closed door, "Edith!"

"Yes?" Brosnan hears from the other side.

"Are they here yet?"

"Yes sir."

"Send them in," Wolcott announces.

The giant Wisniewski ducks through the doorway, but behind him—

Brosnan pushes up on the chair and labors to his feet, "Daniel!"

Wisniewski passes Brosnan and immediately walks to Wolcott's desk and places a hand over the police-issue revolver.

"He is not here to hurt me," Wolcott assures the giant.

Daniel comes forward when he notices his father-in-law, "Dad, what are ya doin' here?"

"I uh—" Brosnan colors up with shame.

"Why's ya revolver out?"

"Son, I only want to help," Tingles crawl through him. "I. . . I love ye so much, son."

"No ya don't. Ya love Doirean," Daniel broods and looks off. "I got no illusions on that. The thing is, I don' need ya help no more. I'm on my own on this. It's time ya let go, ol' man. Ya can spend more time wit' ya daughter an' grandchildren now. Ya time's passed."

"I uh. . ." a pain rushes through his body as the room begins to twirl. The porridge Doirean made him this morning wiggles in his keg belly as he leans on the back of the chair and cautiously sits.

Daniel turns his attention to Wolcott, "Meehan's been released."

No, no, Meehan can't be released. It's all fallin' apart on me. No. A wave of heat runs through the old man, yet his skin is prickly cold.

"Are ye sure, Daniel? Ye're sure Meehan's released?"

Across the desk, Wolcott smiles at him and steeples his fingers under the loose skin of a double chin. "Oh he's out alright, Pakenham from the daily was here this morning and was off to add it into the afternoon edition," the fat man says, then turns his attention to Wisniewski. "But you and Barry left the Hoyt Street Headquarters for the Meehan home at dawn. Is there nothing left of it but ashes and embers by now?"

"No," Wisniewski lips. "They hads guns, ands we did not."

"Who is *they*?" Wolcott demands.

Daniel steps forward over the desk, in front of Brosnan, "Harry Reynolds, Liam Garrity and Thomas Burke."

Wolcott stands, "Show me who they are."

Daniel turns the wheeled chalkboard round where there is a large chart of opposing gang members by name written on it. He then unfurls a large, leather-bound atlas of the waterfront wards from the Navy Street down to Red Hook. Focusing, Daniel pushes on the location of the Atlantic Terminal as if he were crushing a bug with one finger. "Harry Reynolds is right here, he is the dockboss o' the Atlantic Avenue Terminal for the White Hand."

Wolcott mumbles, "I know of him. Notorious as 'The Shiv.' He is lethal with a knife. The quiet one, the outsider."

"Sure but—" Culkin casts doubt on Wolcott's assumption, then runs a finger north along the East River, up the atlas to Bridge Street's Dock Loaders' Club where Dinny Meehan's name is listed at the top of an index card. "He's been wit' Meehan longer than any other livin' member. They met in Elmira Reformatory back in nineteen oughtfive."

"He's loyal then," Wolcott admits. "Watching over his incarcerated boss's home."

"Very loyal," Culkin agrees.

My son knows what he is doing, Brosnan realizes as he listens to them bat round the gang's inner workings. *My son is coming into his own.*

Daniel grabs a book of mugshots and flips through. "Here, this is William Garrity, also known as 'Liam' or 'Poe.' He didn't come off the boat 'til nineteen fifteen."

"Yes, I believe he came with Meehan one time when I was with the New York Dock Company," Wolcott says as Wisniewski nods his head, remembering the face.

Daniel agrees, "His uncle was Joe Garrity, the ILA recruiter loyal to Thos Carmody who was killt after a melee in a saloon that was burnt to the ground in the Donnybrook in Red Hook, 1916, six months after the kid arrived."

"So Poe Garrity murders his uncle and gains status, interesting."

"Seems that way," Daniel agrees. "Before Meehan was released from the Poplar Street Station today, Garrity ran the Jay Street Terminal and the Fulton Ferry Landin' to fill in for the loss o' their leaders."

"On the way up, I see," says Wolcott, one hand spread across his belly, the other strokes a drooping jowl. "And the last one, Burke was it?"

"Thomas Burke. Low level," Culkin says. "Got four kids, one of them's a cripple. He lives below Garrity in an Eighth Avenue tenement."

"Pakenham said an old friend of Meehan's paid his bail?"

"Tanner Smith from the West Side o' Manhatt'n, Meehan's old haunts. An' Dead Reilly representin him in court."

"How does this Tanner Smith fellow come up with that amount of money?"

Daniel looks at Wiz the Lump, then back to Wolcott, "Not sure o' that."

"And now Lovett's back," Wolcott pinky-points toward Red Hook on the pencil-colored colored atlas, then points it out the window. "And most like by now he has asserted control over all of Red Hook. We must hand it to him, he chose to strike at the moment the Black Hand in the Erie

Basin were least likely to be able to defend it. How many men support Lovett?"

"Fifty, I'd say. Meehan's got over a hundret he can call up, but here's the catch; Dead Reilly works for both Meehan *an'* Lovett," Daniel walks away from the chalk board and opens up the book of mugshots to a man with one eye. "If Reilly can get Pickles Leighton out of Sing Sing, then Lovett would have a lot more men. Parolees an' scofflaws, but still lots o' men."

"We need to even up the odds," Wolcott smiles and the extra layers of skin under his chin jounce like bulbous folds of blubber as he laughs. "Go to Reilly and find out what he needs to ensure the trial ends in Pickles Leighton's release."

"Will do," Daniel assures.

Wolcott points to the mugshots, "Concurrently, I need you and Barry to hunt down Harry Reynolds and Liam Garrity."

"We will come at them when they least expect it, an' they'll never know who hit them."

Jesus, Mary and Joseph, Brosnan thinks. *My son is evil.*

"Oh woe betide the unwary," Wolcott smiles. "What is Lovett calling his gang?"

Daniel raises his eyes up to Wolcott and smiles too, "The White Hand."

"Perfect," Wolcott turns toward the window, "I couldn't have asked for a better name. Let them fight over the title and control over the headquarters in Irishtown while from above divine providence will reign fire down on them all."

Daniel clears his throat, "We need more guns. But if we wanna make all the groups in Brooklyn turn against each other, an' we make sure it turns into a true blood feud, we need to—" Daniel gazes at his father-in-law but walks away and flips the wheeled chalkboard and pushes it into the corner. "I have a plan, but—"

"Bollix," Brosnan bellows and stands tall, his chest puffed out. "Ye're in over yer head, Daniel. Goddamnit ye don't even know what's at stake here. Ye're my daughter's husband. Daniel! Think o' yer children, are ye thick? The weight o' that fam'ly is on yer shoulders. An' on top of it all Doirean is heavy with child, ye gobshite eejit, ye."

"Dad, ye just don' understand. I ain't like ya. Never was. Time's're changin' an' ya ain't keepin' up. Ya worked for the gangs all ya life. Now I'm movin' past that. This is the future," Daniel raises both palms and looks round the executive room. "This is my future. An' I'm makin' it my own. Wit'out ya."

"Jaysus ye're a dryshite, ain't ye? I never wanted a copper penny from that god'amn gang," Brosnan repeats and holds his stomach as his voice cracks. "I was forced to go on the tug."

"So what did ya do wit' it all, donate it to charity?" Daniel moves closer.

Saving it for my little Doe to have, Brosnan thinks and turns away eyeing the black smoke through the window until he notices the white moon that watches him from the blue sky beyond. *It's time,* he recognizes. *It's time I speak my mind. My time.* "Daniel," Brosnan towers over his son-in-law. "Daniel, the mayor's civil pension commission has met—"

Wolcott interrupts, "And have concluded that pension funds for the police, firemen and teachers are bankrupt."

"Ye make yerself quiet," Bronsan roars at the fat man. "That was a few years ago, last year the commission proposed a new retirement system thanks to police commissioner Enright. It's the most scientifically devised system ever created in America. It'll pass the assembly next year, I'm told, an' at that point I'll be eligible for a payout since I'm superann... Superann..."

"Superannuated," Wolcott finishes the sentence and touches Daniel's sleeve again. "Also-known-as too old for service. Obsolete. And it is this same police commissioner that you quote who is compelling the older generation of policemen, such as yourself, to resign to his vaunted retirement system."

"I'm eligible to retire, Daniel," Brosnan corrects.

Wolcott laughs.

"Whether I'm alive or not, next year, my family is eligible to receive my pension—"

Wolcott's laughs turn to sniggers now.

"Keep laughin' ye fat-arsed bowsie glutt'nous smug cunt ye. While the people down in Brooklyn are starvin' half to death, ye're up here rollin' round in laughter. But go ahead, then. Cackle it up while ye can, 'cause what ye're about to hear's gonna choke ye! I hoped it wouldn't come to this, but all along I've had an ace in the hole. Ye're a greedy fecker though, I know ye'd rather peel an orange in yer pocket than share a slice, ye stingy bollix. But I'd be a fool an' a terrible detective if I hadn't foreseen that ye'd hoard the harvest and leave my fam'ly mere scraps."

"My weight should have no bearing—"

"Ah lookit, don't get upset about fat jokes, ye're much bigger than that."

Wisniewski shyly smiles at that one.

"When I found my retirement money could be left for my family, I marched directly into Captain Sullivan's office and filled out a report concernin' the illegal payoffs the Waterfront Assembly has been forcin' patrolmen and detectives to take."

"Ya did what?" Daniel cuts in, though Wolcott just watches with a veneer of a smile on his face.

"But that ain't the all of it," Brosnan leers at the fat man. "It appears not all reporters at the daily are like yer Pakenham feller. I met a cub there who said he'd love to write a feature article on the topic, and so I've provided them him with damnin' evidence. Ye know Wolcott, it might take ye a year or so to get used to the prison food up in Sing Sing, but ye can always give sexual favors to the other prisoners for extra rations. They like the soft. They'll love wrapping their hands round the hips of a big, pink girly-lookin' chap like yerself an' thrustin' their seeds up yer hole, one after another." Brosnan bears his teeth and pounds his fist on the executive desk, "There's only one way ye can convince me not to go forward with my complaints to Captain Sullivan an' the daily. Only one thing ye can do to save yerself now, fat man."

Wolcott happily stares back, "Let me guess, I should allow your son his leave of my service?"

Brosnan turns to his son-in-law, "With the money I've saved, I bought a house for yer family, Daniel. On top o' that, I've secured yer transfer to the Peekskill Police Department, where the house is four blocks from headquarters."

Daniel shakes his head and touches his forehead, "What do ya mean? Ya. . . Ya can't do this, Dad. I'm in charge o' my fam'ly. Doirean is my wife an' I make the decisions for our fam'ly."

"It's a new life for ye Daniel," Brosnan presses forward. "The house is paid in full, ye just gotta pay the taxes annually. It's a two-story home with three bedrooms an' two bathrooms, a front yard *an'* a back yard an' warm water heated by a brand new electric-goddamned-boiler. An electric boiler, Daniel. Ye can't tell me Wolcott's offer is better than mine. Now this is what we're gonna do," Brosnan puts his hand on Daniel's elbow, apprehending him, and turns to Wolcott. "Daniel an' I are leavin'. Ye owe me a rake o' money for jailin' Meehan, an' ye owe Daniel more for scarin' up Garry Barry. But we'll call it even, then. And ye'll let us leave in peace. Now."

Wolcott moves his eyes from Brosnan's to Daniel's. The fat man rubs his knuckles gently and bites his plump lip. He looks again over to Daniel and smiles, then slowly opens a palm toward the door. "How can I argue with the superstitious?"

Unexpected, Unannounced

March 1919

I make sure that we are between cars and wait in line for the train car door on the left, allow others to go ahead of us, then pull Burke's sleeve to enter the car on the right.

"Why'd ya do that?"

"Don't look round."

"Why?" He cranes his neck round the train car.

"We're going to be the first ones off the train when we stop at Atlantic, then we're going to run to Fulton Street Elevated at the Flatbush Avenue station, understand?"

"Why?"

I wish Harry were here, not you.

But the plan seems to have worked and I no longer feel eyes watching.

A few blocks from Borough Hall under the barren scarecrow trees that sprout from the sidewalk, we walk toward Atlantic Avenue, until—

There it is again, that feeling.

Just then a sullen face emerges from a three-foot space in a shadow between two close-cropped buildings.

"Liam?"

"Jesus wept," Burke whispers with eyes big as pies.

"Liam, I ain't here to hurt ya," he gives me his palms as if to show he is unarmed. "Just wanna talk is all."

There is something familiar about the man's face. The dark rings under his impassive eyes and the shards of hair falling out the side of his flat cap offer up a bewildering presence. His shirt is buttoned up to his thin neck and the dark rust-brown stains on it are evident since he wears no tie. But it's his eyes that give him the haunting look. And when he speaks, the words don't seem to relate to the vacant expression in his face.

"I'm just here to pass on a message, is all," says he.

"Darby?" I lower an eye at him. "Darby Leighton?"

"Bill's back," he says. "I'm sure ya know that by now."

Burke glares into Darby's eyes as if it were the shadow of a man. "What. . . message?" Burke manages.

"Bill's gonna come to the Dock Loaders' Club. Around quittin' time. Peaceful-like though. No bad blood. He comes under a white flag and requests safe quarter an' drink. Rules o' hospitality, ya know?"

"White flag? Hospitality?" I mock. "What happened to Mickey Kane?"

Through skeletal cheeks, Darby glares into the distance with a stark stare.

"I'm just hear to tell yaz we're gonna come by tomorrow. Shake hands maybe."

"So why do you follow us round? Why can't you just come up and say that?"

"I. . . I didn't mean to startle yaz. I'm just here to say—"

"Alright, you already told us."

"Listen Liam," Darby struggles with words. "I. . . I don' want trouble either. Like ya'self. But ya know, The Swede'n Dinny, they done some bad things on us. The Swede beat me to death's door, ya know. Ya seen me runnin' from him before, remember?"

In truth, that was the only time I ever saw Darby Leighton.

He continues, "Times'r changin'. Maybe it'd be best Dinny an' his followers walks away, ya know? His time's passed. It's Bill's time now, an' he's red in tooth an' claw."

If he is nervous behind those lifeless eyes, I can't tell. Yet he mumbles and stammers as if the words are new in his mouth and his own voice is strange to his ears.
He's been away for too long. Unmoored and alone too long.

"The storms have come and left this place stricken, its people hungry," he says in a distant voice as if reading or repeating. "Only the cruelest can survive. Can ya plunder? In the grand scheme, it's all for the best that yaz step away. Does that make sense? Sometimes the worst acts are the most benevolent."

"It does make sense," Burke nods. "Not all o' us have that ability to plunder."

"There's only one person who cares about the people what need caring for," I say as Darby leans an ear in my direction. "That's Dinny Meehan. I heard what you did to Sadie. Your own cousin. You and Anna harangued her and her son. Threw rocks through her window. Didn't you go round telling people that Sadie had been forced to marry Dinny? Was that a lie, or are you after stalking mothers?"

Darby watches my mouth closely as I speak, and when I finish he turns his eyes away in thought. A clacking sound comes from his teeth. A strange thing since he does not seem particularly cold, or nervous.

He speaks, "I bet ya never knew that I was a disciple o' Meehan back when we was just little water rats livin' under a rotted pier. We needed a new leader when the old one off'd hisself, an' I felt like Dinny had destiny on his side. But my little brother Pickles is the begrudgin' type. He wanted Dinny outta the way, or dead," Darby turns back to me with wonder in his eyes. "What do ya do when caught between ya own beliefs an' ya fam'ly's?"

I know that feeling all too well.

"A man's s'posed to make his own mind," Darby says. "But that decision was made for me. My fate may well be to bear the weight o' my brother's ills, but my cousin Sadie is Dinny's hostage. Mark it."

"In no way has Dinny ever held Sadie hostage. I lived with them. You're lying."

"Ya weren't here when everythin' when Christie the Larrikin was murdered back in 'twelve, nor for the trial in 'thirteen when Pickles was set up for it. I played a role in Dinny's ascension. Even Judas Iscariot was an apostle, right? Have ya ever talked wit' Sadie about them days? Have ya? Nah, ya haven't. She only chirps out parts o' her verses, never the chorus. Things ain't always as they appear, Liam. An' sometimes the caged bird sings a love song for her captor, an' that's the truth about Dinny an' Sadie."

"I name you a liar," says I.

"Then why'd she marry Dinny ain't even—" the words catch in Darby's mouth until he swallows them.

"What?"

"But ya can't ask her about it now, can ya? Ya opened her cage and let the bird fly away. She told ya Anna an' I threw rocks through her window, eh? Maybe it was the perfect time to make her escape while her captor was away. But she'd need someone naive to pay for her passage, just like when I paid for her passage back in 1910 from London. She duped us both, Liam. She hides innocent-like behind all them feathers. But ya can't stay innocent forever."

"Is that true?" Burke turns to me.

"No."

I had underestimated Darby Leighton. He looks a sodden mess, but his ploy to plant the seeds of distrust grow. The wound of doubt sticks in my belly like a shiv.

"Things ain't always as they appear an' history ain't nothin' but stories told by victors," dead-eyed Darby flings kernels of yet another story to pollinate. "Maybe my Pickles didn't kill ol' Christie Maroney the Larrikin, as a jury found. There was a witness to the murder, ya know. But she lied on the stand, which turned history in Dinny's favor all on account o' the witness was bulled by The Swede. Imagine it. Imagine the witness told the truth about what she saw. My life'd be very different right now. All o' our lives'd be different. But here we are. Me, I'm tryin' to right a lie, an honorable pursuit. While the both o' yaz want to maintain a lie, the most dishonorable thing anyone can do."

My hand goes quickly to the pipe in my coat as I grit my teeth at those words.

"An' they call Dinny a fam'ly man? He ruined mine. The Leightons are scattered, an' its because o' Dinny Meehan. We'll see who wins though. I got Dead Reilly on the case an' Pickles' got a re-trial an' we're gonna prove Pickles' innocence. Guess what then? A hundret or more parolees immediately become soldiers in Wild Bill's army the day they let my brother outta Sing Sing."

Burke turns again to me, "Is that true too?"

Darby leans in close, "Gather ya fam'lies an' leave Brooklyn. Ya don' wanna be the guy that defends a lie. An' ya don' want ya mother to end up like Mrs. McGowan, Liam, wit' a dead son to mourn. Or in ya case Burke, ya wife'll be left a weepin' widow wit' a cripple kid."

At that the pipe comes out and I swing, though Darby has retreated. Quickly he ducks under an overhang and falls through the narrow darkness of a passageway and disappears. Above, he slips through the shade of a half-open window. One leg trails through.

"Knowin' things is what I'm known for," an echo rises in the narrow confines of the alleyway. "An' I'm the guy waitin' in the long shadows to use them against ya. Leave Brooklyn while yaz can. Hear it."

I tuck the pipe back in its place inside my coat and angrily turn for the waterfront and Atlantic Terminal with Burke in my ear.

"Should we leave now?" He looks up sheepishly. "Like leave Brooklyn?"

"No."

"But ya heard him. We got fam'lies to worry about, Liam. I'm scared o' goin' to war wit' Bill's guys—"

I cut him off, "Dinny was there for us when we needed someone. He's the rightful leader. . . And he is honorable."

I think. I hope. If I am making a terrible mistake, would I know?

I pound out my doubts further, "Don't believe Darby Leighton, he lies."

"Uhright," Burke manages with a sad-eyed stare.

Do I really know if I am doing the right thing?

The rail yard of the Atlantic Depot separates the waterfront world from the abutted tenements and factories and storehouses. Further north toward Brooklyn Heights there is a forty-foot bluff that separates our area from the public. And up toward Irishtown it's the approaches to both bridges. The Navy Yard has an old wall at the east end of Irishtown to keep outsiders out, and a gate that bars entrance.

But in the Atlantic Depot black-faced men armed with coal shovels to feed locomotives tip their caps at us as we hop over the hodgepodge of criss-crossing freight rails. A hundred platforms with metal sheds, sloped overhangs and dark doorways face the water where the goods unloaded from ships are directly loaded into train cars by laborers. No teamsters are needed at the Atlantic Terminal as the loaded trains clank with metallic shrieks through cobblestoned streets directly into storehouses and factories through arched shutter doors. The goods can also be hoisted through yet more arched windows above, and beyond the skyline of lower Manhattan reaches high into the obscuring mist across the water.

Close on two hundred men have gathered by the long torso of a steamship in hopes of being picked by the White Hand to unload it. But only half that is needed, the rest are left with no more than a promise from Dinny Meehan to be chosen next time.

"Where ya been?" Dago Tom asks as Burke and I shoulder through the crowd. "Dinny's been waitin' on ya."

"Long morning," I shake my head. "Looking forward to getting back to work."

"Go see Dinny first, g'ahead," Dago Tom's eyes are downcast and disquieted.

Why does Dinny wait for me. Is there something wrong? I've had enough problems for one day.

Spread out under the looming steamship, Dinny's inner circle of dockbosses and chosen few stand as if a public execution is at hand as the New York Harbor moans and rattles with a thousand cascading sounds. Barge horns bleat low and long on the water and provides a bass line for the whistling harmonies and trebled yowls of the working class Brooklyn melody.

To Dinny's left, Vincent Maher leans against the ship door on the long dock with arms folded. His handsome face stares coldly ahead with the handle of a .38 snub-nose protruding from his tight pants and unbuckled belt, thick hair falling over ears in pointy black shards.

To the right is the horse-face of The Swede, sallow and cruel-eyed. As he notices me his milk-white, feathery hair moves with the windy currents atop his ugly mug. At a height of some six-feet and five-inches, he is inhumanely tall for our day.

I turn to Beat McGarry, "What's going on?"

"Ya don' know? I thought ya was one o' them now?" With his lips, Beat points in the direction of Dinny across the dock, then moves away from me.

To keep warm amidst the bitter East River drafts, we jostle and stamp in place. I am among one hundred loyal White Hand men who face Dinny and his inner circle on the raised dock. Before I can push through to join them, Harry steps forward halfway between as if sequestered. He faces Dinny with his back to us and his hands clasped behind in supplication.

"Harry Reynolds," Dinny's voice booms out and a silence comes across the waterfront until far to the south we can hear a pier whistle shriek in the distance.

Harry throws a hard glance over his shoulder in my direction, and my stomach turns.

What's happening?

Ahead the ship towers over us all along the terminal where Harry Reynolds has silently and dutifully led under Dinny Meehan's command since the White Hand came into power some six years ago.

A squeaky shed door opens at the end of the dock from which appears Tanner Smith, who pridefully stands next to Dinny himself. Men mumble round me at Tanner's presence. Chiding whispers, are they. Borne of his betrayal of both Dinny and our ILA ally, Thos Carmody.

Harry breaks the silence and calls out, "I only meant to help ya fam'ly."

"By going to my home again? When I'm locked up?" Dinny stares coldly.

"What is this?" I turn to Dance and Dago Tom.

"Ya big day, Liam," Dago says.

"What does that mean?"

But I'll have none of it, I won't. I step forward and to Harry's side in order to face consequence with him.

"Man," I address Dinny, "It was me that sent Sadie away—"

"Shh," Vincent hushes without moving his eyes from Harry.

Cinders Connolly steps forward next to me, "Man, I asked Harry —"

"Quiet," The Swede yells.

The sea air twists and turns, unsettled. At first it comes from the East, then shifts to the south as we await judgment.

"I had already told ya not to go there under any circumstance," Dinny says.

Standing next to me Harry does not blink or look away as a tugboat spouts in echo in the waterway distance.

"Most o' us here know what ya'd done," Dinny says. "All o' us know the pledge ya swore. An' ya betrayed it at the worst time. . . Now it's time we part ways."

Harry's eyes slowly move up to Dinny's, "I swore two pledges. An' cannot abide by the allegiance to one without betrayin' the other."

I turn to Harry, "What pledges?"

"I told ya, Liam. Quiet!" Vincent says.

Why won't anyone tell me what happened back then?

"We'll go through the men for a vote," Dinny announces

The Swede comes to Dinny's side and looks at Harry, "Can't never trust a man who breaks his promise."

"Vincent, ya're next" Dinny calls, and Vincent walks up angrily to stare at Harry. But it is obvious that he is tortured by the decision as tresses of windblown hair fall in his eyes. Vincent knows the temptation to defy Dinny Meehan, as the Italian Black Hand has regularly offered him to switch allegiances. Here, his face hardens again on Harry. He clears his throat and speaks a single, somber word, "Go."

Dinny summons Cinders Connolly.

Cinders shakes his head. "Harry's too valuable. An' Liam's far too young to take over the Atlantic Terminal."

I turn to Harry, "What did he say? What did Cinders just say?"

"Ya gonna be the dockboss o' Atlantic now," Harry looks me dead in the eyes.

"I can't be a dockboss. I'm not ready for anything like that."

Dinny walks up when he hears Harry and I, "Yeah well, smooth seas make slipshod sailors. No one's ever ready. Change always comes unexpected, unannounced, stirrin' up fear and doubt. But we have to move wit' it. It doesn't serve to struggle against change. Our time is short in this world, but ya were born for this, Liam."

Both Dinny and Harry hold stares at me until I turn to Dinny angrily, "You speak of change? The man who all call a luddite?"

"Liam," Harry touches my arm. "That was Wolcott said that. Ya quote Wolcott against the man?"

"You weren't even there."

"It's done, Liam," Harry says.

"Done means done," Dinny confirms.

But Cinders is not done, "Harry made a mistake goin' to ya place again. But lucky he did. If he hadn't made that mistake, Garry Barry'd've burnt ya home to ashes."

"Whadda ya say," Dinny turns sideways to request Cinders' vote.

Normally an affable and generous fellow, Cinders bares his long eyeteeth, "I say it ain't Harry's fault that Mickey Kane was killt. We all know Mickey was the future o' us. But wit'out him we must not only mourn one o' our own, we must also reconsider the future. But this? *This*? We weaken ourselves even further wit' this. We gotta keep Harry Reynolds. I hate sayin' this, but it's gotta be said, Liam don' hold sway like Harry. It's a fact," he turns to me with sorrowful eyes.

Dinny turns to The Lark.

"I say what ya'd say yaself, man. My vote's aye," The Lark mumbles with his arms crossed over his chest. "Ya say he goes, he goes. Liam ya're up, but ya gotta square things wit' Petey Behan at the least."

The sting of pride burns me. When a man loses a fistfight in Irishtown it's said the winner takes ownership of the loser's repute. It's an old notion, but old notions still ring true here and feeds the flame of pride in men.

Dinny quickly nods toward Red Donnelly.

"I vote aye on Harry, but ya can't send the kid to the Atlantic Terminal, it's too dangerous for him. He ain't proven," Red says. "No one'll wanna listen to a fella whose manhood is owned by another. Liam's also know for bein' a murderer o' kin. That can be good, but not if he don' own his own manhood."

Again with my uncle's memory. Will I ever get past that?

"An' look what Richie did to ya," The Swede calls out, turning Red's cheeks redder. "He beat ya to sleep, remember? Yet ya hold down the Navy Yard just fine."

I shake my head at that. I never thought the day would come when The Swede would argue my case.

"Liam's only worked the Jay Street Terminal for a couple weeks," Red yells back. "He did well, and that's fine, but if Lovett comes up from the south? Forget about it."

The Lark throws out his chest, "They first gotta come through the Baltic Terminal to get to Atlantic. They do that, an' we'll crush them. Plus we're so close we can give him support if Liam needs it."

"If yaz won't accept Liam, then I'll take over the Atlantic Terminal," The Swede points angrily into his own chest.

Red tilts his head, scared to say the truth; The Swede is not what he once was.

"Ya couldn't kill Garry fookin' Barry," Cinders pops off. "Now look at ya, Swede."

"I vote aye as well," Big Dick Morissey jumps in with a baritone voice and takes the floor since it is his turn for a vote. "But ya need The Swede by ya side, man. Since Liam's repute is sufferin', I can take over the Atlantic Terminal. Ya know I'm as good as The Lark, an' maybe my day's come now. I think the world o' Harry. But if ya say we gotta know who's loyal, since we're about to go to war wit' Lovett, then maybe it's time I step up."

"Yaz don' even understand what's happenin'," Cinders looks at Big Dick, Red and The Lark.

"Vote's over," Dinny turns his body in Harry's direction. "Harry Reynolds, ya hereby eighty-sixt from the White Hand."

Cinders shakes his head, "Fuck."

"Go to New Jersey. Go upstate," Dinny ticks off. "I don' care where ya go. I see ya in Brooklyn an' I'll kill ya myself."

"Jesus," I drop my crossed arms. "I didn't even get to vote."

"It's already outta ya vote's reach," Dinny assures. "Five to one. Five to two makes no difference."

Harry nods his head solemnly. He had not shown any emotion during his indictment and does not now either. He takes a shiv from inside his coat pocket, then reaches into his trousers and pulls out a nine-inch knife and drops them both on the ground in front of him. He pushes his chin forward and quickly turns round and walks through the mass of one hundred men with nary a sound.

"Harry's always been there for ya," I argue.

The Swede points at me, "Ya keep ya mouth closed."

Before walking away, I leave Dinny with one last thing, "I know you gave Harry an order. And I know he broke it. I also know that there's no one here as capable as Harry Reynolds to fill your shoes now that Mickey's gone."

"If ya leave, ya don' ever come back," The Swede warns me.

Vincent stands in front of me to block the way. He places a hand on my chest and nods toward Dinny over my shoulder, but there is no order forthcoming.

"Let me pass," I say under my breath.

Vincent rolls his head to one side and shrugs, then steps aside. As I bang through the men waiting to unload the steamer, I feel their eyes on me. Burke joins me too, and keeps up as I break into a dead run through the trails of entwined rail tracks and hop through two linked storage cars. At the corner of Henry Street and Atlantic Avenue I catch up to Harry along the sidewalk in front of the Atlantic-Pacific Mfg. Co under the sign that reads "Life Preservers and Ring Buoys."

"Harry."

He does not turn round, but looks in the direction of my shoes from the side of his face.

"I don't understand what just happened."

Still he says nothing. He just stands there in his dark gray suit, black tie and Hanan boots.

"Where will you go?"

"Dunno," he manages.

The wind from the bottom of the street crawls up our backs as sheets of half-crumpled paper and candy wrappers dance along the corner of the building and settles eventually in the slushy grates of a sewer on Henry Street.

"Harry."

"Don' thank me," he says, well aware of what I am about to say. "Ya already did that by comin' after me."

"But what did you do?" I dare to come close to his shoulder. "Back before I came to Brooklyn, something happened between you and him. What was it? Tell me."

A deep growl rumbles in his chest, "We all got things we done. Things that we're not proud o' an' don' want nobody to know about. There are things ya did too, that I know ya don' wanna talk about. That ya don' want ya mother an' sisters to ever know about. I'm no different. We're all just tryin' to survive. Any way we can. Ya did a terrible thing so that ya could get ya fam'ly to safety. In the end though, overall, it's not so terrible, is it? What ya did? In the end, it's nothin' to be ashamed of."

"Well—"

"I've stuck to the pledges I've made as best I can, even when they contradict each other. For the rest o' my days I'll honor them. 'til the day I die, at least."

"I know you pledged your loyalty to Dinny, but what's the other one?"

Harry shakes his head, "If it's all about fam'ly, it's alright, right? We just want a better way. A better day for them. We'll sacrifice ourselves for the hope that they'll have a better life. That's why ya did what ya did, right? Fam'ly?"

"But—"

"Some o' us got no fam'ly. None. No parents. No siblin's. No kin whatsoever. For people like me it's a dream, havin' a fam'ly," he turns his head in my direction without looking at me. "It's all I've ever wanted. That's the only thing I've ever wanted. This? What we have? This was my fam'ly. Or as close to my fam'ly as I could get."

"Ya're always welcome in my family."

He shakes his head again and begins to speak, then runs fingers through his hair.

"What?" I step closer. "Say it."

He shakes it off and turns his eyes to mine, "It's ya time to step forward now."

"I can't be a dockboss. It's a jape to think I could do that job. I'm not ready for it. I have to tell them—"

"I already taught ya everythin' ya need to know," Harry says.

"But I worry that I put my family at risk and if—"

The most important thing of all.

"If I'm doing the right thing. If what *we* are doing as a whole is good or benevolent. Like, are we the villains that people say we are? Or do we fight for good?"

Harry ponders that for a moment, "They never wanted this work, they just want to control it so that we can do nothin' but shovel shit against the tide. They vilify us for what? Ensurin' our fam'lies are fed by controllin' the labor racket? Controllin' our own destiny? If that's a villain, I don' wanna be a hero."

He takes a deep breath and lays a hand on my shoulder, "In a rotten world, good eggs stink. Ya're a good egg, Liam. To them ya smell rancid. Take heart an' be sure o' this; the White Hand does good too. An' just now it honors ya. It'd only be bad if ya refused the call."

"It also honors Tanner Smith, doesn't it? While dishonoring you."

Harry points into my chest and taps three times, "Don' believe everythin' ya hear."

What does that mean?

But Harry turns round to walk east on Atlantic Avenue away from the terminal.

"What about what I see?" I call to his back. "A witness is he who saw."

"Don' believe all that either."

"Will I ever see you again?"

But Harry has gone. He walks in front of a wain just as a gust of wind had kicked, and caused garbage to tumble across the cobblestones and up into the opposite sidewalk. Harry had gone and did not look back.

Life is Due

The cast iron gray clouds move slowly above like a river of molten ash. Below it, white plumes of mist spill along the water and obscure the distance with chalky and churning bluffs. The Statue of Liberty's shape comes into view here and there, only to be swallowed again by the veil.

"A deal is a deal, it's done son," Detective William Brosnan assures his son-in-law Patrolman Daniel Culkin.

"I'm fine wit' it, dad. I don' wanna work for Wolcott no more. We pick up the last payments on the tug this mornin' an' tell Lovett about that thing. Did ya tell them already? The thing?"

"I did."

"Who'd ya tell, Bill hisself?"

That's not your business, son. It's mine, Brosnan runs the back of his hand up the stubble of his cheek in thought. When you make a move in Brooklyn, you run the risk of losing the piece of meager ground you hold. But violent moves risk life and limb. Bill's invasion and conquest of the South Red Hook Terminal could not go without an Italian response, Brosnan had learned from a few gumshoes. Paul Vaccarelli, the old leader of the Five Points Gang hired a young gun by the name of Scarfaced Al, a two-hundred pound, twenty year-old to exact revenge. Lovett's new gang may have won for the time being, but the Black Hand's next move could cleanse Red Hook with Irish blood.

"Bill deserves fair warnin'," Daniel says.

"It's done, son. That's all there is to know. Why do ye care about Bill Lovett anyhow?"

Daniel bites his lip and growls under his breath, enough for Brosnan to hear. *He's too young to be making demands. Too excitable. His time is coming soon enough. He need but wait, as my time draws to an end.*

"Daniel," Brosnan reaches for his son-in-law's arm to turn him round.

In civilian garb they stand beneath the length of freight-rail platforms along the Atlantic Terminal. On the shorefront, the young and gloomy-eyed riverine laborers of the Atlantic Avenue Terminal watch wordlessly at the two plain-clothed policemen amidst the criss-crossing freight tracks.

"What?" Daniel flippantly responds.

Brosnan touches his floppy cap at the men on the Atlantic Terminal, then looks down down to Daniel's eyes, "I want ye to know somethin'."

"What, say it then."

"I know ye're not a Brosnan."

Daniel shrugs impatiently.

"But I want ye to know that my home is yer home an' that. . . The dignity o' my house is. . . It's the strength we hold in our name, the Brosnan way."

Daniel's eyes wander until they come up to meet Brosnan's, "Thanks Dad, I uh. . . I really appreciate that. Means a lot."

The old man's eyes fill with water and goose-prickles gather on his arms. A sad sort of happiness lumps in his throat and the tears he hides from his son-in-law are wrought of joy, not pride.

My little Doe will have her children's father by her side long after they put me in my hole, he smiles while thinking of the home in Peekskill he bought for them.

"Did ye hear talk o' the Garrity buck taken over the Atlantic Terminal?" Brosnan calls ahead to his son-in-law in a chesty voice.

Daniel nods as he strides a subgrade of railway track.

"They're cute when they're kittens, but lions grown want for blood," Brosnan surmises.

"But why'd they boot Reynolds?"

"For once in my life," Brosnan takes a deep breath. "I don't give a fiddler's fart."

"Maybe Reynolds killt Mickey Kane?" Daniel wonders.

"If I'm to believe Lovett's camp, Dinny Meehan killt his own cousin."

Daniel laughs, "That's my favorite one." But the young patrolman's eyes go dark.

Does he think I tipped Meehan that Wolcott put a target on Reynolds? Brosnan wonders, then speaks up, "Tanner Smith's back by Dinny's side, maybe that bowsie bastard had somethin' to do with it,"

But Daniel gives him a squiggly mouth to show his doubt, which injures Brosnan's pride and sends his thoughts tumbling, *the underworld stirs to life as resources grow scarce. More murders are undoubtedly coming. I hope I'm doing the right thing for him. But if my move is made with love in my heart, how could I be wrong?*

Out on the water, to their right, tugboats negotiate through the mist with warning blasts like blind and bleating goats in a foggy Irish valley. Tall above them all, obscured by passing sheets of vapor, the craggy peaks of the Manhattan skyline come into view in dream-like outlines.

"Son, do ye remember back when ye asked me for Doirean's hand in marriage?"

"Course I do."

"Did ye know that I tore holes in my socks on purpose, so I could intimidate ye?"

"I remember how ya propped ya feet up on the dinin' table, but I didn't know ya did it on purpose."

Brosnan giggles with a chesty timbre, "Doirean lost her head over it. She screamed at me for that one. But outta all the boyos that'd come for her, ye were the only one she liked." Brosnan lies. "She said that, ye know. Truly. She loved ye from the start. I don't know why, ye were a damned nuisance."

Daniel laughs, "I was. . . eager, as ya like to say. I'm sorry Dad. If I've caused trouble—"

"Ah stop with that, will ye," Brosnan slaps a delighted hand on Daniel's shoulder. "I was once a hellion myself with the broth of a boy, o' course. All young men are. But a man's gotta strike his own path."

"That's true," Daniel mutters.

"Ye're makin' the right decision, son," Brosnan announces as he lights a *Na Bocklish* and whips out the match. "This house up Peekskill-way is a beaut. I want ye to know, Daniel. The future is comin', do ye know what I mean, like? An' it's not here in this city. No sir. It's out there. Out in the new world. The suburbs. My god, I can't wait to see the look o' her face tonight when we tell her about the house."

"It's got a new boiler in it, ya say?"

"Paid for it myself and then had to pay for the damn yoke to be installed on top of it," Brosnan proudly glances sideways. "Oh the fireplace works fine, o' course. But the house has new pipes and it's all controlled down in the basement. Upstairs there're three bedrooms. The master bedroom is yers and the two children can stay in their own rooms. When the baby comes, there's a small room, like a nook, in the master bedroom for a newborn."

"Where're *you* gonna sleep, Dad?"

In my hole, Brosnan thinks. He hadn't put much thought into devising a scheme for all to believe he would be coming with them. He has other plans. Plans he could never talk about again for fear of being called psychopathic. Or superstitious, as Wolcott named him. *No, I'm not going to Peekskill, a deal is a deal, even if I forced Wolcott into it,* he thinks. *They will know when they find my cold corpse next to Dinny Meehan's when I sacrifice myself to this devilish destiny. I will go right up to the Dock Loaders' Club and do the deed, then. . .*

Brosnan peers down at Daniel, "I can stay on the sofa downstairs. Or maybe we'll put a mattress in the basement. We'll see."

"Nonsense," Daniel waves off. "Ya can stay in one o' the bedrooms. Little Billie and Daniel Jr.'ll stay in the same room together."

"Ye're a good lad," Brosnan allows. "I'm so glad for ye and my Doirean. Truly, I couldn't be happier for ye both."

Up ahead, through the maze of dock sheds and pierhouses and the hole-in-the-wall shops for rope craftsmen, tug repairmen and junk dealers, the two policemen in civilian garb come upon the Baltic Terminal. There, The Lark and Big Dick Morissey supervise a few longshoremen as they load an automobile truck. One of the workers has his pants round his ankles and unwinds silk from a large spool round both of his legs. When he sees Brosnan and Culkin his eyes dip downward as he pulls his trousers up and stands in front of the silk spool, as if hiding it.

"Bunch o' gypsy thieves," Brosnan shakes his head. "Speakin' o' which, did ye know that strange feller Darby Leighton snuck up on me a few days back?"

"Oh yeah?"

Now you know who I told about the vengeance from the Black Hand and this Scarfaced fellow.

Brosnan looks down toward Daniel, "Scared the bejaysus outta me, he did. Darby Leighton was a recluse livin' in the back arse o' nowhere for so long his mind's gone soft. He doesn't know how to speak natural, like a normal person, like, ye know? He just tilts his head an' stares sideeyed at ye. No handshakes, no 'hi, how are yez,' just threats from the gobshite tool."

"What did he say?"

"If I wanted help overthrowin' them lot o' diddicoy culchies that follow Meehan because Bill Lovett's the rightful leader o' the White Hand an' this that an' the other thing," Brosnan's face blanches when he realizes that he may have given too much away.

"What did he say then?"

If you're moving to Peekskill, what's with all the questions about Brooklyn Brosnan looks away, "He said he knows where we live an' if I don't get my priorities straight, he can't promise our safety. Ye know how them yokes work."

"An' what did ya say to that?"

Brosnan shoulders uncomfortably in the civilian garb, clears his throat and turns to Daniel, "I told Darby there's no bleedin' difference between Meehan and Lovett and that the real threat to them all is Garry Barry. Well ye'd think I took his last drink o' water 'way from him when I said it. He didn't even know Barry was still alive."

"That's good," Daniel looks away when he is speaking. "Someone should take care o' Garry Barry some day."

He truly has turned away from Wolcott.

Brosnan rolls his eyes and bellows, "Darby was askin' me who poked that little feral she-hound, the Lonergan hussy. Apparently she's reached the age that she can feel the heat twixt her legs. But if that one's gonna start whelpin' pups, ye're leavin' at the right time, Daniel. Her mother squeezed out fifteen, for god sakes. An' all o' them bite too. Well maybe that Tiny Thomas wasn't so rabid, poor child. That little sweet moppet, aye, he died 'cause his thick mother still believes hospitals will give ye the black bottle if a Protestant needs the bed. The child steps on a nail and is done-in by the infection. The ignorance o' these back-arsed people, ye know what I mean, like?"

"Why would Darby be askin' about Anna Lonergan?" Daniel wonders.

"The Leightons are a flock o' dingbats, don't forget. The only one who had any sense in that fam'ly was the eldest brother, Frank, an' he's leavin'," Brosnan turns the conversation away from Brooklyn. "Ah sometimes ye just gotta build a bridge an' get over it. Ye're right to move away from Garry Barry, son. That's a troubled soul, believe me. Troubled to the core o' him. I'm proud o' ye. Ye know how much I care about my little Doe. But don't ever forget that ye're part o' our fam'ly, as I said. An' ye always will be. I remember yer father. The story he told me about what happened to yer grandparents on the ship from the ol' country was a damn tragedy—"

"I don' wanna talk about that," Daniel turns away.

"Why, I was only—"

"The past is dead," Daniel says with bitterness on his mouth. "An' the dead don' talk so there ain't no use lookin' back to them. If I never hear anythin' about County Mayo and that fookin' famine again, I'll be happy."

"There's a lot to be learnt from the past," Brosnan says softly.

"Only if ya're a prisoner to it. I'm a free man. What about ya'self, ol' man? Are ya imprisoned by the talk o' the dead? Are the ghosts o' the past drawin' ya inward like the infirm to the house o' god?"

He knows. Wolcott must have told him. Damn that Wolcott to an eternal hell. Brosnan clears his throat, "Ye don't know what I know about Garry Barry, son. Or what I've experienced."

Daniel grits his teeth and clenches fists as a wet, foggy wind sweeps through an an alley one block away from the water and ripples through their civilian garb. Under a lean-to they pass a chandler who drops a wick into a greasy tallow mold and catches a glance of them. The small man croaks something in their direction and sweeps a shaky arm along his wares like a starved salesman. And next to him is a cooper in a dark room who swings a mallet onto a chisel to lower a metal hoop round the beveled staves of a barrel.

"Dad," Daniel says without looking up at him. "I'm sorry. Ya're probably right. It's just that. . . It's hard to remember sometimes that I'm young. An' I know we're doin' the right thing t'day. After we meet Wisniewski, for the last time, we'll be through wit' Brooklyn. But Wolcott owes us for services rendered. I got him Garry Barry an' ya got Meehan jailed for the boot theft at Hanan's. After this, we're square wit' him. An' I know, in the heart o' my heart, that movin' up to Peekskill is the best for us."

"Ye're a good lad," a lump grows in Brosnan's throat and his eyes threaten to boil over with tears of happiness. "A pain in my arse, but a good lad. Ye're doin' what a man was made to do. It's our duty to arrest the bad guys. But our true callin' as men is to ensure our fam'lies are safe. All else pales in comparison." Brosnan stops Daniel with a hand to his arm again, "Tell me I'm right, Daniel. What is a man's true callin'?"

Daniel stares back at his father-in-law's demanding eyes, "A man's true callin' is to take care o' his fam'ly."

Satisfied, Brosnan strides along the wharf's edge where Meehan's territory ends and Lovett's begins at Union Street, "As an older fella who learned his lesson many a-year ago, I take great pride in helpin' ya do the same. If this is all ye ask in return," he raises his hands toward the tugboat. "I'll gladly come along. Most policemen in Brooklyn are on the tug. It's been part o' the job since before I joined the force back in '88. Christie the Larrikin had me meet him at the end o' Gold Street when he became boss in 1900. When Meehan took over, he moved it over by the Fulton Ferry Landin'. Now Wolcott has us way down here on the Union Street dock. At least it goes quickly. Get on the tug, take the envelope and get off."

"Well who was the King o' Irishtown before Maroney?"

"Eh?" Brosnan is taken aback by the question and has to think on it for a moment. "Yeah well, no one rightly knew, to be honest. T'was shrouded in their code o' silence. There were rumors o' some feller by the name o' Sean Dream, but I never met him. In them days I used to meet the gangs on a tugboat near the Jay Street Railyard, but it was the Dock Loaders' Club where they were headquartered. Meehan re-opened it in 1913, an' that was that."

"Dad?"

"Yeah?"

"Back when ya started, how did ya learn about the handouts?"

"The hard way. Captain Sullivan was a detective back then. He took me in an' gave me the chance when I was off the boat from Dublin. Just as I brought yerself in. O' course I had my own philosophy on life an' took a moral position on the whole affair, as youngsters tend to do. 'I'm a man o' god,' I told him. 'My duty is to serve the law an' I won't be corrupted.'" Brosnan laughs at his younger self. "I thought I knew it all. Well ol' Sully took me by the neck an' told me outright, 'If ye don't take the yoke from the gangs then ye can ask His lordship His very-fookin'-self upon the pearly gates if he agrees about yer moral fookin' position. Ye wanna survive? Get on the tug.'"

"That's what he said?"

"That's what he said," Brosnan confirms. "But from what I hear about things up in Peekskill, the longshoremen gangs an' the unions don't pay the police off."

"That's good to hear," Daniel peeks up to Brosnan. "What about the businesses? Fact'ry owners'n shippin' companies an' the like?"

Brosnan groans, "I dunno. Ye'll have to find out when ye—we—get up there."

The two plain-clothed policemen turn up a wooden dock and high-step over the gunwale of a tugboat where the giant Amadeusz Wisniewski sits with a scrawny hand-rolled cigarette between his fingers. The stink of diesel comes from an exhaust pipe and mingles with cheap tobacco. When Wisniewski sees Brosnan he stands in the back of the boat a head-and-a-half taller than the bear.

"How ya, Wiz? Let's get this over with ye big lump," Brosnan says. "Hand her over."

Wordless, Wisniewski reaches into a breast pocket and hands him an envelope, but drops it just out of Brosnan's grasp. On the main deck's flooring is two inches of saltwater that quickly soaks through the envelope.

Brosnan looks up to Wisniewski, "That envelope's empty."

Wisniewski taps on the window behind him with his wedding band and the engine is suddenly floored.

"Where're we goin'?" Brosnan bellows, catching his balance.

Two men appear from the wheelhouse above and descend backward down the bridge ladder next to the single round smokestack. Brosnan recognizes the first man, but can't put a name to the face. The second face causes his right hand to move for his police issue revolver. But before he can draw it, he feels another gun press against the skin under his ear, cold and hard.

"No Dad," Daniel Culkin says from behind as he holds his own revolver to his father-in-law's head with his right hand and gently takes Brosnan's police issue from the holster with his left.

Garry Barry walks toward the stern and worms in close to Brosnan with what appears to be a bail hook in his hand. Barry gazes up into the bear's eyes as the bulkhead of Brooklyn is left behind. The scar that runs from above Barry's eyebrow down through his left eye still seems swollen and has blackened with a greenish-yellow color underneath. One eyeball is black, while the other is a pale gray. As the smell of infection and puss comes to Brosnan's nose, his mouth fills with water and his stomach turns. Barry's scar then runs below the left eye and forms a v-shape, going up into his bent and bulbous nose and ends just over his upper lip. Brosnan had learned that while Barry was in the hospital, doctors had hastily opened his face to repair the broken bones in his sinus cavity and orbital. Then haphazardly stapled it back together, convinced he'd hemorrhage and die. But that was months ago. More than a year, even.

Brosnan notices Barry also has a hole in the left shoulder of his coat and a red glistening wound beneath. It is not a bail hook he holds, but a scythe wrapped with leather straps round a piece of wood. The fetid stench coming from Barry's mouth reeks of putrified, rotted skin. When a maggot wriggles from Barry's nose unnoticed, Brosnan almost gags.

"I. . . I saved ye life twice," Brosnan manages to say to Barry over the sound of the struggling diesel engine and the gargling propeller. "When I found ye in the collapsed tenement, then again after the White Hand beat ye on Hoyt Street. Daniel, tell him."

"No Dad," Daniel says from behind. "I'm not here to save ya. Wolcott told us all o' the crazy myths about death exchanged for life durin' the storms an' whatnot."

Life is due when death is wrought, the words ring in Brosnan's head.

"Ya crazier than ya lead on, ya know that? But it turns out ya was right, I s'pose. Someone does have to give their life after all. A Brosnan. But ya can't undermine destiny. That ya can't do."

"Daniel, the house in Peekskill—"

"Luckily we haven't told Doirean about it yet," Daniel keeps himself out of the view of Brosnan's eyes. "She'll never even know when I get power o' attorney over the property. Ya know how it is ol' man. The less ya tell that little Doe, the better off she is. We got that in common, at least. Now get on ya knees."

"No, I can't let ye do this son."

Wisniewski steps forward and with two giant paws, he forces Brosnan to his knees. Saltwater in the bottom of the tug wets Brosnan's pant legs. Wisniewski then ties his hands behind him as out on the water a lighter barge is being dragged north through the fog toward the Brooklyn Bridge. But no one is on the deck to see him, *hoo-hoooo* goes the harbor tug up the old river.

James Cleary rolls an empty wooden barrel on its side to the stern of the tug and rights it next to Brosnan.

Is that from the cooper by the Baltic Terminal, Brosnan wonders.

Above, Garry Barry winds the hand-scythe behind his head and swings down toward the old man with a grunt.

The world goes upside down and twirls at least four times until Brosnan is able to focus again. With one eye submerged in the two inch saltwater at the bottom of the tug, he sees his headless, flaccid body twitching a few feet away as it reddens the saltwater.

I never knew, death was always my duty. My role cast in memory, Brosnan thinks, then closes his eyes and mouths the words, *my little Doe, life is due you.*

Fear of A Blood Feud

Dinny's chair sighs when he sits at the desk between the two big arched windows. A low groan rumbles his chest as he holds court from the perch overlooking the East River and Manhattan's skyline, "They may try an' make our ways illegal accordin' to their laws an' send us the way o' the dinosaurs, but as o yet they haven't. I called yaz all for a meetin' 'cause we have to thresh out the wheat from the chaff on a few things—"

Blam, blam, blam, someone bangs on the door and scares me half out of my boots.

"I have news!" we roll our eyes when we realize it's the old man Beat McGarry's muffled voice on the other side. "Ya gotta know this! It's important!"

The Swede wears a terrible air and plaintively declares, "Fookin' useless as a one-legged man at a shit-kickin' contest."

The men in the room look to Dinny, "Let him in before he hurts himself."

Vincent saunters over and fiddles with the chain, but before letting him in he looks back at us with a wry smile, "Who is it?"

Big Dick Morissey's laugh grinds like a winch engine and The Lark barks out, "We ain't buyin' no bibles t'day!"

The two burly longshoremen giggle like school girls as they had when they used to prank Lumpy Gilchrist, the savant. All nine of us in the room smile and for a moment we are our old selves again. But since The Swede's left arm has withered, he cannot cross them over his chest as he was known to while standing to the right of Dinny. With Harry banished, I can't enjoy much of anything. I want answers about his departure, and I plan to get them. The new face among us, replacing the beloved Harry, inspires nothing but unease; Tanner Smith.

Tanner cloaks himself off to the side in the office above the Dock Loaders' Club. Better off obscured if you ask me. He is not well-liked here. In his early thirties and older than the most of us, he wears a soiled cravat at his neck and a coat that hides his suspenders and outlines the muscle in his upper arms. His dark hair curls at his forehead and the cleft at his stubbly chin where his powerful jaw meets gives him a jaded countenance in the half-light.

Beat McGarry pounds on the door again, "Ok, ok, jape's over. Let me in. I have news."

The Lark's belly jiggles and Big Dick's laugh grinds away at each of Beat's whiney solicitations.

"Just let him in," Red Donnelly cries in Vincent's direction as his righthand from the Navy Yard, Henry Browne watches with nervous eyes to take note of all round him.

Vincent hardly has the chain undone when Beat bursts in, "Listen, listen—"

"Brosnan's gone missin'," Dinny finishes the sentence.

Beat stands upright, out of breath, "How'd ya know it?"

Cinders Connolly stands up to throw a hand-rolled cigarette out an open shutter window, "I saw'r all the tunics outside their tenement early this mornin'."

"Oh, any idear where he is?" Beat prods.

The Lark snorts.

"Do me a favor," Dinny says.

"Anythin'."

"Go downstairs an' help Paddy behind the bar."

"Well Din I thought I'd be more of a help decidin' things up here wit' ya guys. See, I gotta lotta experience wit'—"

"Get out!" The Swede yells. "Every time ya mouth breaks wind the whole fookin' room smells o' shit."

Beat glowers at The Swede and slowly turns where Vincent ushers him out.

When the door closes, I speak up, "There's only one thing to do here. And I'll do it myself. I'm going to go talk to Patrolman Daniel Culkin, alone."

"Really?" Red tilts his box-head.

"What would ya say to him?" Cinders asks.

"I'll talk to him, man to man. He needs to hear that we have nothing to do with his father-in-law's disappearance. I'm sure he'll appreciate it, too."

"Naive," The Swede says.

Dinny clears his throat, "Don' rush in, Liam. Think it through first, eh?"

"Why? Culkin's mostly quiet, right?"

"Beware the quiet one; when ya rest, he strikes."

Cinders mumbles his grief, "Brosnan's daughter Doirean; she's the real victim here. I feel so bad for her. She was a puddle this mornin'. We gotta help her."

"How?" The Swede shows disgust on his long face. "More importantly, why? Brosnan arrested ya three times, like, remember?"

"He was just doin' his job."

"She's a tunic's daughter who's married to a tunic to boot? We got bigger fish. Forget about Doirean Culkin."

"I won't. On top o' all the things she's goin' through, she's in an interestin' condition, ya know what I mean?" Cinders motions with a circle in front of his belly. "It hurt seein' her like that, cryin' an' whatnot. Johanna gave birth four times an' thank god she never had nothin' so disturbin' that she had to cry like that. Sobbin an' losin' her breath an' shit. If we don' help her she'll go stir crazy. She was close to her father. People need people an' she's all alone up there. No matter if she's a tunic herself, she's still Irishtown born an' bred. Some o' yaz've known her since ya was kids, Big Dick? Lark? Red? Ya just gonna leave her alone in her time o' need now?"

"What do ya want we should do?" Red shrugs.

Cinders was waiting for that question. He turns to Dinny, "God is good, but he couldn't be everywhere, so he created women. I wanna send Johanna, my wife to help her wit' the kids, cookin', laundry, ironin'. . . an' a shoulder to cry on. At St. Ann's Father Larkin brings Johanna in to help people through their mournin' when fam'ly members die, like Mrs. Lonergan, ya know? She understands people, my wife, like inner thoughts an' motives, like. She read that ya gotta bring ya repressed conflicts to consciousness, right?"

"Ya what to where?" The Lark side-smiles.

Dinny nods, "It's a nice thing ya offer, but Johanna can't get in that home wit' Connolly as her last name. Her maiden name though, it's Walsh right?"

"Yeah."

"Tell her to just drop in, but not wit' Father Larkin since he knows she's married to the White Hand. Her name's Johanna Walsh for this. Tell her an' she's got my blessin'."

The Swede says nothing, but nods when he puts it together that we'll have someone on the inside of Patrolman Culkin's home. A better idea than mine.

Cinders nods to Dinny, "This mornin', when Doirean was so upset, the red head Maureen Egan shows up. Like a wild woman, she was. Wit' a cast on her arm. Moanin' like a banshee. But all the tunics kept her from speakin' to Doirean an' hurried her away."

"They was best friends at primary school, them two. Moe an' Doe," The Lark says, tapping Big Dick's arm. "Remember them two?"

"The most beautyful girls in all o' P.S. Five. Most popular too. But that was a long time ago. They went in very different directions afterward."

The room turns to Red Donnelly.

"What? We all make mistakes, right?"

The Swede's face pinches, "Red on red. They should make it a punishable offense. A redhead's got no business marryin' another redhead. Ya shoulda known better, Red."

"I shoulda, sure, but I ain't no catch."

"Then why do they call ya Cute Charlie?" The Lark sniggers.

Red looks with reproach toward The Lark, then bows his head ashamedly, "An' anyway, she was—"

"Sleepin' around," The Swede interrupts. "Ya was one o' many, but somehow ya thought givin' Moe a ring would change her ways. A woman may love a ring, but it don' magically turn vice into virtue."

"She's troubled," Dinny says. "Ya don' kick troubled people, ya help them up."

"I'd feel bad for her if she hadn't made me look like a fool," Red says.

"That don' take much," The Swede mumbles.

Big Dick voices in with a baritone, "I hear Moe just wanders around now. Some say she lives in Green-Wood Cemetery. But not long ago she was datin' Garry fookin' Barry the day we beat his head in on Hoyt Street. A year or so later he was pimpin' her outta their room when a tunic an' a big man came durin' the storm. Left her wit' a broken arm an' took Barry an' Cleary wit' them."

"She was a bedraggled mess this mornin'," Cinders says. "But why would she show up at her ol' friend's home when Brosnan disappears? She know somethin' we don't? Is that why the tunics shut her up an' hurried her off?"

"Maybe we should ask her," says I. "Where does Maureen Egan live?"

"Nowhere, she just wanders around," Red says with bitterness on his mouth. "Don' waste ya time on her. She ain't reliable. She hears voices, ya know? She's just. . . She's just a person who brings misfortune to all around her. Like a witch. It's best to steer clear. Everything she touches bursts into flames an' turns to ashes. Some people create. Some destroy. Them people ya just gotta stay away from. Let Moe Egan spread her black magic to others so *they* can suffer the misfortune she conjures."

A cold wind slips through the iron shutters and runs up my legs and into my back. The smell of old and damp wood fills my nose as Dinny speaks, "Brosnan is our biggest concern. We may see him as a tunic an' a souper, but when a policeman goes missin', the earth shifts beneath our feet."

"Hate to say it, but Brosnan probably went the way o' Mickey Kane," Cinders shakes his head.

"We need to hit back at Lovett once an' for all," The Swede says. "He takes out Mickey, annexes Red Hook from our partner an' disappears a tunic? He's outta control. We'll look like heroes for takin' him down."

"Ya sure it was Lovett did this to Brosnan?" The Lark wonders.

"Lovett comes back from the war an' the bodies start pilin', who else would it be?"

"Hold on," I step away from the window, "What if it wasn't Lovett?"

Dinny leans back, "G'on."

I turn to The Swede, "Think about it. Last year Wolcott got a reporter from the Daily to write a piece on police corruption in Brooklyn, remember?" I look to the rest in the room. "After that Brosnan refused to go on the tug with us any longer. Maybe he wanted to break clean from Wolcott too? A fat man gets angry when someone at his table doesn't ask to be excused. We have to put it all together," I realize my earlier mistake. "There's too much to lose here. I lose sleep thinking about what would happen if we lost what we have. Or worse. They know where I work. Where I live. What would my Mam do if. . . I can't even say it, but we need to puzzle this out. When Maureen Egan had her arm broken, a tunic and a big man took Barry and Cleary during the storm, right? Well which tunic was it?"

"Dunno," Big Dick says. "Short fella. Some kids witnessed it from a window above Hoyt Street. They said it was a short tunic. But everyone's short next to a big man."

"So who was the big man?" I interrupt, but get only shrugs. "Was it Wiz? Wolcott's lump? Because we saw Wisniewski with Barry together *after* the storm."

The Swede cuts in, "Where ya goin' wit' all these questions? Ya're always wit' the questions, Liam. Where's ya little buddy Burke? We summoned everybody t'day. Burke ain't everybody?"

"Don't worry about him," I answer, but in truth I don't know where he is.

"Not that it'd matter, that fookin' little poltroon is nothin' but a empty coat."

"Stop changing the subject," I raise my voice at The Swede. "If we don't figure this out, we're done."

"Now he's a expert, look at him," The Swede motions.

Beat McGarry bangs on the door again, *blam, blam, blam.* "I have news!"

"An' this fookin' guy," The Swede points at the door. "Can we have a moment o' silence for him? He's dyin' for attention."

Beat is allowed to pass and rushes in like a flood to drop the afternoon edition on Dinny's desk, "There's a long article about Brosnan in the papers. They're blamin' his disappearance on us. Captain Sullivan says that Brosnan reported to him recently that the gangs offered him a whole rake o' money, but he refused."

"We didn't offer him nothin'," The Swede says.

"Brosnan's daughter Doirean is quoted too, she says the gangs must have done somethin' to her father," Beat looks up. "But we didn't do it, right? Did we?"

A silence takes the room until Beat turns his eyes back to the newspaper and points at the print, "Look here, it says Daniel Culkin is headin' up the investigation."

"Culkin? He's just a patrolman," I grab the paper.

The Swede laughs, "Ya still plan on talkin' to him man to man?"

Underneath the article there is another about a cub reporter that was stabbed to death with some strange weapon, maybe a sickle blade, in his own room downtown. He had been chopped up, and parts of his body were strewn across his room and a hand was drawn on the wall in white paint.

"Jesus wept," Beat says.

Cinders slams his fist onto the paper, crumples it and throws it on the floor. "They're tryin' to dump it all on us."

The Swede begins pacing in the room, "They're closin' in. Fuck, fuck. . . We didn't do any o' this."

"Let's just keep calm. Let's figure this out," I say. "The day before Brosnan disappeared, I saw him at the Atlantic Terminal."

The Lark speaks up for both he and Big Dick, "We saw'r him at the Baltic Terminal too, wit' Culkin. They kept goin' south."

"Together?" The Swede demands. "A day before Brosnan's daughter reports him missin'?

I sit in the chair and lean a finger on my temple, "They're against us too."

"The law's always been against us."

"Not when we paid them off. Now they're coupled up with the Waterfront Assembly. This is a big move," I point to the crumpled paper on the floor.

"Ya don' know that for sure," The Swede cuts in. "Ya whole argument's based on the fact Culkin kills his own father-in-law. An' the Captain o' the Poplar Street Station's in on it too? All the way up to Wall Street? No fookin' way. Ya really want us to believe that?"

"What I am saying is we have to *know* who is behind it. There is great danger in not knowing what we don't know. We're trying to survive here, as a group. All of you in this room understand that if we don't keep things together, we lose everything?"

The Swede raises his voice in the echoless room, "We understand it, Liam. But tunics, they get the benefit o' the doubt. Ya gotta have evidence before ya make a claim like that. The fact is we didn't do this an' that's all there is to it. The truth sets ya free, not lies."

The Swede and I both move our eyes from each other, to Dinny. The rest of the room does as well.

"Anyone have anythin' else to add?" Dinny looks at each individual in the room, then folds his hands together on the desk when he receives no answer. "We should assume Wolcott an' the Waterfront Assembly are behind the Brosnan thing—"

"There's no evidence o' that," The Swede cuts in.

"They want us gone, that's evidence enough. Bill's got as much motive as we do," Dinny says and nods toward me. "Let the kid speak, he's got more to say."

The room turns to me.

"Say ya peace," Dinny signals in my direction. "G'ahead, I know what's really botherin' ya."

I lean a hand on the desk, "You banished an honorable man, but you let another in who dishonored you. Dishonored all of us. What did Harry even do to deserve getting banished? We can't afford to break ourselves apart before even we get started fighting Lovett or. . . or dealing with this Brosnan question. Now that we know we have enemies everywhere, we need to be united. Without Harry, we're weaker. The White Hand has never been this weak. Thousands of people depend on us. We owe it to them to make sure we're ready to fight and able to provide for them."

"I'm ready to fight, why ain't you?" The Swede swings his long lantern jaw in my direction.

Cinders stands between The Swede and myself to address Dinny, "Ya deserve only the truth from those that are loyal to ya. Harry'd've given ya that, if only ya asked. An' he was more loyal than any o' us."

"Speak for ya'self," The Swede interrupts.

Cinders' eyes glint at The Swede, "We know ya're loyal. But not everyone in this room is."

"What? We got a tout in our midst?" The Swede says. "Who is it? Point him out?"

All in the room turn their eyes on each other and wonder.

"I agree," Tanner Smith's gravelly voice sounds off as he emerges from a dark corner and steps into a shaft of light where dust dances round his muscular build. "Get rid o' this ILA tout an' we'll be better off. Henry Browne ain't loyal. He's ya man, Swede. He's loyal to Thos Carmody an' the ILA, not the White Hand."

Cinders chimes in, "Tanner. Ya took a rake o' money from us to do a job; get rid o' Thos Carmody. But we're still talkin' about him to this day, ain't we?"

"Yeah, we're all ILA now," Red says. "What's it matter if Henry Browne's in here if we're all part o' the longshoremen union?"

Cinders makes his case to Dinny, "Instead o' doin' the job, Tanner took the dime for himself an' tried to muscle his way into union leadership. He backstabbed ya, boss. Yet ya reward him for it an' eighty-six Harry? What's happenin' to us? If we're goin' to war, I want Harry Reynolds by my side," Cinders flicks the back of his hand toward Tanner. "Not this fookin' schemin' bastard."

"I'm tellin' ya right now," Tanner looks about and slowly moves from the amber light that files through the arched windows. "Quick Thos was in the same infantry division as Bill Lovett an' Non Connors an' I hear they're married to the same notions now too. We gotta cut ties wit' the ILA. The ILA can't have us both. Thos is gonna choose Bill's side against ya, Dinny. I swear it. The ILA's against the White Hand too, ya just don' know it yet."

"Hold on a second," Vincent comes forward from the door. "Ya're the one's gotta feud wit' Quick Thos, not us. An' that's only on account o' he wouldn't let ya buy-in wit' the ILA when it was us ya sold-out. I hear he called a blood feud on ya too. One o' yaz gotta die, an' I wouldn't bet against Quick Thos, never."

"I always heard ya an' Thos were buddies," Tanner points at Vincent. "Some say ya spend all that time down at the Adonis because ya're a tout for the Black Hand."

Vincent's eyes go cold and he leans his angular body toward Tanner, pulls the .38 from his belt and extends it at the end of his arm, "Ya question my loyalty?"

In a quick move, Tanner grabs Henry Browne from behind in a choke-hold with the curved, keen point of a bowie knife held along the thin skin of the jugular, "Here's ya tout, it's Browne. Look at him, the tout for Thos."

Everyone sitting quickly stands. The rest stare at Tanner and look for an opening to bring him down. But Tanner is a wire of nerves and jerks his catch in the direction of anything that moves. By the neck, he drags a petrified Browne backward and into a corner.

"Tanner," Dinny moves slowly round his desk and leans against it, "Ya not gonna kill him, so put the blade away."

"Get outta the way, Vincent," Tanner says. "Go stand by Dinny.

The Swede cuts in, "He's all talk an' no trousers."

Though Henry can't afford to believe that.

"Tanner," Dinny repeats softly, with a morose and distant smile on his face.

But Tanner's eyes have desperation in them, his mouth downturned in anguish, "Remember when I saved ya back when? Ya think I forgot? Look at all the things I done for ya, Din. I was there when they had the hit on ya, the Hudson Dusters an' the Strong-Arm Squad. It was 1900-even an' ya was what? Ten? Eleven?"

"I remember that," Dinny nods, his eyes focused toward the floor.

"I gave ya money. To go to Brooklyn 'cause I knew a guy. Coohoo Cosgrave. I told ya who to talk to, didn't I?"

"Ya did."

"He helped ya. Made sure ya father got a decent burial, didn' he?"

"He did, ya're right."

"Then ya was in jail an' all o' Irishtown was gonna starve, until I helped ya. I risked everythin' to help ya, Din. Everythin'. I told ya if ya don' give me quarter in the White Hand, I'll tell everyone, I will. I will."

Dinny smiles through a nod, "Ya did what ya could, Tanner. I feel bad. I really do. Ya tried to do the right thing as best ya could."

"Don' give me that shit, Din," Tanner's double-edged blade quivers over the jugular, spittle turns out of his mouth in small, shooting thrusts as he speaks. "I did right by the White Hand. I posted a bond on ya behalf to secure ya release. That's what ya needed, so I got it for ya. Just like when ya was a kid, I helped ya. I proved my loyalty, twice over."

"Tanner."

"Tell me what else I can do? Tell me. Tell me an' I'll do it."

"It's time—"

"Don' turn me out. I'll die out there. They'll get me. Ya know they will, Din."

"It's time we talk about a punishment, Tanner," Dinny leans against the desk with one hand.

"Punishment?"

"I know ya tried, Tanner. But bailin' me out was on ya own terms. Nothin' overcomes betrayal, see? Ya know how the old codes are," Dinny's voice is low, almost to a whisper. "It's a warrior clan's oath we take. It goes back a long way. To the Fenians. It's so deep that it even reaches into the ancient myths an' the Otherworld. Maybe that's not how it's done in Manhattan where it's every man is for hisself. Here? Brooklyn? We're not like that. We remember. We remember the old ways. Take a look around ya," He spreads his arm out along the many of us. "Every man here has a job, an' does it. But if he breaks trust wit' us? Breaks the bond that keeps us strong an' I do nothin' about it? Ya leave me no choice, Tanner. A public punishment's in order."

"Fuck that," Vincent's arm is still outstretched with the snub nose .38 pointed in Tanner and Browne's direction. "He pays wit' his life t'day?"

"No," I cut in as Tanner inches toward the door. "We're not killing anyone."

"Brand him a tout," Cinders says. "Brand his face. I'll get the blacksmith farrier to make a 'T' for tout so all know him as such."

"Yeah, beat an' brand him," The Swede says as the rest of the men agree with a "Here, here."

"I have a way for him to prove his loyalty," Dinny says.

"I'm leavin'! I'm leavin' here," Tanner's eyes are big now and sweat has moistened the curls along his forehead. "Get away from the door, Vincent. I'll bleed this fool white, right here in the office. Move, Vincent."

Vincent lowers his gun and steps away as Tanner yanks his prey toward the door. Henry Browne's heels drag on the wood floor ominously.

"I risked everythin', Din," Tanner yells out. "I'll tell them. I will!"

"G'ahead then."

Tanner looks at everyone in the room, "I got a deal wit' Johnny Spanish the shylock."

"Well that explains a lot," Cinders flits a finger at Tanner.

"An' the vigorish on it is t'rough the fookin' roof. Ya banish me an' I got nothin' to pay him back wit'. Yaz think ya're hard. Yaz're nothin'. Think he won't go after my fam'ly? Johnny Spanish shot his own pregnant wife in the belly back in 1911, remember? Remember? An' wit' Thos Carmody callin' for a blood feud on me? Quick Thos is a killer now. Sixty-seven confirmed kills over there in France. Shit, if I don't pay Spanish, then the *two* most dangerous men in Manhatt'n will want me dead. I can't even go back to my own neighborhood."

Tanner reaches behind him to open the door, "Yaz don' know the shit I'm in now."

He shoves Browne into the room, slips out the door and slams it behind him until we hear his boots pounding down the stairwell. Cinders makes it to the door first and yells Philip's name down into the saloon as we all rush out.

Downstairs Tanner's gravelly voice is calling out, "Get off me, get away! I'll slice ya!"

A scuffle takes over the saloon and the crowd of men swirl and surge round Tanner like a riptide to pull him under. When we finally elbow through the men, Philip Large has his little legs and arms wrapped round Tanner on the floor like a constrictor snake and is bending him backward.

Cinders then pushes through us and comes to his knees by Philip's ear. He whispers gently and pets the feeble-minded man's hair as if he were a puppy and without delay, Tanner is let loose.

"Grab him," The Swede mumbles. "Hold him."

Dance, Eddie and Freddie have Tanner by the arms and legs as Tanner tries to catch his breath. Men had climbed up the mahogany bar to get away from the waving bowie knife but can now come down again. Two appear to have been cut, but not badly. Even Philip is bleeding from his ear, though he doesn't realize it.

Behind us, footsteps creak on the stairwell. It is Dinny, descending.

"Make way," someone says, and the crowd of cold-eyed men do.

Standing next to me, Dinny looks down to Tanner, "Eighty-six him," I advise. "Forever."

"Kill him," Vincent knuckles his .38.

"Beat an' brand him," The Swede's voice falls on Tanner like a gavel. "Treachery is the righthand o' wrongdoers."

Tanner wriggles to free himself as Dago Tom hands Dinny the hunting knife.

"I have a better idea," Dinny calls out so all may hear. "The debt ya have taken on Irishtown's behalf is not proof o' loyalty. Loyalty is the kin o' honor. To prove ya'self on our terms. . . I got a job for ya, Tanner."

"What job?"

Dinny addresses the room, "Pickles Leighton has a retrial in May. If he's released Bill will have a brigade o' scofflaws to go along wit' his Trench Rabbits an' the Lonergan Crew," the men round Dinny cast slurs in the memory of Pickles. "Bill's tryin' to build an army, an' that'd even the score. It seems Pickles won't give him those soldiers until he's released. Otherwise Bill'd have them already an' they'd be at our door."

Cinders begins to chuckle when he figures where the conversation is headed as Dinny turns his eyes down to Tanner, "Make Pickles done in Sing Sing and Bill never gets his scofflaws. Those are our terms."

Tanner's sharp eyes turn dull, "Ain't that how—"

"McGowan was killt, Dinny's first righthand," The Swede finishes Tanner's sentence and crosses himself. "God rest his soul."

And god rest his sister Emma McGowan's soul, I cross myself too. *My first love.*

Dinny shifts with dauntless mannerisms until he speaks aloud, "Make up for what ya done, Tanner. The men in this room don' respect ya for backstabbin' us when we sent ya to do a job last time. Make up for it an' ya will be rewarded wit' quarter in the White Hand."

"How am I supposed to do a job McGowan failed at? An' now Pickles has an entire army in Sing Sing."

"The difference is Owney Madden," Dinny explains. "Pickles has a group that follows him inside, but so does that banty rooster, Madden. Ya was once close wit' him an' the Gophers. Back before he killt Little Patsy Doyle an' got a stint for it. I've been in touch wit' him already. Everyone remembers Eddie Gilchrist, right?"

"Lumpy," someone responds.

"Lumpy the Lamb."

"Madden has offered Gilchrist protection," Dinny explains, then moves his eyes down to Tanner again. "An' he knows ya're comin'. McGowan took one eye from Pickles. Tell Owney Madden ya there to take the other. That's ya job. Ya do these things an' I'll talk wit' Thos Carmody about droppin' the blood feud he put out on ya. Also, the White Hand will assume the debt to Johnny Spanish, an' finally. . . I'll name ya dockboss o' Red Hook."

"Red Hook?" Tanner wonders. "Ya divvy up territory that ain't yours?"

"It will be when we crush Lovett an' his band o' lost boys."

A cheer goes up at those words and a big toothy smile is back on Cinders' face. Even The Swede, born and reared in Red Hook, nods in agreement.

"What about the Black Hand," I whisper to Dinny. "They'll want it back."

But Dinny does not answer. When the room settles again, he has one more question for Tanner, "Do ya know what done means?"

Tanner nods, "Done means done, Din. I know."

"Let him loose," Dinny orders.

As Tanner comes to his feet, Dinny puts a hand on his shoulder, "Ya gotta outstandin' gun charge for violatin' the Sullivan law, right? Turn ya'self in. Plead guilty. Ya'll be out in a year. Probably less."

"A new war for the inside!" Cinders beams. "Gee whiz if this was a movin' picture, I'd watch it. Better than The Musketeers o' Pig Alley. I tell ya what, Din. I shoulda never doubted ya. That was unlike me. I'm sorry about that. I was wrong."

"It's fine," Dinny says as he looks into each and every one of our eyes. "Remember though, it's a silent war. Wars for the inside o' Sing Sing always are. That information never leaves this room."

We all nod.

Dinny points a knuckle at Tanner, "Go."

Tanner wipes down his togs and straightens his black tie. All eyes are on him as he opens the door. Outside the city scrapes like metal shearing against iron until the door closes and Tanner's shamed face disappears from the window.

"Dinny," I whisper in the gray light that illumines us and casts two long shadows on the floor between the bar and the long wall. "About Red Hook, what will Sixto Stabile think if we give it to Tanner. We could lose our deal with the Black Hand."

He hesitates before answering, "That's the thing, ya never lose fam'ly. Friends come an' go."

"But Tanner—"

"Helped me when I needed help. Now look what I've done to him," He stares out the window. "Sent him on a dark journey."

When I turn to look out the window with him, a mass of men round the corner at Plymouth and Bridge streets. Their clothes ripple when the waterfront wind hits them and all hold their caps. At the head of them all is a face I have not seen in some time, though it appears different. Bill Lovett's eyes are circled with black and his face seems pale and bloodless. To his right Non Connors strides in our direction and to his left is a one-armed man, all clad in military garb.

"Here comes the bride," The Swede nods toward Bill, then moves to Dinny, "Our weapons are upstairs."

"Gillen, Eddie, Freddie," Dinny says. "Pat them down before enterin'. Trouble, an' we'll bring fire from above."

As Dinny turns for the stairwell, I call to him, "But how many people would die if we come down with all those weapons—"

"Shut it, Liam," The Swede bumps passed me.

Merged in the Moonlight

She feels a tap on her shoulder. And a voice that calls her name. A woman's voice sweet and caring. A friend. The voice shook her by the shoulder but she could not wake, even as she tried with all her strength she could not move her legs or her body in the paralysis of sleep.

"Anna, Anna," the woman's voice calls as soft as wind through trees.

Anna Lonergan opens her eyes and can see, though her body feels bound by the coma that still grips at her.

"Anna are ya alright?"

She moves her eyes up to Grace White. Knowing there is safety, she closes them again until finally her body begins to stretch out a great yawn. But the back of her head pounds to the rhythm of her heartbeat and bile has settled in her throat.

"Ya was banjaxed last night like I never seen a woman get banjaxed before," Under her shift Grace's breasts shimmer as she moves her weight off her knees to her backside.

A long ash at the end of Kit's paper cigarette threatens to break as speaks, "Ya almost drank ya'self under the bartender."

"We had to carry ya upstairs," Grace has a hand on Anna's shoulder. "An' when we put ya on the sofa, ya fell off an' ya wouldn't let us put ya back, so here ya slept all night on the floor."

Anna sits up and feels that her underclothes and the bottom of her dress are wet. She pulls the cover off to reveal a dark halo stain on the rug round her thighs.

Kit Carroll points with her cigarette at the bathroom behind Anna, "Just missed."

"Not again!" Grace runs to the kitchen to fetch a bucket of soapy water.

"Go in the bathroom an' take that dress off," Grace commands. "We'll bring ya a new one. If Sixto finds out ya wet his rug he'll send us to hell."

"We're already in hell," Kit growls. "Ya think stumble-bums, fuckwit's an' drunken clowns have the freedom to prey on women in heaven?"

Grace and Kit scrub the rug in unison as Anna pads to the bathroom. The mirror shows that the black and blue mark Bill Lovett had given her is gone now. The mirror also reveals a raggedy, damaged girl.

Good, Anna thinks. *I just want to hide in the Henhouse by day. And by night, hide in dreams with Neesha, my love. My prince.*

But she remembers his words when she told him she wants to visit him to live in her dreams forever, 'That is not how it works,' he told her. 'You must surrender.'

But what does that mean?

'Continue on, an' ya will learn, I promise,' he answered.

She unbuttons and slips the dress over her shoulders to let it puddle on the ground at her feet. Her wet underclothes fall over the dress on the floor as she steps out of them and looks again at the wretch in front of the mirror.

I don't want to be a queen, I just want to be left alone. I want everyone to call me Anna the Loveless. Anna the Lost Princess.

Throughout her childhood it was prophesied by the augurs in the oldest section of Irishtown that she would grow to be Queen of the Brooklyn Waterfront, Queen of Irishtown, her beauty unrivaled, her ancestry royal, in a gravelly New York kind of way.

How could they have ever thought that? Anna wonders. *We Lonergans are infamous as the lowest of the low in Brooklyn.*

But to the survivors of the Great Hunger, the original settlers of Irishtown, Anna Lonergan was always greeted with a bow and named a princess when seen on the street with a snot-nosed grimace, balled fists and thick hair flailing in the waterfront wind behind her like a crimson cloak.

In their telling, Princess Lonergan's bloodline included an uncle on her mother's side named Jimmy Brady. Better known as Yakey Yake, Brady was a vicious Lower East Side gang leader that fought off the Swamp Angels, Monk Eastman's Gang and even the renowned Five Points Gang to saunter up and down Catherine Street and adjoining alleys where the Yakey Yake Gang virulently ruled. Anna's father, John Lonergan was Yake Brady's muscle and enforcer. A bareknuckle prize fighter of some renown in the 1890s, he is no more than a drunken foot soldier for Bill now.

I don't want for any of that. I've done all I could to tear down their expectations. Now look at me. I'm nothing, nobody.

Pain shoots into the back of her head and she leans on the sink, dizziness overtaking her.

Anna had never been in a proper bathroom before. She grew amidst the rattle of the Manhattan Bridge in the slums of Johnson Street; the southern edge of Irishtown. In the Lonergan tenement there are only shared water closets and privies outside of their room. Twenty times a day she would march her siblings outside while her mother scrubbed floors in the mansions of the old Anglo-Saxon and Dutch ascendency, her father nursing a bottle of whiskey somewhere, anywhere but home.

I became a mother before ever having sex, and a slattern without ever selling my body, she laughs in the mirror.

A proper bathroom is strangely enticing since it is within the flat. It would have been a great convenience growing up with a proper bathroom having fourteen siblings.

There is even a window in the bathroom that overlooks Green-Wood Cemetery to the south and east. Outside a sigh of wind sends the cluttering leaves of a thousand trees into a gentle sway over the walkways that wend down the rolling bends and embankments. The grass on the steep-sloped hills, the weeping willows and the wildflowers move in the currents too. But the leaning tombstones and copper crypts that have turned green with rust just sit there motionless.

Trundling up the hill of Twenty-Fourth Street a black horse with a crimson bridle pulls a casket coach toward the Yale & Stabile undertaker downstairs. Its forelocks of jet black hair partially cover its eyes while it bobs its head to haul the weight along the inclining street that is hemmed in by rows of black wrought iron fencing and obelisk posts.

Anna's mother had buried two children in that cemetery, which caused Mary to regress into a mixture religion, mysticism and macabre folklore.

More to hide from.

At the burial of Anna's little sister in January, Mourning Mother Mary had entered a state of reverie. She told Anna that cemeteries are like icebergs and, "underneath Green-Wood is a portal to the Otherworld. Below, it's five thousand times as large as what the eye can see above, bigger even! All those people await Him. Await the Messiah's comin'."

In this state of reverie over her daughter's grave, Anna's mother raised her arms to the sky, "When the mist descends an' the veil between the livin' an' the dead is thinnest, the chosen souls will writhe in their graves. An' when storm comes an' unearths the burial mounds, they will rise an' set out among the livin'!"

Over the hole, a terror had come across her mother's face. Men with soiled jumpsuits and paper cigarettes that dangled from cursing lips began shoveling dirt callously into the grave. And Mourning Mother Mary fell as if struck by a bolt of lightning.

"The blood!" She screamed and held her wrists, then reached for her ankles.

The gravediggers stopped their work, Father Larkin halted his sermon, Anna's siblings reared back in horror as their mother rolled on the frozen ground.

"The Messiah! The Messiah has granted me the ecstasy o' his sufferin'!"

Her mother's black dress had cinched up to her waist as she flailed in the fresh dirt and goose droppings. If it hadn't been for Richie grabbing hold of her by the feet, Mary might have fallen into the grave with her daughter.

"Ma, what's wrong wit' ya?" Anna slapped her. "What's wrong?"

"Look," her mother bore her wrists in plain sight. "The blood! The pain o' the Messiah is gifted me. See the blood?"

"I don't see no blood, Ma."

"They come from the Otherworld, they do," Mary screamed at them. "The storm! An'. . . an' a hero will arrive like the risin' o' the moon. Five an' t'ree will come to make seven. It is prewritten, their wet souls will writhe, relived. A great an' horrific spectacle is comin'!"

For close on two weeks Mourning Mother Mary was inconsolable and spouting incoherent stories. Anna never did fully understand what it was that drove her mother mad. But then came the storm in February, just as she'd foreseen in her reverie.

And little did Anna know, the storm would bring yet more calamity to herself even; the greatest tragedy Anna Lonergan would ever know. Worse even than losing her siblings, she had lost Neesha, her love.

In the bathroom Anna looks in the mirror.

I will not cry. You cannot cry if you have no love.

But the thought of leaving her young siblings in the care of her psychopathic mother and drunken father makes her bite at her cuticles again.

I'm being selfish by hiding here, aren't I?

Out of the corner of her eye Anna sees something move in the cemetery. She goes up on her tiptoes to see out the window, beyond the black wrought iron fence.

In the distance she can see the back of the towering gothic-style castle gate entrance, but someone is walking shoeless down a steep knoll as if in a trance. It is a red-headed, emaciated woman, though her hair is curly and unkempt, her dress torn and ratty. Anna squints to get a better look when the woman wanders behind a tree. When she reemerges, the woman stops and stares back.

There's no way she can see me through the window, across the street. No way.

Yet the red-haired woman is fixated as if she has found what she had been looking for all along.

Is that me? In the future?

Anna pants and loses her breath as she comes down to the heels of her feet away from the window. Quickly she goes back onto the balls of her feet for another look, but the red-haired woman is gone.

That didn't happen, Anna convinces herself. *I just imagined it. I'm still drunk, that's all.*

Anna takes a deep breath and sprinkles water over her face.

Or was it Neesha that sent her to draw me out of my hiding? To show me what will happen to me if I refuse to surrender to my love?

Anna turns the water pressure up as high as it will go and rinses handfuls of water over her face now.

I am going mad in here. There's too much peace. Too much time to think.

Out in the parlor the door opens and men's voices come to Anna's ear. Quickly she picks up her wet dress and steps into the tiny closet, but she can't close it all the way.

Kit's protesting voice comes to her, "What, ya can't knock?"

"*Silenzio, puttana,*" is the response.

An Italian man, Anna mouths in the cramped closet.

Sixto Stabile, who owns the Adonis Social Club and half of the undertaker business downstairs rarely speaks Italian to the girls, so it must be Frankie Yale. But then she hears the voice of three men. The third must be the man named Lucy, the one who comes to pick up Grace and Kit every morning at eleven A.M. and drives them to the Adonis.

Naked, Anna holds the wet dress against her body. But the smell of it changes her mind. Quietly, she opens the closet and drops it into the tub.

Then the bathroom door opens.

Anna bites on the cuticles of her hand as the sound of a man pissing into the toilet fills the room. *If he sees me, my hair will give me away as the sister of Richie Lonergan, a lieutenant for Bill Lovett.*

Word has it that *Pulcinella,* as they call Bill, has a target on his back. A big, young fellow was hired to take back Red Hook and kill the Irish leadership there.

But if they find me now, they will kidnap and ransom me. That's what they do, they're Black Hand.

The sound of the man's zipper makes Anna's eyes bulge. The closet door can't close all the way with her in it, so if he tries pushing it, she will be found. Footsteps inside the bathroom make her shiver as she covers up her breasts with one arm and her private area with her other hand.

The man growls and sniffs into the air.

"Puzza de piscio qui," the man calls out in a deep voice to the others in the parlor.

Around the edge of the door she can see the man's profile and knows it is Lucy by the big bend in his nose. Again Lucy sniffs over the tub where her dress lies crumpled and wet with piss.

He must be telling them that it smells of piss. He's going to find me. What am I doing here naked and hiding? I am putting Richie and Bill at risk. I've lost my way.

"Sangue, sangue," Anna hears Grace and Kit yell in unison outside as Lucy growls again in the small space of the bathroom.

Inside the closet Anna shivers. Her lungs long to be filled with a scream, so she takes her hands off her breasts to cover her mouth. Without washing his hands Lucy opens the door and promptly steps out.

Anna takes a deep breath, then listens to the five of them speak out in the parlor. Anna had learned that the only time Lucy could be turned away is if Grace and Kit sang those magic words in Italian, "Blood, blood."

Sometimes, even when they had their blood, Lucy would come back to explain in broken English that a man wished to feed on her blood.

"All men have different appetites," Grace had explained to her last month when their moon had last come.

Then Kit said, "I've played the virgin victim an' the domineerin' dame, but nothin's ravin' mad like a man wit' a red mustache."

"Madness," Grace had agreed. "What are ya supposed to say after a man asks ya to dress up like his mother an' take advantage o' his innocence?"

Kit answered with a shrug, "It was business doin' pleasure wit' ya?"

Anna had heard stories as a girl about how Italians eat their own children in a blood sauce. It was her father who said it mostly, but her mother did not trouble to correct him. She had been told that Irish-American men are wholesome and healthy, strong and just. But both Grace and Kit disagreed. And if the stories she heard about McGowan's wake were true, Dinny Meehan drank the blood of his dead righthander in front of one and all.

Men are beasts, Anna shakes her head in the mirror. *I should have been one.*

The door opens and Grace passes a dress through while Anna exchanges it with her wet dress. "It's Kit's. She's more ya size than I am."

"They're gone?"

"They're gone," Grace assures. "Ya know ya prolly shouldn't—"

"I know," Anna stops her. "I shouldn't be here."

"We need to talk, Anna," Grace slowly closes the door. "A real talk."

Anna holds the dress up to inspect it. It is fringed with a shiny gold lamé round the sleeves and at the hemline, but is made mostly from linen and low quality cotton. The stitching along the waist meanders and there are stains that had been rubbed out with some crude soap and a brush.

I don't want to think about where the stains come from.

The shoulders puff out and the neckline is too low for her taste. Grace had once told Anna that her breasts are a small man's handful and her hips were not the kind most Italian men prefer. She also told Anna that although she is extraordinarily beautiful, she could never be a whore because she couldn't act demure. Not enough for most men's taste, at least.

Anna slips into the dress and enters the parlor room where Kit sits on a sill blowing cigarette smoke out an open window.

Grace turns from the washboard and walks through the parlor with Anna's soiled dress in her hands and clothespins in her mouth mumbling of how the dress will take hours to dry. She leans out the window where Kit smokes and attaches it to the line that stretches fifteen feet across to the neighboring building to the south. Outside Anna sees the piss-stained rug slung over the wire as well.

"I. . . I'm sorry about—"

"Oh stop," Grace turns from the window with her hands on her hips. The two of them take deep breaths in unison and stare at Anna. Grace then takes the cigarette from Kit and draws from it, then hands it back. "Anna?"

"Don't."

"Anna ya worry me."

"Is that right?" Anna stares back at the two and raises an eyebrow.

"Anna last night after ya passed out, ya were talkin' in ya sleep about this Neesha person again. Callin' out his name an' whatnot. Who is Neesha? Ya asked about him when Bill hurt ya that day after the storm. Then last night ya were so drunk down at the saloon Kit an' I had to tell all the men that ya couldn't be bought. One man tried to carry ya off, ya know. Ya passed out on the toilet an' he walked in an' scooped ya up wit' ya under clothes around ya ankles."

"Everywhere I go I have to tell men I ain't no slattern, so what? Everywhere men take bets on who rode me. Now I even dress like a slattern. I don' fookin' care what anybody thinks, understand me? I don' fookin' care. I ain't beholden to that shit."

"Anna," Grace walks in front of her and puts two hands on her shoulders.

"Don' touch me," Anna's eyes flash with blue fire.

"She's gonna cut ya wit' that sharp tongue," Kit advises.

But Grace shushes her, "Uhright, uhright. It's just I love ya, Anna. We both do, see? Why do ya put ya'self through so much? What's wrong? What's on ya mind?"

Anna looks away stubbornly. "I know ya love me," her voice cracks and her eyes glass over with water. "But I can't talk about—"

Grace pulls her close for a hug, but Anna's arms remain limp at her side.

"Ya're touchin' me again," Anna growls.

"Say, if I tell ya a secret that. . . that hurts so bad. . . that I don' ever wanna talk about. Oh never mind," Grace changes her mind.

"What?" Anna perks up and pulls away. "What kinda secret do ya have?"

Grace bites her lip as Kit tosses the cigarette out the window, "Can we sit down at least?"

Anna sits on the floor in the whore's dress cross-legged. Grace and Kit follow suit, the three of them sitting in a circle, holding hands.

Grace takes a deep breath. "I lied in court. To a judge."

"When?"

"Well the trial was in 1913, but the murder I witnessed was in 1912. Actually, the murder Kit an' I both witnessed."

"I didn't see nothin'," Kit shakes her head.

Grace turns her head to Kit and rolls her eyes, "Ya saw what I saw, but ya just said ya didn't see nothin'."

"Yeah, 'cause I know it's better to let sleepin' dogs lie, but *you*?" Kit lowers her eyes. "Ya even told them ya real name."

Anna turns to Kit, "What did ya tell them ya name was then?"

"Peggy Kelly," Kit holds her hand two feet above the ground. "Ever since I'm this high I been told never to tell the tunics my real name. The boys say Patrick Kelly, but my Ma always said, 'them tunics ask ya name? tell them we're all Peggy Kelly, because Peggy Kelly means shut ya fookin' mouth.'" Kit thumbs at Grace. "This one didn' learn her lessons."

Grace rolls her eyes again, "Kit, ya're a ol' biddy already. I never even see ya laugh."

"I am what I am. A whore should never laugh unless she wants a soft cock an' a hard fist."

Anna laughs, until Grace turns on her, "If I tell ya this story, ya gotta tell me yours."

Anna's eyes flick back and forth between Grace and Kit, "Maybe."

Grace sighs through her nose.

"What did ya lie about, in court?" Anna prods.

"Well, Dinny an' McGowan were already in Jacob's Saloon."

"Don' say that name," Kit warns.

"No one's here to hear me," Grace snaps. "Anyway, Dinny an' McGowan were already in Jacob's Saloon, which was between the bridges, it's burned down now—"

"I know it's burned down. Everyone knows that."

"Uhright, let me talk."

"G'on."

"So Dinny an' McGowan were frisked before they came in. They were facing the front window while Kit was dancin' wit' Christie Maroney an' I was singin' a song. I have a beautyful singin' voice, ya know. Everyone says I do."

"And?" Anna had only heard rumors of the story about how the White Hand came to power in Brooklyn when she was eleven years old.

"The sun was startin' to come up. We'd been blowin' dust all night an' drinkin' too. Christie's hand was up Kit's dress while she blew dust from his pinky nail."

"I was what? Fifteen?" Kit strikes a match against the floor and lights a handrolled cigarette. "But older than most already."

"Anyhow, my singin' caused Dinny to start cryin'."

"Cryin'?" Anna sits back.

"I swear he was cryin' when I was singin' *Dear Ol' Skibberreen*. Then we hear some shoutin' outside o' the women's entrance. It was Pickles Leighton. All night long

Christie had been talkin' about makin' the newcomer Bill Lovett's gang fight against Dinny's to make sure that he could keep power to hisself. So Christie was confused when he heard Pickles challenge him to come outside. But as soon as he did, bang. Shot between the eyes. I watched the whole thing. I even saw'r blood shoot out from the back o' his head. The thing is, Pickles hadn't killt him."

"Wait, Pickles hadn't—"

"No, I swear I saw'r it. Pickles was standin' off. Vincent Maher shot him."

"An' ya told the jury on the witness stand it was Pickles did it," Anna nods.

Grace looks at Kit, then back to Anna, "I did. I said it was Pickles."

"Why?"

"The Swede."

"What about The Swede?"

"The Swede told me that if I tell the truth to the jury that Vincent shot Christie Maroney, then he'd kill me an' Kit an' my mother an' everyone else. That sayin' it was Pickles was the only way I could save us. So I lied. I'm a liar. But while I'm alive I should tell the truth and shame the devil," Grace's eyes go white. "But ya know me, Anna. I'm not a liar. Am I?"

"No, ya the sweetest person I ever knew."

"But I lied on the witness stand, they call that perjury. I looked it up."

"Ya did it to save ya mother, Grace. It's no crime if ya lie for ya fam'ly. It's not even a sin."

"I. . . I don' know, but now there's this," Grace sits up and walks over to a drawer in the open kitchen and takes out a piece of paper, then sits down cross-legged again. "A patrolman served me it."

"What is it?" Anna looks at it.

"It's a subpoena. Patrolman Culkin had me sign for it."

"Culkin," Kit repeats as if she were spitting out a rotten piece of meat.

"Yeah, ya favorite customer," Grace turns from the subpoena. "The one that makes ya wrap up his testicles in leather bounds an' wallop them with his own blackjack."

"What?" Anna recoils. "Is that true?"

Kit's eyes roll upward as she shrugs, "He says he needs to be punished. I dunno."

Grace goes on, "Anyhow Patrolman Culkin told me he is head o' the investigation behind his father-in-law'r's disappearance."

"An' ya signed ya real name, didn' ya?" Kit hisses.

"Well I can't lie no more," Grace opens her palms and shrugs. "I don' wanna go back up on the witness stand. I don' wanna see The Swede's face ever again."

"But doesn't Vincent come to the Adonis all the time to see ya?"

"See me, she says," Grace laughs. "He sees me alright. He's my best customer. He pays twice what anybody else does, an' ya know why he does that, right?"

Anna and Kit nod.

"He came to see me at the Adonis the other day an'," Grace looks to Anna. "An' he asked about ya."

"Me?"

"Yeah, he said somethin' about how ya 'full-fledged' now. He likes to call ya a ripe tomato an' he says, 'tell Anna I'm the Queensolver.'"

"What does that mean?"

Kit snorts, "It means he only thinks wit' his little head."

But Grace just shrugs and rolls her eyes, then wraps her long, thin arms round her stomach and bends forward, "I'm scared."

"Ya have to tell them ya were intimidated," Anna says. "Tell them it was The Swede. His real name is James Finnigan. An' ya should ask for protection. Ask Patrolman Culkin an' Reilly to provide protection."

"Then what? I have to move from here? I like it here."

"I. . . don' know, maybe?" Anna wonders.

"I was just a kid back then, they shouldn't make me go back up on the witness stand again."

But if you do, Pickles will get released and Bill will get his army, Anna realizes. Her thoughts run quickly. *If I can convince her to do it. . .*

"Ya should make right for when ya lied, Grace," Anna advises.

Kit looks at Anna sideways, "Yeah, g'ahead, we'll put that on ya gravestone, 'I told the truth, look where it got me.'"

"It's the only way to fix the guilt that looms over ya," Anna says.

"What about The Swede?"

"Ya're right, the tunics aren't gonna provide protection for ya. I got another idear though. I know someone who can help us."

"Really Anna? Who can help us?"

What am I doing? Do I really want this? Do I really want to end my hiding?

"Let me worry about that," Anna stands.

"Wait," Grace touches her hand. "It's ya turn to tell me a secret. I told ya mine, now ya gotta tell me why ya get so shattered wit' the drink and who Neesha is."

Anna lowers her eyes.

"It's only fair," Kit says.

"I know that ya father is. . . He's not a good man," Grace's voice is near a whisper as she looks for Anna's eyes. "Did he take ya purity first?"

"No," Anna pulls away. "He's guilty o' a lotta shit, but not that. But I did see him carry off my mother. . . A lot. An' every time I saw'r her belly big wit' another child, well—"

"It made ya sad?"

"No, angry."

"Anna, why do ya let people think that ya prostituted ya'self? When Bill called ya a slattern in front o' ya brother, ya didn't say nothin' back. Now everyone thinks ya sold ya'self to pay for ya fam'ly."

"That wouldn't be a sin, remember?"

"Well, but—"

"People believe what they want, not what's true or factual. The whole world's built on lies by men. I ain't a slave to their idears an' I ain't a slave to the word 'slattern.' Let them think what they want, it don' matter. Anyhow, I want them to think less o' me."

"Why?" Grace's mouth goes small in disbelief.

"Because I wanna—" Anna stops herself, then takes a deep breath. "Because I just wanna hide from all o' that now. An' the best way to remove myself from expectations is to let them think the worst about me. Better that way."

"But why do ya wanna hide? From ya fam'ly, o' all people?" Grace turns to Kit. "If only Kit an' I had a more o' a fam'ly, maybe we wouldn't be in the pickle we're in t'day, holed up in a house for whorin' hens. But ya throw away the gift o' fam'ly?"

Damn you, Grace. Damnit that hurts.

"Ya don' know what it's like to have so many in ya fam'ly thrust all kinds o' expectation on ya everyday—"

"I wish I did," Grace interrupts.

"Same here," Kit agrees.

"Who is Neesha then?" Grace asks.

Neesha, my love. My prince.

Anna's stomach turns when she hears his name, and she bites at a loose piece of skin on the cuticle of her middle finger, "I can't tell ya."

"Anna? Ya promised."

"No I didn't. Anyhow I already told ya a secret, that I'm hidin' here," Suddenly a rush of pain shoots into the back of Anna's head again and everything starts to spin. Black spots appear in front of her eyes and sounds come from her that she had never heard herself utter before. Moans of fear. Laments of grief. Pain so deep that the ache reaches far into her chest. Before she can gain control of herself again, she is prostrate on the ground with big tears dropping onto the wood floor.

"Sweetness," Grace's voice goes soft and is colored with a sympathizing tone, which makes Anna's chest heave. Her sobs are so strong now that she must take deep breaths to fill her lungs with air while salty tears stream into the corners of her mouth. Kit scoots closer to her when Anna curls into a fetal position. Grace lifts her head and puts it on her thigh and softly wraps strands of Anna's red hair round her ear, soothing her with gentle strokes across the scalp.

But I want to tell them so bad. I want to. I want to.

"Ya were in love," Grace realizes. "Was it real love? Was it true?"

Anna bursts into tears again. Spittle lands on the wood floor in front of her. She nods her head and turns her eyes to the ring on her left finger. It's amber color shines in her wetted view. It looks like a wreath of laurel that wraps delicately round her finger. Gold like her lion's mane.

Crown me king, and you will be Queen, he told her. *I live inside another now. But who?*

The realization sparks joy in Grace's eye and she grabs Anna's hand and pulls her ring finger close, "Ya got married? Is this a weddin' ring? Ya told me it was passed down in ya fam'ly. But there ain't a diamond? Anna?"

"I. . . I almost got married, but he—" The words are too heavy in her mouth. They bear so much weight that she struggles to lift them to her lips. She had never said the words aloud since Neesha had. . . died. She had never said his real name since that terrifying morning when she found out. Only in dreams does his name exist now. And keeping the secret of their secret love is all that gives her heart.

In dreams. That is where he lives forever, in dreams. He is a myth now. Neesha, my love. My prince. His real name was. . . I can't, I can't even think it.

She sits up at the thought that the man she fell in love with so quickly and so deeply. . . still lives. Yes, he lives, even more beautifully than ever, and it scares her. Shocks her so badly that she fears she is losing her grip and that she may fall. Fall to him. Again. In the Otherworld.

If I surrender to him, then I will know I am mad.

Too many nights she had woken up in belief that she was with him. So many times that she blurs the line between dreaming and wakefulness. She prefers dreaming, of course, where she could see him. His big face and flaxen mane. His hands brushing against her like the wind, their bodies merged in the moonlight as they had been in real life. It felt so good to have him inside her again. So close that she could feel him from within. With words, when he was alive, he poured his heart into her ears like molten gold. Pouring so truly that she had let go of the hate that had kept her alive through the countless trials and tragedies of her childhood.

Now, when they are together in her dreams, every muscle in her body relaxes and she drifts away. Even begins to surrender to him. But at the precipice, she would look up and see another man's face. A grotesque man with a black mask that half-covered horrific scars. Scars that leak pus onto her. Into her mouth. It had happened so often in her dreams now that she no longer trusts herself to give in because as soon as she does, her Neesha turns into a monster.

In the dreams where Neesha turns, a snowstorm rages outside and dawn cuts across the eastern sky like a razor on skin bleeding orange light. She longs to drift away again and surrender to his loving words and live there forever, but it would mean her sanity.

She looks at her two friends.

I'm ready. I trust them, she thinks to herself, then finds their eyes and speaks.

"It was Mickey Kane. Neesha is Mickey Kane."

"Ya were in love wit' Mickey Kane?" Grace's eyes go big. "That's why ya dragged us down to Red Hook after the storm? An'. . . He gave ya that ring?"

She nods and struggles to get words from her throat, "I told him once that I thought it was beautyful that a passionflower could grow outta somethin' as ugly as a simple vine." The tears boil out of Anna's eyes again. "He said that was what made me more beautyful than anyone he'd ever met because. . . because I grew outta the trash heap o' Brooklyn. Then he got me this as a symbol, it's a wreath-o'-vine."

"But why do ya call him Neesha?"

She swallows and palms at her wet eyes, "It was dumb. Borne o' the imagination lovers have, I s'pose. So silly, but so meaningful to me. The stories I heard growin' up like the ol' Irish myths an' whatnot, ya know? There's this story o' two lovers who run away together. Dierdre is her name, Neesha is his, but it's spellt different. I think it's Gaelic spelling."

Kit tilts her head, "I remember that story. Dierdre o' the Sorrows, it's called."

"Yeah, her sorrows are mine now. Just like in the story, he gets killt. Ya see," Anna clears her throat. "I hung on his neck like fox fur on a golden prince, but what I didn't know was that I am, in truth, an albatross. We were gonna get married an' run off forever, but then the storm. . . Then—"

Kit holds her heart and shakes her head slowly in realization.

Grace covers her mouth with both hands and speaks through them, "Ya own brother, Richie. Richie killt' him!"

"It wasn't his fault!" Anna screams and holds hands over her ears. "It's not Richie's fault!"

"An' Mickey paid for ya fam'ly. That's where ya got the money from. I can't believe—"

A knock comes to the door that halts Grace in mid sentence. She and Kit wheel toward the sound, then look at each other.

"Who could that be? Lucy again?" Anna comes to her feet and wipes the memory of Neesha from her eyes.

Grace tiptoes to the door on long, thin legs and touches it gently with painted fingernails, "Who is it?"

A younger man's voice comes through, "Anna, we know ya're in there. Ya can't hide forever."

In Mockery of Honor

"I'm John Carter!" The boy screams and jumps on the hotel bed with the big book open and above his head.

Sadie Meehan's concern turns to a smile when she sees her son look to her. She then turns back to the window and moves the curtain to the side where a collection of black motorcar taxis roll into the car park below. A gaggle of women spill out and bunch together in the cold like winter geese. They wear gowns and cabbage rose hats pulled tight with chiffons, even mink stoles, and are not accompanied by men, save the drivers.

"I'm a super hero," Sadie's son calls out again. "I'm John Carter!"

"Let's just keep it to John," Sadie turns a half-smile to him again.

"Uhright."

"An' where are we?"

He raises the book over his head again and announces, "We are in the Valley Dor, in the Barsoomian afterlife!"

"An' why can't we leave?"

"We're prohibited, but we can escape if we—"

"Later, John. Later, alright? We're to stay 'ere for a bit, yeah?"

"Uhright."

To convince her son to accept a name change, she had to turn it into a game. The Name Game. She explained to him that while they are "on holiday," he could pretend to be someone else. Someone new. Instead of L'il Dinny, as he'd been called all his life, they would call him John.

The Gods of Mars is John's favorite book. It is also the most complex story she has ever read to him, but he is able to keep up with the plot. And the more he learns, the more he wants to learn.

"That kid's got the smarts," Happy Maloney crutches out of the hotel bathroom with shaving cream on his face. "He's already a better reader than I am an' he's only six."

Since she could not use her married name while in hiding, they lied and signed the hotel receipt as "Mr. Maloney, wife & son."

Here, in the Barsoomian Afterlife I am the wife of a Great War veteran, Sadie snickers as she watches the women in the car park below the hotel window.

In the real world Happy Maloney lost his leg in France. Happy earned his nickname from being happy-go-lucky, and he still is, but a dark twinkle had appeared in his eyes since a landmine exploded close to him that left his leg in ribbons. She had only seen that dark shadow in his eyes two or three times since living together in the hotel. He hid it well, but took orders from Sadie with a happy-go-lucky willingness.

What choice has he? I'm the wife of the King of Irishtown and he is but a finger on the White Hand. Here to protect me. Or is he?

Instead of checking Sadie's identification, the hotelier shook Happy's hand and thanked him for his service. That was when she saw the newspaper article on the hotelier's desk about her real husband, Dinny Meehan:

*The Most Desperate Gang Leader
in Brooklyn Incarcerated*

When Happy had turned away with John, she followed without acknowledging the hotelier's staring eyes. That was when she felt a hand grab at her arm, startling her.

"Please let me know if there is anything I can personally provide for ya, mam," He began to lift her hand to his lips until her son John called back to her.

"Mummy! C'mon."

The hotelier quickly let her hand go, smiled a three-toothed smile and scuttled back toward his desk. When he disappeared behind a partition wall, she snapped up the newspaper.

Dinny had been arrested for robbing the Hanan & Sons shoe factory. Since then he'd been released. But with Detective William Brosnan now missing, the investigators have named him a suspect as well as the recently returned "Wild Bill" Lovett.

No, she cannot use her married name. She has to hide that too.

The women in the car park below the hotel window continue to talk and linger and laugh. Nothing seems to worry them as if their numbers protect them from the predators. As if they haven't a care in the world, other than petty pleasures. And where their children are, Sadie could only guess. She has always been chained to her child. A woman is never free of her children, but for the mother who abandons them comes the enslavement of scorn. But the women below seem free enough, even from guilt.

I have got to get out of this room, Sadie looks away from the window. *I'm getting cabin fever.*

How many months had she been locked up in hiding, she can't even remember. Time is passing quickly, though she seems to imagine things more now. Fantasize about the outside world, she turns inward. Fictions arise.

That's what happens when you're imprisoned like a woman in a tower cell. You start seeing things that aren't there.

Even before she escaped Brooklyn Sadie was confined to her Warren Street Brownstone tower while Vincent Maher stood guard downstairs. Dinny said Vincent was only there as a precaution, but Sadie could never tell if he had her on a pedestal, or in a cage.

She turns her eyes to Happy Maloney and clenches her teeth.

My husband's men are always nearby to guard the woman in the tower.

But sometimes that could be a good thing. When a man tried to shame her on the street in Brooklyn for marrying the White Hand, Vincent dragged him away. She heard later that Vincent had shoved his .38 up the man's arse and threatened to shoot it if he ever troubled her again. Of course, she never saw the man after that.

Still, it's hard not to think of yourself as a possession when all you see is your own walls and your child. A sheltered and protected life is better than the itinerant poverty of her childhood, but it was not her choice.

As a little girl back in East London, her wild-eyed mother told stories of the old world. One of those stories was about a woman locked in a tower.

Her mother Rose was half Romani, but because of her mixed blood, she was berated and deemed a "diddicoy." The Ulster Irish side of her mother's family had pushed her away as well, rebuking her as "tinker scum." That was why the Leighton clan swaddled up their little ones and emigrated to East London within earshot of the bow's bells when Sadie was a baby. There were forty-four Leightons altogether that had made the trek, her cousins Frank, Darby and Pickles among them.

In her mother's story, Mary, Queen of Scots was left in a tower prison for eighteen years.

Men love to acquire and enslave a woman's body. It makes no matter if the manacles are made of chain, or lace.

But what's worse, it was the Protestant Queen Elizabeth who held the key to Mary's gaol door.

In my end is my beginning, Sadie remembers the words her mother repeated while telling the story. The words that were sown into the dress of the imprisoned Catholic Queen. *In my end is my beginning*. Strange words that had naught to do with rebirth, but of life after death.

Upon execution, Mary, Queen of Scots wore a beautiful petticoat made of velvet with a black satin bodice and long gloves, ready to die for her devotion. Her gloves, in particular, were in the liturgical color to show she was content to be martyred for the Catholicism: Crimson brown. When Sadie was little, the story had convinced her of the purity of Catholicism and that Mary, Queen of Scots wore those long, blood-red gloves because it represented that she had reached into the deep heart of faith and was willing to trust that death would immortalize her. That in her end, was a beginning.

"I'm a hero!" John calls out again.

Fantasies, Sadie shakes her head and takes a deep breath. *I need to get out of this hotel room. Just for a bit.*

"Sadie?" Happy calls out as her eyes follow the women from the car park to the office below the window. "Sadie, are ya gonna go over John's lessons this mornin'? He's gettin' antsy."

"No," Sadie lets the curtains close. "I want him to read to yu this mornin', 'appy. I'm goin' for a walk. I 'ave to get some air."

"It's cold outside—"

"Maybe I'll just walk around the 'otel."

Happy crutches closer to her in front of the dresser and mirror and shields the revolver from John's eyes, "Take this?"

"I don' think I need it—"

"Ya never know, ya might."

Sadie looks at the 1905 Colt revolver in his palm. It's long, dark blue barrel with a rounded wood grip has a fixed blade sticking up at the end which Happy calls the "sight." She had never shot it, but Happy had taught her how to use it. Though only in theory. In reality, where she rarely lives now, the revolver scares her. She does not want to use it. She does not want any of this fakery and hiding out, but she had made a choice. A terrible choice, but the safest. She chose her son over her husband.

"Just take it."

"No, I won't need it, thank you though."

She walks to the closet and takes out a shawl and covers herself with it, "John?"

"Yeah?" The boy looks up from his book on the bed.

"I want yu to read to 'appy, understand? Work on the things we went over, alright? If yu don't know a word, use the dictionary."

He looks back down to the *Gods of Mars* and mumbles, "Uhright, but—"

"Yes?" She quickly turns round.

"I kinda forget what daddy looks like. Do ya remember him?"

Happy chimes in, "Ya daddy's very handsome an' muscle-bound. He's a leader o' men. We coulda used him in the Army, I tell ya. . ."

Sadie slips out the door.

The tourist hotel in Rockville Centre, Long Island had emptied for the winter months. Days transformed into nights. Then nights to days while the cold kept them inside the room with nothing to break the monotony. Walking alone down the stairwell, past the lobby and down the long hallway, she is overjoyed with the feeling of having broken free. Even from her own child, who she loves more than anything, though she needs a break. She needs freedom.

The conservatively dressed women from the car park have collected in the open convention hall on the first floor that had been empty for months. She sneaks downstairs to spy on them from behind the double-door entrance from the hall. Inside the guests are flocked between the seating area and the stage where a large banner above them reads, "Carry the Nation to Dry!"

Sadie had never seen so many unaccompanied women in one place before. They are an impressive lot, too. Exceedingly kind to each other and without a single male escort among them. No children demand their attention. No elderly in need of care. They are free to do as they please. Free to speak about what they choose. A family of women together to strengthen women's interests, a mesmerizing notion.

"Are you taking part?"

Sadie gasps and whirls round to meet the voice behind her, "Eh. . . No, I was just wonderin' what all these women was doin' gatherin' togeva like this."

"Togeva? Oh, do you mean together? Are you from England?" The woman reaches out with a bent wrist and gently touches Sadie's arm with two fingers. "We'd love to hear your perspective on the movement. We all know England paved the way."

"What movement?"

A smile comes to the woman's face as if she were confiding in Sadie, "The anti-saloon movement."

The woman wears a light blue and white hooped prairie dress from the last century, a wide bow round her neck and a bonnet with lace and white cloth gloves that reach up to the bend in her arm, just like Mary, Queen of Scots, but not Catholic.

"My name is Eleanor, Eleanor Allerton. I am President of the Woman's Christian Temperance League It's so nice to meet you."

"Em. . . 'Ello Eleanor, I'm Sadie," she stammers. "Sadie. . . Maloney. I'm 'ere wif' me son. Me 'usband is—"

"Lovely," Eleanor waves her gloved hands as if to shoo a fly. "We came a long way here. Some of us, like myself, are from Kansas."

"What is Kansas like?" Sadie interrupts.

Take my son and I there. I want to go to Kansas. Wherever it is.

"What's Kansas like?" Eleanor repeats the question in a way that leads Sadie to believe she does not like to be interrupted. "It's fine. But we've never been to New York before so this is a bit exciting, if it isn't too bold of me to say. Please, will you join us? We are having a roundtable discussion. Two New York state senators and five Long Island mayors are in attendance this day. Mamie White Colvin is here to speak, she ran for Lieutenant Governor of New York just last year, you know. A true inspiration. We're making great progress upstate, but the city is, well—"

A jungle of street and river gangs.

"A bit more of a challenge," Eleanor finishes with a pretend smile. "We have an uphill battle, but we need good wholesome women to spread the word of god our Savior who preaches temperance and moderation in the Good Book."

Sadie watches the woman's eyes move up and down her gray dress, stopping at her hair.

I'm a disheveled mess, Sadie realizes and smiles shyly while pushing at the wrinkles in her old house gown with a sweaty palm. She collects herself and looks past Eleanor toward the banner, "What do yu an' the ova woman wish to accomplish?"

"We've already accomplished what we wish. Now it's time to see it through to the end," Eleanor says with wide eyes and a mocking smile. "Only a couple states are left to ratify the Eighteenth Amendment to the Constitution, and women's suffrage rides along with it. A vote to prohibit alcohol is also a vote to advance us women the right to vote, isn't it wonderful? A year from now the Eighteenth Amendment will take affect and saloons across the entire country will be shuttered. We are confronting the notion of people simply being an extension of their urges, you see. What would happen if all of us ended up giving in all the time? That would make us animals. But we have to lead with dignity and act responsibly, in accordance to inalienable values. With god's hand to guide us, the women of today can make life better for the women of the future."

Sadie wraps her mind round it all, but just as she is about to ask a question, Eleanor strikes up again with bright eyes and a saccharine smile, "But it won't be easy. We need strong women to tow the line and help men get out of the saloon and into the home. It's the alcohol that causes men to act evil, not the men themselves. Worse, it stains the purity of women too. Did you know harlotry is much more likely among drunkenness in women? By cleansing them all of alcohol, we cleanse their souls and open them up to god's word."

Eleanor takes Sadie by the arm and draws her near, "Come with me. I'll introduce you to some of the ladies. They'll be so excited to meet you."

What am I doing? This is all too much. I just wanted to get away for a moment.

Sadie stops and pulls her arm away, "Me 'usband owns a saloon."

"Oh?" Eleanor tilts her head and her mouth puckers. "And where is he now? I imagine you are here with your son, of course. A woman is chained to her children, while men gallivant about with the drink coaxing them into sin. Pray tell where your husband is now?"

He is gathering for war.

"I'm sorry," Sadie turns away and calls over her shoulder. "I 'ave to be goin'."

"Mrs. Maloney?"

Sadie almost forgot the ruse of her name, but turns as Eleanor approaches.

"Mrs. Maloney, what about the vote. Votes for women?"

Sadie lowers her eyes in shame.

Eleanor steps back and opens her arm toward all the women gathered by the stage under the banners, then steps forward and lowers her voice, "In May there will be a vote in the House of Representatives. If it passes it will go to the Senate. Now more than ever we need women to help pave the future. Mothers even more so. I understand if your husband would not approve of his wife lobbying to close down his saloon, but would he approve of his wife having a say in a democracy? Would he?"

"I. . . I believe he would, if—"

"If what?"

Sadie shakes her head, "Yu seem to 'ave time and money to burn in order to think o' other people's future. It's admirable, but I. . . I live 'and-to-mouth. My worries are wif me son. Makin' sure 'e 'as food in 'is belly. I want 'im to get an education. I'm not opposed to what yu doin', really I'm not, but I 'ave to stay safe. For me son's future. Think of a way to include poor women. Poor mothers in yu pursuit, an' I'd be 'appy to 'elp. Until then, I thank yu in advance for keepin' us in mind."

Eleanor slowly shakes her head as her shoulders slump and hands settle around her clean and newly pressed gown. As Sadie walks away, a speaker steps onto the stage behind Eleanor and is calling out politely for attention.

"We are all set to begin, ladies. Thank you all for coming—"

"Sadie," Eleanor calls again.

Sadie stands with her back turned as Eleanor comes up behind her.

"Sadie, you are a good person," Eleanor announces in a lowered tone. "And you are very smart, but it's not your intelligence I question."

Sadie shifts to face her.

"The problem is. . . You're ignorant. You're uneducated, isn't that correct? I can't save you from yourself, unfortunately."

Sadie bites her lip as her eyes fill with water.

I will not cry.

She corrects her posture and takes a deep breath, but when she turns, Eleanor has gone.

As the women begin to sit for the speaker, Sadie sees a lone man standing off from the crowd. When she recognizes him by his strange eyes, she jumps behind the double-doors.

Darby. He found me. But how? How did he know? Who told him?

Sadie rushes down the long, carpeted hallway that leads to the lobby. When she hears the sound of doors closing, she peeks behind and finds that Darby's quizzical eyes emerge from the double-doors to watch her.

Just then, up ahead in the lobby, Happy and John walk toward her without noticing that she is running in their direction. She quickly ducks into a room on the right that is being cleaned by the hotelier's wife.

"Can I help you?" The woman asks.

Sadie closes the door halfway so she can see out, then turns round to the woman. Her hands shaking, she puts a finger to her mouth and with embarrassment and fear on her face, shushes her as politely as she can.

"What's wrong?"

"Shh, please don't speak," Sadie pleads. "I 'ave to 'ide."

Sadie turns to look out the door as Happy and John walk past, right in the direction of Darby.

She covers her mouth so as not to scream when Darby walks by in the opposite direction.

They must have walked directly passed each other, but Darby doesn't even recognize his own kin.

Peeking out the door to the right, she sees that Darby has continued on and walks directly out the front door.

The hotelier's wife comes up behind, "Is there somethin' I can—"

Sadie screams and jumps, then covers her mouth again.

"I'm sorry," Sadie mouths, then runs out the door and goes left toward Happy and John.

Up ahead John is running under Happy's missing leg and laughing between the steeple of the soldier's cruthes. She can't call their names, so she runs to catch up to them when suddenly she is grabbed and pulled into a broom closet.

"Ya cousin was here," a voice says.

It is dark and smells of a wet mop. By the sound of the man's voice she knows him as the hotelier.

"He described ya to a T," he pushes her against a wall and leans his weight on her. "Pretty woman, peasant dress, brown hair, cockney accent. Ya name ain't Mrs. Maloney, is it? It's Sadie Meehan."

"Get off o' me."

"I lied for ya on account o' I knew ya'd be appreciative, but if ya ain't appreciative then I know how to get in touch wit' him. His name's Darby, Darby Leighton from Brooklyn, right?"

"What do yu want? I'll give yu money—"

"I don' want money, sweetheart. I wanna feel what it's like inside ya."

He lowers one of his hands to squeeze her hip and dry humps against her pelvis. She feels his tongue flick at the nape of her neck and a disgusted feeling boils in her stomach. A reminder. She had not felt this feeling in a long time. Not since 1912, in fact. But back comes the memory to overflow her thoughts.

The old leader of the Irishtown gangs, Christie Maroney, had inquired about her as he always inquired about the young, unaccompanied girls from broken families. As she walked past one day, he tipped his tiny derby hat and bowed to her on Sands Street. An ugly, burly man with simian features, Sadie thought him comical at a glance, but she hadn't realized his bowing was in mockery of her honor.

A few weeks later he attempted to speak to her, but Sadie ignored and tried to walk round him. That was when everything changed. Everything. Not just for her, but for everyone in Irishtown.

Gold-toothed Christie the Larrikin had grabbed and yanked her to him, just as she had been grabbed and groped in the broom closet. Maroney held her close with a hand that dug low into her backside. Hip to hip he held her, and reached up into her shirtwaist to pluck at her nipple with his club-like fingers, right there on Sands street where hundreds of people walked by and watched and did nothing.

He would not let go. It lasted for agonizing minutes while his derby hatted galoots stood guard. She screamed many times. She was sure everyone could hear her the struggle in her screams, yet no man found the courage to offer her help. Up close, the Larrikin's meaty lips parted to reveal a pink and gold grin. From behind, he thrust a hand within her bloomers and pushed two ringed fingers up and inside her, lifting her off the ground.

She could feel his manhood grow as he grunted into her ear with a husky voice, "Now that ya wet'n ready, ya can work for me."

In the months previous to the incident, Dinny Meehan had been courting her. So had Harry Reynolds who had even pledged himself to her. But Dinny took initiative when he found her on the street after she'd been clutched and fondled. Her hair had fallen unbound and her dress was torn in two places as he pressed her with questions. Through gasping tears she told him what had happened, though in a disconnected timeline.

Within hours Dinny Meehan gathered all the gangs together. And at a gold-throned dawn the next morning the King of Irishtown since 1900, Christie the Larrikin lay dead with a bullet hole between his eyes in the women's entrance of Jacob's Saloon.

The hotelier's hand had made its way up her blouse too. In the darkness he had grown hard and she could feel it on her leg. With his chest against hers, she is pinned against the broom closet wall. When he presses himself against her pelvis, he reaches behind and grabs a handful of her buttocks.

She screams. Quickly his hand goes from her breast to her mouth.

"Goddamnit," his breath smells of rotten cabbage. "Ya shut ya gob, stupid hussy. Here's what's gonna happen. When I'm done I'm gonna give ya cousin's contact information to ya, an' we're even steven, see? I'll just dip it in for a bit, then ya free, uhright? Tell me that's the plan. Say it."

With his hand over her mouth, Sadie can only breath through her nose and can't speak.

What choice do I have? He'll do it anyhow. I'll just think about something else. I'll make something up. A fiction. I'll think about a story my mother told me. I'm not here. Then it'll be over.

Tears dribble out of her eyes and run down the hotelier's hand over her mouth. She nods at him.

Smiling his three-tooth smile, he takes his hand off her mouth and undoes his trousers. He grabs her hand and pulls it to his penis.

There's that feeling again. In my stomach. Disgust. Think about Barsoom. The Valley Dor. The afterlife. Think about Mary, Queen of Scots. Think about anything.

He lifts her dress in the darkness and yanks down on her bloomers on one side.

"Mummy?"

L'il Dinny?

"Mummy where are ya?"

"Sadie," Happy Maloney's deep voice calls out. "Sadie we heard ya yell. Where are ya?"

"Mummy?"

"Fookin' hussy spawn," the man mumbles.

In her hand she feels he is no longer stiff and the penis flops out of her grasp. Then he reaches down to feel it himself.

"Fuck," he leans his weight against her and grabs for her left hand. In the dark she can feel his tongue wiggle over her ring her finger until she feels her wedding band plucked off. "Tomorrow meet me in room 310, upstairs. Top floor. I'm keepin' this just in case. Ya don' show an—"

Sadie nods and straightens her clothing.

"Don' fookin' say nothin' or else. I'll wait in here a couple minutes, hurry up."

Sadie falls out of the broom closet and onto the hallway carpet. She looks at her left hand minus her wedding band and pulls herself back up again and straightens her hair. When she looks behind her, Happy and John are not there. She then turns in the other direction, toward the lobby.

"Mummy! There ya are!"

Sadie runs toward her son and falls to her knees to embrace him on the carpeted hallway.

"Oh my god I love yu so much, Li'l Dinny," Sadie holds his face.

"I'm John Carter," he says.

"Yu are, John Carter. Mummy's little hero."

"Where were ya?" Happy says. "We was lookin' from pillar to post for ya. Ya know there's a whole bunch o' women down the hall an'—"

Sadie doesn't hear the rest of what Happy explains. As the three walk down the hallway, they come upon the broom closet where the hotelier hides.

She stops and pulls Happy down for a whisper, "D'yu 'ave that revolver?"

"Sure I do."

Sadie looks at the door and clenches her teeth.

Not My Enemy

"Bill wouldn't just come to. . . to kill us like he did those people down in Red Hook, would he?" I wonder aloud.

By the barred door Vincent huffs on his .38 and buffs it on his waistcoat while Henry Browne turns the bowie knife back and forth in front of his confounded face. A collection of cudgels and brickbats are wielded by the other dock-bosses in the light of the arched windows.

I toss my pipe onto Dinny's desk, "He wouldn't do that, would he? If not, we need to make peace with Bill and all his."

The Swede palms the grip of a bail-hook and stares my way, "Petey Behan owns ya an' ya look the other way. Bill kills Mickey Kane an' ya turn the cheek. The war ain't even started an' ya cry for peace. Are ya wit' us or are ya a craven scamp?"

"I just—"

"There's no time for just. Let's go."

I speak to The Swede's back, "Every move we make has to be thought-out. If we take unnecessary chances we risk losing it all. The seat of power," I turn to all. "Our families. Everything."

Vincent mumbles while eyeballing his pistol, "Let's finish it now then."

"Wait," Dinny stops the men from going for the door.

Downstairs a rumpus of men's voices come to us to the tune of dragging stools and drink requests. Then songs begin to waft up through the floor boards. The first round goes down quickly and only whets their appetite for the second, and from up here in the office we are besieged by a sing-along that Bill seems to be leading.

Don't you ever laugh as the hearse goes by,
For you may be the next to die.

Dinny says, "Paddy ordered extra whiskey for the shelves. Let them get lubricated. We call him Minister o' Education for good reason."

"That's right," I remember the words told me when first I came to the Dock Loaders' Club, "There's many a slip 'twixt cup an' lip, an' all that is spilled in Paddy's bar ends up in Dinny's ear."

They wrap you up in a big white sheet
And cover you from head to feet.

"Don' sound like they're talkin' much, just singin'," The Swede says. "Let's go."

"Leave the weapons up here," Dinny orders. "If Bill's men came wit' weapons, we'd've known by now."

The Swede snarls through clenched teeth, "We could end this right now. Who cares if Bill didn' disappear Brosnan. If people think he spilled the ol' tunic's blood, we'd be heroes for cleanin' it up, right?" He nods in my direction. "An' this boy'll stop pissin' his trousers."

"No violence!" Dinny stands from his desk. "We got twice the men they do. We have to offer them our hospitality. If they don' respect it, then and only then do we come out swingin'."

"Shootin'," Vincent corrects.

"But we go down as one. Let's be clear about one thing, Bill is here to recruit men," Dinny points a finger into the desk. "This thing. This room. Upstairs, under the bridge. The power in it. He wants to harness the lightnin' an' turn its power against our own people. This," he points again.

"This is all he wants. An' he'll give up anythin' to get it. So if we give him any idea that there's dissent among us, it'll be blood in the water."

Through the flooring the voices reach up.

> *They put you in a big black box*
> *And cover you with dirt and rocks*
> *All goes well for about a weak,*
> *Until your coffin begins to leak.*

The dockbosses are first down the stairs. The bar is shoulder-to-shoulder with men. In the back by the stairwell are dour faced followers of Dinny while Bill's men are cramped round the mahogany trough by the front door, spilling outside. The street is filled with more of Dinny's men, who surround the visitors but Bill's baying hounds bear their toothy grins to keep the factions separated.

As Dinny makes his way down the stairs, Bill is shaking hands with Beat McGarry who tries to pull his hand away. But Bill won't let go. He holds Beat's shake sternly and smiles toward Dinny. Eventually he lets go and Beat scurries off. Just then the song careens toward its chorus and Bill pounds on the bar to the rhythm. His men follow suit, stamping on the floor and laughing it up.

> *The worms crawl in, the worms crawl out,*
> *The worms play pinochle on your snout*
> *They eat your eyes, they eat your nose,*
> *They eat the jelly between your toes.*

As we approach, Bill's lieutenants form behind him. His Army uniform is newly pressed with a warn sheep's pelt over it, though he makes sure that everyone sees the Distinguished Service Cross that is pinned to his chest. Upon his neck, above the uniformed collar, blisters weep pink puss. Some are scarred over. Never a handsome man, Bill repulses now. A face sculpted by morbid and sullen assuredness.

As the two gangs slowly face each other, Darby Leighton slips in the front door as it closes. He rights his coat as listless eyes pan across the inside of the Dock Loaders' Club.

"Get that one outta here!" The Swede bumps ahead of me. "Eighty-sixt means gone for good an' ever. White flag or no, he goes."

Bill casually looks back at Darby, who freezes at the attention paid him, "He's wit' me, Swede. Like all the other lost soldiers the White Hand tossed away."

The Swede turns incredulously to Dinny, who waves it off with a slow turn of his hand, "Let Darby darken the air wit' his lies so that all the men here can see the light o' truth. Eddie, Freddie, pat him down. If he means to sneak a weapon in here, then this meetin' will be short-lived."

Eddie Hughes slaps at Darby's hand to make him raise them faster while Freddie Cuneen rifles through his pockets and palms his cock and balls. When it's found he is clean, the two shoulder back through the slew of young labormen to Dinny's side.

"These the scarpers that couldn't finish off Garry fookin' Barry?" Non Connors snarls and turns his eyes up to The Swede. "An' yaz got them runnin' security? In our gang we don' raise up them what don' succeed."

Big Dick Morissey growls behind me as Dance Gillen is halted from speaking out when Dinny places a palm on his chest. Meanwhile, Needles Ferry nods out, high from a recent fix. His long, narrow fingers reach across the small table while his mouth gapes like a man in his last gasps.

The Swede turns his rage to the bone-thin junkie, "Fookin' guttersnipe catchpenny," and gives him a kick. But Needles' slack body just slivers bonelessly to the floor until someone drapes him over the table again like a suit on a hanger.

I find myself face to face with bantam Petey Behan, who is even smaller than I remember, yet casts a long shadow over me. Petey and I have a long feud between us ever since he stole a coat right off my shoulders. Dinny wouldn't let me forget about it and made me challenge Petey to a fight on the Belgian bricks behind the Dock Loaders' Club. A fight I lost. Since then I grew taller, while he remains short-legged, though shouldered with broad muscle. Petey has begun to take a leadership role of sorts. He's assumed the mantle of the old Lonergan Crew now that Richie has become a lieutenant.

"Next time ya won' be able to get up, Liam. So this is what I want ya to do. I want ya to put ya lips on it, right here," he holds his crotch. "Open ya mout' see? Up an' down. I see I left my mark on ya too. When ya look in the mirror that scar'll always remind ya that ya're feckless an' infirm. Ya should be sized up for a wooden overcoat now 'cause next time we tangle ya gonna end up in Green-Wood under a tree."

Their side chuckles and crows at that.

I measure his jaw in my mind. I know his moves. He is strong, but I am stronger now. "Next time I'll square things, right like," I glare down.

"Oh did ya first mentor Tommy Tuohey teach ya how to fight? I guess the lessons got cut short though. I was there when that stupit Pavee gypsy took his last breath after I kicked him to sleep wit' all my brothers."

"If you were confident you wouldn't threaten me, Petey. I see you."

"Ye're payin' yer own way, ye are Bill," Paddy suddenly declares. "Ye think ye can galavant in here with a few thick navvies an' call the shots? Sure ye haven't the shame in ye to cause a *rúla búla* an' then on top to if, summon free drinks fer yerself?"

"Fookin' disrespectful o' vet'rans," Non Connors sneers. "Ya breakin' ya own rules already?"

Bill leans across the bar at Paddy and points at Darby's buttoned, rust-color stained shirt, "Ya see these men in here? They got the blood o' I-Talians on them. We took back Red Hook. Ya can use that as payment. Ya're fookin' welcome."

Paddy fires back, "I don't feckin' care if ye killt Oliver Cromwell *and* Queen Elizabeth as the cherry on top, ye're payin' yer own way in this feckin' bar!"

Bill shrugs and removes some crumpled bills from his pocket and slams them on the bar, "Drinks for everybody!"

A roar is sent up at those words, and not just from Bill's men.

"Bill," Dinny's voice can be heard as he slowly raises his head to the rebel leader. Dinny's shoulders partially obscure Bill from my view, but to compare the two would be fruitless. Dinny has a thick trunk, wide neck and the small ears of a fighting dog, while Bill is slight of build and four inches shorter.

"Yeah," Bill runs his tongue over his teeth and goes to his tip-toes to see the many men behind Dinny. "I come here t'day to announce that I am the new leader o' the White Hand an' will take my place upstairs. We need not draw blood or go to war. All that can be avoided. Wit' a handshake, I pledge to Dinny Meehan twenny percent o' all profits gained from tribute for ya to distribute as ya see fit. The men that wanna work. . . They will come to me from here on out."

"Stop sayin' that name," The Swede's bloodshot eyes stare down into Bill's.

"Twenny percent? For doin' nothin'?" Dinny asks.

"For steppin' aside, peaceably."

"All because ya announce it?" Dinny says loud enough for all to hear. "Ya must think ya'self some kinda god, amblin' in here wit' those words on ya lips."

"We are not your sheep any longer. We will not follow ya over a cliff. Me? I am fated! The signs are unmistakable, an' they all point upward. I will sit atop Irishtown soon enough, even as ya send dagos against me," Bill rounds on him in a black fury and shows everyone the bullet scar that cut through the hair over one of his fawn ears. "That's from one o' ya I-Talian assassins. An' if that wasn't enough, ya had me charged wit' murderin' him. Then I took the plea an' joined the Army where I inhaled enough mustard gas to kill a stegosaurus," Bill addresses the entire room with an arm extended into Dinny's face. "This is how ya sheepherder rewards his drove."

"Ya rebelled against Irishtown an' killt one o' my enforcers," Dinny too speaks to all in the room. "Would anyone here've honored my dignity if I looked the other way?"

"So ya make a deal wit' the Black Hand against ya own people?"

"I got no qualms wit' anyone willin' to work wit' me," Dinny announces, then faces his opponent directly. "Bill? We worked together in the past. We need to think as one on things again. The true threat to us all is on the rise an' in the wise words o' Detective William Brosnan, the real enemy will leave us all in a welter o' our own blood an' bones. . . Ya come to our headquarters to recruit my men, an' I allow it. But I want ya to know I'm here to recruit you. Come back to us, Bill. If ya don', we'll all be wiped out an' hist'ry will never know Irishtown existed. To come back to us, I offer ya inside information. There is a true threat on ya head, Bill. This Scarfaced Al comin' up from the south."

"It's true, Bill," Vincent leans back against the crook in the bar with both thumbs under suspenders. "I got it from a good source."

The Swede buts in, "Don' confuse him wit' facts, Vincent. His mind's already made up."

"He's after blood vengeance," Dinny picks it up. "If ya join us again, I can talk Sixto Stabile an' Frankie Yale outta sendin' him after ya."

Bill snarls, "Sounds like a bribe."

Bill doesn't like it when power is taken from him. Even when it's in the form of caring.

"This guy ain't like other I-Talians," Dinny continues. "This guy? He's on the up. Two hundret pounds. Meat fists. An' surrounded by a group o' maniacs. Besides," Dinny looks out the window, then back down to Lovett's eyes. "Some things should be kept between us, ya know? Outsiders got no business in our territories, even if we fight amongst ourselves. Don' matter, right Bill?"

Bill looks round as slow nods come from both sides of the room.

"Here's my second thing," Dinny presents his offer. "Ya will have autonomy in Red Hook. Give Irishtown fifty percent o' the tribute money ya earn, an' we will provide ya more strength against any future I-Talian incursions. I will even name ya to my council wit' an equal say alongside The Swede. Accept these terms an' the enemies o' the White Hand will tremble again when the worst thing possible happens; Dinny Meehan and Bill Lovett shake hands. A united Irish-America right here in Brooklyn."

Bill looks down at Dinny's extended arm, then looks beyond Dinny to the men who stand behind him, "For six years he has sat upon his throne upstairs. A throne he won wit' blood. He will tell yaz, as he told me, that wit' every vict'ry, there will be losses. He won that chair not only wit' the blood o' Christie the Larrikin, but by throwin' Pickles Leighton under the trolley. Yeah, he rules t'day, but he will fall like the rest an' when we string him up an' the swains who support him, I will turn to the rest o' yaz. An' I promise I will *personally* separate the sheep from the wolves. Unlike this guy who would put a crown o' thorns on his own head so the world could see him as a victim. I will reward the wolves, while the sheep will be slain. Ask ya'self this; what are ya? A follower o' a fake messiah, or a wolf ready to join the new pack? 'Cause if ya're a sheep, ye'll be slaughtered."

Dinny steps forward, "Slaughtered? Just like my cousin? That's what most people around here are sayin', at least. Ya seen him around, Bill? My cousin Mickey Kane? The dockboss o' Red Hook."

Bill's coal black eyes turn to Dinny. His lips tighten angrily until a hyena smile appears on his face, "We heard he went for a swim durin' the storm."

Dinny lowers his voice and moves even closer, "Ya killt'em, didn' ya Bill?"

"Nah, I heard ya did it ya'self."

Opposite me, Petey Behan sniggers and one-arm Joey Flynn quarks in response, *caw, caw, caw*.

"Bill," Dinny says. "I'm askin' ya, man to man. . . Is he dead? Should I tell my aunt to stop believin' he's gonna come back? Did ya kill him?"

"Nah, I didn't kill him," Bill looks round his men and slowly raises a pointed finger. "Richie did."

We all turn our eyes to Richie Lonergan behind Bill's left shoulder, but the teen is undaunted. As his head slowly swivels toward us, his eyes change from gray to blue when the light that sprays through the front window reaches them.

"I guess ya made ya choice between Bill an' I, eh Richie?" Dinny nods toward him.

Richie shifts his weight from the wooden peg to his one good leg without a suggestion of shame in his distant, high-cheekbone eyes, "Guess so."

Vincent tosses hair off his eye and puts a hand on Dinny's shoulder, "Richie, if it wasn't for this man, ya little brother an' sister would be in pauper's graves right now. An' he's always made good for ya Ma all these years. Paid the rent for ya place on Johnson Street an' the bike shop on Bridge Street—"

"Bribes," Bill interrupts. "Don' listen to him, Richie. They made a fortune in graft an' tried to buy ya loyalty. Ya made a decision to join me based on respect, not payoffs. All o' these men here t'day what support me and my claim do so outta respect. They was lost before, an' they come to me. Ya set them free Dinny, 'cause ya had no use for them. An' now they're found. They summoned me to lead them. Understand? An' if ya don' move outta the way peaceably," Bill raises his voice. "I say put the crown o' thorns on his head an' we'll nail him to the Brooklyn Bridge so the rest o' us can get on wit' the future."

"Bill, ya ain't my enemy," Dinny turns round and raises his voice. "Bill Lovett ain't our enemy. I ain't Bill Lovett's enemy. We are two sides o' the same coin. Two factions from the same clan. The real enemy is out there an' we gotta come together to fight it shoulder-to-shoulder. Now look at what's happenin' t'day. Look around, Bill. Everywhere. The signs. The symbols. We are headed for a bloody downfall if we fight amongst ourselves. I ask ya to set ya differences aside an' join wit' us against the real enemy who haunts us; Wolcott an' his patsy errand-boy, Garry fookin' Barry. Ya're my fam'ly, Bill. We're fam'ly. Because ya fam'ly was side-by-side wit' mine down in Jackson Hollow."

"Where's Jackson Hollow?" Bill lowers his eyes.

"Jackson Hollow was where our fam'lies squatted when they got off the boat in the 1840s. They came shoeless. In rags, but they survived. My father was a child an' only a few shacks away from ya grandparents in the empty lots. Ya see, we're cinched by blood, Bill. Back then the newspapers compared our fam'lies to pigs an' wild dogs, thievin' monkeys. They still do, yet ya bow to them. There's a lotta shit goin' on around Brooklyn, but what do the papers choose to write about? Tilda's Tears? They talk about one guy that ya beat up instead o' all the wrongs that are done by the businesses in Brooklyn to the strugglin' fam'lies who have to break the law to put shoes on their children's feet. That's because the newspapers *are* businesses. An' both o' us? We're the enemy. We are the enemy o' the Waterfront Assembly who wants nothin' more than to have us fight each other. Do ya need to rule so badly that ya'd accept the support o' our true enemy. They've been doin' this to our people for generations. Dividin' us, to conquer us. Do ya hear me? We come from the same mother, we do. We have our differences, but if we're gonna survive we gotta work this out between us. Here Bill. I offer my hand in truce," Dinny pushes an open palm toward Bill again. "Accept my terms, or ask for better terms. Do as ya think is right, but ya're not my enemy, Bill. Ya never were."

Bill looks at Dinny chancing an arm for peace. He turns his head as if to recall some long-forgotten memory from a past life until his eyes move up to meet Dinny's. Non Connors goes to his ear, but Bill glares at him as if he were a stranger, then looks out into some distance over Dinny's shoulder. Darby then comes to Bill, though he keeps staring off. Finally, Abe Harms noodles in from behind and whispers no more than three words into his ear and suddenly Bill snaps his head back and forth.

"It's weakness what causes ya to ask for peace from the man who killt ya cousin. Ya want I should join forces wit' weakness?" But Bill appears shaken and holds two fingers to his temple, "How. . . How'd ya know about my fam'ly? When. . . When I was in France, I had a vision. I saw'r everythin'. It all came to me. The journey o' the Lovett fam'ly from shoeless an' unknown to all-powerful. I saw'r my grandfather stick fightin' in a place similar to what ya describe, but also I saw'r myself upstairs, leader o' the White Hand an' all the territories. I had it. It was mine. An' everyone followed me! That dream. I mean, it was a vision.

It is my fate. An' the moon. The mornin' moon. It foretold my ascension."

"The moon foretells what your heart requests. The desperate turn to fate or destiny as their claim. But nothin's prewritten, Bill. Here's what I do know, the Black Hand wants revenge," Dinny looks round to all in the room, "If ya choose our enemies to help ya, then ya no better than the Butlers o' Ormonde," His eyes glint with intensity. "Ya can't be happy when a fellow Irishman takes the war to our enemy an' succeeds. Nah, instead ya begrudge them, because nothin' cheers up the cheerless like misfortune upon the cheerful."

Paddy the tender chortles in agreement.

"The FitzGeralds o' Desmond rebelled against the English because they wanted to rid the world o' Gaelic traditions an' turn us out. *Twice* they rebelled. The FitzGeralds an' the Butlers were fam'ly, neighbors. Like we are. Related by marriage and blood," Dinny nods toward Darby. "But the Butlers wouldn't stand wit' the FitzGeralds because they saw'r opportunity, see? So they joined the English against their own kind. Because o' that, thousands died o' disease an' hunger, famine and malnutrition as the English and the Butlers scorched the earth, burnt crops an' drove the livestock. Women, children, the sick an' the old were put to the sword. They even butchered those who had yielded an' were sworn quarter. Exiled the rest. Sure the Butlers won, but what was left?
The English took the most tillable land an' gave it to those who were loyal to their crown. The Munster Plantation they called it. More like the Munster clearing. Ya want that to happen here?"

Bill shakes away the suggestion, "I never heard o' that story before in my life."

"Because ya don' know ya hist'ry. In place o' hist'ry ya fill in the blanks wit' what ya call fate. Then ya bend facts in two an' wonder why only half the world believes ya," Dinny motions to all in the room. "Should we allow this man to lead us right into the teeth o' our enemy? Or should we stand together against it?"

Bill runs a thumb and index finger along his upper lip, then speaks aloud, "He would have us debate the past all day long. But I. . . I will give yaz the future!" Bill looks over his shoulder. "The men that follow me cut a new path, like true-blue Americans. Patriots. They'd never follow him for the riches o' an ancient glory that was lost to the English. What man wants to follow the weak into the past?"

Outside one hundred men stand in the cobblestoned Bridge Street under a slab of ashen gray clouds. Through the front windows I see two boys wend through them but halt when Bill's shit-yellow hound sits up with a tongue lolling out of its mouth.

"I made ya an offer, Bill."

"An' I did you as well."

"Do ya refuse me?"

"I do. Ya refuse me?"

Dinny does not answer that, instead he lowers his voice, "Bill Lovett, I call ya to challenge."

All men in the room stifle a gasp.

Chisel McGuire's eyes go white, "A challenge!" He yells out from behind in his barker's voice. "We have a challenge!"

"A challenge!" Paddy Keenan mirrors and throws down two glasses to fill them with home-brew poteen.

Dinny picks up one of the glasses and holds it in front of Bill. Bill then reaches across to the bar and holds it high against Dinny's, "I challenge ya to a one-on-one fight the ol' way, from the olden days," Dinny announces. "Winner takes the Red Hook territory square up. Do ya accept?"

Bill's face is stone and his ears redden at the proposal. But it is no mere suggestion for him to consider. If refused, a man cannot walk among us without scorn on his name and he will never rise above his station, if he isn't shamed out of Irishtown altogether. I had never seen anyone defy the challenge, but if Wild Bill Lovett is known for anything it is breaking code, if it benefits him. The shot of poteen shakes in his hand and the angered look on his face allows us all to believe he could spill it on the floor to sate his contempt for the old ways. Abe Harms ducks under a few awestruck faces and leaves Bill with whispered words. There is silence in the saloon but outside the sound of snapping dogs and a collection of growls rise and fall.

"I further that challenge," Bill growls and holds his poteen above Dinny's, then labors resentfully through the routine. "I challenge ya to a one-on-one fight the ol' way, from the olden days. But not for Red Hook. No. Winner takes the White Hand an' all the territories, square up. . . Do ya accept?"

"Yes!" Darby yells out.

"Shaddup," Bill snaps.

A sadness comes across Dinny's face that no one would have noticed unless you know him as we do. Dinny has had many challenges. But this is different. This has been in the making for many, many years.

"I accept," Dinny announces.

As the two of them throw back their drinks, the bar explodes in celebration.

"Wait, wait," Paddy Keenan stops everyone. "Wait a second! Where will it take place? Where will the fight be?"

Dinny clears his throat, "Jackson Hollow. Meet me in the field o' honor, an' I will try it out wit' ya."

All eyes blink toward Bill.

He's lost already. His face says it all. He is nervous.

"On one condition," Bill says, but before he can speak his mind, a bubbling cough comes to his throat. When it subsides, he snorts back phlegm from his sinuses and speaks. "We do it in June."

"June? Let's do it today," The Swede bellows. "Do it now."

Dinny nods in agreement, "He needs time to recover from his war wounds. I want no excuses. We do it in June. Next two rounds are on me. Everyone drinks."

But Bill is not festive and neither are those in his inner circle. Tradition has it that regardless of bad blood, on the day a challenge is accepted all are to come together in fine spirit while the whiskey flows. A true man does not begrudge another. A man of honor gives praise to the virility in a rival faction fight.

Dinny has an elbow on the bar and one-by-one greets every man who wishes to be heard with attentive courtesy.

Many go from Dinny to Bill, but all go to Chisel McGuire to place money. Odds quickly are in Dinny's favor, for not only has Dinny never lost a fistfight, but he is bigger, stronger and faster than his foe. When I look at Bill in the corner, he scratches at the blisters that weep down his neck. He seems not to have slept in weeks and the hollows in his face are dark bruises, black as his lightless eyes. When his stomach seizes up and bends him, he grits his teeth to suppress a cough but it bursts out of his mouth anyhow, leaving red strands of spittle to hang down his cyan-colored lips.

I sit with my back to the bar at Dinny's left when two ten year-old boys sneak a peek through the front door.

"Go on," Beat washes a backhand toward them, wishing them away.

But Dinny's eyes are alight and taps my arm to let them pass.

As I pull the door open the rest of the way, the two ogle their eyes up to me, "Whoa, it's Poe, the Thief o' Pencils."

It is rare that anyone calls me Poe, a name given to me because Beat McGarry confused a poem by Walter Whitman for Edgar Allen Poe. And Thief of Pencils, of course, came because I had in fact stolen a pencil.

I recognize his broth-of-a-boy mannerisms as Johnny Mullen's son, one of Dinny's oldest followers who died of the grippe after coming home from the war.

"Is there something we can help you with?" I ask the boy.

"See, he is Irish," he elbows the other boy, whose last name is Sutton. "Ya can hear it on him. Admit it's true, Will."

"Ya right, I thought he was from here, but he's true-Irish," Mullen looks up. "Is it true ya killt ya own uncle to join the gang?"

"No," I move to close the door on them.

"Wait!" the boys yelp. "Harry Reynolds is dead."

I open the door again, "Dead? He can't be. Where did you hear that?"

Mullen, the talker, pushes the door open with a small hand, "They burnt his buildin' down. Over on Atlantic. The firemen've been fightin' it all mornin'. There's five dead so far. Five charred remains o' people at least."

I turn wordlessly to Dinny, who waves the boys over with a smile. Mullen and Sutton tiptoe in and bend their heads up to the ceiling and the walls as if they've just entered Taj Mahal. "Look Will, there's the ol' photo o' Lincoln. It's true!"

"Jee wow," Sutton mumbles and tilts back his floppy cap to get a look.

Like silly supplicants the boys move toward a smiling Dinny Meehan. His thighs are thicker than their chests and he reaches a muscular hand toward them for a shake.

"Ya don' shake a man's hand limp," Dinny says. "Try it again. Dig your hand in deep and grip, then look in my eyes when ya do so. . . That's it. Ya give me a dead fish like that again an' I'll have The Swede give yaz the boot. Ya wanna stick around o' what?"

"Yeah," they agree in unison with big eyes, watching Big Dick and The Lark balance four beer mugs on Needles Ferry's cadaverous head while four lit cigarettes hang out of each nostril.

"This one's been dead from the neck up since birth," The Swede growls.

"Try to shake my hand again then," Dinny says to the boys. "That's it, thrust an' grip. Then give me the eye. I like it. Much better. Harry dead ya say?"

"Yeah."

"Ya saw'r him dead?"

"No."

"Then how do ya know?"

Mullen licks his lips and gathers his courage, "He's prolly the reason they burnt it down."

"Who?"

The boys look at each other fearfully and turn their eyes up, "Garry fookin' Barry."

"He the one behind Brosnan's disappearance too, ya think?"

"Yeah."

"Who else is wit' him?"

"James Cleary an' Wiz the Lump. They work for Wolcott an' the Waterfront Assembly."

"Smart kids," Dinny taps my arm, then addresses the two again. "Who else?"

They look at each other and shrug.

"Why do yaz think they went after Harry?"

Mullen again, "On account o' he's loyal to ya an' they wanna see a changeover. A new king atop Irishtown."

"Anybody else they got their eye on, ya think?"

Mullen turns his downcast eyes in my direction, "The most loyal an' most valuable to ya. Garry fookin' Barry's goin' on a tear an' everyone knows he never gives up. Poe Garrity's next."

Dinny looks at me, then speaks to the boys, "It'd probably be smart if Poe got himself a righthand that's hard as iron. Someone who has a personal hist'ry wit' Barry an' enjoys dancin' on people's faces." He stops for a moment. "An' maybe Poe should carry a pistol on his person, don' ya think?"

"Yeah," they boys agree.

Darby Leighton and his sallow cheeks and dead eyes walk over, "Hey boys, d'yaz wanna meet Wild Bill?"

Mullen shies away and looks back up to Dinny, but Sutton goes with Darby to the corner. Bill doesn't offer to shake hands with the boy and stares at them harshly with black eyes under two thick, arched eyebrows.

"I hope Will gives him a dead fish," Mullen says.

Dinny's tone becomes serious, "Ya first name's Johnny?"

"Yeah."

"I'm sorry about ya father, kid. He was a good man. A soldier for the White Hand an' America, too. Most kids would be proud to have a man like that as a father," Dinny taps me again. "Let the kid sit down, yeah?"

"Sure."

"Paddy, give the kid a glass o' the pure."

"One pure fer the bhoy, t'is," Paddy agrees warmly. "The son o' one our own's always welcome to a drink in this establishment, he is."

Johnny Mullen Jr. raises the glass to his lips and lets it bite him. Breathing fire, he puts it down and fights off the sting of the homebrew. "Fuck, that's smarts," he says

Dinny slaps him gently on a thin shoulder. Johnny Jr. looks back to him and gives a demure smile. Then suddenly tears come pouring out of the boy's eyes that he is unable fight off, but I'm unsure if it's because of his father's death, or that he has finally met his hero.

Dinny jumps off the stool. He pulls the boy by his arm, "Turn around an' look straight ahead at the wall. That feelin' that wells up inside ya? That's anger, passion, feelin'. Hold on to it. Don' let it control ya. It's a matter o' life an' death, see? Get on top o' it. There'll be a moment when ya can use that feelin', but now's not that time. Wipe it away an' put a hard shell on ya mug so no one else can have it. It's yours, not theirs. There ya go. Save it. Save it for later."

Johnny Jr.'s eyes search the room to see if anyone had seen his tears. He scratches angrily at his chin and tucks his hands into fists at the bar, "I'm gonna be a real fighter one day, that's why they call me Whyo. Whyo Mullen, an' I ain't one ya should whistle down the wind at, like Will over there. We used to call him Willie, but there's too many Willie's around. And he can't have the same name as Willie Lonergan 'cause Willie Lonergan's tough and Will is a poltroon. His Ma still writes his name in his underwear. But I'm brave, an' I know everythin' about the gang." he gives a hard stare to Dinny. "An' I can help ya too."

I whisper to Dinny, "Garry Barry wouldn't come here to burn this place down too, would he?"

Blind the Predators

Anna recognizes the voice behind the door, "What do ya want, Matty."

"Matty who?" Grace whispers.

"Martin," Anna rolls her eyes. "One o' my brother's tomfools."

The door opens and the skinny kid with a big adam's apple and pushback black hair steps in. "Hi, um, hey—"

"What do ya want?" Anna stands in front of him with her arms crossed.

But Matty's eyes are full of Grace's breasts that are visible through her sleeveless shift while his mouth is empty of words. He looks at Anna, then back at Grace's breasts.

"Matty!" Anna yells.

"Uh. . . it's ya Ma wants to see ya. She had a fit."

"What kinda fit?"

"Ya father eh, he said somethin' to her."

"What did he say?"

"He said um," Matty faces his shoes, then back up to Anna until he notices the dress. "Why are ya wearin' that kinda dress?"

"I'm only wearin' this 'cause. . . Never mind, what did my father tell her?"

"He told ya Ma that ya're a slattern an' that ya slept wit' a man for dime at the Adonis an' that's how ya got money to pay for rent an' food before the storm."

"She did no such thing," Grace exclaims. "We would know."

Matty tilts his head as if to say that doesn't matter, "Ya Ma says ya're the Mary Magdelene."

"Mary Magdelene?" Anna tries to remember her childhood listening to the homilies of Father Larkin at St. Ann's Roman Catholic Church.

"Yeah, the prostitute in the bible."

Kit grumbles through cigarette smoke, "Laugh Anna, it's a comedy o' miscues we have here. Pure slapstick, Mary Magdelene was not a—"

But Matty speaks over her, "Yeah Anna, but ya Ma says ya been victimized by some sort o' devilish possession an' she wants ya come to her so ya can be saved by penitence. Then at least ya will be known as a penitent prostitute."

Kit chuckles, which turns into a wet cough.

"Penitent fookin' prostitute," Anna balls up her fists and walks toward the window in thought.

My own mother believes me a whore. All I want to do is hide from their slavery, but they yank my chain as soon as I flee. Can't I mourn the loss of my love in peace?

Outside the wind breathes and the heaving trees wade in swirls above the old headstones and sloped walkways as Grace, Kit and Matty await her response.

Anna now completely turns her back on everyone in the room and walks to the window. From behind a tomb in the cemetery the emaciated red-headed woman appears again, shoeless. She stares back at Anna with a mop of hair in the shape of the surrounding willow trees. A tear comes to Anna's eye, but she balls her fists tight until it dries up.

That is me. If I stay here. If I ignore the love in my heart, that is who I will become; an old woman wandering among cemetery stones. Now I understand that I must surrender to the love in my heart, not to Neesha. Neesha doesn't exist. Neesha is just a dream, a story, a symbol of my love. The love I must surrender to. My true love, in real life, is my family. That's what Neesha was saying. Surrender to my love. That's it. Now I understand. I have to go home to my family.

"Anna, what are ya gonna do?" Grace asks.

She quickly turns on her heel, "I need to change outta this. What else do ya have Kit?"

"Other than dresses for the Adonis? I dunno, a white peasant blouse an' maybe a skirt. A long plaid skirt."

"Let me have that instead."

"Ya can't wear that outfit outside, Anna," Grace gawks. "Ya don' wanna look like a gypsy immigrant."

"What do I care?"

Kit takes a drag and talks through the exhale, "Ya don' have to dress up to be pretty in a man's eyes, just make ya'self look half stupit. That's twice as much as he needs."

Grace has loss in her eyes and cries out, "But I don' want ya to go nowhere, Anna. Where ya gonna sleep now?"

"Home. I'm goin' home. Should I let my own mother think I sold myself? Nah, I gotta set her straight, an' everyone else."

Grace looks back to Anna with innocent eyes, "But I thought ya said that don' matter? That people believe what they want, not what's true or factual, an' that ya not a slave to their idears?"

Kit chuckles at that, "A woman is a many-colored creature who camouflages desire to blind her predators."

"Anna, what about what ya was talkin' about," Grace bulges her eyes, not wanting to say the words in front of Matty. "What we was talkin' about, ya know?"

Protection. She is talking about who I can get to help protect her when she testifies in the trial so she can tell the truth about who really killed Christie Maroney.

"I'll get back to ya on that, I promise."

"Oh please, please do," Grace says.

"Until then," Anna grabs at Grace's wrist. "Peggy Kelly, uhright?"

"I understand."

Anna then turns to Kit and holds both her hands in her own, "Thanks for all ya advice, Kit."

"Advice? Ya want advice? Never kiss a frog 'cause he ain't but just another dirty dog."

"There are no princes, are there?"

"Princes," Kit scowls at the notion. "Get outta here wit' that. Princes are for dreams, right?"

"What are yaz talkin' about?" Matty's mouth goes sideways in wonder.

"Girls have secrets, Matty. Ya don' know that by now?" Grace scolds.

"Secrets are dangerous. Girl secrets are the mostest of all."

Outside, with Matty behind her, Anna storms down the long slope on Twenty-Fourth Street as her shadow rushes ahead. Down the hill's steep distance a church spire stretches into the sky while Red Hook's grain elevators and sugar refineries bend over the waterfront. And even further still, the Statue of Liberty reaches up and out of the water to protect the flame. The cornices and rooftops descend like giant's steps on both sides of the street, framing the New York Harbor beyond. Over her shoulders Anna's fox-colored mane whips behind her. Unfurling down her back and snapping like a flag in the gales as she strides downhill toward the Fifth Avenue Elevated Train.

"What's not Richie's fault?" Matty calls up ahead. "I heard ya yellin' that somethin' wasn't Richie's fault. What were yaz talkin' about?"

"Shaddup," Anna hurls back.

Matty had loved her since they were but moppets on the Irishtown sidewalks. She thinks of the time when he first told her while playing stoopball on Johnson Street.

"I love ya," he said and showed her his hairless cock. That had no effect on her since she had many younger brothers with the same bald wiggle-worm as Matty. Before that she was unaware love had anything to do with private parts. A month later he asked her to play stink finger when they were in her basement with all her siblings. Instinctively she refused. But the more she ignored his advances, the more he desired her.

Now, walking down 24th Street she could feel his eyes watching her from behind. That only made her want to walk like a man, but no matter what she did it always only seemed to arouse him.

How am I going to set fools like him straight?

But Matty had proved to be a good source of information. He had told her about how Bill Lovett was going to the

Dock Loaders' Club to recruit Dinny's men. A war veteran always has the right of things amongst the working class. But a decorated war veteran has their hearts in his palm.

On Fifth Avenue they ascend the train station stairs, Matty running up behind her. When Anna sees the train is about to leave, she runs in before the doors close. But Matty thrusts his hand through the doorway and looks down to the conductor. He then pulls the door open and enters as Anna rolls her eyes.

Suddenly Matty grabs her arm, "We could leave together. Go to, I dunno, what city ya ever wanted to see? We could go somewhere an' forget all this. Have a fam'ly. Think about makin' payments on a house so we can pass it down. Our kids'd say they were born in the house they had kids in, ya know? We could start somethin'. Build somethin'. We could ponder the future, Anna. Out in the new suburbs they do a lot o' ponderin' an'—"

"There is no future. There's just now," Anna mumbles.

"Bill said he don' want ya around no more," Matty has spite in his tone now. "Or them slatterns ya hang out wit' either."

As the train slows for their stop, Matty sits closer to her.

"We're almost there, ya can go away now," Anna finally responds to him.

"It's just dangerous for a girl to walk around wit'out a escort," Matty said.

So he thinks I'm a whore but he wants to escort and run away with me anyhow.

Anna flutters her butterfly eyes and looks at him demurely, "Do ya think I really did what they say?"

Matty is stumped, "I dunno."

"Can I admit somethin' to ya?"

"Sure sure."

"I'm still pure."

"Then how did—"

"Matty."

"Wha?"

"Whatever ya heard, it's not true. I may have gotten money to feed my fam'ly, an' I may have friends that work at the Adonis, but never, ever did I sleep wit' nobody. I'm surprised at ya, Matty. Ya've known me ya whole life."

Matty looks down at his shoes and sticks his tongue in his cheek, then looks back up to her, "Ya're pure?"

She shakes her head at him, "Just don' tell nobody, promise? Can I trust ya?"

"Uhright."

You're a puppet and I got hold of your strings, Anna smiles. *Tell them what they want to hear, that's how you set fools straight. Blind them with their own fanciful desires, not your own.*

"But ya can't walk around wit' them fookin' slatterns no more, Grace an' Kit. They're whores, Anna."

Anna stops, "An' in ya world, where am I?"

"What do ya mean?"

"Answer me. Where am I? Are ya above me?"

"Ya're a girl."

"So is that a yes? Ya're above me then? Ya're better than me?"

"I—"

"Ya don' wanna admit that I am, but ya believe it," She walks out of the train at the Sands Street Station along the sloped abutment of the Brooklyn Bridge toward the stairwell.

"C'mon Anna, I mean—"

"Ya're just a thick Brooklyn yob at the bottom o' a teenage gang—"

"I'm not at the bottom—"

"My mother's brother was Yakey Yake Brady an' my father was his enforcer. My brother Richie is the leader o' the gang ya're in, but I'm still below ya?"

"Everyone thinks ya whore'd ya'self, so that makes ya—"

"But ya know it's not true."

"I mean ya told me it's not true but—"

"An' if ya believe it, if ya truly love me, ya'd be a man an' stand up for me."

"Well yeah."

"Good then," she says as Matty tries to catch up to her down the hill on Bridge Street, getting closer and closer to the water now.

"But it don' change the fact that ya're a girl."

"I'm a woman," Anna says without looking back. "I'm eighteen."

"Ya ain't a real woman 'til ya have children."

"I have thirteen children," Anna spits back.

"Those are ya siblin's. An' ya don' even pay much attention to them no more."

"I got thirteen god'amn children, but that don' even make me a women? I'll tell ya what makes a woman. A woman makes up her own mind. Which means there ain't hardly a woman anywhere in this world."

"Yet ya call ya'self one?"

"I do," She spins on her heel. "An' if Bill doesn't want anythin' to do wit' me, then why does he have ya escort me around?"

"He don't," Matty responds. "Richie does."

Richie. My sweet, wordless big brother. He knows me. But does he believe I slept with men for money as Bill told him?

Richie Lonergan may report to Bill Lovett, but Anna knows that he loves her. The best sort of love there is; boundless, unending love. The subtle kindnesses he offered her throughout their childhood had always touched her. Somewhere Richie wants to help, but can't.

He can't even speak on account of all the horrors he's experienced.

The Lonergan fury is in Richie, just as much as it is in her. That much they share. She had seen her big brother brawl many times on the street. When he lets his fists fly, no one can stop him. When Richie was caught cutpursing by three men at the Sands Street Station, he had broken one man's collar bone, another man's jaw and threw the last down a flight of stairs from the third to second floor. Then he slid down the handrail and picked the man up over his head and heaved him down to the sidewalks.

Having one leg meant nothing to Richie Lonergan. When he fought Red Donnelly behind the Dock Loaders'

Club, Anna was there. She saw it all. Red threw one punch and missed. Then Richie's eyes lit up and he attacked like a rabid wolf with the scent of blood in its mouth. Richie beat Red Donnelly to sleep right there on the Belgian bricks.

Richie, she nods her head in silence. *Richie could be my most diligent, loyal ally.*

On the sidewalk outside of the Lonergan bicycle shop on Bridge Street between York and Front streets, the barefoot girls play potsy with a small puck, while the boys hold rocks and paving stones, awaiting a rat to peak its head out of the sewer. The boys with suspenders that hold up their big trousers had laid soggy bread on the grate as bait.

Anna's stomach turns when a sense of deja vu washes over her like waves. Then she looks up above the Lonergan bicycle shop to the three-story pre-Civil War clapboard tenement where many families reside in one-window, musty rooms. Just then, an unkindness of ravens dart across the leaden sky amidst the rooftops.

Neesha, now I remember.

In dream, Neesha had told her something that she had heard before, but couldn't remember from where.

You have the will of a prophetess and the future is yours to shape, he told her. *But it was Mrs. O'Flaherty who said it first.*

Last month Mrs. O'Flaherty from the second floor died. She came to Brooklyn from County Galway way back in 1850. Dinny Meehan had her waked upstairs and paraded her casket through the cobblestoned streets to bury her in a proper grave down in Green-Wood Cemetery. A proper grave was the only thing Mrs. O'Flaherty requested, since three of her siblings and her father had all died on roadsides back in Ireland during the hunger times.

When Anna was younger she would often run "tae" up to Mrs. O'Flaherty, who sometimes spoke in the old language, but always had strange things to say.

Once the old woman touched her hand and looked at her with windswept, bright blue eyes.

"Child," she croaked. "Ye're more than a princess. Ye're a prophetess, ye know it? The Ghost God has touched ye an' will come to ye one day, so he will."

Anna stood with her mouth open in her sack dress with a torn sleeve and old beaten boots.

"It's true," the pitch of the old woman's voice went high. "A child o' a lost tribe who will grow very old, like me. But!" Mrs. O'Flaherty's finger went in the air to procure attention. "Ye may foretell the future, t'is true, t'is true. Because the future is yers to shape."

Now two people have told me the same thing, Anna realizes while still she stares above the Lonergan bicycle shop. *Though one of them was dead and in my dreams.*

Anna looks down and turns her hand so the light can gleam on the gold surface of her wreath-of-vine ring.

She thinks of the stories she heard as a child in the old part of Irishtown, closer to the water. There was "Dierdre of the Sorrows" of course, who foresaw the man she would marry when a raven landed in the snow with its bloody prey. But Dierdre's story ended badly and she killed herself when she was taken as wife of the old king.

Will my story end badly too? Anna wonders.

Then there was the willful and ruthless Gráinne who also had an older man as a suitor. But Gráinne's powers were much more appealing, she had the *geis*, the curse-gift that she put on the younger man Diarmuid to make him fall in love with her. He was a skilled fighter and a beloved member of the ancient Fenian warriors, but he eventually died too. Anna bows her head when she realizes that there is nothing in the old stories for her to learn from.

Or is there? I'll just have to make my own story, she thinks, *though mine already has its share of sorrow and death.*

A swirling, unsettled breeze comes up the Bridge Street hill from the water, carrying with it the brine of the East River. Dead fish and locomotive grease mingle in Anna's nose as she grits her teeth again and flexes her fists at the end of both arms.

Lowering her eyes to the entrance of the bicycle shop, she stomps by her brood of siblings and the scabby-kneed jackanapes of Bridge Street. Without noticing her, the boys suddenly screech in unison and heave their paving stones at a pink nose that had sniffed at the bread from below the sewer grate while the girls stop playing potsy to see about the commotion. With hoarse laughs the children run to look down the grate and see if they hit the mark when a babe of no more than three years belatedly throws his rock, hitting another child in the ear. A flood of angry tears come in response.

Anna pushes through the children to see who is crying, but when it is a dark-haired boy who does not own the surname Lonergan, she pushes back through the slew of street urchins toward the bicycle shop's glass door, leaving the kid to his tears.

"Anna, ya're back!" Her little sisters Sarah and Catherine yell up to her.

"Yay!" Little James and Patrick hug at her thigh through the plaid skirt.

"My little ones," Anna runs her fingers through their windblown, dirty blonde heads. "My children. Yes I'm back. Back for ya. An' I'll never leave yaz again."

"Promise it," Julia screams.

"I promise," Anna smiles until she sees two teen sentries that guard the entrance to the Lonergan Bicycle shop.

They are members of Richie's gang that had been enveloped by Bill's boys when he returned from the war. Short and stout Petey Behan stands with his arms crossed and a smirk on his square head. Timothy Quilty stares at Anna with hands dangling round his thighs and his gob open to show his big buck teeth.

"Ya ma's inside," Matty comes to her ear.

Anna takes a deep breath, "An' so it begins."

A Dire Choice

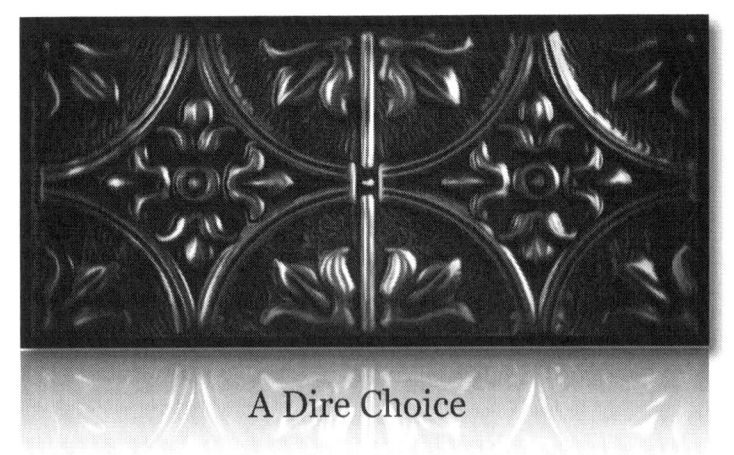

Sadie Meehan could not sleep all night. When the darkness turned to light outside the hotel window, her trepidation piqued. Flashes of unsettling worries plague her now and waves of tingles rush up and down her spine. The hotelier will be up in room 310 soon. Waiting for her. Waiting with her ring.

Two letters had arrived for Sadie at the hotel on Long Island. Though she had sent out many more, only two people responded.

Liam Garrity's letter has twice the amount of money he normally sends. The letter inside simply says, "He's back. Come home. The extra is for passage."

Sweet Liam. Naive Liam. He does not know that my decision is made. I am never going back to Brooklyn.

A choice had been thrust upon her. A simple choice. A horrifying choice. A choice between her husband and her son. And although she questions most of the decisions she has made recently as she sits in the dark on the small chair by the hotel window overlooking the car park, at least this she is certain.

Every time Sadie thinks of her son following in his father's footsteps, her stomach turns. It does not matter that Dinny Meehan's fight is an honorable one, danger is danger.

Her choice riddles her with shame. Yet her choice is final. When it was reported Dinny's cousin Mickey Kane had disappeared in the same area, Red Hook, where Bill Lovett had resurfaced, she knew. And she decided. And she knows now that even though Dinny Meehan had pulled her out of the depravity and poverty she'd known all her life, she could not expose her son to the dangers of her husband's world. But what turns her assuredness to helplessness and finally shame, is Dinny's belief that no child is guilty of the crime of poverty. And he acts on that belief every single day. But it is his selflessness what attracts danger, to be sure.

When Tiny Thomas Lonergan died of an infection from walking shoeless in Brooklyn, Dinny and the gang acted. Within a week every child in Brooklyn wore Hanan boots. In Irishtown Dinny was deemed a hero after that. But even heroes get arrested. Even heroes are targeted for murder. And with Wild Bill back and the Waterfront Assembly and everyone else targeting Dinny Meehan, his son would also be in their sights.

In a moment of clarity and courageousness, Sadie chose her son's future and abandoned her husband's past. *It's easy to make that decision out here though*, she crumples Liam's letter. *But when the money runs out. . .*

Sadie strikes a match, hoping it will not wake her son John who sleeps on the bed next to her. By candlelight she holds the second, unopened letter as if it were a priceless heirloom. This one is from her cousin, Frank Leighton. Postmarked "New Haven, CT." She had saved this one. This would be the letter that would bring safety to her and John.

"We are so sorry," are the first words, which makes her stomach turn again. "Celia and I long for a child in our home. As you know, we have not been blessed with children yet. You must believe us, we are very sorry," her hands shake as she reads on, "But how can we take you and L'il Dinny in without his father's allowing it? We don't want any trouble. That's one of the biggest reasons we are leaving the city. We would love to have you both, but your husband deserves the opportunity to consent."

My husband's consent, she mimics the words silently. *You may look tough, but you are a coward, Frank.*

Sadie and Frank emigrated together by steerage to New York back in 1910. She was nineteen years old then and Frank had turned twenty-one on the day the ship departed from Liverpool. Frank was her best friend in those days. Big and with a flat, pug nose and a constant grimace on his face, Frank was more interested in flowers than fights. He had even memorized hundreds of the Latin names, which helps identify the genus and species, he told her.

On their passage they spent hours arm-in-arm singing on the deck overlooking the expanse of the Atlantic Ocean, sat knee-to-knee playing Cat's Cradle and at night they slept back-to-back in the cot they shared. Frank even waited outside while Sadie used the loo, but never made it seem like he was being protective. It was often rumored that girls who board an Atlantic steamer alone, debark with a base child in her belly. Sadie's own sixteen year-old niece once traveled from Liverpool to Portrush near Coleraine in Northern Ireland, but nine months later she mothered a baby girl.

Though Frank never spoke of such a crude thing, he was keenly aware of their surroundings and scared off would-be suitors with his big head and flat nose. Sadie's mother Rose came with as well, but she spent most of the time getting besotted with the drink until late at night, singing songs with the crew and waking up in their cabins.

Of all her cousins, Frank was the gentlest of heart. "I hate danger," she remembers him saying. A strangely obvious thing to admit, but it explains a lot. Confrontation was something Frank had experienced too much of over the course of an itinerant childhood. Luckily for the both of them that no one on the ship challenged him. Otherwise Frank would have capitulated like the poltroon he truly is.

One cloudless day on deck Frank and Sadie stood next to each other overlooking the expanse of the Atlantic Ocean.

"I'll never go back to London," Frank said in a husky voice, his big club hands wrapped round the railing. "Never. I'm going to get a job an' work until I can buy land somewhere, get married an' 'ave a big fam'ly in a big 'ouse. That's what I want to do. That's what I'm goin' to do. Lots an' lots o' kids, an a big garden too, yeah."

"Yu won't miss East London?"

"Nay."

"What about the rest o' the fam'ly?"

"Like ya mum, Rose?" He snorts through the nose.

"I guess yu got a point, she is a 'andful, me mum," Sadie laughed and laid her head on Frank's shoulder as below them white waves gently crashed against the side of the steamship.

"Ah well," Frank said. "It's not that yu mum's stupid. She's quite smart, actually. It's just that she's ignorant."

Sadie dabs at her eyes with a tissue in the candlelight by the hotel window.

I'm as ignorant as my mother.

She covers her mouth as she weeps when she remembers what Eleanor Allerton, the temperance woman in the milk-white and light blue dress said to her downstairs, "The problem is. . . You're ignorant."

I'm supposed to improve upon my mother's generation, and here I am as ignorant as she is.

The embarrassment turns to pain in Sadie's heart. It feels like a little flame and aches with a burning sensation that can't be extinguished.

I've failed. I'm an ignorant person from a half-gypsy, half-Irish family who married a gangster.

When she crumples Frank's letter and throws it in the garbage next to Liam's, she turns to her son sleeping rag-haired on the bed and pushes the tears from her eyes.

My son will go to college. He will be smart. He will go leaps and bounds beyond any other Leighton. And I will make sure of it. But how? I am as much a coward as Frank.

Sadie's stomach turns when she again thinks of room 310, upstairs. The hotelier had groped her, taken her wedding band and threatened to get in touch with Darby unless she has sex with him. With the sun peeking through the curtains, he will be up there now, in fact, waiting for her.

She looks up to the ceiling, *This is what I get for wanting to be an independent mother? This?*

"Mummy?" John rubs at his eyes and yawns on the bed.

"G'mornin', love."

"Mummy I had a dream."

Sadie blinks slowly and takes a deep breath to gather her patience and answers with a flat, almost perturbed voice, "What was it, love?"

"Someone was comin' to kill daddy."

"What? Who?"

John comes to his elbows, "Five men. We were back home on Warren Street an' there was a woman sleepin' in the kitchen an' ya were screamin', mum."

"I was?"

"So loud it hurt my ears an' the earth, it was movin' like a earthquake. Shakin'."

"Oh 'oney," Sadie sits on the bed and gathers him up. "It was just a dream."

Tearless, he looks up at her, "I'm John Carter, but I couldn't save him."

"Sweet'eart, I want yu to understand somethin', yeah? John Carter is not real. In real life there are no 'eroes, understand? That book is just a story, no one lives on Mars. It's unin'abitable, see? An' no one can save anyone. We're on our own an' we're all doin' the best we can, but—"

"Who will defeat the bad guys then?"

"There are no bad guys either," Sadie holds his face. "Everyone has the capacity to do good things. An' everyone can do bad as well. The 'eroes an' villains live inside o' us all. But in stories, we give them names and roles that mirror our own selves. Does that make sense?"

John looks away without answering.

"Mummy's goin' to get ya some new books today, alright? We'll go to the library this very day an' we'll get yu some books about real life. Because real life is a lot more interestin' an' complex than fictions an' fantasies."

John nods, "Should I throw *Gods of Mars* away?"

"No, yu don' 'ave to do that. Yu should keep it to remind yu o' the lessons yu learned from it."

"Uhright."

A knock comes to the door and Happy's voice comes through it, "It's me."

John looks at his mother, "Happy is mostly good, I think."

"I think so too," Sadie says.

"But he can be bad?"

"Well, he was in the Great War. An' in a war yu 'ave to do terrible things, but is it terrible to do terrible things when yu fightin' against worse?"

John tilts his head and scratches his neck in thought, "What's the answer?"

"The answer is, it's complicated," Sadie smiles and runs her fingers through John's hair. "I'll be back soon, then we'll go to the library, yeah?"

"Uhright."

Sadie opens the door and steps out, "G'mornin', I'll be back."

Happy moves his crutches and pivots to face her in the hall, "Ya're leavin'?"

"I'm goin' downstairs. I'll be back," she calls over her shoulder.

When Happy goes into the room and closes the door, Sadie moves away from the descending stairwell, and takes the ascending stairs up to the third floor.

302, 304, 306, the rooms on the left are even-numbered, the rooms on the right, odd. But all of them are empty for the winter months. The only sound is her own footsteps on the cheap carpet and the wood flooring beneath. Three original oil paintings of the Long Beach Boardwalk, the surf and a fishing boat adorn the walls. At the end of the hall, by a sooty window and a ratty radiator is room 310. Sadie steels her nerves as she stands in front of the nondescript, white door. Then knocks gently.

Quickly the door opens and she is greeted with a three-toothed smile.

"I see you're a good girl," says the hotelier. "Come in."

He looks down the hallway before closing and locking the door.

"Drink?" He hands her a small bottle of rum. "It always makes things easier for women, I've found."

"No thanks."

"Such a beautiful creature," he pets her cheek and runs knuckles softly down her neck and over her left breast, resting on her waist. "I love ya accent, too. Everythin' about ya just makes me. . . I dunno, raises me. When I saw'r ya come in wit' that one-legged fella, I knew he wasn't ya husband. I just knew it. No fookin' way that guy's been inside ya. Nah, ya way too gorgeous for a private in the Army. So when ya cousin showed up an' offered me money to turn ya in? I knew he wasn't lyin'. What is he, like a Pinkerton or somethin', ya cousin? He said ya're the wife o' a wanted man. That right?"

Sadie does not answer.

In my end is my beginning. Today, it ends. And begins.

He grabs her by the wrist and slings her onto the bed violently, "Take ya clothes off, Sadie. Take them off an' lay down. I wanna watch ya. Do it slow."

Sadie raises herself and sits on the edge of the bed as the hotelier rubs the outside of his wrinkled trousers and stares at her.

When Sadie unbuttons the third button of her dress, she reaches into her brazier and produces the revolver with the long barrel.

"The fuck?" He says.

She stands up and holds it at the length of her arms and pointed toward the center of his chest, just as Happy had trained her.

"Listen woman—"

"Get on the bed," she commands.

"This is gonna be a big problem if ya continue to—"

"Get on the feckin' bed before I shoot yu, yu know who I am? Yu know who me 'usband is, yeah? Yu fuck wif me, I'll kill yu meself. Get on the feckin' bed."

In a circle, the two walk round each other, trading places. Sadie is now close to the door as the hotelier holds his hands in the air, standing above the bed.

"I'm not gettin' on the bed, woman."

The report of the revolver shocks her. It was just a quick popping sound, but the kickback coupled with the sound, startles her. Happy had warned her, but it isn't until it actually happens, actually pulling the trigger, that she could fully understand the power of the recoil and the clap of the pistol at once.

The hotelier is now on the bed, shivering. Behind him, through the red umbrella in the oil painting of a family beach scene is a .38 caliber bullet hole.

The wood handle of the revolver is hot, Sadie thinks, then remembers Happy's words. *Don't let it go. The handle won't burn you.*

The hotelier pleads, "Listen I got a wife an'—"

"Take off yu clothes," Sadie interrupts.

"What?"

"All o' them, I wanna see ya naked on the bed."

"What? Why?"

"I'm in control. If yu don' do what I say, I'll kill yu. Yu think the police would suspect a woman? A mova? The wife o' a war 'ero? Nay, police love fictions. They wanna believe in good guys an' bad guys an' little women. By the time they find yu body, we'll be long gone. Yu know 'ow common the name Maloney is in New York? 'Ow many Mrs. Maloney's are there, yeah? Let them round all o' them up, they still won't find me, will they? 'Cause I ain't a Maloney, that's a fiction too. Take off yu clothes."

"Are ya gonna kill me?"

"Not if yu be'ave."

The hotelier unbuttons his pants and drops them to the floor. Then takes off his shirt and undershirt and stands in his drawers. With the revolver, she waves toward the floor.

He closes his eyes and drops his drawers too.

"That's it?" She says. "That's what yu was threatenin' me wif? That little thing? That's funny, innit? Innit?"

He covers his groin with his hands and does not laugh.

"Men like yu'self? From now on, if any man makes a mockery o' me 'onor, they will answer the consequences. Now get on the bed an' bend over."

"What?"

"Do it," she yells while digging her wedding band out of the hotelier's trousers. "Get on all fours. If yu do what I say, yu might get off."

Reluctantly he turns round and gets on the bed.

Between her index finger and thumb, Sadie holds the band up to the light from the window. While pointing the revolver with her right hand, she uses the pinky and thumb on her left hand to pull the band back onto her ring finger.

"Now back up," she says.

"Why?"

"Back up so yu knees are at the end o' the bed, now."

He does as told.

Sadie moves forward and with her free hand, she holds his hip. She then points the long barrel of the revolver toward his anus.

"Open ya legs," she slaps his ass. "Open them up."

The revolver goes in much easier that way.

The hotelier howls and scrunches his cheeks.

"Relax," Sadie raises her voice.

"Just. . . Just don' shoot it inside me."

"Then don' move. My finger's on the trigger. Any sudden movement an' it'll go off."

"Ok, ok, but it hurts."

"Me son an' I, an' me 'usband Mr. Maloney are gonna stay 'ere for a few more weeks, yeah? We're gonna pay in advance."

She reaches into the side of her brazier an' throws the cash on the bed next to him.

"If yu even think about sayin' somethin' to anyone, like the police? Or like Darby Leighton? The White 'and Gang will come back 'ere to paint this small town red, burn this feckin' 'otel down to cinders an' leave yu'self laid out in lavender. Good riddance to bad rubbish, that's what they'll say."

"Ok, ok, I won't say nothin'."

"Good boy, yu're a good boy. I think we're done 'ere."

Sadie yanks the gun from his anus as fingers of blood crawl down his hairy inner thighs. The sights blade must have torn something inside him. She goes to the door and opens it.

"Wait," the man cries. "Wait, I need a doctor. Where are yu goin'?"

Sadie turns round and wraps the foul-smelling revolver in a kerchief, "I'm goin' to the library wif me son."

Germanicus Complex

From the shadowy recesses beneath the approach to the Manhattan Bridge, a muffled metallic screech of train rotors haunts me in its mourning moans. Under the great yawning archway that lets out at Water Street, I can't even hear my own footsteps in the moist and musty oceanic air that riffles through the passageway. Within the belly of the keening giant, the thunderous rumblings shake and tremble.

The bridge is only ten years old, yet appears to the eye as some ancient ruin coated in coal dust. During construction a twenty-one inch thick steel cable broke loose from a tower and wriggled like a whip's lash down Plymouth Street by the Dock Loaders' Club. The legend of the riveter Donal McShane had come to my ears many times from the lips of Beat McGarry. McShane was born in Irishtown, the son of an exiled child. While working up on the bridge one morning a pipe of compressed air broke loose and blew him over the edge like confetti. He died at the arch's entrance where I stand now after a one hundred and twenty-foot fall.

My uncle Joseph knew McShane after he emigrated from Tulla to Brooklyn solely for the work on the Manhattan Bridge. For better wages, uncle Joseph took up the call of the longshoreman's union and was promoted by Thos Carmody as an ILA recruiter. Yet he couldn't even convince me to join, his own nephew. And now he haunts me to this very day through the ringing moans of the gigantic banshee bridge that hovers over Irishtown.

As I come out onto Water Street, five attached industrial freight cars spilling coal onto the Belgian brick roadway pass in front of me. A small locomotive pulls it with a leering, blackface conductor. I walk sideways down the hill and the narrow sidewalk along the anchorage. As the hill heads down toward the water, the buttresses of the bridge slope higher and higher until they plain over the East River.

"Liam!" I hear from behind.

I turn round to see Happy Maloney crutching along the cobblestones.

"Why aren't you with Sadie? Is she back now?"

Happy's hair has begun to grow back and he has gained a few pounds since last I saw him when he was discharged from the Army hospital after the war.

He stops in the street and gives a shame-faced tilt to his head, "I uh—"

"Where is she?"

"She. . . I dunno Liam, she just packed up an' left one mornin'. I dunno."

"What do you mean, she left with L'il Dinny?"

"Well she's callin' him John now, but yeah. They left one mornin' wit'out sayin' nothin' to nobody, see? Just gone, like. I was wonderin' if ya'd heard from her?"

"Me? No, I haven't," says I. "I left her in your care because I trusted you. A woman out in this world alone is a terrifying thought."

"I don' think ya should worry, Liam. Sadie can take care o' herself now. She's different than the soft-spoken woman ya remember."

"Really? Do you think she'll be alright?"

"She'll be fine," Happy shrugs over his crutches.

When we turn the corner at Bridge Street, two black motor cars pull up in front of the Dock Loaders' Club. I jump behind the building across John Street in front of the Jay Street Railyard and push Happy back before they see him. The two kids who stand guard outside the door step forward. The Mullen boy cups his hand and screeches up to the second floor, "*Why-oooo!*" The two then run inside and close the door behind them.

A man in his twenties dressed in a tan suit with a large purple cravat, a matching purple kerchief and slippers emerges from the motor car. He pulls the last drag from a cigar and tosses it into the path of an oncoming junk dray that is being pushed up Bridge Street by a homeless man.

"Who are they?" Happy asks.

"I don't know."

An older man dressed more modestly stands next to the man in slippers. He turns and points up to the second floor of the Dock Loaders' Club and says something. A smaller man with an aquiline nose is summoned by the man in slippers. An arm is slung over the small man's shoulder as the gaudily dressed man in slippers speaks with his hands.

"I think they're Italian," I say. "Do you still have that revolver I gave you when you went with Sadie to Long Island?"

"I uh. . . No, she musta took it."

"It's fine, I'm hoping we don't need it. We need to sure up our alliance with the Italians and I'm sure they're upset about losing South Red Hook. We only have the Italians and the ILA backing us. Without them, we're all alone against—"

"Everybody."

Three large Italians pour out of the backseat of one of the shiny black motorcars and go to the boot and pull out boxes. That is when thirty men come piling out of the Dock Loaders' Club with bail hooks and pipes and even spades, and surround the Italians.

I pull my own pipe out of my coat and walk across Bridge Street from behind them as Happy follows.

"I am attempting to explain to you," The man in slippers speaks with an Anglo-American accent, but has a low, thick hairline and black eyebrows. "It's food. Only food. And what is food? We offer you to accept this food as a token of our esteem."

I shoulder through some of our men and open one of the boxes. It looks as though there are bloody worms inside of it. I open another box, but inside there is a cake and little colorful cookies.

"They wanna break bread," Happy sheepishly moves his eyes to me.

The Swede comes barreling out the front door, "The fuck's wrong wit' yaz? Ya don' just show up here wit'out lettin' us know ahead o' time, Sixto. Ya're lucky I wasn't down here when ya pulled up or I woulda started swingin' first an' askin' questions later."

Sixto Stabile? I realize. *Stick'em Jack's son?*

I met them once before at the Fourteenth Street Hotel where the International Longshoreman's Association holds court in West Manhattan. They call Sixto the Young Turk. One of many new generation Italians who believe in fronting with a legitimate business, while washing the dirty money through the backdoor. Jack, his father, is known as an old Mustache Pete. He seems to have aged ten years since I last saw him. His face is gray and haggard and his eyes droop where crow's feet pinch at the corners.

"*Porca miseria*," old Stick'em Jack proclaims to his son with strange words to our ears. "*Stai per rovinare le tue scarpe in questa sporcizia.*"

"What's that mean?" The Swede demands.

Sixto smiles, "Eh, I wouldn't worry about him."

"This place eh-*shangad*," Jack violently shakes his hands.

"The fuck's *shangad* mean?" The Swede yells.

Sixto steps in, "He just questions the location of your headquarters. He says it's like a pig sty. And that bridge is so loud. It leaves a man to wonder how much dirt and soot must that thing stir up around here. It's not good for the respiratory system. Also, my father is aging and has a case of frequency, can he use your bathroom?"

"Bathroom?" The Swede repeats with a dubious smirk.

"Yes, you know, where all the dicks hangout?"

"We gotta trough out back."

"Oh, never mind."

"Sixto?" Vincent Maher comes out the front door with a startled but joyful smile. "What are yaz doin' round here?"

"Vin!" Sixto traverses the cobblestones and steps up to the sidewalk to shake hands with Vincent, but abandons that in favor of a brusque hug and two kisses on his cheeks. "You are still prettier than most women, I see. Listen, the Prince o' Pals Frankie Yale wanted me to say hello to you. He often thinks about you, you know. He really cares about you. Cares in his heart for you. Paul Vaccarelli says hello too."

Vincent blushes as Sixto's palm cups his face.

"Uhright, uhright," The Swede ballyrags Sixto. "If ya take Vincent's cock outta ya mouth maybe then we could understand ya better. What do ya people want around here? Showin' up outta nowheres."

"I thought I might return the favor," Sixto says with a genuine and confident cast. "Your people come to our place of business every week and drop dimes with us. I thought we could come and return the favor. Do you have any ladies upstairs?"

"Ladies? Upstairs? No women are allowed in our headquarters," The Swede bellows.

"So I have heard," Sixto touches his chin with a finger. "What a shame. Irish girls are such charming things. Gorgeous and pure. With skin of mare's milk and hair kissed by fire. And still you people don't give them work?"

"We don' whore out our women like I-Talians do," The Swede's voice is bitter.

"Well I'm glad you are alright with us whoring your women then, because I thought it might upset some of your people. Anyhow—"

"That's not what I was sayin'."

"That's exactly what you said. Grace and Kit," Sixto kisses his own fingers. "Beautiful creatures. And demure. There is nothing sweeter than demure beauty."

I push ahead of The Swede "We'd prefer that you not enslave our women, of course, but we are allies and must work together. I'm glad you have come today—"

"Get the fuck outta here," The Swede pushes back. "Nobody asked ya."

"I appreciate the sentiment, Mr. Garrity," Sixto salutes me.

He remembers my name?

"Hopefully we can work things out like two businesses with common interests," Sixto then politely pivots away from me and touches one of his Italian cohorts. "By the way Mr. Swede, do you remember this man? His name is Lucio Buttacavoli, but we call him Lucy. Do you remember him?"

The Swede looks at Lucy the man with the aquiline nose, "Nah, I don' know him."

Sixto turns to Lucy and says something in Italian. Together they turn their eyes up to The Swede until Sixto speaks, "Lucy says that he remembers you because you killed his cousin."

The Swede had turned away by then, but when he hears Sixto's matter-of-fact accusation, he turns back, "Whad ya say?"

"At the Fulton Ferry Landing," Sixto shrugs. "Back in 1915, Lucy tells me. They had just gotten off a ship from Calabria. They were disoriented. Unsure of where to go. They didn't know the Irish were in the north of Brooklyn while our people were in the south. They were told they could work on the docks, so they showed up. From what Lucy says, his cousin Giovanni didn't want to pay you tribute. He said you were without respect."

"Wit'out respect? An' what happens if a Irish guy shows up at the Bush Terminal? Or at the Grand Army Terminal?"

"We don't hire Irish down there. But you hired the Buttacavolis, which meant you were charged with their care. Instead you beat them. Killed one of them, took their money. Lucy was punched in the throat and to this day he cannot speak well. Do you deny his claim against you?"

"I don' remember it," The Swede turns round and opens the door. "Ya comin' in o' what?"

Sixto lowers his eyes, gives The Swede a knowing smile and speaks in his tongue to Lucy, who responds, though he has but mere wind for a voice.

"What are yaz talkin' about now?" The Swede rolls his eyes.

"I said to him that he is correct, at least about one thing."

"What's that?"

"You are without respect," Sixto smiles and walks in the front door. "Tell me, where is the one named Cinders? Cinders Connolly, is that not his name? The dockboss of the Fulton Ferry Landing the day Lucy lost his cousin?"

"He ain't here right now," The Swede lets himself in the door.

Sixto's father follows him inside, and the large Italians carry in the boxes of food and open them up on the tables and along the bar in front of the dockbosses, their righthanders and all the rest.

"Jaysus, Mary and Joseph," Paddy Keenan swears. "What are these things on me bar here, Black Hand bombs are they?"

"*Mangia*," Sixto proclaims and raises his hand in a half-salute, though the father is much less amiable than the son and still has the milk of the old country on his lips. Sixto, however, is overly courteous and even gives a short bow. "A gift from South Brooklyn to our northern partners. Do you see? Even when you take the territory away from us that was granted in the deal that brought us together, still we come with gifts and neighborly respect. *Mangia, sta andando a freddo, come il tuoi cuore.*"

The men at the bar are unmoved and stare at Sixto and his father Jack and the silent fellow named Lucy with suspicion.

"They don' understand the words ya sayin'," Vincent leans in.

"*Un regalo,*" Jack raises his voice, his foreign language grating against the ears of the white men. "*Un regalo per tutti voi.*"

"I apologize," Sixto says as the men chuckle at his small feet in slippers on the cement floor and the pinky rings adorning both hands. "*Mangia* means eat. It's similar to an Irish blessing, you could say. *Regalo* means gift. My father would be honored if you appreciate the gift of food that we offer you."

Red Donnelly was the first to notice the smell. The Lark and Big Dick and even Ragtime Howard all stand up when they catch wind of the wonderful scents that waft through the old damp, beer-puddled, wood-framed saloon. Soon enough my own teeth begin to swim in my mouth for a bite of it as all the men huddle round the plates of pasta, sweet sausage, eggplant, soups and greens, mouths salivating. Yet no one dares make the first move until Sixto himself makes a plate and tastes it.

"That's a *fazool*," Sixto points at one of the opened boxes.

"A wha?"

"Traditional soup, at least in our village."

"Who cooked all this?" Beat McGarry asks.

"My father did," Sixto points.

The men had a good laugh at that. Men aren't supposed to cook. Men aren't supposed to hug and kiss each other either. Or dress up in bright colors and wear jewelry. Most men had never even seen an Italian woman before, even though they lived in households and neighborhoods only a few blocks away. Some rumors had spread through Irishtown that Italians cook babies and seep them in blood sauce. But by the end of this day some would say that since the men like to do things women do, kiss each others cheeks and even name themselves after women, maybe they enjoy laying with each other too.

"Ya like sausage don' ya?" The Lark asks Sixto.

"Love it," he responds, licking his lips.

Once the first bite is taken by Vincent, the men tear at the boxes of food like wolves.

"Food," a teary-eyed smile waxes across Sixto's olive-colored face. "It's an international language we all speak."

Seeing tears in his eyes, the white men are convinced he is homosexual now.

"Come, yes?" Sixto says. "Where is our Dinny Meehan? Upstairs?"

"Shut ya fookin' face wit' that," The Swede bellows and everyone in the saloon stops chewing and stares.

Vincent leans into Sixto's ear, "Patrick Kelly, remember? There ain't no one here wit' that name."

Sixto smiles a knowing smile, "Ah yes, my apologies. Upstairs is he?"

"Yeah," The Swede growls and leads the way.

Behind us the sound of scraping chairs comes to our ears and Paddy Keenan's voice, "Hey, hey, hey. It's not here ye'll have yer affray."

I turn and see Lucy has Philip Large by the neck against the mahogany. Philip's round eyes are searching for Cinders, his hands open and over his head in supplication.

"That's a very bad idea, fella," Paddy tells the Italian.

"Lucy?" Sixto calls back, then moves through.

Lucy speaks to him in their language, his voice raspy and low, "*Questo imbecille, questo imbecille.*"

"What gives?" The Swede stands over them all.

"It appears this imbecile was there the day Lucy's cousin was murdered."

"So was I."

"Vendetta!" Sixto presents the word as if he were on the theatre stage. "Lucy wages a personal war for justice on those who took his cousin's life. He names you as well in his vendetta Mr. Swede, but this imbecile was there that day and held him in his grip while your Cinders Connolly punched him in the throat," Sixto shrugs as if the vendetta were out of his power to control. "It is mere justice he requires. One of you three must answer to it with a life."

"Today ain't the day for this, Sixto," The Swede points a finger down into his face. "On top o' that, this fookin' guy don' wanna fight Philip."

"Fight? No, he must murder the imbecile."

"Stop callin' him that."

"Well that is what he is, am I right? He wobbles when he walks, he is as wide as he is tall, his face is flat as an iron and his mind is feeble. Look at him, he is a simpleton. An imbecile. An idiot. If that is what he is, why hide the truth? In any case, of the three named in Lucy's vendetta, he is the most worthless to you, is he not?"

"Be careful," The Swede says. "Ya might get what ya want. But I'm tellin' ya, ya don' want what ya want 'cause it ain't what ya really want, after all."

"Lucy," Sixto turns to his man and after a few hand gestures, Lucy lets Philip loose, begrudgingly.

"Beware Mr. Swede, our people have the memory of elephants. It could be years before Lucy resolves the vendetta, but it will happen." Sixto then turns round to see Dinny standing on the stairwell and calls up to him, "May we have a word, your highness?"

Dinny leans on the sloped bannister, "Ya show up to our home wit'out notifyin' us beforehand. It's a dangerous thing, young man."

Sixto Stabile straightens himself.

Dinny continues, "Ya're always welcome in our part o' town, as ya've always welcomed our men down on Fourth Avenue at the Adonis. But this is different. The Black Hand was driven from these neighborhoods when we took down Christie Maroney, who would sell our girls into prostitution an' give our territory away for personal benefit. Those ways are gone from here. Yet we work together now. Ya ever got idears on comin' up Irishtown-way again, ya send a runner first, understand?"

"We work together?" Sixto shoots him a handsome smile and brushes off some lint from his beige and gold suit. "*Pulcinella* would disagree. Wild Bill Lovett has told my people he leads the White Hand in Red Hook, but I have the impression he does not pay Irishtown tribute. The agreement between the Irish in the north and the Italians in the south, coordinated by Thos Carmody of the ILA to both of our benefit, has been breached."

"Ya ain't a judge to decide when a agreement's been breached," The Swede complains. "Thos Carmody is the judge, let's wait to see what he says."

Sixto's dander goes up slightly. His fingers tense together as if he is squishing a bug, "Lovett invaded and murdered five of our men. Then, instead of coming to me yourself, you send me Vincent Maher, an underling. You must understand that our people see that as an infamy. You reproach us when your people have committed such a crime? You must forgive our belief that any and all agreements between us are null and void."

Dinny does not respond and mumbles are heard from one end of the saloon to the other.

"We bring food," Sixto presents with an outstretched hand, though much of the boxes have been overturned and spilled on the floor when Lucy attacked Philip. "If you understand anything about our ways, you will understand that we offer it as the ultimate sign of respect and hope that we can come to a new resolution, together, on the question of rebels in Red Hook."

Dinny nods and points, "Sixto, Jack and Lucy come upstairs. Masher, Swede an' Poe, come as well."

Me? Why me?

I had rarely heard Dinny use our monikers before, but on this day it seems appropriate since outsiders are inside the Dock Loaders' Club.

Upstairs we take our places; Dinny sits behind the desk with two iron shutter windows propped open, The Swede on his right, myself on the left while Vincent mans the door with a paper cigarette in his mouth and his belt unbuckled, his waistcoat unbuttoned.

Across the desk Sixto wipes a chair with a kerchief and sits primly. He then places his hat on a cross-legged knee to reveal the pearl buttons down white linen spats that fasten under his patent leather shoes. It isn't until we are in close quarters that the strong scent of honeysuckle and lavender reaches my nose and his smile makes me think he just swallowed a canary. His furrow-browed father sits behind him on a stool with a half-open mouth.

The man named Lucy collapses into a chair with a pinched moon face and stares about. With the pad of his fingers he pets a red-coral amulet in the shape of the devil's horn.

"What is that?" says I.

Sixto turns to Lucy. When he looks in my direction the smear of a smile appears on his handsome face, "That is a *cornetti*, it protects against the evil eye. He has heard that the Irish are sickly and sometimes envious of our health. That would be bad luck."

The Swede's face looks as if he's on the verge of retching, "Sickly? What the—"

Dinny interrupts, "Are ya now graduated from college?"

"I am, thank you for asking," Sixto grins politely. "Harvard has had Catholics graduate in the past, but not so many as olive-complected as myself."

"Isn't that the name o' Frankie Yale's saloon down on Coney Island? Harvard Inn?"

"Yes it is, the American dream, right? To attend a prestigious, Ivy League University."

"I wouldn't know," Dinny tilts his head.

"You wouldn't know?" Sixto says unbelieving. "This is the land where everyone has the opportunity to succeed. America, land of the free."

"It's free as long as ya act like them," Dinny rests his elbows on the desk and brings his hands together under his face. "Ya seem to've assimilated rather well. I s'pose it's not so hard for a I-Talian to accept the American way. But for us it can be different. For us, the Anglo-Saxon forced us from our homes and when we came here, years before most I-Talians had, we were reviled for bein' Catholic, not allowed to work an' blamed for it as well, the same thing that happened to us, by the same type o' people back in Ireland. Many o' us see no difference between the English in England and the WASPs here in America."

"And yet you have the opportunity to succeed, whereas in Ireland you do not."

The Swede mutters his annoyance, "Opportunities paid for by prostitutin' girls that ain't even old enough to know what's happenin' to them? That the type o' opportunity ya talkin' about? Ya think it's just grand to hold a girl down by her neck so ya can squeeze the dime outta her. No sir, we do not share the same codes as ya people."

"I had heard that Irishtown was once a good place for bad habits, but not during the current regime's reign," Sixto holds a finger to his chin until his eyes turn up in thought, "And I have *always* heard that your people are haunted by the ghosts of the past. Battles that were lost in the Middle Ages are still debated and wrongs done you are rehashed, reiterated, rephrased and repeated over and over again. Like the potato famine—"

"It was only a blight, and but a single crop in a fertile country," says I. "It seems even an educated man, like yourself, is more than happy to swallow English lies if it benefits you. Did they teach you at Harvard about the millions of pounds of grains and cattle that were exported to British colonies from Ireland back then?"

"I don't believe that was high on any of my professors' syllabi at the school of business, I admit. But what is baffling is so many Irish here in New York are happy enough to dream the American dream. The Tammany Democrats have worked tirelessly to get city jobs into the hands of their constituents. You must excuse my ignorance, correct me if I am mistaken, but it seems only a small amount of Irish in the corner of Brooklyn along the waterfront think otherwise."

I turn to Dinny, then look up to The Swede. I could have been a believer in the American dream if I hadn't been plucked off the streets by the White Hand.

Sixto folds his fingers together in his lap and smiles when he does not receive an answer. He tilts his head again and speaks, "I admire you, Dinny Meehan."

"That ain't no one's name around here," The Swede grumbles.

"I apologize," Sixto holds up his palms up to The Swede and turns his cordial smile back to Dinny. "Still, I admire you. You have codes. Powerful and unspoken codes. Your people believe in you. They believe that you will do right by them. And from everything I have seen, you honor them with honesty and forthrightness. The problem is twofold."

Dinny nods patiently and sits back in his chair.

Sixto begins, "Firstly, the Irish are in decline in Brooklyn. This territory was inherited," Sixto explains with a gentle grin and turns back to Dinny. "And you have done an impeccable job keeping it all together as best as humanly possible, I grant you that. But we are on the rise and will one day take over labor from the Irish predecessors." He looks over Dinny's right shoulder. "Why the long face, Mr. Swede?"

Vincent snorts at the jape and mutters under his breath, "Long face."

"We ain't in decline," The Swede protests. "We control labor along the most profitable waterfront docks an' piers in Brooklyn. I hear pretty words comin' from ya pretty face Sixto, but they ain't worth a fiddler's fart."

"Oh no? Even your line of succession has been cut off, didn't *Pulcinella*, the black clown, take the life of Irishtown's heir? I heard Mickey Kane described as the golden prince. Handsome, strong, extremely talented and dead," Sixto continues, "It has also come to my ear that you are in a vast amount of debt with Johnny Spanish an' we all know what he did to the mother of his own child. Before you become irate again, Mr. Swede, think of it in terms of families. The family unit is the most important element in a strong culture. Forgive me, but the Irish family unit has been decimated with alcoholism, disease, the Great War, dissension and flight for many years now." Sixto moves in his seat and speaks with both hands in the air. "Think of it in terms of weddings and funerals. Which do Irish experience more of in these neighborhoods?"

I turn to Dinny. I know the answer: Funerals. I have never been to a wedding among our people, but I have attended many funerals. Especially during the war.

"Let me finish. Secondly," Sixto moves his presentation forward. "There is the Germanicus Complex."

"Huh?" Vincents asks from behind.

"Have any of you ever heard of Germanicus?" Sixto asks the room.

I look to Vincent and Dinny and The Swede, but none of us recognize the name.

"Of course you haven't," Sixto's voice is silken with courtesy as he speaks to Dinny directly. "In ancient times Germanicus was beloved by the people, like yourself. Germanicus was born into the Julio-Claudian patrician society of Rome and was adopted by his father's uncle, Emperor Tiberius. With that, he became the heir to Rome. Fate had rolled out in front of him like a long red carpet and he was destined to one day rule all the land. He commanded many legions of the Roman Army and avenged previous defeats. All that he pursued, became his success. And we all know that nothing succeeds like success, and so his power accumulated. Everything he touched turned to gold and everywhere he went the people threw roses at his feet. On top of all his success, he treated the poor not with the disdain and fear that other Roman rulers had. No, he loved the poor people in their masses. He kissed lepers and yet never lost a limb. He hugged those who had the black death and did not once cough. He sent his personal finances to help the needy and paid particular attention to the mothers who had lost husbands and sons in battle, or were alone in the world. When he arrived in Rome after yet another winning campaign abroad, the streets overflowed to welcome him with adoring, fanatical followers. And what was Emperor Tiberious to make of all this love for his heir? He summoned Germanicus in front of the court and forced him to kneel and kiss his ring. But Germanicus made matters worse. Germanicus showed Tiberius great humility and swore him loyalty to his dying breath. An honorable, selfless act. Can there be anything more infuriating to the emperor of Rome than humility from his rival? Tiberius had lost on all fronts in the people's eyes, so he sent Germanicus East. But Tiberius, stricken with jealousy, had a plan and promised to elevate the governor of Syria if he did his bidding. And so it was done. Germanicus was poisoned and died and the people of Rome never had the emperor they loved, no. Do you know what Rome got instead of the righteous and beloved Germanicus?"

None of us know the answer, and so we return the question with blank stares.

"Rome received Caligula instead, the son of Germanicus, a sadist, sexually perverse and an extravagantly insane tyrant who was so maniacally self-centered that the world would never look back to the likes of Germanicus again. You are doomed, Dinny Meehan—"

The Swede interrupts, "How many fookin' times I gotta tell ya—"

"You are doomed to be forgotten forever and your code of silence will conceal your wonderful intentions like a crypt so that the world will never know you. Your victors will write your history, but mostly you will receive the greatest slight anyone can offer; instead of writing about you at all, you will be ignored. Woe to the vanquished, as they say. But in the meantime, you may be of help. Right now there is a cancer in Red Hook, spreading death. This *Pulcinella* that you call Wild Bill Lovett butchered five of my friends last February when he appeared mysteriously out of the storm. He had murdered Sammy de Angelo and Il Maschio before that. Worst of all, he has taken the territory, breaching our agreement. The only way this situation can be resolved is to grant us our grievance with more territory."

"What are ya askin'?" Dinny responds coolly.

"You and yours are hanging on by a thread and that thread is fraying fast. It would be a mercy if we snipped that thread by invading the Irish territories up to the Navy Yard and pushing you all into the East River so that Brooklyn can get serious about its future."

"Try it," The Swede's gaunt face shows he is keen for the challenge.

"What are ya askin'," Dinny's voice hardens.

"The price is all of Red Hook," Sixto leans back. "It is a small price. Truly small, considering the vast majority of Red Hook is already settled by our people. All but the rich waterfront area. We will provide support from the South and East in an attack on Lovett while your faction of the White Hand attacks from the North."

"We are the only White Hand," The Swede reminds.

"And yet this *Pulcinella* claims the White Hand name for himself," Sixto lowers an eye and wags a slow finger at Dinny. "Tell me this. Is it true Lovett sees himself as Vercingetorix reborn?"

I look to Dinny as I had not heard that myself.

"That he determines his policy based on druidic signs due to ancient connections between the trees and the moon? Relies on a whisperer and sends shadows out to do his bidding? If he sees himself as Vercingetorix reborn, is it not the Italian that he centers his own personal vendetta against since it was an Italian, Julius Caesar who defeated Vercingetorix?"

"I ain't responsible for what Lovett thinks," Dinny says. "Ever since he came back from the war, he's been, I dunno. Different."

"There are some who say you know exactly what you are doing. That you make a big production about how your gang is split up in two, but send *Pulcinella* to take back Red Hook from us. This has lead some to believe that you are behind it all. I have even heard it said that you have dispatched two murderers under the auspices of being banished. That Harry Reynolds and Tanner Smith are killer bees sent from atop Irishtown to attack down in the honeycombed tenements and factories along the waterfront areas to exact your own brand of law, is this true?"

"If ya not my enemy, then ya have nothin' to worry for," Dinny answers.

Sixto reaches across to his father and touches the top of his hand. His father then nods back pridefully. Sixto then turns to Lucy, who pulls a cigar case out, withdraws one and hands it to Sixto.

Sixto holds the cigar as if it were a treasured item and gently leans it on the edge of Dinny's desk and speaks, "I don't believe much in superstition either, but my people do. As do your own. In any case, here is our offer. Together we will crush the rebels in Red Hook and the new border will move from the Gowanus Canal to Union Street. Everything north is yours, everything south is ours. Some will die. Many will be hurt, but the threat to you will be removed. Agree to this plan and Frankie Yale, even Paul Vaccarelli, will be contented and this egregious disrespect offered to our people will be forgotten and righted. All you have to do is pick up that cigar and light it. We will shake hands and eat like kings. And most importantly, a war between the Black Hand and the White Hand will be averted."

Take it. Pick up the cigar and light it, I think to myself. *We have no choice. Irishtown is under siege and needs its allies.*

The Swede chuckles, "Ya owe ya success to Thos Carmody an' us for makin' that agreement that brought us together. But wouldn't it be funny if the first thing ya ever did, is the best thing ya ever do? Or the only thing ya ever did?"

The Young Turk sits back in his chair. His father mumbles something to him in Italian, but Sixto only twists the rings on his fingers, then holds a pinky up in the air to await Dinny's response.

"Ya've done well for ya'self, Sixto. When last we jawed ya had not yet supplanted ya father. I hear ya take after Frankie Yale more than ya father an' ya've gone into business down by the cemetery. Funeral parlor, I hear. Is that how ya wash all that dirty money ya make in prostitution? I hear ya keep ya top earners locked up in a room above it"

"I can promise you that Frankie Yale and I are excellent undertakers," Sixto warns with a cunning smile.

"It's a dyin' industry," Vincent cuts in awkwardly from the door.

"I like that one," Sixto turns and smiles at Vincent, "That reminds me. I want one more thing added to our offer. I want Vin as well."

The Swede scowls, "The fuck's wrong wit' ya? Ya can't *have* him."

"As part of this deal, I want you to give me Vin as a gift," he turns back to Dinny. "Vin is very popular in South Brooklyn and his Irish heart doesn't bleed through the waistcoat like the rest of you. At the Adonis, he would be in my employ."

"More like a prisoner," The Swede says.

"He is much more appreciated by my people than your own, isn't that right Vin?" Sixto turns in his seat and all eyes are on Vincent, who turns a shame-faced frown away from everyone.

"Ya knew about this request beforehand?" The Swede demands of Vincent.

"I don' have nothin' to do wit' nothin'," Vincent pleads. "A guy can ask for whatever he likes, but I'm Patrick Kelly. Always have been."

Behind everyone, Dinny speaks, "Ya won't ever have Vincent."

"Such a shame, he is quite a specimen."

"Fookin' sausage lovers," The Swede growls and throws his lone good hand in the air at the Italians.

"This one over here is very quiet and oozing with innocence," Sixto points at me with curiosity in his eyes. "You should let him speak more. I believe he is in favor of our offer."

Dinny lazily says, "Ya can't have him either. Anyhow, it's my turn to talk."

"You have the floor," Sixto allows a curtsy from the chair in front of the desk.

Just pick up the cigar, Dinny. Just do it.

"What we have here is a difference in values," Dinny folds his hands and leans back, distancing himself from the offered cigar. "We want only what's ours. Wit' that bein' said, ya've overlooked our ways. In fact most people would say ya attempt to subvert it," Dinny's face darkens.

"How have I offended?" Sixto requests.

"Our people have for thousands o' years sought an honorable way to resolve disputes between factions. But even though we were uprooted, we have kept our traditions. Bill Lovett an' I have a difference an' we have decided to resolve it in a way that ya do not care to honor."

"A fistfight? That's what honor is?"

"In an honorable world, the fist is mightier than the gun. An' ya would have me invade Bill Lovett from the North before even we can have a chance to resolve our issues, our way."

"Listen—"

"Two things," Dinny interrupts again. "First thing's this Scarfaced Al fella? Ya better get him the hell outta Brooklyn. That's a warnin' I won't bother to say twice. Bill knows the big boy has been tasked wit' takin' him down. Bill has his men on reconnaissance as we speak an' his lieutenants are devisin' a counterattack. Ya got a few days. I know the man is a tough fighter an' smart as a whip. Don' matter though, no one plays as tough as Wild Bill Lovett, an' there is no one in all o' Brooklyn that can fight like Richie Lonergan can."

"Pegleg," Lucy growls.

"Except ya'self," The Swede says. "No one's ever beat ya."

"Two," Dinny points two fingers into the desk. "We have a common enemy, ya'self an' I, which is what brought us together in the first place. An' it took a smart guy like

Thos Carmody to get us both under the ILA banner. Our common enemy is Jonathan G. Wolcott an' the Waterfront Assembly," he picks up the cigar and Sixto hands him a pack of matches.

"What is your counter offer? Name it? If you have a hard time justifying the loss of all of Red Hook, ask me for something in return. Ask me to take care of your debt with Johnny Spanish. Ask me to help you expunge the charges that loom over your head. Name the price."

"The price is Wolcott."

Sixto turns round to his father, then back to Dinny, "What would you have us do?"

"Go to every business in South Brooklyn and burn down those that are on this list," Dinny produces a piece of paper and hands it to Sixto.

The Turk runs a pinky vertically down the paper, "These are all major businesses with executives that put big numbers on our racket games, spend large quantities of money at the Adonis and hire us as Starkers to take care of personal problems. All the graft we would lose—"

The Swede butts in, "From kidnappin' their fam'ly members for ransom?"

Sixto turns angrily at The Swede, "What happened with your sister was well before my time."

"Blackhanded," The Swede growls.

"This. . . " Sixto slaps at the paper and tosses it back on Dinny's desk. "This would be terrorism. We are not Bolsheviks. This is America."

Dinny languidly responds after working Sixto into a lather, "In a few mont's the ILA will call upon both o' us on a general strike for better wages an' every dock an' pier will be shut down. Manufactured goods will not be able to enter or leave New York. The Black Hand and the White Hand will be wrapped around the city's throat. When this happens Wolcott will attempt to divide the ILA in two, Irish against I-Talian." Dinny leans across the desk. "What I wanna know; does Frankie Yale an' ya'self see Wolcott as an enemy? Or an ally? More importantly Paul Vaccarelli, a vice president within the ILA now on the same level as King Joe Ryan, does Vaccarelli see Wolcott an' the Waterfront

Assembly as the enemy?" Dinny points to the paper. "Do these things I ask now, prove to me who your true enemy is, an' all o' Red Hook will be yours when I beat Bill Lovett, one-on-one."

"This. . . This cannot be done. It would professional suicide."

"No deal then," Dinny drops the cigar and matches and stands in place.

Sixto also then stands and places his hat on his head.

"Wait," I yell to Sixto. "Don't leave yet—"

"Liam—"

"No, we have to work something out, right now."

"Wise words," Sixto stares at Dinny.

"We can't lose allies. If we lose them, we'll only have the ILA and we don't even know whose side Thos Carmody—"

"Liam!" The Swede raises his voice and steps in front of Dinny's desk just as Lucy is standing. But Lucy forgot the horn-shaped red amulet in his lap and drops it on the floor where The Swede accidentally steps on it.

Lucy then speaks quickly, angrily in Italian.

"Wha?" The Swede says. "I didn't do it on purpose."

Sixto says, "But you touched it with the bottom of your shoe."

"So? So what?"

Sixto collects his dignity and gently takes Lucy by the arm, then tips his cap before walking toward the door where he shakes Vincent's hand and touches his face gently, "Farewell, my friend."

Lucy the man turns round and eyes The Swede, mumbling something in Italian to Stick'em Jack.

The Swede barks out, "Hey, what did he just say?"

Sixto smiles and searches for the right words in English, "He says something like. . . Vendetta keeps me hungry, but eventually we all sit down to feast," he closes his eyes and slowly nods toward Dinny, "Adieu, Germanicus. *Vae victis.*"

When the door closes I turn to Dinny, "What are you trying to do? Are you trying to lose everything on purpose?"

Dinny calmly turns his head to me, "If ya ever tip ya cap to outsiders again, I'll banish ya. Ya didn' trust me when it came to Tanner or wit' Harry, an' now this. If ya think ya know better, say so when we're alone, but never show an outsider ya desperate. Ever."

A Commitment

Why can't I even put a name to a face? I'm such an idiot.
    It was just as the sun was setting behind the Statue of Liberty. Darby Leighton climbed a factory on Union Street that abuts the train-house between the Baltic and North Red Hook terminals. When he jumped down onto the sloped roof, he landed soft as a cat. Unheard except for the flight of pigeons that leafed up into the sky, cooing. But no one could see him behind the shadow of a brick chimney. Down below, on the waterfront, a man stepped into the back of a tugboat and was handed a pregnant envelope.
    It all happened on the same tugboat where Darby used to watch Detective Brosnan collect his own take.
    I know I've seen that man before. He must be getting paid off by Wolcott and the Waterfront Assembly because the giant Amadeusz Wisniewski was on the moored tug. Garry Barry was too, and all along I thought Garry Barry was dead. I'm such an Idiot.
    The mysterious man was not wearing a laborer's suit. He looked less like a simple laborer than the type of fellow who represents many laborers. He wore round-rimmed Windsor glasses, a double-breasted dark wool suit with thin, barely noticeable stripes. The mysterious man's trousers were high-waisted and cuffed at the ankle, English style. His face was narrow and he had a commanding way

of speech as if he were a man who gives direction, but does not take it.

Immediately Darby recognized the man's face, but can't put a name to it. An important man. A man Bill will want to know is in Wolcott's employ.

What good is a reconnaissance agent if he can't remember names? I can't find Sadie, I can't figure out who bedded Anna, and now this. Idiot.

Darby grits his teeth. His eyes are fixed and seemingly unconcerned as he stares out the window through the fire escape. Below, down on Flatbush Avenue the black motor cars move silently, as well as the street trolleys in the center lane and the elevated trains. Across the street and beyond the factories are an endless succession of rooftops and water towers with advertisements scrawled across them. Above, slanted smoke belches into the sky from factory chimneys and tenements alike. But it is only the mysterious man on the tug that worries at his thoughts.

A factory whistle calls out, unheard.

It announces the end of a shift across the street, though Darby cannot hear it. Behind, Ligeia mimics the sound of the shift whistle, "*faweep, faweeeeeep,*" she sings with a loving smile to their Colleen Rose in her arms. Lost in the thought of the mysterious man, when Darby sees his fiancé and daughter, only then does he faintly hear the whistle outside and realize where he is; the building where they squat.

The Socony gas factories loom across the busy intersection with trolleys and pushcarts meandering both Tillary Street and Flatbush Avenue. It also has a hundred workers going at it day and night. During a shift change they look like soldiers with floppy hats and lunch pales charging in waves against each other; half of them heading into work, the other half heading home, beat.

Opposites colliding, yet working in unity, Darby blinks that thought away. *It would be good if I got a job there. Punch in. Punch out. No rat race.*

But he knows you have to know somebody who knows somebody to get in at Socony. Recently it had a fifteen-percent reduction in work force, while at the same time thousands apply for any and all openings due to layoffs elsewhere in Brooklyn.

Hopeless. There are less jobs now than I've ever seen in Brooklyn. I need to concentrate on the opportunities I have with Bill's new gang. And I need to put a name to that face.

That night he dreamed he was chasing the man, but he had no face at all. Only when Darby looked into a black, rain-dappled puddle could he see a reflection of the Windsor glasses on the narrow face. All night and into the morning he was plagued by it. But in this tiny room, there is no place he can pace. Darby moves his eyes round the room: The metal bed longwise against a sloped wall, the wooden bassinet with tiny blankets hanging over its side, the brick wall, the window with a fire escape outside, a sink and toilet and a nightstand overflowing with unfolded clothes.

"Darby?" Ligiea says.

But when he does not answer, she eventually walks away.

The building where they squat had been condemned for almost four years. Once upon a time it was a textile factory, but the ceilings had collapsed on five floors since then and most of the window frames had rotted, the glass gone or broken.

When Ligeia told him she was pregnant, Darby had walked into the building, went upstairs, came into a water closet and noticed there was a window in it with a fire escape outside. He then got water and mortar and sealed the entrance door with leftover bricks as if it were one long wall. Even if someone walks into the abandoned building and comes up to their floor, they would never notice that behind the wall a family of three squats in what was once a men's water closet.

Unless they hear the baby within. Or find Darby carrying pales of water up to flush their waste down the toilet.

Behind him he faintly hears Ligeia humming to Colleen Rose. He had forgotten where he was again.

I'm home. If you can call this a home.

He turns to her, "Can I hold the baby?"

Ligeia moves closer to Darby and gently passes Colleen Rose over to him. She rubs a hand down Darby's shoulder, then touches his face, "What is it you think about-eh so much, Darby?"

"Nothin', I'm fine."

Ligeia pulls her hand away stomps off.

"What?" He says to her back.

"I no like when you no talk to me," her fingers make detailed gestures until she waves her fists in the air and raises her voice. "Why you no talk-eh to me, eh? I ask you question and you say 'Nothin', I fine, nothin', I fine.' Is that your favorite thing to say? You lock me up in here with the baby all day, all night I sit around like a cow, feeding her, feeding her. But what about me? I starving in here. In here? Here? No kitchen? Just toilet and window and walls. I want you take me to *ristorante*. I want to go out! Darby, my love, what we do here? We stay forever here? No, no we cannot stay forever here. No, no!"

Holding the baby, Darby stares at her.

"What you say? Anything? Talk to me, Darby. Say something, anything. Please, Darby," she rushes over to him again and grabs his free hand. "Tell me when you come to America, tell me."

"I already—"

"Tell me!"

Darby rattles off the main points, "Yeah, so I was born in Ireland but we moved to London when we was babies on account o' the fam'ly could get work there. We have a big fam'ly an' we all travelled together. Thirty, forty o' us at once."

"Your mother? What she like?"

"I dunno, I never met her. Or my father. When I was five I came wit' my aunt Rose an' my brother Pickles to Brooklyn. But she abandoned us here."

"When you were five-eh year old, abandon you both?"

"Yeah."

"*Come orrible,*" she says in Italian. How horrible. "How do you eat?"

"I learned to steal, we both did. Gangs taught us. Later on, we sent for Frank an' my cousin, Sadie."

"I like Frank. He so nice, that man. He bring flowers when Colleen Rose born, remember?"

"Yeah."

"Frank is older brother, yes?"

"Yeah."

"What Pickles like? Why you call him Pickles?"

"Ah, it's a long story. My younger brother Pickles, he ain't as nice as Frank, that's for sure."

"Why you say he no nice?"

Darby does not want to tell her so much about Pickles that she is scared of him, "Well, when we were kids he always used to say to me, 'Some cause happiness wherever they go; others whenever they go.'"

"That no nice. Why he say that to you, Darby?"

"I dunno, it's a quote from some poet or somethin'."

"What about Sadie, she have baby too?"

"Well, he's not a baby anymore but—"

"Where they now?"

Darby tilts his head, "I'm not sure. I have to find her though."

"Yes, you do. I want to meet her, how can I help find her?"

"She's in hidin'."

"Hide? Why?"

She is scared of me, Darby thinks. *She knows I am after her to pay for Pickles' retrial.*

"Her husband is a gang leader," he says instead.

"Sadie, did she travel from London to America together with Frank?"

"Yeah."

"Where Frank move you say? Conn. . . Connect—"

"Connecticut."

"Yes, Conne-ti-cut, Sadie will go there. She want to be with Frank, her family. The family she trust. A mother go to people she trust."

"I hadn't thought o' that," Darby says.

"See what happen when you speak with words instead of thinking, thinking forever?"

Darby almost smiled at that.

He had never witnessed anybody learn a new language. But Ligeia made it seem easy. Plus, communicating with her is much simpler than with others. Every exaggerated movement of her hands, every large-eyed revelation is easy to translate. From her full lips, he can read all the English words she learned. He had never met anyone who makes their thoughts more obvious in facial expressions and hand gestures than Ligeia. It is a match made in heaven.

They should make a theater show about us, Darby thinks. *And call it "The Lonely Lipreader and the Playful Pantomime."*

The way she speaks reminds Darby of the Italian men he witnessed being murdered when Bill's gang took them by surprise after the storm. But they weren't just Italian men. They were regular, normal men with wives, children, parents, grandparents, aunts and uncles.

Figlia, figlia, the Italian man's words haunt in a trance-like chant. *Figlia, figlia.* Darby remembers when the crier looked back at him with a thankful look on his face when the .45 was pulled away from the back of his head. That was his last emotion, because he never even saw Bill point it at his temple and fire.

Darby looks down on his linen shirt with the rust-colored blood stains.

Italian blood. Ligeia is someone's figlia too.

"Darby?" She comes to his face again and holds it in her palms. "Don't go away, Darby. Stay with me. Sometimes you get a eh-look on you face, and then you go away and talk no more. I no like that."

But he does not answer her. Instead, he looks at the ring he gave her that Frank loaned him the money for. It is so thin that he worries it might snap. It is only a band and does not have a diamond on it. A diamond, Darby could not afford. He reaches with his free hand and holds her ring finger and his fiancé's smile warms him. She walks over to the window to shed light on it and holds her hand out flat.

With Colleen Rose sleeping in his left arm, he goes down on a knee and looks up to Ligeia's eyes, "Will ya marry me?"

"I already say yes, Darby. Stand up, the baby no breath so good like that."

"I'm gonna ask ya every day," Darby's face is an unflinching mask. "Every single day, because I want the commitment we made to each other fresh in my mind until the day comes when we can afford to raise ourselves up from here as a true fam'ly in our own home. This ring represents my commitment to ya, because my commitment is true. But no matter what, we do it together. Ligeia. . . Will ya marry me?"

"Yes, yes, just stand up."

And Darby does, "Ya saved me from. . . From myself. I will always be in ya debt, Ligeia. I love ya so much. I'm sorry I'm still kinda lost sometimes. Ya brought me this angel. An angel o' hope. Now I want to live again. I want to provide for us, but—"

"But what?"

But I think I'm too damaged already. I am an idiot. I don't deserve you.

"But what Darby, tell me?"

"No, you tell me somethin'," Darby says to her as they stand in front of the window. "Where were ya born."

"Ellis Island," she waves a hand over her head.

"No. It's there ya was reborn. We're both immigrants to this country. Colleen Rose will one day want to know o' our lives. Tell me again."

"It's no good, my-eh story."

"I won't tell nobody but Colleen Rose, it's just me an' her, that's all."

"I'm eh-gonna cry if I—"

"I wanna listen."

Ligeia takes a deep breath, "I was eh-born in back of a wagon that carry fresh-picked apricots on a dirt road on border between the regions *Basilicata*, where my peasant mother was born and raised, and *Calabria* where my father, a married politician come from. I was born Ligeia Guida DeSantis, and they say I am not only *figlia de puttana*, a whore's daughter, but also without a region. An *Italiano's* region very, very important, you understand. In America it no matter so much where you mother or father were born or what class they come from or even if they married. But in Italy very, very important. Class, status. And I come from bottom, a bastard. Not even a boy bastard. *Bastardo ragazza. Infamia.* A girl bastard."

Darby reads the words that come out of her beautiful lips and repeats the Italian word he learned recently, "*Figlia.*"

"Yes, *figlia. la figlia nessuno vuole.* No one want this type of daughter."

"I do."

Ligeia gives a half smile and flicks impatiently at a tear on her cheek, "When I arrive at Ellis Island, I never find my cousin who sent for me. I was eh-twenty years old when I step off plank of the big steamer. I search desperate for my cousin but no one hold a sign that read "Ligeia DeSantis." When they pull my ship away from Ellis Island by three loud little tugboats, and a new ship take its place along the eh-pillars that hold up the dock, I worry so much. And I wait so long. Then wait more. I sit on the luggage in a dress that still have the scent of the Italian countryside. One man with a fat belly and paper approach me, 'Where ya goin'? Manhatt'n? Brooklyn? Bronx? Queens? Where?' Ligeia pushes her belly out to impersonate the Ellis Island employee and does her best at a New York accent too. "Where ya goin'? Eh?'

"I never know where my cousin live. My cousin was supposed to *bring* me there from Ellis Island. I never knew the name of the place. Was it Brooklyn? Bronx? The words sound same to me. And back then, I have no English so I say, 'Brooklyn?'

She pushes her stomach out again, "'Take that ferry, g'ahead,' he tell me and walk away.

"In Brooklyn, I see through the fog the big buildings and the Statue Liberty and more buildings beyond. Then I go hungry. So I walk and walk. I walk around the South Brooklyn Italian neighborhoods by day and sleep under stairwells and benches for the night. No one help me. Even they know *infamia* when they see her.

"One day a Sicily woman named *La Sorrisa* come to me on Sackett eh-Street and help carry my luggage. She have a accent in Italian even me no understand."

"'*Ti porterò dal principe*, I take you to the Prince,' she say to me. I did not know America have prince and princesses, kings and queens.

"'*Si, si*, the Prince o' Pals,' *La Sorrisa* say to me again. '*Vieni con me*. Come with me. The Prince o' Pals *always* knows what to do.'

"But this eh-Prince of Pals? He buy me from *La Sorrisa*, then sell me to the family Stabile to work as *puttana* at, oh I forget the name."

"The Adonis Social Club."

"That it, you know this place?"

"Yeah."

"I no work there, I run. Right away, I run. I no *puttana*, you understand? How you say in English?"

"Whore or slattern."

"I no whore or slattern, no, never. I run and that night I find you on stairs when—"

"No," Darby says. "I don' wanna talk about that. That I can't talk about. Listen, the Prince o' Pals is a fella by the name o' Frankie Yale, see? He's Black Hand."

"Black Hand? Oh, I see. *La Mano Nera*, now I know. Now I see."

"An' so is the Adonis," Darby turns to look at her. "I gotta go there."

"For why? You have me for—"

"It's for business. I'm lookin' to find somethin' out."

"Find out what?"

Should I talk to her? Yes, I should. I should tell her everything.

"Well, there's this girl that my boss asked me to find who she had, uh. . . He wants to know who she lost her purity to."

"Purity? *Pureza* eh? Why?"

Darby swallows, "He wants to kill that man."

"This your boss eh?"

"Yeah."

DIVIDE THE DAWN

"Now I see. I have known men like this. They are blind to a woman's *pureza*. Dangerous men, they are. An' he ask you to find this out for him. It's secret, yes?"

"Yeah."

"Ah, well you must do your job, Darby. This man pay for you, me, Colleen Rose so we can get new home. Yes, yes. This girl who lost her *pureza*, who does she have as best friend?"

"I dunno, maybe Grace an' Kit, two slatterns at the Adonis."

"Go to them. They know too. She share with them her story, I know this about women. So here what you do; take knife to *puttanas* and put to their throat and tell them you kill them if they don't give the information. Where Grace and Kit live?"

"The Henhouse. A place where the Black Hand keeps their top earners."

"Go there. Quiet as cat. No go to Adonis, too dangerous there. I know."

"How do you know? How do you know all o' this?"

"*En Italia*, we know things. But Darby, you must be very careful with this boss. He is a bad man. Do not fail him, he will kill you if you fail him. What is his name?"

Darby looks away, "I-talians call him *Pulcinella*. An' from what I hear, he looks for signs in nature an' thinks himself reborn as some warrior chieftain."

"*Pulcinella, eh? La marionette?* I see. They have fear of him. You need to do these things, find Sadie and the lover of Anna for you boss. What else?"

I need to put a name to a face, but maybe that can wait.

"There's nothin' else."

"Then we go."

"We?"

"We go to Conne-ti-cut, you, me and Colleen Rose. Together, yes. After that, you go to Henhouse, let us go now."

"Why do ya wanna go wit' me?"

"I like Frank. He good man. He tell me his wife no can have baby. He cry when Colleen Rose come. He love

Colleen Rose and he say his wife want to see her too. He say this to me in hospital."

"He did?"

"Let us go there now."

"I would, but my boss wants me to come meet him for a secret raid."

"A secret what?"

"Raid, like an attack."

"You no soldier, Darby, my love."

"I could be, maybe."

"No, you no go, Darby. Do not go to *Pulcinella* if you not know this information, Get information first."

"He said I *gotta* go to it, this raid."

"Maybe I go talk to this *Pulcinella* then, eh?"

No, never. You can never talk to Wild Bill Lovett, he hates all Italians.

"Darby, when you have his information, he will pay you? He will give you things, like important title or something? Status among the other men, right?"

"Yeah, he said he'd consider me for Fifth Lieutenant, then I'd make good money."

"Darby, my love," Ligeia takes the baby from his arms. "No go to secret raid, please, my love. If you no have information, he kill you. This secret raid? It no exist, Darby. He will kill you instead."

"But I have to show up, Bill is a stickler on punctuality, a disciplinarian. If I don' show up, he'll send someone to. . ."

"Darby don't eh-leave me here alone in this place with baby. I can't be alone again, no. Darby, Darby listen to my words, Darby, no, no—"

"It'll be alright," Darby brings her close.

"Have you see him kill before? Have you?"

Yes, many times. All were Italian.

"No," he answers and takes her hand again so that he may see the ring he gave her. "I made a commitment to ya. An' that commitment is sacred to me. Is it sacred to ya as well?"

"Yes."

"I will be back, my love. I will be back to fulfill my commitment."

Ligeia takes a deep breath and crosses herself, *"In nomine Patris et Filii et Spiritus Sancti. Amen."*

She pulls the cross from inside her blouse and kisses it, then reaches up to wrap a hand round Darby's neck as she lay her head on his chest.

Mary Magdalene's Blemish

I hope they try and stop me, Anna bites her lip as she approaches the guarded door of the Lonergan bicycle shop.

Petey Behan looks at her with a box-faced smile, "Yo Anna, who was it got a leg over on ya, eh? Timmy Bucks says it was Poe Garrity, but I says no way."

Anna looks at Timmy with his buck teeth protruding from an open gob, "This fookin' muppet? He might be able to eat a apple through a tennis racket, but he don' know the first thing about what a woman wants."

Matty giggles when Timmy's face scarlets.

Anna turns and comes face to face with Petey, then steps closer so that their noses almost touch, "An' you? By the end o' this day, ya will pay for those words wit' blood."

She moves to walk past, but Petey stands in front of the door, "What's the password?"

"Fuck you ya fookin' box o' rocks."

"That ain't it."

Anna wheels round and throws a punch and just as Petey is about to retaliate, her big brother Richie comes out the door and stares wordlessly at Petey until he backs away.

Anna flies into the bicycle shop with the wind as the door crashes against the wall.

Her mother Mary sits at a small desk with tears in her eyes. Forever with tears in her eyes. There are different types of tears that come from her mother. Some are begot by anger. Some from self-pity. Others for the martyrdom of Jesus on the cross. And still more for the all-too rare acts of kindness offered to her.

The begging mother, the mendicant mother, they should call her.

Anna knows all the types of tears Mourning Mother Mary has in her arsenal. But the tears that fill her eyes today are borne of defeat.

Anna slams the door and looks to her younger brother, sixteen-year old Willie who stands next to Richie's most-trusted follower, the curly-haired Abe Harms.

"Go outside Willie," she coldly commands.

"I'm old enough to know what's goin' on around here," Willie protests.

"Get out right god'amn now!" Anna screams and kicks the small desk over that her mother sits behind.

"Ya go out as well Abe. . . go," her voice low now, assured. "This is a fam'ly matter." She turns her eyes back to Willie, "For the elders o' the fam'ly, both o' yaz go."

As Willie walks past her, Abe touches Anna's elbow so gently that she thought it might be a fly. He leans into her ear with breath of cool mint, "Bevare your family's fury," says he. "But a big brother is forever your champion, yez."

"Wha?" Anna turns angrily, yet something compels her to whisper back to him. "I don' need a champion."

"If only a lady might need one to protect. . . or avenge her," he backs away with eyes of supplication.

Avenge? Avenge what? What does he know?

Anna turns slowly to Richie, but cannot get a read on his impassive, pale eyes. Then to her mother. Exposed, Mary is bellowing and jiggling and sagging in the chair that now has no desk in front of it. Mourning Mother Mary sobs like a great shoulder-less pigeon with a long, chinless neck of wattling flesh. Her hands clasp over her face in remorseful shame with breasts that slope low under a plain sack dress. The bun atop her gray-peppered hair is unkempt and falls to her slumped neck like onion skins. Mary drops her hands for a moment to look at her eldest daughter, the burn across the left side of her face revealed.

"Anna," Mary announces in her half-Brooklyn, half-Irish accent. "What are ya wearin'? Ya look a migrant person in them frugal togs, ya do. A peasant blouse an' a skirt? At least pull ya hair back like a lady, eh? What happened to ya? Did a man hurt ya? Was it the man who gave ya money to pay our rent? Oh, nah, nah, nah. . . Please tell me it's lies bein' spread 'bout ya."

"Why would I do that?"

Mary stands up at the same height as Anna, but is much heavier and speaks in a low, calm tone, "Anna, I want ya to know I'll always love ya now matter—"

"Isn't that ya job, Ma? I mean ya love him don't ya?" she points at Richie.

Mother Mary squirms, "Course I do."

"Why would ya consider not lovin' me then?"

"Anna, if ya could just understand. What ya have is a gift from god. Beauty an' youth. Good men want that, but—"

"But what? they don' want me now? An' if they don' want me, then I'm like garbage? Ya think I'm thick as planks and don' see things for the way they are Ma?"

"Ya just left us. Where did ya go, Anna? Where? Even now, where do ya sleep? Oh! It's all lost," Mary cries out. "A woman's weapon is the wound that weeps love. God blimey, if ya don' use it ya're through. Ya're a woman now, Anna. A woman has love in her heart. Ya purity unblemished is the gift ya bestow upon a man who earns it, Anna. I won't believe ya to be the demimonde they name ya. If it's true, ya have to go to Father Larkin, sweetness. Repent, repent like Mary Magdalene. Tell me then, what do ya love?"

Anna turns away in thought, *I love Neesha, forever and always*.

"Ya won't even answer, will ya? No, ya won't. Ya heart is black as coal, Anna an' ya nothin' but a. . . nothin' but a twist! Look at ya'self."

Anna's mouth goes small and her eyes narrow, but she says nothing.

Mary moves to focus on her son, "Richie I told ya to do what the man says—"

"His name's Dinny Meehan, Ma," Anna interrupts. "No one even calls him 'the man' anymore on account o' everyone knows who he is outside o' Irishtown now. We don' have to abide by his codes no more."

"It's lost," Mary buries her face in her hands. "Richie could be up there with the king above the Dock Loaders' Club right now—"

"King," Anna rolls her eyes.

"They're in control o' the waterfront an' the rake o' money it brings, but no. Both o' ya had to ruin our chances o' makin' it. Neither o' yaz would listen to reason. Now Bill's back an' there's war again. It's always the same round here is it not? Since before I even came it's been this way. Gang wars. Fightin' fer control o' labor so to charge the longshoremen the tribute money. I guess it'll always be this way, like we're just a moment in time. We'll be forgotten, surely we'll be forgotten an' they'll be twenny more kings o' Irishtown over the next twenty years, if truth be told. No one'll look back on the year 1919 an' think t'was any different. Another year, another war. I just wanted a future, Richie. A future, Anna. That's why ya have children, is it not? Ya have a future, but it's lost. It's gone now."

Richie wobbles to take the weight off his peg and put it on his lone leg, "Ma, it ain't lost—"

"T'is! Me own daughter uses the lord's name in vain and gives her body 'way like some—"

"Slattern?" Anna finishes. "An' as for our lord, he's got no answers for us either, Ma. Every time I went to talk wit' Father Larkin, he'd tell me to light a candle or pray an' to be quiet an' do my duty an' take care o' the children an' keep my purity so I can attract some hairy-arsed man to marry me an' support me so I can bring more children onto this dirty earth. There's no future that I'm willing to submit to. There's none offered me."

"Oh Anna ya've always been so full o' the vinegar an' with a tongue as sharp as a serpent's tooth."

Anna grits her teeth and grabs her squealing mother by the shoulder, "An' I want ya to know Ma. The man who ya believe I slept wit' at the Adonis Social Club? The man that paid our rent durin' Winter? He didn' take my stupit purity. Brooklyn did. Bein' in this family did. You did!"

"Stop it Anna, please stop it," Mary tries to ward her off with a sign of the cross. "Let me go, don't tell me no more."

"Ya took my blood, Ma!" Anna screams and pushes her mother. "Ya tried to betroth me to that boy Liam Garrity, remember? Sell me off like a farm animal for that future o' yours. An' what about me? What about what I want? Ya never asked. Ya an' Dinny just put together a plan to hurry up an' marry us so that he could inherit Richie's followers an' all the little Lonergan boys like Willie for his gang, an' ya could stand tall as Queen Mother o' Irishtown. It all made so much sense to ya, didn' it? But now? Now ya future's gone 'cause I'm stronger than ya. I won," Anna points into her own chest above Mary. "I won the right to decide my own future."

"Ya mighta won, but we all lost because o' it. The whole fam'ly. An' fer what, eh? So ya could besmirch ya soul in the face o' god? In the bed o' some lustful stranger? So we could pay rent fer a few months? Nah, nah, nah! Ya'd be happy to put ya mother through the depths o' hell to have ya own way wit'out a single t'ought fer ya brothers an' sisters. What do I say to the people what name ya a slattern, Anna? What do I say to them?"

"Tell them the Lonergan fam'ly survived a winter wit'out losin' any more children, an' that ya daughter took matters into her own hands in the face o' her mother and father's lunacy. The fookin' lunacy o' this fam'ly caused all this! It's ya fault Richie lost his leg, ya know. What type o' mother sends a eight year-old twelve blocks for bread in a city wit' streetcars on every block?"

"Anna," Mary swallows the pride that had welled up in her throat. "Anna listen to me, Bill has a black drop in him, ya know. He has it from his grandfather. His father not so much, but his grandfather killt men an' would fight any man until he fought a man twice his size an' was beat to death. The black drop might be good fer soldierin', but ya should steer clear from him, Anna. Mother to daughter, understand?"

"So we should go meekly into Dinny's favor?" Anna waves her mother off. "Just keep ya advice to ya'self, Ma."

"Oh, it hurts, it hurts so bad," her mother is holding her hand at the wrist again.

"What hurts, Ma?" Anna asks.

"I can feel it," Mary calls out and holds her hands above her head. "I can feel ya, Jesus. I can feel ya pain. I have it! I have ya pain in my wrists an' in my ankles where ya was nailed to the cross by the Romans, persecuted by the Jews. The nails! Oh they hurt."

"This again," Anna shakes her head.

"The Great Tribulaton!" Mary screams. "Worse than ever's happent! All the signs are bein' shown us! Our faith is shaken but we must continue to believe. The sun an' moon will darken now an' the stars'll fall from the sky. The Son o' Man will appear in his great glory amidst the clouds. Listen for the trumpet. Ya must *listen*! An' then ya will see his angels accompany him. I have been granted the rights o' prophecy. The saints an' the angels give me visitation—"

"Is she mad?" Anna asks Richie, though he does not answer.

"Anna, can't ya see it? Can't ya?" Mary rushes up to her, but gently strokes down Anna's arm. "Even the auld augurs in Irishtown see it. But they don' know. They don' understand what's really happenin'. They say the moon will rise an' the hero will come, but they're pagans. Somethin's comin' alright, but it ain't no hero or archons or orphans an' all that silliness, nah, nah, nah. I tell ya Anna, I can feel Jesus in me hands an' in me feet. Where they nailed him to the cross, I feel it. I do, I swear it, child."

She is mad, She can't be round the children. Anna looks at Richie. *He can't even communicate. Who will care for our little siblings if their mother is psychopathic?*

"Anna, one night I woke up an' I was bleedin' from the wrists. Look, look, here are the scars. In these days we pass through a final fire, ya see. There've been fires everywhere in Brooklyn o' late. More are to come. An' storms too! Hunger. Death! All the businesses are lettin' men go. No more ships! No more European contracts. That's what all o' this is, ya see. God is puttin' ya t'rough this difficult time to test ya, understand? If ya believe, ya will seek penance like Mary Magdalene. Ya will, ya will. Before it's too late. He's comin'," Mary raises her arms again. "God, send us ya son. I know it is he who comes."

The bell on the door jingles as John Lonergan stumbles in. The room goes quiet except for the snuffles of Mourning Mother Mary. The father walks along the wall of bicycles sideways until he stops. He looks at the desk on the ground, then to Anna and clears his throat, "I've been laughed outta Red Hook. Bill. . . he just laughs. I'm lower than Darby Leighton now. I'm the lowest o' them all."

"The final fires are risin'," Mary mumbles. "An' what about Richie? Can he go back?"

"Richie's Richie," he slurs.

Mary declares "Oh but it's only a matter o' time 'til the man decides not to pay the rent any longer wit' the both o' yaz followin' his sworn enemy. The fires. The fires. "

"Dad rarely works anyway," Anna sneers. "Richie's been the breadwinner for years, an' I aim to help him do even better."

John licks his lips and looks into the face of his daughter, "Is it true?"

Anna's anger turns to shame, and the pit of her stomach tumbles with her father's question.

"That's where ya got all that money over the winter, right?"

Anna looks over her shoulder to Richie. Then slowly back to her father, "Ya're not capable o' supporting a fam'ly, Dad. Step aside so Richie an' I can take care o' things from here on out. Even she's worthless now," Anna says turning to Mary.

John looks to Richie, then back to Anna, "Everything'll be a lot better when ya walk out that door wit' a broken face." John balls up his fists. "That's when everyone outside'll know what happens when a daughter turns into a slattern. Then I'll get my honor back in the eyes o' men. Only then."

Anna moves in closer, daring him. Sticking her chin out.

I don't care anymore. Beating me means nothing. Do it.

"Oh my god!" Mary screams.

John flies at her and grabs a handful of hair, pulling her to the ground where he sits on top of her. Anna claws up at his face but her father's hand closes round her throat. She watches as he winds a fist from behind his ear and crashes it down onto her mouth, breaking the skin.

Anna spits her blood back up at him, "G'ahead, kill me! Kill me!"

John punches her again as Anna sees her mother come from behind her abuser in an attempt to catch the fists before they come down on Anna's face.

Anna can't see her brother, but calls for him, "Richie!" Another punch falls onto her face, "Richie!"

"I'm in charge here," John screams at her. "Richie listens to me, not ya'self."

As John pulls back for yet another punch and lands it, all turns black. Anna's eyes are open, but all is black. She reaches out with her hands to touch something, anything, but she cannot see. Then there is a doorway. It's a pier door and both shutters are open. Outside is the water and beyond she can see the Statue of Liberty. The sound of a gun clap scares her. Then he emerges from the darkness.

"Neesha?" Anna calls. "Neesha, ya're bleedin'? Ya're head is bleedin'."

She holds Neesha's amber hair, but all she feels is the slick blood that flows from the back of his head.

"They killt ya, my love. They killt my love," Anna says.

Anna's eyes blink until she can again focus to see that her father is suddenly pulled off of her. He lands on the ground next to her with a thump. Richie had yanked him by the collar and tossed him aside. Before John can get up again, Richie is in his space, mauling him with lefts and rights though Richie's face is devoid of emotion and he never loses his breath. When John tries to roll to one side, Richie cuts him off and plants knuckled fists into his father's face, five, six, seven times. Upper cuts and back fists and finally a knee up to his nose while Mary is still on the ground rolling round like big baby stuck on its back.

Richie falls to his knees next to Anna and with a strangely placid voice, he asks, "Are ya uhright?"

Anna pulls long strands of hair out of the meaty chunks of skin from her bloody mouth. Her big brother helps her sit up as he squats over her and thumbs blood from under her eye.

Again Anna searches in Richie's eyes, but cannot find much of anything inside. She looks closer still, and still nothing.

"Richie," she says calmly. "Don' ever let no one do that to me again."

"Uhright," he answers.

"Richie," Anna repeats without a sign of tears on her face nor anger in her voice. "Not even Bill."

Richie looks at Anna with a simple stare and nods, "No one'll do this. Never."

"Help me up."

Richie stands and offers his hand until they clasp at each other's wrists. He pulls her up easily, his grip strong as iron. Thoughtless, he pulls her close and looks down at their father sprawled on the ground and puts an arm around her to help her walk.

"I love ya Richie," Anna hears herself say and is as surprised as her brother by it. "Ya my fam'ly an' I'll protect ya too. I promise, Richie. I do."

Richie's eyes move and his mouth wiggles as he searches for the right thing to say.

He is my brother and I don't care what is wrong with him, Anna thinks. *He could never say the wrong thing. Even when he says nothing, it's fine. He is my brother. My blood.*

As brother and sister step outside under a cobalt gray sky, Tim Quilty and Abe Harms step aside. Up the Bridge Street hill a gust of wind ripples through their clothing. Anna's fox-colored hair whips behind her and stands on end and swirls and dances six-and-a-half feet in the air like dragon flames.

"It's true, ain't it?" Petey Behan speaks in the direction of Anna and Richie, though his eyes are at his shoes. "Ya're still pure, ain't ya? Matty told me so."

Before Anna can answer, Richie speaks, "It is true. An' if I hear anyone say otherwise ever again, they will die screamin'."

Petey turns to Anna, "I'm. . . I'm sorry Anna. I was wrong. I didn' know. I'm sorry."

"Me too," Matty takes off his hat and holds it in a hand. "I'm sorry."

"Sorry Anna," Timmy stands awkwardly to the side attempting to cover his buck teeth with his lips.

But Abe Harms offers only a slight, congratulatory smile, salutes her with a half open hand and steps back into a genuflecting curtsy, "My lady."

Vercingetorix Reborn

Inside the covered pierhouse it smells of dead fish and vomit. The arched iron double doors creak on rusted hinges as Non Connors opens them and tells Darby Leighton to sit down in the chair at the small wooden table where a ball-peen hammer lay on its side.

"Don' touch that," Connors commands.

Outside the arched loading doors the New York Harbor moils and churns round Governor's Island. And beyond, the Statue of Liberty reaches above amidst the current of steamers, barges, docked warships and tugboats that crisscross through the harbor traffic's shipping lanes.

Darby sits in the chair and looks at the hammer on the table. On the floor in front of the loading doors is enough dried blood to evidence a murder had occurred.

Mickey Kane.

The name rings through Darby's head. The memory of that night is enough to make him shudder. The storm raged and Colleen Rose entered into this life as Mickey Kane exited. *This is where it happened. Right in here after I gave the gun to Richie.*

Bill Lovett comes in through the pier entrance behind Darby, walks round him, then sits at the chair across the table as Non Connors closes the entrance door behind him, leaving them.

"What ya find out?"

"About Anna?"

"Did ya tell anyone about the secret mission?"

"No," Darby answers as his mouth squiggles slightly.

Bill raises his hand, "Talk."

"Well uh, nobody seems to know much about who Anna slept wit'. People are takin' bets though."

"Bets?"

"Yeah."

"So everybody knows about it, but nobody knows who it is?"

"Not everybody, just the tunics. Petey an' a few others have backed off ever since Richie sorted them out."

"Tunics?"

"Before Brosnan disappeared, I asked—"

"So ya only asked Brosnan?"

"No, I asked others, but only Brosnan was makin' bets wit' his son-in-law'r."

"Dead man's words," Bill growls to himself.

"How do ya know he's dead, Bill?"

Bill eyes him and grits, "Ya name me a cop killer?"

"No, I—"

"What did Brosnan say before. . . Before he disappeared."

"He said he didn' know, didn' care. Here's the thing, Bill. Women, they like to share their uh, emotional experiences in life, right?"

Bill's brow furrows and confusion turns his face blank, "They do what?"

"Ya know, they talk things out, right? That's just what they do. So my next move is to sneak into the Henhouse an' make them slatterns tell me. If someone bedded her—"

"They'll tell ya, I get it," Bill pulls out his .45 caliber and drops it on the table next to the ball-peen hammer with a thud.

He kill you, Ligeia's words echo in Darby's thoughts. *If you no have information, he kill you.*

"So ya still don' know then," Bill puckers his lips and pushes his chin out. "Ya fail me?"

"Nah, Bill."

"Seems like it to me."

This is the time to save yourself, Darby thinks. *But how? I can't even bring up the mysterious man with the Windsor glasses because I still can't put a name to his face.*

Darby stammers, "Bill. . . This kinda. . . This kinda information don' come out so easy—"

"We don' got time for patience, we're surrounded," Bill leans into that word. "*Surrounded*, Darby. They got their fookin' noose round our necks an' we gotta go on raids to weaken their ability to pull it. Because once they pull it, we choke to death, see?"

"I know—"

"Tell me about Sadie, then."

Darby's teeth clatter in his head until he clinches his jaw, "What about her?"

Bill gives a half shrug, "How much money does she give ya?"

"She has given me about two hundret dollars."

"She really wants Pickles released? Why does she want that?"

"Because we're fam'ly. Pickles an' I paid for her passage an' now that she's escaped—" Darby swallows before saying the name, "Now that she's escaped Dinny—"

"Some people think ya're bribin' her. That ya gotta secret she don' want nobody knowin' about."

"Abe thinks that."

"So does Thos Carmody. So it's true?"

"It's a secret. I can't tell ya. It's a *fam'ly* secret."

Bill's hand immediately goes to the big Colt .45 on the table. He palms it, but let's it go after biting back his anger, "Where's she stayin' now, Sadie?"

"In hidin'."

"Where?"

"I can't tell ya that either, Bill."

"Ya fookin' Leighton bastard fookin' asshole cunts," Bill picks up the .45 caliber with one hand and the ballpeen hammer with the other. "The whole fookin' lot o' yaz. Sometimes I think it's the Leightons that hold the noose round my neck, ya know that?"

"Nah Bill—"

"Pickles won't give me the soldiers, ya won't give me information an' Sadie's fundin' somethin' I got no evidence is even in the works."

"The retrial's in May, Bill. It's comin'."

"Oh it fookin' better be," Bill waves the hand cannon in Darby's face, then pets him with it. Darby blinks when he feels it touch his eyelashes.

"Ya know," Bill pets him again. "When I look in ya eyes, all I see is. . . indecision. Ya got no fookin' discipline, no sense o' duty, no loyalty," he stops on that word, then moves on. "I see doubt an' worse, I see ya doubt ya'self. Ya know how that makes a surrounded captain feel? Furious. On the front we executed men who had eyes like yours. Shell shock, some smart guys wanted to call it. But shell shock's just another word for weakness, cowardice. At war, there's no room for weakness. No time for cowardice. So we tied them up an' put a bullet in the back o' their heads an' made sure everyone in the comp'ny watched for the example in it. We all have a fate. Is that gonna be ya fate, Darby?"

The desperate turn to fate or destiny as their claim, the thought appears in Darby's mind, but he can't remember exactly where it came from. *Yet Bill Lovett falls for fate, hook, line and sinker.*

Bill pushes his tongue into the side of his cheek, "I wanna be clear about somethin', so sit there an' listen. I want two things from ya, an' I need them both. One: The man who stole Anna's purity from me. Two: Pickles released. Is that clear?"

"Yeah."

"Here's the thing; if ya don' get me both I'm gonna make ya stand up right there," Bill turns round and points at the dried puddle of blood in front of the arched loading door. "An' let Petey Behan shoot ya in the head. Right in the back o' the head an' ya brains'll come out ya eye sockets an' ya nose an' mouth an' ears. Petey wants to be Fifth Lieutenant, see? But he's never killt nobody either. Well there was that Joe Garrity affair, but it wasn't him that dealt the fatal blow."

Darby again shudders at the memory of it.

"The worst thing ya can have as a soldier on the warfront is a imagination," Bill says. "The thing is, I need ya to prove ya loyalty to me now, Darby. Because I don' see it. My lieutenants don' see it. Even the Shit Hounds don' trust ya. Prove me ya loyalty right now," he pets his face again with the .45. "Prove me it. . . or take a swim wit' Mickey Kane, ya will."

"Wanin' Gibbous," the words come to Darby's lips, but he can scarcely believe he heard them himself.

"The what?"

"It was a sign. A sign to be interpreted by he who sees it."

Bill's mouth opens and his shoulders drop, "What kinda sign?"

"When we all gathered under the stairwell in the snow," Darby sits up in the chair, his eyes aglow. "We thought ya was dead, Bill. I stood among ya men an' heard their words. An' when ya appeared above, they knew ya had been brought by the white mornin' moon over ya shoulder swimmin' in a blue sky, just like. . . Just like the old augurs o' Irishtown had predicted. They been tellin' them stories since. . . Since before even I came to Brooklyn in 1895. They saw ya comin' from a distance, Bill. An' ya men? They knew ya took the life o' Irishtown's prince an' heir. Don' let ya'self think they can't see the symbolism o' that. I know ya believe ya'self a Captain. But the men, an' myself. We know ya as Vercingetorix, King o' Gaul, an' that ya've come back to unite the Celts an' set the Romans straight. They see ya as the seed o' their hope. The seed o' the people. Do ya understand, Bill? We see a king. A king reborn. Ya must forego ya captainship, see," Darby's opens his eyes as wide as he can and whispers. "Become the king. Only a king can sit at the desk, the seat above the Dock Loaders' Club, under the bridge. The seat where power pulses, then emanates down into the Brooklyn docks like blood through arteries so that the money can flow back up through its veins. Ya got Non Connors an' one-arm Flynn to lead the troops, but ya'self? Ya gotta give the men what they have been told since they were little boys. Ya gotta be the man they prayed for to return when Mickey Kane," Darby moves his eyes to the bloodstained floor and nods. "When Mickey Kane was dockboss here, an' the men were lost. Now that they are found, ya gotta give them what they see. An' everythin' that's happened in ya life was but to prepare ya for this moment. Be the king, Bill. "

"I uh," Bill is at a loss for words and holsters his .45 caliber. "I never listened to them fookin' soup stories in Irishtown. Did they really foresee my comin'?"

I think so? They speak of five archons and three orphans who raise up a hero.

"They did," Darby assures.

Bill lowers one eye and shakes a pointed finger at Darby, "You. . . Ya see ya'self as some kinda druid or somethin'? Ya eyes, they look different now."

"I have not changed, Bill," Darby sits back. "It is ya'self that can see now."

Bill laughs, but Darby continues, "I can see the signs too, but I'm ya shadow agent, remember? It's what ya named me. The thing is; how do ya ever prove a spy is loyal? How do ya test it? A spy moves between the enemy an' the ally an' no one can ever tell the difference. The thing is, Bill. I'm not here to show ya loyalty. My message will not always be well-taken an' oftentimes it'll be too difficult for ya to hear the words an' the. . . visions."

Bill sits back down at the table without taking his eyes off of Darby's eyes, "The moon was a sign? To them?"

"It's called the Wanin' Gibbous, a sign o' great turbulence an' a changeover from the old to the new. When the men saw'r it, they knew ya were reborn by their hopes."

Bill reveals a half-embarrassed smile, then turns his eyes back to him, "When? When will it happen? When will I be king?"

"The signs often take time to interpret. We often don' notice them when they occur, it takes the eyes o' a hawk to see them. Ya see, there is a reason why I lost most o' my hearin'."

"Wha? Why?"

"Because when we lose one sense, our other senses become stronger."

"Ya fookin' crazy, ya know that?"

"Bill," Darby stares him down. "I am at ya service."

Bill's jaw moves until he turns round and leans an arm against the arched door, "Ya know when I was in France, I could feel him."

"Who?"

"Vercingetorix, like his bones spoke to me through the earth. A man experiences things in battle, an' I felt him as if we was fightin' together on the same blood-soaked soil. An' where we were in the Argonne forest? It was not too far from where the great Battle o' Alesia happened in 52BC against Caesar. What's two thousand years to a ghost? Nothin', nothin' at all, " Bill grunts and leans his back against the wall now. "Everyone tells me I died there. I dunno. I don' remember that. But there is a long time period where I don' remember anythin' at all. If I did die, I know the soul or the ghost o' Vercingetorix was runnin' round my body, waitin'. Waitin' to leap in an' animate me again so to square things up wit' the I-Talian, see? An' Anna. Anna was there too. Shit, she was just a girl when I left, an' I never once felt a thing for her growin' up here in Brooklyn. But on the battlefield she became my angel, ya know? Like a white angel all pure an' innocent an' uh, matronly an' nurturin' wit' a heart made o' kitten fur. An' Vercingetorix? He was my black angel."

Darby listens closely.

"I need ya to find out the name o' the man who rode Anna, understand?"

"Yeah."

"When I kill him, I will have his soul. An' she'll be pure again."

A silence takes the pierhouse that Darby finds endearing.

We have had a moment together, he and I. A meaningful moment.

Bill shakes off the memories and hoots out with a wild call, "That's the first time I ever talked about that. Fookin' feels good."

Bill smiles at Darby until he suddenly grabs the hammer, "Uhright, but I still need to test ya. Tell me, Abe went over ya role for the raid, right?"

"He did, but I'm not a soldier, Bill. I can't go on raids."

Bill grumbles under his breath, then looks over to Darby with disgust on his mouth, "The more people I know, the more I just wanna be wit' my dogs."

Bill lets that hang in the air for a moment until he looks back up again, "Ya goin' wit', an' that's the end o' it. I wanna see ya prove ya loyalty in the. . . in the real world. Tell me then, what's ya role in the raid?"

"I dunno, Abe said somethin' about keepin' a door closed."

Bill smiles, "Not good enough," he turns to the door and yells. "Non, come in here."

The door opens and Non Connors speaks through the crack, "Yeah?"

"Bring in Richie."

Darby's stomach drops, "Bill—"

"Shaddup, here's the thing," Bill says as he spins the hammer in the air and hands it to Richie. "Pain always helps ya learn things quicker, like. Somethin' else I learnt in France that prepared me for the present. An' on top o' that, ya never fookin' forget it either."

"What do I—"

"Break his finger in half," Bill says.

Without hesitation, Richie grabs Darby by the throat as the table is upended. Next thing Darby knows, Richie is sitting on his chest and holding his finger out. Then the hammer comes down with a smack.

A scream pierces the pierhouse as Richie walks out the door, allowing all outside to hear.

As Darby lifts his hand to his face, bile appears in his throat when he sees his pinky is broken and bent sideways, dangling by thin flaps of skin as blueish-red blood streams down his arm like reaching roots.

Bill jumps on the ground to look in Darby's eyes again, "Now ya won't forget ya role, will ya?"

They Let Us Starve
April 1919

Dawn opens its cloudy eyes to find hundreds of men filed along the shore, restless already. Hungry for work.

"Jab," Dance Gillen calls out, so I lean to the right and let the fist whip over my left shoulder. But he comes back with another left, this one a cross that catches my ribs.

I surge for breath as the cobalt gray morning sky pisses all over us, coming down sideways off the Atlantic Terminal. Out on the dappled currents of the river, scarves of rain cascade in the shape of foraging birds. A thousand waves as white as an old man's beard crest between here and the island of Manhattan where a hundred ships negotiate through the gray darkness along the turgid East River.

"Ya're slow t'day," Dance lowers his fists on the wet dock.

As a sparring partner Dance leaves me bruised and sore. I need it though, as he fights as tough as the Pavee brawler Tommy Tuohey ever had. He may not be the biggest, but he might be strongest and without question he has the fastest fists of the White Hand. He's a natural, and I'm an out of practice seventeen year-old who is in over his head on his first day alone as dockboss.

I take a deep breath, "Bring it back again. The jab and the left to the body."

From behind I hear Dago Tom's voice, "Liam, maybe ya should take a break. This barge'll be ready soon."

"Nah, let's go," I urge Dance. "Swing."

"Ya look tired," both Eddie and Freddie stand between Dance and I.

"Get out of my way," says I. And they do.

Inland, a crowd of some three hundred drenched and hopeful laborers watch on amidst the ballast of stone and gravel along the track bed and the sprawling network of the freight yard with its rolling stock, switches and an engine house with a thirty-foot tower above platforms and freight bays. Out on the echoing anchorage, harbor tugs moan in communication through the darkness, *hoo-hooooo*. Their hawser lines are strung high above and tied to the horn cleats of both the port quarter and the starboard beam of a giant engineless lighter barge. When the diesel engine of the tugboats are throttled, the slack is whipped taught to drag the old barge into dock, while the tug itself is lifted up and out of the water and spun violently. Closer to the pier five more tugs yank at the beast like the lilliputians who fettered Gulliver in the old book while two others push from behind.

I'm in over my head, the thought passes through me. *Petey Behan said I'm feckless and infirm, maybe he's right. If those laborers decide to charge they would butcher the White Hand at the Atlantic Terminal and I would be forever known as the dockboss who gave it up, just as Dinny Meehan had let Red Hook slip away. But at least I have help.*

As the sky flashes with lightning so distant that it is silent to our ears, Dance dances to his right with fists over his face, "Jab."

I duck the jab and move to my right to avoid the body shot, but he comes over top with the left cross this time and it catches the side of my head. For half a second the world falls into a haze as the low mutterings of thunder crackles down the dawn. My head tolls like a curfew bell and then the years flash before me and I am following my father through the turned fields of our Tulla farm. My older brother Timothy is next to me and together we are planting seeds behind Da, children again.

"I'll beat ye bloody an' bury ye in the field," Timothy ribbed me while I pushed seeds into the twisted soil.

"You won't."

"Yeah, ye're prolly right," Timothy flashed a coy smile from above. "Ye'll prolly be buried in some far off place."

"I won't, you eejit," I cry. "I'll be buried on the farm here. Or at least in Tulla parish."

Da stopped when he heard me. "Ye won't be buried on the farm, bhoy. Nor anywhere near the parish. Yer brother tells it right. Ye'll be gone from here by then. Ye may never come back."

I had run into the back of Da when he stopped. I gathered myself, blinked the dirt out of my eyes and looked up to him. "I don't want to go. I'm true to the family."

"I had two sons fer good reason," my father's voice washed over mine like rain does tears. "Yer mother an' I kept tryin' after Sean and Colm, my two bhoys that died durin' the first two winters of our marriage. When Timothy survived I said 'this one will take the fam'ly farm.' An' when yerself came along I said 'let him be close to his mother,' so I did. But great troubles are astir again. The next rebellion will be a bloody one an' ye'll take yer mother an' sisters 'way from here, so ye will. Ye'll not die here, Liam. Ye'll be gone."

"I don't want to—"

"Not up to ye," Da interrupted. "Ye think I'm bein' hard on ye, do ye? Ye don't know the half of it bhoy, for the enemy of us is a heartless savage that is after starvin' our fam'ly to death so to conquer us an' lie about it as if t'were a game. Then they'll write the hist'ry of it so it looks like t'was our own fault from the start of it. That's what they do. But we're not them, are we? I meself could never starve a fam'ly regardless of guilt or complicity. But I will butcher any foreigner that comes to my farm. An' on top of it I'll never repent to no man, priest or god fer it."

You thought you had it all figured out, Da. But you didn't. There was one thing you couldn't have known.

"Liam, ya ok?" Dance shakes my shoulders and quickly I blink my eyes again and I am back on the Atlantic Terminal with rain pelting my face.

You could not have known that New York would be as dangerous as war torn Ireland.

"Liam, can ya hear me?" Dance asks again as I come to my feet.

"I'm fine," I push him away but the bells still toll in my head.

"I'm sorry I hit ya that hard, Liam. I didn't think—"

"Don't worry. It's what I need to get better. I have to get better."

A few minutes later I am told The Swede and Vincent Maher are inside a covered pier.

I thought this was to be my first day alone?

I shake off the rain and walk through the narrow passageway where arched doors on either side offer soft gray light. At the end of the pier I see them both.

"There he is," Vincent smiles. "King o' the Atlantic Terminal."

"Why are you fellows here?"

The Swede does not turn round when I approach. Instead he stares out a rain-soaked window toward the morning skyline. Tiny windows glow in the distance across the East River and as he looks closer, his reflection appears in the window. I can't tell if he is looking at himself or the city beyond, but his grim and gaunt face comes into view.

"I want ya to know I'm always here for ya, Liam," he says without looking at me. "I watched ya come up an' I wasn't always good to ya, but ya made it now. Ya made it an' I'm proud o' ya."

"Thanks—"

"But it's dangerous here. People will know ya're new an' they'll test ya. Push ya. See how far they can get. Don' give them an inch, ya can't trust no one, ya understand?"

"I do."

"What, he can't trust ya either, Swede?" Vincent japes, but The Swede doesn't answer him. Instead he turns away from the window and holds his cruel eyes on me.

"Ya call on me when ya have trouble, uhright?"

"I will."

He pulls me closer with his strong arm and kisses me on the top of my head.

"Why did we let the Italians go?" I look up to The Swede. "They were our allies. Now all we have is the ILA, but Thos Carmody fought with Bill in the war. They're closing in on us, remember when you said that? Remember when—"

"I remember," The Swede begrudgingly admits, then grabs me by the shirt. "Ya're a fookin' kid. Keep that in the front o' ya thoughts, uhright? Ya don' know everythin'. Trust Dinny. Ya just gotta trust him. He's tryin' to help ya. T'day ya grow the fuck up, uhright? Yesterday ya were a boy. Forget it. T'day ya're a man."

But we are going to be all alone against the world soon, though I clench my teeth so that I don't say anything else that makes me look young and desperate.

To cut the tension Vincent announces, "I can't wait for summer."

At that The Swede's face sours, "Summer gives me the shits. Let's go."

Vincent whispers in my ear while motioning to the covered pier, "He don' like it when people know he's a softy."

As we come out into the rain, Dance is awaiting us, "It'll cut the arse off ya, this fookin' rain," he says under a floppy cap with streams of water running down his swarthy face.

"A warm bed an' a hot woman sounds like the cure to me," Vincent hunches his shoulders and somehow keeps his paper cigarette lit under the tilted brim of his cap.

The Swede admonishes. "There's work to be done. This is how we feed our fam'lies. Rain, snow, heat, freeze, we're workin'," He turns his eyes behind us at the hopeful longshoremen that have gathered in the rain. "Too many god'amn vodka-swillin' Polocks an' Ruskies around here o' late. Someone oughta toss lit matches at them so we can see how quick they'll catch. But the ones who call themselves Russians usually ain't, they're coppersmiths, confidence artists an' clairvoyants lookin' to give ya the gypsy-switch. They steal as fast as a plague o' locusts strip a corn field naked. If ever ya hear a Russian describe himself as Master o' Ceremony, ya better guard ya wallet because ya're in for a fight."

"Not t'day," Dance growls at the rain. "This day is for Liam to show all them fucks who the new boss is at the Atlantic Terminal."

The three of them turn to me while Vincent tosses the handrolled into the heaving river.

"Liam!" Dinny calls through the rain. "C'mere."

I walk along the dock with wet boots through the torrent as the eyes watch.

"Help me tie these down, yeah?" Dinny says as two sailors twenty feet above toss down a thick mooring line from barge deck to pier.

As we tie the sopping wet rope round the bollard, Dinny clears his throat, "I know it's ya first day, but we have need."

"Need?"

"No more money from Tanner, an' wit' Red Hook in Bill's hands an' less ships to unload now that the war's over, we don' have the income we once did."

"And?"

"The Leech."

"The landlord? Vandeleurs? What about him?"

"He's workin' wit' the Poplar Street Police Station to evict about thirty fam'lies from Irishtown. Biddy Hoolihan is seventy-nine years old. The Leech would throw her out to the elements," he holds his palms up to the rain. "The fatherless Mullen fam'ly has many children an'—"

"And who else?"

"And the Lonergans."

"The Lonergans," The name puts a sour taste in my mouth. "How long are we going to support them? I agree with The Swede, we should let them pay their own way since Richie is Bill's. Not to mention, he pulled the trigger on Mickey. We should cut them loose."

"I. . . I can't do that. I care for the Lonergans as much as I do the Garritys."

Why? I don't understand why. This is too much for me, I think. *I'm in over my head. Feckless and infirm. Someone else should be dockboss, not me.* I shake my head and look back to Dinny, "So what can I do?"

"Strong work ethic, loyalty, dependability... Those traits deserve recognition, an' ya display them all," He turns to look up to the ship we just moored to the pier. "This ship has eight hundret an' twenny bolts o' silk on it," He then turns round and points toward an uncoupled dark green boxcar in the rail yard. It is on the opposite track as the freight cars we are supposed to load for transport to a nearby textile factory. "I need ya to get fifty bolts loaded onto that single car over there. The green one."

"Steal fifty bolts?"

The switchman tips his cap in Dinny's direction, "I gotta buyer," he says.

"On my first day?"

"Ya'd be savin' thirty fam'lies from eviction. What are we s'posed to do, watch them get thrown out? No, good people come together to help the needy. The Leech is on the board o' the Waterfront Assembly. Even though there's less income comin' through the docks, he's raised rents an' has the backin' o' all the businesses around here. Newspapers'll never write a story about it because they're on the tug too."

Now I put my neck on the line for everyone else?

I give Dinny my grief, "Harry was my friend. Sure he was sulky and silent, but he displayed all those traits you just listed, and look what happened to him."

"We all have different paths we must take," Dinny stands to look at the rope tied to the bollard, then nods to the men up on the deck of the barge as the rain taps on our darkened coats and caps. "He was a good man—"

"And now we speak of him in the past tense. He's dead, isn't he? Just like Tommy Tuohey before him who also brought me up under his wing. Are men cursed to champion me?"

"Ya should be more worried about all the men that stare at ya."

I turn my head back to the hundreds of hopefuls that await our picking them, though we only need about sixty.

"Some need a show," Dinny says. "Ya gotta give them a spectacle. Somethin' they'll remember. Have ya thought about who ya want for a righthand?"

I'm not answering that question. Instead I ask, "Why did ya choose me? Others are not so wet behind the ears as myself. And garner more respect. Petey Behan owns me and—"

"One good man can tame the worst in twenny for a good while. Two, a hundret, an' for longer."

"What are you talking about?"

"The soul o' man is tempest-tossed an' always lookin' to break what's seen as holdin' him down. When they witness a good leader, they see good in themselves an' the beast within is calmed. A tyrant may take power for a time, true. Cruelty often wins, there's no denyin' it, but a good man is one who knows what it is to suffer. A good man has enough cruelty in him as any other, but recognizes that true leadership comes from below, rising up from us. Not from up high. Wolcott lives among the clouds far from us because he sees himself as a god, but ya'self, Liam? Ya come from the earth an' have risen up wit' humility an' honor. I chose well. Ya never asked for this, an' that is most tellin' of all."

Damn you Dinny Meehan. Even though you leave me cold with troublesome tasks, you warm me with words. You always have.

I turn back to the men that watch Dinny and speak on the rainy shore, "If they're desperate, why do they believe they can lead?"

"We all want to try an' steer our own future, even if it means drivin' into a brick wall. These men?" He slowly gives a half turn. "They feel untried. Wit'out opportunity, desire takes hold. Desire is born o' fancy. The flight from fancy to fantasy is not long at all, and soon gives way to action. Most leaders turn to inspirin' fear to tame the tempests. But some can be persuaded by humility an' honor to convince more that there is dignity in our cause. *Those* men can calm hundreds in ya name. The rest must be sated by spectacle. . . Who ya choosin' for righthand?"

"Dance."

"Why?"

"I make my decision based on who is most qualified, not by the trouble I'll have because he is half-black. Dance Gillen is one of us. Always has been. He's hard as bricks, a right scrapper and he can do this without me, if that day were ever to come. He's earned righthand, but he deserves dockboss."

Dinny turns and puts a hand on my shoulder in front of the eyes that peer through the torrent, "Ya put things in motion what most people either can't understand or won't."

I hide the prideful smile that comes to my face, "I'm sorry for sending Sadie and L'il Dinny away. I know she's your wife but you were incarcerated and Darby and Anna were tormenting them. I had to help them."

"Ya did it right. She'll be happier now."

"Happier?"

Dinny's jaw clenches at the thought of Sadie until he speaks in a tone of admission, "Ya spend ya whole life thinkin' ya gotta protect a woman, it ain't until later ya realize the best thing ya can do is let her go. How can I tell her to stay in her tower when its under siege? No, she needs to learn to fend for herself. I love her wit' all the wit all I got, but the only way I can show it is to let her fly away. Good thing is, she an' our son are outta the way o' the terror what's comin'."

"What terror, Pickles' retrial? Bill?"

"Worse."

"Like what?"

He shakes his head slowly and flashes the dark handle of a Webley Revolver to me, "Take this."

"I won't."

"Ya should."

"Harry never needed one. I have the pipe in my coat."

"Harry knew what he was doin'," Dinny rolls up a sleeve and shows me the gunshot wound I saw him take back in 1915. "I won't show ya the others. I'm gonna give this to Dance, then."

"What are we going to do about Bill?"

Dinny shakes that off, "Don' let nothin' stop ya from putting fifty bolts o' silk on that boxcar. Worry about the men who watch ya. By the end o' this day, they will challenge ya. Make them forget about how Petey Behan owns ya. Make them remember how ya killt ya uncle."

"What about—"

But he interrupts me, "The pilgrimage is takin' place on the day o' the fight, in June."

"The pilgrimage," I simply repeat.

Every year there is a pilgrimage from Irishtown to Jackson Hollow and back to honor the original settlers; the survivors of the Great Hunger. It appears this year's will have even more relevance.

Dinny walks on and calls for The Swede and Vincent to come with him.

I turn to Dance, "Are we ready to unload?"

"Yeah."

Dago Tom comes to my ear, "Five hundret bolts o' satin, two hundret twenny-nine various broadcloths, three hundret bolts o' wool an' eight hundret an' twenny bolts o' silk."

"We have to put fifty bolts of the silk on that boxcar over there."

"I know, we know what the deal is."

"The faster we get this done, the better."

Beyond the platforms are warehouses and factories that provide cover for any invader. With Brosnan disappeared, some patrolmen might come to ask questions. Or worse, Bill with his lieutenants and Trench Rabbits.

But Dance growls at the dark green boxcar, "That fookin' thing."

Turning round, Freddie Cuneen walks up to me with the maze of bisecting, intertwined depot rails behind him, "We'll be loadin' on track six over there. The conductor is pullin' her round as we speak. We gotta clean path from dock to train."

"Where's the stevedoring company?"

But just as I ask, three men with a folding table, a coffer chest and chairs appear.

Dance says. "Any more than sixty men an' we'll take too big of a hit. We're here to make dime t'day."

"Walk with me," says I to Dance. "Eddie, Freddie and Dago come up behind him."

There are twenty other men I trust, but my inner circle of dock, deck and hull gangs at the Atlantic Terminal are set. At the end of them all are the two bright-eyed ten year-olds that Dinny had brought along as runners, Whyo and Will. A dream come true for the boys. Now they're making money for their mothers.

We walk through the lines of wet men who would work for me this day, if picked.

"I need sixty strong men!" I yell out to all who would hear. "Courageous men, but you shits can help out until I find some."

A few snickers come from behind me.

"The only thing you have to remember is that the White Hand is your boss and myself and the men that walk with me are all named Patrick Kelly. If you're picked, you will work all day unloading this barge," I point up to where the planks are being rolled down onto the pier that lead to the hull as the long winch arm reaches over me with an empty net connected to it. "The stevedoring company will pay you your day's wage and then you will give us ten percent. If you hear voices in your head that tells you not to pay up, remind yourself that men die out here for doing less."

After that, the picking went rather easy. But Dance came to my ear.

"I got ten guys wanna put two dollars in ya pocket an' mine each for the right to work this mornin'."

"They wanna pay two dollars to us now an' give up ten percent what the stevedoring company gives them afterward like everyone else?"

"Five percent. They're offerin' ya'self an' I money to go around—"

"I know, I understand it. Who are they?"

"Russians, they say."

"Give them an inch and they'll take a mile. Tell them no. They don't get to pay us for the right to get chosen. I do the choosing, and afterward they pay us tribute like everyone else."

"Right."

"Ya seen Burke?"

"Nah."

I don't have time to think much on Thomas Burke. Instead I look up to the barge moored to the Atlantic Terminal, "Let's unload this beast. Dance?"

"Wha?"

"You're my righthand."

He nods and hides his surprise, "Ya're not worried about—"

"I'm not. Dinny supports me on this."

He nods again, "Harry never wanted a righthand. Too much of a loner, ya know?"

"Well I need a righthand. The best. I need you."

~~~

When the job is done and the longshoremen are paid by the stevedoring company, there is trouble.

"Poe," Dance calls while counting out the cash by the stevedore's table with ten men round him.

"These guys say we had a agreement, five percent."

"I didn't make that agreement, remember?"

"Oh I remember, but they remember it different-like. We were just about finished loadin' up that second train car. Ya know the one for Dinny's thing? But we can't finish until the Ruskies pay up."

The open-shirted, swarthy Russians have a mixture of callous looks on their faces, and balled fists. Between thick shoulders, tufts of chest hair peak out of thin linen shirts and unbuttoned waistcoats while a few wear red neckerchiefs and sheepskin caps with scruff on square chins. They all have the same wily eyes that steal looks at us under thick tresses of wavy hair that has dried since the sun came out.

I turn back to Dance and walk with him a few feet away, "What's the difference in our overall take?"

"Not much."

"Yet they want to dig in their heels over a small amount?"

I'm in over my head, feckless and infirm. The voice echoes in my head and the answer back is, *Yes you are in over your head. You should be sized up for a wooden overcoat.*

"You picked them," Dance says. "What do you want to do with them?"

"I know what it means to squabble over dimes. Next time they'll saunter up to the docks with their cocks in their hands, giving me terms."

I turn to look at the cold Russian eyes and gather Eddie and Freddie, Dago and twenty men I trust. In front of the stevedore's table I square off in front of the Russians with my men behind me. One Russian, slightly shorter than myself but thicker in the chest, looks up to me with a stony, hard-bitten stare. I speak first, "You got sand, challenging us. But I've been told courage is only a stone's throw from madness. You guys owe money. Take ten percent out of that envelope you just received and hand it over to me, all of you."

"They don't speak English much," Dance tells me.

I gnash my teeth at them and look round, "Everyone stop!"

Dance smiles and bites his lip. I've seen that look on him before. Dance gets eager moments before he gets to dance with a man.

The stevedoring men plead their case, "Sir, I mean it's just a few dollars. Be reasonable."

"I am being reasonable. Stop!" I yell. "Everyone hand your envelopes back to the men sitting at the table. Now! Do it. Do it!"

"Aw Jaysus—" A man begins until Freddie Cuneen pushes him to the ground and rips the envelope out of his coat and hands it to over the stevedore's table.

"Dance," I call out without losing eye contact with the hard stare of the Russian leader. "Form a circle. Eddie and

Freddie, Dago. Let's go. Get the rest of our men. Where's Whyo and Will?"

Whyo runs up to me, "Here, here. I'm here."

"Your faster than Will, right?"

"Yeah, like the blazes I run."

"Good, blaze down to the Baltic Terminal. Tell The Lark and Big Dick we have trouble and to send men. Now, go."

Whyo runs behind us to the south and disappears between freight cars.

Will steps forward, "Ya want me to go to the Dock Loaders' Club for The Swede?" He stops, then gulps. "Or the Masher?"

I look at the Russians. Do they deserve a beating? Or Vincent's .38? "Get The Swede to bring twenty men."

Will rushes through the enveloping circle toward the Russians, but before he can get anywhere, he is picked up by an arm.

Both my fists and teeth are clenched now as round us the fighters' circle closes. Atop the barge a few sailors point down at us and gather with a bird's eye view. Five men are lined up along the rope ladder that runs up to the ship deck. A few other men climb up to the top of the locomotive that we just loaded and exchange bets. I pull out my pipe and take off my coat and cap.

"This is our territory," I yell to all. "No one gives us terms in our territory. These men have waved the right of honor and do not pay tribute to the White Hand. That means they lose all their earnings today."

The circle tightens round them, yet still they give us lifeless stares.

"Ya wanna fight all o' us, or give us what ya owe? Who the hell do yaz think yaz are?" Dance stands at my right with the Webley Revolver at his hip.

The hard-bitten fellow comes forth to speak for them, though he proves to be a jaunty fellow, "I am Motshan, Master of Ceremony. The King of all Russian, Rumanian, Serbian, Bulgarian, Greek and Turkish families in the United States," The Russians round him nod to each other in agreement while four or five young women step out from behind a platform festooned in gold-coin necklaces, gold-coin bracelets and gold-coin earrings with motley-colored skirts about their broad hips and red scarves upon their heads.

Motshan gives a languid smile, "I hear this your first day? Eh? We fight. But we change mind," he whistles and in seconds thirty men come pouring out from thirty directions beyond the platforms and warehouses to run through the network of freight rails toward us. "We want money from all sixty laborers today and all money from stevedore company. Everybody money. Now! And all bolts on that green boxcar too."

A gunshot goes off, but Dance is tackled to the ground. On the other side of us a Russian falls to the dock with a hand over his shoulder and blood seeping between fingers.

"*Viteza de atac!*" The Russians call out and quickly the stevedore table is overturned. The coffer chest where the money is kept is yanked from them and we are overrun by their numbers.

"Get that chest!" I yell out as Eddie and Freddie swim through the crowd.

But the chest is so heavy that the Russian must drag it away. When the circle closes on him, he lets it loose to defend himself from the punches reigning down on him. We outnumber them four to one, but when the thirty men rush into the fray with clubs and sticks, at least ten of ours are pushed over the bulkhead and into the choppy river. Including one of the stevedores.

From the edge of the water we fight them back. My left fist pumps while the pipe in my right hand connects here and there, but there are too many faces. Then I see five men jump into the boxcar where the stolen goods are held.

"Get those bolts!" I yell out.

Ten of ours break through the line and another brawl ensues along the rail tracks of the depot. One Russian who had almost made it into the car was pulled down by the back of his pants bearing his arse to all. Ten pair of Hanan boots then kick his head and shoulders and torso until he balls up to protect himself.

When I move to fight a man one-on-one on the dock, I have to step over the bodies who have either been knocked out or are partially unconscious. Eddie Hughes is whipping a knife in the air and catches a Russian's forearm, carving it open. A gaggle of Russians move backward when they see blood. Freddie Cuneen is at his side and thrusts a cudgel into the Russians. With a deep cracking sound, it bounces off the top of a man's head. Blood runs down in fingers into his eyes and round his nose until he receives a second clubbing across the face that fells him for good.

The Russians sure up a charge and push us back against the water. My heels are at the edge of the bulkhead and behind me I can feel the void. The drop to the water is only ten feet, but it would mean the loss of the Atlantic Terminal if we are thrown into the East River.

"*Impinge-i*," they yell, which must mean throw them in, or something. "*Impinge-i!*"

They kick at us on the edge. And throw sticks and paving stones too. Three at a time they rush forward to push us in. Two men behind me fall backward.

"We can't hold them off," Dago Tom yells.

Ten Russians lock arms and start a countdown in their language. They have their sights on us and there is no way we will be able to stop their push.

"*trin, duy, yek—*" they rock back and forth, counting down.

But suddenly they are crushed from one side by a wave of men. The Russians with locked arms are pushed to the ground and stomped. The Lark appears and bulls two men backward while Big Dick tosses a man over us and into the water, then grabs another by an open shirt and tears the whole thing off of him. They had brought twenty of their own men from the Baltic Terminal as little Whyo Mullen is howling from on top of a boxcar, jumping up and down. "White Hand, White Hand forever!"

Stepping over victims Eddie and Freddie slash and brutalize more to move us off the bulkhead edge. From the side I see Dago Tom drag one Russian by a leg while the poor fellow takes Hanan boots to the back of the head. The leader of the Russian's face has long smears of blood across it already. The hard stare has disappeared now and his eyes are panicked in self-defense. Now he wobbles to keep himself on two feet.

"Hold him up," I yell to two of our own men who splay him out like Jesus on the cross.

The man's face comes into measuring and my fist breaks his lip open, cutting my knuckle with a sharp cuspid tooth. He kicks back with both legs, barely missing my face until he is felled backward and engulfed by men.

When I look over, Dance is dancing on someone's face. When he is done, the Russian's body moves slow and sloth-like, his eyes dazed and his mouth open. He cannot seem to gain his balance or even know that he is on the ground as his legs are moving as if to walk. Dance then takes off his hat and moves to stomp the man's face again.

"Where's the gun?" I yell at Dance.

He pulls it out of a pocket and points it in the air. All heads duck down when the pistol claps.

"We need to kill them," Dance calls back with fury in his eyes. "At least one."

"No, take the envelopes of the men that challenged us," I command, my hand slick with the blood from a blue and swollen knuckle wound. "Spread their earnings out among all the men that took part in this justice."

The Russians are dragged off.

"Justice would've been one life, at least," Dance confides as order is almost fully restored. The Lark and Big Dick agree.

"Ya don' wanna be seen as weak," Dance pleads.

"No one'll see what happened here today as weak. If anything, they'll see it as merciful."

"Mercy is weak," Dance says.

"I will never kill a man again," says I. "I made a vow and I plan on sticking to it."

"That's an unfortunate vow. Makes things more difficult for all o' us. We may have beat them t'day, but they'll be back tomorrow with even more men."

I hate that he is right. Mercy is considered weak to some of these men. *The men who need to be sated by spectacle.*

"Take all of them that we have in custody here. Drag them beyond the freight yard and line them up below the tenement windows so people can watch."

"And?"

"Break their knees. Break their ankles."

"That's a temporary fix. They won't be able to walk what? Two months? Three? They'll plot to come back the whole time they're laid up."

"What would you suggest? Other than killing?"

Dance thinks for a moment, then shrugs, "There ain't nothin' else. Breakin' their ankles an' kneecaps will have to do. . . Let me see that hand."

His dusky fingers spread the five inch wound open. More blood pulses out and I can feel a heartbeat inside the hand.

When I look at it again, the skin round the deep wound has turned a dark shade of blue.

"Never punch a man in the mouth," Dance turns his hazel-eyed stare to me and let's my hand loose. "Go for the jaw or the nose. It ain't bleedin' too bad that ya need a tourniquet, but it needs to be washed off. Salt water'll help. I'll take care o' the rest here on the dock. At least we still got the goods on the boxcar though, even after all that."

We both turn as the sliding door is slammed shut and the lock latch fastened with a rusty squeak and a clang.

"Irishtown won't starve this week," I say, walking through the men with my hand a glistening red mess.

"Good man, Poe," a voice calls out.

A hand reaches out and surprises me, though it just pats me on the shoulder.

As I am headed to the floating sheds to soak my hand in the river, Eddie announces, "We ain't no fookin' feckless cowards. An' there ain't a god'amn outsider that challenges us wit'out payin' a heavy price for it. We made that clear t'day!"

Freddie says, "The White Hand descends upon them what think they can call us out. No one calls out Patrick Kelly at the Atlantic Terminal!"

"Poe," Dago Tom comes from behind and grabs my arm. "Ya gotta say somethin' to the guys. Ya gotta. Look at them all. They're waitin' for ya."

When I turn, all the men have me in their sights. "Speech! Speech!" They call out.

I turn the rest of the way to face them as Dance drops a stool on the ground in front of me to stand on. When I do, I can see the amount of them as all the men who had been loading the train pavilions have joined. When their demands for a speech quieten, I clear my throat.

"There's no need for celebration here," I call out. "There's no need for speeches. What we done today is not right. But it's necessary. We do what is necessary round here to feed our families. If this were a better world, all of you would be peaceful men. Do not exult. Go to your families and tell them that you love them. Tell them that you do things that you are not proud of to ensure they are fed. But remember that everyday we win, others lose. This is not the world we would choose, but it's the only world there is."

As I step down Dance laughs and shakes his head in comical disbelief, "Ya're more like Harry than I ever realized."

Big Dick's baritone voice chuckles, "I remember when we used to dump him head-first into garbage cans. Now look at him."

I turn back to Dance, "I want everyone from the Bronx to Gravesend talkin' about how a bunch of Russians were maimed at the Atlantic Terminal today. Let as many people see you do it as possible."

"Ya got it, boss," Dance nods.

Beyond the dark and floating sheds out on the pier I lay flat on my stomach and submerge my hand in the East River.

I didn't want this, I tell myself again. *I never asked for this. But what do I want? I've done terrible things today. Horrible things I didn't think I could do. Why do people cheer men who do horrific things? Why do they exult in horror?*

I look across the expanse of the harbor. *My mother, if she knew what I did this day, would think me a monster.*

Eat or be eaten, it's said. Feed your family, or starve. Kill or be killed, that is what this place demands of us all, and I am no longer innocent of it.

A swirling wind travels along the water and rifles through my clothing. Suddenly the sun is overtaken and the sky darkens again. A black mist rolls in from the north and soon the bridges that span the East River are engulfed. The city beyond disappears.

A figure appears out on the water, obscured by the tumbling fog. It is a woman in a gown.

Emma, Emma is that you?

Her hair is unwashed and hangs over her gaunt face. Shoeless, she walks on water. When she looks over to me, her mouth almost smiles.

"Emma!" I call out over the water.

"Liam," her voice is low, yet hurts my ears for its vibration. "Why do you still love me, Liam?"

My chin quivers, but anger bursts out of me instead, "I *don't* love you! I never did. I barely even knew you!"

"I name you a liar," she responds. "Why do I still haunt you then?"

"I'm no liar! It's true! Love is a game of chance and surrender that I've no time play any longer. I have a family that needs me to support them. There's no place for love in me."

"Is family not love?"

"It's not the same as loving someone who is not family."

"Liam, if you do not open yourself to the light, the darkness will close in around you. Just now, archons attack. It is not your fault that they let us starve."

As the dark mist rolls over top of her on the East River, I repeat her words, "They let us starve."

I don't know why she said those words, though they are words I have heard throughout my life. They are words that bounce round in my head and cause the greatest melancholia. "They let us starve."

Feckless and infirm. I am feckless and infirm. Worthless, useless, lazy, not worth the value of the food I eat. Not worth the land I stand upon. I am a monster.

A deluge of large raindrops begin to plummet from the dark and swirling sky. The mist is cold to my skin. I cannot see twenty feet but I hear the waves turning over and slapping against the bulkhead. Behind me I hear a rustling. The dark doorway of a storehouse swings open, but no one is there. Waves rock the sheds on the shoreline, yet still no one comes.

"Who's there?" I yell out, but the wind takes my words and sends them to oblivion.

A scraping sound, like metal on cement comes to my ears. Then a chopping sound like an axe into wood. An unintelligible voice says something. It is garbled with phlegm, wet and sickly.

I pull out the pipe that is stitched in my coat, "Come out!" When I grip the pipe, the pain in my knuckle vibrates and I loosen my hand round it.

A man with a black mask over his face emerges from the shoreline mist at the base of the pier. The mask only covers the upper part of his face, leaving his mouth exposed. The nose protrudes out of the mask and is grotesquely hooked with eyes so close together they look like they almost meet. In the masked man's hand is a scythe, or sickle that drags along the pier's planks. When a winch engine one dock away begins whining, he walks directly toward me, his boots pounding the pier, *pa-pum-pa-pum-pa-pum*. Faster and faster. Louder as he comes closer.

"Stop right there!" though I don't believe he can hear me and there is no way Dance, Eddie & Freddie and Dago Tom can either. "What do you want?"

He is half way to me along the pier when he picks up his sickle in a threatening way, waving it across his face with an athlete's expertise.

I don't want to die. Is this death coming for me? I probably deserve it.

His first swing backs me to the edge of the pier. A backhand swing with the pipe connects with a deep clapping sound to the back of his head, though he turns as if unfazed. We have switched places now, he at the end of the pier. I could run all the way down the pier now, but I do not. Instead I stand and wait.

"You killed the cub reporter with that?" I point my eyes at the weapon in his hand.

A bubbling sound comes out of his throat again, but I cannot make out any words. He gargles again, but it sounds like the thunder that rumbles in the sky. "They let us starve," he says, the thunder crackles and right on top of it a lightning bolt flickers and for half a second it is again day time. When the thunder rumbles afterward, I can hear his voice again, "They let us starve."

He waves the sickle over his head once and thrusts a cross-swing toward my face. I step back again, but he sends another quick thrust, this one a backhand and I can feel the breeze on my cheek.

I don't want to die. I might deserve it though. But I can't die yet, not now.

We swing in unison at each other. Our weapons ring in the air at impact in front of our faces and I notice an old stitched wound under his mask, running down from his nose. The pain in my hand reverberates up my arm and into my brain. My instinct is to let loose of the pipe, but I can't unless I don't mind death. But I do mind it, and grip the pipe harder through the pain.

We swing at each other again, the lead of my pipe and the sharpened metal of his blade make sparks above us that dissipate before touching the water round us. A left-handed punch lands on my cheek. I never saw it coming. I lose him in my vision as I struggle to keep balance. Backing away as fast as I can, I see streaks of him. When I swing wildly for defense, I catch nothing but air.

What am I fighting? Who are you?

When I see him swing again, I duck away but the grip of his blade comes down on the top of my head and stuns me. Lying across the pier on my back with the pipe at my side, I touch the top of my head and see blood in my hand.

But is that the blood from my knuckle wound, or my head?

Behind him the wind has turned to gusts and black clouds twist and turn torturously among themselves in the sky. He attacks again from above. I can only fall to my back and kick up with my legs. The sickle waves behind him and comes rushing down toward my face. In a panic I grab for the pipe again and close my eyes. The sparks are much closer to my face this time.

Kill. Kill. Kill, my mind echoes the words. *Murder him.*

A cataract of rain comes furiously down as if a waterfall is being poured onto us. But the sky is black as pitch and I cannot see where the pier begins and where it ends. We are simply out on the water with no notion of direction.

"I don't want to die," I thrash in anger as he is rearing for another swing.

Somehow he lands on the pier next to me, the water on both sides of us. Without thinking I grab with my left hand at his wrist, which holds the sickle. Then grab hold of the flesh but it is as hard as wood underneath the stained cuffs of his dirty white linen shirt and the coal-colored coat. The old wound above his lip is not bleeding, but it is covered with some sort of yellowish green viscous. On one side of his face is a pattern of little holes. Scars like stars in the night sky while another streaks through his hairline over an ear like a runaway comet. From the ground next to him I swing across and connect on the top of his head. He had tried to turn away so that it did not connect on his face, but the sound that came from the blow was deep and loud.

"Ahhhh!" I yell out with every ounce of murder in me.

Before he has a chance to respond I stand up, still holding his wrist. I kick at his abdomen with my right boot and yank at his wrist to keep him off balance. When his sickle falls in the green and brown water I let his wrist loose and barrage him with the pipe three, four, five times in the back until he slips into the water.

I climb to the end of the pier to look for him, but there is no evidence of a splash nor even a wave. I push the water round with my bloody hand, but I see nothing. There is nothing. Just nothing, everywhere below.

"Poe!" Dance yells from the base of the pier by the sheds and storehouse. "That's prolly enough. C'mon in so we can wrap it up."

When I look up, the sky is cloudless and the sun is at its zenith. A tear drops from my face into the East River, though it feels as though it is someone else's tear. Someone else who uses my eyes to cry. When I look round, I see myself. I see myself at the edge of the pier pulling my hand out of the river.

"How is this possible?" The words spill from my mouth.

But are they mine? Did I just say those words? Or was it someone else who put them in my mouth?

I look round, but Dance had already turned back.

I am alone. Alone in this.

I stand and run as fast as I can. Sprinting down the pier toward the shore and my people.

Equilibrium of Contradictions

Remember your role, Darby Leighton rocks back and forth on the train. *Remember your role in the raid. Remember. Go over it again and again so you don't forget it.*

Darby looks down at the bloody splint on his pinky finger.

After Richie fractured it with a ball-peen hammer, Abe spent an hour going over the details of the raid with Darby again.

"If you do vhat is expected of you, all vill be fine, Darby, my little friend," Abe had assured him.

"But where are we goin'? Who are we raidin'?" Darby asked with agony in his eyes.

Abe said, "All that you need to know is your role, yez. Ve all have our own roles to play, you need only vorry about your own, do you understand?"

I hate when he talks down to me like that. I shouldn't even be here. My role is to get my brother Pickles free and to right the lie, not go on raids. I'm no soldier. But don't forget. Don't forget your role in the raid, Darby repeats to himself as his pinky throbs, shooting pain up his arm and shoulder.

Go over it again and again so you don't forget it. He rolls the knuckles on his good hand across his forehead and grinds his teeth.

Last night Darby dreamt death was closing in on him and he could not seem to stop the bleeding. The more he applied pressure to the wound, the more it spat red. What mystified him was that he did not know what had mortally wounded him. Bullet or Knife? Was it an accident? Had someone done it on purpose, or had he done it to himself?

Darby had to wrestle himself out of the dream, only to wake up in sweats next to Ligeia. There, he sat in bed worrying over the dream, wondering what the weapon was that had killed him. Eventually Darby concluded the weapon was a lie.

I lied to Bill and told him what he wanted to hear. I have lied about Sadie. I have lied about Dinny. But if I hadn't lied, I wouldn't be here right now to right the lie about my family. Is it not devious conceit that drives a liar to right other people's lies?

Anna Lonergan's words suddenly come to his mind, "None of us are pure anymore."

Bill beat her for that. But Anna Lonergan had more courage than Darby could ever wish to summon in himself. But is it courage that helps people lie, or is it cowardice?

The thought comes unbidden, and Darby concludes that everyone is just trying to survive in a place somewhere between dream and wakefulness. Bound to life in the now but with death's freedom on the wing. Lingering betwixt the two sides like dawn amidst the night and coming day. Everyone wants to go to heaven, but no one wants to die, and here we are, trapped, or maybe circling the drain like water bugs trying to stall the inevitable.

But lies. Lies cut us open without our knowing it.

I am being pulled in opposing directions with lies on one side and truth on the other. But are they contradictions? Or do they work together in some equilibrium? Just forget about that. Forget it. Darby shakes his head. *But don't forget your role.*

He looks down at the bloody splint on his finger again, *I just have to get through this raid and prove my loyalty so that I can right the lie about my family.*

Darby then looks round the train, confused, *Where am I?*

Wild Bill Lovett stands and sways in the aisle of the train to address his gang after most of the other commuters had been run off at the last stop. His beetle black hair and the dark circles round his eyes contrast the skin on his face, white as mare's milk. When he clears his throat, everyone sits to listen.

"Men will die t'night," he grimly imparts upon his cortege of followers, which includes his four lieutenants, the Lonergan Crew and ten Trench Rabbits.

But Bill looks worse than ever. After he killed the Italians, his health had improved. But now. Now his eyes are red-rimmed with black bags under them like bruises. The open soars on his neck have returned.

"There will be bodies," Bill announces to his men on the train. "So make sure y'ain't stupit enough to be one o' them. Know ya role, an' ya can survive. On this night we make our move in securin' the Gowanus border an' weakenin' our enemy's ability to strike at us. But we gotta crossover to do it. Behind enemy lines. A covert assault in their own territory, South Brooklyn. But we all know the only way to get a dago outta a tree is by cuttin' the rope."

The boys get a laugh out of that one, but Darby does not smile. Either does Bill, who walks back to the front of the train car.

One-arm Flynn calls back to us, "A dago walks into a bar—"

The boys already start laughing at the jape before even the gag line is delivered.

Flynn finishes, "A dago walks into a bar, holds up two fingers an' asks for five beers."

Bill had gone over the plan and everyone's role in it so many times that he now looks the other way when Petey Behan jumps up and down in his seat. Eventually the leg snaps off of it and Petey runs to open a train car window and toss it into the busy street below. All the teens line up along the windows and howl in joy when they see the leg flail through the air and hit a pedestrian down on the street.

"He looked a guniea too!" Matty mocks with vulgar hand gestures as Tim Quilty stands in his seat and thrusts his narrow hips up to piss out another window.

In the front of the car, the shit-black hound circles in place, then hunches its back and looks sorrowfully at everyone.

"Ah Jesus on a stick, the dog's shittin' on the train," someone announces as old man Lonergan snorts, the florid bruises from his son's beating him still visible.

Petey scoops up the dogshit with a kerchief and slings it out the window where everyone on the train looks to see if he got anyone. Two flatly dressed immigrant women, maybe Scandanavians or Poles in their forties stop when they feel something spray them, then look up. When the train car bursts into laughter, a shock of pain streams through Darby's finger and up into his brain.

"I got some in my mouth somehow," Timmy says with a brown smile. "It's still warm."

Caw-caw, one-arm Flynn quarks in laughter.

Darby sulks in a back corner of the train watching as Brooklyn passes by. The sun has disappeared below the skyline, but the blotted clouds in the west are lit with yellow fire until a five story building along the edge of the Fifth Avenue Elevated train blocks the view with a windowless brick facade. When the train passes the building, the fiery sky appears again above the endless tenements.

At the head of the train Bill sits with Richie Lonergan and listens to Abe Harms while his other lieutenants loiter round and pass a cigarette amongst each other. At Bill's feet are three of his Shit Hounds. One brown, one yellow and the black one with the emptied bowels. Some Trench Rabbits had been brought along for the raid as well, chosen due to their loyalty to Bill and ability to follow orders.

Bill's specific, seemingly meaningless orders are as tactical and precise as a military offensive. If carried out according to plan, none of our own will be killed. That's what's said, at least.

Darby must have heard Bill say it ten times, "We work as one; separate pieces all with easy tasks, but important roles none-the-less."

On the train Petey and Timmy yank out a window frame, complete with the glass intact and run over to the opposite window where below pedestrians walk unawares.

One man had remained on the train while all others had been shooed away. He sits opposite Darby in a boater's hat next to the fraternal twins in his care, one dressed as a boy. The other as a girl. He looks at Darby with the eyes of a concerned father.

Darby turns back over his shoulder at the sound of broken glass on the street and the rousing laughter inside the train car.

"Next stop, get off an' switch cars," Darby advises.

The man does not respond.

He does not trust me. Any time people look into my eyes, they are stricken with distrust. Why though? Why does everyone say my eyes are, how did Abe describe them? Bewildered?

At the Sixteenth Street Station the man scampers off the train with his hands tightly wrapped round the twins' wrists.

Deeper into Brooklyn the train goes. Into unknown territory where Italians and Scandinavians own the streets, and where darkness lowers visibility and heightens the mystery in the soldiers' minds. Darby had heard of how Italians practiced an old-world version of Catholicism that was based on pagan idolatry, animal blood and the sacrificing of children.

"They eat their own babies," One-arm Flynn calls over his shoulder to Bill's boys.

"That's who Meehan makes allies wit'? Nah, we're doin' the whole world a favor on this raid. Do ya job an' they won't butcher yaz, got it?"

At the Thirty Sixth Street Station they transfer to the West End Elevated Train that continues south into distant neighborhoods. Again Darby sits at the back of the train in a dark corner seat, alone with his thoughts.

When Abe sits across from him with a newspaper under his arm and speaks in whisper, Darby cannot see his lips in the darkness.

"I didn' hear ya," Darby answers.

Abe leans in closer, but his voice is even lower now. Instead, Darby reads the expression on Abe's face and the words on his mouth, "Why haven't you figured out the riddle?"

"How do ya know I haven't?"

"Because your mind vould be opened if it had. I can see by looking at you that you are ztill a ztupid dumb person, yez. Repeat it back to me, Darby."

"The beauty o' hidden love inside the heart o' an evil little girl."

"Vhat kind of little girl?"

"Red-haired girl who wants revenge. I only know a couple red-haired girls, but I got no idear why they would want revenge for."

Abe blinks his eyes four, five times while looking up as if to feel the air, "She is getting closer, yez. You should find her before she arrives, but your brain is *fakakta*," Abe says with a wet-lipped smile. "Answer me this instead, does Zadie Meehan ztill pay you for the trial? Ve need that trial to occur before the fight with Dinny, yez. Do you understand?"

Darby answers with a lie, "I already talked to Bill about it, so go away. It'll happen."

"Then Dead Reilly does not vant for money?" Darby can smell the winter mint on Abe's breath.

"It's all set for May."

More lies. Dead Reilly, the attorney, recommended another lawyer to take the case over from him, but Darby would not let him pass it off to a stranger. If he did, Reilly would essentially become Dinny's personal lawyer on the matter and could take up the case against Pickles. That could not happen. Reilly had then demanded a new, more expensive retainer. Two hundred dollars. Two hundred dollars that Darby does not have, and cannot ask Bill for. The gang did not have that much money. The labor racket at the Red Hook terminal is not bringing in the amount of cash Abe had suspected. Too many ship captains are choosing the Baltic or Atlantic terminals when rumors circulated about the murders in Red Hook back in February on top of Mickey Kane's disappearance.

Abe stares at Darby distrustfully and drops the newspaper on the seat next to him, revealing a photograph on the cover of a narrow-faced man with his hand inside of his double-breasted waistcoat as if he were a diplomat. Abe then moves in closer again, mouthing the words, "Do you know the fellow, Cornelius Ferry?"

"Needles?" Darby says, but is looking at the photo of the man in the newspaper. "Needles Ferry? The guy who shoots tar an' sniffs dust? Sure. He's Dinny's. Always has been."

"Yez, well," Abe tilts his head and looks away, but the words that form on his mouth, Darby could hardly believe. "A man fell off a barge yesterday an' vas crushed between it and a steamship. When ve fished this man out of the river, Bill found the dead man's identification. The man's name was also Cornelius, and Bill saw that as a sign."

"A sign?"

"Bill believes in signs, as you know," Abe stifles his own doubts with a look that Darby sees as questioning Bill's mental state.

I was right. I gambled and told Bill I could interpret signs, that's why he believed me.

"So tell me, vhere does Neeedles Ferry live?" Abe interrupts Darby's thoughts.

Why, are we going to kill him too?

Darby explains, "Needles does not live anywhere. But he sleeps in a abandoned buildin' off Flatbush where a bunch o' homeless kids flop an'—" Suddenly Darby breaks off when he notices the narrow faced man in the newspaper photo is wearing Windsor glasses. He turns the newspaper round and shows Abe, "I saw this guy on the tugboat wit' Wiz the Lump an' Garry Barry. I saw'r them together. We should tell Bill," he looks toward the front of the train and moves to stand up.

"Hold on one moment," Abe grabs at Darby's arm with small, pink fingers. "You zaw this man? T.V. O'Connor, president of the International Longshoreman's Association valk onto a tugboat together with Volcott's lump?"

"Yeah," Darby taps on the newspaper's photo. "This guy walked onto the back of it alone an' took a plump envelope from them, then walked off. I couldn't remember who the guy was until I saw'r this photo. It was drivin' me cra—"

"How can you be zure?"

"Listen, maybe I can't hear, but my eyes are like a hawk's. It was him, I'm sure. We need to tell Bill."

Abe grabs the newspaper from Darby's hand that has the splint on the pinky.

"Ah Jesus," Darby yelps, holding it at the wrist. "That fookin' hurt—"

Abe looks at the newspaper, folds it, tucks it under an arm and asks Darby, "I need the address of Mr. Ferry, please."

Darby can feel the veins in his forehead pulse in pain, "We don' have time for that small shit—"

"Petey?" Abe calls out suddenly and waves Petey Behan over.

Petey and Abe are of a similar height and age, but that is where the similarities end. Petey's eyes are set wide apart on a box head and his legs seem too short, his torso too long. From his days as a thief while working the throngs of travelers at the three-story Sands Street Train Station on the Brooklyn Bridge, he earned the moniker Petey Cutpurse.

Petey snaps his finger in Darby's face, "Hello? Ya there? Hello? I just asked ya a question."

"What was it?" Darby asks.

But Abe speaks to Petey instead, "Have ya ever known zomeone who dedicates their entire life an' all their energy to being unhappy? Yeah? That's Darby."

Darby begins to respond, but is interrupted by Petey.

"Darby likes to put his trousers on first, then his underclothes."

"No I don't," Darby protests, which makes everyone laugh even more.

Abe speaks to Petey again, "Darby zays Ferry can be found at a flophouse on Flatbush. Do you know this place?"

"Sure I do," Petey's lip seems constantly turned up on one side of his mouth. "That's where I saw'r Poe Garrity. Stole his coat too."

Petey fiddles with something in his pocket, then lazily removes the Colt .45 caliber and points it at Darby.

"How'd ya get Bill's gun?"

"Don' say any more words," Petey watches Darby's reaction. "Bill promised me a kill t'night."

Darby looks over his shoulder toward the front of the train car but does not see Bill.

Petey's eyes look crude when he smiles, "Ya try to move from that seat an' I'll put a hole in ya. See, we're gonna kill ya an' stuff ya under a seat an' walk out the other side wit' our hats low. People'll just think ya're a Brooklyn bum sleepin' off a jag."

Darby takes a moment to find the right thing to say, but is left to wonder if Petey is serious.

"Thing is, I claimed I killt a guy already, which makes me eligible to be Bill's Fifth Lieutenant, see. But Bill says it was Poe Garrity who struck the fatal blow on his uncle. He said I only thrust a knife into the side of a dyin' man, is all. I don' think that's fair, what do ya think?"

"I think ya're a liar," Darby is shocked by his own courage. "One thing I hate is a liar. Put that gun away, get it? If ya don' I'll call Bill's name right now an' he'll have Richie break ya arm for pointin' a gun at his special agent."

Abe's mouth turns into a smile on one side of his mouth, then turns to Petey.

Petey grips the gun until it shakes. Anger appears on his face and his curled up mouth until he places the .45 caliber in an inner pocket.

"Tell me then," Petey says. "What's ya role t'night Darby?"

"Abe an' I are going to bar the door when—"

"How ya gonna bar the door, Darby? Did ya bring ya dustbroom? Ya could use ya dustbroom. Just slip it through the two door pulls, right? Then they can't get out the door. Did ya bring it?"

"No."

"Fellas," Petey calls back. "Fellas c'mere."

The Trench Rabbits and the Lonergan Crew use the straps to keep balance as they walk to the back of the swaying train car that rattles down the Brooklyn night.

"Listen, Darby ain't takin' his job so seriously," Petey explains to the men standing over them. "Everybody's got a job, Darby. We're tryna do somethin' big. Somethin' important, but everybody's gotta do their job. If one person don' do their job, the whole thing'll fall apart, an' here ya are. Sittin' over here in a corner alone an' ya don' even bring ya dustbroom?"

All eyes move to Darby, "Petey, ya will never be Bill's Fifth Lieutenant. Ya wanna know why? Because ya ain't grown up yet. Ya beat one kid up, a teen. An' that convinces ya that ya will be the Fifth Lieutenant?"

"Oh we'll see who gets it," Petey reaches across Darby where Matty hands him a dustbroom. "Here ya go, we brought it for ya. Quit daydreamin' Darby an' concentrate on ya role."

"Daydreamin' Darby," Matty Martin repeats with a chuckle. "I like that better than Dustbroom Darby."

At Stillwell Avenue the gang disembarks and shoves unwitting travelers against the wood platform wall and down the stairwell. *Caw-caw-caw,* One-arm Flynn quarks as Petey and others make way for Wild Bill and his lieutenants. The streets are filled with all sorts of strange foreigners and gullible tourists followed by evil-eyed pickpockets. Lustful night dwellers appear for some grab-assing and drunkards lean with one arm against corner walls like ancient statues to retch in the narrow alleys. The most well-behaved of all are the Shit Hounds, who dare not trot too far from Bill's thighs even though the scent of cheap cotton candy and rotting garbage wafts through their noses. Bill had trained them well and amidst the Trench Rabbits a rumor had made its way to Darby that Bill keeps human meat in his pocket to keep the hounds' attention on him at all times.

Darby suddenly hears Bill raise his voice at Abe, "Stop talkin' to me for a second. Ya're givin' me a fookin' tumor in my ear."

"I wanna go on the Human Roulette Wheel," Timmy calls out. "Can we? It's the best ride they got on Coney Island."

Petey punches Timmy in the arm, "No, we gotta see the Snake-Skinned Boy an' I wanna watch Chief Pentagal bite the head off a chicken."

Almost every man visiting Coney Island wears a boater's hat, like the man on the train Darby saw. The flat cap Darby wears and the floppy cap Abe dons separates the leisurely class from us, the low. No matter, the gang pushes any and all from their path. Without a patrolmen in sight, no one is safe when Bill's wild boys walk by.

When a woman screams, Bill stops. Then everyone stops. Non Connors had pushed a man out of the gang's way. When the man moved to fight back, Non clouted him with three punches and when the fellow fell to the ground he received boots to the torso and face, whipping his head back. The man was asleep under the dress of his date with a bloodied mouth and nose before she ever realized what was happening.

They move on. Through the crowd of revelers and beachgoers they shove, while Darby walks hindmost, as usual.

I shouldn't even be here, he bites his lip. *I hate carnivals. Too many people in one place. I should be spending my time trying to find Sadie. I shouldn't be here. I just want to go home to Ligeia and Colleen Rose. They're waiting for me.*

Bill had sent Darby down to Coney Island a week ago on another reconnaissance mission to find out exactly where the Harvard Inn was, though that was during a weekday.

Here, on a Saturday night the place has come unhinged. Seagulls circle and swoop above with hungry eyes while a naked man with long arms ambles by. The smell of body odor takes the air and people in mid-sentence bump into Darby. A teen walks by soaking wet and drips water on him. And everywhere, everyone dumps whatever garbage they have wherever they walk. A man with part of his head crushed in at the temple in some old injury leans on his mother with blank eyes. The amount of body types vary greatly but many are drunken, exhausted and flush of face. The air bulges with the chaos of competing conversations and pregnant woman with open mouths wobble past him. Another woman with a forked tongue smiles at him like a snake as again the smell of garbage in the breeze reaches him. Rows and rows of people step over the crushed rubbish that accumulates along the curbs.

"Darby!" One of the Trench Rabbits yells. "Where is it?"

"What?" Darby answers, then points. "Oh, we should go to the entrance to Steeplechase park. The club is down the road from there."

When they reach the entrance, the gang forms a circle under the gigantic ferris wheel and down a piece from the famed Steeplechase Ride where for ten cents you can ride in a mechanical horse race.

Bill's voice rattles, "Take ya caps off."

And so they do.

"Put them in ya back pocket. This part o' Brooklyn people don' wear our type o' caps, apparently," Bill shoots an ugly eye at Darby as if he is angry that he hadn't noticed that detail. "Abe, take Darby wit' ya an' scope out that bawdyhouse, but first take off them Hanan boots. Change them wit' somebody. Everyone knows the White Hand wears Hanan."

That is true, Darby thinks.

The boots were stolen by Dinny Meehan when the Lonergan Crew was still under his wing. Though most everyone in the Irish territory got a pair, Darby never did.

A few minutes later, Darby and Abe walk slowly down Coney Island Bowery, a street where at night good parents would never bring their children. Only a half-block from the boardwalk, it is where men go to gamble, drink and whore their hearts out. Darby hears a plunky player-piano playing an old song from the Spanish-American War while in the saloon next door another piano plays *The Sidewalks of New York*.

"Ya see that sign that says 'Stauch's?'" Darby points with his dustbroom to show Abe. "It's right across the street from the ball room. Look for the guy wit' three scars on his face. If he's bouncin' t'night he'll be at the front door an' we won't have to go inside."

Fear washes across Abe's face. The first time Darby had ever seen it on the little whispering mole. But they are both happy to see Scarfaced Al at the front door, bouncing on this evening. As they walk by, he catches the twenty year-old Italian's eye.

The kid is balding already, Darby notices.

The three scars that run concurrent from his cheek to his neck identify him as their target.

"Keep valkin' an' stop starin'," Abe tells Darby. "He noticed your eyes."

"Let's get back to Bill."

Under the ferris wheel Bill is surrounded by his men while his dogs lay with lolling tongues at his feet.

"He's bouncin' t'night," Darby says.

"That's what we wanted," Non pumps a fist.

Abe tugs on Richie's coat and speaks with concern in his eyes as Darby reads his lips, "He's a big boy. Be careful vith him, yez?"

But Richie gives no response.

"Uhright, everyone knows the plan," Bill's voice is like sandpaper on wood as he fights back a cough. "Richie, Petey, Matty an' Tim. Ya know ya role. Darby an' Abe, follow them from the other side o' the street an' cross over when they get him outside. Then keep the door closed. Ya do ya job an' ya don' die, get it Darby? Keep the fookin' door closed."

"I got it, I got it."

"I wanna kill them, Bill. Ya promised me. Lemme have the gun now," Petey says.

"That ain't ya job right now. We gotta get in close first. Surround them wit' bodies, then we do it. The plan is more important than any one o' us, remember that."

The youngsters move off together. From across the street, through the crowds Darby watches Richie limp down the opposite sidewalk. Suddenly Darby can hear his teeth chatter again.

People will die today, Bill had told them all. Darby clenches his jaw and swallows. But the chattering sound comes back yet again.

Abe's eyes are on him, "Ve have an easy job, Darby, my little friend, yez. Take a deep breath. You can do this."

"I'm fine, shaddup," Darby watches Richie and his three followers from across the street. A slew of college-aged men begin a sing-along beneath the Stauch's sign over the street. A white-walled car winds up its horn and blows to get them out of the way. "Sounds like a mangled duck, for fuck's sake," Darby growls.

"Your teeth are chattering," Abe says. "I can hear them."

"Do ya think this Scarfaced fella carries a gat? I hadn't thought o' that. I bet he does."

"Ve vill find out zoon enough," says Abe.

"I don' wanna die, Abe. Not tonight. No time soon."

"Give me the dustbroom, Darby."

"No."

"Come then, ve must cross now," Abe moves off the sidewalk when he sees Richie is in the doorway of the Harvard Inn.

Darby smells the salt in the air mixed with the scent of rotted rubbish. He and Darby lean against a pole in front of the entrance when suddenly Richie's voice howls out, "An' ya ain't old enough to be a bouncer, ya fuck!"

Darby looks away when he sees Richie's face go flush and his eyes turn from pale blue to red with rage.

I hate when Richie gets angry, it scares me.

"Go'on get outta here," the big boy says, though he is the same height as Darby, his big moon face, round shoulders and keg belly give him the girth he is known for.

"Fuck you," Richie stands up to him, an inch taller. "Come outside an' say that."

Richie steps back into the sidewalk while Petey, Matty and Timmy form a circle so pedestrians cannot get in the middle.

The man with the three-scarred face looks incredulously at Richie, who's peg leg is covered by long trousers.

He doesn't know who Richie is, Darby realizes.

Suddenly Scarface Al flashes a smile and waves out some burly friends from inside the Harvard Inn to even the odds. All four of them are bigger than all four of ours, but no matter.

This is could get very bad, Darby's stomach drops. *I don't like this.*

Darby's eyes begin to wobble. As his legs start to shake he holds the light post to keep his balance.

As Scarfaced Al steps onto the sidewalk, he finds Darby's eyes. Then sees the dustbroom in his hand.

He recognizes me.

But it's too late, Richie has punched the man in the cheek and the brawl has begun. Richie's fists are fueled by some bubbling craze inside of him, thrashing and sick with fury. Before the big boy can respond, Richie is behind him thrusting punches into his side and crashing them across the partially balding head and ear of Scarfaced Al.

Timmy then lands a right cross and then a left cross that breaks the skin over one of the Italian's eyes and drops him while Matty is on his back and screaming for help.

"Let's go," Abe yells at Darby. "let's go. We have to bar the door."

"Wha?"

Abe grabs the dustbroom, but Darby pulls it back and runs for the door. As quickly as he can Darby slides it through two door-pulls and the both of them put a shoulder on the door to secure it.

When Darby looks back, chaos has taken the Coney Island Bowery. In unison, Bill and the rest of the gang swarm the four Italians and land punches and kicks, overrunning them. A long-dressed woman somehow is entangled in the melee and cannot escape. Everywhere men are being beaten with pipes and cudgels and fists and boots. Jidge Seaman backs a man into a parked motor car. As the driver tries to take off, Frankie Byrne whips at the Italian's knees with some sort of weapon. Non and Petey and Joey Behan are taking turns kicking at a man's ass and genitals from behind, laughing all the way. The shit brown hound rips the collar off of an Italian, tosses it aside and sinks its teeth into his forearm but then lunges toward the man's testicles. The other dogs are protecting the perimeter from any would-be hero, howling at anyone who comes near the circle.

Men pound on the door from the inside to get out and Darby screams when his broken finger gets caught between the dustbroom and the door pull. Then the dustbroom snaps in two.

"Ahh! They're gonna get out soon," he yells into the afray that has spilled into the streets and sweeps up unwitting tourists and anyone else caught in the disorder.

Suddenly three men slip through the door before Darby and Abe can get it closed again.

"Oh fuck," Darby cries out. "No, no, no. Shit, they got out!"

One of the men who escaped pulls out a pistol and points it directly at Darby.

I'm not supposed to be here, Darby closes his eyes after he saw inside the tiny hole of the gun's narrow barrel. *I'm supposed to be looking for Sadie before Bill finds out I lost her. I have to find her to get my brother Pickles a retrial. And I need to get back to Ligeia and Colleen Rose, they're waiting for me. I can't let them wait too long.*

When Darby opens his eyes again, the man with the pistol is now pointing the barrel into the air and claps off a warning shot, "Alright, Alright, Break it up before I—"

The sound of the man being tackled and slammed to the ground comes to Darby's good ear. Petey Behan has quickly wrestled the escapee to the sidewalk and presses all of his weight on the soft part of the man's wrist with both thumbs. In agony, the escapee yells out and loosens his grip on the gun.

Amidst the chaos of flailing bodies and wild punches, Bill walks gingerly through the crowd and coughs. "Get me that piece," his voice grinds like gears. "I want it."

Petey takes the German model pistol and holds it out to Bill, but one-arm Flynn intercepts it. As bodies are tossed and punches thrown behind him, Flynn stares at the Luger P08 Nine Millimeter Parabellum as if it were some mystical, cherished gem. He holds it out in his palm and rubs a thumb gently across the handle and the distinctive lug at the base of the grip, which was added to attach to shoulder packs for the average Hun soldier. It was this standard issue model that had wounded Private Joseph Flynn in France, changing him forever. When their brigade was isolated and lost, he was without medical care and the wound festered. To stop the corruption, Non Connors, Thos Carmody and five others held him down as Bill hacked at the arm with a rusted hand axe, then tossed the limb into a ravine. They then poured boiling water on the bleeding stump at his shoulder and burned it with a hot iron before wrapping it with soiled linen.

Somewhere Bill had picked up a boater's hat and slipped it over his head. And there is a toothpick hanging out of his wolfish grin as well.

"*Pulcinella*," a wounded man remarks in a grisly voice, recognizing him.

Richie has bloodied the big boy into submission with the help of Petey, Timmy Bucks and Sean Healy, though Richie has a long cut under his eye that seeps blood onto his dirty collar. The Hanan boot that is nailed to his peg leg holds the Italian to the sidewalk by the neck while others have his arms and legs splayed out.

"Check his pockets," Bill says.

Two men rip the pockets out of Scarfaced Al's inner coat and trousers as his eyes stare up and into Bill's.

"Four hundret dime, this guy carries on him," Joey Behan reports as he hands the bills to Bill.

"Give that roll to the Mole," Bill commands as Behan walks toward the door and places the wad in little Abe Harms' coat pocket.

Wild Bill stands over the scarfaced fellow and opens his coat to reveal the silver handle of his .45, then speaks in a languid tone, "Il Maschio, Sammy de Angelo an' now Scarfaced Al." With one eye closed and the barrel pointed down at his victim, Bill finishes, "They send me three killers, an' I send them three bodies back, that's a trifecta."

Leaning against the door still, Darby puts a finger in the only ear he can hear from so that the .45 blast does not deafen him altogether.

"Ya promised me," Petey voices his complaint without saying Bill's name. "Ya promised me captain!"

A gunshot rings out and Darby flinches. The men inside the Harvard Inn stop pushing on the door and instead press their faces against the glass to see who took the bullet blast.

Two blocks east, five patrolmen are sprinting toward them. Three blocks west there are ten more with gun smoke billowing above them.

"Ya stay south o' the Gowanus," Bill warns the big boy, then throws an eyebrow in Darby's direction. "I got my shadow on ya. I know where ya live. I know ya got a Irish wife, an' I know where ya work. Toy wit' the border again an' I'll butcher ya, ya fookin' guinea-wop slime."

And then they run.

~~~

In the back of the dark and lumbering night train, someone pushes Darby by the shoulder, waking him.

"Bill wants to talk at ya," one of the Trench Rabbits says loud enough for him to hear.

Someone laughs and Darby hears a voice, "Oldie man Leighton can't hear a thing, 'less ya yell an' ya scream an' ya sing."

The night's black face had closed in all round to rob him of his valuable vision. With his good hand he holds a straphanger to keep his balance. At the front of the train, Bill stands in the dark with his legs open.

What now? I just want to go home.

When he reaches the front of the train, Bill tells him to turn round and face the men.

"Darby Leighton," he announces in a growl. "Ya failed me again."

The train goes quiet, all but for Bill's words and the iron wheels on the rails outside, clacking down the night.

"But ya showed courage," Bill calls out. "Ya showed spirit under fire. I understand ya was scared, but ya fought against fear, an' never quit. Ya showed gallantry an' risked ya life when we was in combat against a armed enemy force. Behind enemy lines! On top o' that, ya have dedicated ya'self to an honorable pursuit," Bill puts his hand on Darby's shoulder as the train sways. "Ya committed to rightin' the lie told about ya brother by Dinny Meehan."

Darby's stomach turns when he thinks of the money Dead Reilly demands and his missing cousin, Sadie.

"For these reasons, I want ya to hold somethin' for me," Bill reaches into his pocket and produces a gold cross with an eagle's outstretched wings in front of it and shows it to everyone on the train. "I earned this Distinguished Service Cross in the war for the same type o' valor that Darby showed all o' us t'day. Darby?" Bill turns to him. "I want ya to hold on to this for me. I want ya to hold onto it until the day a judge declares ya brother's innocence an' clears ya fam'ly name in the eyes o' men an' law. An' on that day, which is next mont', when Pickles Leighton is released an' we have a hundret scofflaw soldiers at our callin'," Bill finds Darby's eyes in the dark. "I will name ya the Fifth Lieutenant o' the White Hand Gang."

The men stand from their seats and the train explodes in applause. All twenty rush to the front of the train to congratulate Darby as Bill hands him the medal.

But one person still sits in a seat and has not congratulated him. Petey Behan's eyes are downcast and angry, his lip curled.

"For valor!" Bill yells out.

"For valor!" The men respond.

Darby holds the war medal in his hand. It's heavier than he thought. He looks round him at all the men who love him now and he almost smiles.

Those who Survive are Chosen

In Greenwich Village Thos Carmody walks up to the growler hole at Lynches Tavern and taps on it.

The tender Mr. Lynch opens it, "What can I do ye fer?"

"Ya know what I'm lookin' for."

"Thos feckin' Carmody?" Mr. Lynch's eyes look through the darkness. "Is it truly yerself? Ye look terrible."

"Thanks."

"Come round to the back entrance."

Thos gathers his remaining strength to walk round the side of the brick saloon. Everyday he has become weaker and weaker. Yesterday he forced himself to eat. To chew the food that tasted of metal and alloys in his mouth, then struggled to swallow. But it made no difference. Weaker and weaker he has become.

Maybe I got the cancer? He wonders. *Or the grippe*, as they call it in Brooklyn. The Great Influenza, most deem it, though Thos doesn't have any symptoms in his lungs. Just in his weakening strength.

Just as Thos comes to the women's entrance door, it opens and he slips through.

"I s'pose yer lookin' fer information on Tanner Smith, that right?"

"Ya seen him round?"

"I heard he was sent Sing Sing-way."

"But ya don' believe it, just like I don't."

The tall, rangy man with austere eyes sits at a small table in the darkness where only a small window over a stairwell sheds a long shaft of light between the two in the rear room of the tavern. Thos hides the pockmarks left by the Cricket Ball grenade behind his lapel and beneath a lowered cap. He begins to speak until a door opens behind him.

"Thomas Carmody is that yer very self, is it?"

Thos looks up at Mr. Lynch, who tries to warn his wife, but it's too late. Honora has come to Thos's right side and as soon as she sees his pockmarked face, she screams and almost drops her son, who sleeps on her chest.

"Thomas?" She grabs hold of the table with her free hand.

He looks up to her from his chair with sad eyes, "It's me, yeah."

"Oh," she sighs.

Honora's face nervously comes to a smile as she gathers herself. She then reaches down to him and cups the right side of his cheek and gently washes it against the wounds.

That feels nice.

He leans into her hand, "Good to see ya again, Honora. Been a while."

"I'm so happy ye've come back, Thomas. We missed ye round these parts, we did, ye know. My children still talk out on the street about ye as if ye were the prophet o' Greenwich Village."

"I can promise ye I don' have the staff o' Moses."

"Oh ye've the wit on ye still, I see. Ah well, I've brought a drop o' the pure," Honora places an unmarked bottle of poteen on the table and reaches behind for two glasses. "I'll leave ye bhoys at it then."

When the door closes, Mr. Lynch leans forward, "No, Tanner didn't go to Sing Sing. I would think that out o' character."

He fills the glasses and slides one toward Thos, raising his, "*Sláinte chugat.*"

"To *my* health?" Thos asks. "Nothin' can save that, but I'll take a drop anyhow."

"Just throw it down yer gob, ye dour shite, ye."

Thos drinks it with a nod and twirls the glass in his fingers as Mr. Lynch grits at the poteen before speaking, "Ye heard President Eamon de Valera's comin' New Yarkway, did ye?"

"De facto president," Thos says. "Ireland ain't even a country—"

"The Irish people are on their way up, Thos. Don' shake the ladder on them."

"Famous last words," Thos mumbles.

"My patrons have been savin' up. If I give ye any useful information, I'd prefer ye drop a few dullers in the hat fer Irish freedom," A caricature of Eoghan Ruadh Ó Néill and a black and white sketch of John Mitchel adorn the wall behind the tall County Clareman.

"I will whether it's useful or not."

"Good then," Mr. Lynch crosses his long legs and sits back. "So it's Tanner yer after. I heard o' this obscenity ye throw out onto the street. A Blood Feud is it? Ye Americans think ye know somethin' o' Ireland, but ye don't."

"I was born in Ireland—"

"But dragged up round here in New Yark, ye were."

Thos chuckles, "Blood feud. . . It's a good way o' gettin' everyone's attention though."

"I don't know why ye're so dead set on killin' this feller."

It's inevitable. He was hired to kill me and he didn't. It's either me or him, but getting Tanner is all I can think about it. All that drives me to get up when I long to give up instead.

Mr. Lynch's voice is low and gravelly, "He's scared, Tanner is."

"He oughta be."

"But he's a cornered animal. Ye should keep yer eyes open, Thos."

Sound advice, that.

"He's been avoidin' Manhattan because o' yerself an' Johnny Spanish. Meehan has assumed the debt, but it's also assumed Tanner went into Sing Sing to butcher Pickles Leighton an' start a new war for the inside. Thing is, Tanner's own gangmen in the Marginals are ready to turn on him now. Ye know who they are; Lefty an' Costello an' a few others. They came by here an' left this fer ye, just in case ye came by."

The long man slides a piece of paper across the table into the beaming light as Thos puts back the glass of poteen and growls at the bite it leaves in his mouth.

Tanner's hiding out, but his time is due, call us, Thos reads the piece of paper but doesn't waste time on the number.

"Legitimate complaint or trap?"

Mr. Lynch nods sternly, "They want what all the longshoremen want round here; join the ILA before the general strike. They don't wanna be scabs. Ye're the one's got the ear o' the big shots at the ILA, so there's yer maths."

"Adds up," Thos trades a twenty dollar bill for the message from Lefty and Costello.

"Put it in the hat over there," Mr. Lynch nods toward a counter in the dark that overflows with change and bills.

Thos does so, and the tavern owner stands up with him.

"Thank ye fer yer service, Thos," Mr. Lynch shakes his hand and stares at Thos's facial wounds. "But as ye know, fer Ireland's sake, it'd been better if the Hun won."

A failed idea, that.

No one in the Army had ever asked Thos what he thought the outcome of the Great War would be. He was only a First Lieutenant, after all. But the collective belief system the Americans surfaced with later in the war were new and on the ascent. Their patterns of accumulating change had an overall effect of growth, not decline. Their main opponent, the German Empire was seeped in outdated ideas amidst the great testing ground of war. And although they were aggressive and stormed the battlefield, by 1918 they were blown. In short, their ways were fast becoming obsolete. And Quick Thos Carmody would never fight for a losing side.

Without going into detail, Thos simply answers Mr. Lynch, "Yeah well, the Kaiser's part o' the old world now. He's hist'ry, as they say."

The Irish, Thos's own ancestry, had proven over and over to him that their individual properties and their causal relations, which contribute to their collective emergence, was never worth putting money on. When systems of belief compete for cultural dominance, the Irish never win. An age-old criticism not dissimilar to that Julius Caesar heaped on the Celts in his book *Commentaries on the Gallic War*. Success is simply not ingrained in individual Celtic characteristics, dooming their capability to collectively dominate other groups.

But there is one thing Thos can't get his head round. A defect in his theory that only recently has given him pause. A baffling result that haunts him and undermines his assuredness. The unsophisticated nature of the Irish forecasts their failure, yet beyond logic, they always survive. Reborn from despair, changed but with the same old emergent system doomed to failure, again. And resurrected from nothing anon, ad infinitum.

Mr. Lynch's voice snaps Thos out of his thoughts, "Whose side ye takin' in Brooklyn? Meehan? Or Lovett?"

The way Mr. Lynch grumbles at the word "Lovett," tells Thos he's a Meehan man.

Without answering, he raises the clear liquid to his lips, "Meehan's ways are admirable, sure. An' archaic."

"Ye takin' Bill then?"

"I don' know... yet."

"No? Well everyone knows whichever side ye don' choose will *also* become hist'ry. Quick Thos is never wrong... as they say."

The firm handshake from Mr. Lynch drains Thos of most of his strength. When he tries to take his hand back, the tavern owner grips him harder, then pulls Thos closer, "Ye'd be better served if ye fought fer Ireland, not the ILA. We need a smart feller to sort out the issues 'tween President de Valera an' New Yark's biggest fundraiser fer Ireland, John Devoy. They're already lockin' horns, them two. We need a respected mediary, Thos. Ye were born in Ireland an' all New Yark knows yer talents, to be sure. Come, work toward the creation of a country, not to keep afloat a ship full o' laborers an' scofflaws. Ireland calls, Thos. Ireland calls."

"Ya mistake me, sir," Thos says as respectfully as he can. "Ireland's a part o' my past, not my future."

Outside, bundled up in a long coat with flipped collars and a low hat, he leans on the corner of the brick wall where Hudson and Barrow streets meet.

I'm dying, Thos admits while holding the note in his coat pocket with the phone number for Lefty and Costello. *But before I go, I have to get Tanner. Sixty-nine to one.*

Thos can taste the retribution killing in his mouth. Savory and sweet, as nourishing as food. Something, who knows what, draws Thos back to murder with a great hunger. An impulse, even. A need so powerful that it overshadows his decision between Meehan and Lovett. A deep and urgent craving, but whether it's because he misses the hunt and all the killing he took part in during the war, or something else, he isn't exactly sure.

He should've killed me, because now Tanner Smith must die.

Gnawing at him is the lack of assuredness he has always been known for. Before the war he was the quiet, smart guy. Although no one has noticed since coming back, he is changed. Doubt has crept into him. Fear of the unknown. The one thing everyone could count on was Thos Carmody's unflappable certainty. His acuity and brilliant judgment. All changed now. Lost, there are no answers from him any longer. Only questions that lead to more questions. He is changed, and it has everything to do with his awakening in that field hospital.

Now look at me. I'm falling apart. They should call me Timorous Thos. The only thing I know now. The only thing I feel assured about, is that Tanner Smith must die.

In front of the Fourteenth Street Ballroom in Chelsea, two large men guard the front door. One is Irish, the other a dark-haired, moon-faced Italian, most likely an employee of Paul Vaccarelli who was recently promoted to vice president of the ILA alongside King Joe Ryan.

"Where ya goin'?" the Italian moves to get a better view of Thos's face.

"Inside."

The Irish opens the door for Thos, "Come in, sir."

"Who is he?" The Italian demands.

"He's the guest o' honor, ya fookin' dago-eejit."

"Don' call me that—"

As the two argue Thos lights a hand-rolled and whips the match out as smoke curls over his shoulder in the cool air.

"Quick Thos!" He hears a familiar voice.

Thos looks up to the big dog-faced, baggy-suited, cigar-toting King Joe who elbows through the guards.

"Ya're late, Thos," King Joe says with a fat-tongued Rottweiler smile.

"Ya don' really want me to go in an' ham it up at a banquet, do ya? That's what *ya're* good at, not me."

"Just for a bit," King Joe laughs and slobbers on his coat. "How'd ya find out it's a banquet? S'posed to be a surprise."

"Yeah well."

"Anyway, after a little ham an' eggin' we'll head to the backroom wit' O'Connor an' Vaccarelli for a talk. Where's ya uniform?"

"I gave it to the moths. Everyone's gotta eat."

King Joe wraps an arm round Thos and walks him through the front door, "Ya can't be all business, all the time, Thos. We got whiskey imported from Ireland."

"Fell off a British steamer on the Chelsea piers, I'll bet."

"The best kind! Some things'll never change here in New York."

The Italian doorman points at Thos, "He's got a weapon in his coat."

"Ya're lucky he didn't use it," King Joe belches back, then whispers into Thos's ear, "Ya believe this thing about hirin' Vaccarelli as a VP? Fookin' I-Talians all up in ILA leadership. I'll never get used to it, Thos."

"Gonna have to."

Thos looks through the corridor into the smoky ballroom where thousands crowd, shoulder-to-shoulder. As he is lead through the back, King Joe motions to the stage with his cigar hand where a band strikes up, *Stars and Stripes Forever*.

Then Thos hears T.V. O'Connor at the microphone on stage, his voice crackling through the large speakers on the floor, "Here he is folks, Thomas Michael Carmody!"

The slew of union men roar at the introduction and wave flags in one hand while gulping whiskey with the other. They cheer him and step out of King Joe's way to make a path that leads all the way to the stage.

"I don' want to give a speech," Thos yells in King Joe's ear. "I'm not one for a dog an' pony show."

"Don' worry, just a few words. They wanna hear from the war hero."

"I ain't no fookin' war hero."

King Joe helps Thos to a small staircase on the side of the stage as O'Connor asks the crowd to quieten down. Thos leans on the handrail and struggles up the stairs like an old man. Out of breath he looks over the slew of faces that cheer him. Behind, the band members are clapping too, and the drummer gets up from his set to shake Thos's hand.

"My brother was in the 69th," he yells. "Welcome back!"

Ratcheting up his Irish lilt, President O'Connor yells into the microphone, "T'is me pleasure to give yez the warmest introductions. Ye've heard o' the man-behind-the-man, pullin' the strings? Well in the International Longshoremen's Association he is Thos Carmody, an' without his sage advice an innovative, shrewd idears? We'd've lost the war for the hearts an' minds o' the workin' man to the IWW Wobblies. He is a man who left the ILA as Treasurer o' New Yark for the Army, an' comes back as. . . Ye guessed it, Treasurer o' feckin' New Yark!"

The crowd is wild in patriotic fervor. There are red, white and blue streamers and red, white and blue balls hanging from the ceiling and red, white and blue top hats, and Thos feels as though he's at Tammany Hall's Democratic Convention with all the politicking, backslapping patriotism and drink taking.

"Ye've all heard o' the Army's 77th Infantry," O'Connor continues. "Promised support on both flanks, they were abandoned an' encircled by the Hun. Blown to shreds, starved. Most came from New Yark City, so the fight was already in them. Many died fer their country. Fer freedom, but those who survive are chosen!"

Thos looks at O'Connor when he hears the strange words describing him, *Chosen? For what?*

"The ILA loves America!" O'Connor announces, then lowers his tone. "Loves our veterans. Some say we're a load o' Communists, but we all know that's just an attempt to smear us, right?"

The slew of men laugh, but the ruse must be played up. It's only old-money America what claims ya can't be a socialist *and* be patriotic at the same time.

"Thos Carmody," O'Connor holds the microphone closely, picking up a whiskey and holding it high in the air, as everyone in the crowd follows suit and hushes their drunken gobs. "We salute ye an' the great sacrifice ye made fer this country, a god-lovin' free nation where the right to force tribute is as American as apple pie!"

Overcoming their tears, the onlookers roar again in laughter.

"Speech!"

"Speech!" The longshoremen yell.

O'Connor picks up the microphone stand himself and personally walks it over in front of Thos, then yells into it in front of him, "How 'bout a couple words from the war hero!"

Thos touches the microphone stand and steps up to it. He looks into the crowd. Behind him sit wives with their legs crossed, looking impatient. Drunk men with their hats on sideways smile proudly from the crowd, and wait. Thos turns to King Joe, who opens his hands and motions for him to say something.

"I uh. . ." the sound of his own voice through the speakers startles him. "I thank yaz for all o' the uh, praise. I'm not. . . uh, not one for speeches but—"

Thos wants to say that he is uncomfortable in front of big groups because being exposed like this makes him feel he could get shot at any moment. But that doesn't seem like the right thing to say.

"But I uh—" he speaks again into the microphone. "Ya're very kind to—"

When the grenade went off, hot metal came screaming out of the dirt with a flash of yellow and orange. Then there was the smell of burning flesh. His own, yet the artillery fire, the constant screaming of shells, the thundering cannonades, the wounded calling out into the night in prayer and the endless guns spitting fire, the infernal roar went on, all of it, together, unstopping, unceasing until finally, mercifully he lost consciousness. Then the unemotional face of the field surgeon. The blood stains on the white sheets. The meaninglessness of it all. The disconnected reasoning that has taken over his thoughts. The detached order. Or maybe there is meaning to everything, but for once Thos Carmody can't figure it out.

It makes no sense to him to be described as "chosen."

The doctors would only say he suffers from shell shock and certainly the war ground his strength into powder, but there is something else at play. Something bigger. Trying to piece it all together, he searches for meaning, but fears the worst.

Is that what it means to be chosen? That you have an important role to play despite your own will power? But why do I continue to get weaker?

Just then he sees a familiar face in the crowd.

Tanner?

Thos tries to focus in on the face, then reaches behind him and pulls out his pistol and points it into the crowd.

The women behind him screech, unfurl their long legs and clop in heels through the stage curtains. The drummer and tuba player duck behind their instruments. Thirty men below the stage shift and twist away from the pointed pistol like a school of fish obscuring and confusing a predator. In the scattering movements, Thos loses Tanner's face. He lowers the pistol to get a better look into the dispersing crowd until he concludes he is no longer in danger.

T.V. O'Connor startles him when the president steps in front of the microphone and yells into it, "Thank ye Thos Carmody! We salute ye! The ILA salutes all our Great War Veterans!"

The microphone picks up Thos's muffled voice, "I thought it was Tanner."

King Joe then pulls him from the stage with an arm over his shoulder. When they reach a backroom he asks Thos, "Ya got any readymade handroll'ds? Wanna have a smoke?"

"Yeah," Thos reaches a shaky hand into his coat pocket as King Joe pours him a whiskey-neat.

As he lights a cigarette Thos notices an uneven deck of cards in the middle of the table and fights back the urge to reach out and straighten, shuffle and deal them. Instead, standing over the table, he pulls from the whiskey that bites back at his lips and burns his throat.

As he sits he takes account of the room where boxes of Irish whiskey are stacked along the walls with bolts of silk, perfectly organized sacks of cereal grains and flour, and Yuban coffee, three round metal containers of black ink, half-opened boxes of colorful sweets from a Peruvian company, clothing detergent and photo engraving zinc, five barrels of corn syrup, eight kegs of German beer and four kegs of English black treacle molasses that never made it to their destination, but will be resold for King Joe's profit.

"Ya sure ya're up to all this shit that's goin' down in Brooklyn? Ya look, emm, tired an'—"

"Disfigured, g'ahead an' say it. But when I fall, I always land on my feet," Thos says with cold eyes to cover his own doubts. "I just ain't one for stages, I told ya that."

King Joe nods in agreement, "Ya made a choice yet? Lovett or Meehan?"

Thos feels his hand shake again, "Maybe."

"O'Connor's gonna grill ya on it. Tell ya what though, we're Meehan's last ally. Them boyos'll be friendless an' fuckt if we back Lovett. Ya heard the Black Hand no longer—"

"Yeah."

"Personally, I don' want them to go to war wit' each other. It splits up the north Brooklyn longshoremen. We're caught between two stools on this one. War's not good for business. I don' want war."

Thos reads the headline of the newspaper lying on the table.

Union Rift Drawn Down Ethnic Lines, Irish vs. Italian
The appointment of Paul Vaccarelli
Angers the Incumbent Irish Element

"Yes ya do."

"What? Why?"

Thos takes a long drag and in that moment he makes up his mind, "That's what the shippin' comp'nies'll want," Thos exhales and points to the newspaper. "Wolcott's already fast at work."

"How's Wolcott—"

"They got a reporter on the tug. We might as well use their energy to our favor."

"Thos, we don' want a gang war."

"It's inevitable. In this world the peacemongers are blind an' the one-eyed man rules. Lovett is actually prepared for war an' a politician always knows deep in his soul that god speaks through the army, if ya catch my drift. Lovett's got smart advisors too. An wit' all the defections from Meehan's clan? Lovett'll make short shrift o' Meehan when the time comes. Here's what we do; we talk O'Connor into backin' Lovett. Meanwhile we know what's gonna happen in the ILA when we call the strike later this year. Vaccarelli an' his I-Talian element will be makin' a power move on O'Connor. The ILA'll be split. O'Connor an' the Irish against Vaccarelli an' the I-talians. In Brooklyn where Lovett an' the Black Hand'll fight against each other, O'-Connor'll take the heat for causin' the split as much as Vaccarelli does. An' ya'self—"

Spittle gathers in both corners of King Joe's smiling mouth, "I take the high road all the way to the presidency in next year's election."

Thos nods, "Immigrants are the future o' the union."

"So I'll come in huggin' both sides, blamin' O'Connor an' Vaccarelli for tryin' to tear the union in two. The unification ticket."

"What do we care about a gang war in Brooklyn?" Thos shrugs. "Either way, we'll wait 'til after the war's over, *then* we'll take the winnin' side when ya the President o' the ILA."

"Fookin' brilliant. Ya're fookin' brilliant, Thos."

"That's why I'll be Vice President o' New York."

"Yes ya will, as long as the plan works."

"Famous last words," Thos mumbles to himself, then answers King Joe. "I haven't been wrong yet."

King Joe suddenly becomes sullen and turns on Thos, "But what do ya want outta all this?"

"I already told ya—"

"No, Thos, why do ya go outta ya way to make me president? What do ya want, Thos?"

I want to know why I'm still alive. I want to know why everyone says I'm chosen. I want to know why I'm growing weaker everyday and why I yearn to murder again.

Thos looks up, "I want to win. At everythin'."

King Joe's panting mouth turns to a sloppy smile, "So do I. Ya're a big fish in a small pond, Thos. A kingmaker!"

And Vincent Maher is a Queensolver. Put us together and you got a royal flush.

He turns his eyes up, "Well ya gotta live up to that name, King Joe."

The door handle slowly turns. As Thos watches, he gently feels for the pistol in the back of his trousers and fingers the trigger.

Tanner, is that you?

Conjurer Of Misfortune

Patrolman Daniel Culkin's red and glistening cock disappears like a little bald turtlehead retreating into its shell as he buttons the trousers of his police uniform.

"Imagine, if ya can, two people playin' chess," he tells his prisoner who is chained to the radiator. "But there, I already lied to ya. It's a ruse, they're not playin' against each other, it just looks like it, right? Now imagine Wolcott standin' over them both an' directing each move for both players. When Wolcott picks up chess pieces wit' his chubby sausage fingers, blood floods the board, drowning even the Queen and King. On both sides."

The patrolman then walks over to the window and separates the black drapes with a finger, "Ya never thought our headquarters'd be this close to the Meehan home, I know."

Below is a courtyard where newly sprouted grass has grown into a collapsed dray and through a stack of wood-spoked wheels. Beyond are the backs of other buildings that break the skyline with roofs and chimneys upon lowrise Brooklyn tenements as endless as trees in a jungle, hidden families living in each one.

Chained to the radiator Maureen Egan weeps naked, though her cries are muffled by a bar towel that is taped over her mouth. On her wrist is a dirty cast with browned fabric coming out where it ends at her thin forearm and through the finger holes. Because of the cast, the manacles are cuffed at her upper arms and bolted to the radiator, forcing her to press her bare breasts outward, bending her back. The chain that crisscrosses her chest over both shoulders are also secured to the radiator. Her hair is an explosion of tangled red clumps and the makeup she had applied that morning runs down her heart-shaped face like black blood on orange freckled cheeks.

Daniel speaks without response, "So close to the Meehan Brownstone that if this window was a photograph, I could touch it," he runs a finger along the glass where Dinny Meehan's home stands one block away, partially obscured by a three-story building in the foreground. He puts the Lemaire field binoculars to his eyes and can see where the glass had been repaired by members of the White Hand on the third floor where the Meehans live.

Daniel lets the black drapes fall back into place to cover the window and moves his eyes slowly to his new toy, "Best friends yaz were right? Moe and Doe, my wife?"

Maureen attempts to cast doubt on those words, but can manage only throaty sounds. The chain wrapped round her pale pink chest is tight enough that she must use her stomach muscles to sit up. On one side of her is a metal bed with a dirty mattress and no sheets. A single limp and yellowed pillow lies in the middle of the bed next to Maureen's torn dress. On the other side of her is a barrel with steel hoops round beveled staves.

"Brosnan told me the story," Culkin's footsteps ring through the room as he walks slowly over and drops the binoculars on the dresser next to Garry Barry's hand sickle. Against the dresser he leans on both palms, his long tunic almost completely covers his shiny black shoes. "Moe an' Doe. The most popular girls in school. But havin' a good father is a roll o' the dice, ain't it? Sometimes ya get a good roll; a lovin', soft-hearted an' understin' father who'll do anythin' in his power to help his daughter along, like Brosnan. But when ya roll dice ya can also get Snake Eyes," he turns to her. "A rapist an' a drunk. All those years ya father was rapin' ya an' no one ever knew until ya told Doirean? I wonder though, why'd ya keep it a secret for so long? Brosnan said ya father had been doin' it to ya since ya was a moppet. Why didn't ya say nothin' before? Did ya like it when he rode ya?"

Maureen's eyes darken and she lets herself fall back, allowing her legs to open.

"Close ya legs ya fookin' slattern. Fookin' disgustin'," Daniel averts his eyes. When he looks back, she has opened them even wider.

"Close them," he kicks her thigh until it turns bright red. "Ya think that's power? It ain't! It's a finite power, that's all it is. All any whores got." He walks back over to the dresser. "Ya know my grandmother was raped. Raped by a Englishman. Captain o' a coffin ship. My father told that story, but I never wanted to know it. Brosnan used to bring it up all the fookin' time. He used it against me an' I hated him for it. My grandmother was only fourteen when she came over from Ireland. A virgin, more than likely. Just a little girl from a deeply religious an' tight knit community in County fookin' Mayo," he makes a face and wiggles his fingers in mockery. "It was ravaged by hunger. Fookin' peasants. Couldn't read or write. They all turned against each other in the end. By the time she arrived in Brooklyn she was showin'. The way I see it, rape gave me life, an' thank god for that. Plus, there's basically no biological difference between Irish an' English anyhow, right? So who cares about any distinctions an' particulars, I don't. That reminds me. Who fucked the Lonergan girl? Brosnan an' I were takin' bets. He said Vincent Maher. I said it was Sixto Stabile," Daniel looks at her and waves his hand. "Never mind, don' matter who wins now. . . Brosnan's dead."

Maureen's eyes go wide.

"Yeah, he went over to the other side. Ya didn' know? I guess ya wouldn't. No one knows, really. Ya'self'll get the same as him though. Barry wants to cut ya head off too. We just gotta wait 'til we can get a big strong guy to carry ya down the stairs an' put ya in the automobile truck he's bringin'. O' course, that's after we stuff ya in that barrel."

Maureen's eyes turn to the barrel. She moans and wriggles to free herself of the chains, then kicks at the bed and pounds her heels into the floor. She then attempts to position herself so that she can kick backward at the barrel. Unable to reach it, she screams into the towel with more temper than terror.

Daniel grabs the hand sickle from the dresser and flies toward her, "I'll just kill ya now!"

Maureen closes her eyes and hunches her shoulders. Opening one eye, she turns it up and sees Daniel with the weapon over his head, frozen in place.

He bursts into laughter, "That stopped ya, didn' it? Didn' it?"

He drops the sickle on the floor next to her, "G'ahead, take it. Oh ya can't reach? Oh gee, wow. Maybe if I loosened up the chains a bit for ya? Would that work? Then ya can grab it an' try to kill me wit' it. . . Except I got this," he opens his coat enough to show her the steel nestled into the leather shoulder holster.

Daniel turns round and opens the drapes again, leaving the sickle next to her. "Barry an' Wiz voted to kill ya right off. But I wanted to get a piece o' ya first. I ain't into dead girls. I like them warm. Doirean never lets me tie her up. Besides, she's pregnant. She only wants flowers and surprises an' new sofas an' jewelry. She likes them yokes a lot more than she likes cock. She could go the rest o' her life wit'out havin' sex an' she'd be fine wit' it. Just my luck. I'm the one likes to get wild. I like to experiment. My god, I never knew I'd like fookin' a prisoner that much though. I gave ya what, three thrusts? Ah well, it's not like ya enjoyed it. At least I spared ya the agony o' ridin' ya for an hour. Now. . . I've had both Moe an' Doe," Daniel turns and smiles. "Kind o' a nice feelin', actually. Cleary's gonna go next, if ya don' mind. I'm sure ya don't. Men've been ridin' ya for years now. The only difference is we ain't gonna pay ya t'day. . . We're gonna chop ya up. Ya own pimp is gonna do it too, Garry Barry. How's that for loyalty? Or was he ya boyfriend? Did ya see him as ya boyfriend once? Betrothed? Even though he charged other men to fuck ya? Sad, sad girl."

The black blood streaking down Maureen's pale face thickens and weeps onto her shoulders, down toward her nipples.

"Ya were gonna tell on me, weren't ya?" He quickly turns to face her with his bottom lip pushed out and unhooks his blackjack and rears back.

Maureen closes her red eyes and lowers her head in as much cowering supplication as the chains allow. It sounds like a baseball bat clapping a skull, but it is her shin where he bludgeons her. The dense leather at the end with the lead ball inside had caromed closer to her knee than ankle. There, her leg began to turn blue and swell within seconds. He clips the blackjack back onto the belt of his tunic and watches as Maureen's eyes almost pop out of her pressurized head.

She's in another world right now, Daniel smiles. *I sent her there.*

Her face turns purple in front of him, yet only a few muffled screams and some snorting sounds escape.

Daniel takes an exhilarated breath and exhales through gritted teeth, "Ya came to my home like a wild woman when everyone found out my father-in-law went missin'. Ya had to make a big scene. I s'pose ya thought it was a ya civil duty to report me to my commandin' officer. Surely a citizen can do that wit'out retribution. Lucky for me ya got the reputation o' a itinerant slattern."

He looks her up and down, "Ya dropped that letter off at our home didn' ya? Ya wanted Doirean to know about the house up in Peekskill, so ya slipped it under the door, didn' ya?"

Maureen looks quizzically up at him.

"But why sign it wit' a 'H'? Eh? What's that mean, 'H'"?

Maureen shakes her head in confusion and mumbles through the towel.

"Ya ain't so thick, are ya? Nah, ya ain't. Durin' the storm when me an' Wiz the Lump came an' found Barry and Cleary an' ya'self in that room they was pimpin' ya outta? Ya know, when Wiz broke ya arm? Remember? Ya put it all together, didn' ya?"

He shows her one finger, "Ya knew Barry was capable o' killin' anybody." A second finger, "An' ya knew Wiz the Lump reports to Wolcott." He flashes three fingers and balls them into a fist, "An' me. I was the connection to

Brosnan. I wouldn't call it smart, per say. I'd say ya just smart enough to connect-the-dots is all. But ya gotta lotta words that come rollin' outta that lipless slit o' a mouth ya got. Well, ya know what they say in Irishtown; 'clouts for touts,'" Daniel bends down and picks up the hand sickle and touches the tip with an index finger. "Whoa, that's sharp. I saw this cut right through the muscle an' bone in a grown man's neck. The fookin' head went flyin' an' for a second I thought I saw Brosnan's lips movin'. Like he was talkin' to himself or somethin'. Right now I'm thinkin' why not just do ya now? Why wait for Cleary to come up for sloppy seconds? Ya probably already did it wit' him though, right? Probably lots o' times. I heard he an' Barry used to take turns on ya. Anyway, Cleary don' need another turn. I'll just cut off an arm first. But wait, if I do that ya might get loose. A leg then? That might be too difficult. How deep do ya think I can bury this instrument into ya skull? Ya think I could cut ya head in half? Is that possible wit' this? Maybe Wiz could, he's stronger than I am. But I can try. Yeah, I'll just kill ya now."

Daniel stands over her again and holds the hand sickle over Maureen Egan's head. He grits his teeth and his face begins to turn red. His body shakes until all at once, he bursts out laughing again.

"Oh shit, I got ya again," Daniel drops the sickle and lowers himself to see beneath her legs. "Look, look, ya pee'd. Oh fuck that's funny. Ya really pee'd. Listen, listen. I'm not gonna hurt ya. Men wit' real power don' actually do the killin', see. Animals like Garry fookin' Barry do. I'm gonna go get him, I'll be right back."

Daniel stands and moves for the door, but the sound of Maureen's cries stop him. She whimpers, which leads Daniel to believe she has given up hope. His cock tingles at that. He moves his tunic aside and looks down at his trousers where he notices he has begun to stiffen again. When she whimpers again and sniffles, the lump in his trousers flexes.

It's the sound of her cries, he realizes and turns round to her. *I want to hear her cry. It's too muffled.*

He walks over to her and tears the tape from her face and yanks the dirty rag out of her mouth.

Maureen takes a deep breath. Her face is half-covered with a tangle of hair like a wounded animal peering out from a hedge. She looks up at him, "I already told Captain Sullivan that ya killt Brosnan."

"Horseshit, ya didn't know until I just told ya."

"No, I knew it was the four o' ya," she throws her head in the direction of the door. "When ya came an' took Garret away from me durin' the storm, then later I saw the newspaper article about Brosnan. I knew it was all o' yaz, an' I told Captain Sullivan. I told him."

Daniel's hand goes to his stomach, *Captain Sullivan is coming for me. He is going to punish me. He will probably just beat me up and put me behind bars, but I deserve worse. I deserve to be flogged.*

He turns his eyes to her, "Ya're full o' shit. I know ya are."

"G'ahead an' kill me," Maureen's voice is low and hoarse as she pulls at the chains that cross round her bare chest. "Nothin' I can say can stop that, I just wanted ya to know that ya're gonna die too. They'll hang ya for killin' a detective an' a vet'ran o' thirty years on the force. The thing is, for all that is pleasurable comes an equal contradiction o' pain. Daniel, before ya die, I'll haunt ya. I'll make ya pay for all ya pleasures. I have been raped by my father, prostituted by Christie the Larrikin, dumped by Garry Barry an' after ya kill me, I'll sway over ya for ya remainin' days like a axe over the throat."

A noise from downstairs turns both of their eyes downward.

"See, Sullivan is here."

Daniel's eyes go wide. He rushes to shove the rag in her mouth again. As he grabs for the tape, her teeth snap rabidly in the air at his fingers. Running, he opens and closes the door behind him. Then he stands between the door and the stairwell and puts his hand over his mouth to stop himself from screaming and peers over the bannister. Downstairs he does not see Captain Sullivan and everything is just as he left it after he and Barry and Cleary had abducted, gagged and chained her in the room.

He turns back to the door, but again stops himself. *I should go in and kill her. To stop her from talking. She can't haunt me if she's dead. I don't believe her. She just wants to scare me. But I deserve pain. I deserve to suffer.*

He turns round to face the stairwell, takes a deep breath and moves forward.

The bar is at the base of the steep stairwell and as Daniel comes down, the tender's scared eyes find him between the backs of Garry Barry and James Cleary who are hunched over their drinks at the bar. Daniel's tunic is so long it looks like a dark blue dress with a copper badge as a brooch. When Doirean's father got him a spot on the force, she had to take the sleeves back because they went over his knuckles so that only the tips of his fingers could peek out.

"No one goes upstairs," Daniel announces to anyone who can hear.

The tender drops his towel, "Officer—"

"Whatever ya plan on sayin', make sure ya end it by tellin' all these men at the bar that no one goes upstairs."

The tender's white eyes and stuttered words tell everyone at the bar what they need to know. Before he can complete a sentence, Daniel stands as tall as his little body allows and opens his tunic to brush his thumb across the police issue's handle, "Anyone puts a single foot on the first step o' this fookin' stairwell an' the full force o' the law will be upon them, everyone understand?"

Daniel's threat is met with mumbles of agreement. He leans up to sit on a stool next to Garry Barry and wags his finger at the bartender to approach. The man leans in close as Daniel whispers, "I'm expectin' a friend. A large friend. When he gets here the four o' us will be goin' upstairs for about a hour. Maybe two. We'll come down only wit' a barrel an' yaz'll never see the likes o' that red tramp again."

"Alright but—"

Daniel wags his finger in the air again and brings them to his lips while Garry Barry watches the tender closely, "No questions. Take this wad. It's a hundret an' fifty dollars. Ya've never had a day this beneficial in ya bar. Let it be said that no female ever entered, or has *ever* entered this establishment. No women allowed, am I right?"

Barry growls low like a bitch over her pups as the tender searches for words. He had no choice but to allow them to make his establishment their headquarters, and hasn't had a say in almost anything since. Instead of speaking, he only nods, stands back and slips the bills into his trouser pocket.

"Drinks are on the house!" Daniel calls out to the ten to twelve drinking men along the stretch of bar in the low light.

"T'anks officer," a toothless man tips his cap.

"Don' thank me, it's the bar's tender what's payin'."

Daniel's eyes and mouth fill with water as the stench of Garry Barry punches him in the nose.

My god he fucking reeks of death. What is that, the smell of an infection? Rotting innards?

Sitting on the stool, he looks up to the profile of Barry until it turns to see him in its visage. The long scar that stretches through an eyebrow, down through an eye, up into his nose, down through the length of his sinus finally ends on his upper lip. It seems to be blackening. Loose pieces of dead tissue slough off of it from time to time without Barry's noticing. And the scar is swollen with a yellow and pink discharge that oozes out of the black eyeball, while his pale eye appears normal. The long weeping ulcer on his face drips onto the collar of his coat and has darkened the knot on his tie. His faded clothes look as though they had been bathed in the ocean and new bruises have appeared on the cheek and under his good eye.

Daniel leans in and gently places the sickle in Barry's hand, "She's a foul little red slattern that's beggin' us to put her outta her misery, like the kid was, remember? The cub reporter? Ya know she'd tell my wife if we let her go. Tell her all about what we did to my wife's father too. Have ya seen the red slattern yet? In ya. . . In ya thoughts?"

Barry turns back toward his drink and brings the amber liquid to his lips but says nothing.

"Did ya hear me?"

Barry turns to him unwittingly, "Ya smell smoke?"

"Smoke? No. Jesus, I'm tryin' talk to ya. Have ya seen her?"

Barry blinks, "Nah."

You fucking bedlamite, Daniel shakes his head.

It was Barry's questionable sanity that caused Wolcott to choose him in the first place. For years Barry had been dead-set on the idea he was the rightful leader of the White Hand, even as he had but one follower, had been beaten many times and was left aside when Dinny won the waterfront and bestowed his boons on his fellow men. Still, Garry fucking Barry wouldn't change his mind. And like a bedlamite, he couldn't change the subject either.

Drink, he needs more drink. Pour whiskey on that bruised brain and I can get him to do what I want.

"Tender, two more," Daniel motions in front of both himself and Barry.

"Sir," the barkeep's fearful eyes move close. "It went quick. The money ya gave me, it's almost gone—"

Daniel peels a bill and places it on the wet bar.

Barry shoots back his drink and grits his teeth and stares ahead as if he were watching something closely, beyond the liquor wall, "I see a man wit' a stone face. A bearer o' flames. He is a warrior on a secret mission in the psychic war."

"Psychic war, yeah?" A thin smile forms on his Daniel's mouth as he pushes the whiskey he ordered for himself in front of Barry. "What else?"

Barry stares ahead through mismatched eyes, "Out there, shadows seek to right lies. Conjurers summon misfortunes upon evildoers while mothers hide from heroes. Youthful matriarchs an' starved assassins become kingmakers as poets write stories in blood. All come together in silhouettes against a grey sky, under a harvest moon. An' there, do you see it? There I am! ready to take the seat as the victor o' the psychic war. Ready to become the heart that thrusts new blood through the old territories. An' there! The day I am crowned king! I am bein' escorted by a parade o' devoted revelers an' armed protectorates into the Dock Loaders' Club. An' at my approach, I turn an' look up into the eyes of an evil little girl—" Barry stops himself when he notices a new whiskey by his hand and picks it up and tilts it back. "I solved the demon!"

The words bubble in Barry's throat as if he were gargling pus.

Why doesn't he clear his throat? I fucking hate that. Instead, Daniel asks, "What does that mean? Solve the demon?"

"It don't matter now. I'll say more later. But ya should know," He turns his fractured face to Daniel. "God placed his mark on me."

The only god around here is Jonathan G. Wolcott, you fuck, Daniel scratches his jaw and muscles out a smile. *He has weighed that kingdom, found it wanting and will name you a mere client king while he divides its riches between the haves and the have mores.*

But Barry goes on, "A saint is accepted everywhere, but not durin' his lifetime in his hometown, that's in Luke 4:24. Ya'self an' Wiz an' Wolcott. . . Yaz were brought before me. An' for good reason."

"That bible quote. I think it's a prophet ya're referrin' to—"

"No!" Barry grabs and pulls Daniel so close that he can see the candlelight flicker in his black eyeball. "A saint!"

Daniel feels the cold blade against his neck. But before he can reach into his coat for the police issue revolver, Barry snatches his wrist.

Daniel bites at his lip, "Should we appreciate ya now, while ya're alive. Would it make a difference?"

Barry lets him loose and falls back into the barstool, "Nah. No one can appreciate what I do. Only when I'm gone. They'll write about me. Someone will."

Daniel looks out the front door as if to expect the walrus-mustachioed Captain Sullivan to walk in.

That's not going to happen, he tells himself. *Maureen just wants to scare me because she knows I need to be punished. No, Sullivan is not coming for me. I'm coming for him. But if he comes I'll have to beg mercy. No. . . I'll have to kill him.*

The tender looks away when he sees distress on Daniel's face. That shoots boiling blood through Daniel's veins.

We need to get this done and over with soon.

"Where is that fookin' big lump," Daniel mumbles. "This shit's makin' me jumpy. What if these fucks in here talk?" Daniel spreads his arm along the bar's patrons and whispers angrily. "Why didn't we get rid o' them before draggin' her upstairs?"

"They won't talk," the tender assures with unsure eyes.

"*You* don' say nothin'," Daniel almost jumps off the stool to rip the man in two, but sits back and waves a hand toward the bar. "Gimme a whiskey an' water."

He sits back on the stool, seething. When a whiskey is handed him, he takes a sip and drops the glass in a puddle on the bar and looks at the men leaning elbows on the mahogany.

They're going to say something.

Daniel turns to Barry, "It's time we do this now. We can't wait no more."

"Do what?"

"Are ya fookin' slow? Lemme spell it out. The plan includes me becomin' Captain at the Poplar Street Station. Police Commissioner Enright an' Mayor Hylan are pressurin' Sullivan into their new retirement system. But I can't become Captain if everyone finds out what this red slattern knows."

"That ain't my plan, it's yours," Barry answers.

"It's Wolcott's plan you cunt-faced imbecile. You're as useless as a man's nipple you fucking mental cripple."

Barry nods, "I don' give a fuck about that. It don' do me nothin' to kill her. Kill her ya'self."

Daniel feels the stab of anger. He rubs a thumb against the revolver in his coat and stares at Barry, who has turned to face him.

"Ya're refusin' an order from Wolcott?"

"Wolcott don' even know about this."

"We don' see the same future then, do we?"

Barry leans across the bar and takes Daniel's whiskey and water and shoots it down and runs his tongue along the open cut on his upper lip, moving the fleshy, bleeding flaps back and forth, "Nah."

But just as Daniel is about to draw his police issue revolver he hears a huffing sound upstairs, behind him. Then again, *whoooosh*, and a gust of oxygen is sucked out of the room. Daniel turns round on the stool and looks up. A man is walking calmly down the stairwell as flames lick the ceiling with forked tongues above and behind him.

Who is that?

Before Daniel can react, the man reveals a glass bottle and lights the fabric that hangs from the opening. In stride, he throws it over Daniel and Barry and Cleary where it explodes against the rack of liquor bottles, lighting them afire with a crashing sound and a third *whoosh* of flame. Halfway down the stairwell and the man pulls out a handmade metal shiv with a wooden handle and a .32 pocket pistol and fires while descending the stairs. A blood red splotch bursts out of Garry Barry's hip next to Daniel. Barry covers his face and the next shot goes through his wrist, ripping his left arm over his right shoulder and dropping him to the floor. The third shot takes him under his left arm and leaves him crumpled under the bar among the peanut shells.

On the third-to-last step Cleary flies at the man. But he is quickly thrown off and holds his face in shock as the shiv had made its mark down his temple, slicing his left ear in half.

Daniel reaches with his right hand into his shoulder holster and touches the police issue, but before his palm can grasp it or his finger can wrap round the trigger, he finds himself sprawling across the floor as chairs clatter to the ground next to him. While staring at the ceiling, Daniel touches his jaw and realizes it feels out of place. His tongue runs across his back teeth but he only feels blood and gums and a hole. He then swallows and realizes something hard and pronged had gone down his throat.

Was that a tooth?

The man is above him with a fist wrapped over his ear while an entire shelf of burning liquor crashes to the ground behind the bar in a glass heap. But just as the man is about to swing, he is lifted off his feet high and tossed across the saloon. Daniel comes to his elbows and watches as the stranger bounces off the hardwood floor and jumps and is on his feet quick as a rabid dog.

A woman's laugh comes to a cackle behind Daniel like some rancid, gap-toothed witch. Dazed, he turns to look out the front door to see his red-haired prisoner back in her clothing with a hand on the doorframe and black tears on her face. His manacles have been snapped and hang like crude jewelry upon her upper arms above the cast. The chain that was wrapped round her chest and fastened to the radiator upstairs is somehow still bound to her body within her clothing and bends her back into a grotesque crouch, while the remnants of the snapped chain drags on the ground between her legs like a clangorous tail.

"Fuck," Daniel mumbles, then turns back to the fire and brawl within. The stranger is overshadowed by the giant, Wisniewski, who had just thrown him like a burlap bag of coffee beans. The fires crackle on two sides as they brawl while Daniel wobbles to his feet, watching the fight. Wiz the Lump is grabbing at air and obscures the man so that Daniel cannot get a good look at him until a punch whips the giant's head back and drops him to one knee.

Daniel is holding himself up like a man of an age of senility, his hand wrapped round the back of a wooden chair next to an overturned table. Suddenly the stranger walks round Wiz the Lump and is upon him again.

Harry Reynolds?

As Daniel is lifting his other hand to cover his face, the squalling cackles of Maureen Egan come to his ears one last time, moments before a fist fells him onto his back again, spinning him like a turtle in a tunic. With the top of the chair still in his left hand, he raises his head from the ground to see Garry Barry's sightless eyes staring back at him. Wobbling worse now, Daniel grabs two handfuls of Barry's coat and drags him backward out the door while flames still lick with long red and yellow tongues all along the walls behind the bar and the ceiling. Black smoke chases up the stairwell.

Behind him the ceiling caves in, blocking the doorway. When Daniel lets Barry loose, black smoke fills his lungs. He stumbles. His arm goes through a glass window, next to the entrance. Then he feels a trouser-leg burning. He sits on his rump and slowly, lazily pats at his leg with his palms when he realizes he can't breath, and he begins to fall asleep until he is grabbed.

"Daniel, let's go," Patrolman Ferris yells. "The rest o' the roof's about to cave in. C'mon!"

Daniel dreams. He dreams that he is looking at himself in the mirror with the same old-timey walrus mustache as Captain Sullivan. Then he coughs, but reaches into the mirror and touches the big white mustache. He can feel the hairs between his fingers, but when pulled, he does not feel pain, though he hears someone yell out. Through the mirror, he looks behind and sees the tangle of Maureen Egan's red hair hovering above. When he turns round, the side of his face rubs against cement.

"Daniel, Daniel?" A voice is yelling. "Daniel, Daniel. Patrolman Culkin!"

He looks back toward the mirror again and sees the mustache, but it is Captain Sullivan's face this time, not his own.

"Patrolman Culkin, can ya hear me? Can ya hear me? What is ya badge number?"

It really is Captain Sullivan, Daniel thinks. *It's not a mirror. It's actually him, just like Maureen said.*

Only then does Daniel realize he is laying on a sidewalk outside, and Captain Sullivan is on top of him.

"Daniel!"

"Get away from me," Daniel screams and punches at the captain's hands. When Sullivan lets him loose, Daniel stands and lurches down the sidewalk alone. Across the street firehoses are shooting streams into the wood-framer. As the rest of the roof collapses, the sound of studs popping in the fire turns to great creaks and crashes and suddenly the entire structure shifts to one side and tumbles into Hoyt Street on top of two motorcars and a dog who scuttled away too late. Their headquarters now but smoldering wood in the cobbled street.

"Get him," Daniel hears, but the street is falling away and he can't seem to keep his balance. When he stands again after falling on his knees, five men in tunics are holding Daniel upright against the glass door of a women's clothing store.

Why am I crying? What happened?

"It's ok, Culkin," another tunic hugs him.

Ten more tunics surround and protect him from the eyes of outsiders and onlookers. Then another patrolman dabs at Daniel's eyes with a kerchief awkwardly. It's his partner Patrolman Ferris. Daniel hugs him, bawling, coughing and bawling.

"It's not ya fault, Culkin," Ferris says to him. "I loved him too. I miss him everyday. Every-goddamn-day."

Daniel pushes Ferris away from him, "Who? Who do ya miss?"

"Brosnan," Ferris says.

Another voice says, "He don' know where he is, uhright?"

"Who don' know where he is?" Daniel asks the strange voice, but he does not get an answer.

"Just keep him safe," another voice calls out. "Let's move. Move him out. Ferris, is that ya motorcar?"

"Yeah."

Daniel coughs. He notices his hands are blackened by smoke and that he is between two large shouldered men in the back seat of a car that Ferris is driving.

"Where are we goin', will ya just tell me where are—"

"Fookin' animals, fookin' animals," Ferris yells as he rounds a corner. "These fookin' gangs are tryna bring down New Yawk. Sully, ya gotta take the manacles off o' us so we can fookin' get control o' the streets again. They take down one o' our own, then try to murder Culkin t'day. What the fuck are we doin'?"

Culkin then realizes that Captain Sullivan is in the passenger seat of the motorcar when he turns round with his big mustache, "Daniel. Daniel, do ya hear me Daniel? Who was in there, Daniel? What in the hell were ya doin' in there? Who torched the saloon?"

Daniel realizes his mouth has been open this whole time. He closes it and straightens up in the backseat between the others.

"It was Harry Reynolds. I mean. . . It was Dinny Meehan, yes, it was Meehan," he sits forward in the seat and points a finger in Sully's face. "Ya named me to head the investigation into Brosnan's murder, now let me do the job!"

"Disappearance," Captain Sullivan corrects. "He's disappeared, remember? An' anyhow, I only named ya 'cause o' outside forces made me."

"Ya named me to head the investigation an' ya don' let me question suspects."

"*Question* suspects?" Sullivan indignantly repeats. "Is that why they end up with broken bones and missin' fingernails? Oh no, if ya can't establish probable cause, then they ain't suspects."

"So if he was proven dead, then I could question them, I see."

"Ya're too fookin' eager, boyo," Captain Sullivan roars. "In cases as dangerous as this one, it's best to commit to nothin'.."

Daniel grabs at Captain Sullivan's tunic as the motorcar turns on the rocky cobblestones, "If ya don' let us loose we'll lose these streets to the gangs an' the union Bolsheviks. It's ya legacy ya should worry about, ol' man. Ya let us loose. Are ya American? Or are ya a seditious Red?"

Captain Sullivan turns and catches Daniel's eyes, "One man. I'll allow ya to question one man. Make it worth ya while, Culkin."

Ferris gives a half turn toward Daniel as he pushes in the clutch on the floor and shifts into second gear on the tree.

He was following me, Daniel realizes. *Captain Sullivan had my own partner, Ferris follow me all along. He saw everything.*

The Trap Slams

The ballroom band playing *My Country T'is of Thee* suddenly becomes louder as Paul Vaccarelli opens the door to the back room and steps in. When he closes the door and looks at Thos Carmody sitting at the table, he hits the floor.

"Jesus fookin' Christ Carmody, put the gun down."

"Ya should knock before enterin'."

"I'm Vice President o' the ILA," Vaccarelli protests. "Ya're nothin' but a treasurer."

"He's more than that," King Joe barks and kicks out a chair. "Come sit down, Paul."

Thos keeps his stare on the deck of cards in the middle of the table as he tucks the pistol in the back of his trousers. After Vaccarelli slinks into a chair across from him, Thos looks up.

With a gap between his teeth and hair parted down the middle, slicked back wet and greasy, Paul Vaccarelli looks like a street prince. Once known as the prize fighter Paul Kelly, leader of the Five Points Gang, he taught Frankie Yale everything he knows about the underworld, who taught Sixto Stabile, the Young Turk. Eventually he changed his surname back to what he was born with, Vaccarelli, and became a businessman. Albeit a coarse and crude silhouette of one.

Vaccarelli sits cautious as a cat across Thos, keeping an eye on both he and King Joe.

A coded knock comes to the door that Thos recognizes, "Open that door."

"Who is it?" Vaccarelli looks behind him.

A voice on the other side responds, "A bird from Brooklyn."

Vaccarelli turns to Thos with lowered eyes, "What's that mean?"

"It means open the door."

King Joe opens the door and a small man with a hat over one eye comes immediately to the side of Thos's face and whispers, "The mole in Bill's ear says T.V. O'Connor's on the tug. . . with Wolcott. He was seen."

Thos keeps a poker face at that news, though his thoughts make sense of it. *O'Connor's a politician, that's all. If democracy is the illusion of capitalism, then politicians are official magicians.*

Another whisper comes Thos's ear, "Lovett's foray into Coney Island was a failure. The Scarfaced fella lives. But the show o' force will prolly mean he'll be sent to Chitown."

Thos turns his eyes to Vaccarelli and smiles, then whispers back, "Word on Tanner's whereabouts?"

The little man shakes his head.

Thos's stomach turns, *He could be anywhere. Waiting for me.*

Under the table he holds a twenty-dollar bill between his middle and index fingers, which the small man balls up and fists without anyone noticing.

Thos turns his eyes back to Vaccarelli, "We're here to talk Brooklyn. Most o' ya people are out in Bayonne an' the city dump in Staten Island. Ya got no dog in this fight."

Vaccarelli's finger follows the small man who discreetly heads out the door, "Who is that? What did he say?"

Thos shrugs.

Vaccarelli lights a guinea stinker from a cigar box that has a sketch of Frankie Yale's face on it and the words "The Prince o' Pals," scrawled underneath, then speaks out of the side of his mouth, "I got interests all over New York. Even in Brooklyn, ya know that. Welcome back, Thos. . . Sorry about ya face."

Though he dresses with a crude notion of wealth and with cruder ideas on power, Vaccarelli has succeeded in jumping up off the street and into the boardroom when O'Connor named him Vice President. Feeling under-represented and threatening to create their own union, the Italian element in the ILA got their man in Vaccarelli. With a bowler cap too small for his head and a pinstriped suit with slippers over his sock-less feet, Paul Vaccarelli cuts a mean figure. In South Brooklyn, he is close to Yale in Coney Island and Stabile in Red Hook, who have an undertaker's business together.

King Joe slices through the tension between Thos and Vaccarelli, "Don' worry about him, Thos. He represents half o' the ILA in Brooklyn, ain't that right Paul?"

Wordless, Vaccarelli lowers his eyes over bejeweled knuckles.

"The lower half," Thos snarls.

T.V. O'Connor bursts into the room, "Wow, what a slew we have t'night, eh? What a night! Thos ye gotta work on yer presentation though," O'Connor laughs at his own joke.

He unbuttons his coat like a gentleman would and pulls up a chair at Thos's left. Out of a pocket he withdraws a spectacles case, opens it and places a pair of round-rimmed Windsors over his eyes and wraps the earpieces round each ear. The Edwardian sack suit style of dress O'Connor wears had fallen out of fashion of late, but the Irishman in his early fifties hadn't noticed. These were the suits many Englishmen wore when O'Connor had visited Trinity College in Dublin in the months before he emigrated to Buffalo and Albany, upriver. It was a story O'Connor was fond of telling. So fond, in fact, that Thos concluded O'Connor wished he was an Englishman. Instead he is stuck with his Irish lilting mouth and a wilting English heart.

O'Connor proudly wears the double-breasted dark navy wool togs with its hints of stripes and high waisted trousers with pronounced creases down them and cuffed at the ankle as if he were a Dublin Jackeen from the previous decade. A prisoner to his status among men and the division of hierarchies he can never stop trying to ascend, O'Connor's bourgeois values contrast his Irish brogue; a symbol of the salt of the earth New York working class.

Thos can't help but to distrust him, but then again, Thos can't help but to distrust everyone. But after the bird from Brooklyn's news, he has to do something to get O'Connor to admit he's on the tug, and in Wolcott's pocket, the ILA's mortal enemy.

Set the trap, watch it slam shut.

"Alright then, brass tacks. Thos, what do say?" O'Connor says from a narrow face over narrow shoulders.

Thos begins to speak until a knock comes to the door. O'Connor turns to the door, "Who is it?"

On the other side of the door a man speaks Italian.

"Must be fer ye, Paul."

A man with an aquiline nose and a moon face walks in, looks at Thos, and goes directly to Vaccarelli's ear.

Slower than my bird from Brooklyn, but still effective.

Vaccarelli's hand makes a fist and his lips tighten as he gets the news.

"Well Thos?" O'Connor says as the Italian man leaves the room.

"Lucy, eh?" Thos asks Vaccarelli, then touches O'Connor's sleeve. "That guy's cousin was murdered by Meehan's men, yet Vaccarelli will tell ya the ILA should back him. A weak man's stance."

"An' ya'd back this fookin' *Pulcinella* instead?" Vaccarelli grumbles through clenched teeth.

Thos looks at King Joe, then O'Connor, "I would."

"Why? What makes ya think he can beat Meehan in a fight? Ya seen the odds lately?"

"I'm Treasurer o' the ILA, o' course I know the odds. Everyone in the union's puttin' their hard-earned money on Meehan."

"Then why side wit' Lovett?"

"Look what happened when ya fought Monk Eastman, what was decided then?"

Vaccarelli denies the invitation to talk about the old times and changes course, turning to President O'Connor "I just found out Lovett invaded Coney Island an' beat up someone very dear to me outside a business establishment o' my very close partner."

O'Connor asks, "Who, Yale? An' isn't that a bawdy-house? The Harvard Inn?"

"It's a ballroom an' rest'raunt."

O'Connor nods and turns to Thos, "What's with the change o' heart? Ye were a Meehan man before the war. What happened?"

Careful here, we don't want him thinking I change allegiances easily.

"Yeah well, there's a time to gather stones together an' there's a time to cast them away. Meehan's doomed," Thos looks away from Vaccarelli. "If we're gonna stay on top in Brooklyn, we have to go wit' the eventual winner. Loyalty's for ship captains."

"I know why this fookin' *crosta umana* chooses Lovett, because his feud wit' Tanner Smit'."

"Tanner's on his way to Sing Sing, sir," Thos lies, adding "sir" to cloud O'Connor's critical eye.

"That right?"

"Part o' the deal how Smith an' Meehan kissed an' made up. Meehan was jailed-up for theft o' the Hanan & Son shoe fact'ry on Bridge Street and was bailed-out by Tanner. He got the dime from Johnny Spanish."

"Jaysus wept," O'Connor sits back with big eyes behind little spectacles. "Ye're sayin' Meehan's desperate, I see."

"The most desperate man in Brooklyn," Thos assures, eyeing Vaccarelli. "There are always bitter consequences for acts o' desperate hope."

O'Connor speaks while staring off, "Now he's got the shylocks after him because he can't pay since he's lost all the tribute money from the Red Hook with Lovett takin' it back. That's no way to live."

"Famous last words," Thos winks at O'Connor from the handsome side of his face. "Meehan's a bad investment."

Vaccarelli reaches toward O'Connor, "We made a deal between this guy an' Meehan. Now I'm s'posed to go back an' tell my constituents the ILA is supportin' the man that has invaded an' murdered my people?"

Thos bypasses O'Connor and speaks directly to Vaccarelli, "Lemme put it to ya this way; Meehan's losin' support. I've got a guy on the inside o' the White Hand an' he says it's mutiny. Meehan double-crossed some fella by the name o' Lumpy Gilchrist. They're jumpin' ship on Meehan. Ya ever heard the story about the guy who was abusin' an beatin' an ol' man wit' his fists?" All eyes turn to Thos, "A third guy sees it an' decides to jump in an' help out. . . The ol' man didn't stand a chance after that."

King Joe looks at Thos quizzically, though O'Connor and Vaccarelli get it right off.

Vaccarelli touches O'Connor's wrist again, "T.V., who is the ILA's biggest enemy?"

That grabs Thos's attention. He looks coldly at O'Connor, who answers.

"The Waterfront Assembly."

"Exactly, I hear Meehan sees Wolcott an' the Waterfront Assembly as his biggest enemy too. We got common cause wit' Meehan, why go wit' the guy who has sided wit' our enemy in the past?"

The well-meaning fool just helped me convince O'-Connor to side with Lovett without realizing it. He has no idea the president is on the tug.

O'Connor turns to Thos, "Didn't ye serve with Lovett yerself, Thos?"

"I did, sir."

"It doesn't color yer perspective?"

"It definitely does. I know both o' them. Meehan an' I grew up just a few neighborhoods apart. My decision's based on knowledge o' both. Vaccarelli here knows neither." Thos points lazy fingers at Vaccarelli and O'Connor, "Lemme give ya a scenario; what happens if we take Meehan's side, then Lovett wins the war—"

"War?" Vaccarelli questions.

"There will be war, mark it. If Lovett wins that war an' he's holdin' court at the Dock Loaders' Club, we'll look the fool by askin' him if he'll join the ILA. No, he'll tell us to fuck off. He ain't beholden to the ILA any more than he is to the Waterfront Assembly. Then all we got left in Brooklyn is the I-Talian South. An' right around then our election happens, an' it's O'Connor against Vaccarelli here."

Vaccarelli sits up in his seat, "I never announced a candidacy."

"If we waited for the announcement, we'd lose the election."

O'Connor laughs and pounds the table with the flat of his fist, "Fortune favors the bold, Thomas Carmody. Ye're a throwback, fer certain."

"O'Connor's the man for the job, most of us know that," Thos eyes Vaccarelli.

"Ya got a mouth on ya, Carmody," Vaccarelli tilts his head. "An' what if we take Lovett's side an' Meehan wins?"

"He won't, that's my fookin' point," Thos raises his voice.

"Let's calm down here boyos," King Joe holds his palms up to both Thos on his left and Vaccarelli on his right.

"Why can't Meehan win?" Vaccarelli demands angrily.

"Because I—" Thos stops himself and looks across the table at Vaccarelli. Between the two is the lone deck of cards, leaning to one side.

Time to play.

"Predictin' the future is immensely difficult, I understand ya hesitation," Thos allows Vaccarelli his protestation. "Even the best laid plans o' mice an' men can go awry. In the Dred Scott v. Sandford rulin' o' 1856, the United States Supreme Court concluded that the Fifth Amendment protected slaveholders' property, in this case the property in question were. . . slaves, of course. Therefore, the Supreme Court used the Bill o' Rights to *deny* human rights. Instead o' resolvin' the slavery issue, it caused the American Civil War. They thought they could control the future, but the well meanin' fools paved the way to hell wit' their good intentions. Therefore, in comin' to my decision to support Lovett, I have thought long and hard about ya'self, Mr. Vaccarelli."

"Ya call me a well-meanin' fool?"

Thos holds up one finger, "Well-meanin' as in ya're here to represent the interests o' ya own element within the

ILA." Then a second finger. "A fool because ya arrogant enough to think ya know all the angles well enough to predict the future."

Their eyes meet and hold. Paul Vaccarelli is not a man to suffer disrespect. In Vaccarelli's time as a gang leader he had ordered the death of many men. But now. Here. Staring long and hard into his eyes, Thos wonders if Vaccarelli himself had ever killed a man.

Does he own souls as I do? Does he know that feeling?

Unblinking, Vaccarelli says, "Ya never answered the question."

"Life has no answers, only questions. Ask Socrates."

"*Death* is the answer to life," Vaccarelli muses.

"Yeah but no one wants to hear that," Thos smiles.

In the ballroom outside, the band plays a turnaround and a woman's voice can be heard singing *When Johnny Comes Marching Home*. Thos and Vaccarelli had stared into each other's eyes so long now that it had turned into a contest. Sweat appears on Vaccarelli's upper lip and the Italian's face trembles in anger so slightly that it would have gone unnoticed if Thos hadn't half-expected violence to ensue.

Finally Vaccarelli speaks, "Why am I even speakin' to this guy? I'm a Vice President, he's the Treasurer. He shouldn't even be in this room."

"Paul," O'Connor taps Vaccarelli's black pinstriped coat at the arm, then points in Thos's direction. "When Tanner Smith put that hit on Thos an' he an' I spoke of it up in Buffalo, I told Thos to go back to Brooklyn an' turn it all ILA. We debated how it could be done. To be honest, I didn't think he had a chance, but I had to have someone try. An' since all my Tammany friends called him Quick Thos, the Tenth Avenue Prodigy, I sent him back even though he didn't want to go. Next thing I know he hammers out a three-way deal with the Young Turk Sixto Stabile and Dinny Meehan with all o' their respective followers becomin' card-carrying, red-blooded American union men for the International Longshoreman's Association, which effectively put our competition out o' business. My point is, later this year when we go on strike fer better wages, every single dock an' pier in Brooklyn will not only refuse to work, but will not allow scabs to work in their place. Thos brought us Brooklyn at the first of it, don't forget."

"I ain't forgot," Vaccarelli says. "I was involved in it too."

"Ye could even say that ye have Thos Carmody to thank fer becomin' Vice President today, couldn't ye? Since he singlehandedly raised up the Italian to the level o' the Irish in Brooklyn."

"I wouldn't go that far," Vaccarelli sneers.

O'Connor now puts his hand on top of Thos's arm too and has both of them in his grasp like a man of god, "I would," he says.

King Joe pants and rolls up his tongue, "So would I."

Vaccarelli's head is turned sideways though his eyes remain on Thos directly across the table, "I don' doubt this fella's smarts. He's got a lot goin' on up there an' he likes to play the game. I see him eyeballin' that deck o' cards. He wants to play. The thing is, analytics, weighin' other people's motives an' figurin' angles, those are all important, but that's just the game. Sometimes ya gotta go wit' what ya heart says. I ain't sure Thos Carmody has a heart, but I do know if ya rely on the game too much, ya're liable to come to decisions that can lead to regret afterward." Vaccarelli raises his head and points to Thos with his lips, "Ya ever wonder if ya will regret leanin' toward Lovett? Ya ever wonder if ya will regret havin' no heart, Carmody?"

Thos blinks and looks up to Paul Vaccarelli, "In this business a clear conscience is a sure sign o' a bad memory."

Defeat curls on Vaccarelli's lip.

T.V. O'Connor breaks in, "Alright, let's get to the meat o' the matter. What side is Wolcott an' the Waterfront Assembly takin'? I know it can't be Meehan."

It's time to spring the trap on you, O'Connor.

Vaccarelli looks round, "There's another guy wants to be king o' Brooklyn? One king, two kings, three kings a dollar, all for a war, stand up an'—"

"That's another problem," Thos interrupts.

"Wolcott took Lovett's side before," Vaccarelli fires back at Thos. "Against my people."

"An' lost. The Waterfront Assembly has their own man now. Garret Barry," Thos turns his head nonchalantly to O'Connor, but with a predator's eye staring out from his raised lapel. Searching for fear. Searching for knowledge.

Now it's your turn O'Connor. Let's see how you do.

"Garret who?" O'Connor says timidly, then looks at King Joe. "Do I know this man?"

O'Connor's face had blushed at the cheeks. He looks away again, losing his concentration for a moment until he realizes that he is giving himself away in Thos's discerning eye. That is when Thos knows without a doubt that President O'Connor works with the ILA's mortal enemy, Jonathan G. Wolcott. He can see it on O'Connor's face. The guilt. The shame.

Everything is fixed, Thos thinks. *Even sworn enemies are bedfellows. . . Life is the biggest fix of all.*

Gods and kings and presidents. The one thing they all have in common is their class. The owning class. The ruling class, as they are known. Thos once thought there was nothing worse than the privileged rich, like Wolcott. But now he knows there is something much worse, the reachers of the rich. O'Connor has been reaching up beyond his station all of his life. Forgetting his Irish roots, except when it benefits him, esteeming the English and climbing their ladder. . . O'Connor's deceit should not be a surprise. Yet somehow it hurts. Hurts hard because Thos knows he may have to kill his boss if the angles twist in that direction.

Wolcott though. Wolcott would have offered O'Connor something to make a deal between the supposed enemies. Thos looks again at O'Connor.

What did you get for your deceit of the working man, O'Connor? A house? A motorcar? A promise? Or are you simply on the tug now; an envelope handed over with a wink and a soft elbow to the ribs?

"Nah, ya don' know Garry Barry," Thos answers O'Connor's question solemnly so as to ease his boss's shame and encourage him to continue to walk into the trap and eventually into a losing campaign.

Then King Joe's lips start flapping about, "Me personally? I never trust a fella whose first name rhymes wit' his last name. Ever. Garry fookin' Barry? It's just fookin' wrong, ya know what I mean?"

"What's he like?" O'Connor feigns innocence with an obviousness that Thos had never seen on his boss's face before.

Vulnerable, that's what I see on you now, boss. You're vulnerability.

Thos keeps a cool head and smiles, "Garry Barry is a box o' hammers. An eejit on an eejit's errand. He's always seen himself as the rightful leader o' the White Hand, even wit' only one follower. Meehan beat him in a one-on-one years ago. Now he's got a gruesome scar where the White Hand ripped his face off an' danced on it. But in Wolcott's eyes he's as lovely as a lass. Ya sure ya never heard o' Garry Barry?"

"I haven't," O'Connor says. "I mean yes. . . No I've never heard of him. Yes I'm sure I've never heard—"

Ice cold, Thos keeps up the ruse, "The Waterfront Assembly chose him because he'll ruin the gang, is my guess. If he's given the reins, as Wolcott hopes, he'd immediately run the whole racket into the ground so they can undermine the collective o' workers. Barry's been seen wit' Wisniewski, Wolcott's lump durin' the storm, an' a patrolman."

The fact that O'Connor does not shit ten kittens at the notion of a patrolman involved in the underworld confirms to Thos everything he suspects.

Thos continues, "Barry is employed simply to terrorize the gang, but Wolcott can't say that to him, can he? But if we're gonna back Lovett, an' the Waterfront Assembly is gonna attack Meehan, then—"

"Then we actually have a common interest with our biggest enemy," O'Connor finishes the sentence, his face purple with shame. The trap slammed shut.

"Don't even consider that," Thos turns angrily on O'Connor.

"Ye don't know what I'm thinkin'," O'Connor pleads.

"Ya're thinkin' we should back Barry too an' get rid o' the gangs altogether," Thos says with a lowered eye that hardens his words. "First o' all, we should never make agreements wit' the Waterfront Assembly an' the big business interests they represent. Moreover, remember who the ILA represents; the workin'man."

O'Connor blushes and changes the subject, "Let's have a vote then. All in favor o' supportin' Lovett, raise yer hands."

Thos and King Joe raise their hands solemnly.

"Those in favor o' Meehan?"

Vaccarelli raises a hand while watching for O'Connor's.

"Lovett it is," O'Connor announces. "I like the fact that he is a decorated veteran o' the Great War. The ILA can't be seen as red. The newspapers may call us a collection o' scofflaws an' gangsters, but we're not Bolsheviks. Lovett gives us appeal." O'Connor warns with a wagging finger, "But I want no moves until after this fight. Give the men a chance to work it out amongst themselves."

"What about ya vote, O'Connor?" Vaccarelli grumbles. "I know ya' prefer Meehan an' his honor codes."

O'Connor scoffs, "A smart politician always chooses to run for election with the wind at his back," he nods toward the fat-tongued smile of King Joe, then looks shame-faced at Thos. "Ye'll give Lovett inside information about Meehan's doin's from yer informant, but I want ye to play on both sides o' the fence until this fight, Thos. Are ye goin' to be safe to hold with the hare and run with the hounds?"

"I know how the game's played," Thos says. "But we'll need to be able to move fast after the fight. I need a pack o' ILA men to support Lovett in case war breaks out."

"Ye got it," O'Connor points a knuckle at Thos.

Vaccarelli throws up his hands, "Aren't we gonna talk about this foolishness wit' the dry laws?" He turns to O'Connor, "Do they really think Italians will go wit'out wine? The Irish wit'out whiskey? The Hun wit'out beer?"

"Curse o' Cromwell's Puritanism all over again," Thos answers. "Probably a blessin' in disguise though. We own the ports an' piers."

"What's that got to do wit' anythin'?"

"We'll import liquor. Shit, Irishtown's famous for its home-brew. Ever heard o' the Whiskey Wars o' the 1860s an' 70s?"

"Nah," Vaccarelli keeps a quizzical stare at Thos until he stands. "I gotta head off."

"Famous last words," Thos mumbles.

O'Connor stands from the table too, "Ye goin' to see Meehan tomorrow, Thos?"

"Yeah."

"Ye're not nervous he'll know ye picked Lovett over him?"

You would tip Meehan off, wouldn't you? Now that you know I caught you.

Thos turns a cruel eye at the president, "Why would I be nervous o' that?"

"If someone were to talk to Meehan, then—"

"Let that someone talk," Thos breaks in. "It won't matter."

Vaccarelli cuts in, "What do ya mean it won't matter?"

Thos lights a handrolled, "What we're dealin' wit' down in Brooklyn? It don' make the kinda sense we're used to. They got a different sort o' logic, the Meehan Irish do. When I first met Dinny Meehan I never understood half the decisions he made. But that's alright. What ya don' understand now, ya will later. Life an' death? Success an' failure? Murder an' martyrdom? The Irish down there live somewhere between those idears, understand? They seem to violate the laws o' mortality, even. They die off, yet survive. . . Like roaches."

"An' like yerself, Thos," O'Connor says.

Thos's hand shakes under the table, *Is that true? Yes, I suppose it is.*

"But if Meehan were to find out ye picked Lovett over him, he might—"

"He already knows," Thos shakes it off. "Dinny Meehan always knows."

Vaccarelli throws his hands up again, "Fookin' superstitious barbarians. Their spookt, them lot."

As O'Connor and Vaccarelli walk out, Thos draws on the paper cigarette with leopard's eyes fixed on the deck of cards.

Time to play, Bill. The cards are stacked in your favor now.

Thos struggles to sit up and stumbles until King Joe catches him as the band in the ballroom strikes up *America the Beautiful*.

"Thos, ya can't even get up? What's wrong wit' ya?"

As King Joe wraps Thos's arm round his shoulder to hold him up, Thos reaches his other hand between the buttons in his shirt to feel his own heartbeat, but it is not there. *Vaccarelli is right, I'm heartless. That is what is wrong with me.*

"Can ya stand up on ya own, Thos?"

But he cannot. Thos sits and slumps on an untapped barrel of beer close by the door.

Weaker, even weaker now. The time draws nigh.

He pulls his hand away from his heart and reaches into a coat pocket, and with a shaking hand he unfurls a crumpled piece of paper and reads it, *Tanner's hiding out, but his time is due, call us.*

The Risen

Sometime round the same year the Brooklyn Navy Yard was established in 1801, a Mr. Jackson stipulated in his will that the family property could not be sold until after his son, Josiah died. The property was located a few blocks southeast of the Navy Yard and could have been auctioned for a fortune, but for his father's will. Josiah's ten children, however, did not have to abide by the will of their grandfather. And so they eagerly awaited Josiah's death. But Josiah had a different kind of will, and his was legendary. To spite his eager children, Josiah Jackson lived to a ripe old age. The decades-long impasse left the property south of the Navy Yard vacant, which led the good Christian Anglo-American inhabitants who lived in elegant homes and decadent manses surrounding the area to moniker the lots: "Jackson Hollow."

By late 1847, in what seemed an overnight invasion, thousands upon thousands of shoeless, starved and choleric Irish immigrants appeared like ghosts to haunt in Jackson Hollow. Devastatingly malnourished, these human ghouls were unable to travel too far from where the ships berthed them at the banks of the East River.

As they had in Ireland after the potato went black and the English evicted them, they dug holes in the earth called scalps, or scalpeens to guard against the weather. Soon enough Jackson Hollow became a full-fledged Catholic shantytown in the Protestant city's center.

The surnames of these ragamuffin, raggle-taggle refugees were common enough; Connors, O'Connor, Keenan, Kane, Carmody, Cleary, Quilty, Connolly and Donnelly, to name a few. Lovett and Lonergan too. Meehan, Maher and Morissey, Maroney, Maloney, Mullen, McGowan and McGuire. Gibney and Gillen, of course. Ferry, Ferris, Finnigan and Flynn, Barry and Burke and Byrne and Behan and on and on, and on-and-on.

The newspapers described the residents of Jackson Hollow as "Squatter Sovereigns," because they refused to leave or to assimilate into the Anglo-American culture, clinging instead to their despicable Catholic faith mixed with old-world Celtic paganism. To disburse the occupants from this "wretched shantytown," it was oft invaded by police who wore the tunics of London Bobbies and the Jackeen Constabularies of Dublin. It was reported that the police, "rooted them out" of their "pig-dem" where hogs and dogs and goats and cows lived side by side with the scores of Irish Catholic immigrants, and where "the cradle is seldom empty."

To fight them off, gangs of pride-struck, stick-wielding young Irishmen were formed to violently hold the border against the tunics, such as the aptly-named Jackson Hollow Gang. When the tunics came out in force and breached Jackson Hollow's defenses, every single member of the gang gave the police the same name: Patrick Kelly. And so they were Patrick Kelly, all of them. And none.

Over time, the Irish squatters moved along the waterfront to unload the many cargo schooners, barques and brigs. Willing to assume the backbreaking manual labor the Anglo-ascendency refused, the Irish refugees then formed longshore gangs to protect their jobs against outsiders and to fight for better wages against the ship owners and the local businesses that received the goods.

Beat McGarry loves to tell that story. In the darkening street he raises his arms to the low rise tenements and tumbledown shacks lined along the Navy Yard wall. "From the start Irishtown, this same neighborhood, was the headquarters. An' the Irish have never stopped comin' to Brooklyn. We've *always* welcomed people like ya, Liam. But our origins are sacred to us. They bring us back to who we were, an' to the place that we should never have left but for the cruelty in men's hearts."

But I am in no mood for Beat's stories. My nerves are in rags. Consumed, I am, by what it was that attacked me on the pier. *What if it attacks again? How do I know when it comes? What are the signs of its arrival? Who was it?*

But everything keeps getting in the way. One thing after another. A couple hours ago, after divvying up the day's earnings The Swede and I sat on a table in the Dock Loaders' Club. A shock of pain pulsed through me when he poured vodka on the gash along my knuckles. As the alcohol spilled over the table and onto the floor I picked up the opened letter that bore terrible news from Ireland.

"Be careful," I moan.

"What? Ya read it so many times already ya gotta have it memorized by now. Stay still. I gotta wrap ya hand now."

That was when little Whyo Mullen stood next to us with humiliation coloring his face. *Go away*, I thought when the lad approached. *Go away so I can ask The Swede of my attacker.*

"Mr. Swede," he said, eyes at his shoes. "Poe, will yaz come wit' me?"

But The Swede was focused on wrapping my hand and gives a side-mouthed response, "What for?"

"Not too tight," I said.

"Um—" the lad stammered, his eyes searching for words.

"It's gotta be tight to stanch the blood," The Swede mumbled. "It needs pressure. Look how deep the cut is. It *should* be stitched up first."

"Um, my ma's havin' a baby."

We both turn to the boy, "A baby?"

"I didn't know she was with child," I said.

"Me neither. Ya sure she's pregnant?"

Behind him, Will Sutton appeared with a stifled grin just as Whyo found his courage, "She didn' tell nobody 'cause... 'cause my dad's been dead longer than... Do I really gotta say it?"

The Swede's mouth hung open, "So how's she pregnant?"

Just then Vincent walked by with a shrug and a sly smile, "It's a miracle."

Whyo's mouth frowned at that, "The baby's comin' too early, my Ma says. But it's still comin'. An' she don' wanna be alone."

As has been the case since long before my arrival, the whole of Irishtown shows up in force when a child comes into the world. Mrs. Mullen will never be alone in Irishtown. On the yellowed cobblestones of Hudson Avenue we gather, two thousand strong to lend our support to Mrs. Mullen whether it's to welcome in a new life, or say goodbye.

"Not lookin' good," Cinders nods toward the tenement where the Mullens live across the street while a hundred conversations rise out of the gathering night. "But the way I see it, if anythin' makes sense, that child's gotta survive on the day we find out Liam's father passed."

The letter had come all the way from Tulla to the Dock Loaders' Club. *Da is dead. My father. My family. Dead.* Miko O'Dea, my childhood friend had gotten confirmation from Major General Michael Brennan of the East Clare Brigade that my father had died, "while imprisoned by foreigners."

The war in Ireland hasn't even started, and he's gone already. The letter described how he'd been detained recently during an arms raid at a barracks somewhere in the back arse of nowhere, County Clare.

An Irish soldier's death, I surmise, tucking the letter into my coat. Most like, he was tortured for information. And most like, his secrets went to the grave with him. I make a sign of the cross in hopes of better luck for Miko and my brother. Timothy is head of the farm now. *Sometimes destiny does come true*. As much as I hate to admit, we are both growing into the images our father had painstakingly sculpted.

As darkness wins, the wind flaps through the clothes hung on lines above Hudson Avenue as I look round the many silhouettes of natives below, *Ireland isn't the only place that has secrets.*

"Beat?" I tap him the old fellow on the shoulder.

"Yeah?"

"Have you ever felt so bad, so alone that. . . that—"

"The world goes dark?"

My eyes go wide, *could he too know what I experienced alone on the pier? Has he seen himself from a distance as I had? Has he had someone use his mouth to speak? His eyes to cry?*

"Sure, this one time I forgot to give my granddaughter breakfast. She she said she was hungry, I felt like two pennies half-spent. Anyhow, we used to have our own laws, ya know. Back in the olden times they were known as the Brehon, the laws were—"

But I turn away when I realize my question goes unanswered. *I thought maybe he knew, but Beat knows little-to-naught.* Still, he prattles along.

A few minutes later he snaps his fingers in front of my face, "Liam, are ya listenin' to me?"

"What?"

"Why aren't ya wit' ya own fam'ly if ya father just passed?"

I shrug.

"Oh, ya scared to tell them?"

"I'm not scared of anything, unlike you. You're the coward. You and Thomas Burke, the empty suit. I'm out on the docks fighting and you just tell stupid stories about Jackson Hollow."

"Stupid stories?"

"Maybe they're not, but you make them sound stupid."

"I do?" His head spins, jowls quivering. "I was once a dockboss too, ya know. Before Christie the Larrikin—"

"No you weren't."

"I was too!"

"Who was the leader back then?"

"I can't say."

"He didn't have a name?"

"No, it was Sean Dream."

"What kind of name is that?"

"It's not a name, it's a description. Listen Liam, ya should go to the Bard in ya sorrow. Don' go to Father Larkin at St. Ann's, he'll banish ya to a decade o' the rosary. The Bard would greet ya wit' open arms. He has things to say to ya, he told me. I'll leave ya to grieve, then."

Beat skulks off through the crowd with his pride in his throat as Cinders leans on a skinny tree between slate slabs in the sidewalk.

"Whad ya say to him?"

"Nothing, he's just an idiot that doesn't know anything."

Cinders looks me up and down, "Is that what it is?"

Down the block, where Hudson Avenue turns into Navy Street by the entrance to the Navy Yard, Johanna Connolly née Walsh exits the Culkin tenement. As she steps down the stoops she sneaks a peek our way, but walks in the other direction.

"What's she found out so far?" I ask as Vincent and The Swede come to stand with us on the sidewalk above the crowd.

Cinders mumbles his concern, "Strangest thing. Apparently a letter came about a house up in Peekskill that Patrolman Culkin is sellin'. When Doirean asked about it, he flew off the handle."

"What do ya mean?" The Swede asks.

"Brosnan had paid for it an' Doirean never knew a thing about it, see?" Cinders reaches behind him and rubs a knot out of his neck. "The strange part is that letter had been sent upstate to Peekskill, opened, then slipped underneath the door of the Culkin home. Culkin was livid, but no one knew who delivered it to Brooklyn. There was only one clue, the letter 'H' was written on it. Whoever's behind it wanted Doirean to find out."

The Swede and I exchange a glance, but neither of us want to say what we think.

Cinders says, "I'm gettin' nervous. For a little guy, Culkin's got a big temper. Johanna says he's a monster. He hit Doirean the other day. Dragged her into the kitchen by her hair. She's fookin' big wit' child, ya know? What happens if he finds out Johanna's married to the White Hand, huh? Yesterday Father Larkin shows up outta nowhere an' Johanna had to run out the backdoor before he saw'r her there."

"Speak o' the devil, all dressed in black," Vincent says as the priest elbows through the crowd and ascends the steps of the Mullen tenement.

"Why haven't yez taken the poor women to hospital? She's not a farm animal, is she? But yez'll never change, will yez? Right up to the bitter end ye'll go wit' yer Pavee traveller ways. The whole slew o' yez're but shanty Irish!"

"Father, father!" Mrs. Lonergan screams down from a window above. "Come quickly! It's the baby!"

Father Larkin gives one last smirk at us and spins on his heel.

The Lark, Big Dick and Red Donnelly shoulder through the crowd and approach us on the sidewalk.

"Sorry about ya loss, Liam."

One-by-one they tuck envelopes into my coat pocket, shake my hand and offer good will.

"How's ya Ma an' sisters doin' after the hard news?"

"Don' ask him that," Cinders chuckles. "He'll send ya scurryin' off like he did Beat."

Red blurts it out anyway, "Ya ain't told them yet?"

"Why not keep your mouth shut so I don't have to shut it for you, like Richie did."

"Gee Liam, why ya ballyraggin' me for?"

Cinders leans in to my ear, "Ya ever open up that bank account, like I told ya?"

"I did. That was good advice and I took it. It's in my mother's name too, but she doesn't know about it yet."

"She don'? Well, she will. . . if ever the time comes. Here's hopin' it never does," Cinders tilts his head low with a solemn glare and takes a swig from a flask, then passes it to me.

Maybe he knows. Maybe I can speak with Cinders about what I saw on the pier.

But just as I am about to ask, the crowd begins to cheer. Up on the stoops of the Mullen tenement, Chisel Mcguire is taking bets as a circle opens up in the street.

"They're not fighting, are they?"

The Swede looks at me incredulously.

"When Mrs. Mullen is trying to give birth?"

Vincent smiles and points with a paper cigarette, "It's ya righthand too, looky there."

"Dance!" I yell through the crowd, but he is busy dodging punches from Freddie Cuneen.

The fight spills through the street as Freddie is thrown against iron handrails along a stairwell. He jumps at Dance, who tosses him aside into a gaggle of scattering children. When Dance finishes him off, bloodying Freddie's left eye and ear, Chisel runs up to him, hands him a wad of cash and raises his hand for all to celebrate.

"Dance, come here," I yell.

He gathers himself, and from the street he looks up to where we stand on the sidewalk.

"What are you doing fighting today? It's disrespectful."

"It ain't. I honor them. I honor the birth o' that child wit' a fight, especially if it turns out to be a boy. A newborn needs more than a woman's love. It needs to know brutality too," he raises the money in his bloody fist. "This is for the Mullens. I won it for them."

I point along the crowd and give voice to the anger that boils within, "We have to come together as friends or we'll die together as enemies. Didn't you hear anything we told Bill Lovett? We can't shake hands if our fists are clenched."

Dance looks round at all the eyes on him as Freddie comes to stand at his side, "We are friends. An' fightin' is how I got where I am. Ya want me to stop now that I'm a righthand? Nah, I'll fight to my last breath."

He turns to little Whyo Mullen and hands him the wad, then reaches up to me with four blood-soaked bills, "I'm sorry for ya loss."

I don't want that, I think. *Acceptance is defeat.*

The slew of shadowy faces that await my decision look on with interest. From behind The Swede gives me a slight nudge and when I turn back to him, he nods ahead.

begrudgingly I accept the cash. I have no choice, and immediately the faces turn back to the Mullen tenement. Embarrassment burns through me like fire and I can feel the blood rise to my head.

"Don' let it stick to ya," The Swede leans down to me. "What's right is right. Don' matter who or where it comes from."

"I didn't ask what you think."

His long face turns down to my direction, but quickly his eyes move to something behind me, "There they are."

A young woman in a shapely, low-waistline dress walks toward us with a child at her hand. A small brooch shines in the lamplight on her upper bosom; gold branches that open into four petals with a mat-white pearl in the center to match the thick hair that rolls over her marble shoulders. The shadow of trees along Hudson Avenue seem to herald her arrival and tents of yellow gaslight frames her approach as a nervous smile forms on her face.

I grab Vincent's arm, "My god, she is beautiful. Who is she?"

"That's Helen. Helen Finnigan."

The Swede runs to greet her. He touches her shoulder and looks back proudly. He then leans his lengthy body down like a giant giraffe going to its knees, and picks up the child with one arm. But the smile on his face turns bitter when the crowd sees them.

"It's not right," a voice calls out from somewhere.

"Go 'way with yerself, ye mongrel!" A woman announces.

"Ye Finnigans are not above the teachin's in Leviticus!"

The Swede stands in front of the young mother, but his voice is drowned out by the heckling. Slowly she wheels round in the sight of all and with disdain showering over her by insult, she goes up on her toes to whisper in the little boy's ear held by The Swede.

"No!" the child protests. "I want to stay. I want to play!"

She touches the child's chin in its father's arms, but he kicks and screams. Back up the hill of Hudson Avenue they go, his cries banking off the tenement walls.

Vincent leans in to me for a whisper, "Thos Carmody's back at the Dock Loaders' Club wit' Dinny right now."

"It's about time he come see us. He hasn't been here since before he left for the war. We need allies. We can't hold the line alone."

"He's a good man, ya can trust ol' Quick Thos. But I feel bad for him. What he's been through? He almost died over there an' I think it turned him—"

"Turned him?"

"I don' know, he's different now. I went wit' him on his first hunt when we got Silverman, remember Silverman? Now though, he's a killer."

"Is he backing us, or Bill?"

"He says it's us but wanted a word alone wit' Din."

"I don't trust him. I don't trust anybody anymore."

"Listen, I know what'll help ya through this grief o' losin' ya dad. Come wit' me to the Adonis t'night."

Can you bring Emma McGowan back to life? Because that would be the only way I will ever have sex. If it's not Emma, I don't want anyone.

Vincent continues, "Some o' the guys are comin' too, but don' tell Dinny."

"Do you really think Dinny doesn't know everything we do?"

Vincent straightens out a thin, brown piece of paper and drops tobacco flakes in it, "Sure he knows, we just don' make a big production about it, right? Come wit'. I know ya still ain't never rode a female yet. We can cure ya o' that t'night, I'm payin'. We'll put ya up in a room wit' Grace White an' those big soft diddies. She'll be gentle wit' ya. She knows where the cock goes," he snickers at his own rhyme.

"No thanks—"

"More o' a ass man? I'll have Kit Carroll drop to her elbows for ya. Her hips are like the fookin' cradle o' civilization, them yokes. Some people say Egypt is the cradle o' civilization. Nah, that's a lie. Cradle o' civilization is a woman's hips. Think about it for a second, it makes sense. Ya wanna go then? We're takin' the train."

"I don't think—"

"Oh did ya hear?" He interrupts and points out into the crowd, "They're callin' me Queensolver now. it's one word. Queensolver."

"Who calls you that?"

"Everyone, c'mon," the hand-rolled cigarette is now amidst his teasing grin.

"No one has said it round me."

"It's true though," Vincent elbows my ribs too hard.

"I've heard people call you Masher."

"That's a old word. I'm thinkin' o' the future now. Lemme tell ya somethin' a smart fella once said to me, 'Vincent, ya're a murderer o' men, an' a killer o' virgins.' But I don't like that, understand? I don' kill females, uhright? I solve them like. From their virginity. An' their own feelin's. All they want is love, an' in this world love is hard to come by, the poor creatures. Ya ever watch a female cry? Like really watch it? It's a amazin' thing. Pure emotion that bubbles up from within her. It draws me closer like a moth to light, ya know? Some fellas hate when a female cries. I love it. There's nothin' in this world can compare to the purity in her heart. They're all queens, every last one o' them. An' I'm the Queensolver, don' forget. An' tell people to call me it too."

"I'm not doing that," I say.

But he ends the conversation by thanking me as he has become entranced in eye contact with a girl in a heavy dress and hair pinned in an onion bun atop her head, "I gotta go. There's tomatoes need pickin'."

Up ahead the crowd parts in half as Dinny Meehan walks through with a man by his side. Children pace ahead of them, others sprint excitedly behind like pups nipping at the pack leader's heels. A few men reach out for a handshake, though the women regard his advance breathlessly. When he stops it is to gently hold the back of an elder's hand and to smile with lowered eyes that could be judged as fealty.

The man behind him has a collar or lapel covering part of his face with one eye that stares out and reads his surroundings like a big cat cases unknown territory. He has thick hair; wavy at the hairline and bunches a bit in the back, brown and somewhat oily. The copper-colored stubble on his chin and cheeks highlight the judging eye.

Dinny approaches us on the sidewalk, "Liam, ya remember the ILA's Treasurer o' New York, Thos Carmody?"

Thos and I shake hands, but he keeps one side of his face hidden. He mumbles something vaguely respectful, but keeps close attention to the movements in his peripherals.

Behind me The Lark barks out a laughs and Thos moves to meet the sound. That is when I see the rest of his face. *I know that scar pattern. Like stars in the night sky. The man who attacked me, was it him? Thos Carmody?*

"I know you," says I.

Thos's leopard eye finds me, "Excuse me?"

"You attacked me on the pier. You were wearing a mask."

Thos looks at Dinny, "What's he talkin' about?"

"Liam."

"He had those same grapeshot scars but. . . but he had another scar. Others."

"Don' listen to him, he's been actin' up all day," Vincent grabs my arm. "Liam, this is Thos. He's on our side."

"He's not on our side. He's on the fence, hedging his bets," I move closer to him. "I always hear how smart you are, Carmody. Well you must be smarter than I am because I could never keep up with all the lies you tally. The thing is, if you lie all the time you wouldn't know the truth if it was pissing in your ear. You haven't committed to us, have you? Why not do it now? On your word, go ahead."

Dinny cuts in, "Listen Liam, we just struck an agreement t'day."

"What agreement?"

"I can't tell ya right off, uhright? We gotta keep things low."

I don't like him. I don't like the cunning look in that eye.

Vincent pulls me aside, "Just calm down, uhright? Ya know ya really should consider comin' wit' t'night. Ya're all backed up. Ya need to release some o' them seeds or else ya might turn blue. Thos is a good guy."

"It's alright, Vin," Thos says with cool caution. "I see he's got the balls for brawls. We all know a hard man's good to find."

When Henry Browne comes to shake hands with Thos, he mumbles something to Dinny and skulks alone through the darkness, hands deep in coat pockets.

"He doesn't look like a prodigy to me," says I.

"I told ya he's changed since the war," Vincent tilts in my direction.

"What kind of deal did we make with him?"

Dinny looks at me, then the tenement across the street, "Any word on Mrs. Mullen an' the baby?"

Just then Whyo peeks his head out from the crowd to stare up at us on the sidewalk and seconds later his buddy Will comes out too. But it's Whyo who speaks, "My Ma just asked to see Vincent upstairs."

Dinny and I turn to him as he rolls his eyes, "Why me?"

Whyo comes forward a step, "She says she wants to see ya hold. . . the boy."

"It's a boy?" Vincent yanks out the paper cigarette from his mouth and flicks it behind him.

"Yeah."

"It's a boy!" Vincent yells out into the street.

"Hurrah, a boy!" Some in the back of the crowd overhear him.

"It's a boy?" The news starts to spread as he runs through the slew of people.

"A soldier!"

"A soldier o' the dawn," another yells. "A good omen!"

As Vincent is ascending the steps, a Model-T motorcar approaches the crowd with the driver leaning on the horn, *Ooo-wa, ooo-wa*. The red cross from its service in the Great War had been painted over, though you can still see the outline of it on the ambulance car.

Whyo comes to Dinny's side and pulls on his coat, "They gotta take the baby to the hospital."

"That's not necessary," Dinny says.

Though Whyo's disagreement is plain to see, he chokes back a response.

"Dinny," I whisper.

Mrs. Lonergan is howling as she storms through the crowd, "They want to take the baby to the hospital! The hospital. It's there they'll give the child the black bottle, they will!"

"No hospitals," Dinny confirms.

"Dinny, it's not like it was in the old times round here."

Whyo Mullen swallows and looks up with big eyes, "The doctor said if they don't bring little Vincent to the hospital, he'll die 'cause he came too early. He's not, umm, developed all the way yet."

"No hospitals!" Mrs. Lonergan screeches and stands in front of the boy as all in the street turn to us again. "They don' want Catholics, never have. If they need the bed for a Protestant, they'll give the poor dote a remedy. Then ya will feel twice as bad, won't ya?"

Dinny comes down to one knee, "Whyo, what do ya wanna do?"

Whyo straightens up and licks his lips, "I don' want him to die. I'll stay wit' him an' protect him. I'll stay up all night. . . in the hospital."

Dinny pats him on the shoulder, "Ya're good to ya fam'ly."

"What if Vincent don' wanna take him to the hospital?" He asks.

"Tell Vincent ya're the man o' the fam'ly until someone else steps up. If he don' like it, have him speak wit' me."

The boy runs off and pushes through the crowd with Will Sutton close behind.

Chisel McGuire slaps me on the back, "Let's celebrate! This one's for the Mullen boyo. . . an' ya dead Da, Liam."

Chisel's coat is stiff with dirt from sleeping in empty lots. And even though he is dressed like some flimflam man of the last century in black tails, a broken chain to a broken pocket-watch hanging from his moth-eaten waistcoat and a dusty top hat under his arm, Chisel has a strong and pleasing voice.

High upon the gallows tree
swung the noble hearted three,
By the vengeful tyrant stricken in their bloom,

*But they met him face to face,
With the courage of the race,
And they went with souls undaunted to their doom...*

"Talk to me," Dinny touches my arm and waves the others to stay back. "Poetic words, yeah? That ol' song?"

"They are, but not for a newborn."

A laugh rumbles deep in his chest, "Didn't ya father take part in the risin' in Ireland?"

"No way to know for sure. Da never spoke unnecessary words. But I heard out in Clare they were told to stand down."

Dinny's head turns as he looks closer into my face, "Ya're angry wit' him? Even now."

"He had a plan for me all along. Like he thought he was some kind of god or something. Except he didn't realize—"

"That ya'd have ya own struggles?" He nods and purses his lips in wonder. "What makes ya think ya brother don' have his own problems on the farm? I never met ya father, but I'm willin' to bet he did all he could to help ya both prepare for the troubles o' ya own day the best he knew how."

I stare off into the middle distance, then turn back to Dinny, "The British government claimed he was involved in raids since January when the Irish Dáil declared independence. I believe it. He came from a long line of men who fought the English in West Ireland. His father was a Moonlighter. And back further there were wood-kernes in our line."

*God save Ireland, said the heroes
God save Ireland, said they all
Whether on the scaffold high
Or the battlefield we die
Oh what matter when for Erin dear we fall?*

"He was a warrior. An' still t'day his line continues. Ya're no different, only time has changed. People like ya father, an' people like us? We don' want for *power* over others, we only want to be ourselves. There's honor in ya father's death. Great honor. He went to his doom wit' an undaunted soul. My father would thank yours. My father died o' some sickness after we came to Brooklyn. He was a pious man. A quiet man. Wordless but for prayer. Ya father fought to right the wrongs done to mine. For retribution an' for freedom. An' for that I'm thankful."

I look off again. The anger that had bunched up in my shoulders begins to ease, until I think again of what happened to me on the pier. *No one can know what I saw. No one understands. I don't even understand.*

"I worry for my mother, is all. And for my sisters. Look what happened to Brosnan. And to Mickey. Anybody can die at any time and you just don't know until it's too late."

"Do ya believe in signs?"

"Like from god?"

"Nah. . . maybe. There's so much out there we don' understand. Ya can call it god. Destiny. Fate. Belief. Hope. Even fear, but when it's boiled down to the bone, we don' know if things actually happen for a reason. But sometimes a sign appears. When McGowan died I lost someone I could trust. Then, at his wake," Dinny reaches over and touches my arm. "You appeared."

"Seems like a lifetime ago."

"It was a sign. From where or what, I don' know. The world needs honorable people to fight against the things we'll never be able to conquer, like death. But we're not defined by death. We're defined by what we fight for. Not what we lose to."

I blink through my thoughts, but I don't know how to respond.

"How is ya mother doin'?" He speaks to me without looking and I can feel he is not happy that I have never introduced him.

"I. . . I don't know. How do ya tell a woman she's a widow?"

"Gently," Dinny nods, then glances in my direction. "Just keep her away from Vincent."

We share a smile as the shadows in the street begin to disburse and mumble off into the night while Dinny and I stand together on the sidewalk.

I swallow hard, "On the pier at the Atlantic Terminal after we fought the Russians. I saw. . . I thought it was Garry Barry. Then I thought I saw the same scars Thos Carmody has. And it even had Bill Lovett's bullet through the scalp, but he was wearing a mask. A black mask with a long nose, like one of those old Italian theatre masks." He nods knowingly as I ramble on, "But what does all of it mean? That's what has me undone. I can fight, I know that. I understand that I have to do all I can to hold the line and make sure you stay in power. But it's what I don't understand what drives me mad."

"The Bard says we live in a ghost story," his voice is gravelly. "An' we are the ghosts."

"What does that mean?"

"Maybe it means we're not supposed to know everythin'."

"That doesn't help me."

"I'm sorry—"

"What else does he say, this so-called bard?"

"He says the physical world is but a troupe o' actors recitin' a script. But soldiers rage in war under the surface," His eyes find mine. "In the Otherworld. There, the dead are animate, like in dream, the risen people. Grotesque monsters an' warrior heroes battle in an eternal struggle for the right to claim the souls o' the livin'. An' only a great spectacle determines the victor who takes the right to rule over dawn."

"Ghosts," my voice is seasoned heavily with doubt.

"Pookas," Dinny laughs. "Whisperin' in our ears."

"But that's just—"

"Turf fire gossip."

"Soup stories, we called them. I've always wondered who wrote them. I mean like originally?"

Dinny smiles, "We did. You did."

My stomach turns, "When would I have written them?"

He shrugs at that, "Ah, it was just a jape."

"Jape, yeah. Yeah. For a second there I thought—"

"That I was serious?"

"I don't know. On the pier I. . . I saw myself an' it felt like. I felt. . ." I search for the right words. "Like I was—"

"Dreamin'?," he tilts his head in agreement. "Thing about dreams is, can ya predict what happens? Even better; can ya control what happens?"

"I don't know."

"Well ya better survive at least, otherwise what? Ya will be trapped in this story forever."

I grit my teeth at that. Anger begins to pulse through my blood.

My hand, my hand bears a true wound. A physical wound. And that's not from some psychic battle or a dream.

"You're not helping me. Japes and warriors and heroes and dreams. Look at my hand," I pull off the bandage and thrust it in front of his eyes in the dark. "I don't think I can do this anymore. I can't even convince Dance that we should not exult in beating men on the docks. Or murdering them."

"Ya need him, Liam. For what's comin'? Ya need him."

"What's coming? Tell me?"

"I. . . I can't really say—"

"The Bard and his stories? You banish Harry? The Swede? The Swede is a depraved man, you know. Then there's Bill Lovett, Garry fucking Barry, Thos Carmody?" I turn to him angrily. "After talking with Cinders, I think it's possible Patrolman Culkin disappeared his own father-in-law."

The crowd begins to cheer as Vincent hangs out of the second floor window with the newborn in his arms, its tiny feet dangling in the air.

"It's one thing to fight against factions of your own kind, like Bill. But to take arms against a troubled world? And I'm supposed to risk my mother and sisters in the bargain? No. No, there is too much to lose. I am leaving the gang. I'm done. "

"Liam."

"You should have named Dance dockboss in the first place, Dinny. Now you have an excuse."

A coy smile forms on his face, "Liam, remember. Ya can't be brave until ya're scared. Ya can't be honorable until ya're troubled."

"I know, I know. And you can't sacrifice unless you lose something valuable," I walk away.

"Ya can't escape, ya know."

"What did you say?"

"Ya can't escape," his broad shoulders swivel in my direction and his eyes find mine. "That thing that attacked ya on the pier? It's not some *other* thing. It's ya'self. The enemy is within us."

But I turn my back on him and walk up the Hudson Avenue hill, alone.

"There are more battles for ya yet. Ya journey's only begun," he calls. "Hey! Isn't tomorrow ya birthday? Happy Birthday!"

Rule Over the Rubble

The boys had never *worked* with a hammer before. They had only used them in fights, and it's not so easy to hit a tiny nail on the first shot without practice.

"Ow, fookin' shit on a stick, fookin' damn," Matty drops the hammer and jumps in place as Willie Lonergan laughs. "Look, I broke the fingernail. It's split open an' bloody."

"Put some butter on it," Petey laughs and points to the little bottle with a picture of a man with a fish on his back. "Mrs. Lonergan's got cod liver oil."

All the boys make lemon faces at that.

The wood for the bunkbeds were stolen last night from a lumberyard on Dikeman Street in Red Hook an' driven up to Johnson Street by Bill Lovett's most recent White Hand convert, James Hart, the teamster driver who recovered from the grippe. From there, Richie and Petey Behan had worked the sawhorse for two hours to make slats and posts and beams enough for three bunkbeds. That's beds enough for four boys and two girls to Anna's count. Two more will stay on the sofa, while Richie and Willie will share the second bedroom.

Anna stands proudly, *No one in my family will sleep on the floor ever again. Not if I can help it.*

"Vhere vill you sleep?" Abe Harms asks by way of deduction.

"With the youngest children who need me the most," Anna looks over along the wall where Matty and Timmy follow the instructions Abe had drawn out for them.

Abe's family's business is to build shelving for the thousands of neighborhood Jewish grocery and corner store owners who only contract with people of their own kind. So Abe knows exactly how to design and draw up sketches of bunkbeds for the Lonergan Crew laborers.

Abe folds his little fingers together and turns to Anna, "An' vhen the Leech sees that you've upgraded the room, he vill—"

"Raise the rent," Anna finishes the sentence. "We can pay a little extra now that we're dippin' our fingers into the pockets o' two top earnin' girls. But I'm gonna have to come through for them, ya know. If we're gonna get Pickles out, we gotta get Grace away from the Adonis an' provide protection for her."

"Yez."

"Yez what?" Anna lowers her eyebrows and shows Abe her teeth.

He's been a little too happy to help, this one.

"You don't trust me," he says as a matter of fact.

"I don' trust no one."

"Trust is important to you."

"Yeah, and?"

"I must offer you a vay to prove myself to you," Abe turns to her. "Vhat is it that you vant to do so that I may be of service?"

I want Neesha to come back to me, Anna looks off without answering him.

Neesha had vanished from her dreams. Ever since Richie pledged to protect her against her father and Bill, Neesha had gone. What once was her sole purpose in life, to see him, to be with him again as she had in life, had now fallen into the folds of memory and obscured by time.

I want him back. That is what I want, but Abe cannot help me with that.

It is the one thing in her life she has no control over. And it seems the more she takes control of her waking life, the deeper he has fallen away from her dreams. What did he mean by crowning him king? Or when he said he lives inside another now?

When Anna notices Abe stare at her as she cycles through thoughts, a flood of anxiety washes over her.

He thinks me psychopathic, perhaps I am.

"What do I want, ya ask?" Anna reaches down and picks up her youngest sibling, Patrick. "I want my fam'ly to never know what it is like to be starvin'. I want them never to worry about bein' homeless or that their lives are any less important than anyone else's in this neighborhood or any other."

Abe slowly blinks and bows.

Anna continues, "Ya fam'ly's business has provided the security I long for, so maybe ya don' quite understand exactly how important somethin' like that is. The Lonergan fam'ly's been the butt o' jokes for years an' completely dependent on—" she comes in close for a whisper. "Dinny Meehan. I don' wanna depend on him no more, see? I wanna depend on myself."

"Yez," Abe says. "Thank you for your honesty. It means a lot to me and now I can begin to zee how I can prove myself, and help you."

"Yeah, how?" Anna gives him a doubting stare.

"Vhat you seek is change," Abe leans toward her. "But to create change, you need to use tools. Just as these boys are learning to use a hammer and a zaw, nails and wood to create beds for your family, so too do you need a tool for to create a change. But in this case, there is one tool that may precipitate the type of change you zpeak of. A tool to cause change in one fell zwoop, yez."

"What kinda tool is that?"

Abe smiles and moves his little eyes in her direction, "Revenge."

Revenge, the word echoes through Anna's head. Nothing sounds so sweet as that word. It glows amber inside the wound in her heart like a little fire.

That word, my god. I want it. I truly do. I want to make Bill suffer for what he did to my love.

Anna blinks and turns her attention back to Abe.

He knows more about me than anyone, but how? How does he know about Neesha and I? Did he know that Mickey Kane and I had plans to marry and run away together? If so, did he know Bill was going to come back and have him killed, by my own brother?

"Why would I want revenge?" Anna prods.

"A rebel is not a ruler, because a rebel rides a mad horse and turns all to rubble. Rebels. . . are hotheads driven to take power from those who hold it. *That* is their role. The job of ruling after power is attained is the business of those who prevail with a cooler head."

"Ya didn' answer my question."

Abe slowly turns his head to her again and points at his own eye, "But now you have vision, but vhat you need first and foremost, before you can think of sweet revenge? You must come into your own, Anna. You must become matriarch of the valuable Lonergan family, yez."

Little Patrick squirms in Anna's arms and yells toward the front door, "Mama!"

The rest of the Lonergan brood run through the workers and the lumber that is lined along the middle of the parlor. They scream out for their mother, who walks into the first floor tenement with shock on her face.

"An' what in the name o' Jaysus is happenin' round here, eh? Who's behind this?" Mary says.

"Richie thought it'd be a good idear to get proper beds for the kids," Anna says over her shoulder. "An' his friends decided to help out."

"Richie?" Mary makes a face at that. "Richie t'ought this up? I just talked to Richie out front an' he didn' mention that. Where'd the money come from for all this?"

"Ma," Anna waves a finger at her. "Don' worry about it, uhright? It's all for the best."

"I want all o' these people outta me home," Mary drops her purse on the ground. "Out, out! Get outta me home this instant. I didn' invite ya into me home, but I sure as hell will send yaz away. An' take this rubbish with yaz. Look, the sawdust has gotten everywhere. The whole place is covered in sawdust. Jaysus, I go to Communion an' come back to me home turnt upside down, fer godsakes."

Matty, Timmy and Willie drop their hammers in shame and begin to walk for the door.

"Stop," Anna's shrill scream calls out and rings in the ears of all just as Richie comes to the doorway. And the room freezes in place. Even the many children who can't seem to sit still for longer than half a second, stand motionless but for their darting eyes.

That was louder than I intended, but it worked.

She turns to the children, "Patrick, James, Julia an' all the rest o' yaz, sit down on that sofa this very minute. Older ones on the floor. Except ya'self Willie, ya're old enough to take on bigger responsibilities now. Ya're a part o' the Lonergan Crew, got it? Like the rest o' us, ya report to Richie now. Everythin' goes through Richie, yaz understand it?"

The children jockey for position on the sofa and agree in unison, "Yes!"

Mary turns to Richie, "Ya're behind all this?"

Richie stares blankly back at his mother.

"This is Richie's fam'ly now, Ma," Anna says.

"Over me dead body, t'is. Yer father will have—"

"He has no say here," Anna interrupts. "He never has, in truth. It's ya'self, Ma, who made the decisions for all these years. An' it's ya'self that must now let go o' that role. It don' fit ya no more, ya eldest son is now head o' the fam'ly an' all o' us," Anna turns again to the children. "All o' us must do what we can to help Richie take this fam'ly outta the slums for good an' ever. An' wit' our help, I know he can do it."

The children turn their heads in Richie's direction, leaning against the doorway with a saw in his hand.

"He's just a cover fer ya own idears," Mary says. "That's plain enough to see."

"Doubt will only strengthen us," Anna raises her voice again. "That's ya problem, Ma, ya don' even know a good thing when ya see it. I for one do not doubt Richie. He is the leader we all need, don' yaz agree?" Anna points to the children along the sofa.

"Yay!" They yell. "Richie, Richie, Richie."

"Ya ain't capable o' rulin' over this fam'ly, Ma," Anna continues. "We've suffered long enough, it's time we begin anew. A *new* day has arrived for the Lonergan fam'ly an' we will now take charge o' our own future."

"Yay!" The children scream again as Anna reaches forward with a big smile to poke little Sarah and Catherine's bellies with her index fingers.

"Who wants a root beer candy?" Anna addresses the children as a whole.

"Me!"

"I do, me!"

"Please, Anna. Pick me. Anna!"

"Uhright, uhright, sit still. Sit back on the sofa, all o' yaz," Anna says. "Everyone gets one piece, but when I hand it to ya, do not take it out o' the wrapper until I say, understand?"

"Yes," they say.

"An' don' grab it outta my hand either," she raises her voice at Julia. "Give that back to me."

"Why?"

"Give it."

Julia begins to cry, but hands the candy back to Anna.

"Can ya take it from me like a good girl?" Anna asks.

Julie wipes tears and hair away from her face and nods up and down.

"Nice and gentle, uhright?"

Julia opens her palm and when Anna slowly places the candy, Julia closes her palm equally as slow. The rest of the children follow the example as Anna patiently goes from child to child.

"Ya train them like dogs, do ya?" Mary stands next to Anna in front of the children. "These are me childers, not ya own. They came from me body an' I've cared for them me whole life. I am their mother an' no one, I mean absolutely no one has the right to take childers 'way from their mother. No one!"

Anna's eyes move to Abe, who offers her a slow nod of confidence. She then turns her back to her mother and asks a question at the same time.

"Do ya remember the mornin' we woke up an' found Tiny Thomas?"

"Oh my," Mourning Mother Mary shudders. "Why would ya even bring that up?"

"Who remembers Tiny Thomas?" Anna addresses the young children.

"I do," Willie answers for them. "He was always sick."

"Yes, yes he was. He was too small for his age. At six years old he looked like he was four, maybe. I remember him so well," Anna's voice cracks as she looks up toward the ceiling and draws all attention to her. "He was too good for this earth. But he didn' have to die. That? That was avoidable. Do yaz wanna know why he could still be alive?"

The children are too scared to agree, but manage to nod in unison.

"Because ya Ma let him die."

"It most certainly was not me fault, how could ya—"

"It is," Anna's voice goes shrill again. "The black bottle, ya said. We can't take him to the hospital on account o' the nurses will give him the black bottle if they need a bed for a rich Protestant."

"It's true—"

"It's ignorant superstition, Ma. Completely ignorant, an' that is why Tiny Thomas died. He had a simple infection. An infection from stepping on a nail—"

"He was with ya when it happened, it's ya own fault—"

"Yes, he was wit' me," Anna bites down to push back the tears. "But ya were his mother. The mother that should do everythin' in her power to help her children. But ya wouldn't help him. Ya *couldn't* help Tiny Thomas, an' he died. From an infection in his foot, an' ya know what ya mother put on the foot to help heal it?" She turns to the children.

"What?" Little James asks.

"Butter," Anna stops and look apologetically at Petey. "Butter. Butter. An' now she believes the pain o' Jesus Christ runs through her own body. She says she sees blood on her wrists an' ankles an' she almost jumped into our little sister's grave."

Anna walks deliberately over to her mother, "There will be no more violence in this home, but if ya give us a problem Ma, we will make things much worse for ya."

"Ya threaten ya own mother, do ya? Ya couldn't beat me, I have fifteen pounds on ya."

"Oh, I don' fight, Ma."

Just then, Richie stands behind his mother with a solemn look on his face.

"I'm not built to be a violent person," Anna again turns her back on her mother. "We all have our talents, violence is not one o' mine."

Mary turns round, "Richie, are ya going to hurt me, is it?"

"It's time ya take a deep breath, Ma," Anna warns. "Take a deep breath, step back, spend some time wit' Father Larkin. We will give ya money to go to the grocery store an' we will allow ya to spend time wit' the children, o' course, but do not assume ya can make any decision around here wit'out doin' what?"

Mary looks over her shoulder, "Talkin' to Richie first?"

Anna smiles, "That's right."

"Ya're nothin' but a rebel who thinks—"

"No, I'm not a rebel. I'm a ruler. There's a big difference. A rebel destroys, a ruler creates," Anna turns on her heel, stands next to Richie and folds her arm under his. "Ya love quotin' the bible, right Ma? I got one for ya, 'Every kingdom divided against itself is brought to desolation; an' every city or house divided against itself shall not stand.'"

The two of them stare as Mary bows her head, then looks up along the wall where three bunkbeds are half-built. She walks to them and runs her fingers across the newly cut pine, "This needs to be sanded," she turns her head back to Richie.

"We got sandpaper," he answers.

"When ya father comes home, he will have somethin' to say 'bout all this, an' if I know him—"

"He's in the bedroom, Ma," Anna points. "He's takin' a nap."

"A nap? Wit' all this racket?"

"Yeah," Willie steps forward. "He didn't react so well when Anna told him to hand over the tribute money he earned workin' wit' Bill. So we had to show him how things work now. Things got um. . . ugly. So yeah, he's takin' a nap."

Anna had walked away by then as the boys got back to work. Abe began to follow her, but she waves him away and summons Richie to step outside with her.

"Right there," she points for Richie. "On the sidewalk over there. I fell to my knees in horror. Ma had gone out into the cobblestones wit' Tiny Thomas in her arms. People were watchin' from every window. A thought had creeped up in my mind. I couldn't get it outta my head. It was like a ritual, I thought. A ritual, seein' a woman cry over her dead child. Do ya understand me?"

Richie nods.

"A ritual. Like it's happened so often throughout time, it's like even emotions, the most emotional thing in the world, a mother losing her child, even somethin' *that* emotional is just, I dunno, repetition maybe? Like things repeat through time. I don' know what I'm tryin' to say exactly, but I want ya to hear me, Richie."

"Uhright."

"Here's what's gonna happen," Anna turns and looks up into her brother's pale eyes. "We're to give protection to Grace an' Kit, since they were witnesses to the murder o' Christie the Larrikin. After Pickles is released an' we get the scofflaw soldiers from him, Bill's gonna disappear an' we are gonna take over. The Lonergan fam'ly. Does that make sense?"

"Yeah."

Oh Richie my sweet brother, you are going to be my tool. You are going to bring Neesha back. Revenge for killing my love. Revenge will shake the heavens until he comes back to me.

Richie looks away for a moment. Then back to her. Doubt had crept into his thoughts for less than a second. It was obvious to Anna. That little moment of doubt made her stomach flip and quickly her finger is up to her mouth, biting at the cuticles.

I must be the one that is mad. I can't do this. I shouldn't do this. But my instinct says I should. My instinct says it is the right thing to do.

"Richie?"

"Yeah?"

"Do ya wanna do this wit' me? Abe an' I, we'll work all the things out. So tell me. Tell me. What do ya think?"

Richie looks over her shoulder, into the distance, "I dunno."

His eyes, Anna thinks. *I just saw something in his eyes. An amber glow. My love.*

"First ve must get you close to Bill," Abe Harms walks up behind Richie.

"What do ya mean?" Anna turns to him. "Who?"

"You. . . Of course Bill must be convinced that ya have a vay to help him vin Irishtown, and you vill. In this manner I shall prove my loyalty to the Lonergan cause."

"How?"

"Bill is not the type of person who listens to his advisors," Abe tisks and shakes his head. "Zuch a shame. Those who are driven by fate often cannot reason vith those of us who share this earth vith them. Bill is much more likely to believe vhat he thinks are zigns of his ascension, yez."

"Signs?" Anna's lip curls. "What kinda signs?"

"Like vhen a shadow comes to him and imparts the gift of prophecy."

"What shadow?"

Death of a Fenian

Liam. My name is Liam, which means feckless and infirm.

A horse neighs impatiently as I pass a street stable. Under the enclosure of buildings I offer my palm to the shy mare, but she turns me away and slowly lopes back inside to leave me with the swing and sway of her round hindquarters and the snap of her tail.

No one wants me. I am the bearer of bad news and a quitter on top of it.

Midnight's streaky clouds dim the stars and mute the moonlight. Eighth Avenue is illumined only from the street corners where yellow pavilions of lamplight break the black and creep out into the wet street. Alone I wander, now friendless. *It's after midnight so it's my birthday now. I can feel sorry for myself if I want.*

I curse the keyhole outside the tenement. Somehow I put the key in upside down three times in a row. *Feckless and infirm.* The gas lamp in the hallway on the first floor is not lit and I have to feel my way to the stairwell and lean heavily on the banister only to fight again with key and keyhole to our room upstairs. When finally I turn the lock and swing the door open—

"Surprise!"

Before I know what is happening, I am out the door again with pipe at the ready. My sister Brigid laughs inside. And so are some of the Burke children.

I take a deep breath and pinch myself, then slowly open the door to our room again. Inside my sisters are red-eyed and yawning, but come near to wish me a happy birthday.

"Why are ye so late tonight?" Brigid asks. "It's never this late ye come home."

I quit the gang, I think, but instead I just smile.

They even have presents wrapped in newspaper with blue and pink handmade bows that are leftover from Easter decorations at P.S. 5 where they go to school. Two of the Burke children hug at my legs. The littlest one, Mary Louise, claps her palms up at me to lift her, so I do. She climbs up my coat with her lips puckered and gives me a wet one next to my left eye. The room explodes in happiness and applause for her.

Her father is there, reddened by guilt for not having shown on the docks. Then Mrs. Burke walks in front of him and kisses my cheek too.

"We offer our kindest birthday wishes," she holds my shoulders and stares deep into my eyes. "We're so very thankful for the whole o' the Garrity fam'ly, but especially ya'self, Liam. Ya've helped us immensely an' I'm so appreciative. We all are."

Would you still think that if you knew I am as jobless as your husband?

She pulls me closer again and whispers into my ear, "An' congratulations on ya advancement, lately. I knew ya was dockboss material all along. . . Please don' be angry wit' my husband, please?"

I smile back at her as she pulls away, "Never."

She takes her eyes from me and moves them to her husband, who steps forward, "Happy Birthday, Liam."

"Thank you."

His hand is small in mine. And although he is handsome, his frail frame is proof that work on the docks is too much for him. And it is written all over his face.

"I. . . I'm sorry—"

"We'll talk later," I move from him to his eldest son at the kitchen table awaiting me. "I know this was your idea, Joseph. You're the sneak behind it, aren't you?" Sitting next to him, I hold the top of his hand and grab his lapel with a fist, "You were probably waiting to see the shock on my face, weren't you?"

The room quietens to hear his response. His lips move and his head bobs but the words catch in his throat. "T. . . T. . . True," he manages, but then I see the one thing that makes me happy; his smile.

"I knew it. Say, did you like any of those pulp magazines I found for you?"

His eyes widen and for a moment I think maybe his feet and legs would straighten, his knuckled hands would unravel and he would stand from the table with words to flow out of his mouth. But only his eyes rise and grow fierce with passion, while the words still fight to reach his lips. Again the room falls to a great hush to hear him out, "I like. . . eh. . . the dime novels. . . b. . . best. . . Detec. . . tive Story."

His mother jumps in, "He's read all the stories from the same issue, five times now."

"Five times?" I smile with a look of incredulity on my face.

He smiles too as his mother speaks for him with a hand on his shoulder, "I think he has it memorized by now. The Gilded Eros, it's called."

"Ah, I think that one came out a couple of years ago. I'll get more of them. What about the Walter Whitman book I gave you?"

He gives me a sourpuss glance at that, "P. . . Poetry, ick."

I smile, but I had hoped he would've enjoyed Whitman's love for men's hearts as I had.

"Ya gonna have to help me get him downstairs," Burke says "He's heavy, an' he's taller than I am now."

"Most men are," says I, which puts another smile on Joseph's face.

"Is Mr. Reynolds to come this evenin'?" Brigid asks as Abby hits her with the back of her hand.

Harry Reynolds is dead. But I can't say that.

"He's soooo handsome," Brigid laughs. "He would make such a wonderful husband."

"Shut up," Abby grits at her sister and squeezes her hand.

"Harry is more than ten years older than the both of you," I say coldly. "He had to go on a. . . trip. I'm not sure if he's coming back, just so everyone knows."

Abby's mouth opens as she lowers her head, but she soon catches herself to hide the fact of her first crush. Still though, her eyes wander with thoughts of Harry Reynolds.

My mother then walks through everyone in the cramped room with a cake at her chest. I dread telling her the news, *My poor Mam. She doesn't deserve to suffer. Many have earned it, but not her.*

The cake has eighteen miniature candles that are all lit and dripping wax onto the icing. Back in Ireland, birthdays were not celebrated all that often. With so many children and the cost of making a cake for each one too much for a farm family to bear.

"We're American now," Mam announces. "An' I quite like the idea o' celebratin' birthdays."

"Me too," Brigid says.

"Yay!" The Burke children agree.

Dinny Meehan you are wrong. This is not a ghost story, this is an American story.

The joy of the room sobers me from the flask of whiskey I'd shared back on Hudson Avenue, even as the sugar from the cake does not mix well with it. Abby refuses to sing a song unless Brigid joins her, but we are all glad for it as Brigid has a tender voice. The Burke children quickly pick up the chorus on the second passing to light up our room with merriment.

We open the leaves of the kitchen table and even strike up the American Happy Birthday song. Abby and Brigid aren't strong enough to hold me upside down, but they talk me into laying on the ground so they could bump my head on it eighteen times, like we do back home.

Eighteen years is old, I think, then rub the back of my hand down my cheek. But as of yet no stubble has grown.

Mam is all smiles at the sight of me on the kitchen floor, "The neighbors must think we're wild."

"We *are* the neighbors," Mrs. Burke howls. "An' we've known yaz for crazies a long time now!"

When things begin to calm down and the youngest have fallen asleep, I ask for everyone's attention and stand over the table with one hand on Joseph's shoulder and another on Mam's, "I want to thank you all for thinking of me."

"Oh stop," they wave me off.

"Ya gonna make us cry, Liam," Mrs. Burke dabs at her eyes.

"And I want you all to know that you are also in my heart and in my thoughts all day, every day. I hope this is the beginning of a long tradition in our family," I find Abby and Brigid. "A birthday tradition that stretches to our children's lifetimes, and their children's too. To have you all here with me is a blessing. We work hard for what we earn, and we give thanks." To Thomas Burke I turn now. "May the Burkes and the Garritys live long together as neighbors and close family friends. From this generation to the next, and forever afterward. A thousand thanks to you all."

"Thanks be to god," My mother finishes and everyone crosses themselves.

"I ask only for one thing of you all tonight," I continue. "I must speak with my mother about something very important, alone. If you will."

She stares up at me, terror churns in her eyes.

"We'll do the dishes an' clean up," Mrs. Burke offers.

"Mam, will you come with me for a word? It's not too cold outside. A scarf is all you'll need."

She knows. Somehow she knows. She stands in place, her fingertips still on the table. Abby and Brigid do not have the sense that she has though, and gather up dishes with Mrs. Burke, still singing.

Outside the clouds have mostly parted and the moon is eyeing us as we walk on the wet slate sidewalks. A block away is Prospect Park, though that can be a dangerous place after dark. Instead we slowly walk south on Eighth Avenue toward the tall tower of the Armory.

"He's dead isn't he?" Mam stops when we are a block away. "Yer father. Ye got word? Does yer brother Timothy know?"

The street lamp behind her flutters from the gas flame and sheds enough halo light that her blue eyes loom. Above us are a hundred dark windows, some lit by candle. Along the sidewalk are rows and rows of stairwells and coal holes half-hidden by the night.

I reach out for her wrist, but she pulls away, "Just tell me how t'is, will ye? I don' need to be comforted. I'm sure ye feel the right thing to do is to be gentle to a new widow, but I've been without him for many years now. Just come straight with it, then."

"I received a letter from Miko O'Dea, do you remember—"

"Of course I do, Liam. He reported to yer father in the East Clare Brigade. G'on then."

"Anyway, you have the right of it, Mam. He's confirmed dead. But Miko didn't say how or when."

"He wouldn't," Mam looks to the sidewalk. "Not in a letter, he wouldn't."

"Mam, I'm sorry—"

"Don't be sorry, do somethin' about it instead. Because if ye don't, ye'll be next an' all yer pity'll be for nought, won't it?"

"Mam—"

"I've lost things all me life, Liam. Ye know I was s'posed to marry yer father's older brother, ye know? He died of a sudden, an' then it was yer father's turn. I never chose him. Choice was the first thing I lost. I'm fine with it, ye should know. But I'll tell ye what I won't be fine with. If I have to bury me sons before I go. That I won't stand fer. I put me foot down on that, so I do. I know the type o' men ye run with, Liam. They're the same in Ireland these days. It's all bravery and pledges o' loyalty an' honor killin's. An' I know what ye do all day, every day. An' I know that ye made a bank account in me name in case ye one day show up dead like yer father."

"Mam that's not why—"

"T'is! Ye underestimate people too often, Liam," she points her finger at me. "It'll be the death o' ye, ye know. Ye didn't believe I could think through yer own thoughts. That never came to yer mind, did it? No, it didn't. All that money ye have nestled 'way? Fer god sakes, how did ye make that much? What did ye have to do to get it? An' of late, ye've been doublin' the amount. Ye're in trouble, aren't ye?"

Well this isn't going how I thought. "Burke told you everything, didn't he."

"He didn't have to, I saw it all on yer eyes. An' I saw it in Burke's as well. But most of all I saw it in Harry Reynolds' stoney face. It's his face tells the whole o' the story, it does. But if there's one thing I know about men it's the look in their eyes an' that one had a past on him."

"He was. . . He is a good man, I know him—"

"Sure, but there was a hell of a lot more to that feller than he ever let anyone know. But where is he now? Did he go on a trip to New Jersey? Philadelphia maybe? Or did he get burnt to death in that tenement fire over by the Atlantic Terminal?"

"Jesus, Mam—"

"Say it, is he dead?"

I don't know that because I simply don't know. There is a lot I didn't know about him, even as I lived with him for many months.

"Ye're fightin' against somethin' that's way bigger than yerself, Liam. Too big. Ye're fightin' against change, ye know. Against time itself. Ye cannot stem the risin' tide, Liam. Ye think street gangs will own labor forever? Union thugs are the thing o' the future, are they? No, they don't hold true power round here, child. The true power is somethin' ye don't even get to witness. Ye only feel the repercussions after-the-fact, so t'is. Tell me about this missin' detective, then? Go ahead, Brosnan was his name. A man with a pregnant daughter who has two children. His son-in-law is a patrolman on the force as well. What happened to him? Did Dinny Meehan—"

"Mam, don't say that name. Don't ever say that name."

"Don't ye snarl at me!" Her voice echoes off the brownstones, off the old clapboard buildings and round the tower of the Armory. "Ye may think he's a good man, an' he may've done a great many things to help us get out o' Ireland. I don't know the feller, but I do know that a fish rots from the head down."

"What do you mean by that?"

"Ye've changed, Liam. Ye'll end up in Green-Wood Cemetery where ye can rest from yer labor, but yer deeds will follow, Liam. An' what'll Meehan do for us then? Send us a stipend? We already have money aplenty, thanks to himself. That's not what we need though. What yer fam'ly needs is yerself, Liam. In the flesh, not in memory. I'll weather the death o' me husband, but yer's'll rain despair over the rest o' me livelong days."

"What about Timothy? He's going to be swept up in the wars. Everywhere the papers are reporting raids and that the British are going to send war veterans to the countryside with lawlessness on their side. The whole country is set to explode. What if he dies?"

"He's a married man."

"He's married?"

"A mont' ago he was married at St. Mochulla's Church to the Cudmore girl."

"Jennie Cudmore? She only has one eye and he used to make fun of her."

"No, it's Julie he married."

"Julie? She's younger than I am."

"When a girl has her moon, she is old enough for marriage in West Ireland," Mam declares. "It all makes sense now. Timothy sent me a letter to say he was married, but nothin' about yer father's passin'. The Brits would probably never have let that letter leave Ireland. But ye probably know someone who can get letters out o' Clare, don't ye?"

"I do, a County Claremen's association in West Manhattan. So Timothy knew about Da's death before I did," I realize.

"Logically," she tilts her head. "He's the eldest. An' now he has a wife an' a farm. He's a man in a country that'll be at war soon. Let's hope they have children before he dies."

"So it's alright if he dies, but not me?"

"Liam, yer father knew ye'd not make a good soldier. From the start ye were meant to be mine, ye know."

I know, I know.

"Besides, ye've a free soul. Ye were never one to take orders well. It was all imagination an' stories fer ye, never rifles, death wishes or blood sacrifices. It was a good thing to send ye to America, like yer father did. It was his hope all along to live forever in songs, an' so he may, after all. He wanted *us* to live long though. To go to America an' maybe come back to a free Ireland. He wanted that ye would provide fer us here."

She shakes her head with a hand on her temple, then places the other hand on her hip, "Now tell me, what happened to yer uncle?"

My stomach shifts and flutters, "What?"

"Ye heard me, what happened to yer uncle Joseph? Yer father's brother? Go ahead an' tell it to me."

"I don't know what you're referring—"

"Ye lie to yer mother, do ye? If ye lie to me now, then I'll know ye're already dead to me," she moves closer, her red-rimmed eyes ablaze in anger now. "Don't underestimate me again, Liam. Don't do it. Now tell me what ye did to yer uncle Joseph."

She knows everything. How does she find these things out? What drives her? "I. . . I Won't say it."

The stars pulse above as she draws back. She knew, yet hearing the shame in my voice beats her breath. I grab for her wrist, but again she pulls away.

"Ye were forced to do it," she mumbles. "Ye'd never do such a thing on yer own. Ye had to prove yer loyalty to these men, an' they required yer uncle."

"You don't understand—"

"I understand that if this is the type o' men who ye've given yer loyalty, that we are all in danger. But mostly yerself."

I already quit.

"You don't understand what I went through. I was thrown into the maw when uncle Joseph turned me out. I was on the streets and he. . . they helped me do exactly what my father wanted of me."

"I understand it Liam. Ye did a wonderful job, is that what ye need to hear so to start thinkin' o' the future? Thank ye fer all ye've done. But what are we going to do now? What is yer plan *now*?"

I don't know. I thought I did, but I now I'm lost.

"Ye know what amazes me? That I raised ye to see the difference 'tween right and wrong. Yet ye're blind to the noose that looms over yer head, if only ye'd look up an' see it. I do not grudge ye, Liam. I understand now that the future o' this fam'ly is with its women. It always is, if truth be told. I understand too that my son has no regrets for his actions—"

You don't know that. You don't know the horrible regrets I have because I don't talk to you, or anybody about them.

"But I have one request that I'd like ye to honor," she moves closer and whispers, but there are no tears on her face now. "Before I slip the widow's weeds over me head an' go into silence, I have one last request. I know ye question the faith, but it's the faith ye must have now, Liam. Wit'out it, we're all lost. Father Larkin at St. Ann's says ye've never been to see him for Confession. Go. Go to St. Ann's an' Confess. Go to god. Lift the burden an' look up, son."

No, absolution won't come for what I did. Because I can never feel resolute that I'll sin no more.

Regicide Relived, Regicide Foretold

Darby Leighton's eyes are closed, though he can see. What's better, he can hear with both ears again. But what he hears is nothing. The air is still and his breath frosts in front of his face. The snowstorm had come down sideways in a torrent for days and ravaged Brooklyn. Now, here, he stands among a profound calm, hip-deep in a perfect snow again, untouched, unbroken, unblemished.

I'm dreaming. Yet I've never felt more awake.

Ahead is the Meehan brownstone. Behind him a horse whickers inside a stable and eyes him with distrust.

On a wet brick facade of a four story building, bare ivy vines snake outward. With snow having settled on the vines, it appears to the eye that there are bones strung upon the brick exterior wall in the form of letters. Or words. Symbols maybe. Someone might be able to decipher the secret message, but Darby cannot.

An old man's shaky voice comes to him as the wind suddenly rings in his ears, "Darby," it says. "The time has arrived for ye to make a decision. I shall take ye to the darkness o' the past an' to the light o' the future."

Darby covers his ears, "Who are ya?"

The voice continues unabated, "An' I'll even tell ye what ye should do. But t'will be up to yerself, ye who live forever hoverin' at the clash o' dawn, t'will be up to yerself to alter yer course in the present."

"What do ya mean? Why do ya haunt me?"

"The choices that try our souls define us, an' so ye must choose. But before we go," says the wind, as a darkness black as jet suddenly takes the sky. "Look, look up there."

When Darby looks back up to the Meehan brownstone, a full moon now adorns a starry sky. In the black he sees a figure climbing up the fire escape on the side of the building. Darby moves so he can get a closer look while the horse whickers again.

The figure climbing in the dark then stops and looks down, but Darby instinctively moves to a shadow, unseen. Unheard.

"I already witnessed this," Darby tries to organize his fleeting thoughts. "This already happened. I remember it."

The wind says, "Now ye know that I know yer secret."

Darby's stomach turns, *My secret. The wind knows the secret I hold over Sadie's heart.*

"Now we must go to the past, then to the future so that ye may alter the present."

"Where?"

"To 1912."

Darby looks round. He is no longer at the Meehan brownstone. He looks up at the thirty-foot shadow of the abutment to the Manhattan Bridge a block away to the left while to the right is the abutment to the Brooklyn Bridge. Up ahead, ascending a cobblestoned street, Darby's brother Pickles and Vincent Maher walk together between the bridges.

"We really are in the past," Darby says.

"We are."

"But this is my dream, which means it's my perception o' the past?"

"We all impose our will on the past as we do the future."

"Ya gotta kill him," Darby hears Vincent speak up ahead, then watches him hand Pickles a black pistol.

"This was Pickles' last day o' freedom," Darby realizes. "This is when everythin' changed for the worse. This is the moment." Darby calls ahead to his brother, "Don' do it Pickles! I know what happens to ya. Turn around an' go home. Pickles!"

But Darby's words go unheeded.

"Nobody ever wants to hear what I say," Darby remembers. "Why won't anyone listen to me?"

Between the gas lamp posts that line both bridges, Pickles holds the pistol, then tries to give it back to Vincent as he speaks these words, "Kill him ya'self. I got a feelin' this ain't what it's cracked up to be. I'm just here 'cause Bill sent me as a token o' his agreement wit' Dinny."

"No, ya gotta do it ya'self," Vincent refuses the gun.

The two come upon an establishment where the beautiful voice of a young woman cascades through the barroom. The lament haunts down the street and echoes off the bridges. Since Darby is able to hear with both ears for the first time in a long while, the voice sends chills down him and reverberates through every bone in his body. He stops and notices a darkly painted wood sign above the window that displays its name, "Jacob's Saloon."

"I remember this place before it was burnt to the ground. It used to be the headquarters o' the old Maroney Gang."

Just as the first light blushes against the morning sky, Vincent turns sideways down an exterior hallway between two buildings and opens an alley door.

"The women's entrance," Darby says.

Inside, past the stairwell Christie the Larrikin dances with Kit Carroll. He has one hand on her breast while she sniffs dust from the pinky nail of his other hand. In the background McGowan sits in front of the window, alive again. Darby moves to tap Pickles on the shoulder and tell him that one day in the future he will kill McGowan in Sing Sing during the War for the Inside.

"Pickles!" Darby screams. "Pickles, please listen to me. Leave now, before it's too late. Pickles!"

But Darby's words are still unheard.

McGowan sits in front of the window inside Jacob's Saloon next to another man. At that moment Dinny Meehan turns round to look directly at the shadow that follows Vincent and Pickles. Tears stream down Dinny's face like a faucet as he mouths the lyrics of the song Grace White sings.

DIVIDE THE DAWN

O, Father dear, I oft times hear you talk of Erin's Isle,
Her lofty scenes, her valleys green,
her mountains rude and wild
They say it is a pretty place
where-in a prince might dwell,
Oh why did you abandon it,
the reason to me tell?

"I know that song."

"Get out here ya fookin' larrikin!" Vincent yells through the alley entrance as Grace comes to an abrupt halt during the song and a trolley goes by on one of the bridges overhead, *cha-chum-cha-chum cha-chum*. "I challenge ya!"

Christie Maroney turns round quickly for a big man. Then turns back round to make sure Meehan and Mc-Gowan are still in the saloon by the front window, then again back toward Vincent's voice, who stands next to Pickles in the narrow alley as Grace and Kit watch them all with big eyes.

"Can they see me? They're starin' right at me," Darby wonders.

"A challenge?" Maroney's gigantic, ring-laden fist holds the door open as his broad face peeks through the women's entrance. The man monikered "Larrikin" has a heavy brow shelf and eyes that are set peculiarly wide apart over a muscular monkey mouth that protrudes as if the teeth were trying to escape. When his lips peel back for a gruesome smile, his gold-capped teeth display for all to see his crude belief in wealth and status. As King of Irishtown he sold its girls into prostitution, sold its secrets to the Black Hand, sold its waterfront riches to the union, sold its autonomy to the big businesses and sold its freedom to Anglo-American law. It was from this that Christie Maroney had drawn his wealth while Irishtown had fallen to its knees. Guilty of the crime of poverty again.

Darby had heard the superstitious story before: The old-timers in Irishtown, the original settlers, had summoned ancient prayer for Maroney's removal and the women had keened to bring back the old ways. On this day, their pleas would be answered and a new king would arise. One of their own making, and nothing could stop it. Not even the truth.

With Maroney ready for sacrifice, Pickles holds the pistol at his side as he blanches in shock. When he fails to act, Vincent rips the gun from his hand and points it at the big larrikin.

Darby drops down and covers his ears at the report of the pistol, and when Maroney falls, everyone runs. Just then a glim of light flashes between two buildings into Darby's eyes.

"It really wasn't Pickles after all," Darby's eyes are closed. "Yet he rots in Sing Sing these last six years. It really is a lie. I was right all along, my brother is innocent. An' all the dominoes that fell afterward were based on a deception. An illusion. A trick. Everythin'. This is why I must right the lie. Right it so that the truth can be revealed an' Bill can become King o' Irishtown."

When Darby opens his eyes, he is again out front of the Meehan brownstone.

"I'm dreamin'. Yet I've never felt more awake. . . Wait, I already said that."

The wind again dials up and almost blows his cap off as the old man's wavering voice appears, "Ye've seen the past. Now ye shall see the future."

"I don' understand," Darby says.

"Dustbroom Darby," suddenly he hears Bill Lovett's snarling voice from behind. "Ya never understand nothin', do ya?"

Darby turns but only sees the horse again, staring back with a long, tilted face.

"C'mon, let's go. Ya comin' wit', or what?" Bill asks.

He turns again and Bill Lovett is standing next to him, "Where. . . What?"

"Ya're a fookin' eejit. This is why they call ya Daydreamin' Darby, ya know? Where do ya fookin' think we're goin'?" Bill's eyes move up to the broken window of the Meehan home. "We're goin' up to kill Dinny."

When Darby turns back up to the broken window, he asks, "Is Sadie up there?"

"An' what if she is? Their kid's up there too, so what?"
"Will they die too?"
But Bill does not hear him. Bill had never heard anything Darby said.
"This is what we came for," Bill nods in confidence. "I'm here to lead the lost, remember? Ya've been lost ya whole life, Darby. Ya comin' wit', right? Think o' the terror he's brought to ya fam'ly. Do ya still have the medal I gave ya?"

Darby reaches into his pocket, but before his eyes can fix on the medal, it turns to dust in his fingers and the wind washes it away.

Bill chuckles, "It's uhright. We will win when we kill Dinny. Then ya can be Fifth Lieutenant an' a dockboss an' ya fam'ly won't have to live in a water closet in an abandoned buildin' no more. We'll be rich, but we gotta do it together. It's fate, Darby. It's my fate to be the leader. Don' ruin it for me. Ya comin' right?"

"There's no such thing as fate," Darby mouths the words without thought, keeping his eyes up to the window. His teeth then begin to chatter beyond his controlling them, and his eyes move back and forth again.

"What do I do? What should I do?"

"It's too late for that, Darby. Ya're always one step behind, bringin' up the rear," Bill says as he and three other men shoulder past him until another man joins at the stoops. Together the five ascend and enter the building with weapons in their hands.

"The archons. They are the five archons. Bill an' four others, but who are the others? An' where are the orphans?"

"Darby?" The old man's wavering voice comes to his ears as he stands alone in front of the Meehan brownstone.

"Yeah?"

"Look in yer pocket."

Darby searches, then pulls out the Distinguished Service Cross, fully intact again.

The old man explains, "The choice is yours again. Ye've seen the darkness an' ye have seen the light. In yer hand ye hold the dawn. Keep it an' ye shall die, throw it away an' ye shall live an' the war will never happen."

"I'm confused. Let me get this straight. If I throw it away, Pickles will be stuck in prison forever, even though he is innocent an' Bill'll never be king o' Irishtown?"

"That's right, an' ye will live."

"An' if I keep it, Pickles'll be released an' Bill'll be king?"

"True, an' a gang war will claim many lives, includin' yer own."

"All this on account o' I desire to right a lie?"

"Ye cannot change history, ye can only change minds."

Darby rubs one hand against his temple and stares at the medal in the palm of his other hand, "Ya said ya'd tell me what to decide. That I could alter the course in the present."

"It is a terrible decision before ye, but for humanity to evolve it takes one person to deny vengeance. It is the hope o' a better way, however little our sacrifice may make on our overall improvement. However small, t'is hope against the dyin' light in the darkness that envelopes. T'is a dream to right a lie when the damage has been done. The offer o' a gentlelife is before ye, Darby. Throw the medal 'way an' ye shall live a long time with yer fam'ly."

"Why do I have to choose?"

"We all must, because from the seed o' the fallen will grow righteous vengeance as high as the moon fer all to see, an' on an' on, an' on an' on. Forever t'will repeat, if allowed. By things which are not, bring to nothin', things that are. . . ad infinitum."

"Who said that?"

"Oliver Cromwell, another king killer who became king."

"Ya ask me to turn the cheek when Dinny destroyed my fam'ly? When he set up my brother for a murder he didn' commit? Then had The Swede beat an' banish me to the shadows? But that wasn't enough. He then kidnapped my cousin Sadie an' forced her to marry him. An' to have his child!"

"Kidnapped? Forced? Are ye beginnin' to believe yer own lies now?"

"Why should I be the only one to sacrifice?"

"Ye're not. Dinny too has not killed Bill even though he had every right to call a Blood Feud fer murderin' his cousin. Dinny has opened the door fer ye to join him again. Remember, ye once worked together years ago an' ye held him a high regard."

"So much has changed since then."

"Stop the perpetual cycle o' victims an' victors that change places like life an' death, Darby."

Malice glitters in Darby's eyes, "I will not."

"I see," The old man mouths.

"I *will* right the lie about my fam'ly," Darby screams and closes his fist round the Distinguished Service Medal. "I *will*!"

Upstairs, five gunshots ring out and the screams that come from Sadie curdles his blood and shakes the ground as if the earth had been ripped open and the sky cracked. "Darby! Darby!" Sadie's voice is so loud that blood trickles from his ears.

"It's not my fault," he dumbly responds. "It's not my fault."

"Darby!"

Darby yells back, "I can't, I can't stop myself now. I'm sorry, Sadie."

"Darby wake up!"

When Darby swims to the surface through the amber sky and up into life, he gulps for air and comes to his elbows.

"Are you alright, my love?" Ligeia asks him, her face is so close to his in the dark that he can smell the spices of womanhood in her breath. "Darby? You had the eh, what you call? Night terrors again. Darby?"

"Yeah, yeah, I'm fine."

"You were eh-dreaming. Darby."

Darby drops his head back onto the pillow and screws both eyes with the knuckles of his bent index fingers. When he can't move his pinky, he remembers the dressing Ligeia had put on it when she found him wearing a bloody splint.

Somehow she had collected a few liquids, mixed them with something pulpy and made an unguent. With a meticulous and gentle handling of the skin that had been punctured by bone, she spread the potion with the handle of a boiled toothbrush. Afterward she tenderly draped a clean cloth over the wound which she had cut with a pocket knife to fit round the finger. Then she pulled it moderately tight and wove a hairpin through it to keep it in place as if she were darning a shirt.

Colleen Rose rustles in the bassinet at the sound of her mother's voice. In the dark Ligeia freezes with a big smile on her face and puts her hand over her mouth. Darby begins to smile, but although he believes himself smiling, he actually is not. He doesn't remember how.

Everything Ligeia does fills him with something he had never known. The way she smiles as if everything is an inside joke between them, her accent in the language she has picked up so quickly and the way she mothers him. Joy. Love. It was as if he'd been starved until she fed him. All those lonely, cold years in the shadows. And before that, homeless under a rotted pier like a water rat.

Am I really going to die? Die, and lose all of this?

"Darby," she whispers from the other side of the bed and puts his face in her soft hands. "Darby, what do eh-think about all the time?"

He didn't hear that. As she spoke, he had made his decision final, *If I decide something based on a dream, I would be seen as psychopathic. No, I cannot do that.*

"Darby?"

But is it worth the risk of losing Ligeia and Colleen Rose?

"Darby?"

"Yes?"

"What you eh-think about?"

"How much I love ya," He reaches for her hand and brings the ring to his lips. "Ligeia, will ya marry me?"

"Yes," she answers quickly, "Do you worry? Worry about us?"

His eyes move to the right in thought, "After the—" he stops himself from saying after the fight between Dinny and Bill, and instead he says. "After next week, we will go to City Hall in Manhattan. People get married there everyday. We should—"

"Oh Darby, my lover."

"We will get married after next week. I'll make all the arrangements."

I am not psychopathic. And I do not believe in messages from dreams. I will take all the risks that are needed to make my own way for us.

Ligeia grabs Darby by the shoulders, "What about a dress?"

"I'll get money for that," Darby sits up.

But how, he has no idea.

Chirping sounds come from Colleen Rose in the bassinet across the cramped room and Ligeia smiles. Darby then presses a finger to his lips to shush her. Across the street at the Socony factory a shift whistle sounds off as the bed gives a rusty squeak when Darby inches toward her.

He takes her hand and kisses her mouth, "I love ya so much, Ligeia. We're gonna get outta this hole. We'll get married. We'll get a new room, an' we'll be safe. I made a commitment to ya, an' it means the world to me."

Her mouth opens as he slowly pulls down the strap over the shoulder of her nightgown to spill her engorged breast. A slight gasp comes to her lips when he puts her soft brown nipple into his mouth. A shot of milk shoots down Darby's throat so sweet that it stirs his passion to a stiffened point. In response she reaches down and runs the palm of her hand along his shaft and warms it in her gentle grip. With his mouth he takes her other nipple as she watches with downturned eyes and an open-mouthed exhale.

Darby pushes her onto her back and swings his legs over and between hers, but before he can direct himself inside her, she says, "Remember you promise, Darby. I want go out to *ristorante*. I have a new eh-friend to sit with the baby. You take me?"

"I promise. An' we'll look in the windows at dresses. Then we'll get married."

A few minutes later and the room is an orchestra of rusty shrieks and the angry cries from Colleen Rose. A moan issues from Ligeia. And Darby's neck cranes toward the low, angled ceiling.

Forever Over Dawn

Mam had been to a tailor. Yesterday she had hung a new dark blue suit on the outside of my bedroom door. *How does she know my size?*

Now that she is aware of the bank account, she spends money on the things that matter most to her. And this day I would do what she requests, against my instincts.

I cannot speak of love to her, or any other. My love has been tied up like a prisoner since Emma McGowan died. And bound by the guilt of my uncle Joseph's murder. No, I cannot open up to the kindness and humility that I once naively showed everyone. Now I can only show it by going against my own inclinations, and doing what my mother requests of me.

I run my bandaged hand down the arm of the new coat. The fabric is beautifully woven and the hand-written tag describes it as Bannockburn tweed. Inside there is a matching waistcoat and a paper collar that is scalloped round the ends where they meet to allow view of a striped tie of oranges, yellows and hints of green. A matching muffler hangs elegantly out of the pocket. Brown patent coltskin boots with pointy tips and a conservative hat lined with chinchilla to top it off.

A new man needs new togs to get the feel, I smile. I take a deep breath to allow my new life to settle into my thoughts. The fistfights, the honor codes, the fear of death at every corner, the old beat up laborer's suits and the Hanan boots; all in the past now.

Even the camaraderie, a voice inside reminds. My mouth squiggles at that thought. Dinny had not taken my abandonment of post well. He smiled and wished me happy birthday. But the words that ring in my head the most are, y*a can never escape.*

Dinny Meehan has done terrible things, but to come after those who quit the gang would make him evil. Some say he *is* evil, in fact. *But he is not. I know he isn't.*

When I slip on the coat I notice an envelope inside the pocket without a return address. Scrawled across the front it says plainly, "For Liam only."

I open it quickly. Inside, a piece of paper is folded multiple times over so that the words cannot be read from outside. When finally it's open, it simply reads, "Patrolman Culkin works with Wolcott & Barry. It is Culkin who is behind the disappearance of Detective William Brosnan. You were right."

At the bottom of the letter it's signed, "H."

H? Who is that? This is the second time I've heard about a letter with—

"Liam?"

"I'm here, Mam."

She emerges again from her room quietly tying her robe, again, "How do ye like it?"

"It's fine, well-made."

"I got it for—"

"I know what it's for."

She turns her head and lowers an eye, "Ye're havin' second t'oughts."

No, they are trying to suck me back into the racket. "It's fine, stop worryin'," I pull down the rest of the suit.

"Liam?"

"What?" I answer in front of the door to my room.

"Just remember that—"

"Mam, I don't need you wiping the milk from mouth with your robe strings every time you worry, understand?"

She does an about-face at that and gently closes the door to her room.

I should go to Captain Sullivan with this letter, I think. But the more I ponder that, the more I realize how bad of an idea it truly is. I can't go to the Poplar Street Station because they know who I am. It would be better to go public with this information. But I have to go to someone who does not know who I am or my associations.

That's when it comes to me. I look at the new suit and smile. *After I do this, I'm done. No more gangs, ever.* This last gesture I do for my old friends, and maybe, just maybe it will go a long way in helping me feel better about abandoning them.

An hour later and I am at the Western Telegram and Telegraph Company next to the Eagle Warehouses. Two hours after that and I have an appointment.

"You the guy with the telegram to the Daily?" A man with a boater's hat and sharp eyes with a badly rolled cigarette hanging out of his mouth approaches.

"I am," says I.

"What's your hot tip, kid?"

"Are you a reporter?"

He hears the lilt in my voice and nods, "That's why I'm here, right? What are you all dressed to the nines for? A funeral or a court date?"

I look down at the new suit, "I. . . I work for a law office. I'm an apprentice."

"Apprentice to a lawyer?" He turns his mouth at me in doubt. "An Irishman lawyer? That's a scary thought."

"Really I'm just an errand boy to start, but maybe one day—"

"Uhright," he flicks his collapsing cigarette impatiently. "What do you have?"

"Well, something that is terribly illegal that everyone should know about—"

"Spare me the set up, what is it?"

"It's about Detective William Brosnan, you know—"

"The disappeared detective, yeah I know about him. What do you know?"

"His own son-in-law killed him under the direction of the president of the Waterfront Assembly, Jonathan G. Wolcott. It was Daniel Culkin did it."

A junk dealer atop an old wooden coach sends a ripple through the reins attached to a pair of barrel-bodied percherons. He gives me a stern look then clicks from the side of his mouth and the horses pull him through the street.

"Where did you hear that, kid?"

"I told you, I work at a law office."

He pushes his hat to the back of his head and dabs at his brow with a kerchief.

Aftershave, I smell aftershave on him, I think to myself. *Very strong. Like he bathed in it.*

"So you're giving up the goods on your boss. Not so smart are you?"

"This is bigger than even he can handle."

"What's his name?"

"That doesn't matter."

"What's your name?"

I slowly shake my head at him.

"So you want me to write a cop conspiracy, yeah?"

"I want you to look into it, that's all."

"What evidence do you have for me?"

"Culkin and Barry and Wisniewski were together when that building burnt down under strange circumstances on Hoyt Street. Wisniewski is a known, um, consultant of Wolcott's who recently partnered with Barry," My stomach begins seizing up on me before I can even begin to tell the lie. "A witness came to the law office. Someone who was in the bar when it caught fire. He overheard them talking about Brosnan."

"That right?" He stares, then gives a look of frustration.

Shame washes over me in a wave of tingles. *I shouldn't have come forth like this. I'm in over my head again.*

A patrolman and the president of a business conspiring to murder a detective is a weighty accusation, but the thought crosses my mind that it may be too big to be true. That although dark lies can be spread about the working class on the waterfront in newspapers without accountability, such irresponsible reporting about members of major power structures would be repressed before ever seeing the light of day.

I should've realized this earlier, what's wrong with me?

He continues, "You expect me to look into something without any evidence pointing to your claim other than three guys among many who were in the same place before a fire? That's not what I would call a hot tip."

I think of the envelope in my coat pocket, but that would mean nothing to the reporter, "I. . . It makes a lot of sense to at least put it out there and make them answer to it. The public should be aware."

"I tell you what," he says. "I'll look into it simply because it'd make a big story. A big splash, right? But I need more evidence. Anything. How about a quote from this witness? Or this lawyer you work for, he isn't willing to go on the record?"

"No."

"Did the witness pay your boss a retainer?"

"Retainer," I simply repeat, unsure exactly what that means.

A look of doubt comes across the reporter's face. But instead of confronting me, he just smiles, "I'll look into it, that's all I can say. No promises. Who else have you told?"

"Eh, no one."

"Send me a telegram when you come up with something new," he turns away and steps down into the cobbles, then sidesteps a pile of horse manure.

"I will," says I. "Hey, what's *your* name?"

He looks back with a new cigarette in his mouth as a train rumbles by overhead on the Fulton line, "Pakenham."

Pakenham? I know that name.

~~~

The small screen door is pulled back with a crack. An echo falls through St. Ann's Roman Catholic Church and we assume the aspects of penitent and priest.

Through the lattice window Father Larkin's darkened face assumes the austerity of his position with a low whistling pant through his nostrils. His lipless and collapsed mouth is pinched by years of spiritual certitude and his brow is a bushy furrow of graying, unkempt hairs. I clasp my sweaty palms together and lower my forehead onto my thumbs in the heavily lacquered confessional box. Already my knees ache and I stumble with the opening words, but it all comes back to me quickly enough.

I touch my forehead, chest, left shoulder, right shoulder, "In the name of the Father, the Son and the Holy Spirit. Bless me Father for I have sinned. My last Confession was. . . I think four years ago."

"In Paul 5:16 it's said, 'Confess yer sins, one to another.' Do ye understand that I'm only here to help? Ye do not confess on me today, ye confess to god. Only god can absolve yer sins. I am but his instrument."

"Yes Father."

"God understands that ye may be neglectful at times to confess. Sometimes we do not know the full weight sins bear on our daily lives, and sometimes we sin unknowingly, but four years is a long time."

"Yes Father."

"Release yer sins," he sits back impatiently and dabs at his forehead again. "Tell me how ye've sinned."

"I have sinned, eh. . . I lied to my mother."

His nose whistles through the lattice window, "We will speak o' repentance when ye've finished, what other sins have ye committed?"

Is hating your haughty Dublin accent a sin? I wonder. "I have eh. . . I have beaten men with my fists."

"Is the fightin' necessary?"

"To do my job correctly, it is. I mean was, yes."

"But it is in self defense?"

"It was to defend my honor and authority as a leader of men. I had taken over as a, eh. . . manager of a territory and if men didn't respect my word, many bad things could have happened."

"We usually turn to our work superiors, or the law if our authority is challenged. Why would it be necessary to fight a man? Does yer superior tell ye this is necessary?"

I don't want to be here. I don't want to answer your stupid questions. This is all for you, Mam.

"He does. . . Did."

"This is not self-defense an' ye've sinned," his tone has scorn in it. "Let me ask ye this, my son. An' it is my devout hope that ye answer it in truth... Have ye ever killt a man?"

I have, but the words catch in my throat. Uncle Joseph would not listen to reason. He was a drunkard and a fool who stumbled into Dinny's way. He wanted to recruit our men into the longshoreman's union. I had to convince him to join us or step aside, but he became angry. I had to convince him to help me get Mam and my sisters out of Ireland, but he said family is a burden. I begged him with all of the persuasion I possessed and even offered to leave the gang and join the ILA, but he waved me off. I ran out of time. I failed.

"Son, did ye hear my question?"

I look up through the lattice window. I can only see the silhouette of the priest's face now. Behind him is a light. I think it's a candle over his shoulder that wavers here and there, but mostly stands upright. The outline of his shadowed head moves closer, "Son? This is a question o' mortal sin," his face almost presses onto the lattice in his annoyance.

I ran out of time. Petey and Matty and Timmy had stormed into McAlpine's Saloon through pistol smoke, wielding blades and throwing punches. Men began to fall and the only thing uncle Joseph had to say in his anger was that my mother and father were dead. Even my sisters, 'Dead, all of'em!' he screamed. I was only fifteen years old and I had but one job to complete: Bring my mother and sisters to New York. Yet no one would help me. My own blood, uncle Joseph scoffed at the notion. Only Dinny Meehan would help.

"Son, do ye hear me?"

It was Dinny Meehan who sent me to Mr. Lynch from the County Claremen's Evicted Tenant's Protective and Industrial Association in Greenwich Village. With the help of Mr. Lynch I was able to sneak letters to the farm in Tulla during the war. And it was Dinny Meehan who gave me work. I was able to make more money as a runner and a dockloader than most immigrants in New York, and when the war was over, I bought my mother and sisters tickets for passage. Only Dinny Meehan stood with me in my time of need and to complete the job my father had tasked me with. Uncle Joseph deserved to die. He deserved it, yet still I am filled with the shame. It is wrong, what I done. And yet still it was right. The church says when a child dies unbaptized it goes to limbo, yet I feel I am there already, hovering, fixed over a constant position of change. Forever at dawn, forced to choose.

Father Larkin bangs a fist against the confessional box, "William Garrity, are ye listenin' to even a single word that comes from me, are ye?"

"Yes Father."

Through the lattice window Father Larkin's face is flushed, his eyes ablaze of anger as the light over his shoulder shimmers, "I remember the first time ye came to Mass here at St. Ann's. Ye were a good child then, innocent. But Dinny Meehan's men came in and dragged ye out like sheep to slaughter. I warned them not to hurt ye. But Dinny Meehan fashions himself as some savior and provider for the poor. But the poor already have god, they do. I am breakin' the oaths o' my office here, I know. But it can't be helped. Dark times call for dark decisions, an' I've made mine here an' now. Listen to me closely. Detective William Brosnan, a man who served Irishtown since the day he came off the boat has. . . I remember him so well because he came into his police work in this parish the same year I had become a priest at St. Ann's just months before the Great Blizzard o' 1888."

The priest's voice cracks and he sucks in air through his whistling nose, "He may've lost his faith for an ignorant prophecy that fed on his fears, but he loved his wife like I've never seen a man love a woman. He lost her that year. His faith shaken to the core," he growls and sits up. "It was that damned storm. An' the old world took him back. Ol' Brosnan's body was found in the East River this afternoon," Father Larkin's eyes turn up, and through the dark window he leers at me. "All those years on the streets exposed him to the superstitions o' ye shanty Irish. Cursed him, even. But he still found it in himself to be a good Catholic. An' a better man than even I ever believed god could create, an' what do ye do to him? Ye butcher him, stuff the pieces o' him in a barrel an' dump him."

I made a mistake in coming here. I've made many mistakes today.

"I—"

"A man that was beloved by the community, an' by his daughter, herself the wife of a patrolman, god help them now. She is with child on top of it, Doirean Culkin is. Two others already born. Would ye have their father Daniel butchered as well?"

"You have the wrong man, Father."

"Do I? For a fact I know ye killt yer own uncle. I knew him too. Joseph; he was named for the patron saint o' workers who died in the arms o' Jesus an' Mary."

"Yes he *was* saintly, wasn't he?" I put in sardonically.

Outrage takes his face, "Ye've got a mouth on ye like that? I'll tell ye this once, ye do not talk back to me thusly in the house o' god. Yer uncle was not a perfect man, but none of us are. An' if ye'd kill yer own blood, then why is it a stretch for ye to take the life from an officer o' the law?"

Mam told you about uncle Joseph, I realize. *That was a strong move, Mam.*

Father Larkin's eyes flash in fury, "It's Dinny Meehan everyone blames for bringin' this trouble to Brooklyn. They even blame him for that storm."

"Irishtown does not blame anyone but touts and outsiders," I correct the priest. "But I will say this. He is guilty. Not of murder, but guilty of the crime of poverty. Moreover, guilty of standing strong for the poor."

"Ye talk to me as if I'm a crony on the street? No ye don't—"

"You and I aren't all that different. We're both just trying to survive, aren't we? And both of us are succeeding."

"There is a world o' difference between us, William. I am a godly man, an' yer'self? Ye've chose to follow some other false deity, for in times o' great sufferin', false deities arise."

But I'm trying to free myself of him. If only you could see it.

"I know ye've suffered son. I can feel it comin' off o' ye, but ye must cast off the shackles that Dinny Meehan has put ye in. He enslaves ye by his will, even serves ye the lethal bev'rage that has for so long imprisoned the Irish. Ye have to shed light on he who hides in darkness like the demiurge. For salvation ye must expose Dinny Meehan to the light. I have even heard it said he had his own cousin, Mickey Kane, put to death so there'd be no heir to. . . to challenge his tyranny over and the folly exiles an' raggle-taggle diddicoys in his employ."

Lies.

"Confess for yer mother's sake. She has already lost so much, she cannot bear the weight o' losin' a son on top o' her husband. Beat yer swords into ploughshares and yer spears into prunin' hooks an' come to god an' fam'ly."

I come off my knees to exit the Confessional box until his voice softens.

"Son, I can see that ye had nothin' to do with Detective Brosnan's murder. But to save yerself ye must give up Meehan. Ye must say it. Say it to me, an' ye'll be free."

"Is that the word of god? That to repent, I should turn in others?"

"No son, it's the word o' the law," Father Larkin's voice is calm now, inviting.

"Ye haven't a choice, son."

"What do you mean?"

"Admit to me now an' I can protect ye. There's nothin' left for ye out there. Outside," He turns to look behind him and in the candlelight I can see his profile. "Out there it's all over now. Brosnan's death changes everythin'. But I can protect ye if—"

"Protect me?"

"Yes, speak. Speak son, admit Dinny Meehan was behind the murder."

"I'm sorry," I say. "I don't know anyone by that name."

"God will come for ye!" Father Larkin hisses through his nose, then summons a deep and resonant voice that bounces in echo off the rafters. "He is already here for the malevolent. Now!"

"I hear he comes for us all," I stand again to leave.

"Ye refuse the Lord's gift? Now yer soul must be sanctified. Yer flesh mortified. Officer Culkin!" he calls out.

When I exit the box, Patrolmen Culkin and Ferris are awaiting me in front of the pews with a band of tunics who stroke their twelve inch blackjacks impatiently. Culkin smiles and bites his lip in anticipation.

"No!" I run behind the altar and through a doorway into a long hallway with flagstone floors and a high, barrel vault ceiling. I can hear their clomping boot steps behind, chased by Father Larkin's words. "Atone, my son. Jesus suffered an' died for ye, an' so ye must atone. Atone!"

The hallway has four locked doors, but the one at the end is open. Inside I close it behind me and drop the bolt. *He's going to kill me. He's going to cut me at the throat and chop me up.* A small window allows dull light over a small bed in the dark room. As I pick up a shoe, the tunics bang on the door, though their words are muffled on the other side. The shoe cracks the glass on the window, but does not break it. The second shoe goes right through.

Behind me the door is being battered to pieces and soon enough I can see movement through the boards. I pull out the shards of glass from the window as fast as I can until the door is smashed aside.

"Halt I say!" A tunic yells and four of them elbow at each other to get to me.

Glass sticks into my forearm and belly as I slip through, but just as I think I am free, my foot is grabbed and I am pulled back into the window. *He is going to kill me. Cleave my flesh from the bone.* Kicking backward with the other boot, I scrape at the hands that hold me and connect with a face or two until I am let loose.

At basement level outside I run down a cement corridor where columns that begin at eye-level reach up to a covered garden. I jump up and scramble through rosebushes and a tomato patch among freshly turned earth. The cobblestones of Gold Street stretch out ahead and reach all the way down the hill toward the water. To the right is Hudson Avenue and the Navy Yard wall. *If I jump the wall I can hide in the Navy Yard. He's going to butcher me.*

I scramble to my feet, but five tunics block my path to the Navy Yard. I turn for the water instead as above us, tenement windows begin to open.

"Let him be!" A lone woman screams down to the tunics.

Boys appear on a rooftop to watch me run and shower bricks from a broken chimney down onto the men chasing me. Suddenly the air is filled Irish confetti; kitchen utensils are hurled streetwise, paving stones too, and eggs and heads of lettuce burst on the sidewalk. With a clang, a cast iron skillet bounces off the cobblestones behind me.

"Ya let the boy go!" Another woman yells out.

"Fuck off tunics," a crowd of rag-haired boys and snot-nosed girls screech in soprano as they send dornicks and bottles flying at my pursuers.

When I get to the railyard on the water five more men appear, though these do not wear tunics nor police blue, but are plain-clothed. By now I am exhausted and they run me down. It takes seven of them to subdue me until five more pile on. Three have their knees in my back and two more have their boots on my neck and face until they manacle my hands behind me.

"Looky looky," a high-pitched voice says above me. "The dockboss o' the Atlantic Terminal."

"I am not."

"Ya killt my father-in-law, don' deny it."

"I didn't." *He's going to cut me. He's going to stuff little pieces of me into a barrel and dump me in the East River.*

Patrolman Culkin laughs, "Hey Ferris, let's see how long he keeps singin' that tune. I say less than twelve hours."

Ferris smiles nervously, "Yeah, he'll come to his senses."

"An' if it really wasn't ya that did it," Culkin leans down and swipes some pebbles and dirt from my face. "Then I know ya will be happy to tell me who did, right kiddo?"

Just then it begins raining sticks and metal cans. A garbage lid flies like a saucer in our direction and caroms off the pavement into two tunics. An angry gust of wind blasts over us as thirty, maybe forty Irishtown natives sprint in our direction.

A black motorcar screeches to a halt and five men pick me up by the belt to toss me in the back. Two windows explode all round me, the glass falling like rain as I lay face down in the back.

Outside I can hear Cinders Connolly's voice as something bangs against the motor car.

"Wee-um," Philip Large yells out, though I can't see him.

The car then lurches forward. First gear winds so high that the transmission is about to explode until the driver presses the clutch and grinds it into second.

I wiggle up to the window in time to see that we are on Plymouth Street. As we pass Bridge Street I can see the Dock Loaders' Club down the block.

"Help! Help!" But it's too far away.

In the passenger seat ahead, Patrolman Culkin turns round to face me with excited eyes. He swings once and the lead end of his floppy blackjack ricochets off the top of my head. It takes two or three seconds until the pain comes to the fore. When it does, I feel liquid fingers drip down onto my cheek. Culkin's eyes look aroused, like how Vincent's eyes look when he talks about women. Then he rears back again.

Grey's Faith

May 1919

Darby's boots gently touch the metal ladder of the fire escape quiet as the wind in his hair. When he thinks of the possibility of Ligeia and Colleen being found squatting in the condemned textile factory, his stomach does somersaults. He stops and looks down toward their window. But being on the Sixth Floor, most people wouldn't know to look up. On the shaded side of the building, way up here above Flatbush Avenue, Darby goes unseen, unheard. As usual.

As he takes the last step and jumps onto the roof, Ligeia's words now ring in his head, "I have eh-new friend to sit with the baby."

Does she mean a babysitter? How would she have been in touch with a babysitter when our room is sealed off and the only entrance is through the window? Why hadn't I realized what she was saying at the time?

He chalks it up to some problem with her English as another, more looming concern crosses his mind; Dead Reilly and the money he requires for the trial.

The trip to Connecticut to find Sadie had been a waste of time. Darby, Ligeia and little Colleen Rose had made a day of it and went by train. It was all the money Darby had to buy the tickets, but Ligeia was so excited he couldn't tell her how poor they truly are.

They didn't want to tip off his brother Frank, so they came unannounced. But when they found out Sadie was not there, and had never been there, Darby turned white.

Ligeia was not as upset, however. Instead she had turned her attention to how beautiful the suburban house was. She and Frank's wife Celia walked round for hours talking about electric appliances, electric lights, electric irons, electric heat and how handy Frank had turned out to be, evidenced by the two posts he had cemented in the backyard and strung up clotheslines onto.

And when Ligeia found that Celia had gone to nursing school at Bellevue Hospital and that ten of the current students had died of the Great Influenza epidemic recently, she ran to Darby. "They have eh-shortage of eh-students, I want to go. I will go there to be nurse or," she turned to Celia. "How you say?"

Celia cleared her throat, "They also need midwives."

"Midwifes. I can be that too, Darby. I make money for our family," she turns again to Celia and grabs Darby's finger. "Look, I make this myself. His finger broken and bone come out, I fix it."

Darby pulled his hand away, "It's at Bellevue they give ya the black bottle."

Celia sighed when she heard those words.

The hope on Ligeia's face fell away when Darby said, "Besides, why would ya wanna go where the nurses are dyin' o' the grippe?"

Darby's brother Frank changed the subject by complaining in the cockney accent that seems so strange and distant to Darby, "Yu should really let us know when yu're comin' before'and."

But Darby ignored him. The Distinguished Service Cross that Bill had given to encourage him was turning into a reminder of his failures.

What will Bill do when he finds out I have no money for the retainer Dead Reilly requires.

To make matters worse, when Darby had snuck into the Henhouse to make Grace and Kit tell him who rode

Anna, Vincent Maher was in the room. As soon as he realized the Masher was in there, Darby snuck right back out the bathroom window that faces Green-Wood Cemetery.

I left with my life, but not the information I need. Maybe I will die as my dream predicted. At Bill's hand.

The attorney had been avoiding Darby and here it is only a few days from the retrial. When he learned that thousands of dollars had been sent to Dead to be secured, he sensed something wrong.

Why hasn't he responded when I've reached out?

The money Dead secures is the handle wagered for the fight. From every dank corner and garbage-strewn alley in the city; Queens to the Bronx, Staten Island to Manhattan people are putting money on it, but most comes from Brooklyn. A rumor about Bill coughing up blood had swirled and gave Dinny a wide spread. Then it was said the fight is fixed to Bill's advantage. That lie almost evened the odds, though Dinny remains the chalk bettors favorite. But New York loves an underdog. Most of the money that came from Sing Sing is for Bill, naturally, since Pickles owns the inside.

Darby's mind is elsewhere as he stands on the roof and looks over Brooklyn. *Dead must have been in touch with Abe Harms on Bill's side and Chisel McGuire on Dinny's to hold the total handle, but he never gets back to me?*

When Darby walks to the corner of the roof and looks down over Flatbush Avenue and Tillary Street, a rush of fear disorients him.

I could jump now and I wouldn't have to deal with all of this. If Bill finds out I lost Sadie and I never found out who rode Anna and that Dead Reilly ignores me. . . his stomach flips like a fish out of water before he can finish the thought.

His knees wobble over the building's edge. As he peers down with the wind in his hair, the words his brother Pickles said of him comes floating into his mind, 'Some cause happiness wherever they go; others whenever they go.'

But Ligeia says she loves me. What would she do without me if I never came home? His teeth grind together at the thought. *No, I have to corner Dead Reilly right now and make him talk to me.*

In his coat pocket Darby pulls out the Distinguished Service Cross. *For Valor*, the men had yelled out on the train when Bill gave it to him. *Bill is a product of the romance of valor that swept the world into war, but am I courageous?*

Crossing the roof, an identical building is adjoined to the textile factory on the far side, and so he does not have to jump over an alley. He has but to scale a five-foot crumbling brick and mortar wall. As he crawls over it, the Manhattan skyline across the East River appears through the dense morning clouds while the bridges are obscured by low fog. When he reaches the far end of the second building, he turns round and begins the descent down the fire escape. At the eighth floor he looks round himself to ensure no one has eyes on him and quickly pulls up a rotted window frame and slips in. From there a dark and enclosed stairwell leads to a backdoor where an eight-foot old stone wall blocks any view of his exiting the building. Down a cement stairwell, past a basement door, then up another cement stairwell where underneath a water pump is being used by a woman in a sack dress. She speaks German to a shoeless child who opens the tall wooden door of an outdoor water closet, his undergarments wrapped round his ankles as he shuffles toward his mother.

"*woher kam er?*" says the child as the sack-dressed woman turns round quickly, finds Darby's bewildering eyes and shrieks.

A few minutes later Darby pulls the flat cap over his eyes and slinks sideways between trains in the rail yard beneath the Fulton Avenue Elevated line. He ducks into the last car, takes a quick look at all the eyes on the train, and turns his face toward the glass door where he can see if anyone comes up from behind him.

He departs at the Fifth Avenue Court House and walks to the back of a two-story building across the street. At a brick wall he stops with his back to it and looks at his watch, *seven-fourteen a.m. One more minute.*

When he hears a door open, he moves off the wall and turns the corner.

Dead Reilly drops his cigar and almost jumps out of his pinstripes, "Jesus, Mary and Joseph. . . Why can't you just use the front door?"

Darby stares at Dead, "Ya refuse to see me, that's why."

"That's because I didn't have an update on the trial," Dead picks the cigar up from the ground, wipes it off, then throws it over the stone wall behind the law office.

In the natural light, Darby can see where Dead Reilly had shaved above his pencil mustache that morning. There is even some gray in it, and crows feet splay from his eyes when he smiles or grimaces. His waistcoat matches his suit and trousers, but small food stains appear to have been rubbed out haphazardly, possibly with a wet finger. He certainly has his clothes dry-washed, but not as often as he should. In Brooklyn he became known as "Dead" because anytime there was a body, Dead Reilly would show up. Sometimes before the tunics even.

"Ya won't smoke a cigar that touched the ground, but ya will take a percentage off the top o' the handle for the fight? Now I see how a man like ya'self can afford expensive habits an' suits."

Dead looks at him with lowered eyes.

"I see a lot o' things. Ya know what I see in the future? An attorney strung up by his toes naked an' flogged if he don' make right the lie told about my brother. Pickles is in jail for somethin' he didn't even do."

"Don't joke around like that. It's getting more and more dangerous to carry out the public good with you gangs running around here killing cops."

"Killing cops?"

"Brosnan? Have you read the papers today?"

"Nah."

"They found Brosnan's body in a barrel off of the Union Street docks."

Really? That's where I saw T.V. O'Connor get paid off by Wolcott's lump.

"They're blamin' the gangs for that?"

"The White Hand, that's your gang right? Dinny's too? Since he was found on Union Street, the Black Hand is also suspected along with the ILA union."

Darby scretches at his chin, "I guess he couldn't have been placed in a better spot than right on that border between us all."

"Are you trying to say Bill had nothing to do with it?"

"Bill would never kill a policeman. Say what ya will about him, but he's a decorated vet'ran o' the war an' a American patriot."

"So it was Dinny?"

"No, Dinny would never do that either."

"You vouch for Dinny? You, of all people?"

Darby's eyes wander off as he slowly nods, "I respect Dinny a great deal, even if Bill don't."

"Like a drowned sailor loves the sea, eh? Who was it then? Sixto and Yale down south? The ILA?"

"Why would any o' them kill a detective? Who lives in Irishtown to boot?"

"Because he didn't want to be on the tug any longer. That's what is being bandied about, at least. Whether Bill and Dinny had anything to do with it has no bearing on the situation now."

"Of course it does."

"How do you know? Did you see that too? No, you didn't. They'll have to prove their innocence, you understand? The papers already say they're guilty. And this thing with Pickles? You can forget about him. You say he's innocent too? How? Were you there in 1912 when that happened?"

"I—" Darby stops himself, then continues. "Ya know better than anyone what happened. Ya was Dinny's attorney back then. Tell me this, who will show up when *you* die, Dead?"

"I told you not to joke around. I'm a public servant and I—" The attorney looks into Darby's eyes and takes a deep breath. "Listen Darby, I saw Judge Denzinger in his chambers about another case, and your brother's trial came up in light of recent events."

"And?"

"There's a lot of push and pull on this case. You have no idea. Some influential people had taken this case and moved it up on the dock. Others, like Judge Denzinger, want to see Pickles' retrial disappear."

"Even if he's not guilty? They don' care about that?"

Dead turns his head and lowers one eye, "It's just not that black and white from where we stand."

"Who moved the case up on the dock?"

"Yes, well," Dead runs a thumb and forefinger down his thin mustache and turns a confused eye to Darby. "Strangely enough, Patrolman Daniel Culkin has come to me in support of the trial. Brosnan's son-in-law. And—" Dead looks away.

"And?"

"The Waterfront Assembly."

"The fat man, Wolcott?"

"Him and the rest of the Waterfront Assembly, a powerful bunch not to be taken lightly, I assure you. And the newspapers are all in too, have you read the editorials lately?"

"Why don't they pay ya what I owe, if they want the trial to go forth?"

"That's the thing," Dead's eyes light up with interest. "They were all set to pay, then they decided not to. Culkin told me they have a new gimmick."

"A new gimmick?"

"That's how he described it. Like their plan recently changed. He called it Operation Grey's Faith. When he—"

Darby interrupts, "But the trial is still next week, right?"

"Look Darby, you missed payments and—"

"I told ya I'm workin' on that."

"It's too late."

"Too late?"

"The trial has been postponed."

Darby's stomach drops. He no longer hears what Dead says. The words disappear and dread takes over.

Bill is going to kill me. Abe said this trial needed to be done before the fight.

He turns to Dead and interrupts, "Can it be rescheduled for this week?"

"That's just not the way these things work, Darby..."

The words trail away again.

Should I jump off a building now? Should I run away? Where would I go? Or should I go to see Colleen Rose and Ligeia one more time before telling Bill?

"Darby, can you hear me?" Dead speaks from one side of his mouth as the other side has a cigar in it. "The truth of the matter is this is not a case that is high on the court's wish list. And this case was connected to Brosnan too as he was the patrolman who arrested them all back then. The judges and cops, they don't like this. And now that there's a body, no one wants to smear Brosnan's legacy."

"Legacy?" Darby repeats, then mumbles his disagreement. "Ya think anybody will care about any o' us a hundret years from now?"

"Besides, Pickles has gotten himself mixed up in some murders in Sing Sing and is a known leader of a group of hard scofflaws inside. No one wants him on the streets. I had no choice, Darby. The trial is indefinitely postponed."

"But Pickles is innocent. A trial would prove it."

"Darby, how do we know one of your people didn't intimidate the witness into changing her story? She said she would tell the truth this time, sure. But how do we know she isn't coerced?"

Darby turns wordlessly away from the attorney as butterflies mingle in his belly. His eyes begin to flit back and forth and when his teeth begin to clap against each other in his mouth, he looks up, "Only god can save me now."

Scaffold in the Dark

Patrolman Culkin appears to have an erection. His breathing is heavy and his eyes are smiling. Even the black eye he received recently smiles. Then he opens his tunic and unzips his pants to show me.

"I ain't no flamin' heathen, Liam. I just want ya know how much I enjoy this. I can be honest wit' ya, right? Since ya gonna die."

I just wanted to leave the gang.

Yesterday morning, I think it was the morning at least, he removed three fingernails from my right hand. When he removed the bandage over the deep cut in my knuckle, he dug into it with scissors until I could feel the bone scraping against the sheers. The pain rang up my arm and into the back of my head. And when I gave him an answer he didn't like, he cracked the lead ball at the end of his blackjack against my shins.

For hours now, I'm not sure exactly how long, I've been tied naked to a chair that is tied to a pole in the middle of a room in the basement of the Poplar Street Police Station. I can't speak or scream. My mouth is filled with a dirty rag that is taped over my lower face. And it's cold. So cold. Every hour Culkin dumps a pale of ice cold water on me. And laughs.

"Why ain't ya excited like I am?" He extends the blackjack between my legs and gently touches the head of my penis with it, nudging, nudging. The hand-strap is wrapped round his wrist to ensure the twelve inch club-like weapon does not fall from his grasp. The woven black leather hides the coiled spring inside of the shaft that doubles the impact of the lead ball that weights the end. "C'mon now," he says. "Ya can do it. I want to see it grow. I want to see it happy. Ya know I always get what I want."

My body is confused. My raw fingers drip blood behind me. My shins throb with pain, yet the sensation below. *No, don't think about that. Look away. Pretend it isn't happening.*

"Poe Garrity," he smiles while jostling me with the leather weapon. "Also known as Liam or William. The Thief o' Pencils," He holds up the pencil along with the Saint Christopher my mother gave me. "These yours?"

They mean nothing, I think to myself. *What is sentimental value? It's nothing now.*

Unhappy that he received no response, he looks down again, "Why aren't ya gettin' excited, god-fookin'-damnit. Get excited, now!"

Patrolman Culkin stands over me and rakes the blackjack across my chest with a deep thumping sound.

I try to gasp for breath but the dirty rag blocks my throat. Gasping, gasping again, I have to remind myself to breath in and out of my nose. The rag in the back of my throat makes me gag. *Don't throw up, there's nowhere for it to go.*

"Havin' trouble? Oh? Lemme help ya," Culkin grabs one side of the tape over my mouth. "A little reminder though, no screaming. Otherwise—" he shows me the flaccid leather blackjack with the ball at the end.

All of a sudden he rips the tape off my face along with layers of skin from both my upper and bottom lips. It takes every ounce of will power to stop myself from bellowing out. When I begin to catch my breath I run my tongue along my raw upper lip, but the sting stops me from touching the bottom.

"Where did ya get the barrel to put Brosnan in? Smith & Sons by the Atlantic Terminal, right?"

"No," says I.

"I told ya!" He swings the blackjack again and it thumps to the bone of my upper right arm. "Don' ever disagree wit' me. Smith & Sons then, right? Say yes, say yes."

Pain, I think. *Pain is the price of truth. I must pay it.*

"No, I said."

Culkin rears back again as I hunch my shoulders in anticipation, but all I receive is his cackling laugh. "Ya should see ya'self. We should bring the camera in here. That look on ya face, it should be the mug shot we give to the papers."

He runs up close to me now and whispers, "I can do this for the next year, ya know. Ya seen how much fun I'm havin'. But I dare not ejaculate, see. Climax makes me sleepy. Good boys have to wait. Let's go over this again."

Again? The anchor of silence is sunk deep in me. I won't talk. No matter what he says, I won't talk.

"I know ya didn't kill Brosnan. So who was it, Vincent? The Swede? Or was it Harry Reynolds? Now that Harry Reynolds is a terror. Or. . . Did Dinny himself do it?" He takes a deep breath and squats down to me on the chair, eye-to-eye. "I just gave ya four options, Poe. Four. One, two, three, four. I'm too kind. So here's the thing; ya can admit ya killt Brosnan on ya own, in which case ya'd spend at least twenny years, maybe life up Sing Sing wit' ya buddy, Pickles Leighton. Or— "

Sell my friends.

"One o' the four options I gave ya. Thing is, ya gotta make up ya mind now, understand kid? Ya wouldn't know it, but there's thousands o' people outside that read all about how we fished Brosnan outta the river this afternoon, an' they want blood. Ya see, killin' a cop is. . . It don' get any worse for ya than that. Ya life's about to change."

My eyes are forward, but behind me I can see there is no light coming out of the window above. It's night time, probably close to midnight now.

Mam *will have heard they are blaming this on me. My sisters too. Everyone.*

"Thing is, kid," Patrolman Culkin walks behind me with the scissors and begins working on a fourth fingernail. "Ultimately it's gotta come down to Meehan."

I won't talk.

I wish there was a threshold where pain reaches a limit, but there is none. It just gets worse. He digs into the cuticles of my fingers with the scissor blade. Somehow the pinky hurts worst of all. Black thoughts take me over, *I'll never be the same*. Finally I lose control.

Culkin's eyes go bright, "I told ya no screamin'!"

The floppy end of the blackjack waggles in the air, but straightens when the force of the swing comes at me. Now my ear rings like a tugboat's fire siren and I go deaf. *Did it hit my ear? What happened?*

"Say yes!" He screams into my other ear. "Say yes to me! Cry for me! Cry for me! Say yes. Yes it was Meehan. Say it now! Say it!"

"It was—"

He stands above to hear my confession. Again I can see that his manhood has straightened. With the blackjack he moves his penis from one side of his trousers to the other while his smiling eyes grope at my naked body. When the pain and the tears appear on my face, he takes a deep breath to stifle ejaculation, though his back curls and his mouth makes an O.

"It was you," I say.

He grits his teeth, and swings again.

~~~

I am awoken to the sound of hammering outside in the street.

How can life go on while this is happening to me? What are they building?

Later, much later, I awake again. Still naked. Still on the chair. Four pulsing and dripping fingers are still tied behind me. Blue and black welts have appeared on my arm and chest. I can't see my shins, but they ache with a wretched agony.

"They've erected a scaffold outside," I can hear Culkin's voice in the darkness. "It's for you."

"Where are you?"

"Not since 1871," he says. "An officer named Donohoe was killt by the Battle Row Gang. A fella by the name o' Henry Rogers was hung for it. That's the last time anyone has been hung in Brooklyn, ya know. Until tomorrow."

I hear his footsteps. Behind me the light is so dim that I can barely make out the shadows of bars on the window cast along the floor and the opposite wall.

It's so cold, I'm so hungry.

But there is someone else in the room. I can feel it. But my thoughts run ahead of me in the black room.

The scaffold would probably be made of pine. Yellow pine that they would have gotten from the Navy Yard. They have a lumber yard inside the walls. And there's plenty of rope round.

I don't see anything move in the room, but I know someone else is here. There is something I recognize. A scent.

Aftershave. I smell aftershave and cheap tobacco. Where have I smelled that before?

"Pakenham," I say.

Silence responds. Nothingness. Then a single chuckle and the reporter moves into the soft light in front of me.

"Sorry about your luck, kid," says he, all smiles and concern. "You probably should have thought twice about going to a reporter with information like that."

Patrolman Culkin's black-eyed face turns and mumbles angrily at him.

"It's alright, he won't live long enough to tell anybody I was here. Even if he does, who's going to believe a cop killer?"

Culkin skulks off in the darkness, but Pakenham comes to my ear, "I came to see if you had any last words, Liam. Now's the time. Tell your family that you loved them.

Tell your side of the story. Why you did it. You can tell the world. I can tell your story for you. This is your last chance. But you didn't do it, did you?"

"I didn't—"

"Dinny ordered Brosnan's death then," Pakenham interrupts. "Say it's true and it will be."

I need. . . I need hope to withstand the lies and the pain. Hope. How do I create hope?

"Pakenham, I know that name," I mumble.

"Well I do write for the papers—"

"No," I shake my head. "That name is famous."

"Where?"

"In Ireland we never forget a good story, but we favor the oldest ones. We used to joke that we should erect a sign for visitors that reads, 'Welcome to Ireland, please set your watch back seven hundred years.'"

Pakenham titters at the jape, but I move in quickly, "General Edward Pakenham and his famous Pakenham Punch, now there's a story."

"Punch? There was a General Pakenham? Like he punched through armies on the battlefield?"

"Yes, but he lived in Ireland. He was a politician too, wealthy, to be sure. He came from a great family. The famed Pakenham-Mahon family."

Culkin interrupts, "Uhright kid, that's—"

"Hold on," Pakenham says.

Buy in. I need you to buy in so I can create hope. Hope is all I need.

Pakenham's head tilts in the darkness and he rubs two fingers along the V shape of his pointy chin.

"My family came here as far back as the Mayflower, I never heard of this Pakenham in Ireland."

Yes, now I have you. Hope in the form of story.

"Yes, Ireland. Yes, yes, great man. Famous. But he was not Irish, of course. He was English. A venerable colonist living on a gigantic plantation in County Roscommon. Gigantic, many Irish tenant farmers on his land paid rent. His sister even married the Duke of Wellington, very powerful. Very powerful. He fought in the Napoleonic Wars, but there is one thing he became even more famous for. Very famous. His punch."

The reporter looks at Patrolman Culkin, then turns to me and nods.

"It was the year 1815, just five months or so after the British burnt down the White House. He led the fight during the Battle of New Orleans, in the southern state of Louisiana. The Americans had constructed three lines of defense, but young General Edward Pakenham was on the verge of a great career. Only thirty-six years of age. So young still."

"That's how old I am."

I have you now.

"Are you? Maybe you will follow in his footsteps. Anyhow, the main attack would take place under darkness and fog, but almost as soon as they set out, the fog lifted and the sun came out. When they reached the canal under heavy fire, Pakenham's forces realized they forgot the ladder and fascines needed to cross."

"They forgot?" Pakenham lowers an eye.

"Forgot, yes. It's all a part of the heroic ending, I promise," I say. "It can't be heroic if it's easy. The next assault was repulsed by the Americans and much of the British infantry cowered in a ditch until every last one of them were massacred by grapeshot and musket fire. That was when General Pakenham rose to his occasion and lead the third and most powerful assault. But almost immediately he was wounded in the knee. Then, as he was being rushed off the field of action. . . he was shot in the heart while ahorse."

"In the heart?"

"Wait for it," I mumble, almost out of energy now. "Death need not prove fatal, see. General Edward Pakenham's body was then placed in a cask of rum and sent back to Ireland for a formal British military funeral."

"But—"

"But the dockloaders' in Cobh, Ireland. . . I mean Queenstown, Ireland. . . they saw the cask clearly marked with the name of the famous plantation family on it, crossed it out, and simply wrote 'Rum,' then sent it back to America. Well that cask went to a South Carolina tavern where its patrons pulled heartily from the tap and emptied the cask in less than an hour, until they realized it was. . . still heavy—"

"Where in the hell are you going with this story?"

"The men who drank the cask were shocked and disgusted. They dug a shallow grave and dumped the body in, and all promised never to drink again after pulling on that famous Pickled Pakenham Punch."

Pakenham turns to Patrolman Culkin, "He's evil. He is a villain. Only horrible people would tell a story like that."

"But it's true," I say. "True story."

Culkin steps forward, squeezing the leather of his blackjack, "Brosnan used to tell me all the stories that came outta Irishtown. Ghosts an' whiskey wars an'. . . Prophecies. I bet no one in Irishtown foresaw'r this in the storm or the mist. A public lynchin'. Lucky enough ya just turnt eighteen, ya're a man now. Ya're old enough to pay the price," he chuckles and spreads both hands around his own neck. "Choke to death. Outta all the ways to die, chokin's probably one o' the worst, what do ya think?"

I don't answer.

"Yeah maybe ya're right, kid. Maybe it'll go quick. I tell ya what though, ya Ma ain't gonna take it well. She'll prolly blame herself. I mean it was her that led us to ya, right? An' then there's that little business about. . ."

I blink. Then blink again and slowly turn my eyes to Culkin.

He goes on, "She told Father Larkin that Dinny Meehan wanted ya to kill Brosnan. But ya refused, right? So he had to have someone else do it. Or, he did it hisself. But if ya hang for it, I guess she'll feel bad about bringin' it up in the first place."

"You're lying."

"Am I? Maybe she's the one that's lyin' to try an' save ya. Pin on it Meehan. A mother'd do anythin' to save her own son. Includin' dumpin' the blame on someone else. I guess that means it's up to ya to tell me if Meehan killt Brosnan, or did he order someone else to do it?"

"Neither. . . as far as I know."

"Ya know nothin'?"

"Nothing."

"'Cause other guys seem to know a lot. Cute Charlie Red Donnelly's in the other room, see. He says it was ya'self did it. Even the little kids, Whyo an' Will say they overheard talk that Meehan told ya to do it an' ya did. Ya know what that means?"

I don't answer again, but my thoughts are running.

Red is weak. So are the kids. Vulnerable to Patrolman Culkin's blackjack logic. If they don't want the punishment, they would blame it on someone else. Whoever the police want them to blame it on.

"It means if ya admit to what others say ya did, ya will be hung tonight. But if ya tell who did do it, then ya Ma can see ya again. She's outside now. Ya wanna see her? She's kinda upset, by the way. Word seems to have gotten out that the scaffold is bein' raised for her baby boy. She didn' take that well. Neither did ya two sisters. I guess they really love ya. I have no fookin' idea why they'd love a murderer though. So let's do this. Let's go over it again."

Again? I didn't do it, that's all I know. But I would not go to my doom with an undaunted soul, like in the song. If they swing me from a scaffold, I would cry. I would not have the courage of a Fenian. The world would remember me as a man who cried for getting caught killing a cop.

When the blackjack goes in the air again, I thought it would come down on my head. Maybe a shoulder or a thigh. But no, the lead ball landed directly on my manhood.

"I told ya not to scream!" Culkin yells over me.

His eyes are filled with violence again. A joyful violence.

The scaffold will have the smell of newly cut wood. That slight burning smell of saw's teeth cutting through it. I'm sure they will have built a platform too, with the noose swaying in the breeze off the East River. The mist enveloping it in mystery. The darkness obscuring it from view.

"Ya wanna hang t'night?" He points out the barred window behind me. "It's all set up for someone. Ya heard them constructin' it."

The anchor of silence is sunk deep in me. I can't talk. But maybe I should tell him Dinny did it. That's all he wants. It would be easy.

Like a baseballer, he uses both hands to swing the blackjack again on both shins of my legs.

"I asked ya a question! Someone's gotta die for this!"

Tell him Dinny did it. That's all he wants. It's easy.

"Might as well be a worthless Irish teen in a violent gang that robs honest businesses, takes advantage o' the poor an' butchers policemen. Ya wanna die for it?"

Dinny might have done it, I don't know for sure. Wait, the letter. What happened to the letter that was in my new coat from "H"? I look up to Patrolman Culkin, *He must have read it. He knows that I know he did it. I am going to die.*

"What's so funny? I fookin' asked ya a question!" He rears back again in the black.

A bang comes to the door. As spittle flies through the window light, Patrolman Culkin freezes in place.

"Patrolman Culkin open this door!" An older man's voice. "Now!"

"Talk to Ferris," he yells back. "I told him to—"

"I have Ferris next to me," the voice responds. "Open the door, patrolman."

I slowly look up to the whites of Culkin's eyes in the darkness. *He's scared. I see fear.* Then he smiles again, coy and terrifying as he connects his blackjack to his belt.

When the electric light is flipped on, I close my eyes at the shock of it.

"My god," the older man's voice yells. "Look at the poor boy."

He shoulders out of his tunic and drapes it over my shivering body, "Are ya alive, son? Are ya alive? Say somethin'."

I lick my lips and clear my throat. The bright electric, unnatural light above buzzes. It's cutting shine forces me to squint as I look up to his red pistachio face and big white walrus mustache. He wears a police uniform too. On his chest is a badge.

Sullivan, it reads Sullivan. Captain Sullivan.

He touches my shoulder, "Say somethin' to let me know ya're ok."

"Are they going to hang me?"

"Who?" Captain Sullivan looks behind him, then turns back to me. "Son, what's ya name? Tell me ya name?"

"Patrick Kelly."

He then stands up and gives an order, "Put this young man back in his clothes. Untie him this very minute. Ya've had him alone for two days an' ya've gotten nowhere."

"We can't let him go, he's—"

"What are ya gonna charge him wit'?"

"Murder."

"Wit' evidence? Who named him? Who saw'r him?"

"He said it was Meehan."

"No," I whisper.

I'm so hungry, so cold.

"Son?" Captain Sullivan leans both hands on bow-legged knees and looks me in the eye as Patrolmen Ferris and Culkin mumble frantically. "Did ya do it? Did ya kill Detective Brosnan?"

"I'm bleeding."

"I understand, son. But this is important."

"I didn't. I didn't do it."

"Then answer me this. Choose one or the other, uhright?"

I nod.

"Did Dinny Meehan kill the detective? Or did Meehan *order* him killt?"

I turn an eye up to him, "I never heard that name before."

"Give this young man his new togs back," Captain Sullivan orders.

When finally my binds are loosened and I am free to go, my legs will not hold me and I fall to the wet floor with a slap.

I'll never be the same.

A Shadow Falls

Darby Leighton walks through a factory where teen girls and old women worry at their sewing machines. The floor-to-ceiling windows bring in plenty of light which means Darby cannot hide. A few of them turn from their work when they see something wash by. To avoid their notice he slips through a side stairwell and walks across a foot bridge that connects two buildings over an alley where below he can hear the rattle of garbage cans and the backfire of a combustion automobile engine.

Bill will kill me for this. I lost Sadie and I never found out who rode Anna. . . And the trial—

He flies across row house roofs, shifts through fourth-floor windows and emerges through another on the second floor, bends into coal holes in the sidewalk and roams through a diner kitchen unseen.

Wild Bill's voice bounces through his thoughts, "If ya don' get me both, I'll' let Petey Behan shoot ya in the back o' the head an' ya brains'll come out ya eye sockets an' ya nose an' mouth."

He pushes through a backdoor in a grocer where two cats nimbly skitter over alley puddles when they see a shadow stalk by. He strides sideways through narrow passages and shaded courtyards where two men secretly kiss, and he darts unheard behind five men unloading a freight car onto a storagehouse platform.

When he reaches the building that adjoins his own, he walks past the German woman again who folds clothes now, though her young son does not see him this time. He walks down the cement steps past the basement entrance, and up more cement steps where the door is still open.

Should I gather my family and lam out of Brooklyn forever? Or go to say my goodbyes to Ligeia and Colleen Rose before I tell Bill the truth?

He takes another stairwell up to the eighth floor and crawls out of a window and climbs the fire escape to the roof. He hops the five-foot brick wall and begins to descend down another fire escape as the sun bobbles at its zenith.

He pulls up the window to his room and enters.

"Darby?" He hears Ligeia say.

My god, I love my family so much. We have to run. That's it, we'll run.

"Gather everythin' that means somethin' to ya," he says sweeping up armloads of clothes from the nightstand.

"What? Darby what you do? Why you—"

"There's no time, my love—"

In the corner of his eye Darby notices movement by the bassinet and sees a small, gorgeous girl with a fox-colored crown of woven hair pinned up and falling in wisps down a long and elegant white neck. She holds the baby Colleen Rose close to her embroidered peasant blouse.

"Darby this is eh-Molly Maguire. She is my friend. She come here to sit for the baby, when we go to *ristorante*."

He stares at the smiling Colleen Rose, then up to Molly Maguire's face.

Anna? Anna Lonergan? Why is she holding my angel? And why does she lie about her name? Evil little cunt.

The words rise up in his throat, but in his mind different words are recalled, *the beauty of hidden love inside the heart of an evil little girl. It must be her, she is the red-haired girl in Abe's riddle, not Maureen Egan. It's Anna. Is she here for revenge? But for what? What have I ever done to Anna Lonergan?*

"I can't believe how beautyful this little doll is," Molly Maguire's smile is so genuine, so pretty that for a moment he doubts her knavery. "I'll be happy to help. Ya don' even gotta pay me, I just wanna be close to the baby," she turns confidently to Darby. "I grew up a only child, Mr. Leighton."

"She is eh-so sweet, Darby," Ligeia kisses Molly Maguire on the forehead and pulls her close, cheek to cheek. "I never know a girl with so many, eh, instinct is the word I look for to say? Yes, instinct for babies. She have eh-true instinct for babies."

"Almost like she came from a big fam'ly, right Molly?" Darby asks.

But Molly is all innocent smiles and gives a little virtuous tilt to her head, "Are ya two gonna go out that window? Or is there a door inside here somewhere?"

Darby doesn't answer, then motions to Ligeia, "I need to talk to Molly. I need to know more about her before we leave our baby with her."

Ligeia's eyes move from side to side, "I understand, my love. You are the man of the family and want to eh-protect us."

"Yeah," Darby turns to Molly. "Put the baby in her bassinet an' come wit' me."

Molly Maguire dutifully does as she is told as Darby holds the window open for her, then follows her out onto the fire escape.

"Whatta ya want?" He says through his teeth.

"Mr. Leighton? Ya assume I want somethin'? All I want is to help on account o' I love babies so much," her blue eyes have the gleam of fire in them. "Break any windows recently, Mr. Leighton?"

"Anna—"

"Oh an' I want to talk to Bill," she cuts in. "Ya *will* help me get to him. Or ya won't," she turns her eyes inside to Ligeia and Colleen Rose and looks back up to him with her bottom lip between her teeth.

Darby grabs her arm and their boots clammer on the metal platform outside the window.

"Be gentle wit' a girl, would ya?" Molly says until her innocence dies away. "My brother knows I'm here, so if anythin' should happen to me—" she nods toward the ground six floors below.

The memory of Richie Lonergan's pale blue eyes sends icy blades into Darby's heart. Those terrible, unsentimental gray-blue and see-through eyes.

The redhead then flashes a faultless smile and flutters her butterfly eyes, "Do not refuse me."

"Ya're the evil little girl that Abe told me about. Why not just have ya brother or father bring ya to Bill? Why me?"

"We all have a role," Anna smiles. "Now you have yours."

"Bill don' listen to me no more," Darby lowers his eyes. "I uh, I have failed him one too many times now."

"Then tell him what he wants to hear," Anna says with genuine concern in her voice. "But tell him it's a sign that ya saw'r, like a vision. Bill thinks ya're a, I dunno, a seer or a druid or somethin'."

"What he wants is ya'self, Anna. He has me askin' around everywhere about ya. He wants to know who bedded ya so he can kill that man, whoever it is."

Anna blinks and moves closer, "An' now ya have found the truth. Ya saw'r it."

"What did I see?"

"Ya had a vision that I still have my purity. Ya saw'r it in the shape o' leaves swayin' in a tree maybe?" Anna comes closer. "Listen, Bill's war mad an' Abe says Bill claims he can read the future by watchin' the murmurations o' bird flocks take wing."

"What?"

"He devotes hours to the practice. An' that ain't all. One o' his Shit Hounds came up lame so he plunged a knife into its chest and observed how it convulsed. He studied the pattern o' blood that came out and stared into its eyes to see the future as its life slowly extinguished."

Since when does Anna Longeran use words like observe and convulse and extinguish?

She continues, "He believes he is fated. An' ya'self? Bill trusts ya, Darby. He says ya see wit' eyes an' speak no lies."

Darby's honored eyes float with tears, "He said that about me?"

"Sure he did."

"So why would I work wit' ya," Darby suddenly says. "We're opposites. Like contradictions, ya an' I. We got nothin' in common but Bill. Why should I trust ya?"

"Opposites make movement. Contradictions cause sparks," Anna tosses her hand at the wrist. "An' besides we have one very important thing in common."

"What's that?" Darby's voice is colored with doubt.

"Fam'ly. We both got a fam'ly we need to provide for. So tell Bill I have been seen wit' them slatterns 'cause I'm tryin' to win him income, like I told him already. Grace an' Kit? They're sittin' on gold mines, see? Sixto Stabile's biggest earners down at that bawdyhouse on Fourth Avenue, the Adonis."

"Bill ain't no pimp," Darby's voice is glum and hopeless.

"Strange line for a drug dealer to refuse crossin'."

"Bill ain't no drug dealer either."

Anna looks at him distrustfully, "Ya really don' know, do ya?"

"Wha?"

"Abe got Needles Ferry to switch sides. Now he walks around Red Hook wit' a detail o' Bill's Trench Rabbits. Needles gave out one free taste o' the marchin' dust an' one hit o' the boiled tar to everyone down there. He's even got access to true morphine for the injured vet'rans. Now they got a income besides labor tribute."

"Abe is a sneaky bastard," Darby mumbles.

"Abe has a knack for tossin' up a dime in the air an' catchin' twenny cents. He knows how to make himself valuable. He even got information about Thos Carmody's boss that helped bring the union to Bill's side."

"What information? About the president o' the ILA bein' in Wolcott's pocket? I'm the one that saw'r O'Connor on the back o' the tug at the Union Street dock."

Anna shrugs, "Bill only wants ya to have value, see? An' he only wants to hear what he wants to hear, get it? That's his weakness."

"His weakness?" Darby repeats as if he had thought of Bill as infallible all along. "What do ya know about his weaknesses?"

Anna swallows and bites back the words that had come to her mouth, then looks up to him, "Durin' the trial back in 1913, were ya there?"

"Sure I was. I watched my brother get convicted o' somethin' he didn' do."

"Do ya know who the main witness was?"

"Uh, I don' really remember—"

"It was Grace White, ya fuckwit."

"It was?"

"Yeah, it was. Now listen, ya go to Bill an' ya tell him that I'm pure an' that ya gonna make Grace tell the truth this time in court, that Vincent killt Christie the Larrikin."

"That is—"

"Valuable," Anna finishes his sentence. "Ya tell him that he needs to provide her protection because Vincent an' The Swede are bullin' her again, that way—"

"We can make sure she can help right the lie," Darby realizes.

"An' ya come across as able as Abe."

"A white birch tree," Darby blurts when an idea comes to him.

"Wha?"

"I heard Bill talkin' about how they left him to die in the forest by a bunch o' birch trees, if we tell him I was shown a sign from a white birch tree, he might believe it. My aunt Rose used to tell me about how they had the power to purify an' to start the fires o' Beltane."

"What's Beltane?"

"A Celtic festival to mark the beginnin' o' summer. Bill thinks he's been reborn as a Celtic king."

"Now ya're gettin' it," Anna encourages.

"An' they protect from evil spirits. But is it true?" Darby asks. "Are ya still pure?"

"Yes, of course it's true. I'm just a girl an' I'm not sure what I want," Anna bites her lip again, red and moist in Darby's eyes.

It's not true, Darby's head hurts and he places a palm over one side of his forehead. *It's a lie, she is not a virgin. I know a lie when I see one. Everything I am fighting for is to right a lie, but is it wrong to accept another lie in order to right the lie that has defamed my family? Yes, it has to be, otherwise—*

He looks back to Anna Lonergan to test her reserve, "This is dangerous, Anna. If ya not one o' Bill's followers, then ya his enemy. If ya get caught lyin', he'll. . . Ya only gotta look at Mickey Kane to know what Bill does to his enemies."

Anna swallows again and turns her eyes down and away from him.

"I seen what he done to ya already. If he punches a woman, he'll kill one too. Don' do this, Anna. It's not right. Why does Abe say ya want revenge? He told me that there is power in numbers, but a red-haired girl's revenge is even more powerful. What do ya want revenge for?"

Anna blushes and her eyes begin to blink quickly as she looks down and away from him again.

When she doesn't answer him, Darby says, "Secret. There's a secret that's burnin' inside o' ya, ain't there?

Anna turns on him, "Ya're the one's gotta be careful, understand? Abe knows everythin'."

"Knowin' things is what *I'm* known for."

"Abe knows more than you."

"Yeah well, there's one thing he don' know. An' he keeps askin' me about it."

"Yes," Anna agrees. "Sadie's secret. What is it?"

I'll never tell. Not you. Not Bill, no one. I don't care if it burns me from the inside, I'll die with Sadie's secret.

While Darby's thoughts spin and twist and spiral, he doesn't hear a single thing Anna tells him. When he looks back at her, she suddenly stops talking, smiles and turns her attention inside the window again. "Be very careful, Darby. A baby doesn't earn its wings until after it becomes a angel."

What choice do I have? My brain is fakakta. I can't do this alone. I need help.

In the far-off Darby hears the distant tinkle of a trolley bell down below, but an elevated train clicks and clacks and overtakes it.

"One last thing," Anna says, "Ya know that Abe handles all the gang's income? The thing is, Abe knew about a week ago that the trial was gonna be postponed."

"No he—"

Anna holds up her hand, "It's true Darby, Abe's had someone followin' ya all along. Put the devil on horseback an' he'll ride to hell, he says. Put a shadow on the shadow an' the darkness takes shape. How do ya think I knew where to find ya?"

"Does he know Ligeia is. . . I-Talian?"

"Course he does."

"Does Bill?"

Anna slowly lowers her face to stare deep into Darby's eyes, "No, Bill does not know. . . Yet."

"Bill can't know that, he—" Darby thinks of the right way to say what is on his mind, licks his lips and turns back to her. "If Abe gets too influential, we might have to do somethin' about that."

Anna measures her own words, "Maybe. Until then, consider this Abe's peace offerin'," Anna reaches into her peasant blouse and hands Darby a wad of money, "It's two hundret an' fifty dollars. Go to Dead Reilly an' pay the retainer, then go to Bill. An' when ya get back, take this poor woman out an' buy her a dress."

Darby holds the money while still trying to understand everything she just said, then notices Anna has extended her hand toward him.

"A pact," she offers. "Abe, ya'self an' I will get Bill atop Irishtown by hook or by crook. An' when we do, the king's court will already be established."

Darby shakes her small hand.

Anna then opens the window and bends down, "Then we gotta get to work an' start earnin' money. Ya can't live in this shithole wit' a new baby, what's wrong wit' ya?"

"But what about the fight? Bill can't beat Dinny, one-on-one."

Anna slowly closes the window, "The mole in Bill's ear whispers to him."

The Rusted Badge

Daniel finds his wife on the parlor floor of their Navy Street room. The same room that had been her home all her life. Since the very day she was born, which was the day her mother died. Doirean cries and bawls, flailing on the floor of the home where her father William Brosnan raised her as best he could.

"Doirean, ya gotta get up now," he stands over her with Little Billie Bear in his arms dressed in funeral black but for the white shirt and starched paper collar. "Everyone's waitin' outside."

"Where paw-paw?" The boy asks scratching his upper lip with a fingernail. "Where grandpaw-paw?"

"Ah god please, why, why, *whyyyyy*?" Doirean bawls out when she hears her son, who was named for her father. "Daddy, daddy, what happened to ya? Why did this happen to ya daddy?"

Her face is pressed against the wood floor of the parlor, arms sprawled out. She can't lay straight on her belly because it is full with child, so she is slightly askew. She had pinned her long hair earlier, but it is now peeling off and cascades down her neck like the skin of an onion bulb.

Daniel feels a stab of guilt, *I shouldn't have done this. What have I done? This is what I get for being greedy. I have to control her. I have to take control so that she never figures this out. Nobody can ever know.*

"Doirean?" he lowers his voice to restrain himself. "They're waitin' for us outside, we gotta go, sweetheart. Stand up now."

"Mommy," the little one whines and leans down toward his mother with grabby fingers, but Daniel catches him.

"Where's Johanna?" Doirean cries as spittle bursts out of her mouth.

Johanna Walsh had come from St. Ann's and spent countless hours with Doirean washing dishes, changing diapers and keeping the room clean.

It's probably better that she is gone now, my wife needs to get back on her feet. That Walsh woman made her lazy.

"My only friend in the world. I need her t'day. I need her."

Daniel rolls his eyes, the left one is still sore where he had been punched by the ghost of the madman who blew in with the fire and razed the saloon on Hoyt Street to ash and cinders.

Patrolman Ferris had told him that when all the other tunics saw him dazed and wandering from the saloon fire, it had triggered something inside them all, at once. Empathy, for there is nothing stronger than the brotherhood of men in blue when one of their own is wounded by the loss of a family member, his father-in-law, Detective William Brosnan. They had surrounded and protected him as if he were a soldier who'd fallen in battle, and moved him out of harms way.

I need to harness that feeling of brotherhood, and ride it all the way to my captaincy, Daniel thinks. *But Ferris had followed me. Ferris knows too much.*

"Doirean, c'mon. Ya gotta get off the floor. We gotta go now. They're waitin'."

She moans. Louder now than before. Daniel walks to the window with Billie in his arms and looks outside to the people who have shown for the procession from the Navy

Street tenement to St. Ann's Roman Catholic Church. He opens the window for all to hear his wife's crying.

That will keep my battle brothers thinking right.

Doe almost made it without issue. She was strong all morning. Upbeat even. Or at least strong and upbeat for the childrens' sake. She told them they were going to have a good day. A wonderful day. A day to remember grandpaw-paw. She washed and pinned her hair and applied makeup with a steady hand in the soft red, almost pink lipstick that favored the colors of her skin.

Her belt didn't fit though. It didn't have a hole wide enough for her belly. How many pregnant women need a black funeral gown? You would think there'd be more with the great grippe still taking so many children in New York. It was the belt that sent her into a spiral. She threw her eyebrow pencil against the mirror when she looked at the dress hanging like a sack round her body. Daniel grabbed the scissors to put a new hole in the belt, but by the time he finished she was on the floor and everything on the table had been cleared off with a wash of her arm in a fit of despair.

Daniel's tongue wheedles in the strange hole in his mouth where a tooth was knocked out. It's no surprise to him that Doirean had fallen apart. He knew it was coming, yet still it irritates him.

He takes a deep breath and puts Billie on the ground next to her, "Doirean," Daniel's voice is now edged with urgency.

She quickly turns her head from the floor and finds his eyes.

There it is, that look she always gives me. That look of hatred. She hates me and she doesn't even know the whole of it. She hates me just for being alive. It's not my fault. That's alright, she doesn't need to love me. She just needs to obey me.

"Get up," he tells her.

"What is wrong wit' ya!" she screams and pulls herself up from the floor with a flat fist over her head. "I'll put a clout on ya that'll make ya a hospital case."

"Ya don' wanna do that," he says.

But maybe if I allow her to strike me, I can get control of the situation by way of shaming her.

"Mommy," Billie cries again, his big brother stands next to him now with a finger up his nose.

Doirean collapses in tears on the new sofa Daniel had delivered a few months past.

She better not get eye makeup on the fabric, he grits.

The sofa was bought with the money Wolcott had given him on the tug on Union Street when he decided to join the Waterfront Assembly's cause. A small fortune, it cost. The fabric alone was more than one hundred dollars, but made his wife blush giddy when she noticed the green and purple detailed design of Scottish thistle damask. The oak arms and legs are stained with a deep red lacquer that borders round the back of the frame as well, details she adores.

Daniel watches with a lowered eye as Doirean writhes on it, *She could land a job on Broadway with them dramatic overtures.*

"Tell me what happened to my father," she sniffles, then turns her doe eyes at him.

"I'm still investigatin' it—"

"Ya've been investigatin' it for mont's, what have ya found? Anythin'? Or are yaz so useless that even for one o' ya own ya—"

"That's enough," Daniel interrupts.

"That's enough?"

"Yeah, enough. Ya know I won't suffer no foolery."

"Ya mother did."

Daniel wraps a palm round the handle of the blackjack on his tunic belt in warning.

Doirean says, "From soup to nuts, ya're all class, aren't ya?"

"Ya're scarin' the kids."

"They oughta be scared," her lips fold back in fury. "Scared o' their father!"

"What would the kids need to be scared o' me for?"

"Instead o' bein' an example for them, ya're a damned warnin'. Why were ya out durin' the storm, did ya know my father went out in the snow lookin' for ya? Where were ya?"

"I was workin'."

"Where? Wit' who? Ya shift had already ended by then."

"Not ya concern, Doirean," Daniel looks at Little Billie's eyes to see if the boy can tell he is being mean to his mother. The boy has cold, untrusting eyes sometimes. Just like his mother.

"It *is* my concern, goddamn ya," she says.

"Don' use the lord's name in vain—"

"What do ya care about the lord, ya never go to Mass wit' us?"

"Doirean, we can't make them wait much longer—"

"I don' care about makin' people wait!" She screams. "They can wait all day."

"If ya don' get movin' soon, I'm gonna have to bring in Captain Sullivan."

"Why, is he gonna arrest me?"

No, I'm going to let you shower him with tears so I can control his next move, and yours, Daniel stifles a smile and walks to the door. Outside his partner Patrolman Ferris is waiting in the small hallway by the stairwell. Daniel opens the door and whispers, "Bring in Sully."

As Daniel closes the door, descending footsteps can be heard.

Oh this is going to be fun to watch Doirean run him through the cheese grater like she does me.

"Is he really gonna come up an' talk to me?" Doirean reaches for her purse and pulls out a compact to look and see if her eye makeup is running. She swabs her face with powder and blows her nose.

A knock comes to the door.

"I get it," Billie says with a happy tone, the way he had heard his mother so often say.

"No, I'll get it," Daniel pushes the child by the side of the head and walks by him.

Patrolman Ferris takes his police cap off as he enters and gives a little bow, avoiding eye contact with Doirean. Captain Sullivan struggles up the last steps in the hallway. The old man's face is red. He heaves and leans on the bannister, huffing and puffing through his big white mustache. When he sees the door is open and all are watching him, he shoulders past Ferris and embraces Daniel with a powerful hug. A head shorter than Sullivan, Daniel's face is mashed against the captain's copper badge.

"I'm so sorry, son," his voice cracks. "I'm so, so sorry for ya loss. He was a good man that Brosnan—"

No wonder your Captain, you know how to lie.

Daniel blinks his eyes as the old captain offers lavish praise for Brosnan, "The ol' Dubliner was a great joy to work wit' down at the Poplar Street Station. An altruistic man who stayed loyal to the duties hoisted upon him to keep the world in order. . ."

Brosnan was never so heroic. Never so beloved. He lives in the realm of the divine now, Daniel does all he can to avoid rolling his eyes at the old bow-legged captain.

"Did ya know that durin' his rookie year we had the Great Blizzard o' 1888? That was when—"

"Uhright," Daniel interrupts him and moves to the side. "Why don' ya give her a try, Sully."

Captain Sullivan lowers his eyes at Daniel, pushes the tears from them and wobbles toward Doirean, then promptly sits his considerable rump on the new coffee table that Daniel had delivered with the sofa. The salesman said the Art Nouveau table matched perfectly with the sofa and both came from a Belgian designer. He described the carved curves in the oak as "vigorous, yet as feminine as a flower."

Just like my wife, Daniel thinks.

"What's goin' on outside?" He whispers to Ferris. "Commissioner an' mayor are really here?"

"Yeah, we're just waitin'. We can wait all day, don' matter to us, ya know?"

Daniel looks back toward Doirean and Captain Sullivan and talks out of the side of his mouth to his partner, "I know ya've been followin' me. I know what ya've seen."

"What?"

"Keep playin' stupit, Ferris. Ya walrus mustachioed father-in-law over there is on the tug too. So are you. I know yaz suspect me, but ya're wrong. An' if yaz try to throw me out into the water, yaz both'll drown wit' me," he turns and finds Ferris's eyes. "Wolcott will make sure o' that, see?"

Ferris purses his lips and stares straight forward, wordless.

"Wolcott's got a new gimmick. Now that Lovett's gang is makin' dime hand over fist an' Meehan's men are switchin' sides."

And Brosnan's body resurfacing is phase one, of three.

"We're callin' it Operation Grey's Faith. So keep playin' stupit, Ferris. I don' mind. Just stay that way."

Daniel turns back to Doirean and Captain Sullivan who are exchanging words, "Look at her. She's so fookin' selfish. The both o' them. Look at him rubbin' his haunches all over my furniture like the itchy end of a dog."

The look that Ferris gives him causes Daniel to do a double take. But Ferris keeps his eyes averted in supplication.

Captain Sullivan's nose has the likeness of a blossomed mushroom, bulbous and scarlet red and lined with blue veins. His white wisps of hair encircle the ring on the back of his bald head and his legs are so severely bowed that he appears to be in a constant state of defecation.

The captain reaches into a tunic pocket and produces a folded kerchief and slowly hands it to Doirean, "I thought ya might like to have this for keepsake, Mrs. Culkin."

She holds the kerchief in both hands, chin quivering. She peels the white layers open to reveal a blueish-green metallic object in the shape of a shield.

"Eh. . . it's discolored from the saltwater," Sullivan points at it with a pinky as if it were a collectible artifact.

"The salt water?" Doirean wonders, until the realization comes across her face that her father's body had been fished out of the East River off Union Street. Her hands begin to shake as if any hopes she may have reserved that her father might still be alive were extinguished with the proof of Detective William Brosnan's badge presented to her.

It should have been given to me first, Daniel squints at the charade acted out in his parlor. *I will take away your ability to maneuver around me, old man. I swear I will take everything you have.*

"He swore to protect an' serve," Sullivan says in a proud, but lowered tone. "To respect the dignity o' civilians an' render his services in the engagement o' law wit' courtesy, civility. An' in my opinion, an' in the opinion o' all our colleagues on the force, he succeeded in doin' just that, Mrs. Culkin. He did his time wit' great honor, now may he rest."

Doirean heaves and sobs through a deep breath, but her soft eyes darken and grow severe when she turns them back up to the captain, "Who killt my father? Tell me. Who killt him!"

"Now sweet thing—" the old fellow begins.

"Don' start wit' that *sweet thing* horse shit, ya're the captain around here, ya know everythin' about this case. Tell me, or get ya fat arse off o' my new furniture."

Daniel snorts when Captain Sullivan pushes himself up from the coffee table and runs his fingers round the edges of his cap like a shamed five year-old.

"Ya're are all the same, men, yaz only try to do the right thing when all else fails," Doirean disparages the red-nosed captain. "So why did ya have my husband out runnin' around in the snow after his shift durin' that storm last February?"

Daniel's hands clinch inside his tunic pockets, *Why can't she just be more timid? I have no idea why old Brosnan called her doe, her temperament is as wicked as a wolverine's.*

"Daddy?" Little Billie pulls on Daniel's trouser leg.

"Go lay down," he shoos the boy off.

"Mrs. Culkin—" Sullivan begins.

"Don' call me that," Doirean snaps.

"Don' call ya Mrs. Culkin? Well then, what—"

"I'm a Brosnan an' dignity is the strength we hold in our name," Doriean points a finger at each and every man in the room. "If all policemen in New York kept the Brosnan words, there wouldn't be so much corruption an' crime —"

"Now hold on—"

"I asked my father one time how many men worked on the force in Brooklyn, ya know what he said? He said 'about half.'"

Ferris snorts at that one.

"Laugh it up, why not? All o' yaz. I'm just a woman who has to work twice as hard to be considered half as good, but I want yaz all to know that I'll find out what happened to my father. On my own! *Then* yaz can fight amongst ya'-selves to take the credit."

"I won't have this in my house," Daniel bellows. "We're married. Ya're a Culkin, ya said the words."

"I'll tell ya some more words—"

"Ya keep talkin' an' ya—"

"An' what? Ya gonna hit me again?" She turns wickedly toward Captain Sullivan. "Tell me why there is a house up in Peekskill in my father's name."

Daniel cuts in, "Maybe he had a woman on the side, ya know? He was a lonely ol' fella."

"Ya fookin' lie—"

"Stop cursin' like that in front o' the kids—"

Captain Sullivan cuts in loudest of all, "I can assure ya Mrs. Cul. . . Ms. Brosnan, ya may have an eye for detail, but it takes courageous men—"

"Tell me this then!" Doirean screams over him. "Why does my husband come home wit' a dotted eye? Why was there a fire in that saloon he was in? Why was he even in that buildin'? It's not even his jurisdiction!"

Captain Sullivan turns a stern face round to Daniel, but lowers his voice, "Ya husband was on some. . . reconnaissance mission."

"Was it ya'self that sent him down on Hoyt Street?"

Captain Sullivan bites his lip and stands upright, "I. . . I cannot say—"

"No one can say nothin' around here, ya're as bad as the gangs an' their codes o' silence. My own husband looks at me as if I'm a stranger. I'm all alone in this world now. All I have are my children."

"Stop wit' the self-pity," Daniel is surprised by the words that he lets slip.

"Ya couldn't even protect him," Doirean points at Daniel. "He was old an' helpless an' ya just let him fall prey to... to... what? I don' even know what."

Daniel grits his teeth, *She thinks she's in charge. Time to put an end to it.*

"Cap? Ferris?" Daniel says while staring at his wife. "Do us a favor an' take Little Billie an' his brother downstairs."

Captain Sullivan straightens his tunic, "I'll have a word wit' ya first, son," and wobbles to the door.

Daniel watches Ferris's face as he walks by, then stops to stare at his wife before reluctantly following the captain.

In the narrow hallway, Sullivan towers over Daniel as they stand in the dark, "Ya gotta light for that lantern?"

"Nah, I don' know how it works."

"Ya don' know how... Ah never mind then," Sullivan points a finger in Daniel's face. "Do ya know who's down there waitin' right now as we speak? Police Commissioner Enright an' Mayor Hylan—"

"Do they have retirement papers ready for ya to sign?"

"My retirement? My retirement's none o' ya goddamn business. Don' wave a red rag at me, ya're nothin' but a patrolman, Culkin. The cart don' go before the horse, ya're a private in the army o' the law. A grunt. Ya'd be smart to remember that. No, Enright an' Hylan want to turn Brosnan's death into somethin' good, but they don' know what to tell the papers."

"Why not run it through the reporter on our payroll? Like Pakenham? He can spin it for ya."

"What? Whose payroll? We don' have reporters on payroll."

"Ya know what I'm talkin' about."

Sullivan wipes sweat from his face and takes a deep breath. "Is there somethin' about Brosnan I need to know?"

"Like what?"

"Like why does his daughter suspect her husband has somethin' to do wit' his death?"

Culkin's fists curl up again, "She's a stupit woman, don' listen to her. She's outta her skull right now wit' grief. She's just lashin' out, ya know how they can be."

"What was ya doin' in that goddamn Hoyt Street saloon?"

"I told ya, I was on reconnaissance."

"For what? What exactly were ya reconnoiterin'?"

"I got a tip that maybe the White Hand G—"

"Liar," Sullivan grabs Daniel by the throat and backs him against the wall.

Oh god, Daniel feels Sullivan's big hands round his neck. *Oh god that feels good. Choke me. Choke me, I give in.*

"If ya wasn't buryin' ya father-in-law t'day, I'd beat the truth outta ya. But that will have to wait."

Beat me, beat me, do it, Daniel smiles and is forced to talk through his teeth. "I was proved right too, Dinny Meehan blew in an'—"

"Ya said it was Harry Reynolds at first. An' just so ya understand, ya're the only one who identifies Reynolds, or Meehan or whoever it was."

"Well it couldn't've been Reynolds that burnt down the Hoyt Street Headquarters, he's dead I heard. So it must've been Meehan. There was a fire an' I couldn't see straight."

"Headquarters? Headquarters o' what? Whose headquarters?"

Shit, I shouldn't have said that.

"Nothin'," Daniel mouths self-consciously.

Captain Sullivan lets him go, turns on his heel and lowers himself down the first steep step with one hand on the bannister and the other on the wall, "An' what about that house he bought upstate? If I was ya I'd try an' live up to my namesake an' pull a Daniel-come-to-judgment. Take the transfer to Peekskill before I open an inquiry into Brosnan's death. Then ya will have the devil to pay."

"That's not gonna happen. I ain't movin' upstate."

"Ya better, otherwise I have a feelin' that when my new investigator starts diggin' up evidence, he's gonna unearth somethin' that will shock all o' New York. Now I don' want that to happen as much as ya do. But if ya refuse me, I'll push it through."

"Captain Sullivan," Daniel calls down the stairwell confidently.

The old captain breathes heavily and turns round to look up.

"If ya open that inquiry, I'll have Wolcott send a man to murder ya an' Ferris. Then we'll release information through the newspapers, who are in our pocket, that the both o' yaz have been on the tug wit' the gangs for decades. Which is true, o' course. Then, finally, I'll come into my captaincy," Daniel turns round. "See ya outside. Tell the commissioner an' the mayor I'll be out wit' my little Doe soon."

I will take what you have, old man. Daniel thinks as he rubs at his neck and smiles. *I thought he was going to choke me to death. Now I feel better.*

When Daniel walks in, Doirean does not bother to move her eyes up. She sits on the new sofa with perfect posture as if to accept Communion in the hand. But instead of the bread of Christ, it is her father's rusted badge she holds in her palms.

Daniel wipes his tunic down and opens the door, "Ferris?"

"Yeah?"

"Take the kids downstairs, I need a moment alone wit' my wife."

Ferris turns back to him for a stare that Daniel could not misread.

He doesn't like me telling him what to do, but he better get used to it. We may be partners, but he'll soon be reporting to me.

Reluctantly, Ferris takes the boys by the hand. Little Billie Bear quickly yawns, nestles into Ferris's chest and puts his thumb in his mouth. On the way out the boy's lethargic eyes lock with Daniel's for a moment.

Don't stare at me like that. One day you will understand what it takes. If you don't win, you lose. If you lose, you stay weak and vulnerable your whole life.

The door closes and Daniel moves toward Doirean on the sofa, "Ya fookin' kiddin' me wit' all this drama? All this over a old man? Ya said ya'self he was helpless."

"That means ya were supposed to help him!" Doirean shakes her head back and forth with a hand on her forehead.

"Nah, it means he can't help hisself. He wasn't no charity case."

"He didn't think he needin' help, o' course. But he really did, an' ya couldn't even notice it. Ya only worry about ya'self instead. Just like ya can't even notice I need help now. . . " her words trail off into little pouts.

"Tears," Daniel turns his back. "A woman's weapon—"

"I'm not attackin' ya, Daniel."

"Sure seems like it."

"My point exactly," her head is lowered with a middle finger held between her eyes.

"Ya want the last word, g'ahead. I'll just stand here quiet like a fool so ya can turn the knife in my side. G'ahead."

Doirean sits up on the sofa and wipes tears away. She smooths the wrinkles on her black dress and exhales slowly.

"C'mon, we gotta go downstairs now," he says.

"Daniel," her eyes are closed as he tries handing her the black veil and black hat she persists on wearing, even though she's not a widow.

"What?"

"I just wanna know what happened to my daddy."

Shame pulses through him and raises goose pimples on the back of his neck.

"Ya father. . . He thought he was cursed or somethin', I dunno."

"What are ya talkin'—" Doirean catches herself and changes her tone.

He looks into her eyes, "He was worried about ya. Always worried about ya, Doirean. Ya were all he ever thought about. Everythin' he did, he did it for ya."

Doirean's chin quivers.

"He had some strange notion that if he. . . If he died it would give ya life. He went out after the storm to help me but—"

"But what?" Doirean puts a hand on his.

No, don't say it. Don't admit to anything. I need to find someone who will hurt me for what I did. Then I'll feel better.

Daniel grits his teeth in anger, "It was the gangs that did it to him."

"Ya're sure?"

"Yes."

What was it that Wolcott had said? Let the gangs fight for control over the headquarters in Irishtown, while from above divine providence will reign fire down on them all.

He wheels round to his wife, "I'm so sorry sweetheart. The gangs were after him for years. Dinny Meehan and Bill Lovett. They might be fightin' amongst each other, but they wanted him dead because. . . because he was such a good detective."

Doirean's eyes move from left to right, "So is Captain Sullivan gonna have them arrested? At least questioned?"

"He has us manacled until we can prove probable cause. Maybe ya can talk to him?"

"Yeah, yeah," Doirean nods doubtfully. "I'll talk to him."

She doesn't believe me. She doesn't have to. She just has to do what she's told.

"We should get goin'," Daniel stands.

I've been very bad. I don't deserve to be loved. I deserve to be punished.

Doirean flashes a false smile, "Ya're right. We should get goin'."

Daniel pulls her black coat off the coatrack by the door and holds it as she gently puts an arm through. He helps her put the black veil over her head that is connected to the black hat.

She'll be wearin' this hat again soon if I don't win, Daniel tells himself. He opens the door for her, "Ya look beautyful, my little Doe."

"Thanks," she whispers unconvincingly and walks down the dark, narrow stairwell.

Downstairs Daniel hears his wife gasp when she moves outside the tenement foyer. He opens the door to see what it is. Together they stand atop the outside stairwell as a thousand men in police blue take off their hats in unison while black-clad wives and children offer the same respect. Sad-eyed men. Angry-eyed, burly men. With vengeance on their tight-lipped faces, the men in tunics have overwhelmed the street by their numbers. Along the sidewalks across the street they honor the Brosnan-Culkin family with their bolt-upright stance. They have taken to standing upon the Navy Yard wall across the street too, as behind them looms a coal silo and a twenty-foot pile of coal ash with the Medieval plinths and turrets of the Navy Yard gatehouse to their right. A dry-docked warship reaches over the rooftops of the machine and blacksmith shops and high above them all are gigantic smokestacks that issue smoldering black plumes into the overcast sky.

And there it is: Phase two. Daniel looks across the mass of tunics. *My standing army. Ready to fight for me. Ready to reign fire.*

Family First

The last thing I remember was in the ambulance car. I pulled back a curtain. It was nighttime and very dark on Poplar Street but for the bulbs of gas flames in the street lamps. My mother and sisters were not there waiting outside for me.

"Liam are ya alive?" Suddenly Beat McGarry came over to me when he saw that it was me in the back of the Model-T ambulance behind the Poplar Street Police Station.

"Step away, sir," the driver warned him.

"Beat, where's the scaffold?" I ask.

"What scaffold?" Beat's left eyebrow raises and his head slants sideways to show his confusion.

"The scaffold made of pine from the Navy Yard. The one they want to hang me from."

"No one's gonna hang ya, kid," He licked his thumb and reached into the back of the ambulance to rub it across my face. When he pulled it back, his finger had turned a rust color. "Where'd ya get that fancy suit? There's blood all over it. Is that ya own blood? What did they do to ya?"

"Step away from the car, old man," the driver warned again. "Don' make me drop ya. He did this to hisself."

Behind Beat, out in the street I saw the slew of people that had come to see me hang. Twenty, maybe thirty tunics kept them up on the sidewalk with their arms outstretched.

Made even longer by their blackjacks at the end of their hands.

Beat yells into the back of the motorcar one last time, "Are ya uhright, kid?"

"Tell Red and Whyo and Will that I don't hold it against them. Tell them. They'll know what I'm talking about."

But Beat just looks at me with a quizzical stare as the back of the ambulance is closed.

"Get better soon!" I hear him yell.

They must have moved the scaffold, I thought as the motorcar began to move. *It was there, I know it was. I heard them erecting it. I pictured it. It existed like an itch on a phantom limb. A voice in the head. It loomed in the mist and the enveloping darkness. The platform and the swaying noose.*

~~~

My eyes open. I blink twice and jump up to fill air into my lungs.

"Liam, it's ok."

I turn to meet my sister's voice, "Abby?"

"Mam an' Brigid just went out. They just went—"

"Where am I?"

"Long Island College Hospital, near the Atlantic Terminal."

"I know where it is," says I, collapsing back into the pillows.

I lift my bandaged hands and all of a sudden my body's pain comes rushing up to my brain. Wincing, I pull the covers over my eyes to block the bright light coming through the long windows behind me.

"I'll close them," Abby says until much of the light is blocked.

The room is like a dorm. It is not the same room I stayed in when I contracted the grippe last year, but is similar. Nine people fill the twelve beds in the dorm. Some have no family whatsoever at their side.

"Liam, what happened to ye? Ye told us ye were goin' Confession, but the police said ye ran from them. Why, Liam? Who did this to ye?"

"Is Mam upset?"

"O' course she is. But she doesn't know what happened to ye. The patrolman said it might've been one of Lovett's men that did this to ye. Or maybe an Italian?"

"Patrolman Culkin said that?"

"That's him."

That son of a bitch spoke to my mother? I'm in so deep now that I can't escape, even if I wanted to.

The swaying noose comes to my mind again and I have to shake it off to get it out.

That wasn't real, I tell myself. *It wasn't real. It was just my imagination. But what do I do now? Go back to the gang, or leave?*

I toss the sheets off me, "I can't stay here."

"Liam!" Her voice turns all eyes toward us.

"I'm yer fam'ly, Liam. Just because I'm a girl doesn't mean ye have to keep everythin' a secret from me too. I understand why ye don't want Mam to know all, but I. . . I miss ye. The way we used to be in Ireland, as kids. Sure ye was treated differently because ye're a boy, but I'm only one year younger than ye," She comes closer and sits over me. "Remember when we used to play in the fields together an' we'd always team up against Brigid? Remember it?"

A long sigh comes to me as I slowly ease back onto the bed, "Of course I do. She always got so mad when we hid from her together. She'd say—"

"I can't wait to watch Da massacre ye when they find me dead," Abby finishes.

I can't stifle the smile on my mug, "How exactly was she going to watch if she's dead?"

Abby shrugs with smiling eyes.

For a moment we sit there in silence to look at each other. Then look away. Then back again.

Abby reaches for my arm, "Liam, ye've done so much fer us. But ye've changed. Ever since ye left fer New York it's like I don't even know who ye are. I know the look on men's faces when they don't love their fam'ly, but ye don't have that, Liam. Ye've got the love on yer face all the time, but it's tortured now. Ye always seem so tortured."

You don't even know the half of it, I look down at the blue and black bruises from Culkin's blackjack.

"Liam tell me somethin'. Anythin'. I won't repeat it. I promise. I know the code o' silence."

I turn to her when I hear those words. Then clear my throat, "Do you like your schooling?"

"At P.S. Five? I s'pose so."

"I want you to grow up to have a bigger understanding of things. I'm sure the teachers are droll and the lessons are boring, but you will have a broader perspective than I ever will be able to know."

"Because ye couldn't go to get schoolin' yerself," Abby looks down in shame.

"It's not a bad thing if it's what I want. Mam says the future of our family is with its women. And I believe her."

"Liam, she was just tryin' to get yer attention when she said that."

"It worked."

Abby sighs in frustration, "When did ye get so cold, Liam?"

"Cold?"

"I spent my entire childhood watchin' ye. An' what I know about ye is that ye always had an open heart an' a kindness to ye. A love of all things in life an' a deep interest in learnin' about them. But now. . . What happened, Liam? What happened to yer love? Tell me."

"My love?"

She doesn't answer that question because she knows that I know what she means. I've hardened inside and out and there is no way of hiding that from my sister since one of the most important things in her life is the relationship between us.

If I harden up completely, she will too.

"Emma," I say the words.

"Emma? Who is that?"

"Emma McGowan's her name. Beautiful and soft-spoken and smiled back at me when I smiled at her."

"Is she here in—"

"In New York, yes," I look out the window. "I don't even know if she liked me back. We only spoke a few times and once I even gave her flowers."

"Really?"

I nod with, "She was the sister of a guy who died the same time the White Hand took me in. He was the right-hand of the leader."

"The righthand?"

"The leader's most trusted."

"Oh."

"In fact the first day I met them was at her brother's wake the day I was found. But because her brother died when I arrived, and then just afterward, her and I began to spend time with each other, it felt," I turn to Abby. "It felt destined. Like we were supposed to be together. No one was surprised at the thought of us getting married. Having a family one day. It was like everyone expected it, to be honest. I thought about it all the time. Stupidly."

"Why stupidly? That's the most beautiful thing there is, startin' a fam'ly."

"Yeah well—"

"What, what happened?"

I raise my palms and look up, "When I was brought here with the grippe, I was quarantined for a couple months and I couldn't stop thinking about getting better and going to her. To proclaim once and for all that I loved her. I had it all planned, and when I was finally released I went right up to her door, but. . ."

"But what?"

"She had gotten sick too."

"She died?"

"She did."

Abby's mouth goes small as she blinks through her thoughts.

"All along I thought I knew what my destiny was, but it was ripped away. That's the thing. There is no destiny. There is no fate, either. We're just out here swimming against the tide and some of us die along the way and it doesn't matter. You just have to keep swimming, right?"

She tilts her head.

"What? I told you all of this and now you're just going to sit there?"

Abby's eyes look up and her mouth moves to one side until she finally says, "You needed to say that aloud. Sometimes just sayin' it can help, ye know? That's what fam'ly is for. Not to judge, just to be there for each other. To listen."

I look away when she says that. My eyes begin to well up, but I bite the tears back. When I feel as though my voice won't crack, I turn and speak, "Maybe you should give Mam that advice, because she is after me quitting my friends altogether. They saved me, you know. They saved me from being homeless and brought you to me—"

Abby interrupts, "Homeless? When were ye homeless? Ye came here to stay with uncle Joseph."

"Sure well, he turned me out."

"He did?"

"Then he died," I turn to her quickly, "I tried to quit the White Hand. Just recently. For Mam. I tried to quit, but. . . It's too late. No one believes what we do is good. No one stands up for us, even though we feed hundreds of people who would starve if it weren't for our being there for them. Thousands. All of these families that have lived here for so long would have nothing if we didn't organize the labor work, take from the ships and force tribute. And if it weren't for them, my brothers who picked me up off the street, then I wouldn't have you here either. They helped me when I needed it most and brought my family here to me."

"But what do you mean it's too late?"

"I went to Confession and the priest turned me in."

"Father Larkin?"

I nod and show her my bandaged fingers, "The police want to blame us for something we didn't do. For something *they* did."

Abby looks at me as if to question whether I tell the truth of it. As if to question whether I am capable of lying so boldly about a priest. She had only heard stories of how the church spoke out against the Fenians and the Moonlighters and the Irish Republican Brotherhood and sided with our enemy back in Ireland. But she had never been faced with the consequence of it impacting her own life.

"Liam, it's not. . ." she searches for the right word. "Wise. It's not wise to side against the law and the church."

"I was put in a bad spot. The law and the church weren't going to help me get my family out of the way of the coming wars in Ireland. I was thrust into this, but I fought. I fight," I say, correcting the tense to present. "I fight to feed my family, whether the police say it's against the law or the church says it's a sin, I fight for us."

She shakes her head in doubt and disagreement, which makes me feel I'm on an island, all alone.

"Listen Abby, you said you know the code of silence. Let me tell you this. . . Don't break it."

Her eyes move to the side as she slowly nods, "No wonder ye can't love."

"Why?"

Her eyes are alight with realization, "Emma died an' now ye're after protectin' yer heart. Ye won't let anyone in because ye think it's yer fault she died. An' maybe if ye love someone else, ye'll lose her too."

I hadn't thought of it that way. When we were children she would often name the animals and laugh at their individual personalities. But the day Da made me toss those puppies into the lake is the day I stopped giving any animals names.

"I know that feeling," says she.

"How?"

"Harry Reynolds was just a crush, but. . . I know he's dead now."

I look with sorrow to her, "How did you find out about Harry?"

"I asked round," she laughs, though there is no happiness in it. "We're in the same boat, aren't we?"

"I guess it makes us lovers of the dead."

"No," she shakes her head. "It makes us Irish."

We share a smile at that one, but she concludes, "We just have to move on. If we were to ask Emma an' Harry, they would both agree that we need to find new love while we're alive. We have to love the ones who live, but never forget those who've passed. Liam?"

I look up.

"Between us an' the men who helped ye, who will ye choose?"

"I. . . I want to choose the right thing to do," I say. "I've always wanted to make the right choice. The *honorable* choice. But in this? I can't choose one without dishonoring the other. It's a puzzle that can't be solved. It drives my head into a spin."

"Do ye love them?"

"The men in the gang?" I swallow hard, but I know the answer. "I do. They're good people. They've honored me in ways I could never repay. I do love them. With all my heart. But I love my family too."

Abby gathers herself and straightens her posture. "Back home I was to marry one o' the Cudmore bhoys."

"Which one?"

"Padraig."

"The one that loved to flick donkeys in the testicles?"

"That's him. When I had. . ." her face blushes as she looks up to mine. "When I had my moon, our all-too-grand older brother Timothy made a deal with Mr. an' Mrs. Cudmore that if I married Padraig, we would share profits from our two dairy farms. But not long afterward we got a letter in the mail."

"A letter? From who?"

"From yerself, o' course. An' it had three tickets fer passage to New Yark in it."

Once again a smile comes across my face that I simply can't control. And that's why Timothy married a Cudmore, isn't it?"

"T'is," she says. "Payback fer tryin' to sell off yer sister."

The two of us burst out in laughter at that.

"I was so happy when that letter came. I ran through the fields like I escaped the insane asylum, fer fecks sake."

I put a bandaged hand over hers. In response, she puts her other hand on top of mine as tears drop from her cheek in the light from the window. Across the bed I reach to place another hand atop hers to show my love for her, my sister. My blood.

Through the tears she speaks, "I didn't want to marry Padraig Cudmore an' the way I see it, these men that helped ye out? That saved ye? They saved me too from an unhappy life bearin' children to a man I could never love. Liam?"

"Yeah."

"I know Mam would have ye choose, but I don't think anyone has the right to tell ye who ye can or cannot love. Ye love that fam'ly too, the men in the gang. Ye don't have to choose between them an' us. Ye can have us both, the way I see it."

"Do you really think that?"

"I do," she nods. "Mam werries, o' course. She lost two boys already, an' her two livin' sons are both in danger. But it's a dangerous time, to be sure. An' these men helped ye when yer own uncle wouldn't. Go to them, Liam. They need ye. The pilgrimage comes soon. An' the fight."

"How do you know about—"

"Gather yer clothes, Liam. Before Mam gets back."

Mortal Transgression

Rain drips down Thos Carmody's nose and has soaked through his gray suit, darkening it. For the first time in a while he feels like he is back in France, hunting behind enemy lines, death so close.

But why am I so weak? Why am I dying?

He had forced himself to eat two days in a row. The buttered potatoes tasted like metal, the peas and corn as bland as chips of ice. Still he grows weaker.

The wind twists round him in the black of morn and whistles in his ear with the voice of an old man straining through an Irish lilt, *Ye need to hunt. Ye need to kill.*

Thos holds two fingers to his forehead and strains to stand, and fails to do so. He knows the voice in the wind cannot be right. It just can't be. To hunt and kill cannot cure a man who has already so cold and cruel. A man who has killed sixty-eight people in his life already, if not more. To be that heartless and that uncaring, as Vaccarelli said of him, will only lead to regret, or worse. But not better health.

Maybe that is what is wrong with me? Death is tired of my winning ways and wants its scythe back.

There will be consequences for his need to win at everything. And consequences for choosing Lovett over Meehan.

That is what haunts me. That is why I am slowly dying. Death is due.

As the sky flashes over West Manhattan, then crackles despondently, Thos comes to his feet underneath the budding leaves of a skinny Green Ash tree in a narrow courtyard between two brick buildings. The pulley clotheslines are bare above because of the downpour. And no one sees him from the windows above as the color of his leaden gray suit camouflages him amidst the wet slate slabs.

Hunched under his coat's collar he moves through the narrow alley as the outside of his shoulders scrape along both buildings. Tendrils of rainwater rush down the painted masonry facades like pulsing white veins and collect a foot-deep and run in a current down the alley in search of a grate or sewer. Inside his coat he pulls back the hammer to his pistol, then clicks it back again to practice. At each squishing step he repeats the action and continues doing so as he turns left on Eighth Avenue and ambles northward.

As he walks across Eighteenth Street an echo of sound from an elevated train a block away mixes with the slap of raindrops on the pavement. He lowers his cap and tilts it over to the side so that he cannot be seen by the passenger who sits in a curbed motor car. Inside a man pulls from a pipe but takes no notice of Thos.

They can't see ye, the voice in the wind says to him. *Hunt. Ye must hunt.*

At the south end of the block where his mark awaits death, Thos turns in to another alley, unseen. This one is so narrow that he must walk sideways to fit through. When he gets to the back of the building he flits his eyes up into the rain.

Above, Costello unhooks the fire escape ladder and lowers it so that Thos can reach it.

I can't make it. I don't have enough energy.

Try, the voice responds. *Ye are chosen fer greatness.*

Thos chuckles incredulously at that. *Chosen to die, maybe.*

Keep going. Ye will see.

The metal rungs are slippery. Paint chips pop off and fall to the ground with the rain. Thos comes face to face with Costello on the slatted metal platform.

"He's up there wit' two other guys, playin' cards. Lefty's guardin' the front door."

Thos looks up and reaches for the handrail and plods heavily up the metal stairs, "Welcome to the ILA, Costello," he calls over his shoulder in the morning rain.

When he gets to the roof he swings a leg up and over, then falls into a puddle of water amidst gravel and tar. On his back he stares up at the raindrops that rush down at him. Faces appear in the dark gray clouds above and cry all over him as a church bell clamors somewhere in the offing.

I can't get up. I should sleep. But I haven't slept in months. I should sleep.

He had once grown used to sleeping in the rain when he and seven hundred others were surrounded in the gap. It was not an easy thing to do. Many men had gone insane with the rain and mud and fleas and rats. Not to mention the Hun shelling them with mortar and machine gun fire. It's not easy to sleep in the rain when the severed limbs of your dead comrades float by in the red rainwater. Bill Lovett had no trouble sleeping though. Neither had Non Connors. But now? After the war? Thos simply can't fall asleep at all. If he did, it was hard to notice. Sometimes he was groggy. But most of the time his wounds ache, which keeps his brain grinding away to a nub.

The wind turns the raindrops sideways as the voice speaks again, *Get up.*

Why, there's no reason to. There's no reason for anything. I have done terrible things. I have caused death everywhere I have gone since even before the war. My time has come. I will let Tanner take me. He has a family, I do not.

Get up.

On the roof he gets up on one knee in the rain. Water flows down the end of his nose and over the rim of his soggy cap. He lifts himself and moves off, shuffling like a drunkard round cages of wet pigeons who turn their heads sideways to see him. Then turn away. Four-foot brick walls separate contiguous buildings of equal height. He scales them thoughtlessly. Ponderously. And flails again on his back.

Get up.

He stumbles to the other side of the building. He turns backward at the fire escape and begins to descend. Slowly. But on this fire escape there are no stairs and platforms, only a rung ladder leading down to the first floor. When he lowers the leg that was injured by the grenade, his boot slips. Dangling by one hand he looks down through the dark. Gas lamps out on the street throw long, dimming light through the alleyways, but he cannot see the slate or cement ground below.

Four story drop. If I fall it'll be all over.

Don't fall, says the wind.

He feels his fingers loosening. He could grab with his other hand, but something stops him.

If I die you'll die with me. No more voices in the wind. As far as I know, the world will die with me.

Ye're almost there, don't fall.

Thos smiles. And lets loose.

The drop through the black starts quickly. He flies past a window where a man and woman kiss in a kitchen. Then his foot hits a rung from the fire escape, bends his leg and forces his knee up, which smacks against his right cheek. From there, he cartwheels the rest of the way. Cartwheels just like when the Cricket Ball grenade exploded next to him in France. He does not fight the centrifugal force that pulls his arms and legs straight out and he can't fix his eyes on anything. The world swirls in teetering visions and water until he lands flat on his back on top of a mortar and cinderblock barrier that separates two buildings, bending him in half, backward. The back of his head then whiplashes against the north side of the barrier and all goes black.

Get up, the voice says again.

Thos blinks when he hears a woman's scream. He then hears a man's voice calling down from above. It is the man and woman who were kissing in the window, "Sir, are ya ok? Ya musta fell from the roof, should I call a policeman? Sir, can ya hear me?"

Thos blinks again, *I'm alive, I knew it. I knew it. This is not real.*

Raindrops force his eyes closed. He tries to squint to see where he is.

Get up.

Why?

Ye' will soon find out what ye were chosen for.

Chosen, he smirks. *I shouldn't be alive. It's not right. I think I died on the battlefield and this. . . this is a dream. A nightmare. There's something wrong with me. I'm sick or something. I have no energy. I can't move.*

Ye will feel better soon, let's go.

I can't.

Get up, Thos.

My back. It must be broken.

Get up. Ye made a deal with Dinny Meehan. A deal is a deal.

A deal. The day the Mullen widow gave birth to a boy Thos had sat with Dinny Meehan upstairs, above the Dock Loaders' Club. Thos had never made such a deal as this one. He told Dinny that, when the time comes, the ILA would back Wild Bill Lovett, but that hadn't surprised the gang leader at all. He wanted three things in return; the murder of Tanner Smith and another man and all of the Marginals that still report to Tanner, who will also join the ILA.

A baffling deal, it is. Illogical. A deal that means almost assuredly that Dinny Meehan will lose his power over Irishtown. A deal that admits defeat. Without any allies, his followers will be overrun. Beaten. Murdered by the Black Hand, the ILA, the police, Wolcott's thugs and Lovett's soldiers. Five to one, no one can get out alive against those odds. What does the fight even matter any longer? What anything matters to Dinny Meehan, Thos cannot know. Thos Carmody, the man who knows all the angles and sees five moves in advance cannot see Dinny's endgame here. Because there is none.

Get up, the wind says.

I just want to die.

Ye can't yet. Ye've more deaths to add to yer confirmed kills.

How many?

Four more, until yerself will become the hunted.
Who will kill me?
I will, o' course.

Thos wipes the rain from his eyes to see the old man who will take his life. His white hair shimmers in the wet wind. His aged face contrasts the youth in his eyes. Those eyes. Thos recognizes those eyes hidden in the folds and wrinkles, though he can't seem to put a name to the face.

What will you kill me with?

A pencil, the old man answers, then reaches into his pocket and produces it to show Thos. *The English have robbed us for centuries at pencil-point, an' I wield it now, the first o' me kind.*

Instead of sneaking through the window as was the plan, Thos comes to the front door.

"What happent?" Lefty whispers as Thos stumbles and falls into the foyer.

What did happen? Thos wonders, then raises his head, "I fell."

Lefty chuckles, "Jesus, ya look like a drenched alley cat, Thos."

"I'm fine," Thos walks through the front door and collapses into a chair and looks upstairs. "They still up there playin' cards?"

"Yeah."

Just then Dinny walks in through the foyer with Costello and stands between Thos and the door, then grabs him by the arm, "Ya gonna walk upstairs or I gotta carry ya?"

"Dinny?"

"Well?"

"No, a deal is a deal. I can do it," Thos turns his eyes back up to Dinny. "Are ya gonna kill me? Was that the plan all along? Ya make a odd deal like that, I suspect ya got somethin' else in mind. Am I right?"

"Ya mistake me for a liar," Dinny says. "I make a deal; I stick to it."

"There's nothin' to gain from a deal like that. All ya get is five guys an' Tanner dead. I don' got the energy for the rest o' it."

Lefty comes to stand above him, "Dinny's gonna win that fight against Bill, get it? Dinny's never been beat in a one-on-one."

Thos shakes his head in disbelief that anyone would think anything will get resolved by a fistfight.

Dinny tightens his grip on Thos's arm and looks up. "Ya go up those stairs an' there's no turnin' back, understand?"

"Yeah."

"Ya ready then?"

Ready to die, yes I am. For what I have done? Yes.

Thos pushes up from the chair and wobbles.

"We'll go in first. Wait until ya hear us kick the door in, then come up the stairs. Got it Thos?"

Thos nods as Dinny, Costello and Lefty slowly ascend. Two minutes later, the door bangs open upstairs and there is a scuffle.

Thos puts a hand on the banister. *This was meant to happen.* Three years earlier he had walked into the Marginal Club on Hudson Street, walked upstairs and without his knowing it, his life would change. He had no idea Wolcott had hired Dinny Meehan, who hired Tanner Smith to kill him.

Now look. Strange changes.

Tanner had saved his life by banishing him. But Thos had the audacity to refuse to go along with the deal and never hired him into the ILA, as was agreed.

I deserve to die. I deserve this.

As he takes the first step, a banging sound comes through the foyer door behind him.

"Police, open the door!"

The police? The couple who saw me fall, they must've called the cops anyway.

Thos turns back to the stairwell and ascends them as fast as he can, leaning heavily on the banister.

"Police! Open up. Now!"

Upstairs the door is left half-open and six men stand over Tanner Smith whose face is bleeding.

"Fuck, ya gotta be fookin' kiddin' me, Carmody?" Tanner turns white when he sees the specter of Thos Carmody lurch in. "Oh fookin' Jesus on a stick he looks a ghost! What's wrong wit' him?"

Thos leans on the door frame and points behind with a thumb, "Tunics are here."

"Hurry up, Thos," Lucky waves him in. "We ain't got all mornin'. Hurry up. Get ya pistol out, Thos."

But I thought I was gonna die?

"Think about my wife an' my Ma, Din. I'm sorry. I'll turn myself in t'day to the police. I promise I will. I'll turn myself in an' I'll take care o' Pickles in Sing Sing. The trial was postponed anyway, I got time now, see? That's what I was thinkin'. There's still time, Din."

As Lefty kicks Tanner, Thos collapses on the floor.

"Prop him up in a chair," Dinny orders, then turns his tortured face away. "Ya broke my heart, Tanner."

"Look Din, I can still—"

"It don' work that way. Ya just don' inspire people, ya know? Even ya own men have turned against ya," Dinny sweeps a hand round the room. "In these days, loyalty must be proven."

"Well ya can't kill me."

"Twice now ya've shown that ya don' believe in me, but ya're happy to take what ya can. Happy to lie. I hired ya to kill this guy," Dinny points at Thos. "When ya played that wrong, I gave ya another chance, an' again ya showed no honor. That's contagious ya know, dishonor. When men see ya flaunt me, well, ya understand how dangerous that can be. For the White Hand. For all the peoples o' Irishtown that depend on us."

"Thos ain't loyal to ya, Din. I can promise ya that. Thos fookin' Carmody's playin' ya, Din. He chose Lovett's side."

Dinny turns to Thos, who leans sideways in a chair, exhausted.

"Thos has a role to play, but yours is ended."

"Din what can I do?"

"I need men for what comes. Thos needs men too. We thank ya for them."

The sound of rain fills the void when silence takes the room. Somewhere far off thunder moans and through the window, above the city, a half moon cuts the night sky between the churn and twist of low, gray clouds.

The silence is then broken by the muffled banging sounds from downstairs, "Police, police! Open up this door."

"Have ya ever had to do somethin' that was against all ya know?" Dinny turns his back to everyone and stands in front of the rain-streaked window. "Have ya? Ya're on top of a cliff an' if ya jump, ya die. But everyone says that to jump is the only way to survive," Dinny turns back to us. "From the moment o' birth we're told god is above pullin' the strings, but ya never see him."

Thos struggles to sit upright as a battering ram slams into the door outside with a slow, banging rhythm.

"Sometimes we have to do things we don' believe in," Dinny's voice is a low grumble as outside the gloomy sky crackles again. "Loyalty is the kin o' honor. When I was eleven years old, ya saved my father an' I from certain death by givin' us a loan an' sendin' us to Brooklyn. But that was just the beginnin'. We took a ferry that overturned an', well. . . Since then I have lived by a code: He who helps those in need, shall have my undyin' loyalty. Ya taught me that. An' it was *that* code that won Irishtown."

Tanner simpers, "Ya gotta have loyalty to ya own code, Din. If not, then what?"

Dinny nods, "Thing is. . . In the world we live in, when one person wins, another must lose."

Do you really believe that, Dinny Meehan? Do you?

"That's the game," Dinny continues. "An' Tanner, ya've beatin' me twice."

Tanner pleads, "No, that's not true. Everyone can win. This is America!"

Wrong, a myth. The game is fixed. One person dies, another lives. Yet to transgress mortality. . . But how? Thos thinks back on his biblical studies at St. Veronica's. *It is heretical to attempt a mortal transgression. Only Jesus had the power to resurrect, like Lazarus of Bethany and. . . Himself.*

"To create is to truly rule," Dinny's middle and ring finger go to his temple as he turns back to the window.

"The thing that's drivin' me mad... What does it mean that I have to kill the man that taught me about loyalty?"

"Din, ya don' gotta do that. That... that'd make ya evil an' that's not what got ya to where ya are, right? Ya'd turn ya back on ya own morals just so, what? So ya can keep power?"

Dinny pushes his fingers harder into his temple and grits his teeth, "Sometimes ya gotta jump off a cliff. Thos?"

"Yeah," Thos struggles to respond and pulls back the hammer of the pistol in his pocket. Cocked and ready.

"Shoot him in the back," Dinny says. "Then we'll go out the window."

I don't have the strength to go out the window. This is it for me. This is all.

"Shoot him in the back so that the streets will know him for what he was."

"No!" Tanner yells. "Don' do it—"

Lefty and Costello and three others wrestle to put Tanner on his stomach. They hold his arms from behind and place their boots into the back of his neck.

"Stop, stop!"

Thos pushes up from the chair. *I don't even have enough strength to pull the trigger.* He shuffles over to Tanner with the pistol extended. His back hunched like an elderly man. Raindrops fall from his cap onto Tanner, whose feline eyes peer out from the raised collars.

"No, Thos I'm sorry! I was just playin' the game, but I lost. Ya won, Thos. Just lemme go! I'm sorry. I was wrong!"

The quick explosion in the room opens a red stain in Tanner's back as the pistol drops to the floor.

Downstairs the outside door is broken down and the voices of the patrolman are louder now as they pound on the foyer door, "Open up! In the name o' the law'r!"

"Pick up the pistol, Thos. Put one in the heart an' he'll die. In the middle o' his back, to the left," Dinny says.

"Hurry up," Costello demands.

Tanner kicks and screams and gurgles.

"Don' make him suffer too much," Lefty grumbles. "Pick it up."

Thos leans down, but falls to his knees.

"Get up," Dinny says. "Get up."

Thos picks up the warm pistol and shuffles on his knees toward Tanner and the men who hold him down. Over Tanner's back the pistol shakes in his hand. Thos squeezes the trigger, but can't snap it back. He takes a deep breath, then squeezes again with all his might.

The second shot, at point blank, goes through the left side of Tanner's back.

In the heart, Thos thinks. *He'll be dead soon.*

"Let him go," Dinny orders.

Tanner turns slowly to his side. He points at Thos as he gasps for air, then makes a fist and holds it over his forehead. A cough sprays blood. Tanner pounds the flat of his fist on the wood floor as his mouth gulps for air, but comes up empty.

Still no breath, how long can he hold out?

Thos flops on his side next to Tanner and the pistol falls out of his hand. As his eyes close his body relaxes. Drifting. Drifting away, he begins to sleep as all the men round him try to rouse him awake. Except Dinny Meehan, who watches him from above. Then all goes black.

When Tanner Smith dies, oxygen blasts into Thos's lungs like gale force winds. His eyes bolt open and he quickly sits up on his elbows to look round the room. All have left to flee from the police, but Dinny Meehan still stands by the window. Next to him Tanner's bloodshot eyes stare through Thos and into a great and brief distance.

Thos stands. His back straightens. His wounds no longer pain him. His knuckles crack as he balls his hands into fists.

I have never felt so alive. So powerful. So unbelievably immortal. What? What happened?

"Welcome back Thos," Dinny speaks without looking back.

"What happened? I'm transformed. I can feel every muscle in my legs, my chest, my arms. Oxygen! Oxygen flows through my blood like a rushing river. Ya knew all along, didn' ya?"

"A deal is a deal."

"I thought," Thos can hardly believe how quickly the words come out of his mouth. "I thought my cruelty and my heartless decisions were killin' me. That all the men I'd murdered had come back round to haunt me. That all the game-playin' angles had turned back against me. But it turns out—"

"It turns out that in this world, cruelty an' heartlessness is beneficial, yeah," Dinny finishes Thos's sentence as if he'd plucked the words out of his mouth, though he says them with much less vigor and much more gloom.

Thos's face grins and grits with a greedy lust like a first fix, "I didn'. . . I didn' know. I didn' want to believe that. But this is just a dream or somethin', right? It's not real," He stands behind Dinny at his shoulder in front of the window. "I know that I'm in-dream an' time stands still where I'm dyin' on the battlefield because I both conceive an' perceive this world at the same time. This is a future that never occurred. But now I know that I cannot control the events. This is not my world, it's yours."

"No," Dinny says . "I did not conceive this world. I have a role, just as ya do. No more."

"Then who is in control? God?"

"An' they call ya the prodigy," Dinny moves off from the window and looks down at Tanner Smith's body. "The blood feud is over. His soul writhes inside ya now."

"I can feel him."

"Ya own it. His strength strengthens ya. Only a woman's love could save him now, an' no woman could ever love Tanner Smith," Dinny looks up to Thos. "More importantly, ya've proven ya'self. Ya survived an' ya journey continues."

Tingles shoot up and into Thos's body as the ram pounds at the door downstairs. Vigorous energy vibrates in waves through his fingertips and muscles like the sheets of rain outside that wash against the window.

"Where are we?"

"Some call it the Otherworld, some call it a ghost story."

"Where does it end?" Thos asks.

"End? Well ya know what must be done next, at least. Ya need to kill again, remember the deal we made?"

Of course I do. The deal I thought was illogical.

Downstairs the patrolmen finally break through the foyer door. Chairs are overturned and footsteps pound up the stairwell.

"Tanner's body?"

"Leave him. We'll go out the window."

"An' the voice that I hear. In my head. Am I. . . am I mad?"

Dinny does not answer.

Thos stands over Tanner's body as he takes a deep, powerful breath and jumps out the window to swiftly climb the fire escape up to the roof just as the door busts open.

"Stop, halt!"

Divine Providence

Captain Sullivan, Patrolman Ferris and New York Police Commissioner Richard Enright and even Mayor Mike Hylan stand round the casket behind a black Fresian-drawn hearse carriage. An American flag is draped over half the casket. An Irish tri-colour covers the other half, even as Ireland is not a country.

At the sight of the casket Doirean pivots and buries her face into Daniel's chest. Feeling the eyes upon him he wraps an arm round her shoulder and stares back at the slew of policemen and their wives and children while a foghorn moans dully out on Wallabout Bay.

"I'm sorry, Doirean," the scent of lilac comes to his nose when he whispers to her. "I'm so sorry."

"My sweet child," Father Larkin approaches in mourning garb at the bottom step and then, without being prompted, proclaims, "God found it in himself to devote half o' mankind to the creation o' the garden, so he did. She is the vessel o' life an' must tend it gently, the other half is devoted to destroyin' it."

He looks smugly at Daniel, then with a ring-laden hand outstretched he speaks up to Doirean. "I'd be honored to escort ye to St. Ann's while yer husband walks with the casket."

"Father, where is Johanna Walsh? I need her on this day. I have no one to talk to."

Father Larkin's tufted eyebrow goes up, "Johanna Walsh? Do ye mean Johanna Connolly? They've been married many years now."

"Connolly?"

Why is Father Larkin wearing violet? Daniel wonders. *This is no time for penance. Does he know what I did? Is he sending a message to me through his vestments?*

Doirean demurely walks down the stoops in heels and holds the black metal railing with a black gloved-hand, the other hand tucked under the round of her belly.

Obediently, the crowd steps back and separates to make a path for Doirean and Father Larkin who proceed softly, heads bowed.

Captain Sullivan calls out, "Attention!"

His voice echoes off the tenement walls down Navy Street toward the shore and up the hill along the Navy Yard wall. Every policeman click their heels on the cobbles in unison, turn to face the flag and stand in sharp military salute, caps tucked under underarms. A great many of them know drill commands due to their being trained for battle in the Great War. Most hardened by combat.

The silence enthralls Daniel. The discipline. The quietude amongst a thousand policemen and a thousand wives and more children. They stand solemnly along the far sidewalk and up into the stoops of other brick and low rise tenements. A steam hammer slams in the Navy Yard and rattles the casket on the dray, reverberating in Daniel's chest. As he takes his place aside the hearse carriage, Commissioner Enright touches his shoulder from behind. Wordless, he bends down and gives Daniel a half-hug while shaking his hand. "He was your father, is that right?"

"No, father-in-law," Daniel curls a lip at the commissioner's ignorance.

"Ah, well I'm proud that all the work we did over the past year to improve the policemen's retirement system will help your family."

Daniel nods and turns his eyes to Captain Sullivan, *Why not get his papers prepared,* he thinks, but instead he simply says, "Thanks."

As Mayor Hylan shakes Daniel's hand, flashbulbs pop as photographers jostle for position, elbowing each other in ribs with nary a sound but the shuffle of feet. When Daniel moves to take his hand away, the mayor holds onto it and smiles to allow every photographer to get their best shot.

"Pakenham," Daniel calls out when he sees him.

Pakenham approaches and they shake hands in front of the crowd.

Booooooom, the steam hammer comes down again in the Navy Yard and the remains of William Brosnan shake in the flag-draped casket.

Of a sudden, Daniel's voice breaks the silence, "I have released a statement from our fam'ly to Mr. Pakenham, the most honorable o' all the journalists among yaz."

The other reporters glare at him, but say nothing.

"I want to say a few words now," Daniel speaks out.

Pakenham comes to his ear, "That's not what Wolcott said to do, just let the statement speak for itself, Daniel."

Daniel smiles and whispers back, "I am in charge here."

He then sprints back up the stairs as Doirean gives him a look of shock, as do the captain and the commissioner. Though Mayor Hylan seems unaware.

"Thank yaz all for showin' up to honor the ol' Bear," Daniel yells out as all eyes turn to him, even those in the windows across the street and directly above him.

"Daniel," Doirean whispers angrily.

But he ignores her, "We all know who is responsible for Detective William Brosnan's death."

Captain Sullivan's voice growls under his breath, "Daniel, ya get down from there, now."

"We need no inquiry to learn what we already know," Daniel calls out on his tiptoes. "The White Hand Gang did this to us. Dinny Meehan—"

The name floats down the tenement streets until the steam hammer slams down yet again to drown his words. From the river some seven blocks away comes a breeze as the sun is blocked by cloud cover, darkening Navy Street. In a window two buildings down a woman's voice heckles Daniel while the wind swirls amidst the army of blue and black. A whirlwind then dances above the crowd and sucks loose papers, coal ash, a police cap and a metal garbage lid along with rotted food into a pirouette of refuse. The garbage lid spirals away and crashes against the building above him and falls onto the sidewalk with a clamor.

"Dinny Meehan an' Wild Bill Lovett are behind this as they have been behind many other such murders, double-dealin's, automobile an' fact'ry thefts, beatin's an' much more. He tried to kill me his-very-self not long ago when I was on reconnaissance. I saw'r Meehan wit' my own two eyes on Hoyt Street. He shot up the place an' burnt it down. If it hadn't've been for my partner Patrolman Ferris, yaz all would be here t'day to mourn two downed soldiers in the war to win back Brooklyn from the lawless gypsy gangs that infest our streets," he stretches his arm out. "Ferris is the hero!"

Patrolman Ferris's confused face changes into humility when he is named the hero of Hoyt Street. Though Doirean mutters despairingly, "Daniel, get down from there."

"I also want to thank Police Commissioner Enright for his incredible work in improvin' the police retirement system."

Twenty to thirty people reluctantly clap as the crowd looks round at each other, unsure of where Daniel is taking them.

"It has come to our attention that Captain Sullivan is upon retirement himself an' will be well-taken care of," Daniel notices Sullivan's nose has turned crimson as he stares back. "To replace him we need a man who has gone above an' beyond his job's requirement to hunt down the enemy an' collect inside information about their comin's an' goin's. A man who has good sense an' keen instincts an' is willin' to meet the threat o' the gangs an' their influence over Brooklyn labor," Daniel fingers the blackjack on his belt. "I believe the best man for Captain o' the Poplar Street Station is myself, Daniel Culkin. I stand before yaz t'day humbled that ya would consider me—"

Quickly, commissioner Enright storms the steps and Mayor Hylan speaks over Daniel, "We thank you all for coming today—"

"I'm not done," Daniel protests.

"You can keep your mouth closed," Enright tells him.

But Daniel pushes to the front and yells over the commissioner, "Let us rejoice in the memory o' Detective William Brosnan on this day, thank you! Let's head to St. Ann's now, thank you, thank you."

Down the steps he goes, slapping Father Larkin on the shoulder too hard, "Let's go, thank you!"

Toward Doirean, he sneaks a peek as the perplexed procession begins to move, though he cannot see her face under Father Larkin's round shoulders, who has moved between them. He throws his left arm round Patrolman Ferris and thrusts a right hand into the crowd to shake with as many people as he can, thanking them again and again.

As the cortege turns from Navy Street west on the cobbled hill of Gold Street toward St. Ann's Roman Catholic Church, a rattling sound comes to Daniel's ears.

What is that? Chains? Chains dragging on cement?

He looks behind him but can only see police blue. On either side mourners seem unaware of the ringing.

Is it in my ears only? Can no one else hear that?

The sound may be obscured by horse hoofs and boot steps, but the shake of a chain sends chills down his spine, *cling-clang, cling-cling-clang.*

The street and sidewalks are packed with somber faces that stride along with the trundling hearse, but none seem to hear the shrill ringing. The funeral procession eases and shifts through the streets, sometimes stopping, and still the chains haunt Daniel with a sense of terror and a volatile excitement that churns upward from his groin and backside to his lower belly.

"What is that fookin' noise," he turns to Patrolman Ferris.

Ferris leans forward and points up ahead to the right.

Maureen Egan's ratty hair moves through the crowd, red in a sea of navy blue and black. *Boooooooom* the steam hammer echoes in his chest again.

Fucking red slattern, Daniel curses her quietly.

And then she wails, "*Ahhhhh, Noooo, Ahhhhh, Noooooo!*"

Daniel is sweating now and looks for his wife, but still Father Larkin looms over her with his violet cloak and headpiece.

She moans again with a sound so grating against his ears that he covers them. When he takes his hands away again, she is screaming at the height of her lungs. Maureen's eyes find him through the passing bald spots and slick-back, military haircuts. Mourners walk round her on the sidewalk as she holds up her chains to him and keens again, "*Ahhhhh, Noooo.*"

"For chirstsake Ferris, go get her," Daniel mumbles his fury. "Arrest her. Shut her up."

Ferris runs ahead and grabs three other men who tackle the red-haired woman but fail to shut her up.

"Doe! My little Doe!" Maureen screams. "I did not die for naught! I died to give ya life! When death is due, life is wrought!" Her pitch goes so high that the glass in the windows above rattle in their frames. "It was him! It was him all along! Ya're right. Ya instincts tell it true! My little Doe! The ol' bear died for *you*! Died for *you*!"

Suddenly part of the crowd collapses into itself over Maureen Egan.

"Maureen!" Doirean screeches, but is blinded by the slew of mourners.

Blackjacks wave through the air and the sound of fabric tearing replaces her muffled moans. Daniel watches as Maureen is gagged and dragged behind the casket dray and the crowd back toward Navy Street from whence they came.

Where are her shoes? Daniel wonders.

Her feet bleed from the bottoms, and between her legs a tail of chain-links drag through the yellowed, gap-toothed cobblestones. Her hair is a red tussle of dirty locks and stringy strands like a weeping willow that covers her face and gives the appearance of a head too large for her thin frame. Her dirty sack dress had been torn down the middle, though only the chains that cross her chest can be seen.

"Moe is that you!" Doirean yells out again, then asks Father Larkin. "Was that Maureen Egan? Where is she? What did she say?"

The cortege moves on as Doirean mourns louder now with yawning howls. In the windows above the Irishtown narrows all faces stare upon them.

These are Dinny Meehan's people? Daniel nods.

In the old days gangs like the Velvet Caps would rush and fight them off with shillelaghs and cudgels and fists, forcing the tunics to collect their wounded and retreat. Irishtown was much more violent in those days and would never allow any patrolmen within their imagined walls.

The old bear would oft tell those stories on rainy nights with a *Na Bocklish* between his teeth and a North Dublin accent on his tongue. Gone now, is he. And soon to be forgotten.

Booooooom, the steam hammer drops yet again. Further away now, though Brosnan's casket clatters as if the dead Irishman was banging away inside, struggling to escape.

The old-time Irish in this neighborhood have dwindled over the years, which makes it the perfect time to jettison their feckless ways into extinction for good and ever.

When I come into my captaincy, it will be my first priority to starve old Irishtown and scatter the rest to the wind, he cranes his neck up to the old wood-frame tenements that were built before the civil war. *My captaincy,* he smiles at the thought of it. Captain Culkin of the Poplar Street Station.

No, Captain Culkin sounds silly. I'm no character in the newspaper comics. I won't allow anyone to call me that. It will have to be Captain Daniel Culkin.

Daniel has to wipe the smile off his face when he realizes that a group of wives watch him.

It will happen, it will happen, he tells himself. *It's divine providence. God is on my side. The cruel god that wins, not the fake god that the weak pray to. No, the god who preys on the weak.*

Behind him he hears the howls of Maureen Egan through the click of horseshoes and boots. Then his wife's sobs as the dray struggles over the cobblestones. A cool gust blows off the river lifting more caps into the air along with papers until it whistles his name in a windy whisper.

"Daniel," it seems to say. "The archons."

Daniel hears the wobbly voice of a very old man with words like birds that whistle through the wind. He searches round himself to see if others had heard it too, but the faces of the funeral cortege are still somber and silent.

A hard and lengthy gust halts the procession in place this time, and a police cap slaps against the side of Daniel's head.

"The archons make him known as the demiurgic son," the old man's voice appears again, though it's as loud as a scream in Daniel's ears.

"Who? What?" Daniel calls aloud and pulls off his blackjack, wheeling round and wielding it threateningly. "Who said that?"

"It's just the wind," Ferris says with his hands outstretched, showing palms. "Put that away."

"What's an archon?"

"A what?" Ferris attempts to grab at his wrist, but Daniel pulls away and rears back.

"Get away from me!"

"Daniel!" He hears Maureen's moaning voice, though when he looks it is Doirean who is yelling toward him. "Daniel, put that down."

Captain Sullivan pushes through the crowd and finds him. Then Commissioner Enright and Mayor Hylan appear over both shoulders.

Daniel quickly connects the blackjack onto his belt and gives a sheepish nod, "It's alright everyone. Everythin's fine. No cause for alarm. Let's move out. Move it!"

Towering above is the steeple to the Catholic Church amidst the blacksmith shops, the farriers and the lead paint manufacturers.

Voices. Whose voice was that? Daniel wonders. *Who haunts me?*

Across the way Daniel spots his son Little Billie Bear with both hands being held by policemen as if he were under arrest.

A darkness creeps over Daniel's thoughts, *That boy looks at me as if he knows. Who told him?*

As the crowd in blue and black gather round the steps of St. Ann's, Father Larkin ascends ahead of everyone. A few blocks away the Manhattan Bridge rumbles like thunder in the distance and lingers, mingling for minutes with the keening slumbers of his wife. Then the faint sound of rattling chains comes to his ear again, he gulps and turns to look behind him.

At the top of the steps Doirean stands next to Father Larkin. What is being said, however, Daniel cannot hear due to the wind in his ear.

"You must repent," the wind says.

Next to Father Larkin and Doirean above are some twenty to thirty policemen with their caps under their arms. But one of them, the one standing next to Doirean is wearing civvies. The same clothes Detective Brosnan wore the day he was killed on the tug. And under his arm is not his cap, but his own head.

"You must repent," the voice in the wind says.

"You have no power over me," Daniel mouths while staring Brosnan down.

"I know son, I know," Brosnan's hands move his head up to face Daniel. "That was always the problem. Now I become what ye want, what ye choose to remember. Ye? Ye will remember me for bein' weak because I showed ye that I loved ye."

"I'd prefer someone beat me for what I've done. Ya're nothin'," Daniel refuses to look at his father-in-law's face and curls a lip to show his discontent. "I have to go back to Kit Carroll. When she hurts me, only then I will be repentant. On my terms."

"What are ya sayin' over there, Daniel?" Doirean's cold eyes turn to him.

I don't feel good. I feel very, very bad. I need to be punished soon, he realizes. *If only I could find someone to hurt me, badly. Very, very badly. Only then will I feel better.*

Hoo-hooooo, a tugboat hails from the river.

Inside St. Ann's the echoes come alive. A cough here and there, or the sound of kneelers being dropped whirls in the barrel vault ceiling, rushes round the carillon, careers through the balcony seating and bounces back down into the transept.

Daniel inspects the slew of mourners with a bewildered scowl as if he were looking for a hidden gunman.

You will not awe me, you bastards, Daniel rationalizes before sitting.

In the front pew, Doirean sits to Daniel's right. She keeps the boys away though and nods her face at him to scoot down and make room, and he does so. To Daniel's left is an empty seat on the bench.

At the altar Father Larkin asks everyone to stand and Daniel rolls his eyes.

Sit, stand, kneel, make up your fucking mind, priest.

Irishtown's old Roman Catholic Church is filled to the rafters with well-wishers and weepers and wailers subdued by the admiration of the man all hail as some perfect being, in his absence. Daniel spots five, six others he personally heard speak ill of Brosnan while alive, but the old man can do no wrong in their memories now.

Policemen from every precinct in Brooklyn and many in Manhattan, Queens, Staten Island, The Bronx and even parts of Long Island have come. Overwhelming the old church in Irishtown, they stand three deep behind the pews and along the walls.

My soldiers, Daniel thinks to himself with pride.

Father Larkin raises his arms while reading from the large, open bible, "Day of wrath and doom impending. David's word with Sibyl's blending, Heaven and earth in ashes ending. . ."

In his peripheral vision Daniel feels someone stand next to him on the left with his hat under an arm.

Across the aisle Mayor Hylan sits next to Commissioner Enright and near Captain Sullivan as well as Daniel's partner Ferris and other so-called important figures. Daniel sneers at the onlookers behind who treat them with reverence.

When Father Larkin allows all to sit, the man next to him whispers, "Daniel. . . Daniel."

But Daniel lowers his eyes to look at his own crossed hands and ignores the man.

"Daniel, it's me."

He moves his eyes to the side, then turns to face the man sitting next to him, though the fellow does not have a cap in his lap, but his head instead.

"Dad?"

"I've been sent to talk with ye, son. One way or another, we're gonna talk."

"Sent by who?" Daniel whispers back.

Detective Brosnan's hands turn his face upward in his lap to look in Daniel's direction, then speaks with a gurgling voice, "Do ye believe in ghosts? In gods?"

"No."

The smile on Brosnan's face in his own lap sickens Daniel's stomach.

I have to find someone to hurt me so that this idiot doesn't follow me around anymore.

"Ya're supposed to be in that casket," Daniel points with a nod toward the bier.

"Shh," Doirean angrily taps Daniel's leg, then brings her hand back over to hold her belly.

"Daniel," Brosnan's eyes look up again and a sly smirk appears on his pale face that has lines of dried blood smeared across it. "Daniel, I'm here to make a deal, ye bowsie bastard. I tried everythin' to stop ye from workin' with the fat man, but ye wouldn't listen. I knew there was a curse on my fam'ly, an' I was proved right, damn ye. My daughter will live. Life is due her, but as fer yerself? Yer doomed, like. Fer what ye did? Yer doomed unless ye make a deal."

Daniel mumbles out the side of his mouth, "Ya got no sway over me, ol' man. Ya're time came an' went. Now fuck off."

"It's power ye want," Brosnan's hands straighten his head again next to Daniel on the pew. "Thing is, ye can't take power with ye when ye die like ye can honor. But it's the power ye got the lust fer. An' ye want the captaincy too. An' ye want credit fer takin' power 'way from the gangs an' the unions, am I right?"

Daniel lowers his eyes, smacks his lips and looks down to Brosnan's severed head, "An' how is it ya're gonna get me all that, ol' man?"

"Divine providence ye bleedin' dryshite," Brosnan laughs, then coughs, then laughs again. "It's not about whether or not I can get it fer ye, Daniel. No, no. It's about what ye're willin' to give up, is all."

"What do ya want, one o' my kids? Doirean?"

"No, it has to be somethin' ye care about, like."

"Fuck off, I'll get it on my own."

"No, no ye won't."

"What are ya like a ghost? Or a god? Is that what ya're sayin'? Make up ya mind." Daniel whispers, then his eyes change to show his worry. "The devil?"

"Ha!" Brosnan bellows in laughter. "There are no gods or devils that exist beyond our own capacity, right? We create them. *We* are the gods an' the devils an' they only become animated when we fill them with our worries an' our hopes, d'ye understand?" Brosnan looks over toward Father Larkin, "We are the creators o' all, even mortal power structures. An' we give them leaders with authoritative names such as priest, president, prime minister, chieftain, king. . . But all power structures are created by human bein's to benefit a group o' individuals who remain loyal to its demands. Have ye been loyal to law, Daniel? Have ye?"

"I'm loyal to no one. I make my own way, I told ya. No gods or devils? Fine with me."

Brosnan blinks and moves his head in Father Larkin's direction to hear the echoing words of the funeral homily, "Them that sleep in the dust o' the earth shall awake, some to everlastin' life, an' some to shame an' everlastin' contempt."

Brosnan says, "Ye don't believe in ghosts either, but ye converse with them."

"I got my own plan."

"Ah yes, phase three o' Operation Grey's Faith, yeah?" Brosnan's wry smile is punctuated with a wink. "Alas, t'will be ruined before it can ever be realized, ye get me? Unless ye make a deal with me here an' now."

"How's it gonna get ruined?"

"Daniel, Daniel, ye're a fool, ye know it? All along there's been a spy in yer home."

"A spy?"

"A spy, t'is true."

"Who?"

"Think on it, ye fool eejit. What outsider has been in yer home o' late?"

The realization hits Daniel like a course of bricks, "Johanna Walsh."

"Shh," Doirean hits him this time, and even Little Billie Bear gives him a serious stare from the other side of his mother's belly.

"Ye have it," said Brosnan's head. "She knows all, the woman does. Her name is not Walsh though, it's—"

"Connolly," Daniel remembers Father Larkin call her. "Cinders' wife, now I know where I've seen her before. She's married to the White Hand."

"An' she will tell Doirean an' everyone else now that it's confirmed I'm dead, which will ruin yer plan. She knows what ye did to me, Daniel. An' the law will have its justice, t'will. They'll hang ye like a dog. Make the deal, Daniel," Brosnan gurgles. "Make the deal."

"What's the terms?"

"I'll give ye what ye need if ye give me what I want, otherwise. . ."

"What do ya want?"

"Well yer soul, o' course."

Sean Dream

I kick in the door at the Dock Loaders' Club as the candles gutter violently when the wind whooshes through the open doorway.

"Jesus, he's back!" Paddy Keenan yells.

"No, it's just me, Liam," says I.

But I'll never be the same.

The bar explodes in celebration. Everyone round shakes my hand for congratulations and slaps me on the back.

"Liam, what did I do to ya?" Red Donnelly grabs me by the shoulders. "Beat told me that ya forgive me for what I done an' that I'd know what ya was talkin' about, but I don' know. What did I do?"

At that I have no words, other than, "Never mind."

"An' the kids, Whyo an' Will?"

"I. . . I was delirious or something. I'm not sure," I limp through the old saloon to a stool.

"What did they do to ya?" Cinders pulls my arm up to look at the bandages on my fingers, but I just shake my head.

We all know what it means when police want to "question" you.

The Lark and Big Dick pick me up on their shoulders and parade me through the saloon. Even Feeble Philip

Large is jumping up and down and chanting my name as best he can, "Wee-um, Wee-um."

When they let me down someone scrubs the top of my head.

"Don't," says I, coldly.

Dago Tom responds with a shocked face until I show him the stitches in my scalp.

When I show them the bruises on my arm and chest and shins, the realization of what I'd been through begins to take shape for them.

But I can't show them the worst of my wounds.

"I'm almost healed now. The nurses said I looked like I had been through a tempest when they admitted me."

"Well what happened to ya? Who was it did this?"

"It was just Culkin. The last thing I remember I was looking out the curtain of the ambulance, then nothing for days."

"Get ya a drink, Liam?" Freddie Cuneen asks, but before I can answer him The Swede and Vincent storm down the stairwell from upstairs.

"Liam!" The Swede yells.

But Feeble Philip practically tackles him before The Swede dives in for a hug, "Urt, urt. Wee-um 'urt bad!"

"Whad they do to ya?" The Swede stands off, looking me from shoe to cap.

"Ah he can take it," Vincent says. "Tough yoke, this one."

Next to Ragtime Howard at the bar, a forlorn Dance Gillen elbows up with a drink in his fist.

I scoot in next to him, "How you? What's doing at the Atlantic Terminal?"

"Russians ain't back yet," he half-heartedly nods.

"I miss the docks. And it's only been what? Two weeks since I left. . . the gang."

"This mean ya're back or somethin'?"

"I uh. . . I don't think I have a choice."

"Unless ya leave Brooklyn."

"Do you want me to leave?"

"I didn' say that."

"What are you saying?"

"Are ya wit' us? Or are ya gone? 'Cause everyone here thinks ya're a hero now. There's a big fight comin' up. We could use a *hero*," he ends the sentence with a sarcastic tilt to his head.

"A hero? Come on. Why would anyone say that?"

"Only heroes stick to the code o' silence under that kinda torment an' pain," He waves his drink in the direction of my bruises. "Alcohol might be the truth serum, but pain is the tongue loosener."

You have no idea that I was moments away from turning Dinny in.

"No Dance, I'm not a hero. Not even close. I'm just a soldier."

"Call it what ya will, ya're proven now. No matter what ya do, it'll always seen as heroic. It's like a shit gold coins. I've been workin' on these docks since before ya even came to Brooklyn, an' no one sees me in the same light as ya. Why ya think that is, eh?"

"You're a hard fellow, Dance. A smart guy once told me a hard man is good to find. I stepped away from the Atlantic Terminal knowing full well that it would be yours afterward. Some people have to prove themselves ten times over just to be considered an equal. It's not right, but it's real. Those are the true heroes. You're the real hero here, Dance. In my mind, at least. You keep your head down and your fists up."

"An' ya're weak," Dance says. "Weak on account o' ya care too much about other people, just like Dinny does."

"Yet he's been the strongest man in Brooklyn for six years."

Dance nods in admission, "That's exactly what baffles me so fookin' much. I just wish I had the chance to prove myself like ya did."

"Petey still owns me. I'm nothing, nobody."

"If Petey was smart, an' he ain't, but if he was he'd steer the fuck clear o' the likes o' Poe fookin' Garrity."

I nod and put an arm on Dance's shoulder, "I'm with you. I'm not gone, I'm with you."

"Good to hear, we need all the help we can get because if Dinny loses this fight wit' Bill, all fookin' hell's gonna break loose in Brooklyn, ya know what I mean? That happens an' ya gonna have to move because Bill'll demand us gone or he'll send his lieutenants to kill us all."

"I wouldn't even know where we would go," I wonder aloud.

"Don' worry about it, just know that we can't lose," he says. "No matter what, Dinny can't lose, but. . ."

"What?"

Dance's tone goes dark. "Eddie Gilchrist—"

"Lumpy? What about him?"

"Up in Sing Sing. They found him wit' his throat slit, ear to ear."

Inside my pocket I touch the pencil I stole from him, "Was it Pickles?"

"No one knows for sure, but. . ."

"He didn't deserve that. He didn't deserve anything he got. He was good. He was innocent—"

"He was helpless," Dance corrects me. "He couldn't defend hisself. He never even knew what was goin' on around him. All he knew was numbers."

"Tanner," I ball my fist and watch the stitches strain to hold the skin on my knuckles together. "Tanner was supposed to—"

"Ya know Tanner's dead too?"

"He is? Who got him?"

"The Blood Feud."

"Thos Carmody; the guy who plays on both sides of the fence right out in the open."

"An' does it well," Dance holds a palm open. "We got five o' Tanner's men outta the deal. Lefty, Costello an' a few other galoots. But as soon as the tunics found Tanner's body in the Marginals Club, they had to lam it to Jersey. So now we got nothin' outta it but Thos Carmody's promises. I don' trust that one, Liam. Not one bit. He's proven nothin' to us, but I wanna see if Thos Carmody lines up wit' us when it counts at the fight."

"Jesus, what else did I miss while I was gone?"

"The leaflets."

"Leaflets?"

Dance pulls a piece of paper out of a coat pocket, "Thousands o' them just showed up over night all over Irishtown. Up an' down the territories."

I hold the leaflet close to the candlelight and read.

Martyrdom means an early grave,
Don't live life as a mere squatter.
Come to Bill, be strong and brave,
Or stay helpless as a delicate daughter.

Come to Bill, and everyday you'll eat ham,
While Dinny treats you as cannon fodder.
Remember you're old friend Lumpy the Lamb,
Lumpy the Lamb—who Dinny sent to slaughter.

Take hold of life, see how Dinny is deceitful.
Come to Bill, for Bill is the seed of the people.

I toss the paper to the peanut shells on the floor, "A simpleton wrote this."

"Simple words for simple people," Dance says. "We lost a few more to Bill this week."

"That just makes it less and less likely that Bill leaves when he loses," I look at Dance. "Then what?"

"Then ya step away, Liam. Step away so the soldiers can war. That means killin' people, an' we all know ya ain't got the heart for that."

"When is the fight?"

"Tomorrow."

"Tomorrow?"

"Tomorrow," he drops his whiskey on the mahogany.

I flex my hand. The same hand with four fingernails missing. When I make a fist, the stitches in the wound strain to keep the skin closed. Deep in my bones an ache spreads up my arm and into my shoulder.

I turn to Dance, "What's the plan?"

"Plan?"

"Where's Dinny? The fight is tomorrow and we don't even have a plan? Dinny always has a plan. Why don't we have one? Why haven't we talked about it?"

"A plan for what? It's a fight," The Swede shrugs.

"I seen a hundret o' these," Vincent tosses hair off of an eye. "Dinny used to get challenged everywhere we went. It's just a one-on-one."

I look at Dance and the rest. "I don't trust that Bill will show up without weapons or. . . or do something, I don't know, Bill Lovett's a cheat and we should account for that. Vincent, are you going to bring your .38?"

"Nah, rules are no weapons—"

"Where's Dinny now? Like right now?"

"Where he always is after the divvy; the old section," Dance says.

"We never even considered putting Bill in a box," I stand from the bar.

"No, we didn't," The Swede lowers his eyes. "But me an' Vincent did. Ya didn't want to hear about it. Now ya have a change o' heart?"

Yes, I have changed, without doubt. But how much?

"How many people's lives could be saved if we—" I stop myself, unsure of my own thoughts.

Vincent says, "Bill's as good as a corpse already. Let Dinny do the deed wit' his fists. Afterward, all Bill's men join us or—"

"Die," Dance finishes the sentence.

"But if we lose. . . then what?" I break in.

"Dinny's never lost," Vincent says.

"Nothing is never," says I. "Where in the old section is he?"

"Probably the tavern. Ya've been there before, remember?"

Paddy watches from behind the bar as I rush through the labormen and leave.

Outside the wind rushes into my face and I have to pull the door closed as a train rumbles overhead, *cha-chum, cha-chum, cha-chum*. The metallic churning sound of the Manhattan Bridge overpass echoes off the water and cement, and rushes between the buildings on Bridge Street. It almost sounds like a keening woman. Like a banshee wailing her lament, warning of death.

Stop thinking like that. I'm not superstitious. I'm not going to die.

East I go, and north, deep into Irishtown where the cobblestones are as patchy as an old man's mouth and bite at the ankles if I don't watch my step. The old pre-Civil war shacks sway when the waterfront gusts dial up. They creak too, like the old oak framed hulls of masted barques in the nightmares of the Great Hunger's children. The windows are so covered in coal dust that I can only see shadowy figures pass in front of them over the street. The alleys are unpaved and strewn with weeds and shards of glass. When a tomcat with a gnarled ear senses me, it leaps up onto a ledge and scatters into a broken window. The coal holes are like open soars on the sidewalk and I once heard rumor that below them are tunnels that let out into the anchorage. Where they lead inland I have no idea, but in olden times the moored cargo ships would be pilfered at night and their goods run below Irishtown to be fenced or sold directly to anyone who could rub two coins together.

It's so quiet that my bootsteps talk back to me when the sound of them bounces off the tenement walls, while the wind whistles cryptic words in my ear. Above, up in a window I can sense that someone watches me. But I cannot look. I will not look. I'm too scared to see who it might be. Mostly scared that it is myself that watches as I sneak through the old town. Watching from some other time.

Don't look up, just don't, I think. *I'm not psychopathic. There's nothing wrong with me.*

Yet something stops me. In the middle of the street, I stand as if frozen in time. *What am I doing?* A cool wind tosses my hair about as tingles rush through me like ocean currents. Deathly still, I remain, but the wind and the tingles actually feel like something else. Something more. Like eyes that look me up and down. Like thoughts that see through me.

I'm not superstitious, I tell myself. *I'm not psychopathic. Nobody watches me. No one is there.*

Slowly, I move my eyes up. In a third floor window an old man leans on the sill and stares down at me. A soft smile comes to his mouth when our eyes meet. His features are strangely reminiscent of my own, though his hair is white and stands like a pointed crown that shifts in the waterfront wind, his back has bent and wrinkles sadden his countenance.

"I'm not scared of you," says I while a train thunders in the distance.

"I'm proud of you," says the old man in a strained voice. "When honor becomes the enemy, it must act alone. It is not your fault."

"What isn't my fault?"

But the old man retreats into the room and lowers the window.

"Are you a ghost?"

I look round, but no one is there. Still, the eyes see through me and send shivers up me along with the wind.

Not far from here I was arrested. Children and the aged had appeared in my defense, hurling streetwise anything they could grasp only to disappear again.

Did all of that really happen? I wonder. But my wounds tell the truth of it.

The tavern is covered in lichen from the moist and salty sea air. Gull droppings pepper it as well, and it appears the clapboards had never once seen a coat of paint.

Again I can feel the eyes. *You're not there*, I tell myself. *You don't exist.* But I know that it does. He does. They do, and a gust of wind agrees when it whispers the words in my ear, "They let us starve."

The old tavern is where I first listened to the man they call The Gas Drip Bard with Ma and my sisters just as we listened to the itinerant shanachie back home. I shake my head when I hear myself call Ireland "home."

It can't be home. We're not going back. Brooklyn is our home. Remember that. Remember.

When the door opens an old woman stands in the doorway. She has a very large bosom, spindly legs and eyes as white as the churning clouds over the East River.
"Liam," says she.

"It is, how do you know my name?"

"Liam, bring yerself in, of course, of course, we've been waitin' fer ye. I've just wet some tae, come in to here. Come here to us. The pookas an' the ghouls'll grab ye."

"There's no such thing as pookas," I say to her.

"I know, I know."

Inside it is dark and damp, just as I remember it. The long bar has old men who sit like statues lined along it with amber drinks in front of them amidst quivering candles that have collapsed into hardened, rippled streams of waxy waves that crest over the mahogany and reach for the floor like stalactites in an old cave. From wainscot to ceiling are old and yellowed newspaper clippings and broken-glassed, framed photos. I see Wolfe Tone and Emmet. O'Connell and Parnell and Mitchel and Owen Roe O'Neill as well as depictions of Dierdre and the Sons of Usna, Cuchulain and my favorite from childhood stories, Finn MacCool with Sadhbh and their son Oisín and of course the warriors known as the Fianna. A newer photo shows the profile of Patrick Pearse, a leader of the Easter Rebellion alongside an old sketch of a gaunt and shoeless mother and her two starved and scowling children at her hip; bedecked in rags, all.

In back, embers illuminate the parlor with a low amber glow. In front of the hearth is a ragged rug with moth-eaten holes plaguing it. Strange trinkets adorn the mantle that have collected inches of dust, almost doubling their size. In the darkest area, along the wall, Dinny sits upon an old divan with six children on his lap, over his shoulder and in his arms like a mother possum who carries her newborns on her back. The children, babies even, crawl across his neck, poke at his smiling face and pull the strings from his boots.

"Ya found me," says he with a face lit only by fire.

"I did. Is the Bard here? The Gas Drip Bard?"

"He is, but he's not feeling well. He's upstairs, restin'."

The woman with the cloudy eyes removes a pot from the hob inside the fireplace and comes up from behind and reaches out to touch my arm with shaky fingers. She hands me a saucer and cup with loose tea leaves inside.

"Don't move," she smiles a white-eyed smile.

I hold the cup but it shakes on the saucer. Her contorted, twisted fingers and boney wrist turn the pot slowly in the orange light that reaches up and out of the hearth. Before I can say "when," she stops and searches the parlor for a sound.

"Good, good," she laughs as she shuffles off into the darkness.

But what is darkness to the blind?

"I thank you," says I, but I don't know if she hears me.

"What can I do for ya?" Dinny smiles as a baby crawls up his torso to give him a hug and to rest her face on the nape of his neck.

"Who is that woman?"

"Brigid Hoolihan."

"Oh," I touch my chin. "Have I heard of her before?"

"She's known as Biddy."

I sit on a chair next to him, "Dinny, we don't have a plan for tomorrow. I think we should—"

"Liam," he interrupts. "Not long ago I said ya journey's only begun, do ya believe it now?"

"If you are asking me if I'm back, then yes."

"Ya've had a taste o' what comes, but there are great struggles for ya yet. Barriers ya must overcome, thresholds to cross. In the eyes o' men, ya're proven now. Ya're ready to fight. Ya will never be the same again, I know. But now ya will start seein' it for what it is."

"What is *it*?"

"It cannot be spoken of. There's only one way to know, an' that's to see it. Not everyone can, but—"

"I just want to know what our plan is for tomorrow. We never truly considered cutting the head off the monster, which would solve a lot of our problems."

"Ya mean kill Lovett, I see," Dinny sits back grimly. "That's unfortunate. I thought ya had learned more by now."

"About what?"

"Remember ya vow?"

"Oh, well—"

"A vow is for life. Ya said that after—"

"After what I did to my uncle Joseph, I know."

"That is a threshold ya cannot cross."

"All I know is that we can't lose this fight. If we lose because Bill cheats, what will we do? All the families we feed? Including my own? We'll all be homeless. He'll starve and banish us. Kill us."

"Listen to me, Liam," his voice lowers and a disheartened look comes over him. "No matter who wins the fight tomorrow, we all lose."

"See, I don't know what you're talking about again."

"Ya need somethin' more than what I can offer ya, I know, I know. An' ya're worried about what'll happen, I understand. But if he pulls some prank like showin' up wit' weapons, he'll never command honor. Honor makes us craftsmen, artificers o' our own material world. Dishonor enslaves us in the will o' other men's manufactured reality."

"What does any of that matter if he wins?"

"It means a lot. . . in Irishtown."

"It means nothing, Dinny. If I've learned anything. If I've grown eyes from the things I've witnessed, it's that people go to strength like moths to light. That's how people are."

"Then we must explain to them that that light will burn them."

"They won't listen. Already men are leaving us for Bill. Needles Ferry, James Hart and others. They see strength in Bill, so they go to him."

"Ya're right, they won't listen. It won't do much good. It will do some though. But to fight wit' dishonor is an affront to all that we have been an' all that we are t'day."

"That's a nice theory. But in the real world it doesn't apply."

"Is this the real world?" His palms go up and he turns round. He walks over and peels off some wallpaper, and let's it drop.

"As real as I know it to be."

"Ya've been havin' nightmares o' late. Seein' things too, I know."

"So?"

"Many o' our people suffer this. They turn to the drink to quell the ghosts an' the melancholia. That feelin' o' inferiority," Dinny sits on the edge of the sofa as children scramble for a place in his lap. "But ya've been sufferin' more than others, haven't ya?"

That's not for me to say, I think.

Dinny's face slowly shifts into a slight smile, "This fight is not just against Bill, is it? No, this fight is not in the real world. It's inward-facin'. So the question becomes; how do ya defeat somethin' that exists inside ya'self?"

I haven't a response for that.

"Wit' honesty," he answers.

"But. . . But there's too much to lose. My mother and sisters. Where will they go if—"

"If ya die? Ya mean, if ya kill ya'self?"

"No, what about everyone else? Are you ready to risk everyone's family for your honor?"

Dinny sits back again, "Say I have someone kill Bill Lovett before the fight tomorrow, then what? I'll tell ya; then I become Christie Maroney, the larrikin I took down to become—"

"King?"

"Leader," he corrects. "Is that what ya want if it means ya will survive? Say it now an' it'll be done. Is this what ya want?"

"I don't know what I want. But I do know the world is moving further and further away from honor and leaning more and more toward dishonor."

"That's where ya wrong, Liam. They have always fought. That is why dishonor has always defeated us in battles, yet still we stand, ready to fight again. An' even if we lose? Still they cannot defeat us. No one gets outta here alive, ultimately. It's a big fix isn't it?" Dinny raises his hands. "So why not fight for what is good in humanity, rather than cheat to live a little while longer?"

"So what are we fighting then, dishonor?"

"Wit' Bill, begrudgery."

"And how do I fight that? Too many people with lofty ideas die young. I don't want that for myself. All I've ever wanted was to feed my family."

"That's ya desire, Liam. What is it that drives ya?"

"I don't know, does it matter? Do I have to know what that is? Who cares?"

"It sounds to me like ya're fightin' ya'self too, Liam. Ya just have to believe that there's so much more to know."

I turn away from him, frustrated.

"What are victims?" He continues. "What are victors when. . . Creation is all that matters. We are not animals, but we have not unwound the roots that hold us back. The systems we choose still mimic the animal kingdom as it capitalizes on other peoples' weakness. Like when lions attack a herd o' impala, they do not go for the fastest or the strongest impala. No, the lions chase after the weakest first. The babies or the aged an' butcher them. In the future we want people to choose. To create, because—"

"Because that's honorable. But how is anyone ever going to know what we did here? The newspapers that tell the stories all lie about everything—"

Dinny laughs and picks up a baby from the sofa. He rubs his nose against the baby's nose and kisses a chubby cheek.

"Can we play now? Play horsey? Horsey!" A little girl with hay-colored hair jumps up and down on the old rug.

Dinny climbs off the sofa and goes down to his elbows and knees as the children pile onto his back, screaming. He canters across the parlor and in front of the glowing hearth as they hold on by his hair and his coat. He laughs and laughs, and as children fall off, he helps them back on.

Biddy Hoolihan reappears and is holding the cup of tea I had drained. She tosses the remaining liquid and brings the cup close to her face. Close to her white eyes.

Maybe there is room for everyone, I wonder.

"*Seandream, seandream,*" Dinny sings in Irish as buxom Biddy howls in laughter along with him and the pile of children that ride his back.

"*Seandream, seandream,*" she shrieks and screams. "*Nuair a théarnaigh an seandream.*"

Dinny speaks in whisper from the floor, yet I can hear him plainly as Biddy's keening song reaches terrible climaxes, "Liam, why do they want to kill us?"

"I don't know."

"Why do they want us outta the way?"

"It's their world. They own it. They own the property, the language, the culture, the money, the power. We only pay rent. They let life to us, but when we become too strong—"

"They divide us," Biddy stops her lamenting croon and rummages through her darkness for me with eyes wide open.

"They may own the future. But we have the past. This?" Dinny stands while holding all six children on his back and arms. "These are the days o' our last stand... Again."

Her eyes search blindly, like clouds watch the earth. She has found both of my wrists and holds them gently, "Ye were born fer this, Liam. The child becomes a man. He transcends the dawn and steps through. Behind him the bridge falls away an' bursts into flames. Ahead is the light o' day an' it is known, well known! that there is no goin' back now. No goin' back at all, at all."

"Tell me," says I, my eyes wet with despair. "Tell me I'll survive. Tell me my family will not suffer and I will join you, here and now. I can't tell my mother that I love her. I want to, but I can't. Instead I must show her. Tell me she won't suffer. Tell me I won't leave her to this wretched future."

A smile flickers in the old woman's face. Her eyes widen again, "Yer mammy will have many days. The gentlelife. She'll revel in the gentlelife until a soft and painless passin' comes to her at a great age."

"Will I be there? Will I be there to comfort her?"

"Yes, Liam. Yes ye are there with her as ye saw yerself in the window. Ye have the gift, Liam. The gift!"

"Gift? Are you referring to the ability to see myself as an old man? To see into the future?"

The blind woman laughs, "No, child. Quite the opposite. Yer gift is to see the past. To look back into the now. To witness an' to write an' to revive like a god this story for to tell. The story what was thought to've died. Now, yer journey is hindered only by the mountains o' yer own makin'. An' ye'll make many, many more still. Tomorrow only begins the journey to yesterday."

"The gift," Dinny stands behind the old woman, then comes closer with the blond-haired girl clinging tightly to him. "Ya have ya mother's pragmatic mind. An' ya father's soldierin' heart. Our home is threatened. Our people are under attack. Our ways are on the verge o' extinction. It's time, Liam."

The little girl stares upon me from his arms. She opens and closes her fists and reaches out for me. Gently she settles into my own arms and wipes hay-colored hair from her eyes before she plugs a thumb into her mouth and cuddles deep into my chest. *Her back is so small in my hands.* Then the other children appear at my ankles and claw at my trouser legs to be picked up too.

"Ya've been called to fight," Dinny's voice is now full of resignation and certainty. "To defend ya people an' to save their memory. Save their memory, Liam. That is your gift. Now fight for us."

I will. I will fight.

Trustworthy

"Celia!" Sadie calls over her shoulder into the house with the East London cockney she never could shake.

A muffled voice responds, "Yes?"

"Is L'il Dinny eatin' 'is grapefruit?"

She hears her son's voice in response, "Yes he is. An' my name's John, remember? Just John, not John Carter."

Sadie smiles and looks back toward her cousin Frank, who is sprawled out in a lawn chair next to her. "Do yu think I'll ever be able to pry that boy 'way from 'er?"

"Maybe not," Frank faces the sun that washes him in a golden mid-morning light. "Eventually the boy will believe yu're 'is aunt, not Celia. The thing I can't get over is what a voracious reader 'e is. Never seen it before in all me life. The three detective pulps we got 'im yesterday? 'E read two already. Two issues o' Detective Story in one day. The child is a pro'igy, Sadie. I never knew anyone this smart an' 'ungry to learn."

"Could be yu're a bit partial to 'im, though," Sadie smiles.

The sun shines more often in the suburbs, Sadie tells herself. *Out here, they worship the sun god. And the god of the gentlelife.*

She reaches down from her reclined lawn chair and brushes her palm along the green blades of grass beneath her. Beyond the back of the house, toward the tree line, is an untouched wood. A wilderness of new things for L'il Dinny to learn about and explore. One day Frank had shown them deer droppings on the lawn.

"Deer?" John had repeated, as if the word had described some fictional animal. "In them woods?"

"*Those* woods," Sadie corrected.

"That's right," Frank had kneeled down to the boy's level. "If yu wake up early enough wif' me, we'll come out to the back porch an' while I read the newspaper, yu can read the pulps. An' if we sit still, the muva will wander out first, an' if it's safe, if we've proven to 'er that we are trustworvy, she'll show us 'er fawns."

"Fawns? What are fawns?"

"'Er children," Frank stands with his arms on his hips. "Baby deer are called fawns. The muva is called the doe."

"I wanna see the fawns."

Frank leans his weight on his knees and looks John in the eye, "Are yu trustworvy?"

"I am."

"Well yu 'ave to prove it to the doe first," Frank finds Sadie's eyes, then turns back to John. "Just sayin' it don't mean nuffink."

"Anythin'," Sadie corrects.

"I will, tomorrow mornin'," John promises. "I'll prove it to her, that I'm trustworthy."

Sadie smiles and looks away in thought, Celia is a very lucky woman to have Frank. He is soft spoken, consistently conservative in his decisions and true to his word, Frank Leighton is a man that can be trusted; a great value in this world. He just needs help knowing what decisions to make, Sadie sneaks a look at him from the side of her face.

Before moving to Connecticut, Frank got a job managing the production of roller skates and refrigerators, a new department at the local Winchester Repeating Arms Company after it struggled when production died off at the tail end of the Great War.

Roller skates and refrigerators, Sadie smiles again. *Music to my ears.*

New Haven is not a new city, but Frank had put a down payment on a home in a brand new development outside the city limits. The woods behind the home would eventually be cleared away to make room for more homes.

She turns to her cousin Frank, "I eh. . . I just want yu to know 'ow much I appreciate Celia an' yu'self for takin' us in."

"Well," Frank looks away. "I didn't 'ave much of a choice, did I?"

"It must be a funny thing to be a man," Sadie answers him, her voice thinly veiled by anger. "Men don't really take a woman's word as much as they do anuva man's word. So then, yu were surprised when I showed up at yu door. I told yu in me letter, cousin, that I 'ad made a decision. I chose me son over me 'usband, yu think that's easy, do yu? Yu don't think I'm torn up inside about it? But it all comes down to one thing. I won't 'ave me son endangered by 'is fava's wars. But yu didn't take me for me word, did yu?"

"I don't think yu understand the danger yu're puttin' Celia an' I—"

"I understand that Celia an' yu'self 'ave no children to protect," Sadie's voice is low but bitter. "Yu can't 'ave children, yet everyone assumes it's 'er fault. 'Ow do yu even know it's Celia's body that can't make a baby? Maybe it's yu own body's fault, 'ave yu ever considered that?"

"I 'ave an'—"

Sadie cuts him off so that he cannot disarm her with his grand humility, "Remember when we spent months togeva, yu an' I? On the steamship? Remember 'ow close we were? I 'eard, just as yu 'ad, about women gettin' raped on the passage to America. Yu never said anythin' about it to me though. Still, yu never let me out o' yu site, did yu? Yu even waited outside the loo for me an' slept next to me, back-to-back. Yu protected me, cousin. Tell me then, what changed yu? When did yu stop carin' about yu own blood?"

"Now yu sound like yu mova, Rose."

"Don't compare me to me muva," Sadie raises her voice and sits up in the lawn chair, bare feet in the grass. "I'm sorry I imposed on yu, Frank. But we're fam'ly. We're blood. Yu should try 'arder to remember that."

"I'm reminded everyday," Frank says softly. "I can't even leave Brooklyn wif'out pieces o' me fam'ly followin' along to remind me."

"So yu were just tryin' to get away, were yu? Away from yu own fam'ly?"

"I admit to that," Frank folds his hands in his lap and turns his eyes toward the tree line and the woods beyond. "Darby is a sideshow o' contradictions. An' I 'ate danger, ya know that 'bout me, but me younger bruvas are troublemakers. Darby made a big mistake in puttin' all 'is eggs in Wild Bill Lovett's basket when 'is fiancé is Italian. An' on top o' that, 'e's just plain barmy. 'E'll end up dead in some empty lot or on the floor o' a saloon somewhere, 'e will. An' Pickles is off 'is chump. Best thing for everybody was when 'e was sent up to the stir."

Sadie squirms in her chair.

"Sadie love, I know yu 'adn't many choices back before Dinny took over Irishtown. I 'eard terrible things 'appened to yu that caused Dinny to 'ave Christie Maroney off'd. An' I know I benefited from Dinny offerin' me a jobber at the Soap fact'ry, but I'd change everythin' if I could."

"I wouldn't," Sadie's fingers dig into the lawn chair. "Then I wouldn't 'ave me son."

"An' what 'appens when Dinny shows up 'ere at me 'ome? What will 'e do to me Sadie? What? Will 'e just send Vincent Maher? That man's a killer, yu know. I 'ave first 'and experience seein' 'im kill."

"They won't do nothin' to yu, Frank."

"Yu don' know that. Celia an' I don' want any trouble, but just in case, I'm buyin' a pistol."

"A pistol?"

"This is me property, Sadie. This land's in me name. It's in the American constitution, yu know. The right to bear arms, yeah?"

Yes, which is why I'm going to keep the revolver hidden in the closet.

"What good is land wif'out children? We're not goin' back to Brooklyn, Frank. We're stayin' 'ere. I'm going to get John into a good school. A tutor over the summer—"

"Where yu gettin' the money for that? I know Dinny's not sendin' it."

"Don' worry 'bout that, Frank. I'll give yu money for rent too, not to worry," Sadie looks into the woods with starry eyes. "Yale University is nearby. There are a lot o' universities 'round 'ere. John's six years old now, by the time 'e's eighteen I want 'im ready. I 'ave twelve years to prepare 'im. Yu said yu'self 'e's a pro'igy, yu did. We may 'ave come from the hills o' Northern Ireland an' the streets o' East London only to land in Brooklyn, but me child need never see a cobblestoned street again, Frank. D'yu understand me? I might 'ave been groped on the street, roped into marriage an' kept in a tower like Mary, Queen o' Scots, but me son will 'ave a better life. An' yu gonna 'elp me, damnit."

"Sadie, I don' like it. I don' like it one bit. I moved up 'ere to get 'way from trouble—"

"Yu know, I was wonderin', Frank," Sadie leans her elbows onto her knees to get closer to her cousin. "Some'ow Darby found out we was on Long Island. Some'ow 'e found out the exact 'otel we was stayin' in. I wondered 'ow 'e found out, but now I don'. It was me own cousin that told 'im, wasn't it, cousin?"

"Sadie, 'e's me bruva," Frank said. "An' 'e was tryin' to get me ova bruva outta prison an' wanted money. Money Celia an' I don' 'ave, yeah?"

"So yu turn-in the mova on the run wif a six year-old? I see. I see. Don't matter that ya look tough on the outside, right? That don't matter because on the inside yu're a coward, Frank."

"An' yu're a beggar—"

"I know, an ignorant beggar. Lost like so many in these times," Sadie finishes the sentence. "But it stops wif' me, understand? I've twelve years to prepare that child. It stops wif' me. An' me revenge will be the education o' me son. d'yu understand, Frank?"

"Mum?" John speaks through the screen door with Celia standing above him. "Have yaz seen any fawns yet?"

"Don' use that word, John. There's no such thing as 'yaz.'" Sadie turns round with a smile on her face, "No fawns yet sweet thing."

"Ya have to be trustworthy, only then will the mother let her children come out."

Sadie glances at Frank with a sharp-eyed smile.

Fight

June 1919

Dawn gathers at the darkest hour and the starless sky turns from black to a cloudy gray. Mist mingles among us and the air is fraught with the scent of a cleansing rain. Above us the bridges linger like the great shadows of mythical monsters over the currents of the old river.

Dinny Meehan stands naked and thigh deep where the stony bank and the muddy shore glistens black under the swoosh of saltwater. With his hands he cups water over his shoulders. From behind, muscle ripples in the triangular blades of his upper back. Between his legs the hint of manhood sways thick like low hanging fruit in the spring. He bows his head as water drips from long shards of hair that fall over his ears and cling to his temple.

"Is he praying?" I turn to The Swede.

"Just leave him be."

Vincent exhales and tosses a frayed cigarette, "I hope this goes over well. I was born here in Brooklyn. Motherless, true. Fatherless as well. But I like it here. It's my home, ya know? I don' think I could leave if we. . . lose."

I growl back at him and nod toward Dinny's powerful build, "If anyone thinks they're going to take the seat above the Dock Loaders' Club from that man today, they're going to have to win it from him, square up."

The Swede bobs his head in agreement and taps me with a fist. Yet my belly gurgles.

So why can't I convince my own stomach that he'll win?

"Square up?" Chisel flashes a brown-toothed smile as he leaves through a wad of bills. "An honest guy an' a liar walk into a saloon, 'Can I buy ya a drink?' The liar asks. 'Sure,' says the honest guy. The liar then turns to the big tender behind the bar an' says, 'this guy just agreed to buy me a drink.' The tender begins pouring until the honest guy begs to differ while the liar tosses the drink back. 'Someone's gonna square up for this,' the tender pounds his fist. 'I'm broke,' the liar shrugs. The tender then looks to the honest guy."

The Swede asks. "Who do *you* got money on anyway, Chisel?"

"Why Dinny of course, I am fundamentally against payin' rent."

Behind us are two, maybe three thousand people at the base of Bridge Street and spread through the Jay Street Railyard, while the shrouded city stands tall across the river. The sound of a metal blacksmith's wheel grating against some sort of sword or metal beam takes to the air. Beyond the Navy Yard wall to our right are competing sounds of a serrated saw that tears through wood, the crackle of welding guns on ship hulls and shovels being thrust into piles of stone and dumped into wheelbarrows.

"Some say he died there," Beat McGarry's mouse eyes stare into my own through the melted candle of a face on him.

"The Bard says that," I shake my head.

"All the survivors o' the Great Hunger say it. Some were there. They brought him back themselves."

"Survivors," I repeat without realizing it.

Beat continues, "They squatted in Jackson Hollow, unwanted. Wretches, amassed in the fields of antebellum Brooklyn like livestock. But whereas cattle had use to the Anglo-American, the Irish had none. We were nothin'. We were no one. A place like that? That's from where heroes arise. I was a babe in the belly the first year I went on this pilgrimage an' have been ever since. But I'll tell ya, I've never seen such small numbers."

"Small? There's a lot of—"

"Not like back then,"Beat interrupts coolly. "We had triple this number o' people. There's been an exodus from Brooklyn for many years now an' I fear we're the last o' a breed. The gang is even split in half an' Lovett's followers don' give two shites about the traditions. That's why ya'self an' I are so important."

"I know but—"

"Can ya imagine the people, Liam? Close ya eyes an' think o' the shoeless masses o' us squattin' in fields an' lean-tos an' shacks made o' trash. They had nothin', Liam. Nothin'. . . but hope. Can ya imagine them? Truly? I believe ya can. Of all people, Liam. I know ya can imagine them."

"I do," says I. "I can."

"An' ya will," Beat points a finger in my chest. "Ya're next in line, kid. Behind me. Ya can refuse it all ya want, but ya will still be next in line. The Bard says it, an I myself know it to be true. D'ya have that pencil still?"

"Pencil?"

"That ya stole from Lumpy Gilchrist."

I blink my eyes and search my pocket. My belongings had been returned to me after I was released from the Poplar Street Police Station. Worthless items to all, but myself. The pencil for which I write notes in Whitman's book *Leaves of Grass*, and the Saint Christopher my mother gave me before beginning my journey across the Atlantic Ocean are my treasures.

Beat continues, "I can't read or write, so I'll continue the oral tradition when the Bard passes on. But ya will write it down for all to know."

We both look out on the water.

He taps me, "Dinny died right there, see?"

"Where?"

"There," Beat points. "Where he's standin' now."

The sun fights through the clouds in the east to cast gray light round Dinny in the moving water.

"If he died, how is he standing there?"

"A song," Thomas Burke answers as he comes up from behind. "Don' be so distrustful, Liam."

Beat joins in, "It was prayers to the old gods brought him back. The harvest moon an' the wind an' the trees, because the god we know had ignored them. So they keened to bring back the old ways an' in response a storm appeared at dawn an' overturned a ferry from Manhattan. That mornin' an eleven year-old boy drowned to keep his sick father afloat, an' they knew their prayers had been answered."

"Were you there?"

"Nah, I was—"

"Myths and folklore from a people haunted by hunger, famine, disease and Trevelyan's cold heart," says I. "I wouldn't confuse hope for magic. I used to believe in heroes that came from the Otherworld and itinerant shanachie seers that told eternal tales, but I was a kid then. Now I'm grown."

"Ya're right, it's mere hope that fuels our stories," Burke's tone is calm and agreeable. "Fertile hope, because the most powerful o' all hope springs from despair, the pang o' hunger an' desperation that causes people to hope so hard their brains hurt for the wantin'. It's that hope what shakes the heavens, an' a hero falls out; his wet soul awakened when the old folk pass away."

"Crazy talk," I spit out in their direction. "I'm supposed to tell that story? With a straight face?"

"Liam—"

"Enough," I interrupt. "I've got more than enough on my plate already."

Naked, Dinny trudges through the East River as a soft rain begins to circulate in the air, barely distinguishable from the morning fog. Biddy Hoolihan comes to his left with his clothing over her arm. A stooped man with a full white beard and windswept sea-green eyes comes to his right on the rocky shore.

"Isn't that him? The Bard?" I ask Beat.

Burke nods and Beat says, "But he has the grippe, Liam. A wheezin' cough. It's in his lungs, real bad. His days near an end. An' mine draws nigh. I'll be the third Irishtown shanachie, an' ya'll be—"

"Alright, alright," I tamp Beat's enthusiasm.

Dinny's broad chest and thick upper arms dwarf the elderly woman and the stooped Bard. The dark wet mist that descended obscures the amber morning light, but does not cover Dinny's bare cock to our eyes. And the dark curly pelvic hair between his thick thighs does not seem to embarrass anyone. Slowly he dresses while out on the harbor a distant tugboat sounds off, *hoo-hooooo*. He then walks directly toward me until I stand off from his way. And a clearing is made through the great slew of old Brooklyn Irish assembled this morn.

"Go, c'mon," Cinders gently pushes me from behind.

As the crowd separates, The Swede and Vincent Maher walk directly behind Dinny. Cinders, Red, The Lark and Dance follow with Big Dick, Philip Large and Henry Browne as well as Eddie and Freddie in tow. Behind them gather the bulk of the longshoremen who follow Dinny Meehan's clan out of Bridge Street. In all more than one hundred men and all the families have come out, though mine is not present.

"Liam," I hear a voice.

When I look over I see Mrs. Burke and her children. She is at the head of them and pushes her eldest son Joseph in a homemade wheelchair.

I run over to greet them, then lean down toward Joseph, "Where did you get this chair?"

He says, "It just. . . appeared at our f. . . front door."

"Who made it?"

But Mrs. Burke just gives a proud smile.

"I came to see a real f. . . f. . . fight," Joseph says. "The legend of D. . . Din—"

"Don't say that name," I point into his face and smile. "You don't know no one by that name, understand? He doesn't exist, remember?"

Joseph smiles a big happy smile and nods without another word said.

"Liam," I hear again and look up.

Mrs. Burke steps aside and through the crowd, my sister walks through.

"Abby, what are you doing here?"

"I'm with ye, Liam."

"Is Mam an' Brigid here?"

"No, Mam wouldn't come. She forbid me to come too, but. . ."

"You shouldn't—"

"Liam, I'm tired o' everyone tellin' me what I shouldn't do. This is what I want. When can I start choosin'? I'll be eighteen come next year. Even if I am a young woman, don't ye want yer sister to have the power to make her own mind?"

"Well—"

"I want to be here. I want to be with me big brother who done so much for his fam'ly, even if his own Mam doesn't appreciate it."

"She does but—"

"I know, she werries. But ye can't werry yer whole life 'way, can ye? Ye've risked everythin' fer us, Liam. Let me show me appreciation. Let me choose. I can do anythin', ye know."

I smile and shake my head, "We need all the help we can get."

Our hands come together, but when she squeezes I wince.

She moves her eyes from my hand to my face, "Be careful today, Liam."

The crowd moves through the streets and the newly bloomed trees. Behind us the aged are helped along by their full grown children, and grandchildren. Still in her widow's weeds, Mrs Mullen carries the newborn at her breast while her eldest son Whyo holds hands with his hobbling grandfather. In his other hand is the little girl with Vincent's eyes.

"It's gonna be a fight for all time to tell," Whyo tells his grandfather with Will Sutton shadowing him. "Like 'A Day for Legends' was back in 1916, or the Adams Street Riots o' 1913. It'll go down in Irishtown hist'ry!"

"Ya do what ya can for the king," Mrs. Mullen nods to her boy with a proud smile. "He's there for us. Ya do what ya can for him so he wins t'day, otherwise. . ."

She trails off, but Whyo continues, "They'll call it the Battle o' Jackson Hollow, maybe."

"The Brawl for King o' Irishtown," Will Sutton offers.

"Ye're warriors, all," the Bard calls forward through a wet cough. "Soldiers o' the Dawn."

A smile comes across my face when I see the old fellow again, the Bard. He wears his good intentions round him like a charm for all to see. And when he smiles back at me I look away the shame wells up in me for not having gone back to him, even as many people had asked me to.

I heard tell that he was one of those whose ship berthed in Brooklyn, which was the tail-end of a great and tragic journey. With nowhere to go, he and many other orphans, lost souls and the broken-hearted wandered into Jackson Hollow, then eventually founded Irishtown and every year go back to honor that journey and the great many who were lost along the way, whether in Ireland or out at sea. And although our numbers are no longer what they once were, I can see he is proud, still.

As Cinders and I walk past, I ask, "How many are there? The survivors from those days?"

Cinders looks back to me, "Eight."

"Eight?"

"Last year there were eleven."

"I. . . I didn't know—"

"No one honors them as much as Dinny. He has cared for them since. . . since before I knew him."

Through the morning mist we walk in a great procession. Between buildings on Hudson Avenue through the oldest parts of Irishtown and up on both sides of the uneven slate sidewalks.

"We love ya!" A lone woman's voice echoes from an unseen tenement window and falls all round Dinny, who leads the way.

"Clouts for touts!" A boy yells out. "Give that begrudgin' Lovett what he deserves!"

"Fist to fist, no one can beat the King o' Irishtown!"

The voices gather as we turn on Myrtle Avenue under the elevated train, but every time I hear how unbeatable Dinny Meehan is, my stomach churns.

"They'll never rid the world o' our like," another voice yells, but that turns my stomach too.

"What is right can never be forgotten! Remember!" Someone yells.

To the right is Fort Greene Park. In the 1840s it was Walter Whitman's doing. He had argued for more parks in Brooklyn to break the oncoming industrial revolution. The great monument to the Prison Ship Martyrs towers high above the park's treeline and over the crypt of some 12,000 Americans who died during the Revolutionary War in America. The prisoners were put on ships out in Wallabout Bay by British command and left in horrific conditions to die of starvation and disease on board.

"They let them starve too," The Lark mumbles.

Red takes up the claim, "They sent the Irish to the roads. Evicted us durin' winter where we died in the hundreds o' thousands."

The chants become dense and boom out as the rain thickens and the clouds bend low down into our midst. The streets are cleared for our coming and every window is open with three heads sticking out of each to see the old Irish clans take Brooklyn again through the fog.

In one window I see myself again. Rather, the old man I am to become. He smiles again, proudly.

I must be psychopathic. There must be something terribly wrong with me. How could Biddy call that a gift? I don't want to crossover to that world. I'll never make it back whole.

"He's never lost a fight in his life!" The Swede raises his lone strong arm, and yet again my stomach flips in anticipation.

Nothing is never.

The Swede then bends to kiss the top of Helen Finnigan's blond head, who holds hands with their child. A tear falls from his eye as he focuses attention on the little dote. Soon enough the child is on his shoulders with a bird's eye view of the current of people striding the streets. On this day no one seems to shame the Finnigan family. On this day we are one family, even when it means the notion of family is stretched so wide that it spans into the forbidden.

From the north the crowd turns right on Irving Place. Up ahead a collection of empty lots appear where three buildings had collapsed, though they were only partially cleared as nature has worked her will upon the area to turn the wreckage into a misshapen clearing. It is the only open area in what was once the empty farmland of the Jackson family. The dirt is soft and lumpy and a growth of weeds have overtaken the ruin of rotted wood frames and joists and roof trusses and rafters that linger just below the patchy grass. An old barn door lies flat against a thicket of grass with its rusted handle still intact and the impression of motorcar tires leave circular holes in the overgrowth.

With handfuls of cash, Chisel McGuire breaks out into song, his voice strong and supple.

'Tis many long years since I saw the moon beamin'
On strong manly forms, on eyes with hope gleamin'
I see them again, sure, in all my sad dreamin'
Glory O, Glory O, to the bold Fenian men.

Soon the crowd takes it up and away, and the dewey morning air is celebrated as a blessing and a reminder of the old world.

Some died by the glen side, some died near a stranger
And wise men have told us their cause was a failure
But they fought for ol' Ireland an' never feared danger
Glory O, Glory O, to the bold Fenian men

The brave Johanna, wife of Cinders Connolly and their four children have joined him now too. Her mission was a dangerous one and she only escaped by the black of her nail. More dangerous than we imagined, but she came out true and gave us the facts of Patrolman Daniel Culkin and escaped unharmed.

Dago Tom's family as well is here. And Dance Gillen has a wife and child too that I meet for the first time, as well as Beat McGarry's grandchildren and many more. Even the silently devout whiskey drunk Ragtime Howard is here alongside his personal priest, the tender at the Dock Loaders' Club, Paddy Keenan. But Sadie and L'il Dinny are missing, which leaves a great void in the morning's fight.

I passed on my way, God be praised that I met her
Be life long or short, sure I'll never forget her
We may have brave men, but we'll never have better
Glory O, Glory O, to the bold Fenian men

From the east we see a gang of men walk toward us of about forty. Henry Browne walks ahead to meet them. The man who Henry shakes a hand with first is the pock-marked Thos Carmody. The ILA union recruiter who hired my uncle Joseph to bring Brooklyn under their banner no longer hides his face under a collar. Instead his posture is proper and proud and his health seems to have improved, his confidence returned. By his side are fifty or so other ILA men including the dog-faced King Joe Ryan.

"There he is, the fookin' coward," Cinders says with a nod toward Quick Thos. "Won't walk wit' us, but sidles in afterward. They won't pick a side, either. They said they'd make their appearance, then go so as not show favoritism. When Dinny wins, we should keep their earnin's, don' ya think Chisel?"

"Nah, the big money's on Bill, if. . ." Chisel doesn't bother to finish that sentence.

Coming up behind that group from the south is a gaggle of swarthy Italians togged in colorful raiments. Though some are dressed as laborers. Sixto Stabile leads that group and is surrounded by Lucy Buttacavoli, he of the aquiline nose. Sixto's father, Stick'em Jack and the two big men that drove the motor cars up to the Dock Loaders' Club a month ago shadow them. Then there is another group of Italians surrounding the Prince o' Pals, Frankie Yale, who could not find it in himself to put boots on and instead tiptoes through the uneven field in slippers, hands bedecked with rows of rings.

Paul Vaccarelli crosses from the Italian group to the ILA and shakes hands with King Joe as a courtesy, the both of them being vice presidents, but only nods at Quick Thos.

Behind us, up on a mound of swollen trash and reeds and underneath a five story tenement are three young women. One of the girls is ahead of the others, her fox-colored hair streams like a cloak in the wind behind her. She wears a peasant blouse that clings to her lithe build with a separate skirt that is high enough over her ankles to show the stolen Hanan boots she sports.

"Anna fookin' Lonergan?" Vincent bites his lip. "Damn that's a nice ride."

"Can't she afford hair pins?" Someone voices a complaint.

"Nah, she's free as a filly gallopin' through the purple heather," Vincent smiles. "That tomato's ripe an' ready. Hot-blooded I tell ya, wit' that fookin' fierce stance on her."

Behind her is the buxom Grace White and Kit Carroll who are gaudily tinseled with fluffy dresses. Grace is festooned with fake gold necklaces like some top-heavy gypsy queen while Kit drags from a smoldering paper cigarette with a disinterested, cat-like glare.

"Grace & Pretty Kitty," a mischievous smile forms on Vincent's face.

"Jesus on a stick," The Swede mumbles his displeasure, then yells up at them. "Go find ya'selves some good Irish-American men to take care o' yaz!"

"God knows we won't find none here t'day," Anna howls back, her crown of hair flaring like tentacles in the strong currents. "Especially you, ya fookin' limp-limbed tomfool."

Some of the men can't help but laugh at those words, but the jape is cut short when from the south comes a large band of labormen walking in unison and flayed out like a phalanx with Wild Bill himself at the tip of the spear of men. The two war counselors on his right are the contrarian Non Connors and One-arm Joey Flynn. On his left is the limping Richie Lonergan and Frankie Byrne too.

"What if they come wit' weapons?" Burke whispers into my ear.

I am of the same mind.
This could end quickly.

My eyes search their waistcoats and trousers for the impression of pistols or bail hooks or cudgels, but I don't see any.

"Whoever wins today must do it honorably," I answer him.

Burke's mouth wiggles as he stares at Bill's approach, "I want to believe that too. I heard Bill killt one o' his own men yesterday an' it wasn't just to send a message. He says it makes him stronger, killin'. An' he wanted a boost before the fight."

The Lonergan Crew, who have melded into the Trench Rabbits, march behind Bill's lieutenants through the low hilly ground and overgrown weeds.

"Their numbers have grown," Cinders takes notice. "Looks more like eighty than fifty. An' over there's, it's Needles and James Hart, the teamster."

"We still got them outnumbered more than two to one. We're up to about one-seventy t'day," The Lark murmurs as the enemy approaches and takes up a position along the eastern part of the lots.

"Make a half-circle," Bill commands his men, some of which have to stand on the gable of a crumbled rooftop amidst the reeds.

Dinny nods at both sides of his force to do the same when the gray mist thickens and clings to our clothes and skin. Enemies meet on both sides of the ringwall and the fighter's circle closes in a low-lying area. The women and children, as well as the aged stand outside of it, behind us, up on the mounds of sunken garbage and overgrowth. All then turn to watch the middle where the two melee fighters meet and shake hands and return to their respective sides.

All goes quiet as Lovett surveys the lots and spits without breaking his stare on Dinny Meehan.

Chisel McGuire breaks the silence to announce in his carnival barker's best, "We meet here t'day as men met in the ol' days. The old ways remain here. On these grounds seventy years past came our forebears who first survived a famine, then the cold heart of the English in an attempt to break our spirit and turn our people against each other. Man versus woman, young versus old, North against South. If that weren't enough, those who could flee Ireland entered ships that would become their coffins. When the survivors came here, there were no homes to be had. No jobs to earn food. Nothin' for our like but the words, 'No Irish Need Apply! We are honored by their presence," Chisel yells out and turns with a bow. Standing upon another weedy hill are the last of the aged survivors of those dark days. The eight haggard faces, five women and three men. In response they nod graciously in Chisel's direction at his respectful words.

"Let's get this thing started," Bill suddenly says, dismissing the pageantry.

"Don' ever forget the past," The Swede yells across the fighting circle. "Ya're own grandparents squatted in this self same field we stand in t'day!"

Bill smirks and mumbles something behind him until Darby Leighton comes to his ear. He points up to Anna Lonergan on the hill and says something until the little curly-haired Abe Harms whispers something in support. At that, Anna and her followers disappear on the other side of the hill. Darby and Abe then withdraw behind Bill's gang as well.

Dinny nods at Chisel, whose voice carries across the empty lot and beyond, "We're here t'day to decide who will lead the White Hand an' take his rightful place above the Dock Loaders' Club at Twenny-Five Bridge Street. The loser will be gone wit' himself!"

"Yeah!" Bill's men explode in celebration at the words and begin chanting, "Kill! Kill! Kill!"

"We aren't here to kill," I yell across.

"Yes we are!" Bill yells in a raspy voice once, then twice until his own followers quieten.

He steps forward to the middle of the circle and addresses all.

"Loser will not be gone," he extends his arm straight out and turns it to Dinny Meehan. "I declare a Blood Feud here and now!"

"Yeah!" His men explode again.

"The loser will die!" Bill groans. "T'day."

"That's right!"

"Kill! Kill! Kill!" His men call out

Chisel is taken aback, as we all are. He turns to Dinny and speaks in a lowered tone, "Do ya accept these terms?"

"Say his name," Bill demands. "Say his name so we know who accepts the challenge!"

Chisel speaks over the chant of Bill's men to ensure all understand, "A Blood Feud is an ancient passage. Between two men, one will own death. The other will own the soul and the spirit of the dead he defeats," Chisel turns to Dinny, who nods back at him in acceptance. "Dinny Meehan, do ya accept the challenge?"

Unless you had known the man, you would never know that the face Dinny makes upon that challenge is a sad one. It's the saddest I have ever seen him, for he has already lost. *We all* have already lost, as he tells it. His goal has never been to beat Bill Lovett in a fight. He only sought to outsmart him and weaken Bill until he could convince him that working together made us all stronger.

"How can he refuse?" Red Donnelly mumbles.

"Dirty trick to pull this here at the last second," The Lark says as Big Dick stands behind him.

Dinny raises his eyes to Bill, "I do," he says. "I accept."

The crowd gasps as I look back to find my sister Abby.

She's not ready to see a dead body. When finally I find her on the hill above, she has pushed her shoulders back proudly as if to say, *I am ready. I am ready for everything that you have seen, brother.*

Chisel calls out to the gods and anyone who can hear, "One man will die t'day, one man will live!"

Only Bill's side celebrates, the rest behind us; the mothers and children, the longshoremen and laborers who watched Dinny rise up. Who saw him defend their honor. The people of Irishtown who love him for his generosity and humility, hang their heads.

"Have the aged taken back to Irishtown," Dinny requests. "The children too. There's no need to have them watch this."

A few men run back, but the old Irish-born, original settlers refuse to move. Quite a few of the parents decide against staying, however. They take their children and walk away to Bill Lovett's delight.

"We say right makes might," the Bard calls down to Dinny with a face of pallid and fragile constitution. "An' that we brought ye back for good reason. An' as the timeless universe o' symbols has not collapsed in us, at least," he sweeps his hand among the stooped augurs. "Yer risin' is not yet accomplished. We say ye won't die this day. We say, fight!"

The Swede's horse head nods his agreement.

"How does Bill even think he can win?" Cinders whispers in my ear. "I don' trust him. I don't."

I look over to Dinny where his profile is against the backdrop of tenements that are shrouded in mist. He has removed his coat now. He has unbuttoned his shirt. Now he is more beast than man. The muscles in his shoulders and upper arms pulse in and out as if he is inhabited with some spirit. When he sees me, he whips a shock of hair from over one eye and grabs me by the back of the neck, "I have loved ya wit' all my heart, Liam," he says. "All o' it, since the day ya showed up at McGowan's Wake. Don' ever think that was a accident. Understand?"

"I understand."

"It's not enough they want to remove us from power so we can't help the people in these neighborhoods. No, they want to take our name too. To remove us entirely from hist'ry. No one'll ever know about this day, ya know that? It'll just be a memory, unsung. An' when everybody here dies, it'll be gone an' people'll just go on believin' we were animals who drank an' stole things because we were bored or stupit. But ya can change that, ya know. Ya can. Go to the Bard, Liam. Go to him with the excitement o' a boy runnin' through the slanted fields o' the Otherworld. Go back. Tell me ya will."

Dinny pulls my head closer and our foreheads meet.

"I will," says I. "I will if you want it."

He turns away and lets me loose from a fierce grip, "Good. Make us human."

"The stakes have changed!" Chisel breaks into a singsong voice as he removes his top hat and his dusty coat tails wag in the wind. "We will need a few minutes, for the odds will be settled. Who believes Wild Bill's odds have improved?"

"No ya don't," The Swede pushes Chisel. "This ain't no carnival show. Dead or lost, makes no difference—"

"Why not let the man do his job," Non Connors calls out from Bill's side and nods to Chisel.

"Ya shut ya gob. Challengers make no terms," The Swede answers him.

"I'll put ya down myself, ya sister-fookin' mongrel," Connors points. "Some say ya're haunted, Swede. Is that why ya hover over ya sister all the time?"

One-arm Flynn caws out a laugh as Non starts in with more talk until Bill mumbles something over his shoulder that quietens him.

Dinny steps forward and The Swede, Vincent and myself come together with the rest of the dockbosses and righthands behind us. Across the circle Bill comes forth to meet his opponent.

Chisel has two fingers in his green and yellow checked waistcoat and nods back at Connors in thanks, then wheels on his heel and extends an arm in the direction of Bill Lovett, "The challenger! is the grandson of a Kerryman, son of a sanitation worker an' a decorated veteran o' the Great War! He has many war wounds from his time in France, but even more from the battles here in Brooklyn. To his own kind he is known as Wild Bill. To the Black Hand he is known as *Pulcinella*, but t'day he supports the notion o' change. Is he the light o' the future? The man o' fate what he so proudly claims? Or is he no more than a begrudger as his opponent asserts? T'day. . . we will know."

"A little faster Chisel, there's a lotta people here waitin' for some action," The Swede cups his mouth with his one good hand.

Chisel offers a sham smile and continues, "The Champion! an' current leader o' the White Hand since 1913." He spreads his arm toward Dinny. "Some simply call him 'the man,' some dare to use his real name, but all know that to the soul o' him, he is Patrick Kelly!"

A roar of approval comes from behind us.

"Some, in the oldest part o' Irishtown say he was reborn."

"Bollix!" Petey Behan calls out, then stares across the circle and blows a kiss at me. *I own you*, he mouths in my direction while pointing into his own chest. *I own you.*

Chisel twirls his blackthorn cane in the air to continue, "An' that he was summoned to help the needy! To heal the horrible wounds an' honor the agin' settlers through the winter o' their lives. He has put himself at great risk by raidin' the local shoe fact'ry and passin' out boots to one an' all. An' there ain't a-one person here t'day who has not been touched by his generosity—"

"Don' start cryin' over here," Connors growls.

A voice behind me responds, "Undefeated! Our champion has never lost—"

"I think we had enough, Chisel," The Swede says.

"Challenger and Champion, please step back to ya respected areas," Chisel calls out as both little Whyo Mullen and Will Sutton struggle through the crowd with a gigantic bronze bell. A hammer is handed to Chisel and he looks longingly into the crowd. The bell is then thwacked with the hammer and a shrill and trebly reverberation scares Whyo, who falls back on his duff until he recovers and drags the bell away through the reeds and clumps of rotted wood that has been swallowed by wild grass.

Dinny and Bill circle each other.

"Ya don' wanna do this, Bill," I hear Dinny say.

"Yet here I am."

"I told ya that ya're not my enemy."

"But ya're mine."

"No," Dinny says.

"Yes," Bill responds and steps forward with the threat of a straight right.

Dinny jogs to the right, unfazed. The slew of revelers become unsettled and push from behind me. In the fighting circle, Dinny's hands are held loosely under his chin and his head is on a swivel, waving back and forth in confidence. Without even a single punch thrown, Bill is becoming winded. His cheeks redden and he is breathing out of his mouth.

"What's Dinny's plan? He just gonna wear him out?" Vincent asks.

"He didn't tell me anything," I yell back.

Suddenly, like two wild dogs that break into a vicious dance, Dinny and Bill bump chests and let fists fly. It goes so quickly that it's hard to tell who came out with the best of it, but most are surprised Bill is still standing. Then a right cross from Dinny sails over Bill's head and again the two exchange thudding punches.

Bill now has a lump on his forehead and steps back to rip off his shirt and tie. With an undershirt and a belt that keeps his pants high, he enters the fray again and moves toward Dinny who also sports an undershirt, but suspenders hold his pants up.

With all of the shoving, the ringwall of the inner circle clenches and palpitates like an arsehole, and the rain has softened the ground even further as we slosh round the brown mud.

"Get back!" The Swede yells behind us. "Dockbosses an' righthands! Keep the slew back!"

There are dozens of people on rooftops behind us and even across the cobblestoned street and every window has four heads peering out now. Beyond the fighting circle there are low hills strewn with rusted nails poking out of decayed two-by-fours from tumbledown tenements where onlookers jostle for position. Bill's hounds are wriggling to free themselves from their chain-collars and it takes six men to keep the three of them at bay, for they long to brawl for their master in his time of need.

Again Bill and Dinny come together and snap upper cuts and long-armed jabs into each other. Dinny's ear has reddened from a blow, but it's become evident that Bill's lip is swollen as he wipes blood on his forearm.

"Kill! Kill! Kill!" Bill's side calls out in unison.

"This is gettin' outta hand," Vincent screams across to me, though I can barely hear him.

DIVIDE THE DAWN

Then Dinny has Bill backed up against his own men and thrashes him with a left cross that comes from below. Then two quick rights that stagger him.

"It's almost over," The Swede calls.

But Bill spits blood at Dinny and fights him off with wild lefts and rights that miss their mark. Bill is out of breath but steps forward when Dinny makes his move to the inside of him. Three body blows and a right upper cut stun Bill, and as he moves to turn away, Dinny grabs hold of his trousers by the belt and pulls him close again, where he can inflict more damage. Dinny's fists land square and full force into Bill's chest and ribs. The impact of each blow heard twenty feet away. Then he moves up to the head, blasting knuckles off Bill's forehead and temple and then on the top of his head when he ducks. Dinny is now only bleeding from his hands, while Bill takes punch after punch.

"He has a gun," Someone yells from among Bill's men. "He had a gun the whole time!"

Caw-caw, One-arm Flynn quarks in laughter and points to the ground by Dinny's feet where a pistol lay in the mud. It's an old German model and has a round hole in the bottom of the handle and a narrow barrel.

"No, that's not his," I yell. "He would never—"

"Meehan breaks his own code o' honor," Non Connors stands forth. "He came to kill our leader wit' that pistol."

Richie Lonergan then steps forward behind Dinny and crashes a right hook under his jaw. Dinny drops to his knees in front of us all. He never saw it coming. But before we can even respond, the Shit Hounds are let loose to sprint across the fighter's circle past Dinny and all three dive into The Swede, Vincent and myself in unison.

As the mist turns to heavy drops of rain, then a deluge that soaks the earth, a bugle sounds off in the distance.

"Charge!" Connors and Flynn stand over Dinny and thrust arms across the circle to point the way.

A phalanx of men swarm past Dinny and crash into our lines, trampling me while a yellow dog yanks with a frenzy on my trousers at the ankle.

"Dinny!" I yell out.

Through the crowd Bill's lieutenants kick and punch down into Dinny. Bill then crawls through the mud to search for the German model pistol.

I grind my boot against the yellow dog's eyes, but it just tears back and forth, its neck muscles flexing at each turn.

"They're gonna kill him," Burke yells at me.

"Don't let that dog bite my cock," Vincent screams.

Through the slew I see a punch that jolts Dinny, blood and spittle fly from his mouth. He is on his knees taking punch after punch, but I cannot get up. A wall of men has formed in front of us by the Trench Rabbits and others that block our path to Dinny. Though we have the numbers, we are outmaneuvered and outflanked. A boot takes me by the back of the head, but when I look up Big Dick has torn the dog from my trouser leg and tosses the rabid animal twenty feet into the distance. But he is then kicked from behind by three others and is blocked from the area.

Across the way Richie and Connors take turns on Dinny until Flynn and Byrne get their shots in. Bill has found the German pistol and struggles to stand. Through the melee I see him raise his arm and point it at Dinny's face.

"Bill's got the pistol!" I yell, but I am useless to help, blocked in by ravenous dogs and a wall of trained soldiers.

I try to jump through their line but I am thrown back and booted. Beyond the wall Dinny's hands are held behind him and he is made to kneel. He moves his eyes up to meet the barrel.

"No!"

A tiny smile appears on Dinny's face, but just as the pistol claps Bill is tackled from the side. Dinny jolts backward in response and his head whips behind. On his knees his body flops to one side, but Bill is now on the ground again.

Someone tackled him, I realize. *Someone is beating Bill with fists.*

Suddenly the pistol is ripped out of Bill's hand and tossed thirty feet away.

"Who the fuck's that?" I hear.

The unknown man then swoops into the lieutenants so fast that there is no time to react. He lands a shoulder into Richie's back, doubling him over. An elbow explodes under the jaw of Connors, dropping him. Before Byrne can react he is sent tumbling back onto his rear and receives a Hanan boot across the side of his head. The stranger then simply stares one-arm Flynn away.

"Harry!" Whyo Mullen's screeching voice calls out from somewhere. "It's Harry Reynolds! Harry fookin' Reynolds! It's him! It's really him!"

Behind the wall another dog is kicked in the hind area and limps off, yelping at the air. A punch sails over my shoulder as I get up. Before I realize it, another lands on my temple and yet more on the top of my head. Big Dick picks up the yellow Shit Hound for the second time and slings it over our heads again.

Seventy of their men stand in our way, three lines deep. The nearest line attacks, throwing punches and kicking at us. Then a voice calls out a signal and that line steps back. The second line steps forward and again kicks and punches to keep us back. After a time, the next line comes to the front, fresh and ready to fight.

In the chaos, I am tackled again. As I lay on my back, a fist continually pounds down on me until I catch the arm. When I look at who owns the arm, Petey Behan's box head stares back at me. He gnashes his teeth to pull his arm back as I kick up under his face with a boot. I struggle to stand and take another punch to the head before I have my balance. He swings again and connects but I am at his throat and have grabbed hold of his right wrist with my left hand to stop the beating. I throw him back at the neck and yank him back at the wrist to slam an elbow across his face. As he steps back from the blow I am plowed into by The Swede who has been tackled. When I can't find Petey, I turn to look behind me twice, then three times.

Behind me Vincent screams as a Shit Hound ravages at his cock, "Get it off me! Get it off me," he howls.

Some of our men have have run off screaming, including Burke. And even a few gang members loyal to both sides stumble away holding their sides and their heads. For the rest of us it is blood and fighting. The Lark takes a man by the back of the neck, flooring him into the mud. I believe it is the younger Quilty brother. Dance is in the air, his knees almost touching his own shoulders. As he stomps on face and gullet simultaneously, he struggles to keep his balance. Squat, short-armed Philip Large wrestles a man and catapults him up and behind, a pair of legs trailing afterward. Vincent Maher bleeds from the grommet but has gathered his wits and swings down on a man who can't stand from his knees.

At the next signal, the refreshed wall of men breaks formation and attacks with a ferocity not yet seen. Eddie and Freddie tackle Jidge Seaman, Sean Healy and old man John Lonergan and pummel them. Five Trench Rabbits take turns booting Ragtime Howard, Henry Browne and Dago Tom Montague. The older brothers Behan and Quilty take Philip Large to the ground and don't allow him to get up. The younger Quilty, Timothy, has regained himself and hurls upper cuts and straight-lefts into Red Donnelly's bloodied face like a true boxer while Matty Martin circles behind and kicks him. Cinders Connolly attempts to help but is taken down from behind.

Dago Tom is flung and lands next to me on his back as a mud puddle splashes across my face. He kicks up at his attackers and looks over to me, "He's dead, Liam. Dinny's dead. We should fall back."

"No he is not!" I cry. "No!"

"Yes he is," Red's voice sounds almost sad. "They shot him in the face."

As I come to one knee, bantam Petey Behan stands over me with a glinting weapon in his hand, "There's nothin' to fight for. Quit an' I might let ya live."

The wall of Bill's followers stand over us, supported by two other lines. The violence comes to a sudden halt and a silence pervades old Jackson Hollow. Beyond the wall Harry falls to his knees, exhausted after fighting against Bill and his four lieutenants while Dinny is face down in the mud, motionless. Up in tenement windows and on top of the hills of reeds and trash and the ruin of toppled buildings, the remaining viewers watch and listen, shocked by the events.

Chisel, my sister Abby, Whyo and Will, the Mullen family and the many families of Irishtown await a decision. Even Biddy Hoolihan and The Bard stand among a small group of elders to hear a decision.

A black smile comes across Petey's half-muddied face, "It's over, Liam."

"It's never over," I yell out to all who would listen. "They let us starve! Yet still we endure! Dishonor has always defeated us in battle, yet still we stand and fight, and in so doing, we command honor in order to create. That does not die with Dinny Meehan. That must go on to live forever. White Hand men, come to your feet, now!"

Petey Behan steps forward with a shiv in his hand, "Now it's time to die."

"No!" Abby yells out in the distance.

"You can kill me, but you can never kill our ways," I raise my arms.

"Weapon!" The Swede yells from the ground, holding his clavicle. "He has a weapon!"

"So what," Petey talks through gritted teeth. "Ya boss came wit' a pistol."

"Lies!" I yell. "Lies, lies, lies. Drop your weapon and fight me, one-on-one."

Petey nods and looks round him, "This is the real world. Ya gotta death wish? Wanna be a martyr? I'll make ya one."

He rushes me and swings the shiv, which opens up my shirt at the shoulder with a red wound. Then kicks to the back of my leg. Quick as a badger he is on my back grappling for my neck. Piggybacking me. The sharp cold of the metal shiv slides along my throat to gently open the thin skin.

Ya better survive, Dinny's words come back to me. *Otherwise ya will be trapped in this story forever.*

I splash through the mud fighting for position so that he cannot get his hooks in. The shiv wavers over my throat while my hand holds his wrist precariously.

"Kill him, Petey," Joey Behan cheers his little brother.

A rage gathers inside me. I gain my bearings, then make a quick move to peal him off. I take both of his arms by the wrist and jump backward to push all of my weight into him and wrench myself free at the same moment.

"Yes," The Swede calls from the ground. "Don' give up, Liam."

At impact I wriggle and scrape free. I do not want to wrestle with him so I grab at his coat and pull him backward where he cannot hit me. But with the shiv he swings up and behind him and it scrapes across my arm, opening a sleeve with a gash.

My boots jolt at his lower back as I pull, then kick, then pull again with a fistful of his coat. When he swings behind him again, I catch his arm with both hands at the wrist. Then I wrap my legs round his neck and fall to the ground, shaking his arm to let loose of the shiv. I dig my thumbs into soft spot of his wrist and pull his fingers open until finally it drops in the wet dirt at my side.

Then I jump to my feet and grab the shiv. With blood and mud mingled in my mouth, something terrible yearns to escape from the prison inside me.

Murder him, the words bubble in my ear. *You have him, now kill him. Kill him.*

"Kill! Kill!" The chant of the onlookers takes up the charge.

"Kill him!" Dance yells from our side of the wall that Bill Lovett's men hold.

My heart hurts. It aches to take his life. To have it for myself, always. And I want to give in to it.

How could the heart lie? How could it lie to me? Kill him, my heart answers.

"Cut him open!" The Swede screams from the ground.

"Slash at his face," Vincent says.

"Kill, kill, kill!" My friends chant.

I look at the shiv through muddy fingers. It glints a cold gray into my eyes. Then I close my fist round it, turn away and throw it as far as I can. Through the air it tumbles as all watch it disappear over a roof.

I let loose of Petey's coat to let him stand. When he is upright and raises his fist over his face, I tag him with lefts.

When I swing with a right his forehead bangs against my wounded knuckles and a shimmer of pain slices up through my arm again and into my brain. The old wound reopened, my fists turns a bright red. But pain I don't react to. Not now. I lean into another right hand and he is flung backward, but before he can gather his balance I pepper him with lefts and rights. He then raises up and throws a left jab, but I move to the right, and when he throws a left cross afterward, I see it coming and pull back. The punch whizzes in front of my nose. I flash a quick smile at Dance, then move in on Petey. The empty swing leaves his body unbalanced and unready for my attack. It's his jaw I aim for, but he hides his face between his thick shoulders. Only an upper cut from my left hand will serve now. The impact jars Petey's head back, and it leaves me enough time to land a cross under his jaw that drops him to the mud.

I stand over him between the wall of Bill's men and my White Hand brothers. Four fingernails are missing and the opened scar leaves a blue vein visible through the wound so that enough red liquid soaks my arm to leave the appearance that I had thrust it elbow-deep into a vat of blood.

"And in winning, I give you mercy," Says I. "The ultimate power."

But no answer comes from him. He is unconscious and wordless.

"Swede!" I yell. "Where are ya, lead a charge."

But The Swede is still on the ground holding his clavicle.

Through the wall I see Harry stumble to defend himself against Bill and his lieutenants. Punches rain down on him as he grasps for one of their legs. Richie Lonergan lands punches on the top of Harry's head as Non Connors moves round behind him to boot at his ribs.

"Dockbosses and righthands," I scream. "Fight through the fray. To our leader we go! Fight to our leader, Patrick Kelly!"

Behind me boots begin to stomp in a great push of men that collapses over me in fierce fighting. Our lines form again to challenge the blockade.

"Push!"

DIVIDE THE DAWN

As Dance Gillen brings me to my feet, he looks at me with wild eyes, "Can ya still fight?"

"I can," I yell back, though my right hand is in no shape to land punches.

"White Hand!" I yell out. "We are the Soldiers of the Dawn! In a dark world people are drawn to the light and will forever fight against the enveloping black," I point through the wall of men toward Harry. "Onward!"

Together we thrust at the blockade with our shoulders, then follow them up with punches. The momentum it creates allows for our men to fill the space. More then ram into the back of us. When I break the first line, I stumble into the second and take body blows and pot shots off my skull. But from behind I am pushed through again and fall to the feet of their third line. I duck a boot that was about to kick my face and again the push from behind collapses over me, falling forward. Our numbers overpower their organization. Our passion smashes their tactical cohesion. Holes in their lines allow some of us to break through. Within minutes there are four and five men that squirm out and rush to help Harry. Then finally I am out.

Vincent, Eddie, Freddie and Dance plow into Bill and his lieutenants, then ten, twenty more of us plow through to overwhelm them entirely.

"Are ya ok?" I swing round to Harry, who is on his knees now. He grabs hold of my shoulders to avoid falling. His face is painted red. A deep and weeping wound gushes from over one eye that is the size and color of a purple plum. "Harry? Are you ok?"

Harry struggles to bring words to his lips, but finally says, "Ya're a good egg, Liam. I'm fine, is Dinny alive? I tried to. . ."

Behind us Dinny lies motionless, his face turned away. Body crumpled. As I move to turn him, I am blindsided. Without clear lines now, chaos reigns round me. Harry crawls over and turns him. He wipes mud from Dinny's face, then sits back on his knees with a hand over his mouth.

"Is he dead?" I yell out, pushing men off me. "Tell me, tell me!"

When finally I am able to crawl to Dinny I see that his chest is moving. Mud obscures his face, but it is clear that he'd been shot. A whole the size of a nickel oozes blood from his cheek parallel to his nose on the right side. The bullet had gone in to his mouth there and had exited through his lower jaw in a downward trajectory. On the side of his neck is a burn mark where the bullet has grazed the skin over his jugular.

"He's alive!" I yell. "He's alive! Alive!"

Still the melee ensues all round me until a whistle blows in the distance. Someone is blowing two, three whistles now.

"Why-ooooo," Whyo screeches out a warning. "Why-ooooo."

From the east and west more whistles blow. From the north and south too. Ten whistles. One hundred. More! all at once. Men begin to look round at the noise.

"Tunics!" A man screams.

"Tunics, a thousand tunics."

Every one of them has a blackjack and a revolver. Warning shots explode in the air as they run over the hilly slopes of mud through the puddles with their tunics buttoned high and their caps pulled low. They sprint round the tenements from three sides and across the cobblestoned street.

"Get down!" They yell. "On the ground. On the *ground*!"

They crash into both gangs without discerning one side over the other. Their leather blackjacks with lead balls at the end whip through the air onto knees and shoulders. Heads and lower backs. One by one we fall as they outnumber us all. As I am at the center of the fray with nowhere to go, I have time to drop to my knees and thrust my hands in the air, only to be toppled by three of them at once. They hold me down on my stomach, until I am about to drown in one inch of muddy water. My hands are quickly tied behind and I am dragged by the shoulders backward to a line. There Bill Lovett sits, who is still alive but exhausted. Through the jumble of legs rushing by me he smiles as if this were the most fun he'd had since the trenches of

France. Petey is still knocked out and motionless on his back when two patrolman trip over him while dragging others.

"It's a fookin' shit show," The Swede growls at me from the ground with a tunic's boot on his neck. "Nobody gets nothin'. That means we assume the Dock Loaders' Club." He then yells out for all to hear. "Irishtown is ours! Still ours! The White Hand!"

"It's Bill's," Non Connors yells as he is dragged by feet through the mud. "Dinny cheated!"

One fellow gently strides through the chaos, his tunic too long for him, but is the only clean one left. "Ya don' know shit, Swede. Either do ya Connors. These streets are mine now."

That is when I recognize the voice. *That voice!* Patrolman Daniel Culkin. Suddenly the pain in my knuckles comes alive. The deep bruises in my chest and arm and shins pulse.

"Revenge!" Culkin yells out angrily as the slew of tunics respond with a resounding, earth-shaking battle yell.

"My father can go to his gentle g'bye in peace now," Culkin calls out for all to hear. "Detective William Brosnan did not give his life in service to the United States o' America for naught! Let it be heard across all o' Brooklyn. All o' New York that the law will no longer be flaunted."

A round of cheers meets him.

"We will not be cast aside while criminals murder us. For the safety o' all New Yorkers, the law must reign!"

Patrolman Culkin then turns to Harry Reynolds and drags him to the center.

"No," Dinny mumbles under his breath. "Let him be free."

"This one is more than a simple criminal, he is evil an' un-American!" Daniel turns round so that all can hear him and holds Harry by the back of his collar. "They call him 'The Shiv' for good reason. He cut-up Detective William Brosnan, my father-in-law, stuffed his body parts in a barrel an' dumped him in the East River! But in this country, justice always prevails!"

A thousand voices crawl up through the rain and low cobalt clouds in joyful victory. Daniel then whips the leather and lead blackjack across Harry's face, dropping him into the mud.

"Detective Culkin!" A tunic calls from behind us.

Detective? I repeat silently. *Has he been promoted?*

"This one ain't movin'," the tunic explains to Detective Culkin. "He ain't breathin' either."

When I turn round, it is the old-timer, Beat McGarry. One of our own. His wrinkly face and mouse eyes have come to rest, but a large blue bruise over a temple is raised and gives his head the appearance of being lopsided.

"I think he's dead, sir," the tunic says, pushing the flaccid body with his boot.

Dead? Beat is dead?

The last words I remember him saying; *Ya're next in line, kid.*

"Harry," I mumble with pain in my voice.

But Harry is dragged off.

"Abby!" I turn my attention up to the muddy hillside, but she is gone. Everyone is gone except for those that fought White Hand versus White Hand, lined up in the mud on our knees.

"And this one," Detective Culkin stands over me.

The sound of leather tightening comes to my ears again. The sound I hate so much. The blackjack droops from the weight of the lead ball inside the spring loaded shaft.

"Kiss it," Culkin dangles the twelve inch leather in my face. "Kiss it an' I won't hurt ya no more. I promise. Just pucker those lips an' give it some love. I want ya to look at me when ya kiss it, ya hear me? Look up at me, sad an' obedient."

"Daniel," I whisper. "An invisible hand has written the amount of days in your rule, and they do not add up."

"That was a dumb thing to say," Detective Culkin raises his weapon in the air and grits his teeth. Behind his head I see it against the slate-colored sky, until it rakes downward. . .

The Ghost God

She bites at the bloody cuticles with her front teeth and tears a piece of skin off all the way up to her knuckle.

A whisper comes from the black of the stairwell above, "Keep ya head down. Always keep ya head down, Anna. No one knows we're comin'. Best for them an' us that we ain't seen."

The only light comes through a soot-covered stairway window. Quick as a ghost he slides up the stairs where his shadow gently passes like a flicker, rifling up through the cross's reflection upon the wall from the window muntins, disfigured and slanted.

He crouches and turns to her with the eyes of a lost soldier, "I'll go up first, but ya gotta stay low. Crawl on ya belly. Ya shouldn't o' worn a dress."

I'm not wearing a dress, it's a skirt. And what else am I supposed to wear? If I wear anything else they'd shave my head and burn me alive or something.

Darby Leighton reaches up through the silence of the top floor and lowers the wooden extension ladder. As it unfolds in three sections, a flight of pigeons flap over Anna's shoulders and through her hair. She does not scream though and turns her eyes back to Darby with her hand flat against her mouth.

The wood-framed, pre-Civil War building had been condemned and empty for two years and all of the door handles, jake pipes and tin ceiling tiles had been stripped and sold by junk dealers, the bannisters and parts of the floorboards used for firewood. But for Darby it is yet another hidden lair to obscure himself.

I'm the one known for knowing things, Darby had once told Anna. And it was for places like this that Darby had gathered knowledge by observing others like a deviant peeping on the disrobed.

When he opens the roof hatch, she shields her eyes from the sunlight that spills all round her. She then steps forward and puts a boot on the first rung. But when she puts weight on it she can feel that the wood is rotted.

"Hold tight wit' ya hands when ya step up," Darby calls down from the roof hatch. "Distribute ya weight evenly. Don' put all ya weight on the rungs, they'll bust."

But when she grabs the ladder a splinter slips into the side of her index finger. Anna grits her teeth to keep silent, pulls the splinter out of her finger with her front teeth and holds the ladder tight with both hands. At the top rung she slips, but Darby catches her by the wrist and hoists her up with a grunt.

He is stronger than I thought. Ligeia must be fattening him up. His eyes are not as dark as they used to be and his lips are not so white and chapped, though he still has that look of bewilderment to him.

On the roof she crawls through the tar and black puddles and sun-bleached rocks to the crumbled cornice along the edge.

The two of them slowly peer through decayed crenelations like scouts along a parapet. Anna's stomach turns when she sees the cobblestoned Bridge Street below. As the wind sings a mean song in the rooftops and whistles through her hair, she suddenly feels as though she is falling.

"Look, there they are," Darby whispers.

A big man lumbers across the street behind a tunic in police blue and two others. Behind them is a gang of some twelve more tunics who lead a retinue of some fifty or sixty faceless laborers.

The two boys who serve as scouts outside the Dock Loaders' Club scream out. Their childish voices reach Anna, "Why-ooooo!" Afterward they run inside when they see the four men approach, while the rest form up across the street with clubs and spades directly below.

"Who are they?" Anna whispers to Darby.

"Look," he points and whispers. "Some o' them are wearin' Brooklyn Grain Terminal jumpsuits. They were recruited!"

"By who?"

As she turns back to the scene below, her gaze fixes on one of the four men ahead of the retinue who holds some sort of sickle at the end of his arm. As if he felt her eyes on him, or knew she would be there, he turns his head up from the cobbled street and finds Anna's eyes above. Darby and Anna both hide behind the cornice when they realize they've been spotted.

Anna begins to shake uncontrollably. She has her back against the parapet wall and her boots out ahead of her on the rooftop gravel. Darby crawls over, but dares not touch her.

"Ya uhright? Anna? Anna, what are we gonna do now? Everythin's lost."

She had always welcomed Neesha's touch. But no one else's. During her childhood and into her teens she had warned anyone and everyone never to touch her. And no one dared. Not her mother, not her younger siblings unless she touched first, not even Matty Martin, who longed to feel her skin. "Watch out," her father once told an unwitting customer at the Lonergan Bicycle Shop. "The bitch bites."

Only Neesha. His hands were large and warm, his eyes the color of morning light. Neesha could touch her. Even with words.

The wind blows through her red hair and with it comes a memory. His words are memories now, and they will live there, and there only, for the rest of Anna's life. Now his voice is the wind that whistles softly through the rooftops.

"We're like two lost spirits takin' wing against the tempest," Neesha had said to her before he'd died. "My body is strong, sure it is. But ya spirit is so much more powerful than mine. It is a great gift, what ya have Anna. A gift from the gods. An' if ya lead the way, I will reinforce ya. Together we can cross over to the next world," he dropped to both knees and held out his palm. Slowly, he looked up into her eyes. "Anna, will ya guide us? I vow to ya, forever and always, I vow ya my soul, however weak it may be, and I vow my body to ya. Take this ring, an' we will fly together."

You live in memory now, Anna brushes at her eyes in thought. *Not even in my dreams. But why? Why won't you come to me in dream any longer?*

Only Neesha could touch her. When he was alive, the feeling truly was sublime. And when his flaxen mane brushed against her cheek as he took her breast in his mouth, she let go. Surrendered. The deep tingling sensations from his mouth on her breasts had given cause to allow herself to be released from the violent stance she had always maintained. Her muscles had slacked. Her mouth opened to a natural position. When Neesha had slowly mounted her, she allowed him to take down the moistened underclothes that clung to her inner thighs. She was ready, and when she felt his warm breath on her eye and his stubbly cheek, she let go.

What was it? That feeling? Anna thinks. *Was it trust? Trust is. . . treacherous.*

In her dreams, every time she allowed the beauty of trust to overrun her, she found another man was on top of her. A man with a horribly disfigured face wearing a black mask over his eyes with an obscene nose. Down the middle of his face was a long, blackened wound. On his neck were bloody smallpox sores and over an ear a long bullet scar. The dream had turned to a nightmare when he grunted into her; his wounds weeping into her mouth and creeping down her throat, wending through the whole of her body like an infection. Like death.

She looks down at the wreath-of-vine ring on her hand.

Neesha, come back to me. Something tells me to seek revenge against your murderer. That it would shake you out of the heavens so you can come back to me? Is this true?

"Anna, what's wrong?" Darby comes closer.

"I... I will never trust again," she points down to the street. "The man down there? That's the face I saw'r in my dreams."

"Who, Garry fookin' Barry? Ya saw'r him in dreams?" Darby signifies his interest with a tilt of his head. "What kinda dreams've ya had? Anna?"

Darby's voice trails away until it becomes a mere echo to her.

On the roof ahead of them an old man appears. He sits slowly rocking in a wooden chair. His hair is white as snow and stands up like a crown swaying in the breeze. His wrinkles are deep wavy lines that make his face appear sorrowful.

"Who are ya?" Anna asks. "Ya're not Neesha."

"I'm Darby," Darby answers.

"Shaddup, I'm not talkin' to ya. I'm talkin' to him."

"Him who?"

Anna, the old man's wavering voice whispers as the wind gently stirs, mingling with the creak of the wooden rocker. *Shake dreams from yer mane. Let it out. Glory in instinct, fer t'is yer instinct that has the right of it. But one thing ya have wrong; Bill does not have Neesha's soul.*

Anna sits open-mouthed as she had when old Mrs. O'Flaherty told her she could shape the future like a prophetess. She tries to place the old man's voice, but simply can't connect it.

I've heard that voice before.

She turns to look at him, "What do ya mean?"

I can only open the door, ye must enter an' find out fer yerself.

"Are ya the Ghost God that Mrs. O'Flaherty told me about?"

I... I am trapped here, he stammers. Even as he clears his throat, his voice strains but is so disparately memorable. *I did what honor bound me to do, but in so doin', in the eyes o' men an' women, I became dishonorable. Ye see, if the past is as unknown as the future, it is alive, and therefore volatile. But ye can free me. Ye can free us all to become the most powerful person in all o' Irishtown.*

"Me? I'm only a woman. Young an' damaged."

An' ye would not be the first. If ye succeed, ye will have a golden table that overflows with bread an' meat fer yer fam'ly. An' if t'were that the whole o' yer siblin's were to eat from the table fer a twelvemonth, the bread an' meat would still be in the same form, so it would. Forever the Lonergans would eat, Anna. Forever and more.

"Ya're dead, aren't ya?"

We all die.

"Have ya seen—" Anna's voice catches. She gasps twice to hold back her grief, then swallows.

Have I seen Neesha, ye ask?

She nods.

Neesha... is not dead.

"He's alive?"

He cannot be dead. Yer love sustains him, Anna. But not inside Bill.

"My love? I'm evil, my heart is black as coal. Everyone says it."

He lives, my child. He lives because o' yerself. Ye were asked to surrender. To come out o' yer hidin' an' surrender to yer love. Ye could not've known exactly what it meant, yet still ye did it, ye went back to yer fam'ly an' saved him because o' it. He lives, Anna, owin' to the beauty o' hidden love inside yer heart, t'is true, t'is true.

"Then where is Neesha's soul now?"

The old man's crown shifts in the wind as he sits up in the rocker. A flicker of happiness flashes in his sad eyes as he speaks, *A great battle is underway in the Otherworld. The archons are turnin' against the demiurge, one by one. Two are yet to be made, but three have been named. Ye have seen them in dreams! They're tryin' to turn ye, Anna. Turn ye away from love forever. Ye cannot let them win. Ye must not lose yer love, we desperately need it. Ye must continue to surrender to it.*

"But... but where is Neesha?"

He is caught between the darkness o' the past an' the light o' the future. But his soul does not writhe. It is as pure as a cloud in a mountain shroud... Inside the hope o' the future king.

"Who is the future king?"

In life Neesha was the golden child, the prince an' heir to Irishtown, the old man's tone becomes formal and salutary. *T'was his fate to become king, an' yers to be queen, but t'was fate that was taken. Ye, only ye Anna, can reclaim him. For now he lives inside the pale blue, see-through eyes o' yer elder kin, as t'was he who took yer love's fate. Neesha vowed ya his soul an' asked ya to lead the way, remember? Only ye can save him now, Anna. Only ye can save us all! With that ring ye can reclaim his soul an' fulfill his ascension, but if ye forsake trust and renounce love, ye will fail an' the archons will win. We will all fail unless ye trust yer instincts an' crown him, King o' Irishtown!*

"An' what will *you* get outta it?" Anna sneers. "What am I savin' *you* from?"

The old man struggles to stand from his rocker, then raises his hands as the wind catches his words and whisks him away.

To revive this story for to tell.

"Wait!"

Keep going for a sneak preview of the next book (if there is a next book)

DIVIDE THE DAWN

Eamon Loingsigh
Photo by Mitch Traphagen

DIVIDE THE DAWN

An Enduring Labor Solution

July 1919

Jonathan G. Wolcott blushes as he steps up to the stage and the oak podium as a string quartet lay their bows across laps and gently clap into gloved hands.

The room stands in unison to applaud the President of the Waterfront Assembly for his greatest accomplishment.

"It's been a long-time coming," Daniel Culkin hears the fat man yell into the crowd. "A long, long time."

Next to Daniel, Dead Reilly leans into Patrolman Ferris' ear, "He looks like he's gonna cry."

Just as the applause begin to die down, it strikes up again when one of the Board of Directors, Mr. Vandeleurs yells out, "Bravo, well done, sir!"

Daniel rolls his eyes, *You'd think we were in church for as many times we have to stand up to give praise.*

The smell of new-carpet mixed with brass polish and window cleaner comes to his nose as he waits for everyone to stop clapping. An architect and contractor had been hired to renovate the room on the bottom floor of the Empire Stores building to celebrate the victory.

Well in advance of their arrival, a red carpet had been rolled out over the sidewalk and into the cobbled Main Street where carriages delivered well-fed, middle-aged men and women clad in palatial gowns and stately garb. Daniel had never seen anything so ridiculous.

A caterer had been hired as well, and a staff of tuxedo-clad servants and coat-checkers from an exclusive Lower Manhattan club. They were contracted for the day to serve the four-course meal on shimmering silver platters. All members and their wives even had to choose their lunch two weeks in advance from an a la carte menu.

Each seat has its own rare crystal rocks glass, six-piece silver utensil setting and napkins that are folded into the shape of a white swan. Even the ice water is served in wine glasses.

Five executive tables made of solid wood had been bought and brought in through the arched, iron doors solely for this occasion. They are lined vertically in front of the stage and podium so that all Daniel can see from behind are rows of balding crowns and graying buns with rolls of neck fat pinched upward by collars and coats in the shape of packaged white sausages.

Upon inspection three days before the event, the scent of rotting summer garbage came to the fat man's nose. And so he sprung into action. He hired a team of White Wings from the Sanitation Department to clear out areas along the water where trash rolled in the tide. As a stipulation to their contract, they were required to work overnight before the gala to remove any and all trash cans within a square distance of four whole blocks.

Out the arched, brick windows, beyond Wolcott and the chamber quartet, a skiff lists west toward the Brooklyn Bridge in the East River summer breeze.

"It's horseshit we gotta sit in the back row," Daniel growls at Charles Pakenham on his right who scribbles on a notepad busily. "We're the ones out there fightin'. We should be up on that stage introducin' Wolcott. At least I should be."

When Pakenham finishes his note, he puts his pen down and turns to Daniel, "Is it true Harry Reynolds escaped?"

Daniel's hands ball up into fists, "Ya're not gonna put that in the paper, are ya?"

Pakenham shrugs, "Tomorrow all the gang members will be arraigned in front of Judge Denzinger. Except Reynolds. The public will know by then."

"No they won't. He's got no fam'ly. No one cares about a fookin' motherless rowdy, so no one will know if he ain't there 'cause no one even knows he exists."

"The Coal Hole Robber," Pakenham says, recalling a headline from the year 1905. "It was my first year as a beat reporter. He was stealing through the coal holes, sneaking up through the fireplaces in the basements an' picking tenement door locks, then quietly creeping into bedrooms and stealing little valuables to resell in pawnshops. He would've never been caught if he didn't leave coal soot all over his bedsheets at St. John's School for Boys. I was there when Judge Denzinger sentenced him to Elmira. That's where he met—"

"Dinny Meehan, I know the story."

Pakenham smirks at Daniel, "My editor will want a quote from the lead investigator of Brosnan's death after the arraignment. Especially if they're released."

When he hears those words, Daniel feels the pain rush up from his groin again where Kit Carroll had made him repent for his sins a few days ago. She had bound his cock and balls in the leather strings of a cat o' nine tails so tightly that his gentiles had turned a blueish purple. The gag he had given her stopped him from crying out and if he moved too quickly, it would touch the back of his throat, causing great discomfort and fear of choking. But that was not enough. No. She then took his blackjack and raked his bound testicles so that the lead ball crushed them. After the tenth time she undid the gag.

Through the tears of groin and abdominal pain, Daniel said, "More, I've been really bad lately. I have to get better. I can't carry this weight. Ya gotta make me pay, Kit. Please, make me pay."

Daniel turns his eyes up to the cheerful fat man who is soaking up his victory. Then a champagne cork pops and Daniel jumps out of his seat.

Harry? Is that you?

"What's wrong?" Patrolman Ferris says with one hand on his revolver.

"Jesus Culkin, sit down," Pakenham complains.

"Shaddup, you."

Father Larkin leans on his staff and turns to look back at Daniel too.

Mind your own business, priest.

As the applause again dies down, Wolcott's tremulous gut clenches as he raises his voice so all can hear him.

"First, let us thank our host, my former employer; the New York Dock Company."

Again with the applause, jeez.

"Now if you will allow me to thank the speakers that preceded me this afternoon," Wolcott clears his throat and steps aside to extend a stubby arm to a man sitting behind him on a leather Queen Mary wing chair. "First; our keynote speaker. A Brooklyn-born genius and National Academy of Sciences member, Dr. Charles B. Davenport."

Again the applause builds up, then dies down.

"Dr. Davenport, with funding from the Carnegie Institution of Washington, has completed the most groundbreaking research at the Station for Experimental Evolution. His findings have informed us immensely. We thank you Dr. Davenport for you wise words this day."

Again the many men on the executive table drop their cigars in their mouths, or in crystal ashtrays to clap and shout out polite encouragements, while their wives share smiles and whisper to each other.

"Hear, hear!"

"I also must recognize our guest speaker. Mrs. Marian K. Clark, Chief Investigator of the New York Bureau of Industries and Immigration. Her tireless advocacy for the deportation and sterilization of defective aliens will help us create a healthier America.

"Two other groups that we invited in to give information must be underscored as well. The National Americanization Committee has done incredible work compelling immigrants and their children to assimilate, creating conformity to American patriotism and loyalty to our national ideals.

"And finally, please help me in thanking Eleanor Allerton of the Woman's Christian Temperance League. With her great work, along with many others comes a truly remarkable, extraordinary occasion when by this time next year, alcohol will cease to be a great determinate in worker accidents, harlotry and inefficiency."

A final round of applause echoes through the room as pudgy fists pound on the tables. Unwittingly, the hired staff even clap into their white-gloved hands if only to join the momentum.

Outside, through the arched windows Daniel sees a dark figure amidst the working men near the Fulton Ferry Landing.

Who is that? Is he wearing a mask? My god, what have I done?

As the sound in the room dies down, Wolcott smiles humbly and shuffles hidden papers on the podium in front of him, then looks up.

"The future," he begins with a long pause.

DIVIDE THE DAWN

artofneed.com

Other Characters (in alphabetical order)

Sammy de Angelo - Black Hand assassin, murdered by Lovett 1917
James Behan - Trench Rabbit, Petey's older brother
Boru - Mr. Campbell's horse
Henry Browne - Red Donnelly's righthand, Thos Carmody informant
Joseph Burke - Thomas Burke's disabled son
Giovanni Buttacavoli - Lucy's cousin, murdered by The Swede 1915
Mr. Campbell - Boru owner, lives across street from Meehan brownstone
James Cleary - Garry fookin' Barry's lone crony
Johanna Connolly née Walsh - Wife of Cinders, Spy
Costello - Member of the Marginals, Tanner Smith follower
Freddie Cuneen - Whitehander, best friends with Eddie Hughes
Dierdre - Tulla farm dog
The Dropper - Manhattan shylock, labor slugger
Needles Ferry - Drug addict
Abigail Abby Garrity - Liam's sister
Brigid Garrity - Liam's sister
Da Garrity - Fenian, Liam's father
Joseph Garrity - Liam's dead uncle
Mam Garrity - Liam's mother
Timothy Garrity - Liam's older brother
The Gas Drip Bard - Irishtown shanachie
The Ghost God - ?
James Hart - Teamster truck driver, quarantined with the grippe
Sean Healy - Trench Rabbit, Frankie Byrne follower
Quiet Higgins - Whitehander, died in WWI
Biddy Hoolihan - Blind woman at Irishtown tavern
Hotelier - Owner of Rockville Centre, Long Island hotel
Ragtime Howard - Whiskey drunkard at Dock Loaders' Club
Eddie Hughes - Whitehander, best friends with Freddie Cuneen
Mayor Red Mike Hylan - Mayor of New York
Gimpy Kafferty - Whitehander, died in WWI
Mickey Kane - Cousin of Dinny Meehan, Murdered by Lovett in 1919
Paddy Keenan - Bartender at Dock Laoders' Club, Minister of Education
Feeble Philip Large - Cinders Connolly's righthand
Lefty - Member of the Marginals, Tanner Smith follower
Celia Leighton - Frank Leighton's wife
Colleen Rose Leighton - Darby & Ligeia's baby
Frank Leighton - Darby's older brother, Sadie's cousin, Thos Carmody informant
Pickles Leighton - Darby's brother, in Sing Sing since 1913
Rose Leighton - Sadie's mother, Darby's aunt
John Lonergan - Anna/Richie father, former Yake Brady enforcer
Tiny Thomas & Ellen Lonergan - Died from infection & grippe, respectively
Willie Lonergan - Anna/Richie younger brother
Honora Lynch - Wife of tavern keeper
Mr. Lynch - Tavern keeper, Greenwich Village
Happy Maloney - One-legged World War I vet, Sadie's escort

Il Maschio - Former Black Hand leader, murdered by Lovett 1916
Christie The Larrikin Maroney - Former Brooklyn gang leader
Charles McGowan - Former Meehan righthand, murdered in Sing Sing, 1915
Emma McGowan - Liam's first love, died of Spanish Influenza in 1918
Chisel McGuire - Flimflam man, singer & barker
John L'il Dinny Meehan - Sadie's son
Dago Tom Montague - half-Irish/Italian Whitehander
Big Dick Morissey - The Lark's righthand
Motshan - Master of Ceremonies, gypsy king
Johnny Mullen - Whitehander, WWI vet, father of Whyo, died of grippe 1918
Widow Mullen - Widow of Johnny, Mother of Whyo and Vincent's child
Mrs. O'Flaherty - Lived above Lonergan bicycle shop, original Irishtown settler
Timmy Bucks Quilty - Trench Rabbit, former Lonergan Crew member
James Quilty - Trench Rabbit, Timmy's older brother
Miko O'Dea - Liam's childhood friend in Tulla
Jidge Seaman - Trench Rabbit, Frankie Byrne follower
Shanachie - Itinerant storyteller in Ireland
Silverman - Wolcott's thug murdered by Vincent & Thos in 1916
Whitey & Baron Simpson - Whitehanders, died in WWI
La Sorrisa - Italian recruiter of prostitutes
Johnny Spanish - Manhattan shylock, labor slugger, gave loan to Tanner Smith
Tommy Tuohey - Irish gypsy, Liam mentor, murdered by Lovett 1917

For more art, character backstories, the Divide the Dawn soundtrack
and more:
artofneed.com

Printed in Great Britain
by Amazon